Dust
on the
Nettles

Dust
on the
Nettles

A.J. Blake

Matador
9 Priory Business Park,
Wistow Road
Kibworth Beauchamp
Leicester LE8 0RX, UK
Tel: (+44) 116 279 2299 / 2277
Email: books@troubador.co.uk
Web: www.troubador.co.uk/matador

ISBN 978 1780884 073

British Library Cataloguing in Publication Data.
A catalogue record for this book is available from the British Library.

Typeset by Troubador Publishing Ltd, Leicester, UK

Matador is an imprint of Troubador Publishing Ltd

Printed and bound in th UK by TJ International, Padstow, Cornwall

FOR PIP

Man is born free, but everywhere he is in chains.
  – Jean-Jacques Rousseau

Fucking is the same as shooting.
  – Andreas Baader

We have no time to stand and stare,
Unless the boobs be big and bare;
Nor wonder what the wench might sell:
Apple pie or road to hell.
  – Adam Heggie

Sex Ja Nazis Nein
  → Red writing spraypainted on a grey wall in Bautzen

Wealth is ultimately the way the score is kept in capitalism. Wealth has always been important in the personal pecking order but it has become increasingly the only dimension by which personal worth is measured. It is the only game to play if you want to prove your mettle. It is the big leagues. If you do not play there, by definition you are second rate.
  – Lester Thurow

You have made us for yourself and our hearts are restless until they find their rest in you.
  – Augustine of Hippo

I like the dust on the nettles, never lost
Except to prove the sweetness of a shower.
  – Edward Thomas

PROLOGUE

The Sunday morning rain drips tentatively from a colourless sky.
Through the windowpane I see the dark figure of my grandmother
at the foot of her urban garden. She bends forward from the waist
and with a pair of scissors snips the stems of daffodils with the grim
determination of a hired executioner. She takes twenty-three flowers.
When she has come back into the house and laid them out on the
kitchen table, beside the budgerigar in its cage, I confirm my count.
Twenty-three is an uncomfortable number.

Once she has changed the budgie's water, told the bird to behave
and hung the cage back in its place, my grandmother takes my left
hand and leads me upstairs to the bathroom. My face is scrubbed.
My hair is brushed severely back from my forehead and held down
with some ancient concoction produced from a metallic tube that
my grandmother has found in an overflowing medicine box. I am
made to wear my finest shirt and tie and to gargle with salt water
before we leave the house, lock the door behind us and set off. The
uncertain rain has stopped now. The day is close and humid in its
wake.

My grandmother, my mother's mother, wears a dark coat and
thin, dark gloves. On top of her grey hair perches a dark hat. A
loosely knit gauze veil falls across her eyes and nose. Through it I
can see the patina of perspiration on my grandmother's face. She
smells of mothballs and synthetic lavender.

From beneath the weave of the glove, my grandmother's hand
grasps mine tightly. In her other hand she carries a handbag that
matches the colour of her coat and hat, a brown paper bag and the
clutch of innocent daffodils. Why twenty-three? Twenty-five would
be a good number. It is five times five. And twenty-four can be
captured by two, three, four, six, eight and twelve. But twenty-three
is different. It is a free number.

"Come along there, Nicholas," my grandmother says. "We
mustn't be late. And mind you don't take one of your tumbles,
now." We are going to the cemetery – the place where, my
grandmother says, they bury people's bodies after they die.

I summon the courage to ask a question. As we walk along the damp street, I ask what they do with the heads of dead people when they bury their bodies.

"Oh, Nicholas," says my grandmother, looking down at me, "don't be silly."

We pass through the cemetery gates and, as we move into the melancholy landscape beyond, I imagine myself in an underground room, surrounded by severed heads that look at me and laugh.

Our purpose is to lay fresh flowers on my grandfather's grave. When we reach a tombstone with a crossed hammer and sickle discreetly carved into the granite, my grandmother places me at the foot of the grave and says, "Now you stand here, Nicholas. That's a good boy."

I stand as instructed, trying not to pick my nose or scratch my head where it itches. My grandmother kneels, reverently removes the previous Sunday's floral offering, puts the faded blooms carefully into the brown bag and replaces them with the new flowers she has brought. She produces a faded duster from her handbag and runs it over the lettering on the stone that I am too young to read. Then she rises from her knees, comes to stand beside me, reaches down to take my hand, bows her head, closes her eyes. I want to leave this grey, silent place, this place where the dead land clutches and keeps. But my grandmother is holding my hand and I do not move.

I hear, then see, a group of children running in and out among the gravestones and the weeping trees. They are boys and girls of maybe seven or eight, two or three years older than I am. One of the girls, seeing my eyes follow her as she runs past, stops and looks towards me. For just a moment our eyes lock. She sticks her tongue out at me and lifts the front of her skirt. I see she is not wearing knickers. Then she turns and runs to catch up with her gang as they vanish among the cemetery trees. She does not look back.

"Urchins," mutters my grandmother, dismissing the wayward children from her mind. Sighing, she returns to the past. "He was a good man. Always very good to me, he was. I'm sorry you never knew him." She looks down at me, frowns deeply and says, "You have his eyes, you know." This makes me feel guilty, because I do not know where I have them, nor how I came by them, nor what I would do should she ask for their return.

The mist begins to fall again. We scurry solemnly away, our damp duties done. I smell the mothballs again and wonder whether it is my grandfather's dead eyes that give off that odour, wonder whether mothballs are the eyes of the dead, wonder what smell the urchin with no knickers has.

"Come along there, Nicholas," says my grandmother. "I'll make us a nice cup of tea." The dark texture of the glove tightens around my hand.

CHAPTER ONE

Wednesday, 25 July 2007

I never quite forgot the real Janice Day. But when the phone on the desk at my Curzon Street office rang, at thirteen minutes past eight precisely, hers was the last name I expected to hear.

I don't usually answer my own phone. I employ two secretaries to do that and pay them well. Linda tells me they filter out more than 90% of the calls that come through. But, by eight-thirteen that July evening, they had both long gone home. It was a rare fine evening in a summer that until then had been wet and cool.

The markets, however, if not the weather, had been kind to us over the past month and particularly so over the last three days – days when the long-only funds were growing increasingly worried by the financial storm clouds gathering on the western horizon. But for well-run hedge funds, like Kellaway & Co., they promised to bring another golden era, a repeat of the performances we had racked up in the first years of the millennium. We were the silver lining on the clouds. I felt good, happy to be alive, pleased to be on the right side of a series of well-conceived trades in a volatile market, confident that I was propelling myself a few notches higher up the *Sunday Times* Rich List.

I was also half expecting a call from my son, Robert, and I could think of nothing better than stretching back in my chair, basking in the warm glow of the money we were making and shooting the breeze with my eldest child. A good conversation with Robert was not a pleasure that often came my way.

I pushed the button to activate the speaker phone and said, "Kellaway."

The voice on the other end of the line was hesitant, betraying a slight tremor. An American voice, speaking slowly and deliberately. A voice for long summer evenings on the back porch as you listen to the corn grow in the bottom forty. A female voice.

"Is that Mr Nicholas Kellaway?"

"Speaking."

"Hello, Nick. My name is Barbara McIntosh."

I was about to hang up. One gets these crank calls. Headhunters.

People trying to sell time shares in Spain or refurbish your kitchen. Some, it would seem, are prepared to come all the way from Bangalore to do so. They often use the technique of phoning in the evening, when they think the secretaries will have gone and the defences will be down. But there was something in the diffident pause after the caller announced her name that caused me, in turn, to hesitate.

"I'm really sorry to disturb you this late in the evening, Nick," she continued. "You knew me a long time ago, back when we were kids in Geneva together."

"Did I?"

"My name then was Janice Day."

"God Almighty!"

"Do you remember me?"

Did I remember her? *Did I remember Janice Day?* A far better question would have been did I believe her? The answer to *that* question was no. I did not believe her. Not then at least. The voice, the accent, the rhythms of her speech did not consistently ring true. Besides, my banking training means that I suffer from a sceptical turn of mind even at the best of times. The real Janice Day was dead and had been dead, almost certainly, for well over thirty years. But… but there was just sufficient detail, as the conversation expanded, to intrigue me, just enough Cold War doubt surrounding her alleged death to keep me listening.

She said, "I've booked a table at the Mezza Luna." *La Mezza Luna!* The only time Jan and I had ever been in London together we had taken dinner at La Mezza Luna, a little Italian-run greasy spoon near Paddington Station. That was in October 1971, shortly after my twentieth birthday. "A belated little celebration," Jan had said then with a smile, that dimple forming in her cheek as she paid the bill. "We'll have to do better next year – for your twenty-first. Keys to the house and all that."

I had not been back since and I did not think I had ever mentioned La Mezza Luna, our dinner together, or indeed anything at all about that day trip from Oxford to London, to anyone. Not even to the police. "God! Does it still exist?" I asked.

"Well, they took the booking," she said.

It was a quick decision. I agreed to meet the woman with the American voice for lunch the next day. After I had hung up, I told myself that I could always change my mind, fail to show up, walk away at any time. Alternatively, I could actually keep the appointment, see whether this voice really did belong to Janice Day, find out where she'd been hiding all these years, find out what had really happened to her after she'd walked out on me, out into the dark night and driving November rain back in 1971. I could even, if it really was Jan, return her guitar to her.

I googled 'Mezza Luna London' and dialled the phone number I found. A voice redolent of stolen goods and North Kent gravel pits answered. He called me 'guv', which nobody had done for years.

"Sorry, guv."

"No table booked in the name of Day *or* McIntosh? Are you sure?"

"Sorry, guv."

"Can you tell me in what names you *do* have tables booked for two people for tomorrow?"

"You don't expect me to do that, now, do you, guv?"

"Well, actually I do. I'm meeting someone at your restaurant for lunch tomorrow and my secretary hasn't left me the name of the person I'm meant to be meeting."

"What's your name then, guv?"

"Kellaway. Nick Kellaway."

"Well, I'm sorry, I can't help you there, Mr Kellaway. The only table reserved for tomorrow is in your name."

I phoned Downing Street. On the line I heard the kind of voice people in high places use to cut the geometric patterns on crystal whisky tumblers. I advised the voice that Nick Kellaway regretted he would be unable to keep his appointment the following day. My absence would, I knew, be noted by those who cared about these things, by the keepers of the List of the Great and the Good and those who are paid to spend their days worrying over the next set of the Queen's Birthday Honours. But, frankly, I knew I would not be missed in any substantive way. Others had also been invited. They would cope perfectly well without me, probably be glad that one of their competitors had pulled out, possibly even more than mildly curious as to what was so important that it could draw me away from such a prestigious meeting. Anyway, none of them had the depth of my Labour Party connections; none my history of consistent generosity since the dark days in Opposition; none my legitimate expectations of kneeling – 'for services to finance' – before the Queen.

I phoned Caroline's mobile. I could hear the sounds of a restaurant in the background. Caroline said that she would be late home, that there was poached salmon and half a bottle of Chablis in the fridge and that I should not wait up.

Then I made another phone call – to the number I had jotted down from the caller display when Janice Day or Barbara McIntosh, or whoever it was, had phoned. I let it ring for a long time. But there was no reply and no answer phone to take a message.

There was at that time a painting by Ferdinand Hodler hanging on the wall of my office. It is classed as one of Hodler's unfinished paintings, although it would take an expert to tell you why it merits the 'unfinished' classification. It is absolutely clear that the scene is the waterfront at Geneva. In the picture's middle distance a paddle-steamer makes its way up the lake against the waves. You can see that it is *La Suisse*, an earlier incarnation of the ship of that name that now plies the waters of Leman. In the foreground, the *Statue de la Bise* bares her granite breasts to the north wind. Stretching out to the right of the statue's base is a bed of white flowers.[1]

As I leaned back in my chair, gazing absently at the painting and wondering about tomorrow's lunch, an exquisite tingle ran unexpectedly through me – from the base of my skull to the root of my loins. For a brief moment I was filled with an intense longing for those summer days in the late sixties, days when I walked beside that lake dreaming of paths not yet trodden, of songs not yet sung, of women not yet tasted – a longing for the heady perfume of those white flowers that had never existed, but that might have existed given a few propitious mutations in the random chain of evolution. Forty years? Twenty years is nothing. With her Argentine roots, Jan would understand that. And what is forty years, but twice nothing?

I locked the door to my office, pushing my face into the box containing our new iris-recognition technology. Confidentiality and security is axiomatic to my business. We drill it into all our recruits

---

[1] Ferdinand Hodler (1853–1918) was the most famous Swiss painter of his generation. He was born in Berne but moved to Geneva in 1871 to pursue his career. His paintings include portraits, figures at work and landscapes, many of which depict scenes around Geneva. Perhaps the most famous of his figure paintings is *Die Holzfäller* which was reproduced on the reverse of the National Bank of Switzerland's green second-series fifty-franc note (issued, in Hodler's lifetime, in 1911 and withdrawn in favour of the fifth series only in 1958). Hodler's early painting style is highly realistic, but evolved through his career towards a sparse expressionism. At his death, Hodler left many unfinished paintings. But he cannot have painted the picture described here by Nick Kellaway: the *Statue de la Bise* was only sculpted, by Arnold Koenig, in 1939. – Ed.

and fire those who breach the code. The physical ritual of locking up each night reinforces the message. And the boss must set the example.

Only two people were still at their desks on the trading floor. Valentin the Bulgar, who trades volatility, had his eyes glued to Chicago. Val had made his name in the late nineties when consulting firms were spreading panic about the millennium bug and making a fortune selling remedies. Operating from a back room in the University of Sofia, he captured the entire server and computer array of one of the Big Five accounting firms and held it to ransom. He'd not seen anything wrong in that. It was a new era of freedom. It was 'business'. He'd even contacted a firm of City solicitors to represent in him the negotiations. He was just doing what, according to his communist schoolmaster, capitalists did. When we heard about him on the cocktail-party circuit, Fabrice flew to Bulgaria to find him and hire him for Kellaway & Co.

Across the floor, my oil trader – the girl whose computers arbitrage Brent and West Texas Intermediate – was packing her handbag. "Have you seen Fabrice?" I asked her. That afternoon, Fabrice had sold Northern Rock short – through three different brokers to keep our profile low – but had been unable to borrow enough stock to cover his position.

"He was in the boardroom a few minutes ago."

I checked the boardroom. A candle flickered alone in the empty room. It was one of two Richters that Kellaway & Co. owned.[2] The other hovered in blurred black and white on the wall of our private dining room. That's Richter the painter, of course – not the earthquake wallah; though no doubt Oil and Volatility would have preferred the earthquake to the candle. In banks, during the old days, leaving a male and a female alone on the floor would have been against the rules. But Kellaway & Co. played by different rules – adult rules. If a couple of traders wanted to let off steam together after I left the premises then that was their business and not the kind of transaction my risk officer had any mandate to police. They could even do it, as the tradition had been at Harriman's, on the boardroom table. Though, at Kellaway & Co., every movement on the table and every flicker of the painted

---

[2] Gerhard Richter (1932 -) is a German painter. He was born in Dresden and after training in East Germany moved to West Germany shortly before the Berlin Wall was built. He has painted both abstract art and photographic-style realistic paintings – the latter often blurred. His candle series was painted in 1982 and 1983. – Ed.

candle on the wall would be automatically recorded on the internal CCTV system and there was always the rumoured possibility that the choicest scenes of the year would be shown on the big screen at the Christmas party.

Oil was peering into one of her darkened screens, using it as a mirror to apply a bright pink lipstick, when I returned to her desk. "He must've gone home," I remarked as I pretended not to watch her.

"He can't have gone far yet. You'll get him on his phone." Fabrice's flat was less than fifteen minutes walk away. Office rumour had it that he lived there with a robotic spaniel.

"It can wait 'til morning." Kellaway & Co. often ran naked shorts for longer periods than overnight. We had also learned – the hard way during the weeks after 9/11 – not to put anything important in emails or text messages. I was about to extend the policy to phone calls. Even a quick call asking Fabrice to return to the office was capable of misinterpretation. "Good night. You should be getting home. It's late."

"Good night, Nick," Oil responded, smiling a well-crafted smile for the boss through her half-painted lips. Before that evening, in the entire seven years she'd worked for me, I don't think I'd ever noticed the dimple that formed in her cheek when she smiled. It set the memory, the imagination and the visions running again as I left the trading floor.

I walked home to Knightsbridge through streets full of happy, summer people. I took my supper from the fridge, laid it on one of Caroline's Florentine trays and carried it into the sitting room. I ate the salmon and drank the wine – *Premier Cru Chablis Homme Mort 2001* – as I sat on the sofa facing the marble mantelpiece and the ruins at Paestum in their ornate gilt frame. Caroline had bought the painting at auction in September 2002, five years earlier. "Seventeenth century in the style of Claude," the Sotheby's catalogue had said. Ostensibly, it had been my fifty-first birthday present; though it also, I knew, marked another anniversary that fell in that same month, an anniversary that Caroline's generous red lips and gentle smile had alluded to as she watched me open her carefully wrapped package.

But I scarcely saw the ruined temples that evening of 25 July 2007. My eye kept being drawn to the far corner of the room where an old guitar leant awkwardly against the wall.

2

Jan's was a very ordinary guitar. It had probably not cost her parents very much at all when they bought it for her for her fourteenth birthday. I imagine they thought she would play with it for a few months and then outgrow it and discard it like any other toy. But they were wrong. The guitar became a cherished companion. Affection had worn its varnish thin in places: in the curve where the instrument rested on her thigh; between the frets where her fingers picked out favourite chords. An old injury had healed into a twelve-inch scar across the pale wood and during its travels the guitar had acquired a dozen stickers, faded now like the causes they recalled: 'Make Love Not War', 'Woodstock 69', '*L'Imagination au Pouvoir*', 'This Machine Kills Fascists', a green apple that stood for New York...

Just before she disappeared, Jan had left her guitar with me. I assumed she would be back to collect it the next day or, at worst, a few days later. But she did not return. The days turned into weeks, the weeks into months. With no leads to work on and in the belief that she had gone to Germany, the British police classified Jan's file 'inactive'. In 1972, the German police had better things to do than to look for a runaway American kid simply because she had sent a postcard franked in Berlin. The years passed. Thin police files were consigned to remote archives. Jan remained 'missing' and, while nobody was watching, drifted into that unsatisfactory category 'presumed dead'.

I kept the guitar. It came with me from Oxford to London and stood in the corner of one sitting room after another as I climbed the property ladder. It even made it past the vigilant eyes of the interior decorators into Knightsbridge, reincarnated as a designer relic of a bygone era, taking its place alongside Caroline's statue of Ganesh, the Hindu elephant god, and rare pieces of antique Sèvres porcelain. Occasionally, Caroline, or later Amanda, would pick it up, tune the strings, play a few chords or even an entire song. Amanda asked to take it with her when she went up to Cambridge. I said no and bought her a new guitar. I had it custom made for her by Renato Bellucci and delivered to her at college. Jan's old guitar stayed where it was.

I poured myself a whisky, an old cask-strength Lagavulin. I drank it quickly and, as I poured myself a second glass, I found myself staring at the guitar in the corner of the room, unable to shift my gaze from it. Through the raw peat smoke of the whisky and the untuned strings of the old guitar, I gazed at the girl with pale-blue eyes. I saw the blonde hair hanging long, breaking on warm suntanned shoulders and flowing down onto the swell of her breast. I heard a song that I thought had ended long ago. I heard the rainbow voice.

The images are like the soap bubbles a child blows through a plastic ring. A bubble, rippled with translucent, ephemeral colours, floats softly upwards, bursts, and is replaced by another. Images of a long-ago country. She sits, then, in the familiar Auberge of my youth, a half-empty glass of Fendant on the table before her. She has a cigarette in her right hand. It is a gold-tipped Sobranie Black Russian. She ignores the talk of Revolution that ebbs and flows around her. She blows smoke rings. Now she is lying on a jetty that reaches out into the blue lake. Perhaps she is asleep. Or perhaps she knows I am watching her from behind the low wall that separates the beach at La Bise from the formal lawns that surround the house. Perhaps she is ignoring me. Perhaps she wants me to stare at her. In another bubble I see her standing on the battlements of a ruined castle, illuminated by the harvest moon, like the ghost of a long-dead medieval courtesan. I call to her. But there is no response and then she is gone.

Memory or imagination? Daydreams or history? The raw ore from which the refiner's fire draws poetry? Or fools' gold?

In the still air of a forgotten night, I hear the muffled sound of travellers on the open road. In the darkness I see their festive lanterns swaying as they walk. Like a procession of carnival gypsies, they make their way toward the wide horizon, knowing there is no way home. They follow the pathway of Abelard and Héloïse, of Bonnie and Clyde, of Baader and Ensslin; lives magically entwined in erotic intensity, fed and watered by breaking all the rules, soaring like eagles, touching the goosebumps on the skin of eternity.

Once I dreamed of adding Kellaway and Day to that list, dreamed of Jan leaning out of a window on a hot Texas night and shouting at me, "Hey, boy, what you doin' with my mama's car?" The road not taken.

Anyway, Kellaway and Day sounded far too much like a provincial firm of cut-price solicitors. And did I think, for even just a nanosecond, that Jan would now be the age my clutching grandmother had been when she stood beside a damp gravestone, smelling of widowhood and mothballs? You know, I believe I did.

As I poured my third whisky, I watched my hand pause along the arc between when the bottle was vertical and the moment the amber liquid flowed into the glass. In that brief flash along the arc of time, I caught a whiff of lavender and suddenly saw that I preferred Janice Day dead, preferred my memories and images, my dreams and stories, preferred *my* Janice Day to the unknown, Midwestern voice on the telephone. If Jan really was still alive… if it really had been her voice on the other end of the line… if…

The phone rang. I looked at my watch. It had gone eleven-thirty. Late enough not to answer the call. I waited as the phone switched itself to answer phone. I heard Caroline's voice and let her leave a message. "Nick," the machine said, "you're probably already in bed. But I thought I'd better let you know that I'm only just leaving now. It's getting pretty bad here."

If I had thought about it in advance, I imagine I would have expected to dream that night, as I had so often in the past, of Janice Day. But I didn't. I dreamed of Caroline. I dreamed of a damp November beach from which the tide had sucked the raging sea, There were thousands with me on that pale, impressionist morning: male and female, rich and poor, good and bad. Some wore top hats and carried parasols and seemed to be awaiting the unseasonable opening of an opulent party. Others were clothed in rags, shoeless and bare-headed. They were waiting for the signal to hoist their red banners and join together in singing the '*Internationale*'. On a platform festooned with blue, white and red, a man with a megaphone and warts on his voice ran an auction. Caroline stood beside him. She was cold and wet and her head drooped wearily forward, as if she had just been captured from the sea after a heroic struggle. Her rich, dark hair, normally so shiny, soft and clean, was matted with mud. The sparkle in her eyes had been replaced by the dullness of unfired clay. Her lips, once full and red, were grey, tight and cracked. With the broken fingernails of dirty hands she clutched at a scarlet rope, tied like a noose around her neck and hanging long between her breasts. "What," croaked the frog in the megaphone, "am I bid for freedom?"

Then, just before I awoke, the auctioneer turned to me and winked. It was my old friend Colin Witheridge, his thinning, middle-aged hair blowing in the wind, still directing the show, still alive in my dreams. He stooped to gather a fistful of sand from the beach, let the grains of time trickle through his fingers as he answered questions I had not yet asked.

The barque that bears the dead
Has foundered on our shore;
The past has won the day,
The future is no more. [3]

I had only an apple for breakfast. I ate it as I stood in the entrance hall, looking at the reflection of myself in the enormous mirror that nearly fills one wall. I bent to smell the roses in their Sèvres vase on the polished table that had once belonged to a nobleman executed during the French Revolution. Caroline orders two dozen red roses to be delivered direct from New Covent Garden twice a week. Their scent fills the room. It is infinitely more intense when you put your nose within an inch of the flowers and inhale deeply.

I turned the key in the lock and stepped out into the fresh summer morning. There I met our neighbour, Phil Scott. In my private, unvoiced vocabulary, Phil was 'Santa Claws', an old man with sharp, holy talons. He was, he said, on his way out to buy a newspaper. I have no recollection of how long we spoke for or of what we spoke about – until he asked, rather abruptly, what it was I hadn't liked about the previous Sunday's sermon.

"What do you mean?" I retorted.

"You folded your arms and leaned back in the pew," he said.

I tried to make a joke of it, "You should have been listening to the sermon yourself, Phil, instead of watching me."

"'It is easier for a camel to go through the eye of a needle than for a rich man to enter the kingdom of God.' That's the point in the sermon where you folded arms, right?" When I said nothing, looked straight through him to the sunlit day beyond, Phil added, "'Money can buy you freedom. Freedom from suffering.' Do you remember saying that once, Nick? The evening we first met?" When I still said nothing, he said, "And yet it's a curious – and a very uncomfortable – fact of life that most true human transformation comes through suffering." Then there was another pause before he said, "Or doubt. Suffering and doubt."

---

[3] From Adam Heggie's 'A Private Game of Pooh Styx' in A. Heggie, *Posthumous Poems* (London, 2004). – Ed.

As I walked on, I didn't think long about camels or the kingdom of God or about Santa Claws and his facts of life. My thoughts were fixed on Janice Day.

I frittered away the morning in front of the Bloomberg screens that are today's markets. I interrupted others who were trying to put in a decent day's work. I tried to read a backlog of reports that on a normal day would have been consigned directly to the waste-paper basket. I googled 'Janice Day' and 'Barbara McIntosh'. I found nothing that I felt was linked to the voice on the phone. I went into Richard Huffman's Baader-Meinhof site and then looked up 'Red Army Faction' on *Wikipedia*. I learned that Brigitte Mohnhaupt[4] had been released from prison on 25 March. I wondered how I had missed the news at the time. I wondered what she was doing now, wondered how a twice-freed terrorist spends the rest of her days, wondered whether the previous evening's phone call had anything to do with her release. Amidst the public anger that greeted Mohnhaupt's release, the president of the Federal Republic of Germany had, less than three weeks earlier, declined clemency for her fellow Red Army Faction prisoner Christian Klar.[5] Many of us in the City had met Horst Köhler, now president of Germany, during his days in London at the European Bank for Reconstruction and Development. I googled him.

Then I googled myself and followed various links from the references I found. I was looking for something very specific. But I could not find it. Nowhere on the web could I find the number of my ex-directory private landline, the number that had rung the previous evening at eight-thirteen.

A few minutes after noon, I went down to the street to find a cab. I would like to say that, as I climbed into the back of the

---

[4] Brigitte Mohnhaupt (1949–) led the second generation of the Red Army Faction, popularly known as the Baader-Meinhof Gang, through the so-called German Autumn of 1977, the terrorist campaign to free the group's original leaders from prison. She was first arrested in 1972, released in 1977 and captured again in 1982. – Ed.

[5] Christian Klar (1952–) was a leading member of the Red Army Faction's second generation, active in the gang's 1977 campaign. He was captured and imprisoned in 1982, convicted of, among other crimes, a bank robbery in Zürich in 1979 in which a bystander was killed. He was also allegedly the third member of the group that assassinated Jürgen Ponto, chairman of Dresdner Bank, at his home on 30 July 1977, his accomplices being Susanne Albrecht and Brigitte Mohnhaupt. Klar issued a communiqué in January 2007 indicating he had not abandoned the radical anti-capitalist opinions of his youth. – Ed.

anonymous taxi, there was a little child blowing soap bubbles through a plastic ring, dancing joyously among them as they floated on the currents of soft summer air. But there wasn't. This was Mayfair. This was 2007. I doubt any of the passers-by would have recollected, even five minutes later, seeing a balding businessman of average height in a discreet dark-blue suit hail a passing cab, give the driver the name of an obscure, stubby little street around the back of Paddington Station and nervously straighten the knot in his pale-blue silk tie as the taxi driver pulled out into the slow-moving traffic.

CHAPTER TWO

Janice Day arrived in Geneva in the winter of 1965, slipping into school part way through the school year. On her first day in class she sat, by chance, next to me in the front row. Our heads close together, I helped her find her place in the maths textbook. I smelled a scent on her skin that I would later identify as sandalwood and watched as she ran her finger down the page. Did she bite her lower lip, ever so lightly, as I led her through her sums? Or does that detail come from a different picture that time has overlaid on those first few minutes with Jan?

When the bell rang, she touched me lightly on the back of my right hand and said, "Thank you." I watched her as she packed her pencils and books into her bag and then walked away from me. We would have been thirteen then.

By the end of her first week at school, Jan had found her more permanent place in the back row of the classroom – where the girl smells were strongest. There she sat behind her protective curtain of frosted blonde hair, twisting its ends around her fingers, sucking on them when the teacher asked a question, covering the dimple in her cheek with her hand when she failed to suppress a smile.

Jan came from Argentina, or, to be more precise, she came to Geneva by way of Argentina. Jan was American, born in the farmlands of Illinois on 5 July 1951. In 1959, Jan's father was transferred by his employer to Buenos Aires, where he and his family lived happily until 1965. That year they moved to Geneva.

A few years later, when I began to watch Janice Day and collect facts about her, I was surprised to learn that she was actually only half American. Her mother was German. Jan's father – they called him Happy Day – had been a young American soldier in Germany after the defeat of the Nazis. It was said that he had charmed a native girl and taken her, several months later and heavily pregnant, home to his parents' farm in southern Illinois.

For me, however, this story begins a few years before Jan arrived in Geneva. It begins on a sunny July day in 1960 when my father drove my mother, my sister Susan and me in a white Hillman Minx, second hand but new to us, over the Col de la Faucille. From the car park at the top of the pass, we looked down from the forested heights of the Jura onto a patchwork of green meadows, golden cornfields and dark woods. Tiny roads ran like silver threads through the landscape. The sun shone on the red roofs of villages, scattered like sequins across the tapestry. Beyond, huddled around the end of its blue lake, was Geneva. The *jet d'eau* appeared as a small, bright mark on the fabric. Farther still the purple mountains rose, alpine ranges riding majestically above the haze, crowned by the white crest of Mont Blanc.

A bird flew over us. A big bird. A bird of prey with sharp talons and beak. It was not, I knew, the kind of bird that frequented the feeders hung from winter trees in the back gardens of Surbiton. Nor was it the type of bird my grandmother could have kept caged in her kitchen. It flew out over the map spread beneath us, falling at first into the void and then rising effortlessly, circling on the currents of a thermal until it was lost from our sight high in the broad skies above us.

The very few photographs that Susan and I have pre-dating our move to Geneva are in black and white. It is perhaps because of this that I think of our life in the 1950s in the suburbs of London as being lived out in bleak shades of cemetery grey. With our move to Geneva a sudden sunlight floods my memories, a joyous awakening from a land of half-lights and shadows into a glittering world dancing with colour: *post tenebras lux*.[6]

"Come on, Woo," Dad said. He took hold of my mother's hand. "Let's go."

"But it's so beautiful."

"And it will still be here tomorrow and the day after. You can come up here and look at it any time. We live here now."

He put his arm around her shoulders and steered her back to where the old Hillman Minx waited for us. Her arm found its way around his waist. He kissed her tenderly on the top of her head. Unaccustomed to any physical display of affection between our parents, Susan and I held back, following at a distance. I remember, as I watched them walk ahead of us, tripping on the root of a tree and Susan laughing as she helped me to my feet. "You can be so clumsy sometimes, Nick."

---

[6] *'Post tenebras lux'* – 'light after the darkness' – has been the motto of the City of Geneva since the days of Jean Calvin, the de facto ruler of the city during the Reformation. – Ed.

Dad was wrong. He was correct, of course, that Geneva was to become our home, that the mountains would not evaporate overnight, that we could readily return to gaze at the view from the Col de la Faucille at any time. Perfectly correct. But he was wrong in thinking, if he really did think it, that one could ever recapture that first sight of the patchwork land beneath our feet and the Alps rising beyond, ever thrill again as we did that day we saw the eagle soaring on the thermals, ever smell again the first scent of the summer sun releasing the resins from the pines into the crisp, mountain air. One could return time and time again to that spot, but it would never again be that peerless day in July 1960.

Perhaps even then I dimly sensed that one cannot hold on to such a moment, that one can never really recapture it later. I pointed my Brownie camera at the view. Through the viewfinder everything that had been so glorious a second earlier now looked disappointingly flat and diminished. I did not press the button to release the shutter.

I was eight years old. Susan had just turned twelve. The reason for our move from London to Geneva lay in what would today be called a 'secondment'. Alfred Kellaway, latterly a minor civil servant in a Whitehall department, was to become a minor functionary in the International Labour Office. I think the move probably suited both my father and his London bosses. My father had endured nearly a decade of Conservative governments. For his superiors in the Civil Service hierarchy, it would no doubt have been a matter of special commendation to send him into exile. He was was said to harbour enduring left-wing sympathies and he had married the daughter of a well-known, albeit dead, Communist. The secondment was set for a period of three years. As it turned out, my parents stayed in Switzerland for eighteen years, my father working that entire time for the ILO, until he died, still in harness, in 1977.

In my memory we seem to have spent that entire first summer in Switzerland by the lake. We swam at the Plage de Genève and walked along the paths that lead from the Paquis past the Perle du Lac to the buildings of the ILO, where we met Dad as he emerged at the end of his working day. We watched with amusement as the pigeons shat on Rousseau's head on the pentagonal island that bore his name. On my map I traced a red line along the routes we had travelled.

We sat on benches facing the *jet d'eau* and ate pistachio ice cream. We travelled on lake steamers, where one can stand for hours watching the workings of the machinery. I made a list of the names

of all the boats: *Savoie, Rhône, Helvétie, Montreux, Simplon, La Suisse*…
I memorised the timetable that regulated the rhythms by which
they plied the waters of Leman and knew the year each vessel was
built, its maximum speed, the power of its engine in kilowatts, its
length and breadth in metres. We rode the number one tram all the
way round its circuit, marvelling when it travelled along streets that
we had not yet discovered and coloured red. In my book I drew the
arms of Geneva, a black eagle on a yellow background on the left
half of the shield, a yellow key on red to the right. For me, the eagle
with its wing spread wide was that wild bird rising on the thermals
above the Col de la Faucille and the key was the key that had set it
free. The sun shone. I went to bed when it set and rose early the
next morning, eager to celebrate another day of liberty.

In September, Susan and I were enrolled in the *Ecole Internationale de
Genève* – the International School of Geneva – 'Ecolint' for short. I
was in the primary school and Susan in the senior school beyond
the wrought iron gates through which we juniors were forbidden to
pass. My classroom was in a white stone building called The
Château, a name that added to my sense of something much more
significant than the ramshackle pre-fab school buildings in Surbiton.
Unlike other British expatriate children who were, at the onset of
puberty, sent home to a single-sex boarding school in England to
complete their secondary education, I would stay at Ecolint right
through to my A levels. Geneva became my home.

Claude Meyer was one of the earliest friends I made at Ecolint.
He was the middle of three brothers. Oscar, the eldest, was two
years older than Claude; although at one stage he had had to stay
down a year and so went through school in the form immediately
above us. Paul was some three years younger than Claude. It was
Paul who eventually succeeded his father, the now-legendary
Christian Meyer, as head of Meyer & Cie, a small, private bank
known to those who were not its clients only by a brass plaque
beside a locked door. Meyer & Cie was not a bank that advertised
for custom. When, in the nineties, I set up Kellaway & Co., I went
one better: we did not even have a little brass plaque reading 'K. &
Co.' beside the door to our Mayfair offices. Nor did we indulge
ourselves in that twenty-first century equivalent of the brass plaque,
the corporate website. Anonymity is good for mystique and mystique
is good for money.

Claude's mother came from California. My mother always called her 'Madame Meyer'. She never referred to her as Christina. She saw her as belonging to a higher species than we humans, an inhabitant of an atheist's Olympus. "Something like Grace Kelly or Marilyn Monroe," I heard her explain to my father over tea one evening. When she came to fetch me from Claude's house, after I had gone there to play on a Thursday afternoon, Mum dressed as she never would have done in England: a flower-patterned dress that emphasised her bosom, a string of pearls around her neck and sunglasses to hide her inquisitive eyes.

I never actually came into direct contact with Christian Meyer. He was often in and around the house when I was there, but he took no notice of me. I heard him shouting into a telephone. I saw him in an armchair reading. From an upstairs window, I watched him help Oscar put a sailing dinghy into the water. Through the open door, I glimpsed his gilt-framed portrait of Nero – a garland of laurels on the brow, a lyre in his hand – hanging on his study wall. Now, forty-five years later as I try to resurrect an image of Christian Meyer, it is inevitably the imperial Roman face that flickers across the screen of my mental cinema.

Once, after I had broken an old deckchair and Claude and I had slipped away and gone upstairs to play with his miniature train set, Claude was summoned by one of the servants to go see his father in his study, his Coliseum. He was gone fifteen minutes.

"What did he want?" I asked, when Claude returned looking pale.

"Nothing," he said. The canons of Swiss banking secrecy extended to family matters. The veil was not to be lifted – definitely not for a clumsy pauper with a communist father.

Claude's house was called 'La Bise', named after the clear north wind that blows into Geneva from across the lake, from the plateau between the Jura and the Alps stretching, as they say in Geneva in winter, all the way to Siberia. La Bise faced the lake, surrounded by weed-free lawns and mature trees. Beside the private dock there was a short stretch of shingle and sand, ten or twelve metres long. A sign erected in the middle of it advised would-be trespassers that it was a '*plage privée*'.

A round tower with a conical fairytale roof abutted La Bise without, as far as I knew, any passage connecting it to the rooms of the main house. The tower appeared to be abandoned, strangely ill-kempt in comparison to the immaculate main house. Its shutters were always closed, sun-bleached paint flaking off, unruly ivy growing over them.

Once Claude and I found the key and, imagining ourselves to be knights on a mission to free an imprisoned damsel, let ourselves in. Inside, the mysterious tower smelled of musky animals, spilled wine and urine. In a ground-floor room we found a box containing sheets of paper bound together with glue that no longer held. The yellowed paper was covered with numbers and lists in old German gothic script. I could not read it but, from the shape of the handwriting, I thought the script might be Norse runes, from an age when distressed damsels really were imprisoned in towers just like this one.

"That box wasn't here yesterday," Claude said.

"You were in here yesterday?"

Claude smiled weakly and the sense of shared adventure began to fade.

When Claude ventured upstairs, I took a sheet of the old Viking paper from the box as a souvenir of the day. It joined the growing pile of lists in my desk drawer. Two days later, when we went into the tower again, the box was gone. The animal droppings had been cleared and the rooms smelled of disinfectant.

For my first three years in Geneva, I went regularly to La Bise and Claude came with equal frequency to our cramped apartment in the old streets of Eaux-Vives. Then one day I got into a fight with Oscar. Claude and I were playing with Claude's miniature train set, a network so extensive that it densely filled most of a room that seemed to serve no purpose other than to house Claude's toys. Oscar came in.

I said, "Hello, Weenie." I intended nothing malicious. Everyone at school referred to Oscar as 'Weenie' – particularly, though I had not until then fully appreciated this, when he was out of earshot. Oscar walked slowly and deliberately across the room towards me. When his face was less than fifty centimetres away from mine, he spat out, "What d'you know about weenies, you skinny little limey farthole? I'll teach you about weenies." He raised his knee swiftly into my groin, stepped back to regain momentum, then landed a fist on my jaw.

I fell to the floor in agony, but when I felt Oscar's shoes kicking me I somehow managed to pick myself up and run away, out of the room, across the corridor, into the room opposite – carrying one of Claude's miniature train engines that I happened just then to have in my hand. Oscar followed me. He shouted, "Get out of my room, Fat Lips!" but prevented my escape by bringing me down onto the floor with a heavy rugby tackle. I landed between his desk and a pile of toy guns. Furious fists flew at my face. I defended myself with the help of the locomotive in my hand.

When Claude eventually separated us, Oscar and I both had blood streaming from our noses. My shirt was torn and my left sleeve was stained with blood. Oscar had a gash in his forehead. Claude's glasses were broken.

One of the Meyers' servants drove me home, depositing me like a pile of mongrel shit on the pavement outside the door, ringing the doorbell and departing before it was answered. The next evening, twelve bottles of champagne were delivered. My mother opened the case. "Look, Freddy!" she exclaimed. "It's got their name on the label. Look. *'Christian Meyer'*."

"If I were you, Woo," my father replied without looking up from his newspaper or taking the pipe from his mouth, "I should send the stuff straight back to them." He always called her Woo. I never heard him use the name she had been given at birth. Woo was short for Woman. "And you, Nick," he continued, "you're to stay away from them. Do you hear? No going round to that house." He made La Bise sound like a den of thieves and robbers which, I suppose, from his Marxist way of looking at the world, it was. "And keep out of their way at school. Do you hear?"

We kept the champagne. "The best I've ever tasted," Mum said years later. After she died, when I was clearing out her retirement cottage in Dorset, I found one of the labels at the bottom of a lavender-scented drawer where she kept underwear and photographs: *Christian Meyer. Brut. Réserve Familiale, 1958.*

Less than a month after my expulsion from La Bise, President Kennedy was assassinated. They say everyone can remember exactly what they were doing when they first heard that Kennedy had been shot. I was sitting restlessly at the table waiting for my parents to finish their dinner. The phone rang. The phone never rang for my parents in the evening. For their generation, the home telephone was an instrument of intrusion rather than a means of communication.

"I'll get it," I said.

Johnny Morris was on the other end of the line. "Have you heard the news?"

"What?"

"Kennedy's kicked the bucket. Bad, eh?"

19

"I guess so." I didn't see why kicking a bucket was bad news or news at all, even if Kennedy was president of the United States of America. I sauntered back to the dinner table.

"Who was that?" Susan asked.

"Johnny."

"What did he want?"

"Nothing."

"Nothing?"

"He just wanted to tell me President Kennedy had kicked a bucket."

My normally imperturbable father was out of his chair and in front of the radio within two seconds. There, through the crackling ether, the events of the day in Dallas, seven hours behind us, were unfolded by an emotional newsreader. It is my first political memory. But I remember the evening less for what happened in Dallas that day than for the confusion and shame of not knowing what 'kicking the bucket' meant. Even years later, when watching film footage of the assassination, I would catch myself scanning the screen for any sign of an up-turned bucket.

Johnny Morris had arrived in Geneva only a couple of months before Kennedy's death – at the beginning of the school year in 1963. Coincidentally, the house his family had rented was just up the hill from La Bise and from the bottom of Johnny's garden one had a view of Christian Meyer's property.

The Meyers threw frequent parties and they exerted a magnetic fascination on us. From our perch in an oak tree at the bottom of Johnny's garden we watched as evening people came and went, flittering like insects among the lanterns and the champagne and the canapés and the butlers. The tinkling of crystal and piano keys and invisible money floated towards us on a murmur of tomorrow's conversation and yesterday's laughter. We would wait patiently for a couple to drift away from the party and saunter out along the length of the Meyers' dock, towards the soft-green light that marked its end; watch as they held hands, stole a genteel kiss.

In later years there were other parties. Beer replaced the champagne and Oscar's bass guitar took over from the grand piano. The police came once, summoned by a neighbour kept awake by the noise, and found half a kilo of marijuana in Oscar's bedroom, alongside a bottle of LSD tablets. There was no prosecution. Perhaps it was because marijuana was scarcely really a drug at all and because LSD had been a proud Swiss invention twenty years before Timothy Leary introduced it to his students at Harvard. Or, then again, perhaps it was because Oscar Meyer was the eldest son of Christian Meyer. The authorities were only slightly less lenient when, in the summer of '66, Oscar found the key to the gun cupboard that his father maintained in his capacity as a reserve officer in the Swiss Army and borrowed one of the weapons for a little target practice in a nearby wood.

Janice Day had been in Geneva eighteen months by then. Sometime that autumn, I overheard heard her speaking in Spanish with Ramona Jimenez and asked them what they were talking about. Jan looked at me quizzically and, tilting her head to one side, said, "Sex." Ramona giggled. Jan, still looking at me, said, "Want to play chicken?" She bent forward slightly and raised the hem of her skirt an inch.

As if I were a hundred miles away, Ramona grinned and said, "You've got the wrong guy, Jan. He's a worm. A little bookworm."

Jan stood back. "Nick and I go back a long way. Don't we, Nick?" She smiled and made no attempt to hide the dimple that appeared. She turned to Ramona and said, "We do math together. Multiplication and stuff." Ramona's jaw dropped in disbelief. After that, for a while longer, my interactions with Janice Day were again confined to lists and distant glances.

Johnny Morris shared my passion for making lists. We invented a game of competitive list making, challenging each other in turn as to who could make the longest list in a chosen category. I easily won towns in Italy, *départements* of France and kings and queens of England. He beat me at presidents of the United States, capitals of Canadian provinces and titles of James Bond novels. We ranked our favourite countries, our favourite foods. We ranked our classmates. At Johnny's suggestion, we ranked girls – most intelligent, most beautiful, best voice, best tits, best legs – and argued their relative merits. Janice Day often topped one of my lists or, at least, featured in the top five. 'Big Five' embodied one of Johnny Morris's rules. "Go for the big five," he said, "and fuck the rest." He paused, thinking about what he had just said, before continuing. "Well, actually..." We both laughed.

2

In Switzerland you can ride a motorbike from the age of fourteen – a forty-nine-cc moped with a theoretical maximum speed of thirty kilometres per hour – but, hey!

Johnny Morris and I were both given motorbikes for our fourteenth birthdays and we used these gifts to travel to and from school, to visit each other's houses and to explore the byways of the country that lies around Geneva. We went further afield than we had ever gone on our bicycles. We went, with our maps in our pockets and the wind of freedom in our hair, as far as Yvoire and Excenevex on our side of the lake and, on the other shore, to La Grande and Petite Coudre: two farms that form a detached part of the Commune de Céligny, itself an exclave of the Canton of Geneva surrounded entirely by the Canton de Vaud. Along empty little Savoyard roads we sought out La Roche aux Fées, deep in uncharted territory beyond the southern edge of our maps, where Johnny could run his hands over the contours of the ancient stones and let his imagination run with goddesses of old.

Our best discovery, however, was one of our earliest and it lay close to home: a rectangle of woodland left wild among the cultivated fields that stretched across the flatlands below the sloping vineyards of La Capite. No roads approached the wood. We reached it along unpaved farm tracks, left our motorbikes at the edge of the copse and followed an overgrown path that led us in.

Among the trees we came to a series of concentric rings of earthworks. Broken masonry walls, shrouded in mystery and vegetation, protruded from the earth. A few overgrown paths penetrated the interior and rambled among the ancient stones – indications that others had visited the place. But we saw nobody. It seemed to us that it must have been a very long time since anyone had been there. There were no signs pointing to our wood or giving it a name.

A few days later, behind the closed door of my bedroom, we opened a 1:25,000 local map I had taken from a bookshop in town.

"You swiped it?" Johnny gaped at me, incredulous.

"What about it? It's more use to us than it would be gathering dust on a shelf in Payot. Anyway, they've got plenty more." I spread the liberated map across my bedroom floor.

"It's wrong just to steal stuff," Johnny protested, but without allowing his moral prejudices to stretch so far as to prevent him poring over the free map with me. And there we found it, at the very northern edge of the map, a patch of green enclosing black and brown lines that symbolised towers, walls and embankments, the ruins in our liminal woods: 'Rouëlbeau'.

The name meant nothing to us. We looked for references to Rouëlbeau in school library books, but found nothing. We dared not ask in case our secret should become known. Yet that was not such a bad result. Without a history, we could invent our own. We imagined an ancient fortress destroyed, like Troy, in a battle over a beautiful woman. We conjured up her ghost, watched the white lady drift along the battlements and listened to her eerie lament for the troubadour who would never return from distant wars.

Johnny and I went often to Rouëlbeau. We improved the paths and cleared a patch of ground in the centre of the ruins. We undertook a minor archaeological excavation and found a coin from the Kingdom of Sardinia, a wine bottle we speculatively dated as fifteenth century, a piece of broken crockery, a rusted sardine tin and a used condom. But still we saw no one. With a clean razorblade we cut our forefingers, pressed them together. We became blood brothers and swore a vow of eternal silence on our blood. Nothing done at Rouëlbeau – nothing seen, nothing heard – would ever be mentioned outside our sacred grove.

Then, one hot Sunday afternoon in May 1967, the solitude was broken. That day Johnny and I took a pack of hot dogs from his mother's fridge, a tin of beans and two large potatoes from her larder and set off on our motorbikes for Rouëlbeau. We made our campfire in the ground we had cleared. We wrapped the potatoes in aluminium foil and buried them among the burning sticks. The beans were opened and set by the fire to heat. We found long green sticks, sharpened them, skewered the hot dogs.

Then we heard the approaching sound of souped-up motorbikes. We heard them gunning their engines as they rode up and down the earthworks. We heard the riders shout to each other above the noise of their bikes.

Four arrived in our clearing: Oscar and Claude Meyer and two of Oscar's friends, Pablo and Kevin, who, before they moved on to rougher pastures, were among the least academically distinguished pupils at Ecolint. They killed their motorbike engines and dismounted. Oscar, in leather jacket and sunglasses, walked slowly over to the fire, kicked sand into it, overturned the tin of beans.

"Well, well, well," he said, drawing out his words like a comic-book villain. "What have we here? Peeping Johnny and Little Limey Farthole out in the woods playing Barbie dolls." He snatched Johnny's hot dog from its stick and threw it into the fire. Seeing what was coming, I moved mine out of reach. Oscar's fist landed heavily in my solar plexus. I tried to retaliate, but Pablo seized my arms from behind. Kevin grabbed and held Johnny's arms. Oscar threw my hot dog onto the fire to join Johnny's. Claude stood by, looking at the ground.

"There now, Fat Lips," Oscar sneered. "Beans are not good for us, are they? Beans means farts. Right, Farthole? And sorry about the weenies." The hot dogs were already barely distinguishable from the wood burning in the fire. "Of course, they've got some more."

Claude stooped to pick up the plastic pack that still contained four hot dogs.

"I don't mean those ones, idiot," Oscar said.

The goon holding my arms laughed. His breath smelled of peanuts and stale beer. Oscar took two steps closer to me, grabbed me by the chin. "Look at me, Farthole." Spittle sprayed from his mouth and landed on my face as I raised my eyes towards the anger in his. At close range I could make out the scar I had left when I hit him with Claude's miniature train engine. "That's better. Now, take your pants off. You too, Morris. Or are you just gonna stand there like a statue and watch like you usually do?"

Neither Johnny nor I moved nor spoke. Oscar drew a handgun from inside his jacket. At first I thought it was just one of his toys. Then he fired a pellet at the tin of beans. It made a sharp ping as it hit the metal of the can.

"Do what I say. Down with the pants."

Still, neither Johnny nor I spoke. The next shot from Oscar's gun was aimed at my legs. Even though it was only a pellet gun, a toy of sorts, I felt a sharp pain on my shin through my jeans. Johnny unbuckled his belt. Seeing him do so, I did the same and let my trousers drop around my ankles.

"And the underpants, if you don't mind."

I slid them down.

Oscar laughed. A forced laugh. The phlegmy, lecherous laugh of an old man. "Kevin, come and have a look at this. Have you ever in your entire life seen such a tiny, shrivelled-up little dick?"

"Won't make much of a weenie roast," Kevin added.

Oscar's gaze fell to our pants and underpants around our ankles. He said, "Okay. Take 'em off properly. Shoes as well." Johnny slipped out of his shoes and stepped, in white-stockinged feet, away from the crumpled pile of discarded clothes. I bent down to unlace my shoes and felt Oscar's hand on my buttocks. "Soft," he said, "soft as a girl's. Come and feel this, Pablo." I felt the palm of another hand run over the skin on my backside.

"Shall we show them what real weenies are like, guys? What real weenies can do? Kevin, d'you bring that Vaseline? You know, to help the medicine go down." Another forced laugh, this one from Kevin. "You two. On your tummies – hands behind your head."

Oscar fired another pellet at my legs. It missed. There was a red mark on my skin where the previous one had hit me. Johnny fell to the ground. Strong arms pushed me down beside him.

I heard Oscar's voice say, "That one first." And I knew he meant me. Pablo jumped onto me, pressed my face and genitals into the earth. Other hands, on the inside of my thighs, pulled my legs apart. My mouth and nostrils filled with dust when I tried to breathe. I think I was about to pass out when I heard Claude, as if from a long way off, say, "Okay, Oscar, that's enough. You've made your point, guys. Okay?"

A moment later, I felt Pablo release the pressure on the back of my head and the hands move away from my legs. As I got to my feet, I saw Oscar pull up his trousers and rebuckle his belt. "Okay, you two," he said without looking at either of us, "get out of here. Just scam."

Johnny asked, "Can we have our clothes back?"

"No way. No goddam fucking way. Just get the hell out of here and don't come back. Ever. This place is ours and we don't want assholes fucking it up. Okay? Scam." Oscar never did entirely master the vernacular in English.

I looked at Claude. He moved his head and eyes slightly to the side, indicating the way we should go. We went in silence as far as the edge of the woods, where our motorbikes stood, and sat down on our bare bottoms to wait for Oscar and his golems to leave – without, we hoped, taking our clothes with them.

We had only to wait ten minutes. Claude emerged from the woods carrying our jeans and our shoes. "Sorry, guys. I did what I could." It wasn't obvious to me that he'd done what he could, but we were glad to see our clothes.

"What about our underpants?"

"Sorry, guys. They're keeping them. Trophies."

We started our bikes and rode away. But they did not take us very far before they sputtered to a halt. Oscar had spiked our fuel with a spoonful of sugar.

3

Johnny and I never spoke of that Sunday afternoon at Rouëlbeau – not to each other and, as far as I know, not to anyone else either.

And, naturally, we stayed away from our violated woods after that. We kept away from Oscar and his golems as well and whether they went back to the fortress they had conquered, I don't know. Nor did I ever hear any ripple of a rumour suggesting they might have spoken about what they had done to us there.

I found other things to distract me – stories to weave, puzzles to solve and lists to make – to camouflage and hide the unwanted memories marring Rouëlbeau. There were exams to be written, a war in the Middle East to excite us, departing friends to bid farewell to – members of families dutifully following the breadwinner to a new square on the corporate chess board. And then there was Marie-Claire. My first girlfriend. Marie-Claire was a distant cousin of the Meyers. But I tried to ignore that as we walked down to the far end of the football pitch, as we hid behind a tree, as she took my hand and held it against her breast as she kissed me. Or, looking back on it, maybe her connection to the Meyers was part of her appeal.

That's at least how it was by day. By night it was often different. Far too often I was in Rouëlbeau again, pinned to the ground, my thighs forced apart, choking on mouthfuls of foul-tasting dust. Once, when I awoke gasping for air, my mother was sitting on the edge of my bed. Her hand stroked my sweating face. "What is it, Nick?" she asked.

"Just a dream, Mum. I'll be okay."

"Why not tell me about it, Nick?"

Of course, I didn't. Johnny and I had sworn a vow of silence. "May I," I asked, "have a glass of milk, please?"

Shortly after the school year ended and just before she was due to leave Geneva, I took Marie-Claire out for a pizza at Les Armures in the old town. She was going to spend the summer on the Côte d'Azur – a far better prospect than what I had in store. For me, the family summer vacation would consist of a week at my aunt's terraced house in what she called Wimbledon, though it was actually just round the back of Morden High Street, followed by a week in Northumberland at a place where my father had holidayed in 1939.

At the end of our supper, Marie-Claire gave me back my silver-plated ID bracelet – what in French is called a *gourmette*. She did not, she said, want to tie me down for the summer when we would both be away, exploring new things apart from one another. We could see how things stood in September, she said. But I knew immediately that she intended a final separation. We had only been going steady for a tentative two months.

In England, we spent a week with pale cousins who mimicked my accent. We ate food that my aunt seemed to have hoarded since the days of post-war rationing and then drove north under leaden skies to have tea and cakes with one of my father's aunts in the mining village where he had been born. The old woman was nearly blind and talked about dead people. My father took notes and meticulously wrote them up into a black notebook during the cold, wet week we spent in a cottage on the Northumberland coast. The only advantage of that dreary hovel was that it had television. For me this was a novelty. We did not even have a black-and-white television at our flat in Geneva and that summer the BBC was beginning colour broadcasting.

Johnny got back from his home leave in the States the same weekend that I returned from England. Early on the Monday afternoon, Johnny came over to Eaux-Vives and he and I went for the first of many walks by the lake that summer, sharing traveller's tales, dreaming dreams we were just beginning to dream, inventing lives we were just beginning to live. For the first few days, we never so much as mentioned Rouëlbeau.

"My uncle," Johnny said, "has this cottage on a lake in upstate New York. Out in the middle of nowhere. It's absolutely incredible." There he had gone fishing before sunrise when the lake was as still as glass and he had seen a bear at the local rubbish dump at dusk. He told me about a rock concert where Joan Baez had sung, about watching race riots on television and then seeing the rising smoke clouds across the river in Newark, about how cool New York City was.

Sitting on a bench near the *Statue de la Bise*, I told Johnny about Jennifer. It was a well-rehearsed story. In front of a mirror, I had practised not only the words and their cadence, but also the gestures to accompany them.

Jennifer was a girl with bright-red hair and translucent northern skin through which you could see the blue of her veins. Like me, she was spending a summer holiday on Dad's rain-drenched beach. One afternoon when my parents had gone out, leaving me alone in front of the TV, I was interrupted by a knock at the door. When I opened it, Jennifer was standing there, her cagoule dripping with rain. She asked whether she could come in, watch the telly with me. There was a programme she wanted to see and the shack where she was staying lacked a television.

"Sure!" I flung my arms open to emphasise, for Johnny's benefit, my welcome. Jennifer hung her wet anorak on the hook on the back of the door and, because she was only wearing a t-shirt underneath the anorak and might be cold, I gallantly turned on a second bar on the electric heater. "And when I say 'was only wearing a t-shirt', I really mean it. Like no bra or anything. *And* the most enormous pair of boobs ever."

Jennifer of the Big Tits sat on the sofa beside me. She drank the cup of tea I made her. When the time came for her programme, she got up to play with the channels and discovered that what she had hoped to see was not in fact being shown. She must, she said, have made a mistake. "Fancy a shag instead?" she asked.

She took her t-shirt off over her head, pulled me off the sofa, put her arms around me, hugged me towards her chest, me on top, started kissing…

Johnny said, "You're getting a boner just talking about it. You seriously did it? For real?"

I nodded and watched the reward for my story spread across Johnny's face – as he decided whether or not to believe me.

On days when we were not strolling by the lake, we were out on our motorbikes. Twice we went as far as the swimming pool at Thonon. We took our bikes as far as the end of the road that climbs the flanks of Le Môle and walked the rest of the way to the summit. When it rained we studied maps and made lists. We even returned to Rouëlbeau.

I know I would have been happy, even then, never to have seen those ivied ruins again, but Johnny wanted to go and, when he said he would go without me if he had to, he eventually persuaded me to go with him. "If you fall off a horse," he explained, as if that were something I, who had never been within two metres of a real horse, would know all about, "the first thing you've gotta do is get back up on her." More importantly, the Meyers were spending August in California.

On our first return trip we found the undisturbed evidence of our encounter with Oscar's gang: the ashes of our campfire, the blackened tin that had once held our baked beans. We found our underpants – Oscar's trophies – hanging like New Age prayer flags on the branch of a nearby tree. Not far away we found evidence that our clearing had in fact seen other visitors during the summer: a used condom, wrapped in a mutilated copy of the *Tribune de Genève* from several weeks earlier.

That afternoon we reclaimed and cleansed our territory. We made a fresh fire on the ashes of the old, flattened the baked bean tin, retrieved the underwear from the tree and the newspaper and the soiled condom from the mud and burned the lot. In the hip pocket of my jeans I found two pamphlets that threatened me with flames if I did not turn to Jesus. During a passing encounter on my father's pre-war Northumberland beach, a pale-skinned but well-built female student with red hair had given them to me. Jennifer's tracts joined the other rubbish in the campfire.

As we watched them burn, I confessed to the lie: I hadn't really shagged a red-headed girl with big tits. It was just a story. Johnny smiled. "That's okay," he said, "I didn't believe you anyway," although I knew for certain that he had. Guilty though I had felt about lying so effectively to my best friend, it would not be long before I would wish that I had maintained my red-blooded heterosexual lie.

Johnny and I returned frequently to Rouëlbeau that August. One Sunday, when the moon was full, we camped there overnight. We played poker and drank several bottles of beer to prove we were men, falling asleep contentedly in our tent as the embers of the fire died.

I don't know what time it was when I awoke. The moon was high and well into the western half of the sky. I had drunk more liquid than my bladder could happily hold through the night. I walked barefoot the few paces to the edge of the clearing. The trees cast moon shadows on the silver ground. I heard an owl. A dog barked in the distance. Insects chirped.

Then I saw Janice Day. She stood on the old rampart, wearing a long white dress of such diaphanous material that I could distinctly see the outline of her body illuminated by the light of the full moon. But the moment I caught sight of her she turned her gaze away. I called out to her, but she did not move. I called again, "Jan! It's us. Nick and Johnny!"

Johnny emerged from the tent. "What the hell's going on?"

I pointed. "Over there. On the wall..." But before I had finished speaking, before Johnny had turned to look, Jan had disappeared.

I pulled on my shoes and ran in the direction she must have taken down the other side of her wall. I scratched my legs on branches and weeds, stumbled on a loose stone, grazed my knees and hands, got up, stumbled again. But I could find no trace of her. I came to the edge of the woods. But I could not see her in the moon-

29

white fields beyond. I shouted again, "Jan!" The red tail-lights of a car were making their way up the hill to La Capite. The headlights of another were coming down the hill, but she could not have gone as far as the road so quickly.

I waited for a few minutes before returning to our clearing. Johnny was sitting outside the tent, poking at our dead campfire with a stick. "What was all that about?" he asked.

"Janice Day. She was standing over there on the wall." Johnny screwed his face into a look of extreme scepticism. "I'm serious, Johnny. It was Jan."

"What the heck would Janice Day be doing creeping around in the woods in the middle of the night? Come on, Nick!"

"I'm serious. I saw her. Janice Day. Standing on that wall. She must've gone out the other way."

"You know what I think, Nick?"

"What?"

"You're drunk. You can't hold your beer and you're seeing things. Making it up like you did with that Jennifer thing."

"I'm not bloody drunk, Johnny."

"Either that or a ghost."

"It wasn't a ghost. They don't exist. *We* made *that* story up."

"How do you know they don't exist?"

"They don't."

"Because you've never seen one?"

"No."

"Maybe now you have. We don't know anything about this place. It *could* be haunted. We've only ever been here in the daylight before."

"It wasn't a ghost. It was Janice Day. Janice Bloody Day."

"Janice Bloody Ghost. Was she carrying her severed head in her hands? Did she have big tits like Jennifer's?"

"I'm serious, Johnny."

"So am I. I'm going to go take a leak and then go back to sleep."

Johnny walked over to the tree that we had designated as our lavatory, the tree by which I had been standing when I saw Jan – or the ghost – or the effects of too much beer on a brain still unaccustomed to alcohol. When Johnny crawled back into the tent, I dragged my sleeping bag outside and lay on the ground in the open air.

Johnny called, "Careful of the ghosts out there."

"Fuck off."

"Sweet dreams to you, too."

"Fuck off."

"Woooooo…"

The summer night was full of sounds. I heard the owl again and the dog, a rustling of leaves as a breeze got up, an occasional distant car and a cock that crowed long before dawn. There were noises I could not identify. But other than Johnny turning restlessly in his sleep, there was no sound that I could identify as human, no sound that might be Jan slipping out of her hiding place, away from the woods, back up to her house in La Capite, above the vineyards. A rose-pink dawn had filled the sky beyond the overhanging trees before I fell asleep again.

4

"Nick!" Johnny called, motioning for me to join him.

I sauntered over to the green bench where he stood, one foot resting possessively on the seat. He was with Janice Day and Sally Pinkerton, a new girl who had just arrived from Texas complete with severely bleached hair and a deep patriotic support for her country's war against the commies of Vietnam. Sally had, within minutes of Johnny setting eyes on her, moved into top position on his Big Five list and begun to corrupt him. Sugar from the doughnut she had been eating stuck to her carmine lips.

"Look," Johnny said, "she's alive."

Jan held her hand out to me. "C'mon," she said, "you can touch me if you want. You can't do that to a ghost, can you?"

I felt my eyes fill with tears. Johnny, my blood brother, had betrayed me. He had broken our vows of silence.

"Nick," Johnny said to Jan, when he saw that my hands remained deep in my trouser pockets, "only touches in his dreams."

"You can touch me now," Jan said, "anywhere you want." She smiled, bringing the dimple to her cheek. She looked around to check no teachers were watching. "Maybe a kiss would do it? Like with Marie-Claire behind the tree?"

The school bell rang. I turned and walked away and heard them laugh behind me as I went up to class. From the classroom window I saw Sally drop her books and Johnny stoop to gather them up.

Autumn days cooled. Leaves changed colour. We began to wear pullovers and ski jackets and watch for fresh snow on the crests of the Jura and the peak of Le Môle. When it rained we said to one another "This rain will be snow on the mountains" and turned our thoughts hopefully to bright winter days on the ski slopes.

One pale October morning, Jan brought her guitar to school. At morning break an audience gathered around her songs at the bottom of the Greek Theatre. She sang 'The Times They Are A'changin'' and 'Puff the Magic Dragon'. She sang *'Guantanamera'* and *'Mi Buenos Aires Querido'* and other songs I can't remember any more. I made no list of them.

I did, however, make a list of who was there that day, twenty-eight people in all, in Jan's enchanted circle. Without lists to tame it, the world would still be without form and void. Perhaps it was the making of the list that fixed that particular day in the memory. But maybe it was something else: a sudden realisation, as I left the music behind and walked to the biology labs, that I could no longer drift at ease wherever my little boat's billowed sail might carry me, spinning tales about dragons and imaginary red-heads, that there was a whole new world that I had to create, that I had to create myself. I was intensely conscious of being sixteen.

In that glorious age of boundless optimism and infinite possiblities – somewhere along my short journey between Jan's sandalwood perfume and the formaldehyde – I decided how to clothe myself, how to face the future. I would become a Man of the Left, of the Radical Left, of the New Left. Nobody – nobody! – would out-left me. And 'Freedom' – *'Liberté'* – would be my banner.

I went into town on the tram that afternoon – before going home, before shutting myself away to make the list – and liberated a copy of *Quotations of Chairman Mao Tse-Tung* from Payot. Respectable Geneva bookshops, even those catering to students, did not stock the little red plastic-covered editions printed in the People's Republic of China and distributed by its agents with missionary zeal. Mine was a version published by Seuil and printed at Bussière Saint-Amand (Cher) in the depths of rural France: *Citations du président Mao Tsé-Toung*. It was not quite as cool as having the genuine Chinese article. But hey! As far as I knew, nobody else at school owned a copy of the little red book in any edition whatsoever. And the fact that it came from the Cher seemed somehow significant. The Cher was the country of *Le Grand Meaulnes*. I had already seen the film twice. It had been released less than a month earlier.

The other day, while going through old papers that I thought might be useful to me as I began to write Janice Day's story, I found the little red book I bought that October day. From its shiny cover the visionary icon of Mao still, even in 2008, gazed out at some elusive distant object. Tucked inside the book I found one of my old lists, the one I made the day I became a Man of the Left. As I read the names each face came to life. I caught the scent of Jan's perfume and watched autumn leaves falling and swirling in little wind-blown eddies across the shifting mosaic of my world…

You watch the light catch loose strands of Jan's hair and break into rainbows. The autumn wind caresses them, frolics with them like a lover careless of time. The guitar is balanced on her thigh. Her right breast rests gently in the curve on top of the guitar. She has stuck the peace symbol, the white dove's foot, on the wood of her instrument.

Jan sings 'Puff the Magic Dragon'. Some join her in singing. Brad Barton, who comes from Detroit and plays basketball with the senior team, sits on the step beside Jan. He says, "Damn fine song." You wish you could say "damn fine song" the way Brad does. You wish you could play the guitar and sing.

All your Big Five are there: Polly Page and Eva-Maria Bocardo-Griffin sit on the step below Jan. Marie-Claire Dufraisse, who has begun her moves to the centre of the circle, stands beside them. Johnny Morris holds Sally Pinkerton's hand. Then there is Sammy Blum, awkward, cadaverously pale, and thin. He lost thirty-two close relatives at Auschwitz and Treblinka. He stands beside Jean-Louis Alteschläuche and Edward Reader.[7] Both their fathers are senior diplomats at the United Nations.

Joshua Fulton has inserted himself in the space between Melanie Mudford, whose family skis with J.K. Galbraith in Gstaad, and Ramona Jimenez, whose family left Cuba with Batista, Lansky and a large pile of cash that is said now to be dwindling ominously. They pretend to ignore him.

Elizabeth Merrifield-Hayes, whose father admires Bernie Cornfeld, is there. She is standing by Kathy O'Neil. Kathy has only just arrived in Geneva and a rumour has begun to circulate that her father is a spy. You know all about it because you were party to making up the story from fragments of an overheard conversation: Iran at the time of the coup against Mossadeq; Cairo when the Suez Canal was nationalised; Berlin when the Wall was built in 1961; and in Berlin again this past summer, apparently in

---

[7] Edward Reader (1950–) could not have been present in Geneva in October 1967. He had moved from Geneva to Bonn, with his family, in July 1967. By October 1967, he was in the lower sixth at a boarding school in England. This error gives reason to cast doubt on the claim that this list is drawn from contemporaneous notes. – Ed.

his old friend the Shah of Iran's entourage, when a German student was shot dead.[8] *Kathy is a dull, moody girl, young for her years, but your rumour has given her a patina of reflected glamour. Spies are definitely cool.* You and Johnny Morris have read The Spy Who Came In from the Cold *and, using Ecolint identity cards with false birth dates, you've seen* Goldfinger *and* Thunderball *at the cinema.*

From where you stand on the outer edge of the circle, you notice that the pale-blue plectrum with which Jan strums her guitar matches the colour of her eyes. Both match the colour of the autumn sky. You notice that Johnny's hand has moved onto Sally's thigh and that she has not resisted. You notice Brad Barton looking at Marie-Claire with a look you cannot yet identify...

The school bell rings to signal the end of morning break. Obedient to its call, you scuttle away to double biology, stumbling up the steps. Jan ignores the summons to class and begins another song.

> There is a house in New Orleans
> They call the Rising Sun.
> It's been the ruin of many poor girl,
> I know, oh Lord, I'm one.

Some go with you up the stairs of the Greek Theatre to their books and their allotted classes. You hear her voice as you go.

> O mother, tell your children
> Not to do as I have done
> Spend your days in sin and misery
> In the House of the Rising Sun.

During that October half-term, when Sally was in Rome with her parents, Johnny and I returned to the ruins at Rouëlbeau. We found three tents pitched in our clearing and a group of boy scouts – *éclaireurs suisses* – oblivious to Oscar and his gang and to the ghost on the battlements – meticulously preparing their campfire beside a pole from which their pennant flapped. We stood, unseen, in the

---

[8] Benno Ohnesorg was shot at close range during a Berlin demonstration against the Shah on 2 June 1967 by Detective Sergeant Karl-Heinz Kurras of the West German Political Police. Benno Ohnesorg was a religious pacifist taking part in a demonstration for the first time. The date 2 June 1967 marked a change in the political thinking of many Germans. Many on the radical left looked back to that date as the one that set them off on their 'struggle against reality'. – Ed.

shadows of the trees, a wind blowing in from the lake through the paper-dry leaves covering any sound we might have made. For a couple of minutes we watched the interlopers. Then we left.

As we travelled back to Johnny's house, it occurred to me that we would probably never together return to Rouëlbeau, for time moves relentlessly onwards in one direction only; that the domain among the trees was no longer ours; that the barbarians had breached the walls and planted a strange flag on the ancient tower; that Rouëlbeau was itself without history and without future; that it was a mere palimpsest on which each successive generation wrote a small portion of its private story, working out in draft its hopes and dreams and fears, oblivious to those who had gone before and to the scribes who would follow and write a different tale. Only the ghost Johnny still insisted I had seen remained. Or perhaps, he said later, it was an angel. Or maybe just the play of moonlight among the trees. But it most certainly was not Janice Day.

> *The castles now in ruin lie,*
> *Alien flags from towers fly,*
> *Captured widows mourn and cry,*
> *Rememb'ring us in dreams.*[9]

I saw less and less of Johnny and felt the loss keenly. Oscar Meyer had, however, been sent to a boarding school renowned for its austere discipline and had not returned to Geneva after his summer in California. With Oscar out of the way and Johnny increasingly occupied with Sally Pinkerton, I began, warily at first, to spend more time with Claude again. Neither of us ever mentioned Rouëlbeau. I spent a cold weekend with him at the Meyers' old wooden chalet at Les Sornettes, in an isolated meadow near the railway line that runs up from Montreux to the Rochers de Naye and, in due course, I would be invited to the new mountain home among the ski fields of Crans-Montana. But I was not invited to go to La Bise again. I would see Christian Meyer's château in the Champagne and stay at the beach house in Malibu before I was able to return to that enchanted domain by the lake.

Oh, I saw La Bise from afar during those years after we had

---

[9] These lines are from Adam Heggie's 'Samson Hedonistes' in *Posthumous Poems* (London, 2004). – Ed.

outgrown spying on it from Johnny's tree. Once, I saw the house from the evening deck of a lake steamer making its way north up the lake. The electric lights of the house blazed with pre-climate-change exuberance and I fancied I heard the sounds of genteel party music drifting towards me across the waters. But it was neither the brilliance of the lights nor the imagined tinkling of piano keys and crystal flutes that made me certain that the place passing by on the dark shore was La Bise. It was the solitary green light, suspended in the night below the house. That was unmistakeably the light that stood low on the lakeward end of the Meyers' private dock.

5

In the closing months of 1967, I began to assemble the wardrobe of a foot-soldier of the New Left; new clothes designed to carry me to the centre of the crowd, to the place where Jan sang songs from New Orleans and the boy from Detroit could confidently pronounce 'Puff the Magic Dragon' to be a "damn fine song".

A few months earlier, during the Six Day War, I had gone with a group of schoolmates to give blood at a Jewish centre in town. By Christmas, I was a fervent Palestinian complete with a black-and-white *keffiyeh* just like Yasser Arafat's. I replaced my Swiss-made jeans with a pair of genuine Levi's. I let my hair grow. I could quote Mao Tse-Tung (in French). On my bedroom wall I hung a poster of Che Guevara, recently martyred in Bolivia by auxiliaries of the CIA's Special Activities Division. I cut a two-metre length from a roll of wallpaper and painted the seven letters of *'LIBERTÉ'* on it in bright red – the colour of fresh blood. I hung the sign on the wall above my bed. I could have written my banner in English: 'LIBERTY' and 'FREEDOM' also have the requisite seven letters. But the 'É' at the end of *'Liberté'*, with its three prongs and its *accent aigu*, held greater appeal, openly pointing, as they do, into the free unwritten future and standing ready to embrace it.

As I fell asleep that first night beneath my new banner, Liberty became a woman. The woman had frosted blonde hair and a dimpled smile that spoke to me more eloquently than my seven red letters. She sat on the far bank of a river. A guitar was balanced on her thigh and its trembling strings beckoned me to cross over into the Promised Land.

My father lived in the quiet zone of one who had lost his faith but kept his Party membership card. He kept, too – loved and cherished – his library. There, among the yellowed classics – Feuerbach, Marx, Engels, Lenin, Shaw… – I found bright copies of Herbert Marcuse, Ivan Illich and Wilhelm Reich[10]. I read voraciously and kept a list of the books I devoured. I read *Moby Dick*, *Steppenwolf* and *The Great Gatsby*. After reading Sigmund Freud's *On Dreams* I began to keep my own dream diary. The first entry is dated 19 December 1967. In that dream I was in Rouëlbeau again, but alone this time, without Johnny. The lady in white moved along the ruined ramparts, flitting between one realm of unreality and another. I wanted to go to her, to touch her, to follow wherever she might lead, but Oscar and his golems pinned me to the ground and my screams were stifled by a handful of dust.

One cold January day, I joined a protest march against the American war in Vietnam and, when I had tired of chanting "Ho, Ho, Ho Chi Minh", I stumbled into the Landolt. At the wooden table where Lenin himself had once sat, I found Marie-Claire. Her Parisian boyfriend, who, as I would shortly point out, had *not* just taken part in the demonstration, was expounding the reasons for Lenin's 1903 rupture with the Mensheviks. In the argument that followed I demonstrated to my own satisfaction that I was more informed, more radical and far harder than Marie-Claire's boyfriend. I also established, beyond reasonable doubt, that he was not at all the Left Bank student he claimed to be. His was one of those campuses known by number rather than name and he lived, despite his reputation as the scion of a noble French family, in a single-sex dormitory out among the *bidonvilles* of Nanterre.

When it was clear that I had won the argument, I told a story drawn from the protest march. I laughed at myself showing a policeman a fake Ecolint ID card, the one that had got me into cinemas to see prohibited films. It was, I said, the one with the face of a monkey where mine should have been. I took it from my pocket and passed it round the table.

Marie-Claire held out a finger and touched my lips. "I like the way you tell a story, Nick," she said as she put on her coat and Jean-Daniel led her towards the door, still his captive. I had marched in

[10] See, for example, E. Reader, 'Foundations of New Left Thought' in H.A. Frankland and F. Honeychurch (eds.) *250 Years of German Political Theory* (Oxford and Berlin, 1993). – Ed.

the cold. I had told a good story. I had won the argument. My shoulders sagged as I watched them go. Marie-Claire's liberation would have to wait for another day.

Politics became my lifeblood. I cheered the newscaster when Alexander Dubček was elected leader of the Czechoslovak Communist Party and spring came early to the politics of Prague. My pulse quickened when news filtered through that US troops had massacred civilians at My Lai because the accompanying polls showed US public opinion turning against the war. When Lyndon Johnson decided he did not want to be president any longer, I ordered a bottle of champagne to be brought to us at Lenin's table in the Landolt. Although I did not notice it at the time, and I doubt that Janice Day or any of my contemporaries in Geneva noticed it either, Andreas Baader and Gudrun Ensslin planted a firebomb in a wardrobe in a Frankfurt department store.[11] It was intended, following a pamphlet published in Berlin, as their protest against the war in Vietnam.[12] They were arrested for arson. The teenagers drinking champagne in the Landolt were not yet ready for that sort of thing.

4 April 1968 – Martin Luther King is assassinated at a Memphis motel.

11 April 1968 – Rudi Dutschke, student leader of the left-wing German extra-parliamentary opposition, survives an assassination attempt.

23 April 1968 – Columbia University is shut down by anti-war protesters. There is at least one Ecolint alumnus among the leaders of the peace movement there.

27 April 1968 – In Nanterre, Daniel Cohn-Bendit is arrested for publishing a recipe for Molotov cocktails.

---

[11] Kaufhaus Schneider; 2 April 1968. – Ed.

[12] Several leaflets on the same theme were published by members of Kommune 1 in Berlin following a fire in a Brussels department store on 22 May 1967 in which some 300 people died. The first leaflet was entitled 'New kind of demonstration tried out in Brussels for the first time'; the second 'Why do you burn, consumer?'; and the third 'When will the Berlin department stores burn?' Kommune 1 was probably the most notorious of the New Left communes in Berlin in the late sixties, famous for such well-publicised actions as removing the doors from the communal toilets. Its prominence in the public mind rose noticeably when Uschi Obermaier, sex symbol extraordinaire, moved in. Ed.

10/11 May 1968 – Paris: the Night of the Barricades. Students on the Left Bank, *lycée* students – kids our age! – prominent among them, build barricades from trees they have chopped down and cars they have overturned. They throw petrol bombs and cobblestones at the riot police. Marie-Claire is there. She has smuggled herself to Paris to be with Jean-Daniel. With skirts swirling and a wine bottle in her hand, she stands on her barricade, throws back her head and laughs. Captured in a black-and-white photograph, Marie-Claire becomes one of the iconic images of *Les Années '68* – the one later to be captioned *'Le Temps des Cerises'* and sold as a poster in Athena.

12 May 1968 – I decide I must travel to Paris. Because public transport is not functioning in France, I plan to hitch-hike. My father forbids it. My O levels loom. I say that from now on O levels won't matter and quote Mao Tse-Tung. My father smiles indulgently. I make do with a clandestine visit to Annemasse. I take the number twelve tram to the end of the line and walk across the unguarded border.

3 June 1968 – After school, over a glass of Fendant in the shade of the great plane tree in the garden at the Auberge in Grange-Canal, I analyse the French student movement, expound a list of its strengths and weaknesses. Janice Day plays her guitar and sings 'Love Is Just a Four-Letter Word'.

5 June 1968 – Bobby Kennedy is assassinated.

20 June 1968 – Marie-Claire's father – a veteran of Verdun, who made his fortune in the teeth of Algerian adversity – takes fright at events in his native land and moves from Divonne across the border into Switzerland. The new villa is on the lakeshore beyond Nyon. Its basement – apart from the compulsory bomb shelter which Madame Dufraisse will dutifully keep well-stocked – will be devoted to housing Monsieur Dufraisse's gun collection.

27 July 1968 – Marie-Claire phones. She is not spending the summer in the South of France this year. Her mother wants to settle into their new home and her father has bought a boat to complete the establishment on the lake. She and Jean-Daniel are taking it out for the day. Would I like to come and bring a friend? I phone Jan. I try to speak slowly, avoid the tremble in my hand from communicating itself down the telephone wires. To my enormous surprise she agrees to come with us.

28 July 1968 – A day sailing on Lake Geneva with Jan. Marie-Claire's mother packs a lunch for us to take. Jan brings enough marijuana to stone an elephant and says to call her 'Juana' and to call Marie-Claire 'Mari'.

We sail toward La Bise and see Claude and Paul Meyer in their dinghy in the middle of the lake. "Oscar," says Jan, "comes home tomorrow. He's been walking somewhere in the mountains with his dad." I watch, unable to move my limbs or shift my gaze, as Jan unbuttons her shirt, takes it off and throws it casually onto the deck. She unzips her shorts and pushes them down her thighs. Underneath, she wears a light-blue bikini that comes loose as she dives into the water. After a few seconds I gather myself together and dive in after her. Jan is a stronger swimmer than I am. I resolve to improve my swimming.

In the early evening, as I leave Jan at Rive where she gets the bus home, she says, "Whatever you do, don't tell my mom we went sailing. It's the one thing I'm, like, not allowed to do." I return to Eaux-Vives, walking several inches above the surface of the pavement, basking in the lingering glow of a perfect day on the water. Later, I wonder why Jan's mother would forbid her to go sailing, wonder whether I should classify the entire day as a dream and duly assign it a number.

3 August 1968 – We leave for a fortnight's family holiday in Italy. I spend a considerable amount of time swimming in the Adriatic.

20 August 1968 –Winter comes early to the politics of Prague. Blaming the Jews for the inclement weather, Russian tanks invade Czechoslovakia. I have a long discussion with my father about Soviet foreign policy. He disagrees with my thesis that students are now the vanguard of the working class.

22–30 August 1968 – The police brutally break up peace demonstrations at the Democratic National Convention in Chicago. Hubert Humphrey, the candidate of the establishment, a running dog of the imperialists, the incarnate continuation of LBJ's war mongering, emerges as the Democrat's standard bearer for the presidential election.

3 September 1968 – Monsieur Dufraisse's collection of guns arrives at his new villa on the lake. It has taken more than a month to ensure each piece is properly disabled and then to clear Swiss customs. The month of delay was the month of August, when not even the bullets of Monsieur Dufraisse's staccato machine-gun voice could stir the slumbering blood of vacationing functionaries.

4 September 1968 – Claude and Paul Meyer and I help Marie-Claire and her father unpack the guns. Each is wrapped in protective swaddling cloths. "Like baby Jesus," the old man says. There must be more than a hundred guns. There's even a Maxim Gun that saw action in the Zulu Wars in the collection. I quote Hilaire Belloc: *'Whatever happens we have got / The Maxim Gun, and they have not.'*

"Ah, mon petit Nicolas," says Dufraisse, pausing in the assembly process. "Therein lies the difference. Now what has happened is *they* have the guns and *we* must disable ours."

We leave him among the machine gun's scattered parts, cradling one of his baby saviours, a Nagant M1895 revolver that allegedly once belonged to Nikolai Yezhov, whoever he was. When he is out of sight we smile at the idea of a white-haired septuagenarian on the barricades brandishing his Kalashnikov as he waves his fellow pensioners forward. Claude gives his cousin, Marie-Claire, a light tap on the bottom.

28 September 1968 – My seventeenth birthday. Johnny Morris and Sally Pinkerton buy me a joint present. I can no longer remember what it was, only that the card attached to it was signed by both of them. I think I still have that card somewhere. After school Johnny shows me a photograph he has developed in his father's darkroom. It is a full frontal picture of Sally Pinkerton in the nude.

2 October 1968 – The Tlatelolco Massacre. In the Plaza de las Tres Culturas in Mexico City, government gunmen kill students and other civilian protesters. The official death toll is twenty-five. In reality, more than ten times that number have been murdered. The Mexican authorities are particularly keen to keep down the numbers of those officially dead because the Olympics are about to open in Mexico City.

10 October 1968 – The Detroit Tigers win the World Series. The next day – when Edward Reader's nasal whine insists that America's national baseball championship has no right to the title 'World', that they should at least let Cuba compete and that Fidel Castro is a first-class baseball player – Brad Barton lands a left hook to the side of Edward's head, breaking his jaw and knocking him momentarily unconscious.[13] Brad Barton is suspended from school for a week.

When Brad returns he claims that, during his week away, he has

---

[13] Since Edward Reader had left Ecolint over a year earlier, this event is, *prima facie*, unlikely to have really happened. See A. Petzke and B. Schmendrick, *The Wishing Well: Memory, Imagination, Dream and Wish Fulfilment in the Construction of Fictional Narrative*, New York, 1966. – Ed.

laid three girls: the daughter of his parents' Spanish housemaid, the English au pair in the house next door and Janice Day. "One week; three women; three countries," he says. Few fully believe his boast.

14 October 1968 – The American government announces that 24,000 soldiers are to be sent back to Vietnam for involuntary second tours of duty in the theatre of war.

16 October 1968 – American Tommie Smith sets a new world record for 200 metres at the Mexico City Olympics. White Australian Peter Norman takes the silver medal and American John Carlos the bronze. On the podium at the medal ceremony, the two Americans raise their gloved fists in the Black Power salute. Peter Norman stands by them wearing the badge of the Olympic Project for Human Rights. The two Americans are expelled from the Olympic Games at the insistence of Avery Brundage, President of the International Olympic Committee.

Sammy Blum, who has never before been known to comment on current events, says that Avery Brundage is a Nazi. 'Nazi' is, for us, still a term that has specific reference rather than just the all-purpose insult it is soon to become. So Sammy backs up his accusation with tales from the 1936 Berlin Olympics. But his stories are so boringly told that anyone who might have listened has drifted away long before he reaches any conclusion.

18 October 1968 – At the Auberge, I eloquently argue that, with a choice between Humphrey and Nixon, Americans have been deprived of any real opportunity for change at the next election and hence deprived of their democratic rights; that, as a consequence, direct action, violent if necessary, has become totally legitimate. Jan asks, "Nick, have you ever been to the States?"

I say, "No."

"Then," she says, "shut your mouth. It talks like a hooker's cunt."

6

I don't think I spoke to Jan again that school year. It was her last, her senior, year at Ecolint. Twelfth grade. At the end of the year, the Americans, and those who had yoked their academic destinies to the American college system, would disperse to campuses across the United States. The rest of us would stay behind for another year – our schoolboy noses, theoretically, deep in our A level textbooks.

It seemed to me that, in her mind, Jan had already gone. She spent the minimum time possible at school that year – arriving slowly, departing quickly. She never brought her guitar, never sang, rarely spoke. If she still played her guitar she played it for other audiences, in other theatres. From time to time I heard whispered third-hand tales of those midnight places, listened intently to what was said to have happened there. The first dark stirrings of the Janice Day legend.

Three or four times I saw Jan around Geneva, away from school. In August, a day or two before she left for college in Illinois, I saw her standing alone leaning against the railings by the lake. She was wearing a red t-shirt. The words 'Eat Forbidden Fruits' were spread across her breasts; across her back, 'Class of '69'.

Her gaze was fixed on the water and I don't think she saw me. I walked by and did not stop. My fingers were entwined with those of the girl I was walking with. As my eyes rested just for a moment on Jan's red shirt, I felt Kathy O'Neil's gentle tug on my hand.

It was Kathy's idea that we go to her flat in La Gradelle. Her parents would both be out, she said. We took our shoes off at the door and stepped barefoot onto the Persian rugs that covered the parquet floor. "My dad," Kathy explained, "brings them back from the Middle East. He spends most of his time in Iran."

Kathy showed me the rug in her bedroom – classic Bokhara pattern, she commented, made on a traditional loom by Uzbek tribeswomen. There were three Persian rugs on the floor of her parents' bedroom, all woven of pure silk, with some enormous number of knots per square inch. A hand-embroidered Afghan bedspread covered her parents' bed. An elongated nude, in provocative pose and coarse wooden frame, hung on the wall above the bed: "My mom," Kathy said. Translucent alabaster urns filled a cedar cabinet in the living room.

Kathy put the soundtrack from *The Graduate* onto the turntable and lowered the needle. Sitting on the sofa listening to 'The Sounds of Silence', I put an arm around Kathy's shoulders and imagined myself in Ali Baba's capitalist den of spies and thieves. The Inevitable Revolution would put an end to all this; but in the meantime…

Kathy heard the noise before I did. She was off the sofa and out of the room before the key turned in the lock and the front door opened.

"Hello, Mrs O'Neil," I said.

"Nick! Hi! What a nice surprise. Is Kathy here?"

"She's in her room getting changed."

"Maybe you could help me bring the groceries up while you're waiting."

We went down to the underground garage in the lift together. As she unlocked her car, Mrs O'Neil said, "I hear you're the smartest kid in the school. A regular genius at math." I didn't respond, didn't know what I was meant to say. She handed me two Migros bags. With my arms immobilised by her groceries, she looked me in the eye and ran a fingernail along the ridge of my nose. "And so handsome with it. A powerful – dangerous – combination." The finger moved from the tip of my nose to my mouth and lingered there. "Such erotic lips. Such... You have witchcraft in your lips, Nick."

Mrs O'Neil was dressed like a bee: a black-and-yellow striped shirt and black shorts so short that, when she bent into the car boot to lift out another shopping bag, they revealed the crease between her buttocks and the tops of her thighs. "Be careful how you spend your capital, kiddo," she said as she handed me a third bag. "Kathy's still a virgin, you know. She's not on the pill and she's only just turned sixteen."

Kathy's mother and I shared a birthday. I was a month short of my eighteenth and Karen O'Neil a month from her thirty-ninth. Well before the celebrations, however, Kathy and I had broken up. Her parents, she said, had insisted. "My dad found out you and your family were communists."

In September, a letter and two books in a brown paper parcel arrived from the United States. Johnny's letter was long, full of the thrills of America, his new life as a college student and... "Guess who was on the plane to New York. Janice Day! We sat together. She slept most of the way. Head on my shoulder."

The books were *Mere Christianity* by C. S. Lewis and *Escape from Reason* by Francis Schaeffer. Johnny and Sally had spent a week at Schaeffer's commune near Villars earlier in the summer. From his armchair across the room, my father asked, "What's that you're reading, Nick?"

"Some stuff Johnny sent me."

"Johnny Morris?"

"Yeah."

"Johnny never struck me as religious."

"He seems to be going that way."

"Just remember you've got exams coming up."

"Yeah."

In October, I went for long weekend with Claude Meyer to the chalet at Les Sornettes. In November I sat my Oxford entrance exams. In December, I went to Oxford for interviews. In January, Claude invited me up to the family chalet in Crans-Montana for the last week of the Christmas holidays.

Paul, his younger brother, was also there with a friend. Christina Meyer was there. Christian himself, the *pater familias*, was away – in Bonn attending a government meeting on the flow of Jewish funds out of Germany in Nazi times. There was no sign of Oscar.

After I had been in Crans two days, Marie-Claire arrived. She came and went as she pleased, Claude said; always welcome because she was his father's favourite god-daughter, the much-indulged daughter he'd never had.

This January, to the Meyers' evident discomfort, Marie-Claire came with her Parisian boyfriend and moved with him into her usual room on the other side of the thin wall from the room Claude and I were sharing. Jean-Daniel skied badly and, after a day on the slopes with him, Marie-Claire consigned him to ski school and skied with Claude and me. Skiing with Marie-Claire was a joy. To stand at the top of a slope as Marie-Claire skied down in front, perfectly holding her line, her tidy little bottom wiggling rhythmically from side to side around it…

At night, after Claude had fallen asleep, I lay in my bed, hard against the partition wall, holding my breath as I listened to the sounds coming through from an imagined future on the other side.

When I arrived home from the mountains, the letter from Oxford was waiting for me. It offered me a place to read Mathematics and Philosophy starting in the Michaelmas Term of 1970.

My mother kissed me on the cheek, which she had not done for years, and whispered, more to herself than to me, "The flower of British youth, Nick. You'll be with the flower of British youth."

My father set his pipe down in its ashtray, laid his hand on my shoulder and said, "Well done, old chap."

I was more than ready to go. The Auberge and the Landolt were being colonised by a younger generation. Most of my friends were already gone – most of them to the United States. The mountains, the wall of the Jura to the north and the teeth of the Alps to the south, once the beautiful frame around paradise, now only served to hem me in. News of the world beyond came through *The Herald Tribune* and letters from Johnny Morris.

6 March 1970 – A bomb being built by members of the Students for a Democratic Society explodes prematurely in a house in Greenwich Village. Three of the prospective bombers die. Two escape.

17 March 1970 – Peace movement tactics force the US Army to charge some of its own officers with suppressing information about the massacre they carried out at My Lai in Vietnam.

12 April 1970 – A former Ecolint student tells me in hushed tones, as we sit among the flowers on a bench by the Duke of Brunswick's monument, of a plot to bomb federal buildings across the US. Only weeks later do I understand that his references to 'weathermen' had nothing to do with conventional meteorology.

22 April 1970 – The hundredth anniversary of Lenin's birth. I pay my awkward respects (with two others) to the plaque on the house where he (*'Fondateur de l'Union Sovietique'*) once lived.

29 April 1970 – The United States invades Cambodia.

4 May 1970 – At Kent State University in Ohio, the National Guard fire on students demonstrating against the invasion of Cambodia. Four die.

6 May 1970 – Eva Bocardo is photographed topless on a campus in California. In her left hand she holds a burning bra; in her right, her boyfriend's burning draft card. Eva's amply endowed chest ensures wide circulation of the picture. Eva is charged with obscenity, is threatened with deportation from the United States as an undesirable alien. She tells the press that she once slept with the police officer who arrested her.

8 May 1970 – Manhattan construction workers attack students in New York who are protesting against the killings in Ohio.

9 May 1970 – Claude and I go to Les Sornettes for another long weekend. We clear the cobwebs that have formed over the winter and open shutters and windows to let the sunlight in and purge the smell of damp. We run the Swiss flag up the flagpole. By tradition, it flies whenever a Meyer is in residence.

By day we stride through narcissus meadows and climb to heights where the snows have not yet melted. In the evening we rest our mountain-weary limbs by a big log fire in the hearth and drink wine that comes from the vineyards on the terraced slopes stretching down to the placid lake below. As the embers die, Claude tells me the stories Oscar used to tell him and Paul when they shared a room here, before the new chalet in Crans-Montana was built and claimed first place in the family's affections. Tales of robbers and murderers and vampire madmen desperate to slake their thirst with fresh blood from the slit throats of little boys. More than once, Claude says, Paul crept out of the room to seek the security of his parents' bed and refused to look at Oscar the next morning. We laugh and Claude fills our glasses with kirsch because the wine bottle is empty.

14 May 1970 – In Jackson, Mississippi, police fire on students protesting against the American War in Vietnam and Cambodia. Two die.[14]

21 May 1970 – Weather Underground issues a communiqué saying it will attack a symbol of American injustice within two weeks.

27 May 1970 – Pictures of Eva Bocardo in the nude appear in *Playboy*.

9 June 1970 – Weather Underground bombs a New York police station.

In the spring of 1970, I began to spend time with Elizabeth Merrifield-Hayes and through her I met her father. Lizzie was beginning to market herself as a socialist intellectual and no doubt thought it would enhance her brand if she associated it with mine. We went to tiny unknown cinemas together to watch avant-garde films. I followed Lizzie when she walked out midway through a tedious play by Samuel Beckett. When we were alone all that happened was that we spoke in French.

Lizzie came frequently to our apartment for supper. We spoke of how the rich were growing richer and the poor becoming poorer. My father said the only remedy was a strong socialist government imposing a highly progressive tax structure and strongly redistributive policies.

Equally often, I supped *chez* Merrifield-Hayes, only a few streets away, but with an expansive sitting room that overlooked the lake

---

[14] On the same day, in West Germany, Andreas Baader escaped from custody. He was assisted by Ulrike Meinhof, who had arranged a meeting with him at a site away from his prison. Both Andreas Baader and Ulrike Meinhof went underground from that point. The legend of the Baader-Meinhof gang was born. – Ed.

and genuine oil paintings, instead of prints, on the walls. We spoke of how the rich were growing richer and the poor becoming poorer. Clive Merrifield-Hayes said the best approach to ensuring one was on the right side of this equation was to manage the wealth of the rich, charge them 1%, or more where you could get away with it, make money for yourself whether markets went up or down. "You humbly pick up these little scraps from the masters' tables," he said, "and hey presto: suddenly you're investing your own funds alongside theirs."

Bernie Cornfeld was his hero. The IOS Fund of Funds was, he said, a stroke of genius. Bernie had seen a market niche and had exploited it brilliantly on the back of acute jurisdictional arbitrage. From his origins as a poor immigrant boy in the slums of Brooklyn, he had become one of the richest men in the world. The salesmen at the top of his pyramid were also becoming seriously rich. And Bernie's investors, Clive Merrifield-Hayes said, were doing famously.

- "It's marvellous the way he delivers constant and consistently high returns. Exactly what investors want. They don't like things going up and down, out of control all over the shop. I suppose that, very occasionally, he might have to borrow just a little from new investors to ensure the faithful established investors continue to make their return, what? But it's all for the greater good, of course."
- "Bernie once told me he was a socialist when he was young. They say – don't they – if you're not a socialist at the age of twenty you have no heart, if you're not a father at the age of thirty you have no balls, if you're not a capitalist at the age of forty you have no brains and if you're not rich at the age of fifty you're a fool."
- "He has this marvellous château. You know the sort of place the hoi-polloi visit on coach tours, what? Except Bernie has *his* place all to himself. And his girls, of course. And his friends. He has oodles of friends. Knows everyone."
- "He's shacked up with this absolutely gorgeous little thing. Can't be any older than you and Lizzie. Bernie born in Turkey and this little doll born in Japan, he tells me. All very cosmopolitan, what?"
- "Money maketh the man."

"Manners," corrected Lizzie.
"What?"

"It's 'Manners maketh man' not 'money'."

Clive Merrifield-Hayes clamped his jaw and furrowed his brow. "No," he said. "I disagree. The Wykehamists got it wrong. Take half a man's money away from him and you reduce him to a snivelling dwarf. A homunculus. Take all his wealth away and you destroy him utterly. Manners and all."

Bernie Cornfeld was near the end of his reign. In May 1970, he was ousted from Investors Overseas. Rumours of fraud began to circulate. Legal charges followed. Clive Merrifield-Hayes, however, remained faithful. He was one of the few who still believed in the Cornfeld magic, who continued to be in contact with the man when the money began to ebb away and the good-time friends disowned him. He even visited his fallen idol in St Antoine prison.

When my mother had to go to England – to take care of her mother who had had a small stroke, fallen and broken her hip – Lizzie came round even more often. Sometimes she cooked our dinner. Afterwards my father would abandon his evening pipe and guide her through dog-eared volumes in his book collection. I think he was falling in love with Lizzie's puppy-dog looks, her soft, brown eyes, her big-lipped mouth that curled downwards at the corners, her eagerness to look at books yellowed with years and tobacco stains. Once I saw my old-fashioned socialist father put his hand gently on her studious shoulder and then withdraw it again almost immediately, apparently surprised at what he had done. Years later, when Lizzie published her *magnum opus* on the Durham coal field, Alfred Kellaway was mentioned prominently in the acknowledgements. Dad, however, was dead by then. And by the time I'd banked my first million, Clive Merrifield-Hayes was dead too.

In the early summer I saw Janice Day again. It was the day I sat my last A level paper. I believed I had done exceptionally well and skipped out of the examination room feeling lighter than a helium balloon.

I went to the Auberge to see whether any friends were there to celebrate with me and found Jan sitting alone at a table, a carafe of white wine and single glass before her. I sat without requesting permission and offered her a cigarette.

"You still smoking these commie black sticks?" she asked, taking one. I lit her cigarette for her. She sucked in the smoke, blew a smoke ring as she exhaled.

"How's college?" I asked.

"Good." She was looking at something in the middle distance over my right shoulder.

"I'm going to the States for a month."

"Yeah. I heard. With Claude, right?"

"Yeah."

She blew another smoke ring. It held its shape as it drifted upwards. A perfect zero. "You'll enjoy it. It'll be good for you," she said. "Who knows, you might even get yourself laid."

CHAPTER THREE

"Bloody hot in here," said the sweating suit as he plonked his large posterior onto the seat beside me. The breath that propelled his words towards me smelled of lunchtime wine and a diseased gullet. When a disembodied voice announced that the flight to Geneva was to be delayed for a further forty-five minutes a collective groan rose from the waiting crowd. I watched my fellow passengers loosen their ties and fan their damp faces with folded copies of *The Times*. The fat man turned awkwardly towards me and spluttered, "Typical."

I smiled the smile of a foreigner ignorant of the conventions of English weatherspeak and fraternal moaning. Then, from behind my protective copy of *Le Monde*, I returned to the world that I had left only two hours earlier. From the vantage point of that Heathrow departure lounge, I weighed the past nine months and concluded that, on balance, I had had a very good first year among the flower of British youth.

I had joined the Humanist Society, the Nietzsche Society, the Labour Party and the Oxford Revolutionary Socialist Students. I had hung a banner from my window commemorating the hundredth anniversary of the Paris Commune, found a recording of 'Le Temps des Cerises'[15] and broadcast it out across the quad at full volume. A photograph of my banner had appeared in *Cherwell*. I had organised an anti-war demonstration, spoken twice at the Union, rowed in the college's third boat in Eights' Week, made new friends and impressed my tutors.

For the first time in my life, people (at least two) referred to me as 'cool'. So cool was I that MI5 had even tried to recruit me. Or so I gently let it be understood among those who manned the reputation

---

[15] *'Le Temps des Cerises'* ('The Season of Cherries') is a song written in 1866 by Jean-Baptiste Clément and set to music by Antoine Renard. The song is irrevocably linked to the Paris Commune of 1871 and became – with its overtones of nostalgia for an era of liberty, joyful solidarity and resistance to the forces of the Right – one of the most captivating and enduring anthems of the French Left. It was sung at the Place de la Bastille memorial service for President Mitterand in 1996. – Ed.

mills. I thought the rumour had a certain ring of probability about it. It matched my marginally exotic Geneva persona and chimed with my stories. I told of a meeting at the Café de l'Horloge with a mysterious Russian woman who wore a Blancpain watch and mistook me briefly for an undercover compatriot. Another time I wove a tale around clandestine conversations under the Passage Malbuisson clock among white men in dark suits. The conversations had taken place at the time of the Biafra War and they were discussing the profitability of 'the Africa trade'. They fell into a guilty silence when they realised I was eavesdropping. It was all so much more sophisticated than campfires and ghosts at Rouëlbeau, a first cigarette at the Auberge de Grange-Canal and a stolen kiss at the far end of the football pitch.

But neither the approach from MI5 nor, of course, my acquaintance with espionage and gun-running among the timekeepers of Geneva was true. Nigel Bickleigh, a fellow first-year undergraduate and university Labour Party member, with impeccable establishment credentials and a face to match, *had* been approached to keep an eye on the more radical elements on the party's left-wing fringes. His job, they told him, would be simply to file occasional reports with London. Despite being a committed heterosexual, Nigel was exactly the type of candidate you would imagine the masters of British espionage trying to seduce. But he declined the honour. As a matter of principle, he apparently said, he would not spy on his friends and fellow citizens. I never actually heard Nigel say he had refused the first rung of a ladder that would have turned him into James Bond; but that was the message the mills of Oxford ground out and he was widely lauded for his stand.

Although only in his first year, people had begun to speak of Nigel Bickleigh as a future cabinet minister; "And – who knows?" Colin Witheridge said with an expansive gesture of his arms as we walked through a mush of sodden leaves, past rubbish bags left to overflow and rot by dustmen on strike, "Maybe even prime minister. He could sort *this* lot out for a start."

So, in order to capture a small share of the praise for myself, I quietly allowed word to get about that Nigel Bickleigh was not the only potential spy to have been targeted by the grey men in London and to have spurned their advances. Then, one evening in The Bear, Colin Witheridge said, "They never asked *me*."

Nigel and I laughed. We had by then only known each other a few weeks. But impressions form quickly and the idea of Colin as a spy seemed utterly absurd. "They'd never take *that* risk," Nigel smiled.

"What d'you mean by that?" Colin asked in tones that left it unclear whether his offence was real or in jest. He set his quickly emptied pint glass on the bar. "It'd be *me* taking the risk."

"You don't know what risk is," Nigel retorted.

We had already, more than once, watched Colin wander with a shrug and an ever-broadening grin into territory where we and the rest of the angelic host would have feared to tread. Yet nobody would have called Colin Witheridge a fool. He had a growing reputation for being fearsomely clever and was said to be destined for a First. He was, moreover, the only person any of us knew who typed his essays rather than scrawling them out longhand. And, as befitted his subject, he had a Russian typewriter as well as an English one.

Although you would never have guessed it from his public-school accent, Colin came from the farthest northern reaches of England – somewhere up near Jennifer's translucent beach. His mother came from even farther north, from Orkney. He had a mop of tousled hair, sparkling blue eyes and an open, freckled face. Perhaps all that, together with his natural ability to charm all but the most taciturn members of the university, was why he acquired the nickname 'Balder'.[16] In accordance with the tenets of correct English behaviour, his intelligence was well hidden: he gave the impression of being a loveable buffoon. From the first time I met him I decided I wanted to spend time with him. Wherever Colin was, laughter promised to be not far away. Once he came to a Labour Party meeting dressed in the green mask of a Hollywood extraterrestrial. An earnest Welshman tried valiantly to thwart the theatrical entrance. "This is the Labour Party not the Fancy Dress Party," he said.

"It's all right, boyo," the green man replied, "I'm a friend of Karl Marx. I'm the alien in alienation."

More conventional minds might have seen in Colin's behaviour a lack of serious commitment to the cause. Colin didn't. To his way of thinking, he could be a stalwart Labour Party member and a Martian simultaneously. It was all just part of the gentle art of being in two places at the same time. Colin believed in God *and* he was an atheist. He was vegetarian *and* a carnivore. "If my dad can be a barrister, a

---

[16] Balder – 'Balder the Beautiful' – son of Odin and Frigg was the best-loved of all the old northern gods. He was the god of the summer sun – a fertility god dying with the season each autumn and rising again each spring. In later years, Emma Somerwell (née Emma Wallace) would claim that she had been the one originally to bestow the name "Balder" on Colin Witheridge. – Ed.

husband, a father, a golfer and a sailor all at the same time, well..."

"But," I protested, "those things your father is, they're compatible. The things you're trying to be at the same time are mutually contradictory."

The big smile spread over Colin's cherubic face. "Don't be so simplistic, Nick. You know that bit in Marx where he says that come the Revolution a bloke can be a hunter, a fisherman and a worker all in the same day? Well, you know, we don't have to wait for the Revolution and the withering of the bloody state. We can just get on with it now. All it takes is a little imagination, a little mental dexterity. Notions like meaning, contradiction, compatibility, integrity, all that sort of stuff... it's just in the petty bourgeois mind, and in your constipated little philosophy books. You don't have to *live* like that. Come on, Nick, you're always on about Liberty: fling it all to the wind and claim your freedom *now*."

He told a story of spending a night with Caroline Carter, then fast becoming the University Labour Party's pin-up girl. The next day a plain girl called Judy rushed in to Colin's room and began to cover Colin's neck with kisses. When she paused for breath, she gasped, "Thank you *so* much, Colin. That was *the* best sex *ever*."

"So? Who was right?" I asked.

"That's the thing. We both were. In Judy's very pedestrian mind I'd screwed her. In mine I'd had a fantastic night with Caroline. It's all about being in two places at the same time."

Well before my first Michaelmas term was out, I realised that impressions were also forming around me. I was becoming, I noticed, something of a curiosity, if not a minor celebrity, among the wide-eyed first-year undergraduates of Oxford. Coming from Geneva bestowed on me a certain cachet that was not granted to the natives of Bolton or Tunbridge Wells. For the first time in my life, being an outsider did not seem to me an entirely bad thing. Paradoxically, it seemed to be my path to the centre of the crowd.

I sat through political meetings, adopting the pose of a visionary with gaze fixed on higher objectives, neither knowing anything of, nor caring anything for, British Labour Party lore. Life in James Maxton House in Keir Hardie Close was unknown to me. My antecedents in the Durham coalfield and holidays in dank Northumberland beach huts failed to convince when set alongside the ability to list, in geographical order from north to south, all the communes of the Côte d'Or between Dijon and Beaune. In fact, I was so New Left and unaccustomed to the ways of my native land that I publicly imagined a trade union to be an English translation of the French *trait d'union* and a trade unionist to be someone with a double-barrelled surname. In pubs, I amused my drinking companions by ordering a blonde or a brunette instead of a lager or a bitter. Colin Witheridge retorted, "Once you've had black, you'll never look back." He left it ambiguous as to whether he was referring to beer or women. Colin was a Guinness drinker; but he also claimed to have magnanimously lost his virginity to a Zulu prostitute in Durban – his contribution, he said, to the noble fight against fascism and apartheid.

As if this New-Left-Swiss-James-Bond exoticism was not enough to see me through the damp Oxford winter nights, I happily embroidered California Dreamin' tales onto the rough, denim fabric of my Greyhound travels in the United States. I spoke of the days Claude and I spent at the Meyers' house on the beach at Malibu; of a commune in Oregon where love was free and marijuana plentiful; of meeting Kathy Boudin, the Weatherman bomber who had gone into hiding, at a safe house in San Francisco.[17] "*Boudin*," I added enigmatically, "is French for blood pudding."

"*Black* pudding," Nigel corrected me. "The correct English term is black pudding."

The meeting with the Kathy Boudin and my nights at the Oregon commune *were* lies. But hey! They fitted within a bigger pattern that was true or, at the very least, was becoming true. I sang 'If you're going to San Francisco', dreamily drawing out the 'a's in 'San Francisco'. Once, when I'd had a little to drink, I even remembered to wear some flowers in my hair.

As I contemplated my first year at Oxford from the departure lounge at Heathrow, however, I was acutely conscious of one aspect

---

[17] Kathy Boudin (1943–) was born and raised in New York City in a Marxist family. During her university years she spent a year (1964–5) studying in the Soviet Union. Following her return to the US, Boudin became an active member of Weather Underground, a left-wing terrorist organisation that carried out attacks on government and corporate targets in the United States. She was one of two survivors of the Greenwich Village explosion on 6 March 1970 when a Weatherman bomb intended for an army base in New Jersey exploded prematurely, killing three would-be bombers. Boudin, who was on bail at the time, disappeared. She resurfaced in 1981 as the driver of the getaway car when a group from Weather Underground and the Black Liberation Army robbed a Brinks armoured vehicle. Boudin was imprisoned for her role in the deaths of a Brinks employee and several policemen who died in the incident. There were also Weatherman casualties in the shoot-outs following the robbery. Boudin was released on parole in 2003 and took a job in an HIV/AIDS clinic. – Ed.

in which I had failed, of one vital garment still missing from my New Left wardrobe. My quest for truth, beauty and goodness had not progressed beyond its platonic phase. Although I would have denied it if asked, I was still a virgin.

Sexual mores were changing in Oxford as elsewhere. In a blatantly meaningless world, virginity and monogamy had become socially inadmissible – and nowhere more so than among the self-appointed vanguard of the Revolution. But Oxford was not Berkeley or Berlin or the Bois de Boulogne. Here the nocturnal voyages of discovery that gave rise to the raft of unverifiable sexfarers' tales still took place behind locked door and drawn curtain. There was, as far as I was aware, only one full-blown, free-love commune in Oxford in the early 1970s. It was in East Oxford – on the site, I think, where the mosque now stands. There they ate nut rissoles and raw vegetables and, by report, copulated like bonobos. They gave the inevitable children Sanskrit names and daubs of red and yellow paint on their pale foreheads. By the time I went up to Oxford, however, the glory days of the Cowley Road establishment were already well in the past. It had fallen under the spiritual directorship of a dominant alpha male who drew up and enforced rotas governing childcare and cleaning the lavatories, cooking, washing up and who could have sex with whom and where and when. He vigorously protected his captive yonis from passing predatory lingams.

Emma Wallace was then in her second year, reading French and German at St Anne's. She used to invite me to dinner in her college and to her room for coffee afterwards in order to speak to me in grammatically impeccable book-French.[18] The walls of her room

---

[18] Emma Jane Featheringham Somerwell (*née* Wallace) (1950–) was born in Paris to expatriate British parents and educated at Cheltenham Ladies' College and the Universities of Oxford and Poitiers. She taught modern languages in English girls' secondary schools from 1974 to 2006. Her publications include *Le Mal, La Mort et Le Néant: The Nihilist Current in French Literature from Baudelaire to Bataille* (1979); *Nietzsche and Postmodernism in Contemporary French Poetry* (1986); *The Phoenix Song: The renaissance of Eros from the ashes of Athene's funeral pyre* (1987); *The Impact of Nietzsche on the Twentieth Century French Novel* (1992); *Roads to Freedom: The Life and Times of Léon-Robert de L'Astran* (1999); *La mort érudite de la veuve Sophie* (with Charles-Henri Bonneville de la Tour de St Jean de Tholome, 2001); *Liberty and Licence: Breaking Nietzsche's Bounds of Freedom* (2002); *The Philosophy of Murder* (2003) and *Jericho House* (2006). Under the pseudonym Jane Featheringham, she contributed the controversial article 'Nietzsche: Nazi or Humanist?' to H.A. Frankland and F. Honeychurch (eds.) *250 Years of German Political Theory* (Oxford and Berlin, 1993). Emma is married to Thomas Percy Somerwell, a merchant banker. They live in London and have four adult children and two grandchildren. – Ed.

were festooned with reproductions of Manet's *Déjeuner sur l'herbe*, Cézanne's *Grandes Baigneuses* and Picasso's *Demoiselles d'Avignon* and with an assortment of provocative posters bearing legends such as '*La libération d'une femme commence par sa libération sexuelle*' and '*La femme est née nue mais partout elle s'est vêtue dans les fers*'. I formed the not unreasonable notion that I might achieve my apotheosis beneath those starry banners.

So, one wet evening, I arrived at St Anne's with a bottle of Beaujolais and a pouch of cannabis I'd bought from a dealer in Jesus. I listened patiently to Emma's discourse on what Marx might have said had he addressed the issue of gender; but the proof of the pudding is in the poking and when it came to translating theory into practice – or *praxis* as Emma insisted on calling it – I was ushered to the door.

It was raining hard as I walked back down the Woodstock Road. I consoled myself with the thought that there were many women in Oxford, many more attractive than Emma Wallace and her Avignon sisterhood and more deserving of my attentions. Neither that thought, however, nor the rain-sodden west wind dampened my ardour. I could have turned right, walked towards Jericho, knocked on the door of the last remaining brothel in Oxford – the only one not yet driven out of business by cut-price competition from the women's colleges. I could have paid for a whore and drowned my virginity in her warm, commercial embraces. I knew the way to Whisky Willie's door and I had enough money in pocket to pay the price he would ask for one of his girls. But I didn't turn. I went on, back to my room. I switched on the electric fire, stripped off my wet clothes, lay naked on the floor and got by with... well, you know... a little help from my hands.

None of this fitted my developing image. Suffice it to say that by the third week of Trinity Term I had abandoned all thought of shedding my virginity in Oxford and pinned my hopes on sunnier climes during the long vac. To that end I began planning a trip to the Greek Islands. Nobody – nobody! – had ever been known to return from the Aegean without getting laid. My travelling companions would be Nigel Bickleigh and Colin Witheridge and we would meet in Athens at the beginning of August. Colin, 'Balder the Beautiful', had no trouble attracting women – if you believed his banter. And they swarmed around Nigel like, as Colin once infelicitously remarked, flies around a pile of horseshit. Even, I reasoned in my gloomier moments, the crumbs from their taverna tables would be enough for me.

As things turned out, I did not have to wait for August in Greece.

2

"And, oh yes," Mum said, "Claude Meyer dropped in yesterday." She turned her face towards me, taking her eyes off the road – the road that leads from the airport, past the United Nations, into town.

"Claude? What did he want?"

"He said he thought you would have been home by now and I told him he was a day too early. He's invited you out to La Bise tomorrow... What do you think of that? He's left a note for you... It's been such a long time since you were invited to La Bise, hasn't it? Since that time you had that fight with that horrid brother of his and Madame Meyer sent the champagne round afterwards. Do you remember that? You can't have been much more than twelve at the time. Still wearing short trousers, you were. We had just moved to Geneva, then, and you and Claude Meyer were such good friends. He's grown a lot, you know."

"He *is* twenty."

"I suppose he is. And you'll be twenty before the end of your holidays. I hope you don't mind me asking, Nick: is there anyone special? I met your father when I was twenty..."

The lake appeared before us, white sails becalmed on its blue surface. There is just a split second, as you drive down that hill towards the lake, when you can glimpse La Bise across the water and as we passed that spot I felt a sudden undertow of excitement pulling me towards that house again. I had been to the other Meyer properties – Malibu, Champagne, Crans, Les Sornettes – but since that distant day of the fight with Oscar, I had not returned to La Bise. In my imagination La Bise had become more than just a rich man's house by a rich man's lake. It had become an enchanted realm. Somehow the passing years had washed away Oscar's taint and La Bise had emerged from the cleansing as my own *domaine perdue*. I had not seen Claude since leaving him at Los Angeles airport the previous summer. Yet I found myself more excited by the prospect of a return to La Bise than by the thought of seeing my Californian travelling companion again.

Among the letters awaiting me at home was one from Johnny Morris.

He wrote plaintively that he would "not be coming home to Geneva this summer". His father had been transferred to Chicago ("for an East Coast family like us this is one stop after purgatory on the B-line to hell") and would be leaving Geneva in June. Johnny hoped to spend a week or two with Sally in Texas, but for most of the summer he would be at his new home in the suburbs of Chicago – "learning to hang out at the malls and drive a pick-up truck. I see more of Janice Day (take that any ole way you want) than is good for me. A couple of weeks ago we spent an hour walking by the lake (Michigan not Leman, alas!) talking about old times. I guess I'll be seeing quite a bit of her over the summer and when I do I'll sure give her a big kiss from you."

That night I dreamed of La Bise again. In my dream, I owned the house by the lake. I walked from room to room, surveying my domain. I looked for the people who should have been there with me. But there was no one there, no one but me. My throat tightened. I became increasingly anxious, wondering where all my people were. My breathing became laboured. I smelled burning rubber. Sweat broke out on my brow. A phone began to ring. I wanted to answer it. I felt a desperate need to hear a voice, even if it was on the other end of a telephone line. But I could not find the phone. Nor would it stop ringing. Then I realised that the house was on fire; that its walls and ceilings were crashing down around me; that there was no escape. I tried to scream, but no human sound came from my gaping mouth. Echoing in my throat was the sound of the phone that would not stop ringing.

Does everyone always awake from a dream just before they die? I do. If people do not wake up when they die in their dreams, do they die in real life as well? Or do they simply awake unharmed from the dream in which they die and get up and go about their normal business?

I got out of bed and sat at my desk in my pyjamas. It was three in the morning. I wrote the dream out while I could still recall it and titled it 'Fire at La Bise'. 'Fire at La Bise' is dream number fourteen in the *Dream Diaries*.[19]

---

[19] E.R. Puddington, B. Smynacott and W.J. Chapple, *The Dream Diaries*, Wichita, 2003. A selection from Nick Kellaway's dream diaries was published under the auspices of the Kansas Institute for Sleep Science (KISS). The introduction, analysis and commentary fill four times as many pages as the dreams themselves. The anonymous dreamer is identified only as a now fifty-year-old, bilingual, London-based professional who has kept a systematic record of his dreams since the age of sixteen. – Ed.

Christina Meyer opened the door when I arrived at La Bise the next afternoon. She wore a loose dress with pastel-coloured flowers printed boldly on it, gathered together at the waist by a broad leather belt.

"Oh, you're looking for Claude. He's not here just now, I'm afraid."

She looked at her watch, an antique Blancpain. "He shouldn't be long. It's such a lovely afternoon. Why don't you wait for him down by the water? I'll tell him you're here the moment he gets in." She led me through the entrance hall and pointed me to the open French windows that gave onto the terrace and the lawns beyond. "You know the way, of course," she smiled, obliterating eight years of absence.

I stepped out onto the terrace. Was La Bise the same as it had been when I had last been here? It seemed smaller, of course, but also strangely tame and domesticated. Wrought-iron tables and chairs, lavishly scattered about the terrace, seemed each to know its place. Roses bloomed to perfection.

As I stepped onto the grass just beyond the crisp terrace edge, the round tower with its dunce's hat came into view. Once upon a time, a fairytale damsel had been imprisoned there and two young knights on a rescue mission had fought their way in. They had found nothing save stale animal droppings and a box of yellowing papers. Since those days, however, the tower had been restored. The ivy had been peeled back from the walls and the stonework repointed. Newly painted shutters were open and boxes of geraniums hung from the windows.

I looked up, over my shoulder, back to the main house, recalled which window had been Claude's, which the toy room, which Oscar's – the room where I had given him the scar on his forehead.

I remembered the low stone wall at the end of the front lawn on which Claude and I used to sit many years earlier dangling our legs, a parapet above lapping waters of the lake. I sauntered away from images of Oscar towards those happier childhood memories. I had installed myself on the wall before I looked over to the beach and jetty below.

On the dock, lying on her back, on a large blue towel, was a woman. *Naked.* She wore a pair of sunglasses, but no other article of clothing shielded her body from the sun.

We were not yet generally accustomed to public nudity in 1971. I had never been near a topless beach. I had studied the anatomy pages in *Encyclopaedia Britannica*. I had seen naked women in photographs in *Mayfair* and *Playboy*. I had cut out the one of Eva Bocardo that appeared after her Californian protest and Blu-Tacked it to the wall of my Oxford room. I had looked, carefully hiding my amazement, at the grainy black-and-white picture Johnny Morris had taken of Sally Pinkerton. I had gawped, with no attention to artistic merit, at nudes on the walls of galleries and museums – and at the one above Karen O'Neil's bed. I had lingered by billboards displaying scantily clad, well-formed girls to advertise all and sundry consumerist baubles. I am absolutely certain, however, that this was the first time I had seen the completely naked body of a fully grown woman in the flesh with my own eyes.

Except for the slight movement of her breathing, the figure on the blue towel lay absolutely still. Perhaps she was asleep. Or perhaps she knew someone was watching her. Perhaps she was ignoring me. Perhaps she wanted me to stare at her. For whatever reason, I had ample time to imprint the vision in my mind and allow it to settle into the deep recesses of my subconscious. I drank in the long neck, the rounded shoulders, the breasts and their rose-coloured nipples, the flat stomach, the mound of pubic hair, the long thighs… How long did I sit there staring at her? I don't know. Five minutes? Maybe ten?

Then she moved. She stretched her arms above her head, arched her back, raised her knees, sat up. Only when she took her sunglasses off and shook her hair did I suddenly realise that I had been looking at Janice Day. *Janice Day, completely nude.* Still, she did not seem to see me. She pulled a t-shirt over her head – no bra. She pulled a pair of cut-off jeans up over her long legs – no knickers. I slipped from the wall, out of her line of sight.

Janice Day came up the steps from the lake moments later. I was, by then, sitting in a garden chair, nonchalantly reading a book, waiting for my heart rate to drop.

"Nick!"

"Oh, hello, Jan."

"What are you doing here?"

"Waiting for Claude."

"Right." She sat in the chair beside me, took off her sunglasses and peered at the book I held in my hand.

"How are you, Jan?"

"Okay, I guess. You go to Cambridge now, don't you?"

"Oxford, actually."

"Oh. Sorry. Right. Still pretty good."

"You still going to that school in Illinois?"

"Yeah. I guess. It's a shit hole."

"Really?"

"A God-forsaken shit hole. I get away from it as often as I can."

"Doing what?"

"You don't want to know."

"Try me."

"Sophisticated stuff. You don't want to know anything about it. Sophisticated, meaningless shit. God, I've been fucking sophistocrapped to death."

"D'you still play the guitar?"

"Guitar?" A pause before she continued. "No. None of that any more. Listen, Nick, you've always had your head screwed on. Even with all that communist shit, you've basically got your head screwed on. So stay away from all this crap. You're a bright kid. Cambridge and all that. Must be great. Just hold on to it."

Janice Day was beginning to sound like my mother after one gin and tonic too many, but, whereas my mother would have looked me in the eye and demanded that I meet her gaze, Jan stared vaguely above my right shoulder at something in the distance. She got up from her chair, kissed me on the cheek, her breast pressing against my shoulder. She rested her hand on my thigh to steady herself. Scents of sandalwood and suntan oil enveloped me.

"Good night, Nick. Gotta get some shut-eye."

I watched her cross the lawn as she went towards the tower and entered the chamber of the Viking runes. I stared for a few moments at the door through which the distressed damsel had gone and then got up and walked down to the dock where she had been lying, out to the light at its far end, back again and then along the pebbly beach. I kicked the post that held the *Plage Privée* sign, pushing it a further centimetre towards its eventual demise.

"*Salut! Ça va, Nick?*"

"*Oui, et toi…*"

Claude and I spoke of many things, of things past, of things present, of futures we would create. At some point we switched from French to English. We reminisced about our time together in California. We exchanged information about mutual friends. Claude had seen Johnny Morris's parents before they moved to Chicago. They had come down to La Bise for a farewell supper the Meyers had organised. At some point I overcame the rising taste of dust in my mouth and asked him about Oscar.

"God knows! He's meant to have a job at a bank in San Francisco. Dad fixed it up for him. But on Saturday he turned up here. And then, yesterday, he was gone again. Took Dad's Ferrari. Didn't say where he was going. Dad doesn't know yet."

"Where's your dad?"

"Walking with Paul in the Grisons."

"You didn't go?" Claude's love of the mountains was legendary.

"No. This is Paul's trip. I went two years ago. Oscar two years before that. Same route. Huts along the Austrian border. Family ritual. A kind of coming-of-age ceremony. Remember when we made a list of all the Swiss Alpine Club huts?"

"Yes," I confessed.

"Seen anyone since you got back?"

"Janice Day was here a few minutes ago."

"Doesn't surprise me." Claude looked at me, as if considering whether to tell me more, before continuing. "She's always hanging around. Got some problems at home with her folks. She was here this morning baking cakes with Mom. Then she was okay. Wearing an apron. Up to her elbows in flour. But other times she's not so good. Poor kid's stoned out of her mind half the time."

"She seemed okay just now."

Okay. More than okay. Much more than okay.

3

I came to the stone tower under cover of night, through the garden of Johnny's old house, where no-one was living now, and over the fence by the old oak tree. I lingered in the darkness, until the last light in La Bise had been turned off. Then I crept across the black lawn, round to the front of the tower. From a window a warm light streamed into the thick night, sparkling, as if through a stained-glass window, with rubies and emeralds and sapphires. Through the window I could see a children's party, a white-faced clown and, in the middle of the room, an elegant woman sitting with her back to me playing the piano. Her blonde hair fell and curled on her shoulders. I heard laughter. Happiness was only the thickness of a stone wall away.

I left the window and went to the door. But there was no door. I pushed on the stones. I kicked at the wall. But there was no way in. I stretched my arms wide to embrace the sacred tower, to hold it close – and awoke from one of the many dreams that gnawed at my sleeping and my waking hours in the days after seeing the woman in sunglasses on the dock at La Bise.

I did return once to La Bise in the flesh during those broken days, and when I asked Claude about Jan he said, "I don't know. Haven't seen her since the time you were last here. Why?"

I phoned Jan's home. A vaguely Teutonic voice I took to be her mother's answered and, when I asked for Jan, said, "I'm sorry, she's not here just now."

So absorbed was I in fantasies about Janice Day that I almost forgot that a stream of visitors from Oxford was due to pass through Geneva during July. When I came in one evening, I found Priscilla McGinley and Caroline Carter in the sitting room, sipping gin and tonics with my mother. They were on their way to the socialist paradises of the East. One evening, over a glass of sherry in Caroline's room at LMH, and before I knew Sill was to be travelling with Caroline, I had suggested Geneva as a convenient stopping point between the Channel and Yugoslavia.

"Forgotten we were coming, then?" Sill sneered.

Sill was the person who, during Freshers' Week, had signed me up to the Labour Party despite my predictable misgivings that it was far too bourgeois an institution for one committed, as I was, to Freedom and the Brotherhood of Man. "We'll change it from the inside," she had argued.

Sill was ostentatiously working class, exaggerated her Liverpudlian accent to the point of incomprehension, wore her hair cropped short, had eyes the colour of the underwater ice that sank the *Titanic* and swore like the proverbial trooper. When asked what her middle initial – 'C' – stood for, she routinely replied "Cunt". A persistent *sotto voce* rumour had it that she was a card-carrying lesbian. I heard that once, when asked the question outright, in a pub where the reputation mills ground most finely, she had replied, "I'm a category mistake."

Caroline said, "We've just been having a very interesting chat with your mother about Venice." She got up from her chair and gave me a kiss on each cheek.

When I first saw Caroline, at a Labour Party meeting in my early weeks at Oxford, I was startled: *what's Marie-Claire doing here?* Like Marie-Claire Dufraisse, Caroline was small, dark and fine-featured.

She had shiny black hair, warm sparkling eyes and dressed with a precision that most students professed to abhor. Her voice was like strawberries and cream on the riverbank at Henley before Events Management arrived with their well-heeled corporate clients intent on rape and pillage. In Colin Witheridge's infectious fantasies, Caroline was a Sunday-school girl who had sung solos in her church choir and public-school chapel. "I mean," he had said, "what do *you* think about during the sermon if not about fucking the choir girls."

Caroline had lived in India as a child and kept a stone statue of Ganesh in a corner of her room. An old leather-bound copy of the *Kama Sutra* sat prominently on her bookshelf, among Penguin editions of nineteenth-century English novels. Perhaps as part of her affection for all things Indian, Caroline wore the same sandalwood perfume as Janice Day.

On her first day in Geneva, Caroline woke with gastric flu. Mum happily assumed nursing duties and insisted, when Caroline was no better the next morning, that Sill and I continue alone with the plans I had made for the day. She handed me the car keys.

I had hoped, when I made my plans, that it would be Caroline and I going off for the day, that Sill would prove true to what I had once heard her say: "I don't do outdoors." But, as it happened, it was Sill and I that set off for the mountains that morning, with, on my part at least, a significant measure of reluctance and a dim sense of foreboding. At Sill's request we stopped at an *épicerie* in a small village beyond Annemasse. She emerged with three one-litre bottles of *vin de table*.

"This stuff's cheaper than petrol," she said with a triumphant grin as she got back into the car beside me.

"And no more fit for drinking, either. It's pure gut rot."

Sill looked at the bottles cradled in her lap. "Gut rot," she said, "from the German *gut rot* meaning 'good red'." Then, with no warning: "D'you fancy Caroline?"

I did not reply.

"C'mon," she insisted. "Have you ever fucked her?"

"No, Sill. I haven't."

"She's got a wild sex drive," Sill leered.

I concentrated on my driving.

"Have you ever fucked *anyone*?" When I still didn't answer Sill continued, "There's a nasty rumour been going round Oxford that the great Nick Kellaway is actually a virgin. I didn't believe it, of course."

I resurrected Red Jen and she rode to the rescue. Jen of the Big

Stacks and the Wet Working Class Coast and the Phantom TV Programme. Jennifer the Good Red.

"God! How romantic! I was raped when I was eleven by my uncle." I had heard the story before. It would go on to become one of the foundation myths of the Jericho House.

From where we parked the car to the isolated meadow just below a south-east-facing ridge is normally a walk of less than an hour and a quarter. When the sky is clear there is a splendid view of Mont Blanc from that ridge. In early July, the meadow flowers at that altitude are at their best and lend their sweet scent to the pure mountain air. Dad called the meadow 'Blueberry Hill' after the wild blueberries that grow there in abundance.

Sill was, however, so physically unfit that our walk to Blueberry Hill took us more than two hours. She was drenched in sweat when we arrived. She sat, flipped the plastic cap off one of the bottles of wine and took a long draught. Mont Blanc appeared distant and indistinct, only just visible against a sky that was turning a pale grey – almost the same hue as the snow. A *foehn* was beginning to blow, a warm moist wind from the south that muddles the senses and causes depression and suicide rates to rise in the valleys north of the Alps. In less than ten minutes, Mont Blanc had disappeared.

Sill and I ate our picnic and drank her wine. Sill expounded a hypothesis that there had always existed egalitarian communities in the mountains that had been well armed and defended their women, their livestock and their liberty against the encroachments of feudalism in the plains below. It was a Marxist version of Switzerland's founding myth. It was nonsense; but I was too uninterested in political debate with Sill to say anything. We lay on our backs on either side of the picnic debris and I wondered how long it would be until the rain set in. I fell asleep.

What is it that brings on dreams? All of us, by the end our first year at Oxford, had read, or pretended to have read, Freud. We were able to give a coherent analysis of the contents of specific dreams. We recognised a phallus when it appeared in mufti and all flat and circular shapes were unequivocally female. What, though, is it that brings certain dreams on at specific times? The pressure changes brought about by the *foehn*? Red wine? Cheese? All of the above in combination with the heady scent of crushed Alpine flowers and the sour smell of an unwashed woman lying beside me? The early stirrings of the bacteria that would in the fullness of their own time erupt into a bout of gastric flu?

Another dream of Janice Day filled my head. You can find this one as dream number sixteen in *The Dream Diaries*.

I see her lying on the dock at La Bise. The sunlight is sparkling brightly on the dark surface of the water beyond. She sits up. She sees me sitting on the low wall that defends the Meyers' house from the predatory waters of Leman. She waves. She comes towards me. She is tall. Her breasts are like biblical towers. Her thighs are strong. Her pubic hair is like a flame that will consume me. She comes up the steps from the lake and puts her arms around me, draws me close to her naked breast, kisses me, whispers my name, "Nicholas." Then we are in a white room where there is a picture of a grey, turbulent sea on the wall. Jan says, "Help me, Nicholas. Please." She is leaning over me. I want her more than anything in the universe. I will help her. I'll do anything she asks. She says, "Thank you, Nicholas," and lowers herself onto my waiting body. I erupt in a volcanic orgasm. Then melt away like an ice cream in the sun.

A wonderful wet dream on a bed of pale-blue mountain flowers? Ah. It wasn't, alas, that simple.

Before I was fully awake, I sensed my belt being unbuckled and zipper undone and Sill's hands on the flanks of my hips pulling my shorts down. She had taken off her jeans and was unclothed below the waist.

"Come on, Nick," I vaguely heard her say. "We can't let this go to waste."

She mounted me and pulled my dream-wrought erection inside her. My back arched up to meet her. My hands on her buttocks involuntarily held her against me. Then… it was finished as quickly as it began. Finished almost before I emerged from the dream, before the white room and the grey seaside and Janice Day vanished in the sunlight.

When, after a few long seconds, I opened my eyes, I felt the palm of Sill's hand slap me hard on the cheek. "You complete bastard, Kellaway. You fucking bastard," she said. "How dare you take advantage of a poor working-class girl like that. You bring me up to the middle of bloody nowhere and treat me like shit. God damn you. I'll have you for this, you fucking bourgeois bastard." She put her discarded clothes back on: knickers, jeans, socks, Susan's boots. She put the piece of kitchen paper she had used as a napkin at our picnic inside her pants, tightened her belt and set off down the hill.

I watched Sill stumble, regain her feet, rush on, disappear over the crest of a little knoll lower down the meadow. Five minutes earlier I had been a virgin, dreaming of a glorious consummation in a white room at La Bise. This was not how that phase of my life was meant to end. It was the wrong script.

I pulled my shorts up, tidied the remnants of our picnic into my rucksack, and followed Sill down the mountainside. I found her lying on her back in a slight depression at the bottom of the meadow, her eyes closed, her jeans and pants around her ankles, her knees spread wide, her middle name exposed to the elements. When eventually she saw me, standing looking down at her, she said, with only slightly less ferocity than a quarter of an hour earlier, "God damn you, Nicholas Kellaway. I've had to bring myself on by hand."

We walked back to the car in silence. A light shower fell, wetting us through because we did not stop to put on our waterproofs. On the damp, silent drive back to Geneva, I stopped at a *boulangerie* in Annemasse to buy two loaves of airy French bread, which my mother preferred to the heavier Swiss variety. Sill stayed in the car. She was snoring when I came back with the bread. I had a headache brought on by the cheap wine and the *foehn*.

Caroline was up and dressed, though still looking pale and fragile – and no less lovely for it – when we returned. My mother beamed at her patient's progress. "Such a nice girl," she said. "We've had a lot of good chats today, haven't we, Caroline? I hope you two had a nice picnic. It wasn't spoiled by the rain, was it?"

Caroline said, "I broke one of your mother's special glasses, I'm afraid."

"It doesn't matter, dear," Mum said. "It was an accident."

"It was very clumsy of me. They were all lined up on the table and I knocked one of them with my sleeve."

"Don't worry yourself about it, dear," Mum said soothingly. "It was an accident. It doesn't matter."

But I knew it did matter. The broken glass was one of a set of six my mother had bought in Venice in 1961. They were decorated with gold leaf and each was made of a different colour of glass. We had gone over to Murano and watched glass animals being created. Mum had bought her set of glasses in the adjacent shop, spending nearly an hour deciding which ones to buy. The ones she eventually chose found their home in our Eaux-Vives flat, in a Victorian vitrine, behind bevelled glass, dusted and polished periodically, but never used for drinking, rarely even coming out to queue up on the table to be admired. It was the pale-blue goblet Caroline had broken. The remaining five had been replaced safely on their usual shelf.

Caroline went to bed soon after supper. Sill, too, went to bed early. She was tired, she said. I announced I was going to go out for a walk. I needed the air to clear my head.

"You're restless, Nick," my mother said, "always wanting to be going somewhere. Why not just settle in for the evening with a nice book? You've been out all day. It's still raining."

Dad looked up from his newspaper. There was in his expression neither encouragement to go nor encouragement to stay, simply a curiosity to see what I would do. I went out. I walked down to the lake, brushed the puddles of rainwater from the shiny surface of a bench by the *Statue de la Bise* and sat there for more than an hour, staring into the empty gathering gloom, staying on long after the murky orange had faded in the western sky and the drizzle had begun to fall again.

By the next morning the weather had turned fine again and Caroline was well enough to go out for a walk in the afternoon. Sill, having had enough fresh air the previous day, decided to stay in. I was pleased to have at least one afternoon alone with Caroline.

We walked slowly. I pointed out sights and monuments and told her things that had happened at the places we passed, bestowing human significance on the trees and stones and tarmac. I wanted to take her hand as we walked, but I could not bring myself to do so. She made no attempt to take mine. I wanted to stroke her silky hair and hold her close. But we walked on, looking at… things. I wanted to tell her what had happened up on the mountainside the previous day. I wanted Caroline to hear it from me before she heard a distorted version from Sill. In due course, I did tell her everything. But not that afternoon. I could not find the words. I had not yet found the voice in which to tell the story even to myself. It was, in any event, not yet the end of that little story with Sill.

At some point during the night Sill came into my bedroom. She must have walked along the corridor past the door of my parent's bedroom that was always left ajar at night. She woke me as she came into my room and closed the door behind herself. She was wearing an old dressing gown that she had borrowed from my sister's wardrobe.

I must have performed more satisfactorily than I had on Blueberry Hill. When we had finished and the first colouring of the new day was beginning to appear beyond the drawn curtains, I received, instead of a slap across the jowls, a light kiss on the forehead. Then she was gone, wrapped in Susan's dressing gown, back along the corridor past my parents' open door.

Caroline and Sill left for Italy soon after breakfast. Caroline sent my mother a thank-you letter, posted in Venice. She apologised again for breaking the glass. "She's such a lovely girl," my mother said. She looked at me, transparently hoping for a response. I gave her none.

Just before I left for Greece, I received a postcard from Caroline. It was a picture of the old bridge in Mostar before it was destroyed in the Balkan Wars of the nineties. I still have it. It is propped up on the desk beside me as I write. Nothing ever arrived from Sill.

4

"Hey, kiddo. Nicky. Baby."

"What?"

"Slow down." She lifted her knee, expelled me from her groove, rolled out from under me, left me lying face down on the Persian rug as she stood up.

There were Persian rugs in every room in the apartment – except the kitchen and bathroom. There were dozens more in storage in Bethesda. All top quality, all handmade on traditional looms. Something about knots per square inch. Descriptions I had heard before. Tom bought them from the best merchants in the Teheran bazaar. He paid a fortune for them, she said, gently relegating him to the category of unreasonable husband.

I rolled onto my back, felt the heat of the late afternoon sun on my skin as it flowed through the open doors from the balcony. I watched her naked body move as she crossed the room. A record was playing rock music: insistent beat, heavy bass. She lifted the needle from the vinyl, searched the collection of records on the shelf beside the gramophone, took one out of its sleeve and put it on the turntable. The soft voice of Art Garfunkel echoed the command to slow down, suggested I make the morning – or afternoon or evening or whatever it was – last.

She came back to the Persian rug, lay down on top of me. "Okay, Nicky," the teacher said. "Rocky Mountains. And I get there first."

She had her own vocabulary for sex. She had a groove and I had a horn. Her equivalent of my feeling horny was her feeling groovy. Her orgasms were the Rocky Mountains. Mine were tolerated as an inevitable part of the process. Semen was honey, as in "Hey, Nicky. No honey before the Rocky Mountains."

Once, on our second day, I made the mistake of casually referring to what we were doing as making love. "Get that one out of your head, kiddo," she said. "Screwing. Fucking. Call it what you want. But don't mix it up with love."

She always played music when we were having sex. The record player had a mechanism that lifted the needle at the end of the last track and brought it back to the beginning to play the whole side through again. We screwed to 'Scarborough Fair', 'Mrs Robinson' and 'Love is Just a Four-Letter Word'. We fucked to Mussorgsky's 'Pictures at an Exhibition', Ravel's 'Bolero' and Beethoven's 'Choral Symphony'. There was even an old, scratchy recording of American tent-meeting, revival hymns that she once put on the gramophone.

On the morning of our fourth day we were lying across her big double bed. I had just led her through a choreography of several orgasms and was feeling particularly pleased with myself when the phone that crouched on her bedside table rang. She stretched out an arm to answer it. I could hear the loud voice of another American woman on the other end of the line asking her questions.

"It's great," Karen answered. "You kinda forget how guys are at nineteen. The horn's always full. The honey flows like water and before you know it they're up for an encore. Plus this one's got gorgeous lips."

"Where's your little man right now?"

"Funny you should ask that. He's lying right here beside me, waiting for you to get off the phone so we can get on with it."

"Yoo-hoo. Karen, you're so crazy."

"And I bet you just wish you were crazy, too."

I think, looking back on those July days, that Karen O'Neil was a serial adulteress. Tom spent weeks at a stretch away in the Middle East, in Germany, in anonymous cities behind the Iron Curtain. That had been the pattern for years. She never knew when or where he was going, when he would come home, knew better than to ask. Other than scraps about his love for Persian rugs and that he was a "man of no opinions but many habits", she told me very little about the absent, arms-dealing husband who had perhaps once been, and maybe still was, a spy. Kathy, the daughter, was never mentioned.

Nor did Karen tell me much about herself – other than what she liked in the way of sex ("beware of monotony: it's the mother of all the deadly sins") and that she had once been a schoolteacher. I think she had taught English. The few bookshelves in the apartment were inhabited by the classics of American literature. She said nothing about other men. I guessed at other affairs only because I felt like the latest in long line of ghosts. At times I was a memory; at others an undressed rehearsal. I wondered, with rising discomfort, whether she had picked up other boys outside Migros, asked for their unsuspecting chivalrous help with her shopping and lured them into her lair while Ali Baba was away.

Once she lifted the veil she had drawn over the past just enough to say that I was her first Englishman. "It feels," she said, "deliciously like double treason."

"What d'you mean?"

"I married an Irishman."

"I thought he was American."

"Boston Irish. More Irish than a Connemara leprechaun. *And* you're a communist. "

The leprechaun phoned one morning when I was in the apartment. Karen waved me out of the bedroom and closed the door softly. Tom was in Teheran and phone calls between Teheran and Geneva were rare in those days.

"When's he coming back?" I asked when she opened the door.

"When the Shah signs the deal."

"When will that be?"

"Maybe tomorrow. Maybe the next day. How the hell should I know?"

"Will he give a warning?"

"The Shah?"

"Tom. That he's coming back."

"Probably not."

She showered. I watched her dress.

"I have things to do, Nicky," she said.

I put my clothes on, went on my way, virtuously telling myself as I left the apartment that I would not cross Karen O'Neil's threshold again. Revolutions are not made in the palaces of absent spies. I had made plans to see Claude Meyer at the Café du Commerce that night. Yet when Karen phoned inviting me to her apartment "for a peaceful drink" I told her I was free, pulled out of the evening on the town and went to her like iron filings to a magnet.

Over the wine we eventually got round to drinking, she put the question Sill had asked on our way to the meadow. I reluctantly abandoned Red Jen, told Karen about the mountain walk and the *foehn* and the wine and the unripe blueberries. If Karen bothered to think about whom I had been with in the mountains that day, she would, based on the image I painted for her, have pictured Janice Day rather than Priscilla McGinley – the dream, not the reality. Karen knew Jan's parents. She saw them regularly at contrived social events among the expatriate Americans of Geneva. She had undoubtedly met Jan herself.

Why did I tell Karen anything at all about Blueberry Hill? Why – when I knew that if I had asked her the same question all I would have had for an answer was a sphinx-like smile? Why did I not stick with the impersonal safety of hieroglyphs and lies? I cannot answer that any more than I can tell you why I was drawn back to La Gradelle time after time that week.

If my story of the mountain picnic did bring thoughts of Jan to Karen's mind, she did not give voice to them. She simply expressed astonishment that I had got through Ecolint and then an entire year at college with my virginity intact and a mild disappointment that she had not found me a week earlier. I think she was pleased to learn that I had not screwed her daughter, though I felt she was less interested in Kathy's chastity than she was in the idea that she had triumphed over a rival.

Kathy was due home on Saturday. Her arrival, Karen and I both knew, would bring our eight-day affair to an end – if it had not been brought to an end earlier by Tom's return. Then, three days later, Karen and Kathy – and Tom, if he had returned by then – were due to fly to the States.

On Friday, for the first time, I spent the night with Karen. We slept little, but were nevertheless out of bed before six on Saturday morning. We spent three hours cleaning the apartment, ridding it of the smell of sex and Russian cigarettes. We changed the sheets and towels, put bleach in all the drains, sprayed foam on the rugs and hoovered them intensely. We disposed of empty wine bottles and sprayed an air freshener, marketed as smelling of alpine flowers, into every nook and cranny. Before ten o'clock that morning I was turning the key in the front door *chez* Kellaway.

Lizzie Merrifield-Hayes stood in the kitchen by a steaming kettle making a pot of tea. She was wearing a white blouse that was too big for her and a pair of bell-bottomed blue jeans. From beneath the bottoms of the bells bare feet protruded. Her nails were painted scarlet.

"Hi, Nick," she said. "I was just making a pot of tea for your dad and me. Would you like a cup?"

Dad came into the kitchen. "Good morning, Nick."

Lizzie put the pot of tea, three cups and a small jug of milk on a tray and carried it into the dining room.

"Where's Mum?"

Dad looked at me quizzically. "England," he said.

"Oh."

"Nick, you were here when the call came about your grandmother. We agreed she should go."

"Oh, yeah."

The three of us sat at the dining room table. Beside the tea sat a tape recorder and a pile of papers. The top paper in the pile was covered in my father's spidery handwriting.

Dad said, "Lizzie's just going to record some of my memories. You're most welcome to stay if you'd like."

"I'm doing some research on mining families," Lizzie explained.

She pressed the button on the tape recorder. My father started what sounded like a speech he had prepared long ago and then found, when he came to deliver it, that the lecture hall was empty. Now, to his relief and evident pleasure, here to listen to him was young Miss Elizabeth Merrifield-Hayes, Cambridge undergraduate historian with eager eyes.

"The name Kellaway," he began, "came to England with the Normans. The surname originates either in Caillouet, a small Normandy hamlet near Evreux or in a place in the Risle valley near the town of Brionne called Callouet. When the Normans conquered England in 1066, they became the ruling class. But as far back as I have been able to trace my own ancestors, our Kellaways have always been working class and poor. My great-grandfather, John Kellaway, was born in 1837, in Ludworth Parish, County Durham..."

I finished my tea and left the room. Through the open doorway to my parents' bedroom, I saw the unmade double bed. My newly opened eyes saw men like trees walking, red toenails and the architectural incentives to immorality. I went to my bedroom, closed the door and lay down. It was after four in the afternoon when I awoke. The flat was quiet. Both my father and Lizzie had gone.

5

Colin Witheridge, Nigel Bickleigh and I spent as little time as we honourably could in Athens. We paid our respects to the Acropolis and the Agora, to the Areopagus and the Acepheleion, and then moved quickly on to Piraeus and a ferry bound for the islands. We had not come to Greece to look at old stones, nor to tread the streets of Socrates, the paths of Plato or the alleys of Aristotle, nor to hear tales of yesterday's goddesses, preternaturally wise and perpetually virginal. Our quest lay elsewhere. And you know what? I was embarking on it without L-plates slung around my neck.

The flower of European youth descended on the beaches of the Aegean that summer of 1971. Female flowers – young women of our generation, women just waking to the dawn of the world, women who came from climes where the sun was elusive – shed their inhibiting petals and spread their welcoming thighs.

Nigel, scion of the British establishment, was the first among the three of us to score. Two hours out of Piraeus he disappeared with a Belgian girl into a lifeboat that in an emergency would never have left its rusty harness on the deck. The girl came from Antwerp and her aim was to reach Kastellorizo, the farthest of the Far Isles. She listed in gentle cadences all the islands that lay between Pireaus and her eastern goal, islands floating like dreams on a sea of uncertain reality. She spoke of Kastellorizo in soft, respectful tones, as if it were a mythical archipelago somewhere over the horizon, a land beyond the limits of the known world, a place where you might find Ulysses holed up with a runaway siren or Jason and his Argonauts waiting for the next ferry homeward bound.

Our first island was Mykonos. Our days were hot and shadeless. Ignoring the consensus that it was a bourgeois, consumerist pretension, we bought suntan cream and applied it liberally. By night we spread our sleeping bags on a beach and covered our heads with our towels to keep the mosquitoes off. Our beach, however, was too close to a town that had pretensions to a higher form of tourism. The police woke us, shining torches in our eyes, and apologetically moved us on. They patiently ignored the curses we called down on them from Mount Olympus as we shook the dust of their town from our shoes.

We spent a week on Ios, where Homer's grave is said to be, where retsina flowed, where clothes were a useless fashion accessory, where you could get high merely by breathing deeply as you walked along the beach at sunset. After a midnight dance at a ramshackle taverna, I began a three-day liaison with a buxom Norwegian lass called Hilde that ended only when she left the island to connect with her flight home.

After Hilde left, I took a book and went to read at the far end of the beach. In the late afternoon, another Aphrodite of the Eastern Isles (name Rosa Winkel, sunburn to match) came out of the sea, walked up the beach and asked, in tremulous French, whether I was the guy selling cannabis. No; but I shared with her the small amount of dope I had. Rosa told me she was called after Rosa Luxemburg.[20] I asked her whether she came from East Germany.

Rosa smiled at my naïveté. "From the Saarland," she said, "just two kilometres from the frontier with France. My parents moved to Germany from Alsace after the war." Her elder brother, she said, had originally been christened Adolf, but when he was three he had had his name changed to Karl, after Karl Liebknecht.[21] I laced another of what Jan had once called my 'commie black sticks' and offered it to her. That evening I added the fourth entry to the list I had begun on Blueberry Hill.

We met more Germans than any other nationality in Greece that summer. In the space of twenty-five years, West Germany had risen from the bombsites of the defeated Reich to become the most prosperous country in Europe. Its young people seemed able to remain students well into their late twenties, the job market only a

---

[20] Rosa Luxemburg (1871–1919) was a Polish-born German socialist. She broke with the German Social Democratic Party when it supported the German war effort in the First World War and founded (with Karl Liebknecht) first the pacifist Spartacist League and then, after the war, the Communist Party of Germany. On 15 January 1919, Rosa Luxemburg was extra-judicially executed by the Freikorps called in to assist the Imperial Army in putting down the so-called German Revolution. Her body was dumped, together with those of other executed workers, in the Landwehr Canal. Rosa Luxemburg's *Dialectic of Spontaneity and Organisation* and her prophetic criticisms of the Russian Bolshevik revolution of 1917 made her a popular figure with the New Left in the second half of the twentieth century. – Ed.

[21] Karl Liebknecht (1871–1919) was a German socialist lawyer and founder (with Rosa Luxemburg) of both the Spartacist League and the Communist Party of Germany. After the German defeat on the western front in the First World War, he instigated, without the support of others members of the Communist Party leadership, the left-wing uprising that came to be known as the German Revolution. He was captured in Berlin by those defending the newly established Weimar Republic from the Revolution and executed without trial. – Ed.

distant nightmare. Their degree courses appeared to be infinitely flexible, allowing them to come and go as they wished, and, at a time when the British were still restricted to £50 when they left the country, the Germans had money.[22]

I had never been to Germany. My knowledge of the country was limited to what I had read in Tacitus, seen in war movies and tasted in the odd sip of Liebfraumilch. My understanding of the language went no further than the translations on the trilingual packaging of Swiss consumer goods. At school, when the time came to take a third language, I had opted, following my father's prompting, for the mathematical certainties and academic prestige of Latin, leaving the living joys of German and Russian to others. It did not matter: the Germans we met spoke good English.

Leaving Ios, we joined a group of German travellers at the stern of a ship that was travelling south. They were travelling from Naxos, they said, bound for Santorini. One of the German women meticulously spoke, like an incarnate Baedeker, of Santorini as the prototype for Plato's story of Atlantis. She kept each item in her rucksack wrapped in its own individual waterproof bag. She pulled one out to show us. It contained a box of condoms.

Our German shipmates were mostly female. The leader of the band was male – but only just. He spoke with a lisp, had long hair streaked with grey gathered into a ponytail and wore colourful bangles on both wrists. He was also the guardian of the wine cellar that the Germans had brought on board with them and kept a set of six crystal glasses which he polished frequently with a linen tea cloth. Before opening a bottle he would take from his rucksack a pair of white silk gloves and pull them onto his long, bony hands. Corks emerged from wine bottles with the flourish of a magician producing yet another white rabbit from a top hat. He poured an inch of wine overboard before filling the glasses for his waiting acolytes: "For Poseidon." His name was Markus Holzschifter. He had, he told us, once taught English in a *gymnasium*.

Markus's opposite in the group was Karl-Heinz Kupferhoden: blond, close-cropped beard, muscled, tattooed. Scars on his face and

[22] As the era of the 1960s *Kommune* in Germany wound down in the early 1970s, large numbers of German youth (for example, Uschi Obermaier) began to travel widely, some in search of 'experiences', some for more overtly political reasons. Of Uschi Obermaier, Rainer Langhans is reported to have said "I would betray any revolution for this woman." It was, however, with Dieter Bockhorn, that Uschi Obermaier travelled the world. – Ed.

his hands did not speak of the good life. Most of the time he sat brooding, hiding from the sun under a railwayman's cap that he kept pulled low on his brow, passing a silent sentence of damnation on the world. After a glass of wine he would become aggressive. "Are you American?" he asked, pointing an accusing finger at me.

"No," I replied, "English."

"You sound like a fuckin' Yank."

I produced my dark-blue British passport and waved it in front of him. Kupferhoden snatched it from my hand, opened it at the page with the photograph. He seemed to have difficulty reading. Then he said, "This guy's only nineteen. 'Nicholas Alfred Kellaway, born London, 28 September, 1951'. Nineteen." He made to toss my passport over his shoulder into the foaming wake behind the ship and it would have joined Markus's drink offerings there had a small, dark-haired girl – we later learned to call her Anna Schmidt – not grabbed his arm and caused the flying passport to land on the deck.

We – the Germans, Colin, Nigel and I – disembarked at Santorini and made our way to a beach of grey sand on the east side of the island. Our new companions treated us courteously. With the exception of Kupferhoden, they always spoke in English when we were around, even to each other. For our part we were careful not to mention The War or the 1966 World Cup. Markus Holzschifter and company felt no such inhibitions. "For most of us," he said, "it is a closed period of history. We know more about Pericles and Alexander. Our fathers are silent and the books are not published."

"My father," Karl-Heinz Kupferhoden added, "was very silent. He was killed in 1944. By the Americans." Daylight had first illumined young Kupferhoden's countenance six months after his father's death.

"I only learned of the Judaeocide when I was twenty-two. In 1964. When the Auschwitz trial[23] began," continued Holzschifter. "There were all these pathetic little men on trial. Tight-assed,

---

[23] Following the Nuremberg trials after the Second World War, a number of senior officials involved at the Auschwitz concentration camp were handed to the Polish authorities and tried there in 1947. A second Auschwitz trial took place in Frankfurt in the Federal Republic of Germany beginning in 1963. Most of the twenty-two on trial (from a total of some 7,000 SS personnel estimated to have been involved at Auschwitz) were medium ranking officers. The proceedings of the court were public and served to bring the detailed mechanics of the Holocaust to the attention of many in West Germany for the first time. – Ed.

bourgeois little men, just like my father. If these twenty had been feeding Jews to the ovens, what had all the rest of them been doing? What had *my* daddy been doing?"

"Bourgeois families lead to sexual repression. Sexual repression leads to fascism, and fascism leads to genocide," said Kupferhoden, like a sullen schoolboy reciting a memorised formula to the ticktock of a New Left metronome. "It's axiomatic."

"Their lips are as tightly buttoned as they pretend their trousers are," added a girl called Petra Steinhauer, her hand resting on Nigel's arm. It was that hand that would end Nigel's hopes of a career in politics.

Our Baedeker nodded vigorously. For her the ubiquitous 'Make Love Not War' t-shirt was not just about an alternative way to spend an idle Saturday evening. It was fundamental theology. "Genital people are," she said, citing learned references and footnotes, "psychologically incapable of evil, also."

I heard Colin's voice – in light mocking tones – say, *"Axiomatisch."*

"They killed him, you know," said the Baedeker.

"Who?" I asked.

"The Americans, of course."

"Who did they kill?"

"Ah. You mean *whom. Whom* did they kill." She paused as if waiting for confirmation that 'whom' was indeed what I meant. "Wilhelm Reich. They burned his books, put him in prison and killed him. Of course, they said it was natural causes. But ya, sure – what do you expect them to say?"[24]

Day and night we learned about German politics, about the Grand Coalition and its break up, about the extra-parliamentary opposition and the role thrust upon student cadres as the proletariat forsook its historic mission. "The particular task of our generation is to ensure that the seeds of fascism never germinate again," Anna explained. I alone laughed at the pun. Every eye fastened on me. Anna looked as unamused as Queen Victoria on a state visit to a nationalised brothel. Karl-Heinz glowered beneath his proletarian cap.

We heard of Germans undergoing training in revolutionary practice in Palestinian refugee camps, of communes in Berlin that

---

[24] See W. Coldridge, *Sexual Repression, The New Left and the Myth of Wilhelm Reich's Execution*, Edinburgh, 1974.

were giving birth to a just and free society. We heard names that would later become familiar: Gudrun Ensslin, Horst Mahler, Holger Meins, Brigitte Mohnhaupt, Andreas Baader... We heard about Petra Schelm. The police had murdered her in July.

"Like Wilhelm Reich?" Colin probed – the light mocking tone again.

"No," answered the Baedeker. "The German police. She was driving her car and the pigs pulled her over and shot her dead. It could have been any of us." Petra Schelm had been a friend of our new friends.

Markus asked, "Have you heard of Ulrike Meinhof?" I had not. "Ulrike is no longer just writing history in ink." He spoke of Ulrike Meinhof in the same reverent tones with which he addressed Poseidon when pouring his oblation into the wine-dark sea.

"We slept in a lemon grove on Naxos," Markus said. "We were sleeping on Ariadne's beach near the town. We could see the ruins of Dionysus' temple from there, but the police moved us on. The lemon grove was better than the beach. The smell when we woke in the morning was like heaven."

One night Markus pointed out Ariadne's sign in the sky: the Corona Borealis, the stars Dionysus, the foreign god, had hung in the black dome of the night sky as a wedding gift to the bride he found, abandoned by Theseus, on a Naxos beach. "Dionysus is my favourite god," he began. "He is the god of the people who are outside the walls of our logical society. That is why in classical times it was women who were his chief worshippers. Ask Anna. She is a devotee of Dionysus-Sogol, like Dionysus-Zagreus, the Cretan incarnation, the bull, the goat... You know, maenads in a frenzy, heads thrown back, fucking whatever man they find. Then tearing him to pieces with their bare hands, eating his flesh and drinking his blood. I think I prefer the Dionysus of our lemon grove on Naxos, Dionysus-Dendrites. The gentle god. The god of the trees."

"Are *you* going onto Crete?"

"I don't have the time." Markus buried the stub of his dead joint in the sand. "Back to Germany, I'm afraid. Everything's finished in Germany now. All hope is gone. Inevitability is going to have to wait for another day. Now, what I would love best of all is to find a good woman – a 'soul mate' as you say in English. We would get in a boat and sail away as far as possible, my woman and I. That, for me, would be true freedom. Like the morning scent in the lemon grove, only going on and on for ever. Touching the goosebumps on the skin of eternity." Markus turned his gaze from the horizon where the sky met the eastern sea and looked at me. "A dream? Maybe. Maybe like the Revolution. Maybe like Abelard and Héloïse. Do you have any dreams, Nicholas? Do the English dream? What does a mathematician dream about?"

The electrification of the Greek islands had not yet been completed in 1971 and the taverna on our Santorini beach was among those parts still in the dark ages. It was lit by kerosene lanterns and smoky candles. Thirteen of us – Nigel, Colin, me and ten of our German friends – sat around the table, drinking wine that had been made on the island. Good wine. The first wine I had tasted in Greece that was not flavoured with pine resin. The waiter had cleared the debris of our moussaka and chips and brought us another three bottles. A storm lantern, suspended from the rafters above our table, cast wobbly shadows on the walls. Colin Witheridge and Anna Schmidt had moved to the far end of the table. They had discovered that they both spoke Russian.

The rest of us were talking about the war in Vietnam. About the American military bases in Germany. About the increasing dominance of the world economy by American companies who made their profits through products such as Napalm and Agent Orange. About how evil capitalist advertising agencies had even, according to our Baedeker, hijacked Sex for their own nefarious ends.

"One evening in Wiesbaden," Petra Steinhauer said, "my friend and I found four American cars parked outside a brothel. Nobody guarding them. Nothing." The two girls had let the air out of the cars' tyres. When the American soldiers returned they found Petra and her friend pretending to be streetwalkers. The soldiers kicked their cars, swore, asked Petra whether she had seen who had let the air out of their tyres.

"Two black men," she had answered in staccato English. "US Army."

"Fuckin' niggers."

Petra grinned. "'Yes,' I said. 'But pay is good. We charge black men double.'"

Into the silence after the laughter had died down, Karl-Heinz said, "Nicholas, when did you last fuck the Americans?" When I did not reply, Kupferhoden hammered his fist down onto the table. The glasses jumped. Wine spilled from some of them. "Answer me, Fuckolas," he said. "When did you last screw an American?"

I enjoy telling a story. Even then, at nineteen years old, I thought I was pretty good at it. I enjoy telling a tale most when I have an attentive audience. Just then, I had twenty-four eyes focused on me wondering how I would answer.

"Well," I began. "Funny you should ask that, Karl-Heinz…"

I had already begun to tame the turbulent, contradictory emotions that surged along my arteries whenever I thought of the week that I had spent in and out of Karen O'Neil's flat at La Gradelle. I had made a list recording our copulations, setting out time and place and manner. Now, in a dark taverna on Santorini, I reduced Karen to a character in a narrative, a narrative I controlled, *my* narrative. A story to titillate a holiday party of German revolutionaries. I changed Karen's surname from O'Neil to O'Connell. It was still Irish, which was important, for when I began I did not know whether I would appropriate her Leprechaun of Connemara for my tale. I shifted the location of our trysts from Geneva to London – to Mayfair, which I thought was probably the sort of sophisticated part of London where a rich expatriate might live. Mayfair also had a louche cachet bestowed by association with the top-shelf magazine of the same name. I gave Karen a southern drawl instead of her New England vowels. But I left her as forty-something and married. I described the opulent décor of the apartment as accurately as I could: the finest carpets of Tabriz and Isfahan, Egyptian alabaster, beaten copper from Baghdad, vials of ivory and coloured glass, cedarwood cabinets from the mountains of Lebanon… I told of the Samarkand silver we smoked and the sandalwood joss-sticks we burned, of the Modigliani-style oil painting of Karen in the nude that hung on her bedroom wall…

"This woman," Kupferhoden asked, "she was married?"

I thought I had made that clear in my account. "Yes."

"What was the name of the husband?"

"Tom." I answered. "Tom O'Connell."

"American?"

"Yes."

"What did he do?"

"Do? Nothing. I don't think he ever found out."

"No. I mean he was rich, damn it, what did he do for bread?"

"Oh, that. He was a spy, actually. Worked for the CIA. Sells military hardware to the Shah of Iran now. He was in Berlin with him when that Ohnesorg chappie was killed."

Silence. Then Markus broke it with a laugh. It was as if the incredible claims of my last answer had revealed everything that had gone before to be nothing more than an elaborate joke, ridicule that Karl-Heinz's wine-fuddled brain gradually interpreted as aimed at him. He threw his empty glass at the wall above my head. Shattered shards showered down onto my shoulders.

"You're full of shit, Fuckaway," he said. "Full of fascist shit. All mathematicians are fascists." He knocked over his chair as he stood and walked fiercely out into the night.

It was a dark night. When we left the taverna we found our way only with difficulty to the patch on the beach where we slept. Anna Schmidt said, "Karl-Heinz was three metres away when Benno Ohnesorg was shot. He came to the apartment where I was living twenty minutes later, shit-scared, shivering from head to toe. And, you know, it was June." She had her arm around Colin's waist. Nigel walked down to the water's edge with Petra.

In the clear night air and with no moon or electricity providing rival sources of illumination, the stars were brighter and more numerous than I had ever seen them. I traced constellations that the ancients had named when they had sailed these seas. Lying on my back watching for shooting stars, I listened to waves lap at the beach, at this soft remnant of Atlantis the Violent. I heard cicadas in the fields behind. A dog barked and a man shouted at it until it stopped. A cock crowed a false dawn. A motorbike started. I could not tell how far away it was. Perhaps the sound had carried all the way from the town, down through the sleeping fields. From the presumed tangle of limbs to my right came snatches of Russian poetry and then the grunts and liquid sounds of extravagant lovemaking.

As I lay alone on the sand that night, unable to sleep, my potential for genocide unquenched, I found myself perversely pleased with Karl-Heinz's reaction to my story. The new name – 'Fuckolas Fuckaway' – lingered in Nigel's and Colin's vocabulary for a few days. Sometimes, even years later, it would surface as a term of affection, bringing forth conspiratorial smiles, memories of young innocents abroad. Then, after Colin died, after his body was found in a shallow woodland grave, his daughter spat the ancient nickname at me, accusing me of a long list of heinous crimes – crimes that included complicity in her father's murder.

6

When Nigel, Colin and I left Santorini and moved on to Crete, Anna Schmidt came with us. On the ship, she told us about growing up in the East, in Bautzen, in the shadow of the German Democratic Republic's most notorious political prison. She had escaped to the West when she was nineteen – after the Berlin Wall had been built and at a time when the border guards had orders to shoot potential escapees on sight.

"How," Nigel asked, "did you get across?"

"I am," she replied, "Anna Houdini."[25] She offered no further explanation and we sought none. Later, as the ferry approached land, she said, "My father was here in 1941." We sought no explanation of that either.

We found another beach and another taverna, not unlike the ones we had left on Ios and Santorini. The people on this beach, too, were not unlike those on all the other Aegean islands that summer: young, bronzed and scantily clad.

There was a church at one end of our new beach, a Greek Orthodox chapel, white-washed with blue domes and always locked because tourists steal icons. Anna, who was the only one of the four of us with a camera, took a picture of Colin, Nigel and me standing in front of the church, in goofy, self-conscious poses. I still have the copy of it that she had made for me. On the back of the picture she wrote 'The Three Musketeers, Kreta, August 1971'. Anna had me take a picture of her standing with Colin in the same place. Her arm is around his waist and his lies across her shoulder, his possessive fingertips dangling above her breast. On its reverse, Anna wrote, 'To Colin, With Love, Anna'. But it was years before I saw a copy of that photograph and that inscription.

Perhaps we were beginning to grow bored with life on the beaches, for after a couple of days we decided to make the trip to the labyrinths at Knossos. Anna stayed behind. When we returned to our beach about half an hour before the sun set, Anna was not there. Her rucksack and sleeping bag were still lying on the sand beside ours, in the spot where we had left them in her care. Colin, rummaging, found Anna's passport and her contraceptive pills in a protected interior pocket in her rucksack. The pill for the day had

---

[25] Harry Houdini (1874 – 1926) was an American escape artist and stunt man. – Ed.

not been touched. It was getting dark as we began to look for her. We asked those on the beach whether they had seen her. Nobody had. The family that ran the taverna shrugged their shoulders.

There seemed little we could do as night fell. We agreed to go to the police in the morning if she had not returned by then. I fell asleep thinking of Anna, devotee of Dionysus, the maenad who went on wild, drug-soaked rampages in the hills, looking for men to devour. I felt stupidly envious of Colin Witheridge and hoped, in those moments as sleep overcame reason, that Anna Schmidt was gone for good.

When morning came and there was still no sign of Anna, Colin took her passport and went with Nigel to the police station. I stayed on the beach, never straying far from the pile of rucksacks and sleeping bags. When Nigel and Colin came back in the afternoon, Anna was with them. They had found her at the police station – in a cell where she had spent the night. "Pigs," she said. "Fucking pigs." Anna's Houdini skills must have failed her.

"They arrested her," Nigel said with an ill-concealed smile, "for sunbathing topless too close to the church."

"Can you believe it?" she said. "These people come down in their black robes to ogle at our bodies and then, when one of us gets her tits too close to their holy icons, the pigs put her in prison. Can you fucking believe it?"

Anna plotted the revenge for her arrest slowly, brooding darkly on it during the days that followed. Then, early on the evening before we were due to leave Crete, we put her plans into effect. Once it was dark, we took a hammer Colin had borrowed from the unsuspecting owner of the taverna, two torches and the multifunctional Swiss Army knife that Anna carried in her rucksack and walked over to the chapel that had been offended by the sight of Anna Schmidt's bare breasts. With an expertise that surprised me, Anna forced the padlock on the church. The door squeaked loudly as it swung open on its rusty hinges.

"You two," Anna ordered, motioning to Nigel and me, "stand guard out here. If you see anyone or hear anyone coming, shout."

"Where are *you* going?" Nigel asked.

"Inside."

"What for?"

"To fuck."

We left Anna on Crete. There were promises to meet again and addresses exchanged. Perhaps Colin, even then, had other ideas. But it never occurred to me that we would see Anna Schmidt again. We had also exchanged addresses with Nigel's Belgian wench, with Hilde Nielsen and Rosa Luxemburg, with Markus and Petra and most of the other Germans we had camped with on Santorini, with countless others. As far as I was concerned, however, this exchanging of addresses and light farewell kisses on suntanned cheeks was simply part of a pleasant ritual that signified nothing. I had come to the Aegean in August 1971, so had they. There was nothing more to it than that. These people would be listed and tidily filed away under the label *Greece, 1971*. Maybe I would tell stories about them, add characters, created from the material they provided, into subsequent – improved – accounts of my week in Mayfair with Karen O'Connell. But I would never see any of them again.

Nigel, Colin and I were on our way before sunrise the next morning. Anna poked her head out of her sleeping bag. Mosquitoes had bitten her face during the night. One had given her a badly swollen eyelid.

The three of us walked up past the chapel, its forced door still open wide, its icons unprotected from marauding tourists, out to the road. The first car to pass, a rusting red Simca from the 1950s, stopped to give us a lift. The driver was a priest in a long black robe.

"Hi, kids. Want a ride?" He told us he had grown up in Philadelphia. "The American one," he said. "Not the original Greek one. It's in Turkey now. All the original inhabitants killed or kicked out fifty years ago. Massacred by the Turks." There was bitterness and anger in the words themselves, but not in the tone of the voice. His grandparents, he said, had come from Anatolia. They had escaped.

He asked us where we had been in Greece. We told him: Athens, Mykonos, Ios, Santorini (which he insisted should be called Thera) and Crete. When he asked, we told him where we had slept in Crete. I expected a sermon on the morals of the foreign beach dwellers. But he simply asked, "Did you see a little chapel on the rocks at the end of the beach?"

"Yes." It was Nigel who answered.

"It's a shame our chapels are always locked nowadays. It's because the people think tourists steal the icons. They are cheap, meaningless souvenirs for a tourist, but holy windows into heaven for those who live here. Anyhow, that little chapel is famous throughout Crete for its miracles. Have you heard about that?"

"No."

"Well, you see. It's like this. If a woman wants to have a child, she goes there. She prostrates herself on the stone floor in front of the iconostasis and prays to the holy mother of God. Within a year, a child is born. It always works. I have never heard of a case where it failed. Never."

I looked at Colin. He was not smiling. Was he remembering the teethmarks that Anna, devotee of Dionysus-Sogol, had inflicted on him in front of that same iconostasis, that she had failed to take her contraceptive pill for two consecutive days when she was arrested? Or was I just imagining a layer of pallor spreading beneath the joined-up freckles of his summer tan?

The priest drove us, several kilometres out of his way, all the way to the ferry terminal. Standing beside the car, he hugged us each in turn, his great black beard rubbing our awkward cheeks before he lifted our rucksacks from the boot of his old Simca.

"May God bless you," he said, with a formality lacking until then. "May He accompany you on your journey, boys, and cause His face to shine on you from the magnificence of His creation. In the fullness of his time, may you find peace in the forgiveness of your sins."

I looked back when we had walked about twenty metres. The priest had already driven away.

7

"Died?"

Dad said simply, "Yes."

"How?"

"She had been ill for some time, Nick."

"But..." My voice trailed away. The lake appeared ahead of us. Two sailboats danced uncertainly on its grey surface.

My father had picked me up at the airport on my return from Greece. He had listened, as we drove into town, to my stories of the Acropolis and Knossos, of the chapels on Ios and the spectacular cliffs on the extinct volcano at Santorini... before telling me that my grandmother had died while I was away.

"Your mother is very upset."

"I'm sure she is."

"Upset, as well, that I let you go to Greece and that you missed the funeral."

"Let me?"

"Yes."

"When did she die?"

Dad told me the date. He had flown to London one evening after work and been with my mother at the bedside when my grandmother died the next day. Susan had arrived an hour later. All the other grandchildren were present at the funeral; all of her descendants apart from me. Her ashes were buried, beside her husband's, in the plot she had tended each Sunday morning, beneath the lonely hammer and sickle she had faithfully polished with her faded yellow duster.

Mum scarcely spoke that evening. She served supper with uncharacteristic efficiency and declined my offer of help with the washing up. When I began to tell her about Greece, she sat heavily in her chair, picked up a magazine and hid her puffy red eyes behind her reading glasses.

Pleading tiredness from my journey, I went to my bedroom, kicked off my shoes and stretched out on my bed beneath my old red *LIBERTÉ* banner. As I lay there, thinking about my month in the sun, I watched the April lilacs and daffodils wither and sink back into the dead land, found myself running and skipping with the girl who had lifted her skirts and stuck out her tongue. I felt the gloved hand slowly release its dark brown grip on me.

I calculated that on the day of my grandmother's funeral I had been lying on a beach in Santorini, trying to imagine the discreet charms of the Baedeker Guide to Greece as she accused me of being a fetishist (which is hard to pronounce after half a bottle of ouzo) and predatory parasite on the liberation of women. Regrets? Where would I rather have been? Lying in the sun on an Aegean beach – even if being told I was no better than a capitalist whoremonger – or in a damp English graveyard? Do you need to ask? The bourgeoisie can bury its own dead. For once, I harboured no regrets about being unable mimic Colin's talent for being in two places at the same time. Yet Colin Witheridge was right about one thing: I didn't have to wait for the Revolution. I *was* free. I stood on my bed, stretched my arms wide and, in one extravagant motion, ripped my red banner from the wall and crumpled it into a ball of waste paper. I no longer needed it to preach to me.

A week or so later, on the evening before I was due to return to Oxford, I went for a stroll without any planned itinerary. I walked up past the golden domes of the Russian Orthodox Church and through the streets of the Old Town, past the cathedral and the house where Calvin had once lived. I turned my gaze away from the fearsome profile on the wall plaque and, once I was sure there was nobody but me in the street, sang the opening lines from Bob Dylan's 'Mr Tambourine Man' as I wandered aimlessly on.

Then, going back down to the Rues Basses to catch the tram home, I spotted Janice Day. She stood alone on the pavement outside La Vie en Rose. Although the evening was warm and dry, she was wearing a raincoat and a pair of leather boots that reached almost up to her knees. Her hands were thrust deep into the pockets of the mac. In the pink light of the nightclub's neon sign, her face looked tired and worn.

"I thought you'd've been back at college by now," I said with more than a hint of a question in the statement.

"I'm not going back."

"What?"

"I'm not going back."

"Why not?"

"I'm just not. Maybe next year. What about you?" she asked.

"Going back tomorrow. Term doesn't start 'til the beginning of October, but I've got some stuff to catch up on."

"You go to Cambridge, right?"

"Oxford, actually."

"Sorry. I should've remembered. Anyway." She looked furtively up and down the street behind me.

"What're you gonna do?"

"As a matter of fact I'm going to London next week. D'you know, I've never been to England?"

"Really?"

I tore a blank page from the back of the book I was carrying and wrote my college name, address and the phone number at the porter's lodge on it. "I'll show you 'round Oxford if you want a day out of London."

"That'd be nice. Maybe." She took the paper, put it into the pocket of her raincoat and bent forward to give me a feather-light kiss on the cheek.

I left her there and, deciding against the tram, walked home. I was intensely aware of the place where Jan's lips had touched my cheek. The feeling seemed to give rise to a hope that she would actually turn up in Oxford, would let me show her round, would let me... Well...

Experience, however, had taught me that it was all most unlikely. American girls, I had learned, idly said these sorts of things with little connection between what they promised and what they eventually did. And Janice Day was, from everything I knew, more unreliable and more unpredictable than most.

CHAPTER FOUR

The note in my pigeonhole in the porter's lodge was in awkward capital letters: 'Mr Kellaway. Miss Day telephoned. She will arrive on the 4:30 train.'

I spent the next two hours behaving like a girl, trying to decide what to wear, arranging and re-arranging my rooms. I took down the poster of Che Guevara, put one of Geneva in its place, took that down and put Che back. I lit a joss stick and then opened the windows to get rid of the smell.

Twenty minutes before the train was due, I was pacing up and down the station like an expectant father, smoking one Sobranie Black Russian after another, still not believing that Janice Day was coming to Oxford to see me.

The train arrived on time. I scanned the windows of the carriages. The doors opened. The voice over the loudspeaker system croaked, "Oxford. Oxford. This is Oxford." Passengers alighted. No sign of Jan. Then I felt a touch on my arm.

Shit! Shit! Shit! Priscilla McGinley stood grinning. "Hello, Nick," she leered.

I had heard that Sill was in Oxford, living in digs in Jericho, but I had not, until then, seen her – had not, in fact, seen or heard anything from her since the morning she and Caroline left Geneva. I tried to brush her off. "Meeting a friend," I said.

"Ah. No 'Nice to see you again, Sill' or anything? No 'Didn't we have a lovely time up on that mountain, Sill?' No 'Fancy a shag, Sill?'"

Then I saw Jan, struggling to get off the train with a large suitcase and her guitar. I ran along the platform to her, arriving too late to be of any assistance. She looked pale. Her hair had lost its lustre. She was wearing the same mac I had seen her wearing outside La Vie en Rose. We kissed on the cheeks, like continental bourgeois cousins on a frosty January morning.

"Welcome to Oxford, Jan. Good to see you."

"Good to see you too, Nick."

Then I noticed Sill beside me. She thrust out her hand towards Jan. "I'm Sill. Friend of Nick's."

Jan shook her hand. "I'm Janice. Nick and I were at high school together."

"You a Yank?"

"Pardon me?"

"American?"

"Yes."

"Shit."

I carried Jan's bag across the bridge and out of the station. Jan carried her guitar. She and Sill were walking ahead. I could hear snatches of their conversation. "I was in Geneva in the summer," Sill said. "Nick dragged me up some God-forsaken holy mountain. There I was expecting the Ten Commandments an' all I got was fucked." Sill looked over her shoulder and grinned at me. "Okay with the bags, Nick?" Then to Jan again, "How long're you staying in Oxford?" It was beginning to rain.

"I don't know. I haven't decided yet."

"Where's she gonna stay, Nick?"

"With me."

"Are you living out?" She knew I wasn't.

"No."

"You can't fucking do that. They'll give you hell."

"It'll be fine, Sill."

"It bloody well won't. You'll never even get that" – she pointed at Jan's suitcase – "past the fucking porter. They'll be down on you like a ton of shit."

"It won't be a problem."

"Like fuck." Sill turned to Jan. "Tell you what. You can stay at my place. Nice little house. Four bedrooms. The others aren't up yet, so it's just me. Plenty of space."

Jan looked at me, said tentatively, "It sounds like a good idea, Nick."

Sill said, "We'll get a taxi. It's raining, and anyway, Nick'll kill himself carrying that case all the way to Jericho."

"Jericho?"

Sill and three other like-minded girls, one of them Emma Wallace, had rented a Victorian terraced house in Jericho for their third and final year at Oxford. It was built of red and grey bricks and lay not far from the *faux-romanesque* tower of St Barnabas.

When I was nearing the end of writing this account, I decided that I needed to refresh my memory of some of the places where its events had taken place, to follow the movements of Jan's imagined figure. I wanted, in particular, to stand again on the pavement outside the Jericho House.

So one Sunday morning in July 2008, I caught an early morning train to Oxford. The day was clear and still, the winds and rains of the previous days had moved on. I walked past the walls of Worcester, to which pollution from passing cars sticks mercilessly, and along Walton Street, past the University Press and the eroded Corinthian columns of a temple to Freud, which I'm sure had been a church when I was up at Oxford. I seemed to pass far more shops and restaurants than I remembered. Jericho sparkled in the sun and only a rare car moved through its gentrified streets. Windows that had once displayed their solidarity with the proletarian revolution, now sported signs advocating independence for Tibet and commending a campaign to 'Save Our Boatyard' (by www.portmeadow.com) that I fear had already by then been lost.

The house where Jan lived for a few weeks in the autumn of 1971 had been somewhere near here. When the windows were open, you could hear the bells of St Barnabas and the sound of metalworking in the boatyard. Sometimes you could smell the canal mingling its dank perfume with the scents of tobacco and cannabis, of sandalwood and rose, of frying chips and yesterday's beer. I looked for the house, but I could not find it. Perhaps it had been demolished, replaced by one of the more modern houses that fill the gaps in the old terraces where printers and boatmen used to live. There had once been a plan to demolish the whole of Jericho. The town planners succeeded with a similar plan for St Ebbe's, replacing it with an appalling shopping centre and evil car park, themselves now ripe for destruction. But Jericho was mercifully spared.

I walked away. Perhaps I didn't look hard enough for the house. Perhaps I didn't want to find it. Perhaps the Jericho House, like so much else, lived better in the memory.

I went down Walton Well Road. From the bridge I could see new dwellings looming over the canal, the type that estate agents flatter with the adjective 'desirable'. I disliked them instantly and hoped that the previous summer's floods had irreparably damaged their foundations and that the residents had suffered severe problems with their mortgages in the liquidity crises of the last twelve months.

I walked to Port Meadow and across the Isis to Binsey. The Perch, once top of the list of my favourite Oxford pubs, was barricaded behind a builder's temporary fence festooned with plaques advertising the names, addresses and qualifications of those who were doing the work. I remembered reading that a kitchen fire had reduced The Perch to a charred ruin. It looked as though its resurrection body, taking shape behind the protective wooden panels, would be more glorious than the one I remembered from the evenings when I came out here with Jan – walking back across the river, as the mists rose from the dark meadow, towards the lights of Jericho.

Back in town, I took a late breakfast at The Eagle and Child. Afterwards, on the pavement outside the pub, a group of eager American summer students asked me if this was the place where C.S. Lewis and J.R.R. Tolkien had met to discuss *their* fantasies and, if it was, could they go in and have a look around. I found myself scanning their gum-chewing faces to see whether any bore a resemblance to Janice Day. There seemed to be a part of me that refused, as I stood among those kids, to travel from the past to the present, refused to acknowledge that it was 2008 not 1971. Even after the previous summer's lunch at La Mezza Luna and all that had happened after that, I was still looking for Jan. When I told the girls, with only a little exaggeration, that I had met Tolkien when I was up at Oxford, they snapped photos of me as if I were some sub-species of hobbit.

I walked back to the station, up the steps towards the glass-fronted building. Then I saw her: Janice Day! A girl coming out of the station. Long, off-blonde hair, blue jeans, red t-shirt stretched over her full breasts, khaki-green rucksack on her back, guitar case in her right hand. She walked towards me. I smiled.

She looked past me to where the taxis wait. She passed within two metres of where I stood, rooted in another age, in a past millennium. I watched her put her rucksack and her guitar case into the boot of a taxi and climb into the back seat. She took a piece of paper from a pocket and seemed to read an address to the driver. I watched the cab pull away, stop at the lights, drive on when they turned green. The part of me that lives efficiently – that lives successfully – in the present awoke and urged me gently, *Nick, old friend, it's time to move on. The Paddington train leaves in less than five minutes. Janice Day is dead. You know that.*

On the train to London, I found myself staring vacantly out of the window, remembering the wet evening after Jan arrived in Oxford. The three of us – Jan, Sill and I – ate supper at The Lamb and Flag, across St Giles' from where I had, thirty-seven years later, been accosted by the cameras and mobile phones of the young American tourists. Pies, chips and bitter. "Nosh like this'll put you back to rights," Sill said to Jan. But Jan did not eat much, left most of her beer standing in its glass, said she was real tired and wanted to go back to Sill's to get some sleep. I paid the bill for all three of us and bade the two women goodnight as they walked out into the rain.

2

It was a season of smiling dreams and golden moments on the thin fabric of reality. I saw Janice Day as much as I could over the weeks that followed, though, inevitably, far less than I would have liked. Sometimes four or five days would pass when I did not see her in person. But even during those absent days and nights, she was never far from my thoughts.

Jan gradually lost her pallor. Her hair regained its shine. She borrowed a commoner's gown and a bicycle. She went to a series of lectures on nineteenth-century German literature. "I'd've majored in German if I'd stayed in the States," she said. She read voraciously and asked me well-crafted questions about Marx's early writings and about Antonio Gramsci's analysis of cultural hegemony and social superstructures as a means of repression in the interest of capitalist conformity. I invented what I thought might be plausible replies. I had never heard of Antonio Gramsci.

We had several drinks at The Lamb and Flag but after Jan had read *Jude the Obscure* she would not go back. We had our first curry at a Bengali restaurant in The Turl opposite Exeter after Jan told me she had just begun reading *A Passage to India*. We met for breakfast at George's in the market. We walked across Port Meadow to The Perch at Binsey and once along the river to The Trout. Crossing the meadow at dusk one evening Jan dared me to catch one of the horses that graze there and said she would take her clothes off and ride it like Lady Godiva if I succeeded. I did catch one. But she became coy and reluctant and I did not hold her to her promise.

I think Jan only left Oxford once during the weeks she was there. She had to go up to London on some mysterious errand and I went with her. I rambled around Hyde Park, watching squirrels frolic in the fallen leaves and noisy geese migrating southwards across the grey urban sky, while she did whatever it was she had come up to London to do. Before we caught the train home to Oxford we had dinner at the Mezza Luna. That was Jan's idea; a spontaneous, though belated, celebration to mark my twentieth birthday.

One afternoon, kissed by a warm autumn sun, Jan took her guitar to the Parks. A small crowd of passers-by gathered round her as she sang 'Joshua Fit the Battle of Jericho', 'You've Got a Friend' and 'Swing Low, Sweet Chariot'. I asked her to sing 'Puff the Magic Dragon', but she said no. She declined, too, to sing 'House of the Rising Sun'. "I've been there," she said, enigmatically adding after a pause, "I'd like to think I've kinda moved on."

Once, after we had played a game of tennis and were walking back at dusk across Magdalen Bridge, the bells ringing joyously in the tower, she took me by the hand, then put an arm around me. "Nick," she said, "you're so lucky to go here. So damn lucky. Oxford's just so magical."

"Like Puff?"

"Different, but probably just as good." She pulled me close and kissed me.

Jan had been in Oxford about four weeks when I ran into Colin Witheridge in The Turl outside Lincoln.

"Nick," Colin said. "I've got a problem."

"What?"

"Anna's turned up."

"Who?"

"Anna Schmidt. God dammit. You must remember. Greece? The girl…"

"Why's that a problem?"

"It is. Believe me."

"Pregnant?"

"Get off it. I need to find her some place to stay."

"What's wrong with your room?"

"She was there last night but then this morning the bint got caught prancing about in the altogether on her way back from the shower."

An involuntary smile. "Prison sentence didn't teach Fraulein Houdini anything then?"

"God, Nick. She laid into them. Verbally, I mean. You know, all that Marxist-feminist crap about sexual repression, oppression… Standing there in the fucking nude spitting out all that shit. Ever read Marcuse on surplus repression?"

"And?"

"*And?* Can't you imagine? The blokes were loving it. Absolutely fucking loving it. Egging her on. I calmed her down. Took her back to my room. Then I had to go off to a tutorial and when I got back there was a note to go see the Bursar."

"So?"

"What d'you do with that American of yours? Where d'you keep her?"

"She's staying with Sill."

"Do you think she'd take Anna in?"

So the German girl we knew as Anna Schmidt was moved into the house in Jericho with Jan, Sill, Emma and the other two whose names I can't recall. According to Colin, Anna stayed in Oxford for five days. I saw her only once during that time. It was one afternoon when I'd gone over to see if I could find Jan. Anna was in the house, alone. She stood in the kitchen in front of a bubbling pot of goulash, blood-red from a surfeit of paprika. She offered me a cold beer, an imported German one. "I hate your English beer," she said. "It's like warm piss."

Anna was simmering with anger, not only about the temperature of English beer but about everything and particularly everything male. One of the houses in the street served as a brothel, run as an informal co-operative on behalf of its workers by a Scotsman called Willie. He had, I slowly gathered, propositioned Anna as she walked along the street. We all knew Willie; 'Whisky Willie' as we called him. He was regularly out in the street touting for business for his 'girrrls', chatting up the passing traffic in his broad Glaswegian banter, "Ye cannae be goin' doon thar, laddie. Six lassies in the same wee hoose? They're aw frae Lesbos, Jummie." He was harmless. Just doing his job. The business he ran was on the decline. His market was shrinking as sex became more readily available elsewhere without apparent charge. Gratis. "Now this 'free love', Jummie. That's unfair competition."

"I slapped the bastard's face," Anna said, "hard."

I finished my beer and did not stay long.

Later, after Anna had left Oxford, stories began to circulate about her. Jericho House stories. I heard this one first from Jan. One afternoon, or so the story went, Anna had berated the wearily pregnant neighbour from across the street for her "abject submission to conjugal slavery." The husband had come across the street an hour later, banged on the door and, when Anna opened it, told her to "piss off back to bloody Germany and remember who won the fucking war." The next morning, when the fascist oppressor had left for work, Anna stretched herself naked across the yellow and purple carpet on the floor of the downstairs front room, under the reproduction Renaissance painting of Adam and Eve, and masturbated energetically. The curtains were drawn widely back such that Anna was fully visible to anyone who happened by – and also, not incidentally, to the anxious wife who watched from behind the lace curtains in the upstairs window opposite.

"Modesty," said Jan, "only begins with the knowledge of evil."

"Where'd you get that?" I asked. "The Bible?"

"Rousseau."

"You've been reading Rousseau?"

"No. It was just in one of those classes I'm doing: Revolutionary Political Philosophy from Rousseau to Trotsky."

The following January, Emma Wallace told me a variant of the story of Anna and the pregnant neighbour. It was sufficiently different from the version Jan had told me that I asked if it was true.

"True?" Emma questioned. "Does *that* matter? It's a Jericho House story."

One evening in November, when you were beginning to feel the penetrating cold that hangs in the damp air on Oxford winter nights, Jan came to dinner in college. She arrived with her guitar, slung over her shoulder by its embroidered strap, unprotected from the weather by its usual case.

She arrived half an hour late. We left the guitar in my room and went straight over to Hall. A cold rain was falling when we came out after dinner and we returned quickly to my room. I turned on both bars of the electric heater and opened a bottle of Fendant.

We sat together on the sofa, facing the electric fire as it warmed the room. Jan spoke to me for the first time of her family: of her elder brother who was training in Florida to be a pilot; of her sister who had married the previous year and was already expecting a child; of her parents' marriage, under strain after her mother had discovered that Happy, Jan's father, had had an affair with a secretary in his office; of her mother's childhood in Hitler's Germany...

"Nick," she said. "You're the only person in Oxford who knows where I'm coming from."

Prompted perhaps by the poster of Che Guevara looking down

on us from his position of honour above the mantelpiece, Jan began to speak of her childhood in Buenos Aires, of how she'd been happy there, until… "I feel different when I'm speaking Spanish," she said. "It's like living in another world. It's like the magical world of a child." She picked up her guitar, played and sang 'Guantanamera'. It was, she said, the original arrangement, the one sung in Cuba before Pete Seeger had adapted it for the American left-wing, folk-song canon.

"Dad wouldn't let me sing that at home," she said.

"Why ever not?"

"Because Pete Seeger's a communist. Because it's Cuban. Because it's anti-American."

"Is it?"

"Dad thinks so. We still hold onto a bit of Cuba. Did you know that?"

"No."

"A bit called Guantànamo. That's what the song's about. 'Guantanamera' means a girl from Guantànamo."

Yo soy un hombre sincero
De donde crece la palma…

I sat beside her. Content.

"Listen to this," she said. She played 'Streets of Laredo', but sang her own adapted lyrics. It is a tribute to how clearly that evening is etched in my memory that, nearly thirty-five years later, when I came to write them down, I could still remember each word she sang, each stanza in the order she sang them. As I wrote them out on a sheet of lined A4 paper, sitting in the sun on the balcony of Paul Meyer's villa on La Côte in the summer of 2006, I could still hear the voice that sang them as if it were in the room behind me.

As I walked out in the streets of Geneva,
As I walked out in Geneva one day,
I spied a young banker wrapped up in white linen,
Wrapped up in white linen and cold as the clay…

Breaking the silence that followed the burial of the wayward banker, I asked: "What about Puff?"

"You're a good friend, Nick. D'you know that?"

When she had finished singing 'Puff the Magic Dragon', she

sang, without being asked, the other song she had until then declined, as far as I knew, to sing during her time in Oxford.

There is a house in New Orleans
They call the Rising Sun.
And it's been the ruin of many poor girl,
And me, oh God, I'm one.

She then interposed a verse I had not heard before.

And all you need for travellin', man
Is a rucksack and a gun.
But the only time I'm satisfied's
In the House of the Rising Sun.

It was a verse I would hear again, in other circumstances, after Jan had gone.

Jan took her guitar over to the corner of the room, leaned it against the wall, pulled her pullover off over her head, switched off one of the bars of the electric heater, came and sat again beside me on the sofa. I put an arm around her and, when she did not pull away, I kissed her on the cheek.

"Nick," she said softly. "Please don't. Don't break this friendship we've got going."

But she did not leave her seat on the sofa, did not move away from me, and when I kissed her again, she did not resist. In those days, everyone knew that when a girl said 'no' she really meant 'yes'. I opened her lips with the tip of my tongue and, when I felt her respond and put her arms around me, I let my right hand move up to her breast and touched it gently through the blouse and bra. I undid one button on her shirt and then the one below it. I kissed her neck.

She pushed me back softly. I heard a cold sigh that seemed to come from another time far beyond that warm Oxford room. A hand on my shoulder, a light kiss on my forehead. "Not tonight, Nick. Sorry."

I looked into her eyes. I tried to pull her towards me, gently, as gently as she had just pushed me away.

"Not tonight. Please."

She got up from the sofa, re-buttoned her shirt and walked over to the window. "It's pissing it down out there," she said. She pulled her pale-blue sweater back over her head. "Do you remember, Nick, that joke you told once, *'J'ai un pullo vert et j'ai un pullo bleu?'* I didn't get it at the time. If we didn't speak French, you guys who'd lived all your lives in Geneva made us feel kinda out of it. We got back at you by being so ultra American and ultra cool. You wanted it and you couldn't have it. And then you didn't want it because of Vietnam and you were trying to make out like you were some kind of socialist revolutionary."

She put on her mac. It was the same coat I had seen her wearing as she loitered outside La Vie en Rose the night I invited her to Oxford, the same coat she had been wearing when she got off the train at Oxford station. I lent her my umbrella when she asked if I had one.

"I can't take the guitar out in this rain. Look after it for me, can you?"

I walked with her past the porters' lodge, out to the street. "I'm okay," she said. "You don't need to come with me."

She kissed me. Gently. Tenderly. Once. On the left cheek.

"Watch out for Whisky Willie," I said.

"I've handled worse," she replied and walked away into the filthy night.

3

It was a dark and stormy night; the rain fell in torrents, except at occasional intervals when it was checked by a violent gust of wind… I slept fitfully. Brief snatches of dreaming had an evil smell of sewers and sulphur about them. I awoke from the stench, reached out for comfort from Jan and found nothing, lay awake listening to the window rattling in its frame.

What a wimp I was! What would people say if they ever heard what had happened – or rather what had not happened – on my warm, cosy sofa last night? They would laugh, that's what they'd do, laugh like the overflowing drainpipes gurgling after the storm had blown itself out and lost its potency.

It was mid-morning when I awoke from what must have been four or five hours of sleep. I had missed a lecture and saw little point in getting out of bed before lunch. I did not see or hear from Jan that day. Nor the following day.

Late the next morning, on the third day, I walked out to Jericho.

There was a police car parked outside the house and, inside, two policemen were talking to three of the girls. Neither Jan nor Sill had been in the house for the previous two nights and they had heard nothing from them. The girls had checked at Somerville and learned that Sill had missed two tutorials. They had phoned Sill's parents in Liverpool, who had not heard from Sill since the beginning of term. Emma had found the telephone number for Jan's parents in Geneva, called it and asked for Janice.

"I'm sorry," a voice Emma took to be Jan's mother's said, "she's not living here. She goes to college at Oxford now." Emma said thank you and ended the short conversation so as not to spread alarm and anxiety.

A strange man with psychotic eyes had, a few days earlier when Jan, Sill and Emma were all out, knocked on the front door, claimed to work for the town council and asked for "the Austrian girl." When told she had returned to Germany, he said, "What about her American friend?" Over the following days he was frequently seen loitering in the street, holding an official-looking clipboard and pen but doing nothing obviously useful. Since nine o'clock on the morning of their housemates' disappearance, the remaining girls had not seen the man again.

They had phoned the police.

The housemates introduced me to the police as "the American girl's boyfriend". The policemen asked when I had last seen her. I told them. They asked for details. I provided them; from late arrival for dinner to premature departure. I don't think they believed everything I said. In common with most townspeople, they probably believed that students lived a life of enviable erotic privilege. It was simply incredible that someone described as the American girl's boyfriend would have let her go home unfucked after a private evening of wine, music and whispered intimacies, would not even have walked her home to Jericho. They asked me about Sill. When I gave a non-committal response, I saw a repressed smile cross Emma's thin lips.

While I was still at the Jericho House, one of the policemen found Whisky Willie in the street. He said he had seen "two of the loony lassies frae the lefty Lesbos hoose" leaving in a cab two days before. The police contacted the taxi firm. They checked their records and confirmed that one of their drivers had indeed picked up two female students in Jericho and driven them to the station. At about eleven-fifteen on the morning after Jan and I had spent the evening in my room.

News of Sill's departure spread rapidly through Oxford. She was well known around the university for her radical politics and, to a smaller circle, for her advocacy of lesbianism as the road to liberation. Some said she had been deeply troubled recently by the elitism of an Oxford education, that she had likely gone to live for a few days in an all-woman squat in East London and that, purged of her concerns, she would be back in Oxford soon. Others suspected that she had been abducted by the CIA, casting the mysterious Janice in the role of evil American abductress. *The Oxford Times* picked up the story from *Cherwell* and included a comment from 'William, a neighbour' who added a touch of colour. *The Guardian* took up the thread and showed evidence of independent enquiry – its article mentioned Priscilla McGinley's American companion, but misnamed her as Eunice Gray.

I drifted in and out of lectures and tutorials, half-heartedly tried my hand again at college sports, attended listless Labour Party meetings, drank beer at the JCR bar. Friends – advocates of the forget-and-move-on school of relationships – took me out to the pub and offered me cannabis. Nigel bought me a curry at the restaurant where I'd eaten with Jan. Caroline Carter dropped in, asked after my parents and then stayed only ten minutes, pleading the need to buy a book at Blackwell's before it closed. Colin called in on his way to a party to suggest I go with him; "There'll be plenty on offer, mate. A proper meat market." I declined and, like most evenings, sat alone in my room. I tried to read, to write essays, to solve mathematical puzzles. But I was always distracted by the mute guitar standing abandoned in its corner. I think I probably stared at it for hours. I never picked it up, never so much as touched it. When I found, on returning late one afternoon, that my scout had moved Jan's guitar to another corner of the room, I cried.

4

A photograph of a city skyline at night:

Greetings from Berlin!
Thanks for everything in Oxford.
Will you be in Geneva at Xmas?
Luv,
Jan.

If hearts genuinely can skip a beat, mine did then as I read the skimpy message on the postcard. If there were such a thing as a moodometer, you would have seen mine jump from zero to a hundred in the space of that missing heartbeat. If I had been able to turn cartwheels, I would have turned them all the way back to my room.

I went home by train at the end of that Michelmas Term. I was taking Jan's guitar with me and did not want to entrust it to the hold of an aircraft. In those days, the boat train left Victoria at three-thirty in the afternoon, you boarded the ferry at Dover, joined another train across the Channel in France, were shunted through the sidings of some Paris marshalling yard around midnight and arrived in Lausanne in time to catch the 07:07 to Geneva.

I had made the journey one childhood spring with my parents. I had drawn back the blinds of the sleeping compartment and looked with delight out on the cattle grazing on the rolling Swiss meadows. Early morning mist had hung among the evergreens. Above, the sky had been clear blue. In the distance the sun of the new day had sparkled on the Alps. How happy I had been that May morning to be returning home, returning to Switzerland!

In December 1971, however, it was still night when the train reached Switzerland. It was cold and drizzling when I changed platforms in Lausanne, a rucksack on my back, an overweight suitcase in one hand and a guitar in the other. But never had my anticipation of being home again given me such a spring in my step. My mother picked me up at Cornavin, drove me home and fed me croissants, home-made strawberry jam and real coffee. Over the kitchen table I chatted to her as I had not done since remotest childhood.

As soon as I reasonably could, I phoned Jan's number in La Capite. A voice I took to be her mother's answered. "I'm afraid she's not back from college yet. Who did you say was speaking?"

"Nick Kellaway, ma'am."

"Oh, Nick. How nice of you to call. You know, we have no idea where she is."

"She told me she'd be home for Christmas."

"That *would* be wonderful. I *do* hope so. When did she tell you this?"

"I had a postcard. Oh, it must have been written ten days ago."

"A postcard?"

"Yes. From Berlin."

"*Berlin?*"

"Yes."

"I see."

"When she gets home will you let her know I called, please?"

"Of course. Of course."

I showered and then lay on the bed staring at the ceiling. I felt the moodometer slowly sinking back towards zero. If her parents had not heard from her since she left Oxford, then she would not be coming home for Christmas.

Geneva can be dreary at the fag end of the year: leaden skies, cold rain, empty streets. Lethargy set in. Friends I roused myself to phone had not yet returned. Others were spending Christmas in the mountains or on some distant beach. I spent hours entombed in the old Eaux-Vives flat. The most useful thing I did was help my mother stir her Christmas pudding. I had brought her some of the ingredients from Oxford.

So it was with relief that I took a call from Marie-Claire inviting me to a fondue party in the new flat that her father had bought her. "A house warming," she said, "and a belated celebration of Escalade[26] and Jean-Daniel's twenty-fifth." Claude would be there, Marie-Claire said, if he got back to Geneva in time.

We ate the fondue, drank the wine and smashed the chocolate *marmite*. Marie-Claire popped a red marzipan tomato between my lips when I had gone on too long about Wittgenstein.[27]

"Those lips were made for better things," she said, but then turned away from me and hid her face.

A marzipan carrot failed to stop Jean-Daniel droning on about the systematic state-sponsored persecution of the Yennish. I doubt if any of us, except perhaps Marie-Claire in her more intimate moments with Jean-Daniel, had ever heard of the Yennish. "Their

---

[26] Geneva celebrates Escalade on 12 December each year. The holiday commemorates the successful resistance of the Protestant republic to a night-time attack by the Catholic forces of the Duke of Savoy on 12 December 1602. – Ed.

[27] Ludwig Josef Johann Wittgenstein (1889–1951) was an Austrian-born philosopher. He is often regarded as the pre-eminent philosopher of the twentieth century. Although he taught chiefly at Cambridge, his influence in the philosophy department at Oxford was without parallel in the 1970s. Wittgenstein's major works are the *Tractatus Logico-Philosphicus* (1921) and the posthumous *Philosophische Untersuchen (Philosophical Investigations)* (1953). – Ed.

sedentary Swiss persecutors," Jean-Daniel lectured us, "particularly target the women because they believe that nomadism, like original sin and other dangerous diseases, is transmitted through the women. Of this, you will hear more soon."

"Can't wait," Claude said and uncorked another bottle of wine.

Although half-drunk and barely listening, we snapped to attention and looked aghast when Marie-Claire added homosexuality to Jean-Daniel's list of dangerous, 'female-transmitted' diseases. "It is a mental disorder," she pronounced and gave as her source the American Psychiatric Association's *Diagnostic and Statistical Manual of Mental Disorders*.

Claude changed the subject abruptly and asked about friends from school. None of us mentioned Janice Day. No-one but me knew she was missing and that was not a piece of bread I wished to lose in the communal fondue pot.

Marie-Claire put an arm around Jean-Daniel's Parisian waist and steered him towards her bedroom. "Good night," she said before she closed the door. "Let yourselves out." The record on the gramophone was coming to the end of '*Le Temps des Cerises*'.

I alone among Marie-Claire's other guests stayed. Although I could easily have walked home, I spent the night on the sofa. I let my mind take its customary somnolent path into the arms of Janice Day, then gingerly allowed it turn to Marie-Claire, to her mischievous smile as she placed the red marzipan between my lips. It was the first time since Jan had disappeared that another woman had come near to sparking my imagination. As if imagination was not enough, I then heard, as I had once in the Meyers' chalet in Crans, the sounds of Marie-Claire making love beyond her closed door. I fell asleep only long, long after the noise had subsided.

I was deeply asleep when the telephone rang the following morning. Jean-Daniel emerged from the love nest naked, unaware until then that anyone had stayed the night, answered the phone and then handed it to me. It was my mother on the other end of the line, worried when she had found my bed at home still unoccupied at dawn. Jean-Daniel said, "Nick, your mother." That, however, was the charitable interpretation of what he said. Jean-Daniel, as usual, spoke in French and what he probably said was "*Nique ta mère.*"

On Boxing Day, Mrs Day phoned. "She didn't come home."

"I'm sorry to hear that. Maybe she's just…" I didn't finish the sentence. I couldn't think what Jan might 'just' be doing.

"We'd like to see the postcard she sent you. Do you have it with you in Geneva?"

"I could bring it round tomorrow."

"Oh, Nick. That *would* be nice of you."

I had never been inside Jan's house, but I knew where it was. I had surreptitiously ridden past it on my motorbike more than once, hoping to catch a glimpse of Jan and pretend it was mere coincidence that I happened to be passing. Enjoy a chat with her. Maybe kiss her goodbye on the cheek as I prepared to ride off into the proverbial sunset. It had never happened, of course.

Happy Day answered the door. Happy was a salesman. He had spent his entire career, since his discharge from the US Army, selling farm machinery – first to American farmers in the Midwest and then to the *estancieros* of Argentina and the peasantry of Europe, egging them on to make a purchase with his famous smile and its implicit promise that one day, if they bought from him, they might become as ebulliently American as Happy Day himself. It was said that Happy Day could sell anything: fridges to Eskimos, coal to the miners of Newcastle, subprime mortgages to the canny bankers of Edinburgh. That afternoon, however, no trace of the legendary smile graced his lips. His eyes were glazed over and on his breath I caught the smell of whisky.

Mrs Day – Ursula Day – served tea in the informal sitting room – the 'den' as Happy called it. She probably imagined that, because I was English, I spent each waking hour sipping from teacups. I, for my part, had forgotten quite how well expatriate Americans maintained the illusion of an idyllic Midwestern suburb inside their homes abroad. In the middle of the room a circular rug made from a single, multi-coloured, braided cotton coil covered the polished parquet floor. The walls displayed high school diplomas, a painting of a farmhouse surrounded by flat expanses of cornfields, two needlepoint samplers and photographs of an impeccably bourgeois family. There was a prominent all-American picture of Jan taken when she graduated from Ecolint and another, with similar effect, of Jan's elder sister, Martha. An airman, whom I took to be Jan's brother, stood beside a plane with palm trees in the background. A much younger Mr Day, in American Army uniform, his foreign bride beside him, posed stiffly. There was also a large heavily framed family portrait on the wall, an oil painting rather than a photograph. Each member of the Day family had been scrupulously painted – preternaturally prosperous and amazingly beautiful. Jan was the youngest: about ten at the time, I guessed. The artist had captured a look of eager innocence on her face that had already vanished from those of the other children. Although my attention was focused on Jan, it struck me that there was something about the portrait as a whole that did not tally with the facts I had collected about Janice Day and her family. It would take several years for me to see, in an unexpected flash, exactly what was wrong.

The Christmas tree was brightly decorated. Beneath it, presents remained unopened. I handed Jan's parents the postcard from Berlin.

"She speaks German, of course," her mother said.

"Ursula's German originally," Happy added, "and Jan's very talented in that way, you know. She speaks four languages pretty well fluently. English, of course. German because of Ursula's diligence. Then French and Spanish."

Ursula said, "We lived in Argentina before moving to Geneva."

Happy looked at his wife as if she had spoken out of turn, as if Argentina – where Jan had said she had been happy, where the nostlagic painting of the optimistic family on the wall had no doubt been painted – was something not to be mentioned in polite company.

"Is she just passing through Berlin? Or maybe she is staying there?" Ursula asked.

"I'm sorry. I don't know, Mrs Day."

"This postcard doesn't say she's coming home for Christmas," said Happy. "It just asks if Nick is going to be in Geneva at Christmas." I felt momentarily embarrassed. I would have been even more embarrassed had the Days known that I was credited with the finest formal-logic brain in my year at Oxford. "Did you show this to the police?"

As it happened, I *had* shown it to the police. I had walked down St Aldate's to the police station beyond Christ Church and waited forty-five minutes until they found someone to look at it. The designated officer turned it over casually, said thank you and then handed it back to me. If they had opened a file on Jan's disappearance, the card would no doubt simply have served to close it with all responsibility transferred to the police in West Berlin. "Yes," I said.

"What did they say?"

"Not much. They asked if I was sure that it was her handwriting."

"It sure looks like hers. But even as her dad I can't be totally certain. Kids change so much at her age."

Ursula asked, "Did she give you any reason for leaving Oxford?"

"No. Not at all. She never even mentioned that she was *thinking* about going. She seemed perfectly happy, busy. Always something on the go. I saw her the evening before she disa… left and… no. Nothing."

"Evening before? Sorry to ask you this question, Nick, but you were not living, so to speak, together?"

"No. Not at all."

The mother shot a quick glance at the father. They had been speculating about this. The glance said Ursula had been vindicated. I imagined myself dropping a further notch in Happy's estimation.

"Where *was* she living?" Happy asked.

"In a house with some other girls in a part of Oxford called Jericho."

Ursula looked startled. "Jericho? Like in the Bible? Where the walls fell down?"

"Yes."

Happy showed me an envelope with a letter still folded inside it. It was addressed to her mother only, in the same hand that had written the postcard from Berlin. In the upper left corner Jan had written her return address. "Here?"

"That's it."

I handed the envelope back and Ursula stretched forward to take it from me before it reached her husband's hand. She said, "She wrote to us every week from Oxford. We were so proud of her, you know. After all the problems she had growing up, getting into Oxford… It's a very famous college, Nick. Then," she waved a hand in the air like a magician at a children's party, "nothing." She opened the envelope, pulled out and unfolded the letter. "This is the last letter she wrote. Janice always wrote to us in English. But this one was to *me* and she wrote it in German. She asked a lot of questions about the time before I was married. The wartime…"

"We hadn't replied," said Happy, "by the time we heard she'd left Oxford."

Ursula looked at her husband, as if trying to decide whether to risk contradicting him. "No, Virgil," she said at length, "I *did* answer. In German. A personal letter from a mother to her daughter."

"You did? All those questions?" asked Happy. There was a note of alarm in his voice.

"Yes. Janice has a right to know. I had an obligation to tell her." Then to me, "Nick, I wonder if it was because of my letter that she went to Berlin. If I could…"

Happy interrupted, asked whether they could keep the postcard. I said yes – how could I refuse them? They had more claim on their daughter than I had. I had only reached the second button on her shirt. I had, in objective fact, no claim whatsoever on Janice Day. I just had her guitar. I didn't mention that to her parents and took it back with me to Oxford at the end of the Christmas vac.

5

I walked over to Jericho the day after I returned to Oxford and found that neither Jan nor Sill had returned. Emma Wallace told me that nothing had been heard from either of them – other than the bland message on the postcard Jan had sent me. Jan's parents had been in Oxford four days previously. They had spent an hour with the police and then gone to the Jericho House to see where Jan had been living. Emma had served them tea and digestive biscuits.

Emma was preparing to host a meeting of her Nietzsche Society cell group and asked me to stay for it. In my time at Oxford, Nietzsche was strictly extra-curricular – well outside the authorised philosophical canon. Although I had been press-ganged into the Nietzsche Society in my first term, I had never actually read a single word that he had written. I stayed that evening only because Emma told me that Jan had faithfully attended the meetings during her time in Oxford. There was also, she said, an American who would be joining the study group. Emma thought I might find Sylvia interesting. "She used to live in Geneva and remembers Jan's family."

The cell group took the passage where Nietzsche announces the death of God:

Have you not heard of that madman who lit a lantern in the bright morning hours, ran to the market-place, and cried incessantly: "I am looking for God! I am looking for God!"

"Where has God gone?" he cried. "I shall tell you. We have killed him – you and I. We are his murderers. But how have we done this?

Is not the greatness of this deed too great for us? Must we not ourselves become gods simply to be worthy of it? There has never been a greater deed..."[28]

---

[28] This quotation appears to have been taken from Walter Kaufmann's translation of Nietzsche's *The Gay Science* first published in 1974. Nick Kellaway cannot, therefore, have read it in 1972.

"Nick," Emma asked mischievously, "tell us, what does it feel like to be God?"

When I said nothing, Sylvia encouraged me, "Come on, Nick." It was because of Sylvia that I went back the next week.

The following week we discussed 'On the love of one's neighbour' from *Thus Spake Zarathustra*. One of those present, a historian from Magdalen, latched on to the phrase '...as soon as five of you are together, a sixth must always die.' He said, "Looking at this in the context of what we were discussing last week, how the act of murdering is in and of itself as significant in a person's liberation as the identity of the object of his murder act is, it seems to me that what the text is saying here is that, for the individuals in their little group of five to achieve their own individual higher existence, they must kill the group's sixth member. A sort of substitute for God."

Emma said, "Go on."

"That," I interrupted, "is so obviously not what it's saying."

"What's it say to you then, Nick?"

"It's absolutely clear. Nietzsche is protesting against a morality based on 'Love your neighbour'. He wants us to see, first, that if I love my neighbour, I am not loving myself, not fulfilling my *Ubermensch* potential. Then, second, he is pointing out with this fifth and sixth stuff that if we focus our morality on those closest to us then those farther away inevitably suffer. Look: 'It is those farther away who pay for your love of the neighbour'. It's clear. He is asking what kind of a morality is it where an individual's value is measured by proximity and using the obvious conclusion as a Socratic *reductio ad absurdum* for conventional love-your-neighbour morality." I remember being rather pleased, as a Nietzsche novice, with my speech.

"That doesn't do it for me," the Magdalen historian said. "It doesn't cohere with the whole thing about murdering God."

"But that's not in this bit."

"It is for me. It pervades everything. The only reason Zarathustra is developing a new morality is because God is dead. How do we live a fulfilling life in a world without meaning?"

"But it doesn't mean the five have to murder the sixth."

"It does to me."

Sylvia, who rarely spoke and did everything in her limited powers to prevent arguments, said, "We've got to let the text speak. It says one thing to one and another to another."

"But only one of them is correct," I said.

"Not necessarily. Something that's true for you may not work for Emma or Mike."

"Come on. What did Nietzsche mean?"

The Magdalen historian fixed his small piglet eyes on me. *"Mean?* What are you on? *Meaning?* I don't know why I'm even bothering to talk to you. Meaning is such a fucking fascist concept."

"Does it matter," Sylvia asked, "what Nietzsche meant any more than what it means to the individual who reads the words? We've got to be careful not to privilege one standpoint above another, even if that standpoint is the author's."

Afterwards I said to Emma, "I think that Magdalen guy is mad."

Emma replied, "So was Nietzsche."

I never went to another Nietzsche meeting, but I did see Sylvia again. Sylvia was an American doctoral student and six years older than me. She had done her first degree at Berkeley and lived in Geneva for three years as a teenager, though I quickly established that she had never met Jan and had never even heard of the Days. Emma had invented that. Maybe she had also invented Jan's faithful participation in the Nietzsche séances.

Sylvia's mother had been Chinese and, behind her sallow mask, Sylvia seemed to cultivate a distant, oriental sadness. Her eyes seemed older than her years and her dark lips whispered that she expected little of life and would take what came, good or ill, quietly in her unobtrusive stride. She hoped, but not too fervently, to get a job at GATT[29] in Geneva when she had added an Oxford D. Phil in the economics of international trade to her résumé. She painted her nails dark purple and waxed her pubic hair.

Sex with Sylvia was uncomplicated. She made no demands on me outside the bedchamber, and even there her presence was minimal. As I lay with her, as winter softened into spring, I would summon Brigitte Bardot, Gudrun Ensslin or some other goddess from the outer ether into her accommodating bed. With my eyes shut, however, it was still Janice Day that came to me most often. I was learning Colin's art of being in two places at the same time and I was, despite its comforts, not sure that I was altogether happy with it. Had Freedom, Revolution, the Brotherhood of Man and all my fervent hopes and dreams so quickly boiled down to this?

---

[29] GATT – General Agreement on Trade and Tariffs, the predecessor organisation to the WTO – the World Trade Organisation. – Ed.

6

In February 1972, word began to circulate that Sill's photograph had been seen on a wanted poster in Germany. Articles about our very own British contribution to terrorism in West Germany appeared in the national newspapers. One newspaper labelled Sill a 'Trotskyite' and printed an archive photo of her in a London protest march against apartheid. She was carrying a 'No Arms to South Africa' banner – the slogan that was subsequently and indelibly parodied on the walls of Balliol as 'No Legs to Patagonia'. [30] The article noted – poignantly – that that particular demonstration had turned violent, shop windows had been broken and policemen hospitalised. None of the newspaper stories mentioned Jan.

Nigel Bickleigh managed to get a copy of the German poster and Colin and I went round to his rooms to inspect it. There were several photographs spread across the poster, like one of those that decorate the walls of French railway stations, drawing travellers' attention to the faces of missing children. The caption under Sill's mug shot identified her as *Priscilla Carmen McKinley*. There also were other pictures, pictures I had not expected: Karl-Heinz Kupferhoden, inventor of my 'Fuckolas Fuckaway' nickname; Markus Holzschifter, Poseidon's *sommelier*; and Petra Steinhauer who, posing as a prostitute, had let the air out of the US Army's tyres. Then, of course, unmistakably, was the face of the girl we had come to know as Anna Schmidt. The caption beneath Anna's photograph was 'Anastasia Kuznetsova'.

I gaped in amazement. Colin was the first to speak. "Shit."

Nigel said to me, "Your American's not here."

"So? Why should she be?"

"Theory is Anna Schmidt, Anastasia Kuznetsova, whoever she is, recruited Sill and Jan when she came to Oxford in October."

"Recruited?"

"Nick, look," Nigel said, "these are meant to be mug shots of terrorists. Maybe not actual Baader-Meinhof, but something like that. There are dozens of these groups in Germany."

"Jan's not political," I protested.

---

[30] See Amy Copplestone, *Legless in Patagonia*, Oxford, 1988. The title of Amy Copplestone's account of Oxford in the early 1970s is derived from the graffiti on the walls of Balliol College. – Ed.

Colin added, "Anna was only here for three or four days."

Nigel held up his hand. "Thing is," he said, "the police may want to speak to us. We need to have our stories straight."

"What is there to have straight? How does anyone know we have anything to do with these guys?"

Nigel looked towards Colin.

Colin sighed. "Nick, you remember Petra?" He looked at Nigel. "And I don't want anything about Anna coming out either, okay?"

"Why not?"

"Caroline might take it the wrong way and..."

Nigel interrupted him, "It would just be better that way. Can we leave it at that?"

The police never did contact Nigel or me. Colin said they never contacted him either but now, with the hindsight of nearly forty years, I guess there were reasons other than Caroline Carter for Colin wanting to keep his association with Anna Schmidt away from prying policemen. I guess he had the means to do so.

I spent a day in the library going through newspaper archives, looking again at articles that had appeared when Sill and Jan had left for Berlin. I read the rare articles on Germany that had appeared in the domestic British press. I began to take notes, to build up a file that I would eventually store away under the heading 'Spring 1972'.

28 January 1972 – The *Berufsverbot* becomes law in West Germany.[31] It gives the authorities the power to deny anyone deemed to hold unacceptable political views the possibility of employment as a teacher or a civil servant. Colin says, "In their next law they deny food to useless eaters." Do I detect mocking tones? Sometimes I think Colin is only a Man of the Left for the sake of keeping up appearances.

30 January 1972 – The British Army fires on unarmed demonstrators marching in Londonderry. Thirteen die.

2 February 1972 – The British Embassy in Dublin is burnt to the ground. British facilities are attacked in Berlin. One dead. German radical groups announce their support for the IRA. British installations will henceforth be legitimate targets.

8 February 1972 – A partially decomposed body found under

---

[31] For a survey of the legal machinery built up to defend the interests of the West German state during the 1970s, see S. Cobler, *Law, Order and Politics in West Germany*, English edition, London, 1978. – Ed.

rubble on a Berlin construction site is identified by police as that of Karl-Heinz Kupferhoden. Police say he was killed by a bullet from a Russian-made handgun. The Red Army Faction issues a statement claiming that Kupferhoden was the victim of an extra-judicial execution.

9 February 1972 – The Heath Government declares a state of emergency in Britain. The ostensible reason is a strike by coal miners.

11 February 1972 – Colin Witheridge arrives at my room one morning just as I am about to leave for a lecture. "Nick," he says, "fantasy and reality have become one." He clasps his hands together, intertwining his fingers, and grins. "I'm fucking the choir girl!"

20 February 1972 – Nigel Bickleigh leads a student march through Oxford in support of the coal miners.

21 February 1972 – Bank raid in Kaiserslautern. Red Army Faction members escape with DM 285,000. One of the raiders, Ingeborg Barz, phones home to tell her mother that she wants to leave the gang. She disappears and is believed dead. Andreas Baader is quoted as saying, "Nobody leaves."

22 February 1972 – An IRA bomb kills seven in Aldershot.

23 February 1972 – A Lufthansa jet is hijacked to Aden. The West German government pays DM 16,000,000 in ransom to release the hostages.

27 February 1972 – Police in Liverpool arrest Priscilla McGinley's father. He is released two days later. No charges are pressed.

1 March 1972 – German police machine-gun bullets kill seventeen-year-old Richard Epple. He was underage and driving without a licence. He had no connection with the Baader-Meinhof gang or any other left-wing group.

2 March 1972 – Tommy Weissbecker is shot dead by police in Augsburg. On the same day, Wolfgang Grundman and Manfred Grashof are ambushed at an RAF safehouse in Hamburg. Shots are exchanged. A policeman dies of his wounds a fortnight later.

5 March 1972 – Outside Herschel House, home of Oxford Astrophysics, I stand guard while Colin paints large letters on the wall. They read 'Fidel Castro is a Martian'.

15 March 1972 – Pipe bombs explode outside a British military installation at Niffelheim near Kiel. Two die. Responsibility is claimed by the so-called Kupferhoden Brigade of the Red Army Faction.

16 March 1972 – Pornograffiti appears overnight on the walls of the Northgate Hall. It consists of a drawing that looks like a hybrid between a light bulb and an erect penis, thrusting towards a depiction of the female sex organs. Below the phallic bulb is written 'a light to lighten the genitals'. A Hebrew translation is provided in brackets. Rumours credit a cohort of maenads from LMH with the artwork. Caroline Carter, said to be engaged in competitive graffiti writing with her boyfriend Colin Witheridge, is apparently their leader. The wall is washed clean within seventy-two hours.

29 March 1972 – Shoot out in Bielefeld. Till Meyer is captured by the police.

1 April 1972 – An article appears in the Swiss press on the country's Yennish gypsies. It details the Swiss government's involvement in the fight against the plague of Gypsyism. There is no mention of Marie-Claire's boyfriend, Jean-Daniel.

10 April 1972 – Pipe bombs explode at a British Army barracks at Mönchengladbach. Three die. A Catholic Irishman, originally from County Armagh and living nearby with his German wife, is arrested and charged with being an accessory to murder. He is never brought to trial, but is not released from custody until July.

13 April 1972 – A house in a bourgeois Munich suburb, known to Bavarian police as being rented by a Radical Left sympathiser, is destroyed in a fire, apparently following an explosion. Bodies of four adults, one a pregnant woman, are recovered from the charred wreckage. None of the dead is identified.

3 May 1972 – Sylvia tells me that she has received a letter from Geneva advising her that her application for a post at GATT has been rejected. She accepts the university teaching post in Singapore which she has been holding as a fall-back.

9 May 1972 – I tell Caroline Carter about Anna Schmidt, her possible links to the Baader-Meinhof gang and her more certain links to Colin Witheridge, letting her slowly draw out of me all the graphic details of a hot August night in a little Orthodox church where local women go to pray for babies and men come away with teeth marks on their necks. She tells me she has heard nothing of this. I feign surprise.

11 May 1972 – Andreas Baader, Gudrun Ensslin and Holger Meins bomb a US Army facility in Frankfurt. A US Army officer dies.

12 May 1972 – A Red Army Faction team, led by Irmgard Möller and Angela Luther, bombs the police station in Augsburg.

They dedicate the attack to revenge for the killing of Tommy Weissbecker. On the same day, Baader, Meins and Ensslin, fresh from their bombing in Frankfurt, bomb the Bundeskriminalamt car park in Munich.

14 May 1972 – Colin tells me that he has broken up with Caroline Carter. "It's only temporary, you know," he says. "I'll never let this one go. Never. Not the choir girl."

15 May 1972 – Baader, Raspe and Meins bomb the car of Judge Wolfgang Buddenberg. His wife suffers severe injuries.

18 May 1972 – In North Oxford, a fire destroys a BMW belonging to a right-wing don with racist views on experimental psychology and immigration. His alleged corporate connections are apparently proven by the BMW: he could not afford a car like that on a university salary alone. Colin tells me how it's done – "You leave a cigarette lighter burning against a tyre. You've got plenty of time to get away because it takes a few minutes to ignite" – without actually saying he is the perpetrator.

19 May 1972 – The Red Army Faction bombs the Springer Press in Hamburg.

21 May 1972 – Priscilla McGinley is arrested in Heidelberg. She was spotted and recognised by a policeman as she walked past a house that the police have had under surveillance for two weeks. Sill admits to having had an affair with a high-ranking official (name and gender not specified) in Bonn, but denies stealing state secrets and passing them on to a person or persons unknown via a waste bin in a park by the Rhine.

24 May 1972 – The Red Army Faction bombs the US Army's Supreme European Command in Heidelberg. Three die. Irmgard Möller claims the attack as revenge for the murder by the German police of Petra Schelm in July 1971.

26 May 1972 – Colin Witheridge and two others found MENDA, 'an unprofitable dressing-up and dining organisation for those who claim to have, but do not necessarily have, an exceptionally high IQ (top two percent of the population (or better)).' I decline Colin's invitation to attend the society's inaugural meeting in Lincoln.

1 June 1972 – Following a gun battle in Frankfurt between the police and the Red Army Faction, Andreas Baader, Holger Meins and Jan-Carl Raspe are captured. Baader surrenders only when he is incapacitated by a bullet wound in the leg.

8 June 1972 – Gudrun Ensslin – brains behind the RAF, autocratic muse of the Baader-Meinhof Gang and lover of Andreas

– is captured in Hamburg. She was out shopping for designer pullovers when she was spotted by a vigilant member of the public.[32]

9 June 1972 – Brigitte Mohnhaupt and Bernard Braun are captured in Berlin.

10 June 1972 – Sylvia leaves Oxford. She intends to spend the summer in California before moving to Singapore. "It's been great," she says. "Keep in touch."

15 June 1972 – Ulrike Meinhof is captured at the apartment in Langenhagen where she has been hiding.

17 June 1972 – Markus Holzschifter is captured in Mainz trying to board a Rhine pleasure steamer bound for Koblenz. His rucksack is discovered to contain three bottles of *Trockenbeerenauslese*, a corkscrew, a full headwaiter's costume and a pair of white silk gloves.[33] His companion, Petra Steinhauer, is arrested with him. She has with her a diary in which she has written a detailed account for each day since 1 August 1971. Although Steinhauer is released in early July, transcripts from her diary will end Nigel Bickleigh's hopes of a political career and provide West German prosecution lawyers with several important items of corroborating evidence for trials in the years ahead. Somewhat to my dismay, I am not mentioned in the Steinhauer diaries.

25 June 1972 – German police kill Iain MacLeod in his Stuttgart apartment. They retrospectively try to establish links between the Scottish expatriate businessman and the Baader-Meinhof gang.

There is still no mention anywhere of Janice Day.

---

[32] See dream number twenty-nine in *The Dream Diaries* and E. Anstey and M. Bottreaux, 'The Social Context Behind the Political Dreams in the Wichita Dream Diaries' in *Sex Today*, Vol. 23, Sydney, 2007.

[33] Markus Holzschifter (1941–1991) was released from police custody in August 1972. No charges were brought against him. Later that year he defected to East Germany. Newspaper articles at the time carried suggestions that he had been a spy in the service of the East German state and condemned the West German authorities for his hasty release. Holzschifter became a teacher of English first in a suburb of Berlin and subsequently in Weimar. After the reunification of Germany and the opening of the Stasi files, it was discovered that Holzschifter had been the object of acute East German suspicion and intense surveillance during his years in the East and been prevented from leaving East Germany for Cuba. He committed suicide in 1991. The German political journalist, Socrates Holzschifter (1974 –), is his son. Socrates Holzschifter's *Fernweh* (Berlin, 2005) is a biography of his father. – Ed.

CHAPTER FIVE

In mid-August I left Geneva for Italy with an InterRail pass in my pocket and no immediate destination in my mind. I wandered through the Italian summer, caught the first train to whatever place name caught my fancy on a station departure board and stayed in youth hostels and the cheapest of hotels. I traded travellers' tales and drank with strangers.

In a Florence hostel, I smoked a Dutchman's pot and was kept awake by his rusty snore – like the intermittent travails a superannuated locomotive. Of Siena, I remember nothing other than a striped cathedral and the disembodied voice of an American girl which became, as I dreamed alone on a narrow bunk, Jan's. A Parisian in Assisi told me in lyrical tones of his fascination with mystical death cults, of severed heads, human sacrifice and the ultimate sensations. He wore black Levi's and a black, sweat-stained t-shirt inscribed with 'Ne Travaillez Jamais' – 'Never Work' – and invited me to accompany him on a walk through the Tuscan hills. I declined.

Towards the end of the month I met, by prior arrangement, a group of four Oxford girls in Rome and travelled south with them. I told them amusing, self-deprecating tales, charmed them with apposite quotes from Horace and Virgil, guarded their clothes as they swam naked in the sea and acted the gallant chaperone through the male-infested warrens of Naples. At Pompeii, I stumbled like a clown around the dead streets as we followed the priapic trail from *The Fornicator's Friend*.[34] In a frescoed brothel, one of the girls, a Half Blue in gymnastics, bent over backwards until both the soles of her feet and the palms of her hands were flat on the floor. We laughed at the visual pun. "I hope," Caroline Carter said, "you're not doing that for Nick's entertainment." We all laughed again and then set off for the Villa of Mysteries and its suburban Dionysian rituals. For part of the journey, the archgymnast rode on my back, her legs

---

[34] S. Cadbury and C. Sandford, *The Fornicator's Friend: thirty erotic side trips on your European tour*, Berkeley, 1970. – Ed.

wrapped around my waist and her arms around my shoulders.

Later that day, while we were sitting in the shade at an outdoor café table sharing a second bottle of white wine, Caroline said, "I'm so glad you joined us, Nick." The other three nodded their agreement.

In due course we came to Paestum.

During our exploration of the temples, Caroline and I found a breach in the fence around the ruins. When darkness fell, we left the other three to spend their second night at our campsite on the beach, took our sleeping bags and made for the gap we had found in the defences. We spread our sleeping bags on the floor of the Temple of Hera, lay on our backs, gazed at the stars, listened to the cicadas.

"When we lived in Delhi," Caroline said, whispering for fear, she said, of offending the gods and guardians of the holy site, "we went out to a tiger reserve once. We stayed at an old guesthouse left over from the days of the Raj. It sat on the edge of the jungle facing a lake…" The guesthouse was painted a dusky orange and its roofline was festooned with pinnacles and domes and *chhatris*. In the evening, just after sunset, Colonel and Mrs Carter, Caroline and Imogen would sit on the broad verandah with their pre-dinner drinks, very still, to watch for the tigers as they came down to the lake to drink.

There was an old Rajput fort on one of the hills in the reserve, not far from the orange guest house. One morning, Colonel Carter decided to take his family for a walk up the hill to tour the fort. Guides were arranged and they set off up the stone ramp, through the ruined gates of the ancient stronghold. Certain stones along the side of the ramp had been daubed with orange and white paint. Caroline asked why. These were sacred stones, the guide explained, gods of the people who lived in the reserve. The tiger was also one of their revered gods – a goddess, in fact, except when she killed their goats. Within the perimeter of the hillfort's wall was another god – a tree that was covered with paint and pieces of paper and fabric tied to its branches with string.

"The Hindus," Caroline said, "have 33,550,336 gods." On top of the hill there were also two Muslim shrines, tombs of holy men, and an old Hindu temple precinct. When the dates were auspicious, the temple became a place of pilgrimage. The Muslims were gone now, but the Hindus still ritually passed by the sites where the Muslim saints were buried along the designated route to their temple. Once, the guide said, with an avuncular smile directed at Caroline, when a group of pilgrims was returning through the forest from the holy temple, a tiger had jumped out of the bushes, pounced on an eleven-year-old boy and eaten him. "I was eleven at the time," Caroline said.

A man sat in the narrow temple entrance. He had long, filthy, matted hair and a spittle-drenched beard that fell to the middle of his chest. Yellow paint encrusted his face and his right hand grasped the stem of a *papier mâché* trident. When he stood, barring the way into the temple, the Carters could see that he was completely naked. He was also very thin. Caroline could see every rib. His arms and legs were like the twigs they used for kindling when they lit the evening fire in the guesthouse. His body was smeared with orange and red and what seemed to be excrement and blood. A wildness in the man's eyes seemed to Caroline to be fixed on her. As she looked at him, she saw the sadhu's dangling penis stand up and swell. It grew until it was thicker than his arm.

As the sadhu shook his trident and called down Shiva's curses, Colonel Carter hurried his family away. That evening as they sat on the verandah, listening to the noises of the night, Colonel Carter attempted to explain the naked sadhu to his children. He had not advanced far in his halting explanation when the whole sky, and the lake that reflected it, lit up with a blue light. A meteor raced across the sky, burned itself out. The darkness of the moonless night returned. The man responsible for serving drinks said, "It is an omen, sahib, a big portend."

News reached the guesthouse at breakfast of an attack on the temple on the hill. The sadhu was dead. Under cover of darkness, a tiger had crept out of the jungle and killed him. It had eaten what little flesh hung on his body. The smiling bearer of the news and the breakfast eggs said, "This sadhu was famous throughout all India for the size of his enormous lingam, and – what do you know? – the tiger goddess has devoured it utterly."

When Caroline finished her story we lay watching the night sky in silence. As a faint trace of a shooting star passed overhead, I reached out and touched her hand. Omens and portends. Fireworks in the sky. Volcanoes erupted. The ground on which we lay trembled and shook. Tectonic plates shifted. A new continent emerged… or something like that… if only I read the right kind of novels…

We awoke as the cocks began to crow and the first pink light of day appeared in the east, dew on our hair, still entwined in each other's limbs. We rolled away our sleeping bags, returned to the sleepers in the campsite on the beach and slept until the heat and flies awoke us.

At the café, where we went for a late breakfast, we learned that Palestinian guerrillas had murdered the Israeli team at the Olympics in Munich.

2

Why did I not continue on to Sicily with Caroline? My excuse then was that I had planned to meet Colin in Geneva, to travel with him north through Germany, but was there more to it than that? From a distance of thirty-five years it is difficult to disentangle emotions of the moment from memories woven around all that has happened since. Was I running away? Did I fear that I would never be able to recapture those tectonic hours in the Temple of Hera, that we would droop under the memory of them, listless pilgrims travelling in the time shadows cast by the tiger goddess of the Paestum night?

Caroline asked me to forget my promises to Colin and go with her to Sicily. But she asked only once. Did I already sense that Caroline Carter was dangerous? Dangerous in a way that Sylvia Spurway, in her many guises, had not been? That in Caroline's embrace I risked toppling Janice Day from her carefully constructed and immaculately maintained pedestal? That I risked seeing the world I had created revert to a primeval soup without form and void?

Among the four girls, Caroline alone came to the station with me when I left Paestum. She kissed me goodbye, holding my hand until the train began to move away. She stood waving on the platform until I could see her no longer.

A few hours later, on the train leaving Rome, my fears were confirmed. As I dozed off I sent my daydreams out hunting, as I often did before sleep, for Jan. If a night with Caroline Carter had caused meteorite showers and earthquakes, what might one with Janice Day be like? But it was not Jan they found. It was the tear trickling down Caroline's cheek as she slowly let my hand go.

The train had reached the outskirts of Florence when I awoke. If we had been born thirty years later, I would have got off the train at Florence, phoned Caroline to say I had made a dreadful mistake and caught the next train south again. But in 1972, there were no mobile phones and we had never heard of text messages. Caroline was somewhere in southern Italy... somewhere on a soft beach fringed by palms and lapped by the azure Mediterranean...

somewhere beyond Paestum… somewhere… The cold, grey grip of reason got the better of me and I took the sad train home.

Colin had arrived two days early in Geneva and I found him having supper with my parents. He was telling them about his eight weeks labouring on a building site, about the proletarian brothers alongside whom he had toiled, about his first-hand experiences of capitalist exploitation and about the wages he had proudly earned. I joined them for the remnants of their supper, listened to Dad and Colin discussing the literary merits of Soviet realist literature and afterwards sat in an armchair to open the post that had accumulated for me.

Among the letters was one from Hilde Nielsen, one of the girls from the previous summer in Greece. Norwegian stamp, return address in Oslo on the back-flap. I threw it unopened into the waste-paper basket. I believe that just then I might even have thrown a letter from Janice Day herself straight into the bin. There was a postcard from the Côte d'Azur written in the polyglot babble affected by my Ecolint schoolmates and signed by Marie-Claire, Claude, Paul and two others whose signatures were illegible. Another card came from the death-besotted Parisian lad I had met in Assisi and to whom I believed I had deliberately *not* given my address. Nigel had written and so had Colin – to say he would be arriving in Geneva two days early.

I kept until last a letter postmarked three weeks earlier in Illinois. Johnny Morris wrote to say that he and Sally were getting married. The date was set for April 1973. The place would be a church in Dallas, Texas. Would I, he asked, act as his best man?

In the letters that had travelled westward across the Atlantic over the past nine months, I had told Johnny everything – or, at least, everything I knew – about Jan's weeks in Oxford. With the pen that wrote those letters I had crafted the emotions I felt after that Bulwer-Lytton night when she disappeared. In each of his responses, Johnny had written at least one paragraph about Jan, sometimes empathetic, sometimes reverting to his earlier teasing vein. In this letter there was no mention of her.

When I replied, that very evening, accepting the invitation to stand beside Johnny as he said his wedding vows, I too made no mention of Jan.

Colin and I took the train from Geneva to Bern. We visited the bears and the Young Boys of Wankdorf. From Bern we went on to Basel where we caught a local train across the border to Lörrach. From Lörrach we decided, despite our InterRail passes, to hitchhike. We could not believe our luck when, after only five minutes beside the road with our thumbs out, a black BMW stopped for us. It was driven by a man of about thirty wearing Ray-Bans: the popular image of the leader of the gang himself. The car even bore a bumper sticker that said something about Baader-Meinhof.[35]

Andreas Baader deposited us deep in the Black Forest on the edge of a village that looked like a set for *Chitty Chitty Bang Bang*. It did not appear on our maps and there was nobody in its streets. Dusk was falling and lights were beginning to come on in the houses, curtains were being drawn, shutters closed to control the light, hoarding it for the bourgeois families within.

As we ordered beer and bratwurst in the *bierkeller*, the staff and the other customers watched us suspiciously as if our manifest intention was to violate their wives and daughters or, worse, to steal their cars. No-one spoke to us. Even the waitress who took our order only nodded silently to indicate that she had understood. When we asked whether there was anywhere in the village we could spend the night, heads shook slowly, as if the worst thoughts that rattled in them had been confirmed.

We ate quickly and left the village. At a stand of evergreens along the road, we spread our sleeping bags on a bed of brown pine needles and spent our first night in Germany there, sleeping only when the barking of distant dogs had ceased.

In Heidelberg we visited the castle and went out to the guarded perimeter of the American Army base that the RAF had bombed earlier in the year. We found and walked along the street where Sill had been arrested. In Frankfurt, as part of our terrorism-for-tourists itinerary, we saw the site where Andreas Baader had been captured in June and then made our way through Stuttgart, Ulm and Augsburg to Munich.[36]

---

[35] The bumper sticker was probably '*Ich Gehöre nicht zur Baader-Meinhof Gruppe*' ('I do not belong to the Baader-Meinhof group'). Many cars driven by young people in Germany at the time carried this slogan, a quiet protest at the suspicion with which all youth was regarded at the time of the RAF campaigns. BMWs were particularly prone to being stopped and searched by the police. BMWs were said to be Andreas Baader's favourite car. They came to be known as Baader-Meinhof Wagens. – Ed.

[36] Uschi Obermaier was originally from Munich. – Ed.

"What's wrong with you, Nick?" Colin asked as we got off the train at Munich station.

"Nothing."

"I think you need a good fuck." When I did not respond, Colin continued: "We'll have our pick of the bunch in Munich." He looked at me as if I might have forgotten what planet we lived on, "Oktoberfest?" Despite the massacre of the Israeli athletes, the Olympic Games had gone on. Now the Oktoberfest too was going ahead.

We drank beer from litre mugs, ate sausages doused with mustard, nibbled rubbery Emmenthal cheese smothered in salt and pepper, drank more beer, swore eternal friendship with strangers. We watched buxom bratwurst babes bounce their big Bavarian boobs and brush their brightly burnished bottoms past punters' protruding noses, as if we were extras in a *Carry On* film. We listened to brassy bands; lined up in front of long urinals in the company of a hundred pot-bellied, middle-aged men; joined our piss with theirs and tried to avoid filling our lungs with the ammonia in the steam that rose in front of us.

On our second day, in the early evening, in the Löwenbräu tent, I saw Janice Day.

3

I had lied to Colin. Oh yes, I had told him plenty of summer truths as well, about my sister's wedding at a cosy little parish church in Hampshire, about walking with Claude and Paul Meyer in the mountains, about running into Eva Bocardo whose *Playboy* portrait he had admired on the wall of my Oxford room. I had bored him, I am sure, with details of the family tree branches that somehow connected Eva to me, with the melodic litany of the place names on the slopes of the Wildstrübel, with an imagined scene of Susan and husband fumbling in the domesticated dark of their wedding night. All that, however, was just wrapping paper around the lies that grew thicker the closer the story came to Paestum.

In the realm of lies, I had screwed an American backpacker in Siena, gone for a walk in the Parisian's valley of the shadow of death and ridden a motorcycle around the Piazza Navona at three in the morning with the cast from one of Fellini's films. I had watched the decaying empire's homosexual population emerge from the caverns beneath the Coliseum, once its gates were closed to the tourist trade, to practise their dark gladiatorial arts. Of Caroline I said nothing, nothing more than that I had met up with her and three others in Rome, travelled south and toured Pompeii with them.

"Did you," Colin asked, "stop at Montecassino?"

"Yes."

"Did Caroline tell you about her dad being wounded there?"

"No." It was another lie. She *had* told me. Tears had run down her cheek as she told me about her father's artificial leg. I wiped them with the tip of my finger and then kissed her lightly where the tears had been. I tasted salt. It was the first time I had kissed Caroline.

I changed the subject, retreated into banter about Jan, unemotional speculation about her November flight to Germany and the postcard from Berlin that had, I thought, with the passage of nine months, become safe. But I was not safe from the sight of Janice Day across the tables of the Löwenbräu tent. My heart jumped up and ran after her at twice its normal pace.

Jan – or her Bavarian double – was dressed in a traditional serving-wench costume. She had three full litre mugs of beer in one hand and two in the other. She bent over a table to serve them. Her breasts seem to swell as she leaned forward and a drinker at the table she was serving pinched her bottom. Then she disappeared. I stumbled around the tent looking for her, but the girl – Jan – was nowhere to be seen. I spoke to the man behind the bar who seemed to have charge of the waitresses. He waved me away as you would an irritating mosquito and then ignored me. Colin joined me in the search and, as I became increasingly frantic and the search remained fruitless, tried to calm me. "Probably," he said, "just someone who looks like her."

"Maybe. But we can't even find the girl who looks like her now."

"How many have you had, Nick?"

Colin sat me down at a table and passed me a hunk of bread to eat. Five minutes later, I saw Hilde pass by the entrance to the tent. Colin said, "I thought you didn't want to see Hilde. You threw her letter away."

I followed her through the crowd, but it wasn't Hilde. When I got closer to her it became clear that she did not really look at all like Hilde. Her male escort wore a black leather jacket and, when I approached, he put an arm around her waist and drew her away from me. As I returned to our table I saw a girl selling sausages who smiled at me with Marie-Claire's mischievous smile.

Colin said, "You know, you haven't seen or heard from Jan for nine months, Nick. You can't go on like this for ever. If you don't get yourself laid at the Oktoberfest, you'll never get laid at all."

Colin, as he later delicately put it, got himself laid on our first night in Munich. A Slovak woman with a wart on her chin came back to our hotel with us. I sat drinking coffee while Colin spent some of his hard-earned proletarian labourer's wages in our room upstairs. At least that is what he allowed me to imagine was going on.

4

It was dark, raining and cold when we discovered that the next train to Berlin left at three in the morning. Moreover, the man at Hof station said, there could be no assurance we would be allowed to board the night train for its passage through East Germany. So, in a dim, cavernous restaurant that other diners had already deserted, over bowls of weak broth in which dun-coloured dumplings floated randomly, we abandoned the Berlin leg of our journey. I had long ago lost my initial enthusiasm for this trip through Germany and each day that passed increased my desire to get back to Oxford. Colin stirred his soup and, without bothering to look at me, said, "Fine with me. Germany was your idea in the first place."

The next morning, Colin and I made our way westward from Hof through a dreary, grey landscape sodden with low clouds on the hills and rain beating against the windows of the railway carriage. "We should've gone to Greece again, Nick. Look at this," Colin said as the train sat, seemingly forgotten, outside the station at Lichtenfels. "How was Italy by the way? How was Caroline?"

"Fine."

"Fine? Is that all? We won't be in Frankfurt until the next millennium. Tell me."

So I began to tell him – again. I had not, however, yet met Caroline in Rome, had not yet progressed beyond either the Tiber or the Rubicon, when Colin interrupted, "Did Caroline mention me?"

"Yes," I lied.

"What did the choir girl say?"

"Nothing much. Just in passing."

Colin stared out of the window. Smoke and steam from a factory chimney lost themselves in the cloud and mist. "Sometimes I think you're a complete wanker, Fuckolas. If I'd've been you, I'd've said to hell with meeting Colin Fucking Witheridge and tramping about bloody Baader-Meinhof land in the rain. *I'd* have gone with them. Shit, Nick, four girls on a beach in the sun? They'd've been aching for it. I mean, a gymnast with *The Fornicator's Friend* in her knapsack? You'd've got lucky with one of them at least. Maybe all four." Colin paused and looked out at the derelict landscape. "But if you'd've so much as touched Caroline, you know, I'd've had your balls for *leberknudeln.*"

I picked up the story of my *Italian Journey* in Assisi and spoke again about the strange lad from Paris.

"Yeah," Colin said. "I've heard of that sort of thing. Big in France, isn't it? There's that line from Baudelaire…"

I offered, *"O, mort, vieux Capitaine, Il est temps – Levons l'ancre."*

"That's it. Your Jan was into that sort of thing."

"Janice Day?"

"Yeah, that's the one. Come on, Nick. You must've known."

"Death cults?"

"Well, maybe not exactly that, but similar shit. She used to read those weird Georges Bataille novels."

"Never heard of him."

"Nor had I. I'd've thought *you'd've* heard of him, though. All your French philosophy and stuff. He was a member of some secret society or something called *Acéphale*. Nietzsche. Death cult. That sort of thing. Between the wars. At least that's what Jan said. First I'd ever heard of Bataille and that. I looked it up afterwards and it's all kosher, all there all right, all properly documented. One of the lesbians in the Jericho House was reading French and she knew about it."

"And Jan was into this?"

"Sort of. Egged on by the one reading French. What was that bint's name?"

"Emma."

"That's it, Emma. Emma Wallace. Little mouse of a thing. Anyway, this Emma was going on about the importance of breaking taboos, experiences beyond the limits society has imposed, that sort of thing. Extreme sensations brought about by drugs and violence and sex and, ultimately, by death. Stuff like bringing on the Revolution by shifting the paradigms of the contemporary episteme. You know the sort of crap. Literature of transgression, the transcendental qualities of evil, the annihilation of the individual in primordial eroticism, sex as a window on death," Colin mocked. "Talk. Talk. Talk. It had you wondering whether there was any time left to *do* anything, with all that talking. Then she said and Jan had gone out for a walk in the countryside one afternoon. Do you know this one?"

"I don't think so."

"Okay. So they go out for this walk. Somewhere along the Isis. It's dusk, beginning to get dark, mist rising up from the river. Very atmospheric. They come to a church. Out in the middle of nowhere. Probably a church that once belonged to a village wiped out in the plague, Emma says, as if that had some sort of significance. Then they find this tramp sitting in the porch of the church. He's blocking the way in, filthy clothes, hair matted with dirt, spit dribbling down his beard, smelling of moths and old pig sties. You know the sort of thing. So," Colin went on, "Emma and Jan take the old bugger by the arms and lead him round the back of the church. They feed him some LSD and then Emma takes off her clothes and starts dancing around among the gravestones. Anyway, eventually they strip the bloke's clothes off and Emma fucks him right there on top of one of those big old family vaults."

For a moment, I found myself thinking of Caroline's Indian story. The tramp here instead of the sadhu, the church instead of the temple… Colin must have misinterpreted the look of in my eyes.

"That's what she says," he continued, "swear to God. There's this little mousey Emma, prim as a starched nun, saying, 'It was so fucking perfect: drugs, sex, church, death – what more do you want? Fucking perfect.' And then she says, 'You know what happened next?' You probably read about it in the papers at the time. The tramp's body was found in the Thames the next day. 'Fucking perfect,' Emma says. It's true. True about the dead tramp at least. I went and looked up the papers. A naked body was fished out of the river on the morning of the 10th of October 1971. Male. Between fifty and sixty. Tattoos of snakes and stuff on his arms. Never identified. And Emma's there, telling this story. It was just a couple of nights before Sill and Jan pissed off to Germany."

"You're having me on."

"No, seriously, Nick."

"Where was Jan supposed to be in all this?"

"That's the icing on the cake. You really haven't heard this before?"

"Seriously."

"Jan taking off her t-shirt?"

"No."

"Well, Jan was sitting there nodding quietly, listening to Emma, looking at her with a blank sort of stare in her eyes. She was wearing this t-shirt. Red. Says 'Class of '69' on the back and 'Find Freedom: Eat Forbidden Fruits' on the front, right?"

"I know the one." Jan's 'Class of '69' t-shirt actually just said 'Eat Forbidden Fruits' on the front. There was nothing about finding freedom, but I let that pass.

"Well, suddenly, she stands up and pulls it off over her head. We're all looking at her, right? Every eye in the fucking room. She puts her hand on her stomach and says, 'Eat forbidden fruits.' Emma'd worked out what she was on about, but the rest of us didn't have a bugger's clue. And Jan's standing there with her tits in everybody's face and saying, 'Breakfast anyone?'"

"What time was it?"

"That wasn't the point, was it?"

"What then?"

"Can't you guess?"

"No."

"Come on, Nick. Use your imagination."

From Frankfurt we went down to Mainz and took the river steamer to Bonn – quite possibly, I said to Colin, the same one Markus Holzschifter and Petra Steinhauer had been trying to board when they were arrested. In Bonn, we wandered past a few riverside dustbins that might have been the receptacles for Sill's stolen secrets. A policeman eyed us suspiciously, but that was probably only because Colin had marched twenty paces in goose step and then broken into a falsetto rendering of 'Die Wacht am Rhein'. When the dustbins and the river began to bore us, we left the Fatherland to the depredations of the *Welsche* and went to call on Edward Reader. Although Edward had been two years ahead of me at both Ecolint and Oxford I scarcely knew him; but he and Colin had been at the same college and a tutor had suggested to Colin that he call on Edward. Edward was now doing his D. Phil, or whatever the equivalent is in a German university, on something about the de-Nazification of Germany after the Second World War. We drank his wine, ate his food and slept on his floor. In return for Edward's spartan hospitality we submitted to him squeaking on about his thesis.

"The Baader-Meinhof phenomenon," said the weasel voice,

"couldn't have come at a better time for me. It provides a new angle from which to approach the whole de-Nazification process: the standpoint of the children. What was their reaction when they learned what their fathers had got up to during the war? From the time of the Frankfurt Auschwitz trial, when things began to come into the open…"

Colin asked Edward if he had met any members of the terrorist gangs. That was the term Colin used, 'terrorist gangs', echoing Edward's usage.

"Yes," Edward answered, "more than one."

"The ones in prison?" I asked.

"Yes. And…"

I caught sight of his right eyebrow rising slightly, accompanying a minor twist of the head. From that, Colin and I were meant to infer that Edward had indeed met some of the Red Army Faction still at liberty, that he knew more about them than he was willing to say. We did not believe him, of course. He had too much the air of an academic recluse to be hanging out with wanted criminals. Besides, we wanted to keep our terrorists to ourselves.

Edward said he hoped to interview Priscilla McGinley.

"Sill's dad," Colin said, "is an Irishman who works for the Gas Board in Liverpool. I doubt you'll get much on the sins of the Nazi fathers from her, Reader, old chap."

Edward Reader turned to me, "Nick, do you remember a girl at Ecolint called Janice Day?"

"Yes."

"Well, it seems that when Priscilla McGinley absconded from Oxford last year, she flew over to Berlin with Janice Day."

"Did she?" I said. "How did *that* happen?"

"Actually, I don't yet know. It's one of the questions I shall be putting to Priscilla when I see her."

"You think she'll tell you?"

"I don't imagine she'll have any reason not to. I've been doing some research and discovered that Janice Day's mother was German. Her father was in the American Army in Germany after the war. So, you see, Janice Day was half German."

"I see."

Colin, I was pleased to see, listened in silence to this exchange and later that evening when, from behind the pages of a book, I overheard him re-tell Emma's story of the tramp in the plague-church door, I was equally pleased that he omitted Jan from the account, leaving Emma to arrive on her own at the church. He also stopped short of recounting the sequel in which Jan removed her red t-shirt. Instead, after fetching a fresh supply of beer from the fridge and a volume of Hegel from the bookshelf, he said to Edward, "How do you manage to live here? It's so boring."

"To the contrary," Edward replied, "this is the most interesting country in Europe. I'm serious. And, what's more, it's the most important country and becoming more important every day. Right at the heart of the continent."

Colin said, "You're full of shit, Reader."

"You just watch. By the end of the century – what's that? Twenty-seven years? That's the same time it's been since the end of the war. In a mere twenty-seven years, Germany will be the undisputed master of Europe. The border between east and west will be gone and this little common market thing we're joining will be a proper big country. And you know what? Germany will be at its heart. Geographically, of course, but also… but also economically and spiritually and emotionally… all that. Greater Germany."

"We'll see about that," Colin replied.

"You'll see. You're right, you'll see. What Germany failed to achieve by military means she will achieve by economic and political means. Financial means. Or even by default. Other countries, tin-pot little countries around the periphery of Europe, will be queuing up pleading to join the Federal Republic. The mighty Deutschemark will suck them in. You'll see.[37] By the way, changing the subject, I don't suppose you've ever heard of a woman called Anastasia Kuznetsova?"

Still hidden behind my book, I watched Colin get up to fetch another round of beers from the fridge, even though our bottles were still half full. Edward persisted, "I've heard she was almost certainly a Soviet agent. That's why they've never found her. They got all the others on that poster, you know. All but Anastasia Kuznetsova. 'Anastasia Kuznetsova', that's a Russian name."

Colin laughed. "That's it, is it? Because she has a Russian name she must be a Russian spy? By that logic, Reader old chap, the three of us must be spooks working for MI6."

---

[37] The context of this conversation is obscured in this account. The background is G.W.F. Hegel's *Philosophy of History* in which he divides the history of civilisation and culture into four phases, namely the Oriental, the Greek, the Roman and the German – each successive phase experiencing a higher level and wider extent of freedom: "…the German world knows that all are free." – Ed.

We went to Cologne (cathedral, Beate Uhse's sex emporium – in that order) and then on to Amsterdam. After a day in the art galleries, we went window shopping in the red-light district. Colin spotted a large black woman who took his fancy, reviving his memories of the Zulu woman who he claimed had initiated him.

"What about you?" he asked.

"I'll go have a couple of beers and wait for you in that bar down by the canal."

"What's wrong with you, Nick?"

"Nothing."

"Come on, Nick. A good, old-fashioned, anti-fascist fuck'll do wonders for you."

A stray dog walked by, unconcerned by either the prostitutes in their red-lit windows or the loitering prospective customers who assessed the wares.

"Sorry."

I left him to indulge his African dreams and when he turned up and sat down opposite me, well over a long hour later, I asked him politely how his whore had been. Colin stared silently at the wooden table between us, pushed away the white plastic ashtray that held the stubs of my Sobranie Black Russians.

"Cost too much of the worker's hard-earned cash?" I grinned.

Again, Colin did not reply. From a black box pinned to a white wall at the back of the bar, Jacques Brel (or somebody like him) sang of obscure texts and mistranslations, of Nubian virgins and the white raisins of paradise.

"Let's go," I said and downed the last of my beer. "It's late."

Colin raised his gaze from the table and fixed his blue eyes on mine. "You did it, didn't you?"

"Did what?"

"You fucked Caroline."

I wanted to say, 'Whatever gave you that idea?' But I was not given the chance. Before the words had come out of my mouth, Colin's knuckles landed on my jaw. He knocked the table over as he got up, glass shattered on the stone floor, another fist connected with my face. Then, just before I lost consciousness, I saw, as if from afar, Colin's foot speeding towards my solar plexus. A thought from another part of the bar-room night flashed through my fading brain: *where did Balder the Beautiful learn to kick like that?*

5

During my last year at Oxford I lived at the top of a house in Norham Gardens. I had a large bedroom (under the eaves, dusty red paint peeling off the walls, south-facing window, small but serviceable desk solid double bed in an antique brass frame as centrepiece), a bathroom, a separate lavatory and a galley kitchen. The rent was well above average, but I assumed – rightly – that my paymaster parents would have no clue as to the going rate for out-of-college accommodation.

I had been back in Oxford four days and was walking to Norham Gardens across the Parks in the late afternoon when I saw Caroline Carter running towards me. Until I began to write this story, I had not thought of that moment for years. Then, when prompted to replay it, it came in slow motion, each step Caroline took towards me taking a full second or more. I noticed things I'd not seen before: Caroline's hair was shorter than it had been in Italy, her feet were bare and her toenails painted red, she wore the old 'Make Love not War' t-shirt that I had left behind in Paestum.

She threw her arms around me, kissed me and pressed her body against mine. When she released her hold on me, she put her hands on my shoulders, looked hard at my face and then placed a finger softly on my lips. "I've cried myself to sleep," she said, "thinking about these lips."

"I didn't think you'd be back in Oxford until tomorrow."

"I came early. I got back last night."

I brought Caroline to my digs. On the wall opposite the bed I had stuck a poster, a derivative of the famous First World War recruiting poster. Lord Kitchener's stern gaze looked down upon the bed and his finger pointed at us. Since our country no longer needed us, he echoed the advice on the t-shirt and commanded us to make love not war. My big brass bed was not found wanting.

"I've brought you something from Italy," Caroline said.

I felt guilty. I had not brought Caroline a present from *my* travels. Caroline said, "Forget it. It doesn't matter. You can buy me dinner tonight instead."

"Agreed."

Caroline had carried a cardboard tube back from Italy. Inside was a poster of the Temple of Hera at Paestum. She smiled broadly as she watched me unroll it. "It's not a great picture," she said. "But it's the best I could find."

"It's the place, all right."

In the bottom right-hand corner, Caroline had written, 'For Nick, all my love and affection, Caro'. 'Caro' was underlined with a flourish.

"I didn't sleep with anyone else after Paestum," she said.

"Nor did I."

"Should I believe you?"

"Yes. I'll believe you if you believe me."

She smiled. "A deal." I think that just then each of us took the implicit pledge totally seriously.

We stuck the poster to the wall with Blu-Tack, giving it pride of place above the bed. On either side of it I hung posters from my second year: Che Guevara to the left; Marx, Engels and Lenin to the right.

Caroline held me to my promise to take her out for dinner. We went – her choice – to the Indian restaurant at the top of The Turl where I had once taken Jan. Caroline said she knew about Indian food and ordered for both of us. She told me about Sicily. I told her about Germany. I said that I knew I had made a mistake leaving her even before the train had pulled out of the station at Paestum. I apologised. She said she had stood on the platform long after my train had vanished and that several times every day in her memory afterwards she had watched the train get smaller and smaller as it disappeared northwards.

We walked, happily holding hands, back to my room under the eaves. I think it must have been nearly daybreak when we finally fell asleep. The sun was shining brightly when I awoke – to the sound of the guitar music and a haunting song. In that brief, creative moment between sleeping and waking, when the world is formed anew, I had the vivid impression that it was Jan's voice I was listening to, Jan's fingers picking out the chords.

When I opened my eyes, it was Caroline I saw, sitting in a pool of early autumn sunlight, her dark hair cascading onto her bare shoulders, playing Jan's guitar, softly singing.

There is a house in New Orleans
They call the Rising Sun.
It's been the ruin of many poor child,
And me, I know, I'm one...

She stopped singing, aware of my newly awakened gaze.

"I didn't know you played the guitar," Caroline said.

"I don't. It belongs to Janice Day."

"That American girl?"

"Yeah."

"So how come you have it?"

"That's a long story." As Caroline looked at me with her inquisitive, big, brown eyes, I began to tell it.

"I never met her, you know," she said.

"Really?"

"I stayed away from the Jericho House. It gave me bad vibes. That's what they called it, isn't it? The Jericho House."

"Not that there aren't lots of other houses in Jericho."

"I wonder who lives there now," Caroline mused.

"Who knows. Students. Different students."

"It's silly really, but I sometimes think houses have their own aura. Something personal that stays on after the people you associate with the place move on. I never liked the Jericho House. Sill said that one of the men who lived there the year before had been arrested for rape. A girl, an American postgraduate student I think she was, had just moved in to another house in the street and had gone round to borrow some sugar or something. The guy, all sweetness and light, says, 'Come in.' Then he shuts the door, takes her into the front room and rapes her on the floor – without even drawing the curtains. She went straight to the police, of course."

"Why," I asked, changing the subject, "did you choose to sing that particular song?"

"What song?"

"'House of the Rising Sun'."

"I don't know. It was just the first song that came into my head when I picked up the guitar."

By the second week of Michaelmas Term, Caroline was spending more nights with me in my big bed than she was in her own little bed along the road at LMH and by the middle of term her toothbrush, her underwear and the *Kama Sutra* had migrated in her wake. Using the pretext that the room was becoming overcrowded, but actually concerned that Caro might find its presence somehow offensive, I announced one morning that I was going to throw Jan's guitar out.

"Whatever for?" Caroline asked with evident surprise. "It's a perfectly good guitar."

"Okay," I shrugged, turning away.

Caroline caught my forearm and turned me back to face her. "Nick," she said, "hang on a moment. You can't imagine that I lack so much self-confidence that I can't sleep with you in the presence of a guitar some other woman once played? Can you? You never even slept with Janice Day."

"No. I didn't." At that moment in time, I was very glad it was the truth. The guitar stayed, and the row I feared it might cause never happened.

But there were *other* rows, arguments, fights. Caroline's temper would flare up and I had an artful way of pouring petrol on the flames rather than dousing them with cooling water. Our contretemps, however, rarely lasted long. More often than not, they ended in bed. "Sex," said Caroline, "is a great healer." Another of her mottos was: "Don't let the sun go down on your anger."

"Where's that from?" I asked.

"I don't know," she said, "probably the Bible. I learned it at Sunday School."

"You went to Sunday School?" I asked, incredulous.

She nodded. "And I sang in the choir."

Yet I must not exaggerate the arguments I had with Caroline, however violent and terminal each seemed at the time and however prominently some of them have lingered in the memory. The tempests were quickly passing meteorological phenomena in a season of long, blue-sky days kissed with the sunshine of contentment. There was, of course, a looming decision, a gathering storm of potentially fatal ferocity: what would we do when the time came to leave Oxford? For the time being, however, we successfully ignored the issue, pushed it ahead, month after month, term by term, dreaming separate dreams, laying our own individual plans. Tacitly, by unspoken treaty, we had agreed to get through finals before the question was properly broached.

Caroline and I both took finals in our stride. We watched the tide of panic rise around us, saw signs of incipient breakdowns, heard of friends suffering from caffeine poisoning induced by all-night revision endeavours, prided ourselves on being above it all. We were happily lying in bed one sunny afternoon in the week before finals. The window was open and a soft, warm breeze wafted through the room. "Sex," I said, "is the great healer."

"You misquote me, Nick."

"What do you mean?"

"You said, 'Sex is *the* great healer.' Sex is *a* great healer. Sunshine's a great healer. So's a walk in the countryside. A couple of aspirin and a glass of water is a great healer. It depends completely on the context. Sex can also be a weapon of war or an act of extreme violence. It can be a tool of subjugation and domination. The Russians raped a hundred thousand women and girls in Berlin alone in 1945. In parts of Africa, they use it for the disgusting practice of widow cleansing. When a man dies, one of his blood relatives forces sex on the widow to exorcise…"

I laughed, the first ill-considered drop of fuel on a smouldering fire, "You're beginning to sound like the Jericho House."

Five minutes later the clouds had gathered and the storm was raging at full force. Caroline picked up an unfinished glass of red wine and hurled it the wall. The glass hit the Paestum poster above my head. Red wine and shards of glass rained down on me. Caroline dressed hurriedly, silently, was gone. I cleaned up the debris, changed the sheets, tried without success to settle down to revision.

By nightfall, Caroline was back, unwilling to let the sun go down on her anger, unwilling to let any rumbling clouds destabilise her and jeopardise her performance in her exams. She pulled me towards her and, as we fell onto the bed that had so recently been covered with angry wine and splinters of glass, I said 'Sex is the great healer'. But this time I said it only in the deep, rumbling caverns of my mind.

All through the year, the Jericho House had lingered awkwardly in those dark caverns. I don't believe I had mentioned its presence there to anybody, except Caroline, and even with Caroline talk of the Jericho House was rare. Once, the story of Anna Schmidt lying naked in the front-room with the curtains open somehow came up and Caroline asked whether Colin and I had seen Anna when we were in Germany. She asked whether I thought she really was Anastasia Kuznetsova the terrorist, or whether there might have just been some mix-up with names and photographs. I asked Caroline once whether she knew anything of Emma Wallace, the girl into whose mouth Colin had put the story of the tramp and the graveyard. Caroline said she had known Emma by sight, as a friend of Sill's, but that was all. I did not tell her the story that Colin had told me on the train between Hof and Frankfurt.

But the story continued to disturb me. One evening, my tongue loosened by too much drink, I mentioned it to Nigel. I think I must have betrayed something of my fascination with Emma's tale for he said, "Look, Nick. Just drop it. It's not as if somebody's going to base a new world religion on it or anything, is it? I mean, nobody's even going to build a minor fringe cult on that one. It's more than a year since anybody's heard anything from Jan. What's Caroline make of all this?"

Yet Emma's story would not leave my brain. I ignored Nigel's advice and looked, as Colin had done a year earlier, at back copies of the *Oxford Times*. I found the story of the dead tramp fished out of the Thames. It was just as Colin had described it. As far as I could ascertain the body was never identified. Foul play was not suspected, not even suggested. The newspaper reports mentioned, which Colin had not, that the tramp had significant traces of drugs in his bloodstream – consistent with Emma's story but no real proof of its veracity.

I looked at an Ordnance Survey map that covered the river upstream from Oxford to its source in the Cotswolds. Nowhere could I see an isolated church near to the Thames. All those marked on the map were in, or adjacent to, villages. Could Emma, however, have altered just that one detail? As Colin also had done, I went to the Bodleian to read about Georges Bataille.[38] I discovered new concepts in the theory of liberation and revolution, prisons and escape routes that I had not dreamed of, transformations through the marginal, ecstasy in transgression, the mysticism of the dark pathways that lead away from the strictures of reason and mathematical certainties. The realm of Sogol opened her secret door and a seductive finger beckoned to me. I remembered the Parisian in Assisi and wondered whether I would have found him less strange if I had known about *Acéphale* before I met him. My image of the Jericho House began to alter. I recalled and began to wonder what Jan had been talking about that seminal afternoon when she had come up from sunbathing on the dock at La Bise. *God, I've been fucking sophistocrapped to death.* What did she mean by that?

I had dismissed Colin's sequel to the story of the tramp in the church door as something hewn from a rich vein of golden make-believe. Now I wondered whether Colin might possibly have been telling the truth when he described Jan nodding as Emma told her story, when he spoke of her taking off her 'Eat Forbidden Fruits' t-shirt; wondered, if it was true, what had motivated her to do it. I wondered whether there was anyone still in Oxford who had been there that evening who might corroborate or contradict Colin's story, wondered whether the story itself had died with the passing season. Perhaps I could seek out Emma herself, lost somewhere in the mythical world that lies beyond a radius of six miles around Carfax. I

---

[38] Georges Bataille (1897–1962) was a French intellectual, archivist, philosopher and writer. He founded and/or wrote for a number of journals including *Acéphale, Critique* and *TélQuel*, the latter also being associated with, and having an influence on, postmodernists such as Michel Foucault and Jacques Derrida. Much of Bataille's extensive writing was initially banned because of its pornographic character. – Ed.

would seek Emma out eventually, but only several years later.

Yet even long after I had put my research into Emma's story behind me, even when Caroline was lying peacefully on the pillow beside me, Janice Day contrived to haunt me. [39] Once I awoke

---

[39] In *The Dream Diaries*, dreams thirty-nine to forty-seven are all dated to Nick Kellaway's third year at Oxford. Janice Day – as 'J' – appears in all but one of these dreams. Dreams forty-three and forty-six and their attendant analyses are of particular interest.

Dream forty-three: "I am sitting in the doorway of a dilapidated building. My hat, a grimy cloth cap, is pulled low on my brow and my collar is turned up. It is cold and damp and everything is shrouded in a thick fog. Inside the building a light is shining. I think it must be warm and comfortable there. But nobody answers when I knock. Then I am in a small graveyard by a river and J is sunbathing on the river's edge. I watch her through a hole in a wooden fence. J rises and walks towards me. She looks like the *Statue de la Bise*. The fence has gone now and J takes me by the hand and leads me back towards the building that has become a church. But then the church is gone and we are in a vast municipal graveyard instead. J is wearing a dark hat and gloves and smells of lavender instead of sandalwood. She is also wearing the loose, diaphanous, white gown I saw her wearing once, by the light of the harvest moon, on the ruined walls at Rouëlbeau. She raises her hands to her neck, unfastens the gown, lets it drop to her feet and stands naked before me. She is someone who looks like my long-ago urchin now, but her body is withered by age and corrupted by leprosy and she smells of mothballs and death. She pushes me into a pit full of rotting headless corpses, victims of bubonic plague. She jumps in after me and smothers me in putrid embraces."

Dream forty-six: "I am walking in a place that is like Port Meadow, except that the flat, waterlogged meadow stretches to the grey horizon in all directions. There is no town – only a dim memory of once-sacred buildings obliterated long before. I am alone at first, but then there are others walking towards me. As they near, I see they are women wearing bikinis. I think they are advertisements for something, but I don't know what. One of the women is J. Her bikini is light blue and I think she is about to dive into a pool that is not there. But then I realise she is stretching her arms out towards me. She tells me she is cold. She asks if I will take her to my room, feed her tea and oranges, play gentle Chinese music to her and paint her toenails purple. But then the one who comes towards me with arms outstretched is a headless man. He is naked – apart from a human skull that covers his genitals. The skull says *"Et in Arcadia ego"* and repeats the phrase again and again until I cannot tell whether it is the skull that is speaking or the genitals hidden beneath it. The skull is now J's head. She emerges from between the headless apparition's legs as if he is giving birth to her. She is wearing ski clothes and we are in a mountain cabin, alone in front of a blazing fire. The skull has become the portrait of a Roman emperor hanging in a frame above the hearth. A broken bicycle leans against the wall. I know I am expected to repair it, though I don't know why and I don't know how."

The image of the headless, naked man with a skull covering his genitals comes from the first issue (24 June 1936) of *Acéphale*, the magazine founded by Georges Bataille and a group of like-minded collaborators with the intention of liberating Nietzsche from his appropriation by the Nazis. Nick Kellaway would have come across it in his Bodleian researches into Georges Bataille.

See also F.-X. de Morchard, 'Wichita Versus Vienna: Alternative Interpretations of Sex-Obsession in the KISS Dream Diaries' in *Sex Today*, Vol.18, Sydney, 2004. – Ed.

covered in sweat. Caroline said I had been gasping and screaming. When she asked what I had been dreaming about, I told her it was a graveyard and an open pit full of the rotting corpses, but nothing more. Certainly nothing more.

6

To spend some time with Johnny in the last days of his bachelorhood, I arrived in Dallas a week before his wedding day. In a regular flow of transatlantic letters, I had told Johnny everything: mildly modified versions of Oxford student life, Blueberry Hill (perhaps a little more of the dream than the reality), Karen O'Neil, a summer in Greece, Jan's weeks in Oxford (maybe slightly exaggerated), Sylvia's Legion ('for we are many'), Caroline Carter… I had not, however, seen him for three years. As we spoke it seemed to me that my candour had not been reciprocated. I still craved his approval. It seemed he no longer needed mine. It was only now that Johnny told me he had signed up to join the Army.

"What the fuck! Johnny, tell me it's not true. What happened to the old t-shirt? What about 'Make Love Not War'?"

"I outgrew it, Nick."

"You're crazy. There's a war going on out there, in case you hadn't noticed."

"Vietnam's almost over, Nick. There's been a ceasefire since January. We'll be completely out of there before I even finish basic training. Anyway, they're not gonna send a guy like me over to 'Nam. Engineering degrees are what the Army's looking for these days, not cannon fodder."

"You're selling out, Johnny."

"And they're paying me well for it, Nick. I have all sorts of debts from college and the Army'll wipe 'em all out. Now they're not gonna throw all that away on a Vietcong bullet, are they? These guys do the math. Besides –" Johnny fingered the tiny gold cross that was pinned in the buttonhole on the lapel of his jacket " – there are higher powers than Uncle Sam's army."

"You've been corrupted, Johnny. Fucking corrupted."

Sober grey morning suits, top hats and white gloves were not current wedding fashion in Dallas, Texas. Johnny, the ushers and I were all decked out in pale blue and frills that made us look like a troop of

Disneyland ice-cream vendors. The church could have passed for an airy modern theatre or an upmarket sports hall, had it not been for the cross on one wall and the saccharine banner on another that read 'God Is Love'. Two other banners adorned the walls of God's Texan house: the American flag hung on the wall to the left of the cross and the flag of Texas on the wall to its right.

There were probably 250 people at the wedding ceremony – in a hall that would not have been filled by a thousand. The congregation, however, made up for its paucity in numbers with an exuberance of singing and clapping, punctuating the wedding vows and the sermon with loud calls of "Amen!" and "Praise the Lord!" Had you behaved in similar fashion in an English parish church, you would have been duly arrested by the episcopal police and incarcerated in the diocesan lunatic asylum with negligible chance of parole.

At the reception, in the ballroom of the hotel where I was billeted, Johnny's and Sally's parents said they were delighted to see me, expressed again their thanks for my coming so far and asked about Geneva. "Those were two of the best years of our lives," Mr Pinkerton said. "Sure as hell wished we could've stayed on a bit longer."

Mrs Morris recalled the times that Johnny and I had climbed trees in their garden, sitting up in the leafy branches for hours. She remembered how worried she'd been when Johnny and I raced off into the countryside on our mopeds. "You'd be gone for the whole day out at those old ruins," she said, concerned still with our inefficiency. "What were they called?"

"Rouëlbeau."

The wedding guests, large people in Texan finery, clapped me on the back, refilled my glass, congratulated me on my best man's speech and said things like:

- "This country sure needs folks like Johnny Morris. He's joining the Army, you know."
- "Johnny tells me you're an Oxford man, Nicholas."
- "Sally tells me you were at high school with Johnny and her in Sweden. That musta been nice."
- "Are you saved, Mr Kellaway?"
- "I just love your accent, honey."

This last remark came from the reddened lips of a girl in a sparkling yellow dress, the type of girl Americans call 'cute', one of a dozen Sally Pinkerton wannabes drifting around the reception. This one seemed often to appear by my side and when I asked her some innocuous question, she blushed and said, "Just keep on talking, honey. I adore your accent." She told me that her name was Tilly, short for Myrtle. A myrtle is a kind of blueberry; '*myrtille*' is French for 'blueberry'.

Johnny and Sally left the reception for a life of marital – or should that be 'martial'? – bliss at Fort Something-Or-Other near El Paso on the Mexican border. Once the happy couple had departed and the party began to draw to a close, I took the girl called Cute upstairs to my bedroom, telling her there was something I would like to show her, something from little old England.

There was a simmering anger within me. I was angry at Johnny's incomplete letters to me, at his decision to join the US Army, at his drinking Coca-Cola while I drank beer, at Sally's insidious corruption of his soul, at the maddening perfection of Sally's Texan tits, at the insolent banner that proclaimed God to be Love, at the honey-hued lips, the hearty smiles, the holy happiness, the heavenly teeth provided courtesy of the earthly ministrations of the American Dental Association. Think of a field of freshly fallen snow sparkling in the early morning sun and the irrepressible desire to run across it and leave one's own muddy footprints on the pure expanse. Think of a shining white ceramic bowl made specifically for assholes to shit in. Think of a sweet-smelling field of yellow spring flowers sparkling in the sun and glorying in the name of 'rape'.

I turned the key and held the door open for the girl. It swung shut behind us with a dull thud as its automatic lock fell into place. *Welcome to Randy the Rapist's rutting rooms, Cutie-Pie.* The girl, who called me 'honey', allowed me to undress her without excessive protest, silently standing before me with her arms hanging limply by her side. I unbuttoned buttons and unzipped zippers. Her sugar-spangled yellow banner fell around her ankles. I unhinged the hooks that held the bra. I caressed her breasts with one hand and ran the other slowly down the line of her spine, fingers reaching inside the elastic around the waist and underneath the thin layer of silk that was all that protected her from me. I spoke softly. She said nothing. *Still enamoured with my accent, Cutie? Enamoured as a rabbit is with the headlights of an oncoming car?* Or perhaps it was as if she were a mute sacrificial lamb, as if I were about to lay her on that plain wooden altar beneath the 'God Is Love' banner, plunge the sacred dagger into her bleating heart and watch the purifying blood flow freely. *Where's your loving protective banner now, Cutie-Pie?* When she began to resist I used the minimum force necessary. Sex was quick. It was not without its intrinsic pleasure, but far greater was the pleasure that came as my anger dissipated with each bullet I fired into her, as I asserted my ego and reclaimed my carefully crafted identity.

Afterwards, she wept. She held on to me in a way she had not done before I entered her, lay on top of me and kissed me passionately, bled profusely over me as I struggled to release myself from her grip. Slowly, it dawned on me that I had just had my first virgin.

The girl left me just after ten that evening, still sobbing as she went. I watched from my doorway as she walked to the lift – the elevator. She pressed the button, waited and entered when the doors slid open. She did not look back.

I went back to bed, curled up under the blood-stained sheets and slept badly. Where there had been anger and then the satisfaction of self-redemption, I found now corroded dreams and fear.

Knock. Knock. The door opens. The fast finger of the hotel manageress points at me lying naked and alone on the bloodstained bed. "This is Mr Nicholas Kellaway," she says sweetly. "He deflowers the maidens of the county and pals around with terrorists, you know."

The lynch mob, baying for even more blood to be shed, peers over her shoulder. Cutie's father leads them. They wear white sheets and the pointed white hats of the Ku Klux Klan, little black circles cut for the eyes. There are red stains on their robes from previous bloodlettings. One carries the cross from the wall of the church where the wedding was held and another holds aloft the banner that says 'God Is Love'. They have rubbed the cross with bitumen and set it alight.

"But that ain't no nigger, Mr Cutie's Daddy. That's a white man," says one of the hats.

"That's an Ogsford man," says another.

"He has this really cool accent," says a third.

"I ain't no goddam racist," says Cutie's Daddy. "I don't judge a man by the colour of his goddam skin. This son of a bitch is gonna swing not because he *is* a nigger but because he *behaves* like a nigger."

"Aw shucks, Mr Cutie's Daddy, that ain't really fair now, is it?"

"Knock, knock."

"Who's there?"

"May."

"May who?"

"Maid service."

I jumped from my bed. It was half past nine. "Come back in a couple of hours, will you?"

Through the night I had tossed and turned, sweated and shivered, dozed and dreamt, woken and worried, but in the end I must have slept. I looked around. The blood was still there. On the sheets. On the towels. There was even a trail of red stains on the carpet, leading from the bedside to the bathroom. *What if they've waited until morning to come for me? What if the good ole boys are patiently waiting downstairs, chewing tobacco and patting their holsters?*

I showered, dressed quickly, packed my case, stripped the sheets from the bed, rolled them up with the towels, threw them into the bath and ran hot water onto them. I took the lift to the lobby. I paid my bill, tipped the doorman, took a taxi direct to the airport. *Do not pass Go. Do not collect $200.* At the airport I waited for hours, huddled in a corner until my flight was called. As soon as we were out of Texan airspace I summoned the stewardess and asked for a large bourbon.

When she brought my whiskey, I said "Thank you" and she said "You're welcome, sir" through the broad commercial smile affixed to her crimson lips.

I settled back in my seat and let just a trace of the stewardess's satisfied smile spread to my own lips. *I've got out of jail free. I've got away. I have bloody well got away.* "And could I have a slice of that blueberry pie, please?"

7

"What happened?" Caroline asked. I turned and saw her standing beside my bed – our bed – holding the shirt I had worn at Johnny's wedding. There was a bloodstain on its tail. I told her a mundane story that seemed plausible even to me – a story in which no fifteen-year-old virgin sacrificed in the cause of liberty had even so much as a walk-on part.

Caroline asked, too, why I was taking down the 'Make Love Not War' recruiting poster. I was, I said, sending it to Private Johnny Morris at Fort Bliss.

Caroline said, "You can make both at the same time."

"Both what?" I asked.

"Love and war."

"I know, darling."

I never did send Lord Kitchener to Johnny.

When, in the week after finals, Caroline and I broke up, it had nothing to do with infidelity, nothing to do with my turbulent Janice Day dreams, nothing to do with another woman. The argument was simply over divergent views of the future. To Caroline's amusement and the disdain of other comrades, I had accepted a job with an American bank in the City. Caroline had set *her* mind on training as a solicitor – the kind of Robin Hood lawyer you see on television, defending the luckless and downtrodden. I assumed that Caroline and I would simply move to London, start our careers, share a flat (quite possibly the rather nice one in Chelsea that her parents owned) and live a life similar to the one we had in Oxford – except that I would be worshipping lucratively in the Temples of Mammon and our existence would be uninterrupted by her petulant visits back to that single bed in LMH. The snag was one of timing. Caroline had deferred the start of her law conversion course in order to do a two-year stint with VSO in India.

"Nick," she shouted, "just listen to me. You don't own me. Just because you fuck my body doesn't mean I'm gonna let you fuck my life." An unfinished mug of breakfast coffee shattered against the Paestum poster and, with that, Caroline was gone.

It was no worse a row than several we had had during the year. I tidied the room, changed the sheets, attended to various trivial things that I needed to do before leaving Oxford and bought a bunch of red roses, fully expecting Caroline to return before the late-running summer sun set, fall into my forgiving arms and smother me in the redeeming balm of sex. But she did not come.

The next day one of Caroline's friends from college came with an empty suitcase, instructions to retrieve any belongings Caroline that had left with me and a curt message that Caroline would be leaving Oxford the next morning. When, after allowing a couple of days for her temper to cool, I phoned her number in Norfolk, her mother told me Caroline did not wish to speak.

Colin Witheridge took some considerable satisfaction in hearing that Caroline and I had broken up. "Inevitable," he said. "Of course it was inevitable." His was, however, but a brief gloating before he reached out a hand of friendship and put a brotherly arm around my sagging shoulders.

I had not spoken to Colin all year and had, in fact, seen him only rarely – at Labour Party meetings I was attending with decreasing frequency. After our brawl in Amsterdam, I had spent the night in hospital and, returning to our hostel the following afternoon, I had found that Colin had already left. Back in Oxford, it no doubt soon became clear to him that the accusations he had thrown at me in Amsterdam, along with his fists, were warranted. During Michaelmas Term, Caroline and I had heard sinister reports that he was 'going to deal with' me. But nothing happened. Not then at least.

Four days after Caroline left Oxford, Colin led me on a brotherly pub crawl beyond Magdalen Bridge, starting at the Cape of Good Hope, up the Cowley Road and down side streets to pubs I had never even heard mentioned in polite Oxford circles. He watched as I hurled a brick through the front window of a house in Marston Street and stood beside me as we peed against a wall in Cowley Place. Lifting my gaze from the streams of urine, my eye caught a line of graffiti. Slowly it came to me what I was reading. The prophetic hand had written 'Eat Forbidden Fruits' and in another colour added 'Fuck Forbidden Fannies'. I watched Colin take out a can of spray paint and add 'Fart Freely' to the text. *Subway walls. Tenement halls.* I broke out in the uncontrollable – inconsolable – laughter of the terminally drunk.

July 1973 was wet and cold in Geneva. I found myself adrift there without plans, without anyone with whom to make plans, without Caroline and, of course, without Jan. I slept more than was good for me. I lay on my bed late into the mornings listening to a succulent female voice sing of murder on the banks of the O-hi-o. I sat out forlorn afternoons staring at the lake from my bench by the *Statue de la Bise*. More than one evening I picked up the phone to call Karen O'Neil, but never completed dialling her number. I lingered around the Landolt and the cafés of the Place Molard. When I told Claude Meyer what had happened in the dying days of my Oxford life, he said, "How in God's name did you let a girl like that go?"

"You only met her briefly, Claude," I replied. "You're only talking like that because you thought she looked like Marie-Claire."

Claude proposed a week's walking in the mountains; but the weather forecast showed wet snow falling down to 1200 metres and I did not wish to add external misery to that already gnawing away internally. Nor did I wish to listen to Claude's hearty mountain tales and hear about the girl he was taking to Malibu. I declined.

I wrote to Caroline. She didn't reply. I phoned her home number. Her mother said she was unable to take the call. I phoned again the next day. Her father asked me to stop phoning. Eventually, I gave up and thought I might ask Colin whether I could travel with him to Greece, but when I tried to make contact I learned that he had already departed, that he would be returning only just before he was due to start his job in the City in September.

I mulled over the possibility of going to Greece on my own. We had, after all, met plenty of solitary travellers, both male and female, when we were island-hopping two years previously: Nigel's Belgian in the Boat, Hilde the Norwegian and Rosa Luxemburg among them. Colin himself had, as far as I then knew, just set out for Greece without a companion. I dug out my maps of Italy and Greece and planned a route – hitchhiking down to Brindisi, over to Corfu, down through the Ionian Islands and across to Piraeus. From there I would see what ferries were sailing where across the wine-dark waters of the Aegean, see who was travelling on them. I would gather my own companions, my own crew. We would contend with men and gods and return to our wintry climes with our own legends to embroider by the fireside when the days turned short and cold.

> The Pan pipe on the mountain rings
> Twice-born Dionysus sings
> The dark wine flows and slowly brings
> The Goddess to her knees.[40]

The day before I was due to set off for Greece, Marie-Claire phoned.

8

"There's just one thing, Nick," Marie-Claire said as I stepped aboard the *Phalanstère* in the marina at Antibes.

"What's that?"

"It's my boat."

---

[40] These are lines from Adam Heggie's poem 'Samson Hedonistes' in *Posthumous Poems* (London, 2004) – Ed.

"I hear you."

"And there's only one rule."

"Which is?"

"It's my boat."

Marie-Claire and I were gone for a month and a day. We avoided towns and holiday resorts, lingering in deserted bays along the rocky west coast of Corsica and among the small islands of La Maddalena and Lavezzi. We lived on line-caught fish and on bread, vegetables and fruit we bought in village markets around the coast. I lost weight. My muscles toned. My skin bronzed. I have never felt healthier either before or since those days on the *Phalanstère*.

After our first night at sea, except when we went into ports to re-provision, Marie-Claire and I rarely wore clothes. We anchored in isolated coves, off inaccessible beaches, in the lee of uninhabited offshore islets. We dived from the boat, swam for hours, lay in the sun on a beach to dry ourselves, made love, swam back to the boat, made love again on the deck. I tried to forget Caroline Carter and Janice Day and the nine-to-five job I had accepted at a bank in the City. Marie-Claire had, I told myself, always been my dream woman, my true love since the spring of 1967 when, behind a tree at the far end of the football pitch, she first planted a tentative kiss on my virgin lips. Now, at last, I had the real thing. I loved the softness of her mouth and the sandy, salty taste of her dry skin. *I have come home.* And it felt, like the wind in my hair and the sun on my back, very, very good.

One night we anchored in a narrow cove. At its head was a tiny beach of the finest sand, but in the darkness you could not see it. No light or sign of human habitation was visible. We lay together under a blanket on the deck of the *Phalanstère*, gently rocked by the waves as they moved from untamed deep to untamed shore. Marie-Claire told me her father's story: from son of a poor sharecropper in the Creuse, through the profitable tribulations of thirty years in Algeria, to multi-millionaire with houses on the Côte d'Azur and Lake Geneva and apartments in Paris and New York.

"Does he," I asked, "still have his gun collection?"

"Of course," Marie-Claire replied. "It's one of the finest gun collections in the world."

Like children in charge of the party, we played games of make-believe. We were a tight-knit band of freedom fighters and imagined ourselves to have stolen the guns and made them work again. With muffled oars and under cover of a purple, moonless night, we rowed the guns ashore. If we strained our ears we could hear distant songs of liberation drifting across the water from the jungle campfires where our comrades waited. The drumbeat of freedom on the eve of the Revolution. And the pulse of Marie-Claire's heart in her breast.

The next night, still anchored in the same cove, I told Marie-Claire that she was my Ariadne and pointed out to her the Corona Borealis, Ariadne's diamond necklace among the stars of the night sky. I told her how Dionysus had placed it there as a gift to the bride he had found abandoned on a Naxos beach. Marie-Claire sprang to her feet. In the darkness I could see only her vague silhouette. "Come on, then, Dionysus," she said, "find me on *my* beach."

She dived into the water. I followed. Swimming cautiously through the ink-black water, I could hear the sound of Marie-Claire swimming ahead of me. It seemed to be a long time until I found the sand beneath my feet, stood in water no deeper than my thighs, walked up the gently shelving beach to where Marie-Claire lay on the sand. I nearly tripped over her because the night was so dark. She laughed, then pulled me down into her.

There, I told Marie-Claire more of the story I embroidered on the old fabric Markus Holzschifter had given me, of Ariadne and Dionysus in the lemon groves of Naxos. Of that spring of love, when the winter's chills had gone and all life was bursting forth with desire and fertility. I told her that Ariadne and Dionysus lived happily ever after, that the most beautiful of women tamed the wild, foreign god and bore him numerous children.

"I am not," Marie-Claire declared as she got up and walked into the sea to swim back to the *Phalanstère*, "such a fool. I am on the pill."

We were sunning ourselves on deck one morning, in the lee of the Ile Lavezzi, when I foolishly – very foolishly – asked Marie-Claire what had happened to Jean-Daniel, her former boyfriend from Nanterre.

"Gone," she replied.

"Gone, like, where?"

"Just gone. That's all we need to know. Gone."

A moment later she asked me, "What happened to Jan?"

"Gone."

"Where?"

"Just gone." I did not want to think about Janice Day. For weeks she had been almost absent from my daytime thoughts. On Marie-

Claire's boat, Jan had even failed to appear in my increasingly benign dreams.

Marie-Claire rolled onto her side towards me, propped her head up on her hand, elbow resting on the deck. She said, "One rule, okay?"

"What?"

"It's my boat. You tell me."

"Okay. But I don't know much," I said. "She left Oxford one morning. She and another girl. Didn't tell anyone they were leaving. Just went. Nobody even knew where they'd gone until I got a postcard from Berlin. That's the last I heard from her."

"Jean-Daniel thinks she's dead."

"Maybe."

"He heard from some of his people – you know, people who know what's really going down in Germany – that she'd been shot in a gun battle with the police. Killed outright. They hushed it up, of course, because she was an American." Marie-Claire, speaking in French, used the expression '*Amérloque*'. "It doesn't matter, though, does it?"

"What d'you mean 'doesn't matter'?"

"Dead. Gone. Irrelevant which. Jean-Daniel is alive and well and living with some grimy gypsies as their resident anthropologist. But, for me, he's gone. So he might as well be dead."

"It's different. You know what he's doing."

"How did Janice Day screw?"

"I never slept with her."

"You never screwed Janice Day?" Marie-Claire locked her eyes onto mine. Her voice betrayed genuine incredulity.

"No."

"You're lying, Nick. I don't believe you."

"It's true."

"Come down from your cloud. Janice Day was the biggest whore in the whole school. A calculating bitch. Used her body to get stuff, just like a whore who screws for money. Everybody'd screwed her."

"I don't think that's right."

"I *know* it's right. I know it's right. Do you remember that time I invited you to come sailing on the lake and you brought Jan along?"

"Very clearly."

"Do you remember that stupid joke Jan told, when she said to call me Mari and call her Juana?"

"Yes."

"Well, I was in Peru last year, right? And what did I learn there? That *'juana'* is South American Spanish for prostitute. And Jan was from Argentina, right? So it wasn't as if she didn't know what she was saying. She was saying that she was a whore. There was that Pakistani guy, remember? She took thousands off him. She got hold of his bank account and just sucked away. She was... What do you English call it? Game on? She had breast implants, you know."

"She didn't."

"Stop idolising her. Of course she did. She got them so she could charge more."

"And what about you, Marie-Claire?"

"What!" She cupped her hands around her little breasts. "You think these have implants in them?"

"That's not what I mean. You like screwing, but it doesn't make *you* a whore."

"Me? Me! Nick! I don't need anything. Money and all that shit. I've got as much as I need. Shedloads of it. I do it for the sheer pleasure of it. What d'you call it? A hedonist."

"Was that how it was with you and Jean-Daniel?"

Marie-Claire was silent for a minute. Maybe two minutes. I wished I had followed my instincts, disobeyed the owner of the boat and said nothing about Janice Day. I didn't believe what Marie-Claire was saying. It was all just petty female jealousy. Yet, just then, it wasn't truth or falsehood that mattered. The worst thing about it was that I was watching Marie-Claire slip out of the best dream of my life.

"Let me tell you a story about Jean-Daniel," Marie-Claire answered. "He came sailing with me just after I got this boat, right? He was a complete wimp at sea and when he wasn't being a wimp he was going on about those Yennish gypsies nobody'd ever heard of. And then, because we were on a boat, sailing on the Mediterranean, he started trying to deconstruct *The Odyssey*. Right? Homer's thing?"

"Yeah."

"So I said to him, 'I'll show you deconstruction' and I made him play the siren game. My boat, right? My rules."

"The siren game?"

"I tied him to the mast, arms pinned to his side. And I just left him there. I fed him fruit. I poured wine down his throat. I lit a joint for him. I sang him songs. I just left him there, tied up, unable to do anything for himself. Like a leek in soup garden."

"Are you really expecting me to believe that?"

"Are you expecting me to believe you didn't screw Janice Day?"

"Can we just drop the subject? You can believe whatever you want."

"Thanks. That's very kind of you, Nick. I might just think about doing that. D'you wanna know why I told you that story about Jean-Daniel?"

"Not really. But go ahead if you want to."

"Because it has a moral. Like all good stories, it has a moral."

"What's this one, it's Marie-Claire's boat?"

It was a different lesson this time. Marie-Claire's words were echoes of ones I had heard not many weeks before, in a different country, from a different mouth. "You don't own me, baby. Just because you screw me, it doesn't mean you own me."

But I wanted to own Marie-Claire. I wanted desperately to own Marie-Claire.

"Marie-Claire?"

No reply.

The *Phalanstère* lies at anchor off Cap Corse, rocking, like a much-loved baby's cradle, on the ebb and flow of the sea. I am lying on my back on the deck. The sun beats down on my face out of a blue, blue sky. I can see, if I turn my head slightly to the left, the ruins of a circular tower high on the shore. It is one of the watchtowers the princes of Genoa built around the coastline when they ruled the island. We have seen many of them as we have sailed around Corsica. This watchtower may be our last. Marie-Claire plans to set our course for Antibes tomorrow. Marie-Claire lies on top of me, her head resting on my shoulder, in light, post-coital slumber. I run the palm of my hand along the length of her back, down onto the soft, rounded hills of her buttocks.

I can hardly hear Marie-Claire's somnolent voice, muffled as it is in my shoulder. But I know she says, "Don't. That tickles."

"Marie-Claire?"

"Mmmmm." A noise that suggests she is listening.

"Will you marry me?"

She lies still, breathing softly; otherwise not moving. Her answer comes, spoken into my shoulder: "No."

"Why not?"

"You need a reason? Then let's just say it's because you're not Catholic."

"And *you're* a good Catholic girl?"

"No. A *good* Catholic girl always has the man on *top*."

"Okay, then. Just come to London and live with me."

Marie-Claire rolls off me. She opens her eyes, props her head on her hand, elbow on the deck, looks at me. It is a pose she adopts when she is about to tell me something she considers important. She is suddenly wide awake.

"Why would I wanna do that? What do you think I am, crazy or something?"

"No."

"Well, then! What a question! London! My God! London's a disgusting place, Nick. I've been there. Grey. Wall-to-wall grey. Drizzling all the time. No proper rain. No proper sun. Dirty buildings. Inedible food. Too many people. And they never say what they mean. They have this compulsion to turn everything into a feeble little joke. They value jokes more than truth. And you know what? They all smell. God, do they smell! They don't have heating or baths in their houses, you know. Unwashed people smelling of piss and stale beer. They never clean their clothes. Layers and layers of this disgusting grime on them. Have you ever travelled in one of those smoking carriages on the Underground? Shit! Is this what you're proposing? At night there's this horrible orange glow in the sky…"

I think Marie-Claire must, nonetheless, have given my proposal of marriage some consideration that night. We were up on deck early the next morning. The first turquoise light before sunrise hung above the sea in the east. We were wearing clothes, warm clothes. The end of summer was drawing nigh. The days were shortening and the air temperature was falling. We busied ourselves with silent tasks around the boat, preparing to weigh anchor. The rising sun coloured the rocks above us pink. The rose light of dawn was inching down the ruins of the Genoese watchtower towards us. Marie-Claire put an arm around my waist and kissed me softly on the cheek. She said gently, "Women coming and going, jokers and thieves," and then, before I had thought of a reply, added ,"Nick, don't be offended that I said I don't want to marry you. I'll never marry anyone, you know."

"Don't be silly, Marie-Claire. You're just…"

"No, seriously, Nick. There's only one person I've ever wanted to marry and I can't have him."

"Who's that?"

"Can't you guess?"

"No."

"Okay. I'll tell you, then. Claude Meyer."

"Claude?"

"He's my cousin."

"Second cousin."

"Still." The rays of the rising sun reached the sails of the *Phalanstère.*

"Claude's not Catholic."

"I'd make an exception for Claude. Anyway, he *has* a serious girlfriend. Nice girl. Daughter of a count or something. I expect he'll marry her. He took her to California this summer."

"So you'll be free to marry me then."

"Nick, please. Marry someone you love."

"I love *you.*"

"Nick, really, with respect, you *don't* love me. You love the feel of me on your body, like you love the warm sun and the salty sea and the taste of red wine. You love it for what it does to you. You love the idea of being in love with me."

I stroked Marie-Claire's hair. "I love *you.*"

Two minutes? Three? "Nick, I've really enjoyed these four weeks. I really have, you know. It's not that I'm complaining; it's just that sometimes it does seem like you're sort of making love to yourself. It's okay for a month on a boat, but it's not the basis for a marriage. Not for me, at least."

"Marie-Claire…"

"Come on, Nick. Let's get the anchor in. We need to catch that wind. We've a long sail ahead."

CHAPTER SIX

London undid me. Brown fog of a winter dawn dripping onto the pavement; pulsating white fluorescent light and typist's chattering keys colonising my brain; wet socks eating the skin of my feet; milky tea and a Penguin biscuit bought from Daisy's trolley warding off afternoon boredom; weary bodies scuttling homeward through the black tunnels of the Northern Line… It sucked the blood from my veins and the breath from my lungs. After a month and a day aboard the *Phalanstère*, this was death row – the silk tie and old glove closing darkly around my throat. Illusions of escape came in violet droplets: from lists and mathematical puzzles, from left-wing revivalist fantasies, from alcohol, episodic sex and scrambled dreams.

I had left Oxford with no arrangements as to where I would live in London. As a result I was forced to rely on a Labour Party flat-share scheme run by the slag-heap Welshman who had once tried to evict Colin from the party. His belief that people like Colin, Nigel and me had no right belonging to *his* party was doubtless reinforced when he read on my application form that I was going to be an executive trainee at P.J. Harriman's Bank.

Through the Welshman's efforts, a small room in a terraced house in Balham – north-facing and smelling of damp – became my new home. My window, which rattled in its rotting frame when the wind blew, overlooked a derelict patch of urban nettles and crippled ironmongery rusting in the rain. At night, the 'horrible orange glow' Marie-Claire had warned me of crept in around the cold edges of the threadbare curtains. I hid the peeling wallpaper beneath posters and maps: Che Guevara, a full-breasted Ukrainian woman extolling the quantity of the Soviet Union's wheat production, Geneva, Ios, Corsica…

The house was owned by an absentee landlord, a heavily mortgaged civil engineer working in Saudi Arabia to convert oil sheikhs' camel-skin tents into concrete follies. "Trading with the enemy," said Adam Heggie, my tall, gaunt flatmate living in the spacious, south-facing room at the front of the house. Like me, Adam held down a City job – his with an Arab bank. "Most people know," he said, "that every river has two banks. Mine is a bank with two rivers." His Labour Party links were tenuous and his fame as a poet still lay in the future.[41]

Nigel and Colin had also taken entry-level jobs in finance: Colin with First Manufacturers' Bank of Boston; Nigel with a firm of insurance brokers at Lloyds. They too had put on ties and trimmed their hair. The three of us met one evening after work at The George in Southwark. None of us was enthusiastic about what we had found across the river in the City. There was, however, a certain satisfaction in being able to share with fellow subversives the experiences of revolutionary agents parachuted in behind enemy lines. We had led no strikes. We had robbed no banks. We had planted no bombs. We had assassinated no titans of industry. I don't know how we had done it, but, as we sat at our desks twiddling our pencils and turning the cranks on our adding machines, the whole capitalist edifice began to crumble around us.

- War broke out in the Middle East. The Arabs (I still had my *keffiyeh*) did well. They accompanied their military success with economic sanctions, refusing to export oil. The price of oil quadrupled. In the UK, a speed limit of fifty-five miles per hour was imposed. In Switzerland, driving was banned on Sundays. Bourgeois families strolled along the *autoroute* between Geneva and Lausanne.

- The Dow Jones Index fell 45%.

- The UK stock market – the 'Footsie' as I was learning to call it – fell 70%.

---

[41] Adam Heggie's (1949–2003) poems are collected in four published volumes: *Riding the Central Line to Bank* (London, 1987), *The Land Between the Rivers* (London, 1992), *More Poems from the City of London* (London, 2000) and *Posthumous Poems* (London, 2004). Heggie's prose publications include *Sacred Women: The Transignification of Temple Prostitutes in Ancient Mesopotamia* (Cambridge, 1984), *The Final Solution to the Financial Crises Besetting Pension Provision and the British National Health Service* (London, 1999), *Irak: Das Heilige Land* (Tübingen, 2001) and *In Praise of Paedophilia* (London, 2002). In *The Final Solution,* Heggie argued for compulsory euthanasia at the age of seventy, which at the time earned him a national notoriety extending well beyond his limited poetry-reading public. After the poor reception of his first novel (*Sex with Fat Girls*, London, 1991), Heggie's second novel, *Love in a Market Economy*, failed to find a publisher in English but was published in Italian and German translations in 2004 and 2005, respectively. His biographer, John Washford-Pyne (*Ealing Broadway, Notting Hill Gate and Bank: The Strange Life and Death of Adam Heggie*, London, 2007), skates over the Balham years in less than a sentence: "Apart from a brief three-year interlude in a shared house in Balham, Adam Heggie lived and worked his entire life at locations along the Central Line of the London Underground network. He was born, and lived until his early twenties, in Ealing. From 1975 until his mysterious death in the early days of the Iraq War in 2003, he lived in Notting Hill, commuting along the Central Line to his job as a clerk in the City." – Ed.

- America was losing its war in Vietnam. The military-industrial establishment had lost the battle for hearts and minds on the home front. Watergate distracted attention from war and focused it on deleted presidential expletives.
- While I had been at university, the UK had enjoyed the so-called 'Barber Boom'. The good-time feeling now fell on its bloated face. People realised that capitalism's last years of plenty had been an illusion fuelled by loose credit and other nefarious tricks of the bankers' trade. There were calls to hang the miscreant moneylenders from the lampposts of their beloved City.
- Goldman Sachs, it was said, nearly went bankrupt.
- Twenty years of solid non-inflationary growth – since the end of the Korean War – ended abruptly. By 1975, the annual inflation rate in Britain had reached 27%. Even then, as you tried to spend last year's pay rise on today's goods and services, it seemed that the capitalist authorities were finessing the figures with frills and flattery – like undertakers daubing rouge on a corpse.
- Nigel Bickleigh lost his job. He'd done nothing wrong, it was simply the application of the time-honoured accounting principle of 'last in, first out'. LIFO, they explained, applied to inventory and, in well-run companies, also to 'human resources' – then a new-fangled euphemism for people. "Deadstock and livestock," Nigel said with a wry smile. After the obligatory good cheer of the Christmas party, the gerontocracy that ran the show gave him a dressed capon and two bottles of claret and told him not to return to the office in January.
- With no oil flowing from the Middle East, British coal miners went on strike to augment the pressure on the fuel-starved capitalist nation and, not incidentally, to use the perennial laws of supply and demand to supplement their wage packets. Industry was put on a precautionary three-day week. Electricity was rationed on a rota. On days when we had no power at Harriman's, we worked in our overcoats and woollen hats by weak Dickensian candlelight until four in the afternoon and then drifted about the dark, unswept streets until the pubs opened.
- On a cold, clear Saturday in January, Adam Heggie and I walked miles through the streets of South London looking

for paraffin for an old 1940s heater we had found. Adam said cryptically, "Woe to the man who has no home when black crows fly to the City and start to screech and snowstorms come." He would later rework the lines and incorporate them into his poetry.[42] We rubbed our icy hands and consoled ourselves with the thought that we were witnessing the birth pangs of the Revolution. Heggie pondered this idea and pronounced it not entirely felicitous: we had, he said, joined the other side. Come the Revolution, the victors would look at our smooth, office-honed hands, ignore our pleas that we were once the intellectual vanguard of the Left, laugh at our claims to have been subversive agents parachuted in behind enemy lines, mock everything and anything to do with the pretensions of the so-called New Left, call us lovers of queers and consorts of lesbians, line us up against the walls of the Bank of England, blindfold us, squeeze the trigger.

Marie-Claire never did come to visit. Nor, predictably, did she write. When I asked Claude Meyer for news, his return letters avoided all mention of her.

Through mutual friends I heard recycled stories of Caroline playing the white benefactress in India and touring the Soviet Union for a summer holiday, but nothing direct. Her wine- and coffee-stained poster remained rolled up in its tube, shoved away – out of sight, but not always out of mind – at the back of my wardrobe. Where Paestum might have hung, I pinned a copy of Botticelli's *Birth of Aphrodite*, a poster of Dionysus from the shop at the British

---

[42] The lines
Woe betide the dying man
Who has no home
When City crows start to shriek
And snowstorms come
form part of Adam Heggie's poem 'The Winter of '74', published in his first collection of poems: *Riding the Central Line to Bank*. They are not original. See Friedrich Nietzsche's poem *Vereinsamt*:
Die Krähen schrein
Und ziehen schwirren Flugs zur Stadt:
Bald wird es schnein,
Weh dem, der keine Heimat hat.
– Ed.

Museum and an advertisement for the Compagnie Générale de Navigation featuring one of its Lake Geneva paddle steamers surrounded by sunshine and sailboats.

Janice Day returned. We travelled again on one of those poster boats, past the sunlit dock at La Bise and on out into the beautiful uncharted waters beyond. Sometimes it was on Marie-Claire's *Phalanstère* that we sailed, Jan lying peacefully on the deck, as she had once lain at La Bise by the waters of Leman, as I steered our course between Scylla and Charybdis. Of course, that was only in my dreams – the narrow margin of the unwritten page in which my real experiences were lived.

Sex outside dreams was a random series of one-night stands in rooms as dismal as my own. They provided welcome moments of release in those early London days and added names to my growing list. Even fuck-and-chuck seven pinters are better than masturbation for keeping fascism and genocide at bay.

To the collection of my old Swiss bicycle licence plates nailed to the walls of my Balham room, I added another – one from the Canton de Vaud for 1969: 'VD 69'. It was not originally mine. I had stolen it from a parked bike

2

The Americans finally lost their war in Vietnam in 1975. Sitting on the floor in Adam Heggie's room with Colin, sharing a joint as we watched television images of the last helicopter fly off the roof of the American Embassy in Saigon, I felt curiously detached. Our entire generation had cut its political teeth on anti-war rhetoric, then we had lost interest. The novelty of protest had worn away, the war had become boring and most of us now had jobs.

At the end of that muted historic week, on Saturday 3 May 1975, a letter dropped through the letterbox in the front door of the Balham House: pale-blue, air-mail envelope, American stamp, Illinois franking. I picked it up from the doormat and looked at it in awe: the rounded American handwriting was exactly what I remembered from Jan's postcard of Berlin. I took the letter into the kitchen and sat at the cluttered breakfast table, fingering the crisp, thin paper, sipping coffee, savouring the moment. At length I wiped the butter and jam and burnt toast crumbs from my knife, slit open the envelope and drew out a pale-blue letter.

It was not from Jan. The letter was from Johnny Morris's mother. There, as I read Mrs Morris's steady prose, I learned that Johnny Morris was dead. The letter gave no detail as to how or when he had died and was vague on precisely where. Just 'Killed in action in Vietnam'.

I went for a long walk around the streets of South London that afternoon. If I recall correctly, I ended the evening outside a pub on Clapham Common. Too drunk to find my way home, I must have acquiesced when a police officer invited me to spend the rest of the night in the cells.

Johnny's ghost hovered uncomfortably over the conversation when a number of us – Ecolint alumni and bewildered hangers-on – met in December at the old Swiss Centre in Leicester Square for an Escalade supper (the usual: fondue, Fendant, marzipan vegetables in a chocolate *marmite*...). Sally, although nobody had seen her since Johnny's death, was said to be distraught. "Imagine," said one of the less imaginative females, "being a war widow at the age of twenty-four." Sally was diagnosed, unseen, as needing psychotherapy, a nice lie-down on a couch while a highly paid psychoanalyst with a beard neatly trimmed *à la* Freud made her feel important by writing down everything she said.

I heard that Polly Page had become a banker with Chase Manhattan in New York. I would have forgotten Polly altogether had she not been a name on my Big Five List. Eva Bocardo, another name, had moved on from artist's muse to painter. Claude Meyer, it was reported, was learning the wine trade somewhere in the depths of Gallia Comata. I knew that already. I knew too that his girlfriend was the heiress to a significant Médoc château. Then somebody said that Claude's cousin, Marie-Claire Dufraisse, had married her psychiatrist and was expecting their first child. This *was* news to me. It took me aback, left me confused and momentarily abandoned, wallowing on a beach somewhere between Naxos and Corsica, such that I missed the turn when the conversation around the table moved on to Janice Day.

Wherever two or three Ecolint alumni gathered together in those days, conversation inevitably turned at some point to Janice Day. I think people took a perverse pleasure in inventing and retailing Janice Day stories, knowing that the chances were remote of them ever being proved false. One formed the impression that not everyone had liked her. That evening we had Jan managing an

162

orphanage in Peru, sunbathing topless at St Tropez, running a shelter for homeless vagrants in the basement of a church on the South Side of Chicago, getting pregnant by one of them, disappearing through baggage reclaim at Anchorage airport before the Japanese woman who recognised her could get through passport control. She had been seen in Buenos Aires worshipping at the shrine of Nuestra Señora La Virgen de los Abarrotes around the corner from the Abasto market. She was living in a New Age community in El Bolson. She was shacked up with the sole remnant of a hippy commune in Cloverdale; she was shacked up with a gun-toting lunatic in Montana, or maybe it was Alaska (which would account for the Anchorage sighting); she was the third wife of a gun-toting headman in the Swat Valley in Pakistan; she was a gun-toting single mother in Peoria. I gave Jean-Daniel as my source for thinking she had been killed in a battle with the gun-toting German police in June 1972, around the time Andreas Baader was captured. Edward Reader said he, too, thought Jan was dead; but in his version she had died in a house fire in the suburbs of Munich. He did not provide a source. Edward was becoming his own source; he was writing his dissertation on the Baader-Meinhof view of the de-Nazification of Germany, after all.

Am I right in remembering that Edward Reader was there? In my memory of Escalade 1975, there is no picture of him – simply a rasping, metallic voice adding footnotes to other people's conversations. Yet it is that voice I hear saying Janice Day died in the Munich fire. Now, more than thirty years later, as I listen to it again more closely, I hear him whispering to me that as part of his research he has seen Anastasia Kuznetsova and then asking whether I could put him in touch with Colin Witheridge. Or do I only imagine that I remember? *Like you imagined that ghost at Rouëlbeau?* And I awake with a start from my memories because it is Johnny's mocking voice that has asked me the question and Johnny Morris, my blood brother, is dead in Vietnam.

On Christmas Day, 150 people were executed in the national football stadium in Fernando Poo while the military band played 'Those were the Days' by way of background music. The news upset me – not because I felt any sympathy towards the unfortunates who had been killed (I didn't), but rather because of the use to which a song I liked had been put. A song redolent of the scent of summer flowers on a warm evening under the plane tree at the Auberge de Grange-

Canal, of glasses of cold white wine on the table waiting to be drunk, of life demanding to be lived, of battles to be won and of Janice Day smoking one of my gold-tipped black cigarettes and blowing smoke rings into the still night air.

In the spring of '76 I found a business excuse to go to Texas. Johnny had been dead for over a year and my trip was long overdue. There were also certain ghosts I needed to exorcise. Sally said she would be delighted to see me. The tone of her voice told me the words were not just empty social niceties.

Sally was living in Houston then, a mile or so from her parents. In an attempt to be independent she had rented a modest house – what, in England, those who don't live in one call a 'bungaloid'. It faced a treeless street lined with identical bungaloids, each thin-walled and black-roofed, too cold in winter and too hot in summer. Dripping metal boxes protruding from the windows provided a modicum of air conditioning and relief from the humid heat of the Gulf Coast summer. By May they were already in use.

For propriety's sake, I booked into a downtown hotel and caught a taxi to the address Sally had given me. She had not long returned home from work when I arrived. It was Friday afternoon.

Sally came – barefoot, toenails painted red – out onto the front lawn to greet me. Her hair, no longer bleached blonde, was drawn flat against her skull, gathered into a Presbyterian bun at the back of her head. Perhaps there were wrinkles of grief around the lips and shadows of war around the eyes, but if there were then the US cosmetics industry had camouflaged them well. To me she looked scarcely changed from the newly arrived teenager who had so quickly shot to number one on Johnny's Big Five List. She threw her arms around me, held me tightly, pressed her head into the hollow of my shoulder. "Thank you so much for coming, Nick," she said. "It means a lot to me and it would've meant a lot to Johnny. Weekends can be difficult, you know."

I took my shoes off at the door, peeled my socks off and stuffed them in my shoes. Sally hid them away in a cupboard and went to fry chicken joints and pre-cut French fries and boil a multicoloured cocktail of frozen diced vegetables. I opened the bottle of California wine I had brought. Sally muttered grace and we ate early – American fashion. The wine was surprisingly good. Sally said, "I don't drink much alcohol any more, Nick," but we easily finished the bottle.

At dinner we talked about Johnny. Sally asked me to tell her everything he and I had done in the years before she moved to Geneva. She said, "Johnny just loved those days. He used to talk for hours about you two and your motorbikes. Swimming in the lake in your underpants. The little hills you'd climb and pretend they were mountains…"

I tried to speak about other friends from Geneva days but Sally always returned the conversation to Johnny. When I mentioned that Janice Day had not been heard from since disappearing four and a half years previously, Sally told me the story, from Johnny's limited viewpoint inside the tent, of the night I had seen a ghost at Rouëlbeau. She remembered, too, the morning Johnny had introduced me to her in the courtyard at Ecolint when she was eating a jam doughnut. *Nick only touches in his dreams.*

After dinner, Sally took two photograph albums and a box of Johnny's military memorabilia from a shelf. I found a bottle of Canadian whiskey under the kitchen sink between the bleach and the washing-up liquid. I poured us each a glass.

Sally released her hair from its bun and sat beside me on the sofa. She opened one of the albums, said she kept the whiskey for medicinal reasons, to help her sleep when the loneliness of the empty bed became too much to bear. "I still spend a lot of weekends with my folks," she said. "This kind of thing takes a long time to heal." When I felt she was going to add something about the comfort God provided, I changed the subject and asked where a certain photograph of the two of them, smiling broadly at the cameraman, their arms entwined, had been taken. "Oh, that," she said. "That's upstate New York. Johnny's uncle's cottage. It was the summer before we were married. Just look how happy we were, Nick." She sipped her whiskey.

A loose photograph fell, face down, out of the album and onto the floor. I leaned forward and picked it up. Turning it over, I saw the grainy black-and-white picture Johnny had taken of Sally in the nude when they were in eleventh grade. I handed it to Sally. She looked at it and, with no trace of embarrassment, sighed, "What's that doing in here?" Then, as she slipped the picture back between the pages of the album, she said, "You have no idea, Nick, how much everything's changed."

When we came to the photos of Johnny in uniform, the tears Sally had held back so well began to flow. I put a comforting arm around her shoulder. I smoothed loose strands of hair from her brow, took the empty whiskey glass from her hand and laid it on the table beside mine. I gently kissed the tear the widow shed for her dead husband and held her hand to steady it and, well, you know how it is, one thing led to another and then to another and – anyway – *sex is the great healer*.

When I awoke the next morning I was alone in Sally's bed. It was still early, just beginning to get light. Through the open door, I could see a light was on elsewhere in the house. I pulled on my jeans and t-shirt and walked barefoot towards the light.

I found Sally in the kitchen standing beneath the naked central lightbulb, wrapped in a faded pink dressing gown that had seen happier days. In her clenched fist she held a kitchen knife. Tearstains marred her cheeks. She looked at me as if she was seeing straight through me to something behind my back. A sudden fear gripped me that she might do herself harm. I said the first words that came into my head, "Is this a dagger I see before me, the handle…"

Lady Macbeth did not allow me to finish. "Nicholas Kellaway," she said in a hoarse whisper, "get out of my house. Get out of my house this instant."

"Okay, Sally. Stay calm. I'll just get my shoes and…"

"You'll do nothing of the sort. You will turn around. You will walk to that front door. You will open it. You will walk through it. You will get out of my house." She took a step forward, lifted the knife to the height of her shoulder. It was pointing at me now, the long, sharp blade glinting in the raw, electric light. The knifewoman took another step towards me. "Go! In the name of God, go!"[43]

The door closed behind me. The key turned in the lock. The street outside Sally's house was deserted – a sleepy Saturday morning. I walked away, shoeless, along rough pavements and across unfenced front gardens. I trod in a Texas-sized pile of dog shit and cut my right foot on something sharp hidden in the long grass. A big, pink car slowed beside me. Two large black men in it eyed me, decided I wasn't worth mugging and drove off.

The bouncer at the hotel door tried to keep me out until I produced my room key. When I tried on a pair of shoes somebody had carelessly left in the corridor, I re-opened the wound on my

---

[43] In dream number fifty-six ('Hot Night in Texas') in *The Dream Diaries* this episode is presented as a dream. Sally Pinkerton is not identified as the woman involved. – Ed.

foot and left a bloodstain on the carpet. To relieve the pain I soaked my feet in the bath for an hour.

Fascist cow. She deserved everything she'd got: the cheap bungaloid, the soiled bathrobe, the bare lightbulb, the hidden whiskey, the dog shit on the lawn… She was nothing more than a US Army recruiting slut, a whore of war, seducing Johnny Morris with her pointy Texan tits and sending my very own blood brother to his death – fighting for the wrong bloody side – as surely as if she'd pulled the damn Vietcong trigger herself.

I had a whole day to kill in Houston and I spent it shopping. When I boarded the flight back to London in the late afternoon, I had three pairs of bright new Texan shoes packed in my case and another pair, picked up for free in the hotel corridor, on my bandaged feet.[44]

That was the beginning of the memorable summer of 1976. Harold Wilson was once asked what his main accomplishments as prime minister had been. He replied with something to the effect that when he was prime minister, Britain had two of the finest summers on record. It was just as well the weather smiled benignly. The country was, otherwise, heading to hell in a borrowed IMF[45] hand basket.

3

A few days after returning from my duties in Texas I completed on the purchase of a flat in Islington. Keen though I was to leave behind the seaweed-green encrustations of my rented Balham room, my primary motive for moving was financial. I was learning my trade.

Inflation was running at more than 25% per annum. This meant that asset values, including house prices, would almost inevitably rise in nominal terms – while the capital sum of the debt I borrowed to purchase the asset would remain constant. Likewise, I could

---

[44] See W.J. Drayford, 'Shoes and Shopping Lists: The Treatment of Displacement in the Wichita Dream Diaries' in *Sex Today*, Vol. 19, Sydney, 2005. – Ed.

[45] IMF: International Monetary Fund. The UK's poor economic situation in 1976 resulted in the government calling on the IMF for a loan. The humiliating conditions of the loan included IMF involvement in the country's budget process. – Ed.

expect my salary to rise, both through promotions and, in the unlikely event of no promotions, simply by the application of cost-of-living increases. Having been employed by Harriman's for more than two years, I also qualified for a subsidised mortgage that protected me from exposure to higher interest rates: my effective interest rate would be fixed at 5% per annum, however high market rates rose on the back of inflation. My only real exposure was to losing my job, but I had now been employed for nearly three years and had survived three sets of Christmas purges. I was game for more of the City. Debt – leverage, gearing – is the miracle drug of finance. I stretched my mortgage capacity to its absolute limits.

Yes, I still considered myself a socialist. Outside Harriman's clean capitalist corridors I guarded my image as a Man of the Left. I still prayed to Karl Marx that the Great Proletarian Revolution would come. In conscious parody of Saint Augustine, however, I prayed that it might not come just quite yet.

Heggie, rather uncharacteristically, helped me move my few belongings. "I've never been to Islington," he said, but he ran out of motivation when he discovered the cardboard box full of my notebooks and lists. I found him sitting on the floor of my new flat reading my dream diaries. "This is *very* interesting, Nick," he said. "Do you write down all your dreams?"

"Not all," I replied.

"Interesting."

"Which one?"

"Not any one of them in particular. More the fact that you write them down at all."

"Why?"

"Do you keep a diary? I mean an ordinary daytime diary. A journal."

"No."

"Even more interesting."

"Why?"

"Well, look, one of the key features of dreams is that in the ordinary course of events one forgets them. You don't forget real life quite so readily so you don't feel you need to write it down. *You* don't at least. For most people, forgetting dreams is a good thing, I imagine."

"Probably."

"Forgetting helps to distinguish dreaming from real life. But, look, suppose you don't *want* to make such a distinction. Suppose you don't believe that the waking world *should* be preferred to the sleeping world, that you think what some people casually call 'reality' on the one hand and 'dreams' on the other are equally valid – because, well, there is no rule that says one's better than the other. Right?"

"Okay."

"Well then, writing your dreams down gets rid of that key characteristic: their forgettableness. Through writing you preserve what memory by nature does not. Then you re-read this record of your dreams – years later, when memory of your ordinary unrecorded life is fading a bit. Suddenly, the sleeping world of those times is more real than the waking world. In 1996, you'll look back and see the world of 1976 refracted through the prism of your dreams that year. Could be very interesting, don't you think?"

I roamed around my flat after Adam left, very pleased with my purchase: two bedrooms, sitting-dining room, kitchen, bathroom, even a large cupboard under the stairs that led up to the flat above. All mine. The walls were freshly painted and free from damp splodges and tired posters. The broad double bed I had bought at Heal's took centre stage in the master bedroom. My desk sat in the smaller bedroom along with a stack of unpacked boxes. For now, until a few more pay cheques had come in, the sitting room remained unfurnished and bare. The only item in it was Jan's guitar.

It was probably the daily sight of the guitar in its corner that led to me, at last, seek out Emma Wallace. Through the good offices of her old Oxford college, I tracked Emma down to the private north London school where she taught French.

Emma met me at the school gate one June afternoon. I was surprised to see that she was pregnant, very obviously pregnant under her mauve maternity dress. Her face was red and, as she kissed the air beside my cheeks, I felt a thin layer of perspiration on her skin. "Thank you for meeting me here," she said. "I hope you don't mind talking in my classroom."

The walls of Emma's classroom were covered in posters of France: Loire Châteaux, Eiffel Towers, Ponts du Gard... One in particular, however, immediately caught my attention: *Le Temps des Cerises*. Paris, 1968. How long was it before Emma's voice drew me away from that schoolgirl's swirling skirts? *Now pay attention, Nicholas.* Actually, what she said was, "Nostalgia?" A soft, almost provocative, half-question lingering in the warm air of a Left Bank night I had not known. I don't think I responded. I know I said nothing about the poster girl on the barricades. Marie-Claire's baby would have been born by now. Only a few months older than Emma's.

"May '68," Emma continued as if I required an explanation. "The poster's a good springboard for classroom discussion. The girls now were – what? – nine or ten in 1968. Ancient history to them."

"I see."

"We were rather ambivalent about *les événements* in the Jericho House. That's what you wanted to talk about, wasn't it, the Jericho House days?"

"Ambivalent in what way?"

"Didn't you have your fill of this at Oxford?" Emma asked, a bemused smile on her lips.

"Go on."

"Well. May '68 was very male, wasn't it? Bluntly, in 1967 the French government legalised contraception and a year later it was brought to its knees by demands from male students for access to women. Okay, you see pretty girls on the barricades," Emma nodded towards the poster of Marie-Claire, "but essentially it was a male protest. The women of the Jericho House aspired to being something more than the objects of male sexual self-realisation."

"And," I asked, "you teach this to your pupils?"

"Sometimes. Sixth formers. If the conversation goes that way. If their French can cope with it. Come on, Nick. They're seventeen, eighteen. They know… I mean, how old were you that night you turned up at St Anne's with a bottle of wine?"

I laughed – a forced laugh, "Don't remind me of it!"

"Why not? You oughtn't to take it that way. I was just…" Emma dropped her gaze from me to the floor – or maybe it was to the mauve bump in her midriff. She was not smiling now. "I was," she said, almost in a whisper, "still a virgin."

"You *were*? With all those posters and women's lib slogans?"

Emma nodded. A long pause before she looked up again. "Cup of tea?"

Tea. China teapot. Matching porcelain cups and saucers taken from a corner cupboard. Nice biscuits in an airtight tartan tin. Real leaf tea, not bags. *Post-lactarian, I presume.* Mother.

"You slept with Sill, didn't you?"

"Do you need to remind me of that as well?"

"Only as a way of saying we weren't really a bunch of dykes. If any of us was a lesbian it was Sill, and you screwed *her*."

"Why did you…? I mean…"

"Political lesbianism? That's the name they've given it. It's not quite as exciting when it has a label, is it? Difficult to say now. I suppose, in a way, it was just one of our stories. A way of asserting a marginal identity. We had this idea that society could be changed by stories, by its marginal elements. Something more subtle, more feminine if you wish, than class warfare on the streets. You become marginal through the stories you create: a lunatic, a vagrant, an immigrant. You open your doors to people from alien cultures, homosexuals, terrorists. You tell stories. You live your stories. Lie often enough and you change the truth. Telling stories was the game we played."

Emma sipped her tea. She told a story that Anna Schmidt had recounted during her few days in the Jericho House. Anna and Jan had captured a horse on Port Meadow, taken their clothes off and ridden it naked, Anna in front holding onto the mane and Jan behind clinging on to Anna.

"Was *that* true?" I remembered Jan declining to take off her clothes and ride the horse I had caught for her on Port Meadow one evening.

"True? Truth wasn't a Jericho House concept, Nick. Stories were either good or bad. No, even that's too strong: there were stories we liked and stories we disliked. We liked Anna's stories. Anna said she'd had the best orgasms of her life riding that horse. That worked for us."

Another Anna Schmidt story. One afternoon, soon after she had arrived in Oxford, Anna was lying on the floor of the front room of the Jericho House when a workman carrying a clipboard covered in tiny spidery writing broke in and raped her. She told it so realistically that Sill said she would take her down to the police station. "The pigs?" Anna laughed. "Never. Anyway, I rather enjoyed it."

Sill, Emma said, never really did catch on to the stories game. Jan parried Sill's story of being raped in the cupboard under the stairs by her babysitter with a tale of losing *her* virginity when *she* was eleven to her older brother. "Sill's jaw muscles were working furiously to control her anger. She hated being trumped like that. And the rest of us were sitting there thinking 'dysfunctional family' – in our language all families were dysfunctional. It was tautological, like a round circle. And then Jan smiles, flashes those perfect teeth and says, 'What's wrong guys? It was *me* that seduced *him*. I was the original Eve-child.'"

Emma smiled, "More tea?" and, as she filled my cup, said, "Jan picked it all up *so* quickly. She was a natural story-teller. A natural liar. Behind the pin-up body, she had something profoundly nocturnal about her. She wasn't the straightforward American she looked. Her mother was German, you'll recall. 'A prize of war,' she said. I remember her saying that to Anna, 'a prize of war', and tugging at that little leather cord Anna always wore around her neck. Jan spoke German because of her mother and she spoke French and Spanish because she'd lived in Geneva and Buenos Aires. I was reading Modern Languages, remember? And here is this American from a supposedly boorish, war-mongering, monoglot culture, casually speaking four languages. I had this theory at the time, probably to justify reading French and German, that to speak another language made you a threat to rational bourgeois society because you could see that there were alternative discourses, other ways of saying things, of seeing things."

I added, "My French teacher used to say, *'Bilangue veut dire menteur, comme le serpent.'*"

"Exactly. I like that. Pity it doesn't work in English. Bilingual. Fork-tongued. The snake, you'll recall, was one of the heroes in Jericho House politics. Eve and her serpent in the Garden of Eden. Remember that reproduction Renaissance painting on the wall of the front room? Eve holding out the apple to Adam? There's this wickedly seductive smile on her face. They're both naked, of course. Adam's covering his genitals with his hand, almost as if he's trying to protect his manhood from this gorgeous thing that's handing him an apple. But how the artist has preserved Eve's pubic modesty is much more interesting: the serpent's coiled around one of her legs and its enormous cobra head's splayed across her genitals. It was a religious painting, of course – originally. The Biblical Fall. 'Original', though, is only one aspect of a painting's meaning and usually not its most important one. You could just *see* that the artist's sympathies actually lay with Eve and her serpent. Something pre-dating the original, even if it might have been subconscious. It was almost as if he was trying to say that before Adam knew Eve she'd had sex with the serpent. Very marginal. Very Jericho House. Have you heard of 'Sogol'?"[46]

---

[46] The concept *Sogol* is comprehensively surveyed in R. de Faucigny, *Subversive Narratives: Minority Rights and the Erosion of the Bourgeois State*, Oxford, 1986, and in D. de Lucinge, *Sogol in Revolutionary Theory and Praxis*, Oxford, 1988. – Ed.

"Yes."

"It's 'Logos' backwards," said Emma. She offered me another biscuit and took one herself. "Janice Day, the Eve-child… She even claimed to have killed her brother, you know – the one she'd screwed when she was eleven. Hit him on the head and, when he was lying there unconscious, held him under water until he drowned."

"We can," I said, "falsify that one. The brother is alive and well and working as an airline pilot out of Chicago."

"Well. There, then," said Emma.

I asked Emma about the tramp in the graveyard.

"Weren't you there that night, the night when Jan…?"

"No. I wasn't really all that close to the Jericho House."

"Maybe not. Maybe it was Colin Witheridge. But you *were* there the night we did Nietzsche and that sixth-must-die stuff. I remember you clearly being there that night. And that Magdalen bloke going on about murder as the route to liberation."

"But that wasn't really Jericho House, was it? The heyday was past. Sill was gone. Jan and Anna were gone."

"Nick, it was *pure* Jericho House. If I ever get round to writing these stories down, that night'll be up there with the finest."

"The tramp?"

"Sorry. Yes. The tramp. The tramp *was* real. So was his death. It was in the *Oxford Times*. That was what gave me the idea. A short story I was going to do. Well, that I had an idea for; I never wrote it. Not yet at least. I ran through the outline with Jan and she said she thought it was good and that I should develop it. Anyway, she started elaborating on it and I added details on top of hers and we got a bit carried away with ourselves. We started living it. Living the story. Our minds devoured by our language. We even went out for a walk up the Thames, looking for a church so that we could imagine the details of the setting better. We found one on the edge of a village and all we had to do was obliterate the village, make it one of those wiped out in the plague. Plague was good. It was dusk – also good for stories like this. Murky, Gothic, October night. Nobody around. Jan took her clothes off and pranced about among the gravestones. Totally Sogol. Very lewd. But there was no tramp, of course, and Jan put her clothes back on because she was getting cold. We got a bus back into Oxford. We couldn't stop giggling for the whole journey and this old man, who looked a bit like the tramp in our story, was sitting on the other side of the aisle saying: 'What's so bloody funny, then? If it's that funny, share it, ladies.'"

"But I heard it that it was *you* dancing in the graveyard."

"Yeah, well, okay. Jan was there and it didn't seem right to give every male eye in the room more of an excuse for mentally undressing her. It was only a story. Does it matter who was doing the dancing?"

"But she undressed anyway. In the front room of the Jericho House. Is that bit true?"

"Is that what you heard?"

"Yeah."

"From Colin? Well, it's sort of true. Half-true. Half-undressed. Took her shirt off. Undressed from the waist up. Nothing more than you see on French beaches."

"And then?"

"You heard about that as well?"

I nodded.

Emma sighed. "I think it was probably the most Sogol thing she could think of on the spur of the moment. You find a derelict stranger who's dying of some disgusting disease. You take him away from the church door where he sits forlornly, hoping for redemption. You conceive a child with him. After the vagrant's done his miserable little ejaculation, you murder him and throw his body into the river."

"And then?"

"Then? Come on, Nick. Use your imagination."

"What was she on about?"

"Come on, Nick."

"What?"

Another sigh. "Jan was always doing stories about abortions. You must've heard some of them. Horrific stories. They seem even worse now that I'm…" Emma stood, put a hand on her belly – the gesture Colin had described Jan making that evening in the Jericho House after Emma had first told her story – and began to tidy the books and papers on her desk. "I've got a staff meeting in fifteen minutes, I'm afraid. Thank you so much for coming, Nick. I really must turn some of this into a series of short stories. So much material." She paused, wondering perhaps whether to say more, before continuing. "It's funny, you know. That's twice I've told the story of that old tramp in as many weeks."

"Twice?"

"There was this other bloke who came to ask me about it. In the year above me at Oxford. Doing his doctorate on German terrorists now."

"Edward Reader?"

"Yes." Emma looked at me, apparently surprised I knew the name. "He'd just seen Anna. Been to see her with Colin Witheridge, I think."

"I don't think that can be right." Colin would have told me if he had been in contact with Anna Schmidt.

"Maybe not. Put it down to the pregnancy."

"You told him the story of the tramp? Including the bit about Jan?"

"Of course, why not?" Emma said. "Other stories as well. We talked quite a bit about Jan. He was interested in her for his thesis. He was convinced she'd got caught up in all that Baader-Meinhof stuff. He said he had it on good authority that Jan was dead. Something about a fire in Munich."

"Another story?"

"I don't think so. Ed does history, not fiction." Emma locked her classroom door behind us. "I'll walk with you to the gate," she said. "We can't have strange men prowling about a posh girls' school, can we?"

We walked across the late afternoon courtyard. "Ed wanted to see a letter that Jan's mother wrote to her just before she disappeared."

"*You* have that letter?"

"Yes. You know about it?"

"Her mother's childhood. In German. How did you get it?"

"It arrived a couple of days after Jan and Sill went to Berlin."

"And you kept it?"

"Yes."

"What's it say?"

"Stuff about growing up in Germany in Hitler's time. Not exactly innocent childhood reminiscences, though. More like a teenage girl's experiences – fantasies maybe – of, I suppose, parties – politically sponsored orgies really – with soldiers home on leave from the killing fields and concentration camps. A sort of dance of death and sex. A kind of morality tale embedded in a highly unorthodox view of Nazi sex policies. A frenzied atmosphere of erotic paganism that we don't usually associate with repressed Nazi types."

"Can I see it?"

"You know, Jan always thought her mother was the innocent victim of this sexually experienced GI Joe and when you listened to some of her stories, you could sort of tell she hated her dad for it, a hatred she transferred to the brother, the one she said she'd killed."

"Who's still alive…"

"But it's significant, don't you think? Telling a story where she killed him."

"The letter?"

"According to her mum's letter maybe the original seduction actually ran in the opposite direction. The woman seducing the man. The baby in the belly was Ursula Day's passport to America, her way out of Germany where she was hungry and everything was in ruins around her."

"May I see the letter?"

"No, Nick. It's personal. Very personal."

"The personal is political."

"And bourgeois toilet training creates fascists. Don't insult me with tired slogans, Nick."

We reached the gate, walking the last fifty yards in silence. Emma thanked me again for the visit and, her left hand resting on her mauve pregnancy, sighed whimsically and said, more to a ghost hovering in the warm air than to either me or her baby, "When shall we three meet again…?"

"We three?"

"Anna, Jan and me."

"Not Sill?" I asked.

"Sill's in prison."

"Jan's dead."

"'*Vieux capitaine, je te salue, Voyageons vers l'inconnu, L'ancre rouilée ne tiendra plus.*'[47] Dead's more interesting than prison, Nick. More potential."

---

[47] From the opening lines of Charles Bonneville's (Charles-Henri Bonneville de la Tour de St Jean de Tholome) poem '*L'ancre de miséricorde*' (Paris, 1972). These lines are repeated – in reverse order – as the closing three lines of the poem. Emma Somerwell's English translation of these lines (in *The Rusted Anchor* – Oxford, 1987) was controversial, since it added a sexual connotation absent in the original: 'I greet thee ancient whore; / Sail me to a distant shore: / Our rusted anchor holds no more.' When Bonneville reissued his poem in 1992, however, he changed the final line to read '*Ma chère putain, je te salue.*' – Ed.

4

"Anna? You've got to be joking."

"I'm dead serious, Nick," Colin said.

"You weren't expecting her?"

"God, no! Out of the fucking blue. Five minutes after I get into the flat, the doorbell rings and it's Anna Schmidt. Except she's calling herself something different now."

It was a mild Wednesday evening in December. Colin and I were standing outside The Jamaica, pints in our hands; bitter for me, Guinness, as usual, for Colin. I had not seen him for months, had never mentioned that I'd seen Emma Wallace in June, that she harboured notions he and Edward Reader had gone to see Anna.

Colin had phoned at eleven that morning. I think it was the first time he had ever phoned me at the office. We agreed to meet after work. "For a quick pint," I said.

"What about Gill?" I asked. Gill was Colin's girlfriend then and she was, I imagined, the reason I had not seen him since summer. She lived in Manchester but spent most weekends with Colin.

Colin wiped the foam from his lips onto the back of his hand. "That's exactly it," he said. "She doesn't know a bloody thing about it. She mustn't, of course."

"Two places at the same time?"

Colin ignored my remark. "I've got to get all trace of Anna out of the flat before Friday afternoon. That's where you come in."

"How? D'you want me to be your charlady?"

"You've got a spare room."

I raised an eyebrow. Anna was, as far as I knew, still a wanted terrorist. And I was an increasingly respectable Harriman banker with an even more respectable mortgage.

Anna was curled up on the sofa watching television when we arrived at Colin's Bayswater flat. She stood, gave a small smile of recognition and shook my hand with Central European formality. Her face was a mask of wan innocence. You would have passed her in the street without a second glance, never imagining her role in Cretan rituals, her part in the stories Emma told or her mug-shot staring from a notorious wanted poster.

"Have you two seen each other since Greece?" I asked.

Colin said, "No. Whatever gave you that idea?" and then let slip that Anna had already been in London for a week.

When I asked Anna why she had come to London, she said, "To rob a bank."

"German humour?"

"Is bank robbery in England a funny thing?" she retorted and took Colin's hand. They were sitting together on the sofa like a couple of contented pensioners.

At some point during the evening Anna showed me her new passport. "Are you not afraid I'll throw it overboard?" I said, trying to joke, alluding to the time she had stopped Karl-Heinz Kupferhoden throwing *my* passport into the Aegean.

Anna caught the reference. She said solemnly, "He will never do that again. He is dead. He was a selfist."

According to Anna's passport, she was now Anna Rotten, born in 1944. For Germans born during the war, there was little surprise that birth certificates were sometimes missing. Anna Rotten had made doubly sure there were no such complications when she applied for her passport. She had been born in Scharlevil, then in Yugoslavia, now Serbia,[48] and was entitled to a *Bundesrepublik* passport under a law that gave Germans, wherever born, the right to West German citizenship. The law was heavily used by refugees from the ancient Germanic settlements in Eastern Europe who, when they could, made their way west after the Second World War.[49]

I smiled at Anna's choice of new name. It had been only a few

---

[48] Anna had chosen her new alias well. Scharlevil was one of several *Donauschwaben* villages around the town of Gross Kikinda in the Banat, a former province of the Austro-Hungarian Empire. Scharlevil's original name – Charlesville – together with those of the neighbouring 'Welsh' villages, St Hubert and Soltur, pointed to the French origin of the inhabitants. Peasants from Lorraine had been settled on depopulated lands re-conquered from the Ottomans in the eighteenth century, although they had long since come to be regarded by their Hungarian and Serbian neighbours as part of the German-speaking *Donauschwaben* community. When the Austro-Hungarian polity was dismembered in 1919, the western regions of the Banat became part of Yugoslavia. The area was occupied by Hitler's Germany in 1941. In late 1944 the Soviet Army drove the Nazis out of the Banat and turned the area over to Yugoslav Partisans who, assuming the local Germans to have been collaborators with the occupying forces, massacred the German-speaking population. Among those killed in the genocide campaign was Michael Rotten, parish priest in Kikinda. Others were transported to forced labour camps in the Soviet Union and, if they ever returned west, it was only several years later and then to subsidised housing in West Germany rather than to their expropriated ancestral farms in Yugoslavia. – Ed.

[49] An ironic epitaph to Hitler's *Heim ins Reich* slogan. – Ed.

weeks earlier that The Sex Pistols had released their début single, *Anarchy in the UK*, to a screaming chorus of outraged tabloid headlines. Johnny Rotten was the group's lead vocalist.

By felicitous coincidence, or so it seemed, Colin knew of another person who shared Anna's new surname. His bank, First Manufacturers' Bank of Boston, had a customer called Thomas Rotten, proprietor of a successful machine-tool company in Brazil and of several bank accounts in Jersey and London – external accounts, not subject to the exchange-control regulations the United Kingdom still had in place at the time. A Swiss Franc account held a particularly large credit balance.

"A German in Brazil," Anna said. "Sure to be a Nazi. One who got away." Anna's words sounded mechanical. I recall, even at the time, thinking: *have Colin and Anna rehearsed this story?*

Thirty-one years later, in the spring of 2008, while reconstructing these events leading up to the phone call of 25 July 2007, I googled Thomas Rotten. It did not come as a surprise to find no trace of him in cyberspace. The Brazilian was old in December 1976 and he had probably died long ago, a poorer man than Anna found him. Nor was there any sign of a machine-tool company I could associate with him. Again, no surprise: if his company had survived it would have been unlikely to have done so under the name 'Rotten Machine Tools'.

I did, however, find the personal website of one Thomas Rotten-Diaz and wondered whether, given the Latin half of his double-barrelled surname, there might be some connection between him and the ex-Nazi victim of Anna's little money-transfer scheme back in 1976. If Thomas Rotten-Diaz existed outside cyberspace, he was a twenty-one-year-old American from Fort Bliss, on the border between New Mexico and Texas. Fort Bliss was where Johnny Morris went, after his Dallas wedding, to join the American Army at a time when the authorities were more careless with their recruits than they have since become. Johnny Morris was only one of some 58,000 US service personnel killed in Vietnam. They would never get away with that now.

As I scrolled down the website I found a pencil drawing of a woman. She was naked from the waist upwards. The artist had left everything below her waist to the imagination of the beholder. Beside her on the page were three separate photographs, each of a gun. They stood with their barrels pointing upwards like erect penises of war. The guns were labelled: *6.5 Grendel*; *.50 Beowulf*; and *5.56 M16A1 W/M203 attachment*. Beneath the guns, the lyrics of 'Progenies of the Great Apocalypse' by Dimmu Borgir[50] were quoted at length, stuff about facing the darkness in our hearts and hunting the bastards down.

When I was reminded of Johnny at Fort Bliss, saw the guns and read the lyrics my thoughts turned, not entirely irrationally, to Oscar Meyer and that day at Rouëlbeau. Then, that night, I dreamed of Rouëlbeau. Oscar laughed, "Are you going to go to school like that, with no pants on?" His golems stood beside him. They called their guns Beowulf and Grendel and pointed them at my bare genitals. As I watched, one of Oscar's golems began to take on my features. It was as if I was looking in a mirror and my image was about to shoot me. Oscar laughed again, "It'll serve him right for fucking around with Jan." I pulled the trigger and the mirror shattered. Then I felt comforting arms around me. They were the arms of angels and then they were Jan's arms. Then Jan became Caroline and she was wiping the sweat from my brow with the palm of her hand. She said gently, "It was only a dream." I felt her body pressed close against mine. Caroline is a good woman, but the arms she held around me felt like Oscar's tightened ropes and the words of the prayer she whispered clutched me like a mailed glove at the throat.

Over the days that followed I returned several times to the exquisite pencil drawing of the naked woman. There was a band, made perhaps of leather, around her neck. From this halter a cord hung. It fell between her breasts. Another band was fastened around her upper arm. It was tight, constricting the bicep. Perhaps it was because of the erect guns beside the drawing that I imagined this woman to be a prize of war. According to Emma Wallace, Janice Day had used that phrase to describe her German mother, 'a prize of war', but then Jan had never seen her mother's last letter to her.

I saw this latter-day prize, recently captured, being led by the yoke of slavery that hung gently from her neck towards her new master's bedchamber. She went, I think, not entirely unwillingly. She held her hair onto the back and top of her head with her fingers. Hers were long slender fingers that possessed knowledge of esoteric things, unforgivingly delicious. The nipples on her breasts stood erect. She went, I think, with confidence.

---

[50] See the official Dimmu Borgir website at http://site.dimmu-borgir.com. – Ed.

Then, one day as I stared at my computer screen, I suddenly understood why the image haunted me: the drawing bore an uncanny resemblance to Anna Schmidt.[51]

5

Sometime during the course of Friday, Anna let herself into my flat with the key I had given her. She was there when I got home from work, watching television with the central heating turned up. She was booked on a Saturday morning flight to Zürich. There were just twelve hours between the Friday violet hour and the time she would need to leave for Heathrow.

We went out to supper at a Greek restaurant less than ten minutes on foot from where I lived. There, when the meal was ended and I guessed the time propitious, I asked whether she had ever heard from Janice Day.

"Jan is dead," Anna said eventually.

---

[51] See H. Lector, *A la recherche d'une femme perdue*, Paris, 1979. "I was wrapped up against the cold, damp Buenos Aires winter, hardly aware of where I was going, knowing only that I had a long walk ahead of me and that dusk was gathering, when a drawing in an illuminated gallery window caught my eye, I stopped and stared. It was her. Or, at least, it was as near as damn it her. The Dark One. That was all she was to me before I knew her name…

I was walking around – seven times around, to be precise – the streets of Jericho with a council clipboard, making notes to support plans to demolish and redevelop the neighbourhood. The curtains were open. The Dark One was lying on the floor of the Jericho House, legs spread, mouth wide, breathing deeply, while a pregnant, working-class neighbour looked on from behind the soiled lace curtains in her window across the street…

German? Yes, perhaps. That was part of her story, part of her disguise. But I had marked her down even then in my imagination as Austrian. Viennese, in fact, with whispered connotations of decadence and intellectuals such as Wittgenstein and Schumpeter and, above them all, Freud. I have often wondered whether she was Jewish herself, my diminutive Dark One, a descendant perhaps of Rahab the Prostitute. Vienna was practically a Jewish city in those days. Small, dark, Jewish as well as decadently Viennese…

I tried the door. It was unlocked. I went in. I set my clipboard on the floor, took the sharp knife from my pocket and put it beside the clipboard. There was a poster of Lenin on the closed door to the room where the Dark One lay. He commanded his troops to go forward, to claim the Revolution's victory. I obeyed and pushed gently on the door…"

See also Beatrix Cheldon, *Customs and Excise: An Anthology of Female Circumcision Practices*, New York, 1982. – Ed.

"How?"

"She died in a fire. She was staying with some people who, what can I say? Let's say the police thought they had links with the Red Army Fraction. It was probably arson. Probably the police making it look like someone else had done it. Like they did with Kupferhoden."

"And you're certain Jan was in the house?"

"Reasonably certain. No proof. But there was no word from her, nothing, after the fire and I knew that was where she was staying."

"But before that? Did you hear from her, see her?"

"Yes, of course. She came to Berlin to see me."

"And Sill?"

"In prison, as you know. Priscilla didn't stay long with me. She went away with some others, Difficult people, then I heard nothing until she was captured. Jan stayed longer with me. She was... what do you say in English? My soul-mate?"

We walked back to my flat. Rain was falling lightly. I offered Anna a nightcap. She declined it, said she wanted a good night's sleep before her early morning start, went into my spare room. I heard her turn the key in the door.

I woke just after two in the morning. Switching on the light, I saw Anna standing at the foot of my bed. She was wearing an old t-shirt of mine, one with the print of Che Guevara's familiar face on it. On Anna, the shirt came down to her knees. She held a sheet of paper in her hand.

"Nick," she said. "I'm interested in this paper." She spoke as if we were attending a meeting with the credit department at Harriman's, discussing whether to extend credit to a client whose finances was deteriorating – a slight tone of menace.

"What is it?" I asked, though I could see it was the yellowed page I had taken, years and years ago, when I was only a child, from the boxes Claude Meyer and I had found in the uninhabited tower at La Bise.

"It is a record from a bank. A bank in Geneva called Meyer & Cie. It's written in old German script – which is strange for bank in Geneva. But maybe not, because it is about Germans. 1938 is the date. I think this is a list of Germans who have made deposits at Meyer. Most of the names are Jewish. Then there are long numbers after the names. Where did you get this?"

"I found it."

"Where?"

"Long time ago. I was probably, what? Ten years old. I was

playing with a friend and I found it. He was the son of one of the Meyers."

"Oooh! I see. You have banking going right through you. Like some of your pink English seaside rock. Even Swiss banking. Very impressive credentials."

"Put it down, Anna. I thought you were trying to get some sleep."

"We will crush Swiss banking when we are in power."

"Swiss banks are proving very useful to you at the moment."

"When we are in power that will all be the past and we will crush the fascist Swiss. Switzerland is an affront." A tone of anger. But it vanished as quickly as it had appeared. "I would," she said in her more formal tone, "like to keep this paper, please. It could prove useful."

"No."

"A trade then. I propose to buy it from you." She laid the yellow page on the bed at my feet and in a single flourish pulled Che Guevara off over her head. She stood naked but for the leather band around her neck and the fine red cord that hung from it. She raised a hand, lifted her hair from her neck, piled it up on the top of her head and held it there. The moment remains utterly vivid in my memory. It was as if, years later, that memory had crystallised out of my brain and become the pencil drawing on Thomas Rotten-Diaz's website.

"Anna," I said. "No. Just leave the paper and go back to bed. Please."

Over Christmas, I spent a few days with my parents at their flat in Eaux-Vives. I was lucky to get there. I had not been abroad since summer and, when I came to look for my passport, I could not find it. The efficient people at the Passport Office in Petty France, however, happily issued me a replacement and I was able to catch the flight I had booked.

Those Geneva days were dark and dreary. We had the electric lights burning even at noon. There were few friends in town. Many of the expatriate families I had grown up with had moved away from Geneva by then. The Meyers had gone up to their chalet in Crans. Marie-Claire was, I learned, there also – with her Parisian psychiatrist husband and his baby. I ran into Jean-Louis Alteschläusche in Place Longemalle and, for want of anything better to occupy the evening, spent an hour and a half drinking new wine with him. I also saw Lizzie Hayes. We met in the Old Town for a pizza. She said she was planning to see my father to show him her work on the mining communities of County Durham, but she had arranged to see him after Christmas, on a date when I would be back in London.

Instead of going home after leaving Lizzie outside her door, I walked out along the lake to sit at the feet of my stone muse. Despite the season she stood there still, her buttocks and breasts full and bare. I found myself thinking, as I sat beside her, of that house with which she shared her name and idly wondered about extending my walk farther out along the lake until I came to La Bise. I wondered whether I would be able to get in, even if only to the grounds; wondered whether, with the whole Meyer clan in Crans, that house of lights would be dark; wondered what might have happened had I not hidden behind the wall that day I saw Jan; wondered whether Jan really was dead. Anna had said that there was no proof. Could she, I wondered, still be in Germany, living underground, part of the reconstituted network that was rumoured to be preparing to spring Baader and Ensslin from prison? I wondered how Anna and Colin had got on with their bank robbery; wondered what Anna might have told him about the night she spent at my flat; wondered whether, that night Johnny and I sat on a branch in his big tree, it really was Oscar deflowering Melanie Mudford that we had seen – playing, as subsequent tellings had it, chicken with her and Melanie forgetting the magic word until it was too late; wondered whether Oscar, wherever he was, still believed that there once had been a Latin author called Euphorius whose works included *The Annals of Vagina Regina*; wondered whether he still carried the scar I had given him with the sharp edge of one of Claude's toy trains; wondered whether all those sunny Geneva years had been no more than a dream, full of sound and fury, signifying nothing.

Susan was spending Christmas with her in-laws in Orpington, so it was only Dad, Mum and I who gathered around the traditional turkey, wearing paper hats from the crackers I had brought from England, toasting ourselves in Migros' Clairette de Die rather than Meyer champagne. "I think," Dad said afterwards when we had sat down to read our books, books that we had wrapped up in shiny paper and given to each other as part of the morning's ritual, a ritual obligatory even in an atheist household, "that next year we should go somewhere they don't celebrate Christmas."

Mum asked, "Where do you have in mind, dear?"

Dad did not answer. He had fallen asleep in his chair.

I did not know it then, of course, but that was to be my last

Christmas in Geneva. I would not return to for nearly twenty-five years. A quarter of a century. The return journey, when it eventually happened in 2001, would not be undertaken for reasons of pleasure.

6

14 January 1977 – A drink with Colin at The Golden Gloves in the Fulham Palace Road. The Brazilian has found a large sum missing from his Swiss Franc account and raised the alarm. FNBB has found the metaphorical fingerprints of Martin Broadwood-Kelly, the fall guy Colin set up, all over the operation and the police have arrested him. "Of course," Colin says, "the chappie's protesting his innocence. The bank, on the other hand, is rather pleased. Martin was one of blokes agitating for unionisation and they'd been looking for a way to get rid of him." *And* Anna got away with the money.

21 January 1977 – Jimmy Carter, the new President of the United States, pardons all those who evaded the draft during the Vietnam War.

22 January 1977 – After a long Friday evening home alone, haunted by Joan Baez on the record player, a small pouch of marijuana and two bottles of Fendant, I fall asleep sometime after two in the morning and dream what is perhaps the most wonderful and satisfying dream of my life. I dream that I am in a familiar white room that looks out over a placid grey sea. I stand beside a big, broad bed as I unbutton Janice Day's blouse. She does not stop me at the second button, nor at the third, nor at the fourth… but what is so wonderful is that I seem in my dream to know that I am dreaming and to be able to control my actions as if I were fully awake. More amazingly still, I seem able to control Jan's response, to prevent her – by an act of *my* will – from pulling away from me as I begin to kiss her.

When I wake, after a gorgeous climax, I reach out to the other side of the bed only to find myself alone again. So real has the dream been that I get up and search the flat for Jan or, at least, for some sign of her. I find the stubs of the Sobranie Black Russians that I laced with hash and the empty wine bottles, but the only sign of Jan is her long-abandoned guitar standing mute in its dusty corner.

I return to bed, hoping to recapture Janice Day there, but sleep now is just another empty room in which Jan's absence echoes. When I wake again it is to a pounding head, a mouth filled with dry, infertile sand and an insistent knocking at the door.

It's ten-fifteen and Adam Heggie stands on my Saturday morning threshold. "I brought you these," he says and hands me Mao Tse-Tung's quotations (in French) and Sigmund Freud's *On Dreams*. "I borrowed them before you left Balham."

Adam makes two mugs of instant coffee – mine extra-strong – while I shower and dress and swallow four aspirins. Then, as we sit at the table drinking the dark mixture that passes for coffee in England and as I flick silently through Freud, Adam asks me what I dreamt about last night. Eager to escape the glare of the cold day and to relive the night in the white room, I tell him. I tell him every glorious detail. Adam is a good audience. I tell him even about the sensation of control. "Maybe," I say, "you could make a poem out of it."

After Adam leaves I take off my clothes and lie down on my unmade bed. I must have slept, for I wake with a start because Anna Schmidt is in the room. She wears a red t-shirt with Che Guevara's face on it, points a Kalashnikov at me, demands money to help the prisoners in Germany and then disappears. It's gone four o'clock and getting dark. The vision of Anna vanishing into the Islington dusk sets me wondering whether that December night was perhaps also only a dream.

I go to my desk and open the drawer where I keep my lists and dreams. I look for the Gothic list I stole many years ago from the tower at La Bise. It's definitely gone. On that evidence I decide to update my 'Lifetime Total' list. But I write 'Anastasia Kuznetsova' instead of 'Anna Schmidt' and claim my first Russian and thirteenth nationality. I think about my earlier dream and about adding 'Janice Day' to my list. I hesitate and then put the list back in its drawer without Jan's name yet written on it. Nor do I place a tick beside her name at the top of my 'Big Five' list.[52]

---

[52] The January 1977 dream of 'J in the White Room' (as it might have been titled) does not appear in *The Dream Diaries*. Nick's apparent ability sometimes to manipulate and control his dreams is, however, mentioned and discussed in the KISS commentary on his dreams; but it is ultimately dismissed as an illusion. M. Bottreaux, *Making it Happen: Lucid Dreams and Wish Fulfilment* (Melbourne, 2008) is highly critical of the KISS conclusions in respect of dream manipulation in general and for *The Dream Diaries* dreams specifically. Anstey and Bottreaux elsewhere, however, (E. Anstey and M.Bottreaux, 'The Kiss Dream Diaries: Fact or Fiction?' in *Sex Today*, Vol. 19, Sydney 2005) have called into question the authenticity of the dreams in *The Dream Diaries*. They suggest, based on contextualised deconstruction criticism, that the dreams may be clever works of fiction rather than an accurate record of actual dreams and that the Kansas Institute of Sleep Science may have been the victim of an elaborate hoax. – Ed.

25 January 1977 – My new boss, an American, says, "We like short hair." He also says, "Carter's wrong to forgive draft dodgers. We'll be the laughing stock of the whole goddamn world." I argue that the past should be put behind us; the anti-war camp, I suggest, should also forgive those who sent their friends to die in the jungles of South-East Asia. He eyes me suspiciously and asks rhetorically, "What do you Brits know about anything?" At the weekend I have my hair cut.

9 March 1977 – A group of twelve Muslim terrorists takes control of buildings in Washington DC. They are holding more than 130 hostages.

11 March 1977 – Colin tells me how Anna's money-transfer operation worked. She opened a bank account in Zürich and told the manager that she was expecting a large sum of money from her father, Thomas Rotten, with which she was going to buy a chalet. It was a plausible tale, just the sort of thing a Brazilian might do to launder his money through Switzerland. From Davos and as if from Thomas Rotten, Anna then sent a tested telex to FMBB in London requesting the transfer of SFR 2.5 million into her new Zürich account. The test – the code – had been supplied, or so it would later appear, by union member Martin Broadwood-Kelly in FMBB's money-transfer department. Anna returned to Zürich, withdrew a modest SFR 2.3 million in bearer CDs, drove to Liechtenstein and deposited them in a Vaduz bank account opened in the name of a friend. "Dead simple," he says.

16 March 1977 – The West German government admits it has been bugging the prison cells of members of the Red Army Faction and that prosecution lawyers have had access to the tapes. There are renewed protests that Baader, Ensslin *et al.* have been kept in prison, mostly in solitary confinement, since their arrest nearly five years ago and complaints that this isolation is a form of torture by the proto-fascist regime – an example of the state brutality that gave rise to the Baader-Meinhof phenomenon in the first place.

6 April 1977 – "Oh, by the way," Colin says, "there was an unexplained £50,000 credit to an account in Broadwood-Kelly's name. They've traced the source of the funds to Zürich. He continues to say he's innocent, of course, but the police say the money'll secure his conviction."

7 April 1977 – In Karlsrühe, the Ulrike Meinhof Commando of the Red Army Faction assassinate Siegfried Buback, West German

Federal Prosecutor.[53] I wonder whether this is the beginning of something bigger, wonder how Anna's involved, wonder whether Jan might resurface.

8 April 1977, Good Friday – My father dies of a massive myocardial infarct. Mum and Dad had come to England to spend Easter with Susan. I put on a dark suit and tie and travel down to Dorset on a midday train. It's astonishing, I think, as I watch the countryside rush past the window, that Dad died just this morning. It seems like he has been dead for so much longer.

10 April 1977, Easter Day – Zohair Yousef Akache, a former student of aeronautical engineering at the Chelsea College of Aeronautical and Automotive Engineering, shoots and kills three people who are sitting in their car outside the Royal Lancaster Hotel. The dead are a former prime minister of North Yemen, his wife and an employee of the Yemeni embassy in London. Akache, it is later revealed, flies out of Heathrow on a scheduled flight that evening.

11 April 1977 – I decide to go out for a walk and Susan says she will come with me. Easter has passed us by unnoticed: for atheists there is no resurrection, even when they die on Good Friday. We walk briskly and mostly in silence.

12 April 1977 – I go up to London. I apologise for arriving late, tell the boss my father has died over the weekend. He says, "I'm sorry for your loss." Twenty minutes later he catches me looking aimlessly out the window. "Kellaway," he shouts, "you breeze in late and then spend the rest of the goddamn day staring outta the goddamn window."

In the late afternoon, the boss comes up to my desk and leans over my shoulder, peering at a calculation I am working on by hand – a variation on option pricing theory that bears scant relevance to my current job. After a puzzled thirty seconds, he takes a step back and says, "Kellaway, go home and take a shower. And change your clothes while you're at it. If you're gonna work for an American bank, you're gonna have to smell like an American."

---

[53] Ulrike Meinhof (1934–1976) had died the previous year. She had been in prison since 1972 with, although kept separate from, the other members of the Red Army Faction captured in the spring of that year. She is said to have committed suicide. Earlier she had written, 'Suicide is the ultimate act of rebellion.' The trial of the remaining Baader-Meinhof prisoners continued, Meinhof's name simply crossed off the official list of defendants. – Ed.

When I get back to my flat that evening, I have the impression I am entering a different flat than the one I left in a hurry after receiving the call from Susan on Good Friday morning. Nothing seems to be as it was when I left. It is only then that I cry.

15 April 1977 – Back to Dorset on an early evening train. I sit up with Mum in Susan's sitting room after Susan and hubbie go to bed. Their bedroom is immediately above the sitting room. I can hear the mattress squeaking and the floorboards creaking as they fuck. Mum seems oblivious to the noise. She says, "Do you remember when we first moved to Geneva, Nick?"

"Very clearly," I say.

"Do you remember coming over the Col de la Faucille and looking down on Geneva for the first time?"

"Yes."

"We parked the car and walked over to the edge of the mountain and down below there were all these tiny houses and fields and you could see Geneva and Mont Blanc. It was perfect. You probably don't remember, but there was this eagle soaring free above it all. I didn't want to leave, but your father put his arm around me and he said, 'Let's go, Woo.' That's what he always called me, 'Woo'. He said, 'You can come up here any time, Woo.' You know, Nick, I never did. I never went back."

19 April 1977 – Dad's funeral takes place at a crematorium in Dorset. Attendance is poor. I spot Lizzie Hayes among the few mourners. She shakes my hand afterwards and offers customary condolences.

"And mine to you," I respond.

"What do you mean by that?"

Quickly trying to find some meaning in my automatic response, I say, "He was very fond of you, Lizzie." When she looks at me oddly, I add, tongue disconnected from brain, "Was he…?" and then stop mid-question. My face betrays the unspoken question.

"Nick! How dare you even think such a thing! Your father was a scholar and a gentleman." Lizzie turns on her black heels and walks away. I want to run after her, apologise, begin the conversation again, reminisce on happy school years in Geneva, and invite her to join us at Susan's for the funeral tea. But, captive to funeral decorum, I stand rooted to the spot and watch her go – walking quickly among the tombstones and the mourning trees.

28 April 1977 – Andreas Baader, Gudrun Ensslin and Jan-Carl Raspe are sentenced to life imprisonment for murder.

29 April 1977 – Skimming through a magazine at the dentist's, I find a photograph taken at the Royal Lancaster Hotel on Easter Day when the three Yemenis were killed there. I think I see Colin's blurred face in from the crowd. When I phone Colin and ask him what he was doing there, he doesn't deny it's him. He replies, "I live just round the corner."

"Who's that you are with?"

"I wasn't with anyone, Nick."

Now that Colin has confirmed he was there, however, I am almost certain that the girl standing next to him in the photograph is Anna Schmidt.

30 April 1977 – Tom O'Neil is assassinated in Beirut. His death merits less than three column inches in those British newspapers that see fit to carry the story.

3 May 1977 – Priscilla McGinley is released from prison. She is put on a plane and returned to England, declared a *persona non grata* in the Federal Republic of Germany – the country that has been so keen to keep her for the last five years.

13 May 1977, **Friday the Thirteenth** – Extract from Hansard:

> <u>Mr Brittan</u> *asked the Secretary of State for the Home Department whether he has reason to believe that Mr Zohair Yousif Akache has left the United Kingdom; if so, what was the date, time and place of departure; and under what name and travelling under what documents he left the United Kingdom.*
>
> <u>Mr Merlyn Rees</u> *It would not be in the public interest, while police inquiries are continuing, to add to the reply which I gave to a question by the Hon. Member on 2nd May.*

I have a few pints at a pub near the Angel and am deep in discussion with three strangers when the pub closes. Outside the door the three go one way and I the other. A white-haired, middle-aged man approaches me and calls me 'son'. He has a map of London open in his hands. I trust people with maps. I form the fleeting impression in my inebriated brain that maybe I know him. Or maybe he is just somebody whose disembodied face I have seen on television. Maybe he is nothing more than an anonymous American tourist, lost in London, out on a nocturnal quest for angels. He holds a white and yellow plastic bag awkwardly in his right hand – probably, I think, because he needs two hands to keep the map open in front of him while asking me for directions. Then the open map is pushed into my face and I feel rough hands at my inside jacket pocket. I feel my wallet go. Then I feel the searing pain of the knife going into my chest. The knife was in the Europa bag. That is why he was holding it so oddly. He was clutching the knife through the bag.

7

16 May 1977 – "You're a lucky man," the doctor says. "Another inch and we'd be planning your funeral."

I feel there should be some outpouring of emotion when you've nearly been murdered but survived, but there isn't. Already it's as if the stabbing took place a long time ago, maybe to someone else, maybe in a novel or a forgotten film, maybe in a fading dream that I failed to write down. As it is I am back at work within three weeks and, because knife crime was so much rarer in London then, treated as something of a returning hero by the secretaries, which I rather enjoy. My boss, however, says, "If you wanna be a Harriman banker, Kellaway, you gotta watch who you hang out with."

18 May 1977 – I'm in a room with many people. It's like my dad's study in the flat in Eaux-Vives, but it is also like the front room of the Jericho House. The picture of Adam and Eve hangs on the wall and the old threadbare purple and yellow rug is on the floor. People are telling stories, drinking wine, laughing, playing guitars. Then I am in a field full of flowers, like the meadows around the Meyers' old wooden chalet above the top end of our lake. It is the season when the narcissus bloom before the hay is cut and the cows are brought up from the valley. I am with women who skip and dance among the flowers. One of the women makes a garland of flowers for me, puts it around my neck, kisses me. I try to hold her, but she has already gone ahead, running across the mountain pasture, running through the long grass wet with the morning dew, running towards the ultimate freedom. We come to the edge of the mountain. A great chasm opens before us. Vultures hover in the sky above, sit on the branches of charred trees. Below, in the abyss, there are clouds of dust and a dryness that smells of rotting eggs. A girl comes towards me carrying a cup in each hand. She drinks cool, clear water from one of the cups. I take the other. It is deep and large, full of fire and sulphur and horror and desolation. A hot wind rising from it scorches my face. Hairs and bones and pieces of blackened skin float on the surface of the molten liquid in the cup. It burns my lips as I try to quench my thirst. I call for water. But there is no water.[54]

23 May 1977 – Muslim terrorists from Molucca mount armed attacks in the Netherlands. They take 105 hostages at a school and capture another ninety on a train.

26 May 1977 – The police visit. Two plain clothes officers of the law flash their proof of identify in front of me and introduce themselves just as you see their fictional counterparts do on television. I don't tell them, but I think them much less accomplished at this than most actors in detective programmes.

I invite them in and, while I am making what I presume (from television) to be the customary cup of tea, they inspect the books on my shelves and the pictures and maps on my walls: Corots and Pisarros, Constables and Turners – all copies, of course – and not a socialist subversive among them, unless you regard a Peters' projection world map as subversive. When I bring the tea into the sitting room, one of the policemen hands me my passport – the one I lost last year.

"Where'd you find this?" I ask.

He points to the sofa. "Under the cushions."

I am expecting follow-up questions about the night I was stabbed, hoping they might have inched closer to capturing my assailant. They show me a photograph. "Do you know this person?" the younger one asks. The photo is of an Arab-looking male, probably early twenties. A black-and-white photograph. It looks nothing like the description of the mugger I gave the police.

"No, sorry."

"This one?"

The second photo is of Anna Schmidt. I say, "Yes."

"What's her name?"

"Anna Schmidt."

The junior policeman begins to write notes.

"Have you known her long?"

"I met her in Greece in 1971. We were both on holiday there."

"Have you seen her since?"

"Yes. She visited Oxford a few months later."

"Do you remember who she stayed with then?"

---

[54] This paragraph has been lifted verbatim from *The Dream Diaries*, dream number sixty-one. – Ed.

"People in Summertown. Family friends, I believe."

"And then?"

"Sorry?"

"And then when did you see her again?"

"Last year. In London. November, I think it was. Maybe December."

"Did she tell you why she had come to London?"

"Not really. She did a lot of shopping while I was at work. So maybe it was for Christmas shopping."

"You work in a bank?"

"Yes."

"Which one?"

I tell him. He writes it in his book. I wonder whether he's ever heard of Harriman's.

"And you did not see her between 1971 and 1976?"

"No."

"No correspondence?"

"No."

"And she arrives and stays with you?"

"Yes."

"Isn't that a little unusual, Mr Kellaway?"

"I don't think so. I have a spare room. She needed a place to stay. She'd have done the same for me in Vienna."

"Vienna?"

"Austria? Where's she from."[55]

"Do you have an address?"

"No."

"A phone number?"

---

[55] See H Lector, *A La recherche d'une femme perdue*, Paris, 1979.

"After Oxford, I was her captive, her slave, drawn to her like Newton's apple to the gravitational pull of the Earth. I had to see her again. The ache in my loins drove all my research and where all the powers of the Federal Republic of Germany had failed, I succeeded.

They said she was living underground, but I tracked Annie Kowatsch (as she was calling herself then) down to a sparkling room in the sky, a garret in Berggasse, high above the throbbing streets of Vienna. As I climbed the stairs I heard Strauss being played in one of the apartments and imagined myself puffing up this staircase seventy-five years earlier, when the emperor was still on the throne, when elegant parties were the norm, when this decadent Vienna was inventing the twentieth century. I had always marked my little Dark One down as Viennese. I said the password and she unlatched the chain, turned the key in the lock and let me in.

I go to my bedroom, write a seven-figure number on a piece of paper. "This is the one she gave me," I say. "I don't know if it works. I've never tried it." The junior officer writes the number in his notebook and hands me back my scrap of paper.

The younger of the two policemen looks up. "Did she stay here, Mr Kellaway?" he asks. He speaks with a strong South London accent, an accent I associate with the criminal elements of British society, rather than with those charged with our safety and protection.

"Yes." I reply. "She did. I told you that already."

"Did you have sexual relations with her?"

"I beg your pardon? She was a visitor in my house, a guest. Do you shag every female visitor who stays with you?"

The senior policeman intervenes, "We will ask the questions, Mr Kellaway."

"Sorry, sir."

"Please answer Sergeant Brown's question. Have you ever had sex with this woman?"

"No."

The senior policeman asks, "What is the connection between Miss Schmidt and this person?" He shows me the first photo again, the one of the Arab.

"I don't know. I don't know who he is."

15 June 1977 – A summer evening walk with Colin on Hampstead Heath. We walk slowly. Me because I am still recovering from the knife wound; Colin because he has been drinking. He has decided to leave FMBB. "We've been in the fucking City for nearly four years," he says.

20 June 1977 – A Monday evening and another visit from the police. They are different officers than those who came on the previous visit. These ones have a lean and hungry look that worries me.

"We have reason to believe," says the senior of the two officers, "that two individuals stayed with you in this flat on the nights of the 8th and 9th of April this year."

---

[55] (Continued) 'You've come to interview me?' she asked.

'Yes,' I said, taking out my notebook and pencil.

She said she didn't remember me from Oxford. That was not surprising: you don't remember people who just make up stories about you; a character doesn't remember her author, even if he has raped and mutilated her. She motioned to a well-worn sofa where sunshine from the skylight fell and asked me to sit. 'I've not been out of this flat for a month. I haven't had a man in three weeks,' said Anastasia." – Ed.

"Not true. I wasn't here then."

"Where were you?"

"My father died on the morning of the 8th of April. Good Friday. I took a train down to Dorset that morning and I was not back in London until the Wednesday morning."

"Can you prove that?"

"Of course."

"Does anybody else have keys to this flat?"

"Not that I am aware of. I had the locks changed last October and I still have all the keys that came with them."

1 July 1977 – I have arranged to fly to Geneva with my mother to help her pack up our Eaux-Vives apartment, the rooms that have been her home for seventeen years. Since Dad died she has been staying with Susan. She is now moving into the retirement cottage that she and Dad bought and refurbished, only fifteen miles from Susan and the grandchildren. But I have to phone her, on the Friday evening before we are due to fly, to say I cannot make it. I plead pressures of work, a major transaction at a critical stage. The boss said, "Kellaway, what kind of goddamn loser are you? Off in April, three weeks off in May. Now you're telling me you're pissing off to Switzerland. Don't they have professional packers in Switzerland? Kellaway, either you work here or you don't. Your choice, kid. If I don't see you here on Monday morning, I'll draw my own conclusions." I am glad of the excuse not to make the trip. I do not want to go. I do not want to be party to dismantling the old flat. Susan takes my place on the flight to Geneva.

2 July 1977 – A girl I met at a Hampstead dinner party in June moves into my Islington flat with me. She is, if I understand these distinctions now, lower-middle class with upper-middle class pretensions – toilet h-aspiring to lavatory. She considers books something to be organised rather than read and rearranges them alphabetically by author, such that J.V. Stalin comes to rest between Muriel Spark and *Kama Sutra*. She does the cooking, insists I be home in good time for supper, hides the ashtrays to discourage my smoking, takes my clothes with hers to the launderette, complains that I spend too much time at the pub, proselytises for the discreet joys of pre-lactarianism.

16 July 1977 – From Emma Wallace I learned that Sill has been put up, at British taxpayers' expense, in a council flat less than ten minutes' walk from where I live. She does not have a telephone. I have knocked on her door twice to no response, but on my third visit, on a Saturday afternoon, Sill answers my knock.

Of her sudden departure from Oxford, Sill won't say much – only that she and Jan had gone to Berlin to see Anna, not intending to stay long.

"After a while I was getting bored," Sill says, "and decided to go back to Oxford. I was in my third year, remember? Finals coming up. Then one of the lads in the squat asked me whether I could help out with something. I went with him to Bonn. Then they sent me in to shag somebody in the government. Some papers went missing. Nothing to do with me, but when they started asking questions, I ran. I was in out of my depth."

"Who sent you?"

"You're beginning to sound like the Pigs. I don't know. I told them that for five years. The police suspected some terrorist group. Then they suspected the East Germans or the Russians."

"What did Jan do after you left Berlin?"

"I don't know, Nick. Same as I told the fucking Pigs. I don't know. I never heard anything. She was having a problem with one of the blokes in the squat when I left."

"What kind of a problem?"

"Usual. Smitten by her goldilocks and wanted to fuck her. Poor bugger ended up dead. Jan didn't kill him, though. That was the Bacon."

"Did he?"

"What?"

"Fuck her."

"Christ, Nick! I don't know. I'm just telling you what I heard. Jan attracted rumours. Half of what you heard wasn't true. You know that."

23 July 1977 – I go to Dorset to spend the weekend with Mum to atone for failing to help her move. The girl asks whether she can come, says it would be nice to meet my mother, that she would be "happy to cook and stuff". I say no.

30 July 1977 – Susanne Albrecht[56], Brigitte Mohnhaupt and

---

[56] Susanne Albrecht (1951–) was a family friend of Jürgen Ponto and was thus readily admitted to his house with two friends who were only identified later. Another accomplice, Peter-Jürgen Boock, drove the getaway car. All four escaped. After further training in Yemen, Albrecht returned to Europe and guerrilla warfare, notably the 1979 attempt to assassinate NATO Supreme Commander US General Alexander Haig, before fleeing to East Germany in 1980 where she lived under an assumed Stasi identity until her arrest in 1990 following the reunification of Germany. She was paroled from prison in 1996. – Ed.

Christian Klar assassinate Jürgen Ponto, chairman of Dresdner Bank.

15 August 1977 – Adam Heggie draws my attention to the entry for 15 August 1665 in Samuel Pepys' diary. The bit he is particularly interested in reads: '…something put my last night's dream into my head, which I think is the best that ever was dreamt, which was that I had my Lady Castlemayne in my armes and was admitted to use all the dalliance I desired with her, and then dreamt that this could not be awake, but that it was only a dream; but that since it was a dream, and that I took so much real pleasure in it, what a happy thing it would be if when we are in our graves (as Shakespeere resembles it) we could dream, and dream but such dreams as this, that then we should not need to be so fearful of death, as we are in this plague time.'

"Who," I ask "is Lady Castlemayne?"

"The King's mistress," Adam replies. "His Lady of the Bedchamber. Totally unattainable for Pepys, of course."

"Except in his dreams."

16 August 1977 – Elvis Presley dies. Colin Witheridge phones to tell me. I've never thought of Colin as an Elvis fan. He tells me that, as a consequence of the job market being dead in August, he is going on holiday to California, maybe see some other parts of the country in the four weeks he plans to be in America – maybe Memphis, Tennessee; maybe Joplin, Missouri; maybe New Harmony, Indiana… "Wouldn't you," he says, "just love to drive all the way across the whole country? Imagine it: Ohio, Indiana, Illinois, Iowa, Nebraska, Wyoming, Montana…"

I tell Colin about Lady Castlemayne.

21 August 1977 – Summer holidays. A fortnight in Ibiza with the girl. She chooses the destination, books the package, makes all the arrangements, packs my clothes into her case, buys and brings a large pack (family pack?) of condoms because she wants a break from the pill, makes sure we leave for the airport long before we need to, checks us in at the ticket counter. Halfway through the first week on the island I decide that my relationship with this little fascist must end. The girl doesn't understand, even when she discovers that I have screwed a Swiss woman staying in our hotel.

5 September 1977 – Hanns-Martin Schleyer, president of the Employers' Federation of the Federal Republic of Germany and president of the Federation of German Industry, is kidnapped in Cologne in an armed assault. Those travelling in the cars with him, including his bodyguards, die in the attack. The kidnapping is claimed by the Siegfried Hausner Commando of the Red Army Faction.[57]

6 September 1977 – Schleyer's kidnappers deliver a ransom note to an address in Wiesbaden. They demand the release of Baader, Ensslin and nine other prisoners in return for Schleyer's safe return. The prisoners are to be transported to a country of their choice before Schleyer is released. A second letter from the kidnappers and a videotape of Schleyer are delivered in Mainz the following day.

13 September 1977 – Baader, Ensslin and the other RAF prisoners agree to be flown out to another country: Algeria, Vietnam, Libya, South Yemen or Iraq.

23 September 1977 – Sill has invited me for a drink at her flat. There is, she said, someone she would like me to meet. The tone in her voice has made me think it is someone I already know. I wonder whether it is Jan; wonder why she has chosen this time to make contact; wonder, with all that's going on in Germany, what she wants from me. I spend three days thinking about Jan by day and dreaming about her by night. When I arrive, however, it's not Jan that I find. Caroline stands and smiles broadly. We shake hands. An engagement ring sparkles on her finger.

Sill dominates the conversation. She speaks mostly about events in Germany, believes the authorities will release Andreas Baader and his cronies and fly them to Libya or some such sanctuary. As long as they remain in prison the country will be under siege. The neo-fascist German government cannot tolerate that.

When Caroline and I have left Sill's flat, I ask whether I can buy her dinner. I do not offer to take her back to my place, even though it is only a short walk away, because of the girl still living in it. Nor do I, because of the ring on her finger, expect Caroline to accept my offer of dinner. To my surprise, she does accept. We go to the same Greek restaurant to which I took Anna Schmidt nine months earlier.

I tell Caroline an edited version of my life over the past four years. She tells me about her two years in India. No, she never came home during those two years. Yes, her sister and parents did go out

---

[57] Siegfried Hausner (1952–1975) was a member of the SPK (Socialist Patients' Collective) and a bombmaker. He participated, as the explosives expert, in the 1975 attack on the West German Embassy in Stockholm carried out by the Commando Holger Meins. Hausner was severely injured in the explosion at the embassy and, rather than being hospitalised and treated, was removed from Sweden to Stammheim prison in Stuttgart where he died shortly afterwards. – Ed.

to India – for her first Christmas there. Just before the monsoon broke in 1974 she went, with a Russian girl with whom she was working, to Moscow and they travelled back overland as far as Tashkent. She tells me about her law conversion course, that she is serving articles now at a major City law firm, that she works very long hours. An evening off like this is, she says, a rarity. I ask her about the ring. Her fiancé has, she tells me, recently been made up to partner in another City law firm. He is a Cambridge man, eight years Caroline's senior. He has a successful mergers and acquisitions practice. Neither of us mentions the argument we had in our final Oxford term. In fact, neither of us mentions Oxford at all or makes any reference to the bed we used to share in a house in Norham Gardens.

We exchange phone numbers and I walk Caroline to the tube. We kiss. It is a just a light kiss of friendship but it brings with it memories of more passionate embraces. On the way home I am nearly hit by a car. The driver jumps out and shouts at me. He swears and punches the air with his fist.

When I get home, the girl screams, "Where the hell have you been?"

I don't bother to answer. I pour myself a whisky. The girl says, "You've bloody well had enough to drink already." She grabs at the tumbler in my hand, spilling whisky on the floor. I top it up from the bottle and go to fetch, from the back of my wardrobe, the poster of the Temple of Hera at Paestum, the poster Caroline gave me at the start of our final year at Oxford. I take my whisky and the cardboard tube in which Caroline's poster has been rolled up for the past four years and sit in my armchair. I pull out and unroll the poster. Lord Kitchener comes out first. I had forgotten he was lurking in there. I let him fall to the floor. Then I pull out the ruins of the Temple of Hera, basking in the glow of the warm Mediterranean sun. I hold the poster in front of me like a fully spread-out newspaper, one hand at either side. It still has a wine stain on it.

The girl shouts at me again. "I'm trying to talk to you," she screams. I ignore her. She lunges at me, tries to rip the poster from my hands. I am left holding two parts of the torn poster. I jump at the girl, bring her down to the floor. My hands are on her neck and I think I might strangle her. I want to strangle her. I want her to go away, vanish from my life. Instead of strangling her, however, I find myself screwing her, hammering my loins into hers as she squeals and writhes. No condom. No pill. I have no clue as to what phase of her moon it is. This releases the energy built up during the hours spent with Caroline, as well as the anger boiling up since returning to this unwanted woman. Otherwise it is a big mistake. The girl thinks she has won a victory, that she has won the right to stay. It takes another week, several decibels of argument and a gallon of tears before she leaves.

8

25 September 1977 – Libya and South Yemen advise Germany that they are not prepared to take the prisoners from Stammheim. Refusals from other possible destinations follow. A number of RAF members still at liberty, including those involved in kidnapping Hanns-Martin Schleyer, fly to Iraq. The PFLP offers assistance in freeing the Stammheim prisoners.[58]

7 October 1977 – I meet Colin at a pub near Liverpool Street Station that no longer exists. It has been replaced by the Broadgate complex and either the Royal Bank of Scotland or the European Bank for Reconstruction and Development now occupies the site. He tells me that the job market is far worse than he expected and that he has been forced to take a position he considers beneath himself. We talk about what's happening in Germany and he tells me he has been to see Sill. "She doesn't seem to know anything about Jan."

I tell him I have been twice to visit Sill since her return. I do not mention Caroline. I ask him whether Sill said anything about Anna Schmidt. Colin says Sill does not think Anna had anything to do with the terrorists, at least not anything direct. Sympathy? Maybe; probably, in fact. Opinion polls in Germany, taken prior to the Schleyer kidnapping, consistently showed that 10% of West Germans were sympathetic to the Baader-Meinhof Gang. Quite a few citizens would help them, give them shelter, lie to the police to protect them. I recall the photograph taken on Easter Day outside the Royal Lancaster and wonder about lying to friends. What about the poster?

---

[58] The flight to Baghdad and the involvement of the Popular Front for the Liberation of Palestine became publicly known only subsequently, suggesting that these daily notes, masquerading as journal entries, are not in fact contemporaneous. – Ed.

"A case of mistaken identity," he says. For my part I decide to keep silent about my two visits from our British police and their enquiries about Anna.

In his new job, Colin will be on a lower salary than he was at FMBB. He will be working in the back office with the clerical staff, learning the trade from the bottom up, starting in international money transfers, hoping to move quickly through to the front office. The detailed knowledge of bank accounts and money transfers acquired in the back office would later prove to be very useful to him – and to me. When, some years later, I needed to open a Swiss bank account that had to be kept secret from the UK authorities, it would be to Colin that I would turn for expert technical assistance.

13 October 1977 – A Boeing 737, Lufthansa flight LH181, takes off from Palma de Mallorca bound for Frankfurt-am-Main. An Iranian couple sits in first class. There are another two Iranians in economy. Otherwise the vast majority of the passengers are returning German holidaymakers, the type of people the British caricature as getting up early in the morning to claim the best deckchairs on the beach with their towels. One of the Iranians is travelling on a passport that names him as Ali Hyderi. He was born a Palestinian refugee, in 1954, in the Bourj al-Brajneh camp near Beirut. It is he who leads the hijacking. When he and his colleagues have taken control of the aircraft, he drops the Ali Hyderi alias and calls himself Captain Martyr Mahmoud of the Martyr Halimeh Commando.

The hijackers issue a demand for the release of the eleven RAF prisoners at Stammheim. The plane flies to Rome. The Italian authorities decline the German government's request to immobilise the aircraft. The aircraft refuels and takes off for Larnaca in Cyprus.

14 October 1977 – Geneva lawyer Denis Payot receives message from the Siegfried Hausner Commando holding Hanns-Martin Schleyer. To the demand for the release of the RAF prisoners, it adds the requirement that two Palestinians in Turkish jails be released and USD 15 million be paid.

Flight LH181 flies from Larnaca to Dubai. On the ground in Dubai, Captain Martyr Mahmoud orders a birthday cake and champagne for one of the hijacked aircraft's stewardesses. It is delivered by the Dubai airport authorities.

15 October 1977 – Gudrun Ensslin and the others agree to be flown to Somalia and released there.

16 October 1977 – Flight LH181 leaves Dubai for Aden.

Permission to land is refused by the South Yemeni authorities and the runway is blocked. Running short of fuel, the plane is forced to land in the sand alongside the main runway. Once on the ground, Captain Martyr Mahmoud shoots Captain Jürgen Schumann dead in the gangway of the plane, splattering passengers with blood and brain.

17 October 1977 – The captured Boeing 737 is refuelled and flies to Mogadishu. The body of the dead captain is pushed out of the cockpit onto the runway. After dark, unobserved by the hijackers, a Boeing 707 lands at Mogadishu. It carries the men of German anti-terrorist unit GSG 9 and the equipment needed to mount an assault on the hijacked aircraft.

18 October 1977 – Under cover of darkness, at 02:03 Somali time, under the code name Operation Magic Fire, the German anti-terrorist squad attacks the hijacked plane. The operation is a complete success. Three hijackers, including Captain Martyr Mahmoud, are killed. All the hostages are freed.

Sometime before dawn, in the cells of Stammheim, another anti-terrorist unit is at work. Gudrun Ensslin, Andreas Baader and Jan-Carl Raspe are found dead of gunshot wounds in the morning. The deaths are reported as suicides.[59]

19 October 1977 – The body of hostage Hanns-Martin Schleyer is found in the boot of a green Audi 100 in Mulhouse in Alsace. Forensic experts establish that he has only recently been executed in a forest location by three bullets to the head.

20 October 1977 – "What," I ask Colin after we've watched the television news, "did Anna do with all that money?"

Colin answers, "Nick, just don't ask questions. You're too involved."

"I'm not involved."

"Oh, yes, you are, my friend. The Liechtenstein account was opened in your name."

---

[59] The extra-judicial executions of Baader, Ensslin and Raspe are, of course, disputed. The official German government story is that they committed suicide. Although he is not uncritical of the West German authorities' treatment of its RAF prisoners or its handling of the kidnapping of Hanns-Martin Schleyer, this is also the conclusion reached by Stefan Aust, probably the foremost independent authority on the Baader-Meinhof Gang. See S. Aust, *The Baader Meinhof Complex*, London, 2008 (English translation). He writes: "… the legend of the murders at Stammheim was born outside the group, not in its inner circle. Later, several RAF members made statements saying that they had learned from Brigitte Mohnhaupt, on the day, that the prisoners in Stammheim had committed suicide." – Ed.

I grab his forearm. "You're full of shit, Witheridge."

Colin smiles weakly. "They borrowed your passport," he says.

27 October 1977 – An envelope franked in the City of London arrives at my Islington flat. It contains a folded A4 sheet of paper on which a poem is typed.

> *I heard a voice that cried*
> *"Baader the Beautiful*
> *Is dead, is dead!"*
> *And through the misty air*
> *Passed like a mournful cry*
> *Of sunward sailing cranes.*
> *I saw the pallid corpse*
> *Of the dead sun*
> *Borne through the northern sky.*[60]

Nothing more.

I suspect Adam Heggie of having sent me the envelope.

4 November 1977 – During a two-week business trip to New York, I arrange to meet Polly Page after work. In the dimly lit bar where we meet, I ask Polly whether New York is still suffering from power shortages. There was a black-out in July, rioting and looting under cover of darkness.

"It was horrible," Polly says. "Just awful being in New York then. New York's always murder in July, but that… I mean, it was truly dreadful."

"Thin veneer of civilisation," I venture.

"New York can be pretty rough at any time," Polly says, "but, God, talk about animals. I guess we're all just animals under – whaddya call it? – your thin vanilla civilisation."

The girl who serves our table is oriental and has a slit in the side of her black dress that comes almost up to her waist. Some returning veteran's Vietnamese concubine. A discarded prize of war.

Polly is a nickname of uncertain origin. Her well-concealed baptismal names are Mary Teresa. At school, when we discovered this, we called her Empty Page. "Nothing there," we said. When we were older and Polly's discreet charms began to become more

---

[60] These lines are taken from Henry Wadsworth Longfellow's poem *Tegnér's Drapa* (1850) – with one letter changed: 'Baader' is 'Balder' in the original. – Ed.

apparent we added, "just waiting to be filled." The bar is only two blocks from Polly's apartment.

15 November 1977 – I learn, from Colin, that Captain Martyr Mahmoud's real name was Zohair Yousef Akache. "The bloke," he says, "who killed those three Arabs outside the Royal Lancaster." I wonder, silently, whether even that was his real name. Maybe it was Zohair Yousef aka Che as in Ernesto Guevara aka Che. Does Colin know more? He doesn't say and I don't ask.

Colin also tells me that it was he who sent me the poem in the envelope – the poem about Baader. "It was Emma's idea," he says.

"Emma?"

"Emma Somerwell? Wallace as was. She fancies herself as a poet – or at least as some sort of writer."

"Maybe I should introduce her to Adam Heggie." I never do.

17 November 1977 – Extract from Hansard.

Mr Brittan asked the Secretary of State for the Home Department whether he will make a further statement about the circumstances in which Zohair Yousif Akache was permitted to leave the country on or about 10th April 1977.

Mr Merlyn Rees The Commissioner of Police of the Metropolis tells me that detailed police enquiries have established that Akache, against whom warrants of arrest have been issued for the murder of three Yemen Arab Republic subjects in London on 10th April 1977, left the country that afternoon. He left through Heathrow Airport, using a Kuwaiti passport in the name of Ahmed Badir al-Majid. Soon after the murders had been committed the police and the immigration service were alerted, but the descriptions of the suspect provided to the police were insufficiently detailed to enable Akache to be identified and apprehended. It was not until the following day that urgent and painstaking police enquiries provided evidence linking Akache with these crimes.

22 November 1977 – I hand a resignation letter to my boss. I have an offer from a bank in New York, I say, and intend to accept it.

"Give me twenty-four hours," the boss says. It is the same boss who likes short hair. My hair is shorter than his now. I had it cut the day before I wrote my resignation letter.

The next day I learn that, in order to prevent my resignation, my boss has arranged for me to be promoted and to receive a significant increase in salary. He hands me back my letter. I ceremonially tear it up into small pieces in front of him. He claps me on the back and says, "Correct decision, Nick."

Useful idiot.

9 December 1977 – I go to a dinner party in Notting Hill. The hosts, a recently married couple, say they live in Upper Kensington. The film *Notting Hill* is still far in the future and 'Kensington' sounds, to those who care deeply about such things, much more civilised than 'Notting Hill'. 'Notting Hill' still carries connotations of slums owned by vicious landlords exploiting the poor, and of abortionists and murderers doing away with innocents in unseemly ways.

I know the husband from Oxford where he read PPE. He works at a merchant bank in the City now. He is said to be independently wealthy. I do not think he could afford to live where he does otherwise. The wife was also at Oxford, but two years below me, I'm told, and I didn't know her then. I am surprised I had not noticed her: she is extremely attractive. She worked, in spite of her degree, as a model after graduation and is now training as an actress.

Most of the guests are Oxford. Many are civil servants, mostly Treasury. We drink white wine, nibble peanuts and chat idly about Christmas plans and the esoterica of politics as we wait for one guest who has phoned to say she has been detained at the office. Our host talks about the need to shrink the public sector, deregulate and privatise and, in a vaguely Leninist phrase, "to continuously roll back the state." I believe I would find his arguments easier to follow if he were less liberal with his split infinitives and more so with the excellent Chablis he is serving. The civil servants reply in a language I find difficult to understand. Perhaps it is Mandarin.

A plain woman who works at the Home Office asks me about my plans for Christmas. I say I will be spending Christmas with my mother in her cottage in Dorset, her first Christmas as a widow. Susan and family are invited for Christmas lunch and I will make the brandy butter and help stuff the turkey. "My first English Christmas since 1959," I say.

"God," says the featureless female face, "I'd never be away from this country at Christmas, of all times. Poor you."

I hear the voice of the guest who phoned to say she would be late before I see her. My heart skips a proverbial if not an actual beat. It is Caroline Carter. She kisses the host and the hostess on both cheeks. She seems to know them well. She greets the other guests in turn with a lavish double kiss. When she comes to me I receive, without hesitation, the same treatment. "Nick," she says, "what a wonderful surprise. How lovely to see you." Then, after she has kissed all the others, we are asked to take our seats. As we make our way to the dining room, Caroline comes across to me, touches my hand, asks, "Did you lose my phone number, then?"

Our places have been allotted and our names written on little pieces of card indicating where we are to sit. It is a long table, sparkling with candlelight reflected in crystal and silver. I am seated nearly at the far end of it from Caroline, on the same side of the table as her. This means I find it difficult to see her. Next to me, on my right, sits the Home Office woman who disapproves of Christmas being celebrated outside England. On my other side, at the foot of the table, is the lady of the house, the aspiring actress. I think that Caroline may not be wearing her engagement ring and spend the rest of the evening listening for snatches of Caroline's voice, glancing along the table, endeavouring to confirm whether my impression about the ring is correct.

18 December 1977 – A late evening phone call from Adam Heggie. "Nick," he says, "tell me: was your American… what was her name again?"

"Janice Day?"

"That's the one. Did she ever surface in all this terrorist stuff going on in Germany?"

"Not that I know of. Why?" I don't bother to say she's probably dead.

"Just curious."

"Is that all?" I ask. Caroline gets up from the sofa beside me, places a soft kiss on my forehead and goes to the bedroom.

"Not quite," I hear Adam say as my eyes follow Caroline. "Another question, if I may: how do you decide which of your dreams you're going to write down in that little book of yours?"

CHAPTER SEVEN

When Caroline left me, in the spring of 2001, we had been married for twenty-two and a half years. We had raised three children and I had entered the rich lists and begun my climb up them.

During those years, I thought far less often of Janice Day. She kept, mostly, away from my dreams and nightmares. Apart from a private little investigation I undertook in Buenos Aires, I heard her name only three times: once through Karen O'Neil and then, nearly a decade later, from Priscilla McGinley and Edward Reader in rapid succession. I listened to what they said with almost complete detachment. I was, quite simply, too busy.

Two weeks after Caroline and I separated, I accompanied Colin on a day-trip to France. After filling every available space in his car with his annual haul of cheap booze, we lunched on oysters in a small village west of Calais. When Colin ordered a second bottle of the most expensive white Burgundy on the wine list, I reminded him, "You're driving."

"Fuck that. You're paying. Anyway, we'll walk it off on the beach."

We walked for two slow hours, England floating on the distant northern horizon. When I tried to talk about Caroline, Colin picked up a handful of sand, let it trickle through his fingers. "'All happy families are alike, but each unhappy family is unhappy in its own peculiar way,'" he mused.

"What's all that about?"

"Tolstoy." Colin winked. "*Anna Karenina*. I did read Russian."

"A long time ago."

Colin picked up another handful of dry sand. "A long time ago... remember that bar in Amsterdam? The time I knocked you unconscious?"

"Yes."

Colin threw his fistful of sand into the air. The wind caught the grains of sand and scattered them. "Look," he said, "on the bright side. You've had twenty-three years of Caroline. Twenty-three years with the choir girl. You've been damn lucky. And now..." We watched a couple bent double digging for cockles as the tide went out. "You're not even fifty, you've got money and the world's… well, your oyster. What about your old Big Five list? What about Janice Day?"

"Dead. Dead long ago."

"There's no proof." The same words Anna Schmidt had used twenty-five years earlier. "You've still got her guitar, haven't you?"

I am getting ahead of myself…

I married Caroline Carter on a pale Norfolk afternoon in November 1978. It was a traditional English country wedding. I stood erect at the front of the old church. Colin stood beside me, both of us in finest Moss Bros grey. It had cost me considerable effort to persuade Colin to act as my best man. I thought he would long ago have moved on from our final year at Oxford. After all, that night in the Amsterdam bar was five years behind us. In the end, Colin shrugged his shoulders. "Okay, then. I suppose nobody else'll do it for you."

Caroline and her father walked up the aisle to tunes from *The Best of Mendelssohn*. A major, who had served with Colonel Carter in the ships at Mylae, attempted to whisper to his wife and, after a lifetime of shouting orders, failed: "Lovely girl, what?" Imogen, Caroline's only bridesmaid, suppressed a giggle. Caroline's dark eyes sparkled beneath her white veil.

Neither Caroline, nor I, nor the barking major was prepared to declare any reason why the two of us should not be joined together in holy matrimony. We said our vows and consented to be bound to one another, to love and to cherish 'til death did us part. That, however, seemed a long way off and I doubt many of the smartly dressed supporters in the teeming terraces behind us regarded wedlock as highly as the Prayer Book did. Some of those we had invited still saw it as one of society's more sinister political structures, refused to attend and went to football games instead. "Football's inclusive, mate. Getting married in a church isn't." A wedding had not then yet become simply an excuse to sting the future in-laws into paying for a big party.

We promised to forsake all others. I agreed also to forsake my Sobranie Black Russians. Standing like a condemned man in the damp garden of the house where Colin and I were billeted, I smoked my last cigarette. In the vague distance where the grey land dissolved into the grey sky, I could see the stone steeple of the grey parish church where my marriage would shortly be enacted. Perhaps all men feel as I did that morning. Does each think then along the other paths he might have chosen to walk? Undergo a Robert Frost moment? See visions of the past metamorphosing into alternative future lives?

"She's such a lovely girl," Mum had said when I took Caroline down to Dorset to announce our engagement. "Your father would have been very pleased. We always suspected she might be the one. Ever since she came to visit us in Geneva. We heard her creep along the corridor to your bedroom that night, you know."

We flew to Venice for our honeymoon. One afternoon, we went over on the boat to Murano so Caroline could buy a present for my mother to replace the pale-blue glass she had broken in 1971. Another evening we walked as far as a restaurant on the other side of the Rialto that specialised in squid and polenta. Mostly, though, we stayed near the hotel. Caroline was suffering badly from morning sickness.

Robert James Nicholas Kellaway was born at 2:30 a.m. on Friday, 13 April 1979.

One Sunday, to give Caroline a rest, Colin and I put Robert in his buggy and wheeled him across Hampstead Heath. The sun was shining. The wind was in the southwest and warm.

"Hear that?" I asked. "I didn't know you got cuckoos in London."

Somehow, as it often did, conversation moved to politics and then, as it did less often, to Sill. On the night of the election that had put Margaret Thatcher into Number Ten, Sill and Colin had sat with us in our Islington sitting room watching television as the results came in. As yet another marginal fell to the Conservatives, Sill had thumped an angry fist on the table. A glass of red wine teetering on the table's edge had fallen to its death on the floor below. "It'll be like Germany," Sill had prophesised. "Democracy, like truth and beauty and love, is only of any fucking use when it gives the right bloody result." Later, as the night wore on, and Labour was preparing to concede defeat, she had become more optimistic: "This'll be a fucking fascist regime. You can see the bloody Hitlerian glint in the Snatcher's eyes," she had said. "Th'll be riots in the streets when the masses see what this is really all about. State brutality before you can say Friedrich Disgustus von Hayek."[61] From the perspective of a sunny afternoon on the Heath,

---

[61] Vienna-born Friedrich August von Hayek (1899–1992) was an economist and political philosopher. He won the Nobel Prize for Economics in 1974. His works of political philosophy include *The Road to Serfdom* (1944) and *The Constitution of Liberty* (1960). Hayek's writings were a major influence on Margaret Thatcher's politics and the rightward shift in the Conservative Party's policies under her leadership. – Ed.

it all seemed like dusty words from a textbook on ancient history.

"Funny sort of life," said Colin, tickling Robert under his chin.

"Sill's?"

"The cuckoo's. Laying its eggs in other birds' nests."

We moved to a large end-of-terrace house in Kentish Town when we learned Caroline was pregnant again. When packing, Caroline found the tube she had brought me from Italy in 1972, opened it and discovered within the poster of the Temple of Hera – along with Lord Kitchener who had supervised our student couplings. The poster of Paestum was, of course, torn in two. "What happened?" she asked.

"Oh, it just got ripped. It was on the wall… couldn't bear to throw it out."

"You old softie. We don't need it any more." She crumpled the two parts of the poster together in her hands and tossed them into a black bag with other rubbish we could do without in the new house. Lord Kitchener joined them.

"What about this?" she asked. She was holding Jan's old guitar by the neck.

"We'll keep that," I said.

Amanda Caroline Kellaway was born on 23 October 1980.

Not long before the Falklands War, I made a trip to Argentina. It was a time when the banking system prided itself on re-balancing the world economy by recycling petrodollars. The idea was that OPEC oil producers deposited the surplus cash they earned from inflated oil prices with banks like Harriman's and then the banks made loans to countries like Argentina, skimming a margin as the funds sloshed through. Walter Wriston, the venerable Chairman of Citibank, opined that countries don't go bust and the funds flowed into eager government coffers – from Argentina to Zimbabwe – in quantities limited only by the speed at which generals can change their trousers for ones with more commodious pockets. I went to Buenos Aires in connection with one of these loans.

Buenos Aires was a city of wide avenues and layer upon layer of peeling nostalgia. It had seen better days. For want of anything better to do in the dreary intervals between dreary negotiating sessions, I wandered the streets of Recoleta and played with sepia images I invented of Jan as a child.

After ten days in Argentina, I decided to do some proper research.

The hotel receptionist had long, black, silken hair, deep black eyes and a golden face that had been sculpted when the world was young. She told me she had been a tango dancer, dancing to amuse tourists, before she broke her ankle. The badge pinned to her hotel uniform told me her name was Sabina. She gave me a map and told me how to find the archives of the *Buenos Aires Herald*. There, after an hour and with the help of a white-haired Anglo-Argentinian archivist, I found the following article in the edition of 5 January 1965.

> *American Family's Tragedy*
> *The body of Peter Augustus Day, 19, eldest son of Mr and Mrs Virgil Day, of Palermo Chico, was washed ashore yesterday at San Fernando. Peter Day had been missing since the evening of January 2nd when he was reported washed overboard in a sailing accident. His young sister, Janice, 13, also on the sailing boat at the time of the accident, survived. She was rescued at dusk on January 2nd after floating alone on the upturned dinghy for several hours. Peter Day had not been wearing his life vest at the time of the accident. His young sister described how an unexpected gust of wind had caused the boom to swing across the boat, knocking the unfortunate teenager into the water, before the boat capsized. Medical officers attending the body confirmed the injuries sustained to the back of Peter Day's head are consistent with his sister's story...*

Playing myself in a third-rate film about the life and obsessions of Nicholas Kellaway, I flashed back to Christmas 1971, to Happy Day's den in La Capite. I suddenly saw what had been wrong with that Day family portrait (*Those were the Days*) on the wall: there were *four* children in it. In the list of facts about Janice Day I had collected, there had never been more than three. I made no further enquiries about Janice Day. It's best to leave the dead behind. They will not follow you.

Indeed, it was not Jan who captured my dreams when I fell asleep on the long flight back to London. I dreamt of Sabina, the uniformed girl behind the hotel desk. In my dreams she danced and kissed with a rare passion. We took an evening walk in a wild, sandy country where stunted hollyhocks bent to the wind. We passed through an ancient valley strewn with pock-marked volcanic boulders the colour of dried blood and came to a field where long ago, before the foundation of Rome, some optimistic farmer had planted olive trees at random. Time and the wind had gnarled and twisted them.

When I asked Sabina to marry me she looked at me through her bronze-age mask and vanished silently back down the wind-blown centuries, carrying under her arm the crumpled remnants of my teenage *LIBERTÉ* banner.[62] As I watched it go, I woke.

With the clarity that sometimes comes on sudden wakening, I saw another road. *You don't need to wait for the Revolution. You don't need to wait for the withering of the State.* I held the map of that alternative road to freedom in my hands: my shiny calling-card: *Nicholas Kellaway, Vice President, P.J. Harriman & Co.* The sword of freedom. It took a few months more to learn how to use it.

Weeks later, when I was alone in the house one night because Caroline had taken the children to Norfolk to visit her parents, I did dream about Janice Day and the upturned dinghy. We were drifting on the blue waters of Lake Geneva, rather than on the mud-brown River Plate. Jan, not her brother, had fallen into the water. There was a gash in her head and blood on her white shirt. I held the blunt instrument in my hand and watched her drown.

By the waters of Leman we sat down and laughed.

2

Thursday 24 June 1982

"Kiddo!" The American voice on the phone was unmistakable. I turned my face to the wall to hide my eyes from my colleagues. "How are you?" Talking nervously, listening intently… I don't remember the words. Then she said, "I'm in London. At the Savoy." Somehow, I agreed to meet – "for a quick drink" – in the American Bar.

Had Karen O'Neil changed in the past eleven years? In the summer of 1982 she was, after all, fifty-one and had been a widow for five years. No; as she sat opposite me with a gin and tonic in one hand and a cigarette in the other, I could detect little difference. Even an hour later as we lay across her hotel bed upstairs, staring at the post-coital ceiling while The Eagles sang 'Hotel California', it was not difficult to imagine the Persian rugs and the crudely framed painting on the wall of her bedroom.

---

[62] *The Dream Diaries*, dream number eighty-two. – Ed.

212

"Did you ever screw Janice Day?" The question came, as the Americans say, out of left field.

"What?"

"It's what Happy and Ursula thought. That you were lovers – in the extreme sense peculiar to foreign vocabularies."

"Why were they talking to you about *that*?"

"So you were?"

"No."

Karen smiled. The smile I remember her smiling when I told her I had not fucked her daughter. She shrugged her naked shoulders. "Happy hired Tom to track her down."

"Did he find her?"

"Tom was killed before he finished the report. What he wrote said she was dead."

"You say that as if there's some doubt."

"There was a fire in Munich…"

"I know."

"But there was also evidence that she'd gone east, that she was living in the GDR. Tom's connections couldn't take it further than that. It seems she'd had a minder with links to Russian intelligence. When things got hot they found her a new identity on the other side of the Wall. It made sense. Jan spoke German because Ursula made sure she grew up with it. She could blend in, in East Germany."

"But he told her parents she was dead."

Karen nodded.

"Why? I don't understand."

"You're not American."

"What does that have to do with it?"

"What about 'better dead than red'?"

I phoned Caroline, told her I was doing an all-nighter at the office, spent the night with Karen.

When I was dressing in the morning – yesterday's shirt, yesterday's tie, things that would be noticed at Harriman's – Karen said, "Nick, I worry about you."

"What's there to worry about?"

"Your career. You're thirty. Where are you going in life?"

"I'm a VP at Harriman's Bank."

"And what are you doing with it?"

"What do you mean?"

"Your future. Is there anything other than endless emptiness and the dwindling figure of a man to whom nothing is ever going to happen?" I began to protest, but Karen cut me short, laying her index finger lightly on my lips. "Use what I've taught you, kiddo. Use the witchcraft."

Office affairs occur more frequently than you might imagine. Credible sociological research indicates that at least 35% of male office workers and 25% of female office workers have had one. Some are just seedy half-hour stands. Others dribble on for decades. A few end in marriage. Most end in tears. What is undeniable is that office affairs add a welcome undertone of illicit excitement to the world of in-boxes and gold-plated cufflinks. On rare occasions, the ordinary office affair can also, if played skilfully, be extremely useful.

There is an old adage in the City: 'Make sure you're on top'. The *double entendre* advice is about corporate hierarchy: if you go in for office sex, always ensure that the person you screw lies beneath you in the organisation chart. In these liaisons, one party or other usually ends up suffering and it is the way of City firms to ensure that it is the junior who loses out in career terms. I knew the adage, did the calculation, accepted Karen O'Neil's advice, unsheathed the sword of freedom, took the risk. I was learning my trade: banking is not about avoiding risk, it is about calibrating risk accurately and, where the pay-off looks good enough, embracing it and managing it.

The woman I sought out and embraced was Mary Connolly. Mary was an American, seven years my senior, two rungs above me on the corporate ladder – something unusual in the phallocracy of those days. She was hard working by the standards of the times, related to important establishment figures in New York and Washington, no kids, twice-divorced and had a fondness for iced vodka with thin slices of Granny Smith apple in it. She was also the ultimate signatory on both my expense account and the performance appraisals that formed the basis for both the meagre bonuses paid in those days and promotion up through the system.

My immediate boss then was not a bright man. He had probably risen farther than he should have done – had the financial sector not seen such a rapid expansion in the eighties and allowed time-servers such as him to float upwards on an incoming tide. Nevertheless, he could read the runes, as we used to say at Harriman's, and, with a subsidised mortgage considerably larger than his unsubsidised scruples, wrote an appraisal that he no doubt felt best fitted the emerging situation. Mary countersigned without a qualm.

One afternoon, when she was lying on her Chelsea bed purring like a Cheshire cat, I asked Mary for the swap book. "Such a little thing you ask," she smiled and gave it to me along with a lingering kiss on the forehead.

If swaps were but a little thing to Mary Connolly, it was because she did not see where the world of finance was headed. Swaps were the original financial derivative instruments. Interest-rate swaps address the issue that some borrowers would like to fix the rate of interest they pay on their debt but find it easier to borrow at rates which float with market conditions. In the early eighties, in the Sterling market in particular, many companies had no choice but to borrow on a floating-rate basis – and were subjected to unpredictable and punitively high interest rates as the Conservative government addressed Britain's accumulated economic ills. Under an interest-rate swap, a borrower can exchange its commitments to pay floating-rate interest for an obligation to pay a knowable stream of fixed payments.

When I started in this business, the typical role of a bank was that of a broker: matching a fixed-rate payer with a floating-rate-paying counterparty. The obvious development was for the bank to act in the middle, itself the counterparty to each of two separate trades, taking a spread out of each rather than a fee as marriage broker. From there a book comprising an increasing number of swaps could be built, so that the need to match each and every trade with its opposite could be avoided. Risk could be assessed and covered on the basis of the portfolio as whole. Conveniently, and assisted by the growing power of desktop computing, this meant more profit to the bank. For some reason which I never saw the need to question, we were allowed to calculate the current profit from each trade on the basis of our estimate of the net present value of the future income stream from it. This formula and the means of its calculation became increasingly important to those who manned the swap desk, as we extracted greater and greater percentages of our little business's paper profits through cash bonuses – and I controlled the black box that that calculated the profits. An Oxford mathematics degree nicely sustained the bluff that this was too complex a mystery for ordinary mortals, or even their auditors, to comprehend. As long as the revenue rolled across the bank's profit and loss account, no significant challenges were made. The unreasonable effectiveness of mathematics had struck another blow for Freedom.[63]

---

[63] Eugene Wigner, 'The Unreasonable Effectiveness of Mathematics' in *Communications on Pure and Applied Mathematics*, 13 (1960). – Ed.

The priesthood of swaps became the highest-paid cadre in the bank. We were a tightly knit band of brothers, uncommunicative sphinxes jealously guarding our secrets, our territory, our bonuses. We acted strictly in accordance with our own interests, maximising the pay-out under the formulae we had agreed with a naïve management, which still, when we first settled on it, included Mary Connolly. We stimulated market demand, showed the market risks that nobody had previously imagined, invented and sold products to hedge them. For a while we were able to get away with something we called the 'dog-leg swap'. It worked like this. On day one of the transaction we paid out a fixed sum and on each of a series of subsequent dates we received a smaller fixed amount. The cash flows involved were identical to those for a fixed-rate loan, but our product was governed by swap documentation infinitely less complex than a syndicated term loan agreement and, most beautifully, not subject to the same Bank of England capital-reserve requirements.

We wrote an unnecessarily complex pricing model that showed management what the bank needed to earn on a loan and what on a swap to make a decent return for its long-suffering shareholders when the allocation of capital was properly accounted for. Not surprisingly, the margins needed on the swap were considerably lower than those for the equivalent loan. Bank lenders to prime corporate borrowers were already finding life difficult in the face of a resurgent bond market. Now, we ate their fancy lunches and toasted our success with the best champagne that the City's wine bars could provide – arguing only, in the best gentlemanly traditions of the Square Mile, over whose expense account the champagne should appear on and how it should be disguised.

By then, Mary Connolly had served her purpose admirably and was long gone. Before she left London, we had a valedictory dinner *à deux* at Le Boulestin in Cheapside. That evening, in a candle-lit, red-velvet alcove, Mary proposed to me. She suggested I leave Caroline and the children, move with her to New York, marry and start a family. "You could," she said, the final inducement delivered with the flourish of a toreador going in for the kill, "become an American. With me as your wife, it'd be a slam dunk." I had not expected this. "Well? What do you say, Nick?"

Temptation? Come on! No bloody way! But how – as I watched my elaborate plans crumble to dust and the value of all those mercenary kisses collapse to zero – how was I going to extricate myself from this? I muttered something into my wine that I myself failed to understand.

"You're a wimp, Kellaway."

I squirmed, wriggled, muttered again – something about 'complicated'.

"Complicated? What the hell do you think this is? Secret rendezvous. Hours stolen between work and dinner... shit, Nick. I'll show you complicated. I mean, I could make this seriously complicated for you, kid. One call to that sweet, little wife of yours... I bet you don't get the fireworks at home you get with me, eh? What if I made one sweet little phone call?"

"She knows. She knows about... well... she knows."

"You're not serious?"

I nodded.

Mary took hold of her glass of wine. It was a good Burgundy, a *1969 Chambolle-Musigny Les Amoureuses.* On our first evening at Le Boulestin, several months earlier, I had translated the label on the bottle for her and later that evening had introduced her to a number Karen O'Neil had first shown me in the summer of '71. After that she always asked me to order a 'Sixty-Nine Less Emmerooze' at Le Boulestin.

"My God! This country! Tell me you're bull-shitting me."

I said nothing. Silence was another of Karen's lessons.

"You bastard. You fucking insolent bastard." She flicked her wrist and launched the wine into my face, threw her napkin across her half-eaten plate of food. "You owe your goddamn life to me and don't fucking forget it. I'll have your balls for this."

I knew I'd won the moment the wine hit my face. The next morning I invented a client and put in an expense claim for the dinner. It included a claim for dry cleaning my suit, a new tie and the taxi fare home. Mary Connolly brought the claim form round to my desk personally a day later. "Bastard," she said, throwing the piece of paper onto my desk. She turned, pile driving her stiletto heels into the carpet, and walked away. I looked at my expense claim. Mary Connolly had duly authorised everything. Two days later she was on the flight home to New York.

3

Caroline's third pregnancy was as unexpected as her first.

There was an unwritten consensus in most City firms that if fast-track female employees wanted to have children they should use the technology available to limit the numbers to one or, at worst, two. The first woman to make partner in Caroline's firm had famously had a hysterectomy six months before she was made up. Caroline was definitely partner-track, a rising legal star with a growing reputation among the rich seeking justice (or revenge) through the divorce courts. It wasn't the old dream of fighting for the wretched of the earth, but the money was good and you've got to make ends meet somehow.

Knowing how much Caroline (and I) valued her job, I tried to persuade her to take the reasonable course and have an abortion. I knew I would probably fail: she had refused all my entreaties when she had become pregnant with Robert.

Caroline did, as I had predicted, lose her job. Her dismissal was, of course, disguised to appear unrelated to her extraordinary fertility. If you have any notion of ever practising law again anywhere – and Caroline even then thought she would be back one day – you don't sue a legal firm for wrongful dismissal. She went quietly. Henry Alfred Charles Kellaway was born on 4 July 1983.

Bad though the timing was, it was not as disastrous as it would have been a year earlier. Then we had had, quite simply, too much debt for one salary to bear. The miracle drug can also kill. We may have abandoned debtors' jails and built tourist attractions and gleaming banks along Clink Street, temples to the joys of borrowing, to the instant highs of consuming today that which you cannot afford until tomorrow, but the enslaving power of debt still lurks in the darker corners of that cobblestone alley. We escaped thanks to Mary Connolly. By the end of 1983 her munificence was bearing fruit. An ever-increasing portion of Harriman's London dealing room was under my control.

A year after Henry was born we moved house again – to what at the time seemed like an enormously extravagant pile in the Surrey stockbroker belt. The previous owners had called it 'Great Pines' and announced it as such to the world with a sign in imported Spanish *azulejos* on one of the gateposts. Not long after we moved in, I arrived home one evening to find the vowels in 'Pines' transposed. I rather liked the accolade, putting me as it did on an illustrious par with the world's most successful men, the likes of Don Giovanni, Genghiz Khan and J.F. Kennedy. Caroline, however, insisted we remove the tiles altogether and the house reverted to the discreet number it had been known by before our predecessors discovered the Costa del Sol.

We sold the house in Kentish Town to a limited liability company that Caroline and I established and owned. It was 100% debt funded. Rental income from a French bank, one of whose expatriate executives took up residence in the house, covered 100% of the mortgage payments.

I used a similar financing structure – the single-property, debt-funded, limited-liability company – to buy all the properties we acquired around Kentish Town over the coming years. We had, ensconced in the leafy outer suburbs between neighbours twice our age, become absentee landlords. Caroline managed the business with ruthless efficiency. With our new Weybridge neighbours, we openly discussed its progress. With our friends of longer standing still living in the brick terraces of Camden and Hackney, we kept its profile low.

We had not been seeing much of Colin Witheridge even before we moved to Surrey and it came as a total surprise when Colin phoned a few months after our move to invite us to his engagement party. Claire was six years younger than Colin and an inch taller, blonde, easy on the eyes, a forensic accountant with one of the Big Eight, or however many there were in those days, the daughter of a diplomat and extraordinarily useful on the tennis court.

Within a year of the marriage, Claire produced a preternaturally gorgeous baby girl. They gave her the ridiculously pompous name of Héloïse – Héloïse Aphrodite Lotus-Flower Witheridge[64] – complete with a redundant 'H', and acute accent on the first 'e' and two dots instead of one over the 'i'. She grew, in the full roundness of time, into a preternaturally gorgeous teenager who called me 'Uncle Nick'.

When Héloïse was two, Colin and Claire moved to Weybridge. I wondered how Colin had afforded the property. When I asked him, he shrugged. "You know as much about debt as I do," he said.

I wasn't sure I wanted Colin Witheridge living close by. Caroline, however, saw things differently. "It'll be nice," she remarked, "having some neighbours our own age."

---

[64] See Yoko Matsumoto and Earl Cheriton, 'Peaches, Diesel and Chardonnay: Given-name Cocktails and the Prognosis of Mental Health' in *The Saskatchewan Journal of Childhood Mental Health*, 17 (2007). – Ed.

Stock markets crashed on 19 October 1987 – a day that came to be known as 'Black Monday'.[65] Although a retrospective look at the charts suggests that this was only a small blip in the Great Bull Run, at the time, as the screens turned red, it seemed very dramatic indeed. I was in New York that day, powerless to do anything with my own London book other than to make a series of phone calls to my screen-struck traders. I cancelled my meetings in New York for the rest of the week and caught the last BA flight out of JFK for London. I did not sleep during that short Atlantic night and arrived in London the next morning with a plan.

Caroline and I liquidated our property holdings over the coming eighteen months. We sold into a still buoyant housing market, kept afloat by the government reducing interest rates to prevent financial distress seeping into the real economy. We sold in order to invest countercyclically in the stock market. As a result of my position at Harriman's we had access to asset classes unavailable to ordinary punters. We did particularly well out of investments in convertible bonds. When the stock market fell, convertibles began to trade at the value implied by their interest coupons alone with no additional value attributed to their potential to convert into shares. It did not take long, nor a Black-Scholes[66] genius, to see that such an anomaly would not persist. When the additional value was again attributed, I sold, took my profit and ploughed the proceeds into shares.

When British house prices fell in the early nineties, the asset bubble created by artificially low interest rates punctured, Caroline and I went back into property. By this time, however, we had made a few moves along the Monopoly board. We bought houses in Knightsbridge rather than Kentish Town. I also bought myself a flat in Mayfair for those nights when I had to stay up in town. With a helping hand from obliging lenders, I had enough money not to unwind our long-equities position in order to buy all those shiny little green plastic houses. The profits I had taken were handsome, and bonuses, particularly since Big Bang[67], had been beautiful.

---

[65] Note that this date was the tenth anniversary of the deaths of Gudrun Ensslin, Andreas Baader and Jan-Carl Raspe. – Ed.

[66] Option pricing theory, based on the Black-Scholes model, has formed the mathematical basis for the explosion of the volume of trading in a broad range of derivative instruments since the early 1980s. Fischer Black (1938–1995) and Myron Scholes (1941–) set out the original concept in 1973 in their paper 'The Pricing of Options and Corporate Liabilities'. In 1997, Myron Scholes was awarded the Nobel Prize in Economics for his work on developing the conceptual framework for the valuation of derivatives. – Ed.

[67] 'Big Bang' refers to the deregulation of the financial sector in Britain on 27 October 1986. – Ed.

4

We turned, 300 yards short of where we had turned two years ago and, with the wind behind us now, we could speak without our words being pummelled back into our throats. There were five of us walking the wintry beach. Robert had asked to come with us for our traditional after-lunch men's walk and, when Henry had heard Robert was joining us, he insisted on coming too. Imogen's new husband of five months, still trying to ingratiate himself with the in-laws, tried to hold Henry's hand, but Henry was not having any of that.

We were dressed in the sombre dark greens and blacks of an English country winter: Barbour jackets, tweed caps and Wellingtons – except Henry. Henry wore red wellies and a pink scarf, hand-me-downs from Amanda, from which he would not be parted. He forgot his claims on independent adulthood and held his grandfather's hand as they splashed together through pools the retreating tide had left behind. "I never thought I'd live to see these things," Charles Carter said. Then he added, as if ashamed of his lack of faith, "Despite our prayers."

By 'these things', Caroline's father meant the overthrow of Communism in Eastern Europe. 1989 fell exactly 300 years after the births of de Montsequieu and Voltaire. It was the bicentenary of the French Revolution and the centenary of the founding of the Second International. The edifices built by their ideological heirs were fast being dismantled.

It was dusk by the time we walked up from the beach to the car, dark by the time we reached the Carters' house. Amanda, wearing a flour-dusted apron too large for her body, proudly presented us with the mince pies she had baked with her Aunty Imogen. We stood by the log fire to eat them. We sipped mulled wine and the children drank spiced apple juice. Our cheeks glowed red from the wind and the fire and the alcohol.

Imogen's husband turned on the television. He didn't know the rules yet. One of them was no television on Christmas Day, not even for the Queen. As the BBC reporter recapped the events of the past few days, we saw tanks on the streets of Bucharest and buildings in flames and no one said anything or turned the television off. We watched men carrying rifles running across an open square. They ran in crouching positions to make themselves smaller targets for the snipers. The BBC told us there were secret servicemen still loyal to the old order on the rooftops firing into the square. From the angle of the pictures, the BBC seemed to be up there among the Securitate marksmen. We saw some of the insurgents fall to the government's bullets. Then it was all over. The tanks turned their guns away from the crowd and the people gave the soldiers cups of tea. We saw the dead bodies of Nicolae and Elena Ceauşescu.

Caroline refilled my glass, caught me under the mistletoe, kissed me. "Once upon a time," she said, "we imagined all this happening here – not in the East."

Did we feel unalloyed Thatcherite joy at the collapse of the Communist regimes? At the unexpected answer to Colonel Carter's prayers? Or did some pure iron in our souls still hark back twenty years, to a time of dreams, and tell us this was not how it was meant to be, this was not how Karl Marx said it would be? I don't know. Images are easy. The emotions are harder to reconstitute.

29 December 1989 – Vaclav Havel – writer, dissident and former prisoner of the *ancien régime* – is elected President of Czechoslovakia.

11 January 1990 – 300,000 demonstrate for the independence of Lithuania.

15 January 1990 – The headquarters of Stasi in East Berlin are stormed by a crowd of demonstrators who force their way into the building. There have been rumours in East Germany that the secret police have been destroying their files. The people want them kept intact. After freedom comes justice.

20 January 1990 – Soviet troops occupy Baku. They kill 130 people demonstrating for the independence of Azerbaijan.

I took two days off work, picked a random East European destination and flew to Prague. I wanted to smell history.

Prague was cold and grey. I saw crumbling baroque buildings propped up by rotting timbers, prostitutes tentatively venturing out into Wenceslas Square to sell their free-market wares, a makeshift monument to Jan Palach who had burnt himself there twenty-one years earlier to protest the Soviet invasion, identical sets of grey metal dustbins outside decaying grey doors, rows of grey Stalinist apartment blocks on the hills surrounding the town, bewildered grey policemen standing idly by the roadside, unsure which laws were still enforceable. There was a banner on the tower at the end of

Charles Bridge that said 'Havel na Hrad'. [68]

Other slogans of the Velvet Revolution had faded, or been torn down, as people went back to work to make up for time lost during the demonstrations of November. The air smelled of boiled cabbage, of low-grade coal and drains. In the graveyard beside the church at Vyšehrad, I watched as the remains of a human body were exhumed from the hard ground. A piece of coarse cloth – identical in colour to the cold, brown earth in which it had lain – clung to the bones. In the metro an honour system operated. Nobody paid.

At dinner I drank beer and ate hard cheese and yesterday's bread because that's all I was offered. A German from the Mittelstand told me how the system worked. He had driven across the border to assess the prospects for expanding his enterprise eastwards and was the only other customer in the overheated restaurant that cold January night. "The workers in this restaurant," he said, "are paid exactly the same wage whether they have clients or not. They think this fair because it is not their fault if the night is cold and nobody comes to the restaurant. But then there is no incentive to work and, frankly, there is a big disincentive to work because they are allowed to take home at the end of the evening any food they think is otherwise going to waste, and because it is otherwise going to waste, they need make no payment for it." He could, he said, treble the wages of Czech factory workers *and* more than double his enterprise's profits if he moved his manufacturing base just a hundred kilometres to the east. Instilling the necessary work ethic would be simple: he would pay not by the hour but by results.

I bought a set of twelve crystal glasses for the price I would have paid for a single cheap goblet in London. The girl in the shop told me she had an advanced degree in education and would teach me anything I fancied in the cosy warmth of her flat. The taxi driver who took me back to the airport asked for a fare five times what his meter showed. I tried to complain. "Communist meter," the overweight driver retorted, patting it with his left hand. He then stroked the steering wheel with his right hand. "Capitalist car," he said.

---

[68] Vaclav Havel had been president of Czechoslovakia – resident in the castle ('*hrad*'), the presidential seat – for a month at the time of Nick's mysterious trip to Prague at the end of January 1990. The slogan '*Havel na Hrad*' had, remarkably quickly, become a statement of fact. – Ed.

31 January 1990 – McDonald's opens in Moscow.

11 February 1990 – The idea of freedom spreads to Africa. Nelson Mandela is released from prison.

13 February 1990 – A plan for the reunification of Germany is agreed between its eastern and western parts. *Das Volk* is to become *Ein Volk.*

26 February 1990 – The Soviet Union agrees a timetable for the withdrawal of its troops from Czechoslovakia. They have been there since 1968.

11 March 1990 – Liberty spreads to South America. Pinochet goes and Chile's new democratically elected president takes office.

18 March 1990 – Namibia becomes independent from South Africa.

21 March 1990 – The Soviet Union admits responsibility for the Katyn massacre and apologises to Poland.

16 May 1990 – Priscilla McGinley dies of breast cancer. "Imagine me," she said to Caroline a month earlier, "dying of such a fucking bourgeois disease."

I went to see Sill in hospital shortly before she died. She lay, thin, in her bed. "Do you remember your Marx, banker man?" she asked. "Where he says that when the Revolution comes there will be no more alienation and you can be a hunter and a fisherman and a carpenter and a doctor and a nurse all in the same glorious day?" It wasn't an exact quote, but the sentiment reflected the original accurately enough. "What could Priscilla be? Come on, Nick. You were the king of alliteration. What could Priscilla be? Priest? Pretender? Prostitute? Procuratrix?" She closed her eyes, opened them to speak again, "Funny, isn't it, how people believe in heaven, but not in hell? The Greeks weren't at all like this. For them, hell was for everyone. Heaven was only for the gods. They were much better people for it, Nick... Nick, do you remember Jules de Gaulthier? He said something like 'Imagination is the great weapon for combating reality.' What was it? I've been trying to remember."

"It's 'Imagination is just one weapon in the war against reality.'"

"That's it. 'Just one'. Jules Achille de Gaulthier de Laguionie, a name the very devils in hell will fucking tremble at. 'Imagination is just one weapon in the war against reality.' I got that from Jan, you know. Your friend Janice Day. Imagination. D'you know what the other one is, Nick? Do you? The other is... is death." She turned and focussed her wandering gaze on my eyes. She mouthed the word again, but this time no sound emerged

Sill had lived long enough to see the Berlin Wall dismantled and hear the crumbling of the cringing régimes she and Caroline had toured in the 1971 long vac. "It's a hard road," she had said. "They were all the wrong countries – it needed to start in the advanced capitalist states: Germany, England, America. You don't spank little children for wanting to grow up, do you? At least they tried."

The nurse came and asked me to leave. "Nick," Sill said, "give my love to Caroline. Tell her I'd like to see her before I go. Tell her 'sex is the greater healer.' She'll remember that. Tell her 'Venice, 1971.' She'll remember that as well. They go together. You'll do that, won't you, Nick?"

Sill died before Caroline saw her again.

17 May 1990 – The World Health Organisation in Geneva issues a statement that it has removed homosexuality from its list of diseases. "*Liberté, egalité* and fucking *fraternité*," says Colin when he tells me. "Be no stopping the buggers now."

21 May 1990 – Edward Reader phones. "What were you looking for in Prague?" he asks.

"How did you know I'd been in Prague?"

"Word travels. What were you looking for, Nick?"

"Just wanted to see what it felt like."

"And?"

"I walked around a lot. I saw some interesting things. To what do I owe the pleasure of this call, Edward?"

"Janice Day,"

"What d'you mean?"

"You need to find a woman called Else. I think that's the name. German. She was in Prague in 1972. At the time of the Munich Olympics. Helping people from Eastern Europe get into West Germany. Janice Day may have been with her."

"Hang on, Edward. Where's this coming from?"

"All sorts of things are coming to light. Sorry, I don't have a surname."

"The house fire. The house fire in Munich? You told me Jan…"

"Not her. We have the names now and Janice Day is not one of them. There *was* an American involved, not killed – just involved – but she was called Rose."

23 May 1990 – Colin Witheridge phones. He has taken a new job: corporate banker to his new employer's oil industry clients. For his new bank he is drawing up a list of prospects that includes emerging names in Russia.

May and June are peak conference season in the world of finance. I joined the fun and went to a three-day conference in Rome. The organisers of these events select their venues well. Few among those who spend their days at computer screens under the fluorescent lights of the City's dealing rooms would not relish a few spring days away from cluttered desk and screeching phone. Where better to spend them than in the Eternal City?

I stayed at the conference only for its first day. I had a speaking slot in the morning, chaired a session in the afternoon, shook the hands I needed to shake, distributed my card liberally, joined the cocktail party and the sponsored dinner in the evening, drank abstemiously. Early on the second day, before the bleary-eyed revellers had assembled to listen to the second day's opening speech, I hired a car and drove to Florence. It was only with some difficulty that I found the Villa Sangalletti in Fiesole, where Eva Bocardo lived, but I was nonetheless ringing the bell on her gate well before the appointed lunch hour. Eva came to the door wrapped in a paint-spattered smock, her hair tied up in a scarf. She was bare-legged and barefoot. The nails of her fingers and toes were painted scarlet. She wore no jewellery, pressed her body into mine as she gave me a warm hug.

"Nick!" she exclaimed. "How very good of you to come."

I spent two days with my cousin Eva. When I left my wet portrait was hanging on the wall of her studio. As I drove south along the *autostrada* towards Rome, I felt like one of her painting rags that had been wrung out and left to dry on a wire in the Tuscan sun, scarcely able to keep my eyes open and the hired Mercedes on the road.

There was nobody in when I arrived home in Weybridge later that day. I went to my study, unlocked a drawer in my desk, rummaged among my lists, found one I had made long ago on lined schoolboy paper. *The Big Five: Janice Day, Sally Pinkerton, Marie-Claire Dufraisse, Polly Page, Eva-Maria Bocardo-Griffin.* Sally, Marie-Claire and Polly had tidy little tick marks beside their names. I now added one next to Eva's name. Only Jan's name remained unticked, and, if you believed what Edward Reader had said, Janice Day might not be dead after all.

6 June 1990 – A second call from Edward Reader. He tells me Susanne Albrecht has been arrested. She has been living in East Germany under an assumed, Stasi-given identity for ten years. "There are," he says, "scores of these old terrorists still out there." I remember what Karen O'Neil told me that night at the Savoy about her CIA husband's report to Jan's parents. *She could blend in, in East Germany.*

8 July 1990 – West Germany wins the World Cup, beating Argentina in the final.

27 July 1990 – Belarus declares itself independent as the break-up of the USSR continues.

30 July 1990 – A Provisional IRA bomb kills Ian Gow, MP for Eastbourne, outside his East Sussex home.

2 August 1990 – Saddam Hussein catches the zeitgeist and decides to board the freedom bandwagon. Iraqi forces liberate Kuwait from its decadent feudal rulers and incorporate it as a long-lost province of mother Iraq.

6 August 1990 – Edward Reader phones again. I have done nothing to follow up on Edward's earlier calls. What could I have done? How could anybody comb through 80,000,000 Germans looking for a woman who might or might not be called Else, who might or might not have met Janice Day in Prague in 1972? If Tom O'Neil couldn't find her, how could I? I've moved on. I've not even had a dream about Jan for years. I'm a busy man. If she's hiding in the East, they'll find her eventually, like they found Susanne Albrecht.

"Nick," Edward says. "I just thought you'd like to know that your name has been found in the Stasi files."

"What?"

"You're right. I should be more precise: Stasi had a file on you. They had one on Colin Witheridge as well. There's one on me, of course. I wouldn't have been doing my job if there hadn't been one on me, would I? Mine had my entire doctoral thesis in it. I even had a code name. Yours is quite innocuous, Nick."

"Good. So why phone me to tell me?"

"Well, I just thought you'd like to know. You'll be able to check out what it says – if you want. But, as I say, it's quite innocuous. I've had a look at it. Nothing to worry about at all. I've not had the opportunity to look at Colin's file yet. It's quite a fat file, Colin's. And there might be one on Caroline,"

"Might?"

"It looks like there might be."

"There *might* be one on the man on the moon."

Edward ignores my comment and continues as if I had not spoken. "There is *one* other thing that I think you might be interested in, Nick."

"Which is?"

"Did you ever follow up that Prague lead I gave you?"

"No."

"Pity. I'd've been interested to hear what you'd found. Anyway… there was also a file on Janice Day."

"You say 'was'?"

"Well, there's not much to say except that it's not there now."

Lights on the console in front of me tell me two other external lines are ringing unanswered. The rule in *my* dealing room is that all calls are answered after no more than four rings. I lose patience with Reader's circumlocutions and say, "Then there ain't much to tell, is there?"

"Nick, the fact that the file is gone is what is significant here. You have to understand. Back in January, when they broke into Stasi HQ, it wasn't just ordinary East Germans in the crowd trying to stop them shredding stuff. All kinds of people were there. Stasi agents wanting to destroy incriminating papers, West Germans, people working for the CIA, the KGB, Mossad. How d'you think they'd have got in otherwise? Anyway, one of them must have taken the file on Janice Day."

"And you know who."

"No, actually, I don't. That's the whole point. I *don't* know who took it. Maybe someone who wants her to stay dead. I don't know."

When I hang up I realise that the entire conversation has been recorded on the new system Harriman's has just installed to keep better track of dealing-room trades.

14 August 1990 – Lunch with Colin. "Me?!" he exclaims, when I relay the news that the GDR had a file on him.

I think I detect a tremor in Colin's voice. His career, running for so long, as he jokes, to British Rail time, is at last beginning to move off from the platform. No doubt the last thing Colin wants is to see it derailed by rumours that he is a Communist spy – particularly now that the Communists have lost. Rumours can be potent in the City. Many a promising career has been destroyed for misdemeanours far less significant than being a Communist agent.

Later, over coffee, when conversation returns to Edward Reader's phone calls, Colin asks, "Did he say anything about Anna?"

"No. Should he have?"

"Just wondering… how often do you see Edward Reader?"

"See?"

"Yes."

"Not often, never, in fact. He just phones. I haven't actually *seen* him since you and I were travelling around Germany." I have forgotten his appearance at one of our Escalade reunions.

"1972."

"That's right."

"Eighteen years ago. Eighteen fucking years. Can you believe it? That's half a life time. We'll be forty next year, Nick, forty. Can you fucking believe it?"

5

At the beginning of 1994, after a record bonus, I resigned from Harriman's and set up Kellaway & Co.

Kellaway & Co. is generally regarded as a hedge fund or, more accurately, the manager of a series of hedge funds. Shares in Kellaway & Co. cannot be bought on the Stock Market or elsewhere. I own all the voting 'A' shares and the non-voting 'B' shares can only be acquired by employees when and I allocate them as part of a bonus package. Those who are rich enough can, of course, invest in one of our Cayman Islands funds. With the money confided to us, we place bets on stock markets, currency movements, interest rates, commodities, structured products and all forms of options and derivatives. We take long positions, naturally, but, because we aim to provide constant returns to our investors whether markets go up or down, we also short markets, individual stocks, currencies and so on. Being a hedge fund we hedge the risks involved. That may limit the upside but it also protects our investors on the downside and that is what they want from a true hedge fund. The science lies in getting the balance right.

We have also built a reputation for being on the right side of a number of one-off events. Sometimes we have participated in the buy-out of an entire company where the financial engineering looked promising, behaving more like a private-equity firm than a classic hedge fund. We have been able to influence the destiny of other companies through small shareholdings. An activist track record bespattered with the boardroom blood of a dozen kills means they take us seriously when they see us coming.

On the liabilities side of the equation we have, of course, the money paid in by our clients. We also have debt. We established, early on, generous lines of credit, including one with Harriman's, and borrowed to leverage our investors' funds to their financial advantage. After a few years of trading we had six prime brokers – useful for hiding the source of big trades – and each of them desperately eager to extend credit to us. Debt is the magic dust in our system: sprinkle it on a trade and, if you are on the right side of it, you multiply your returns. Our fee, based on the industry's standard two-and-twenty formula, is what investors pay Kellaway & Co. for usually being on the right side of the trade.

Here's a legitimate question: why would any sober investor put his confidence in Kellaway & Co. and pay us those kind of fees, particularly in those early days back in 1994 and 1995 when we were just starting out and had no track record, no market-beating performance charts to point to? The answer lay in the personal reputation I had built. Two events loomed large in consolidating my reputation. Each of them was known to the market as 'black', but, for me, they were pure gold.

Black Monday was 19 October 1987. It was, and remains, the day on which stock markets fell further than any other day on record. The Dow Jones Industrial Average fell 22.61% that day. For a number that will convey the sense of the panic that gripped the markets, look for the second worst fall in the Dow Jones's record: 11.73% – and that was on 29 October 1929, the notorious Black Tuesday, the worst day of the legendary Great Crash. If you had invested your savings in the stock market a month earlier, in September 1929, and held on to them, the charts tell us that you would have waited a lifetime until they were again worth what you had paid in September 1929. It might have been worth following your stockbroker when he jumped from the top of the Empire State Building. After Black Tuesday came the Great Depression and civil disorder. Within four years Hitler was in power in Germany and then came the most devastating war the world has ever seen. On the morning of 19 October 1987 this terrible sequence was at the forefront of our minds. As if to help our imaginations along, news appeared on our stricken screens that American bombers had destroyed Iranian oil installations in the Persian Gulf.

I was in New York the day the screens turned red, sitting in the margins of a dealing room that was not my own, watching traders for whom I had no responsibility take a constant stream of sell orders. Many potential sellers could not get through on the telephone lines. Systems could not cope with the volume of transactions. The computer-driven index arbitrage and portfolio insurance strategies, intended to stabilise the market at times like these, fuelled the vicious downward spiral. Like debt itself, they began to smell bad running in overdrive in reverse gear. Even the computers, spewing out their automated sell orders, were in meltdown mode, adding to the acrid smell of a dealing room in panic.

I cut short my trip to New York and flew back to London overnight. Black Monday had wreaked less devastation in London than in New York. The FTSE 100 was down *only* 10.84% on the day, but the backlog of trades and the knowledge of the financial hurricane in New York, that continued apace after London closed for the day, led to a further 12.22% drop in the FTSE 100 on the Tuesday. That Tuesday, 20 October 1987, remains in the record books as the day the London Stock Exchange lost most value in percentage terms. Monday 19 October 1987 sits in second place. I stayed up in town all week and hardly slept, but I did notice during the course of the week that John Templeton[69], possibly the greatest countercyclical investor ever, had said, "The bear market might already be over." That was all the back-up I needed for my investment strategies, both personal and for Harriman's.

My ambitions for what would later come to be known as the proprietary trading desk – where Harriman's would trade and invest for its own account rather than those of its clients – were, however, held in check. "This is a bank, Nicholas, not a casino," said my American boss when he called me into his office. Behind his back we called him 'Whiteface'.

"But we're going to make shed-loads of money. Fucking shed-loads."

"Nicholas, cool it, okay? I don't want to have to cut your limits, do I?" Globules of congealed saliva adhered to his lips.

I stormed out of his office. *Bespittled dwarf of bourgeois reaction.*

Whiteface had been a successful young lender in the days when banks expected their corporate clients – or 'customers', as they no

---

[69] Sir John Templeton (1912–2008) was an investor known for the development of mutual funds and investing across a number of markets. He had a reputation as a 'stockpicker' and for countercyclical investing. – Ed.

doubt called them – to be in credit with the bank at least a month each year. They called it 'annual clean-up', as if borrowing was something dirty. Bank lending, in Whiteface's youth, was strictly for working capital purposes. The bank would lend to a farmer to buy seed and would be repaid when the harvest was sold. Corporate financial year ends were set to fall approximately thirty days after the company's metaphorical harvest and well before its next sowing season. Good credits presented annual year-end accounts that were debt free. If bank managers, scarred by the havoc leverage had played in 1929, knew anything about the magic of debt, they saw it as black and satanic.

Whiteface's wife was confined to a wheelchair with advanced multiple sclerosis. He had photographs of her – in better times – and of his three young children on the walls of the office that he kept obsessively tidy. He was comfortable in there, reading and dictating memoranda. When he emerged from his den, you could see the fear in his eyes, the eyes of a manicured poodle going to meet a pack of pit bull terriers. For Whiteface, the flashing screens, the ringing phones, the shouting voices and the heat from the bodies and the ill-ventilated computers would never be anything other than an alien and perilous environment.

Whiteface wrote my performance appraisals. The one he wrote at the end of 1988, by which time we had booked our now legendary Black Monday profits (despite Whiteface's constraints), was glowing. There was, however, an insidious little custom around Harriman's then that every performance appraisal must contain some element of constructive criticism. Whiteface's little phrase was 'Could have been more ambitious with his strategy post 10/19'. *Revisionist prick.*

I placed an immediate call to the chief executive. I named the figure I wanted as a personal bonus. In the January 1989 bonus round, I was paid 25% *more* than I had asked for and Whiteface accepted a generous early-retirement pay off. I was given Whiteface's office when he and his family left it. I declined the offer, electing to stay out in the pit, out where I belonged, among the Rottweilers.

The day that consolidated my reputation in the City was Black Wednesday – 16 September 1992. It showed the world that I was a player across more than one market. Black Wednesday was the day Sterling was ejected from the European Exchange Rate Mechanism, a pre-Euro system that tied minor European currencies to the power of the holy Deutschemark. The UK had been a member of the Exchange Rate Mechanism for two years at the time of Black

Wednesday, but the fundamentals for British membership were altogether wrong. The boom engineered after Black Monday had come to an end and Britain had gone into recession. House prices fell and at every middle-class dinner party talk was about 'negative equity' – the amount by which the mortgage on your house exceeded the value of the asset you'd borrowed against. Norman Tebbit said ERM stood for 'Eternal Recession Mechanism'.

On Wednesday, 16 September 1992, the traders struck. Everyone sold Sterling. It was the Market versus the State. The British government spent some £27 billion bolstering the pound and it failed. The markets won. George Soros[70] made a profit of something over a billion dollars shorting Sterling. Encouraged by my risk controller in the bank, even then a committed Eurosceptic, I joined in the fun. My profit was more modest than what Soros pocketed, but it was nonetheless significant. The profit, of course, accrued to Harriman's: I was still an employee. Despite another fantastic bonus in January 1993, that was beginning to irk me.

6

Client confidentiality requires me to use pseudonyms for my anchor investors at Kellaway & Co. They were two Arab brothers I had known for ten years, Mohammed and Abdullah, whose not inconsiderable wealth came from oil and inherited privilege. The family had been a client of Harriman's for three generations. I had taken the boys to Bangkok not long after they came of age and introduced them to some of the city's finer establishments. Annabel, famous for her body, came aboard soon afterwards.

When Mohammed and Abdullah came to London in early 1994, I took them to a well-known club, not far from my Mayfair flat, where I've long been a member. The brothers spotted her first. Abdullah whispered, "Is that Annabel?" She looked bored, fashionably bored, bored with her muscled companion, bored with her surroundings, conscious of the mute gaze of those around her, practised at ignoring it.

"Let's go say hello," I suggested.

---

[70] George Soros (1930–) is a Hungarian-born American speculator, best known in Britain as 'the man who broke the Bank of England' for his speculation against Sterling in 1992. – Ed.

"Do you know her?" Mohammed asked, wide-eyed.

"She's not wearing knee kazz," added Abdullah.

Once I had worked out what Abdullah had said, I saw he was right. Annabel was wearing a tight, semi-transparent, red dress that left little to the imagination. No bra and, like the runaway urchin in my grandmother's graveyard, no knickers. It was for moments like these that my friends left their sacred desert sands behind.

"Do you know her?" Mohammed asked again.

Without answering him, I walked over to Annabel. The brothers followed me and I introduced them. "… And I'm Nick Kellaway. I run Kellaway & Co., the hedge fund, and these two guys are my very good friends and clients."

This was something of an exaggeration; strictly speaking, Kellaway & Co. had yet to sign its first client or hire an employee. I wasn't sure whom I was trying to impress more, the potential clients from Araby or England's most talked-about woman.

Annabel's companion, spittle spraying from his mouth, said, "Fuck off."

A deep, dark bedroom voice, expressed a subtly different viewpoint. "Hang on," Annabel said, "I wanna talk to these guys."

"What about?" asked muscle man.

"I want Mr Galloway to tell me about hedge funds." (Actually, she said "fudge ends" – but I knew what she meant.) "Tell me," she said leaning towards me, "how much money can you make for me?"

What do you say when England's pin-up asks you that and purses her red, red lips less than two feet away from yours as she waits for your answer? If you've been running a hedge fund or whatever for a dozen years, do you trot out all the statistics, the most flattering league tables, the best out-of-context quotes from the technical press, percentages calculated in ways you need a mathematics PhD to grasp? Maybe not. But if you've just hung up your brass plaque, if you haven't yet gathered in your investors, if you haven't yet even made a single investment… then even that approach is not open to you. I turned Annabel's question to Mohammed and Abdullah. "Ask my clients," I said, "how good I am. I'll get another bottle of champagne."

When I returned with two bottles of the most expensive bubbly the house had to offer, Annabel asked, "Did you really make $137 million in one day?"

"I did."

"Holy shit."

I went home that night with my anchor Arab investors (and Annabel's phone number) in my pocket.

Annabel came to dinner at the Mayfair flat three weeks later. We drank. We ate. We talked. What about? Money? Yes. Her career? Yes. Her diet? Yes. Her childhood? That too. My collections of Egyptian alabaster and erotic Persian miniatures? In passing. Politics? No. Religion? Only if you classify crystals, universal life forces, spirit channelling and Heggie's 'Nice Scene' syncretism as religion.[71] Her likes and dislikes? Yes. Yes. Yes. Then – between the Mayfair lilies and the rose, on the battlements of a caravanserai on the high road to Samarkand, perfumed by frankincense from Ophir and sandalwood from Hind, serenaded by nightingales, surrounded by gold and copper from the palaces of Baghdad and cedar from the mountains of Lebanon, among the deep-red Bokhara carpets and vials of ivory and coloured glass, I added another name to a list that long pre-dates the one of Kellaway & Co.'s prestigious clients.

I never spoke of that night – except once to Colin, who said he didn't believe me. It was more of an achievement because it was unsung, not because it was what I wanted, but because I had had what others wanted. I had possessed the nation's dreams. The night remained deliciously secret, like the monogrammed gold stays that keep my shirt collars stiff. I know they are there, but nobody sees them. Occasionally, someone discovers that Annabel is a client of Kellaway & Co. and asks me how that came to be. I am practised now in my response. I smile enigmatically, say I don't discuss my clients' affairs and let them imagine what they will.

---

[71] 'The Nice Scene Creed' in Adam Heggie, *Posthumous Verses* (London, 2004):
> *I believe in horoscopes*
> *And what the entrails said,*
> *In Buddha and Mohammed,*
> *That Elvis isn't dead.*
> *I believe in Climate Change,*
> *Recycling and the Sea,*
> *Peace on earth, goodwill to men,*
> *That healthcare should be free,*
> *In Gaia's magic crystals*
> *You buy from Krishna's store,*
> *Prostitutes of Babylon*
> *And Horus' holy whore.*
> – Ed.

Despite what he said, Colin *might* actually have believed that I slept with Annabel.

One Saturday afternoon, rain drove Colin and me off the golf course and into the clubhouse. Colin made his way to the bar and persuaded me to join him for a quick drink. I should have known better: Claire and Héloïse were away for the weekend and, predictably, one drink led to another, then another. A dangerous cocktail of the English round buying tradition and frustrated male golfers. Sitting on the supposedly dry side of the rain-streaked window pane, we sipped gin and tonics and watched the long-legged American waitress bustle between the thirsty tables. Colin watched my eyes follow the legs and said, "A damn good tennis player that. Beat Claire in straight sets: six-two; six-love."

"I could go a couple of rounds with her."

"What? Anti-fascist investment advice?"

"Something like that. You'd get a damned good workout. Those legs..."

"Nick, listen, if you think that's good, wait 'til you get to Moscow. Legs like you've never even imagined. Not even in your most spectacular dreams. Or better still, in this weather, Greece. There's this Russian friend of mine with a yacht full of gorgeous long-legged blondes anchored off Santorini. Remember Santorini? The Germans?"

"Of course."

Colin changed the subject, moved it to another – a then famous – pair of long legs. "Did Annabel invest with you?" he asked.

I nodded. Somehow physical gestures did not seem such a breach of client confidence.

"What," Colin asked, "does Caroline make of it?"

"Of what?"

"Annabel. All the others."

"I don't know. It's not something we talk about."

"So you don't think she minds?"

"How should I know? I imagine she'd see it as a sign of virility. Like a big bank balance and points on the driving licence. As long as I keep seducing her, why should she mind?"

"And the choir girl still seduces you?"

"God, yes. Shit. I mean none of the others come anywhere near Caro."

Only Robert was in when I got home later that afternoon. Before shutting himself away in his bedroom he told me that Caroline had taken Amanda and Henry for a spontaneous trip to a London theatre. I was asleep when they returned. Caroline woke me as she slid, freshly showered, into our bed and lay at the far edge of her side. I tried to pull her towards me, but she resisted, claimed she was too tired and rolled away.

Over breakfast the next morning Caroline asked pleasant questions about my aborted day on the golf course, about Colin, whether I knew the new American waitress at the club had beaten Claire at tennis, whether I could spare half an hour to help Robert with his maths homework... I saw invisible dots forming on the table between us and began to draw imaginary time lines between them.

My memory is of specks of dust floating in the warm air, sparkling in the bright spring-morning sun and of an intense desire to be away, away from Weybridge, away from England, away cycling among golden childhood fields, the blue lake somewhere to my left and fresh snow on the Alps to my right, Caroline sits on the edge of the big sofa and, with the palm of her hand, wipes a tear from her eye. "It's not that, Nick," she says.

I put an arm around her shoulders, say, "Are you angry, darling?"

Caroline throws off my light embrace, walks to the window and, looking into the garden, says, "More sad than angry." I am absent too much, she says. I spend too long in the office, too many nights in Mayfair, and when I am home my mind is still in London or God knows where. "It's been going on for years. The children hardly know who their father is. Robert's nearly grown up. He'll be gone soon."

Do I sigh? What can I say? Until I sort out this mess with Gary Rackenford, I *will* be spending long hours in the office, my mind *will* be elsewhere. I have taken this one Sunday out to be with Caroline and the kids. I say, "I'm here now, darling."

Gary Rackenford was one of the first people Kellaway & Co. hired. He was a profoundly private young man who worked with a rare intensity, peering at his screen from deep-set eyes. On the rare occasions he broke his silence it was to speak in a rusty flintlock voice, a voice laden with unintended menace, the kind of voice you would put in charge of the firing squad when the Revolution began to falter. *Pour encourager les autres.* Before becoming one of the City's finest traders he had driven a shiny, mock-Tudor Mondeo, worn bright floral ties and plied a salesman's trade around the industrial estates of Essex.

He came a-cropper in February 1995. He had put on a number of large – and highly correlated – naked short positions. When the gamble started to go wrong, with the price of the stocks he had shorted continuing to rise, Gary doubled his bet rather than unwind it and take his loss on the chin. He doubled up, moreover, in secret, by-passing the rather rudimentary controls we had in the firm in those early days. Naturally, when I found out what he had done, I dismissed him.

We were fortunate to have money flowing rapidly into our funds just then and we were able to use them to ensure that, despite Gary's cock-up, our investors continued to see the constant returns they expected. At such an early point in Kellaway & Co.'s history, our reputation would have been irredeemably harmed had we be unable to protect them. I had to work like a demented Stakhanovite, for long hours after the rest of the team had gone home, to achieve this result.

I replaced Rackenford with a young Frenchman named Fabrice. He had a strong Marseille accent, a very limited trading record and a CV with more holes in it than a prize Emmenthal cheese, but I liked his attitude and gave him a job. The others nicknamed him 'Win-Win' because of his irrationally optimistic view of every imaginable situation. Fabrice – Win-Win – made good profits for us in the money markets, particularly after he worked out how they really worked and got to know some of the people involved in the daily setting of key rates as well as some useful little facts about them that they would never wish to see exposed to the clear light of a sunny morning. He still works for me, my longest-serving and most trusted employee. That was the positive side of Rackenford's departure.

Less than a fortnight after Gary had cleared his desk and walked silently out of the office with his accumulated personal belongings in a black bin-bag, I took a call from his wife. Gary was in hospital, she said. He had tried to hang himself from the rafters in his garage, but had fumbled the attempt. The wife, a former nurse, had found him dangling from the rope but still alive, cut him down and called for an ambulance.

Gary learned the lessons from his failed suicide attempt. He was still without a job in May and tried again. This time he succeeded; he was dead by the time his wife found him. She phoned me again on a Friday afternoon several days later, but I had already heard the news of Gary's death by then and did not take her call. There was something else on my mind.

7

Dear Nicholas,

You did not reply to my last letter many years ago and sometimes I wonder if perhaps you never received it. If you did not then this letter will be a shock to you. I wonder if you remember me and those days we spent on the island of Ios. I am unable to forget you. This is because I have your face before me every day of my life.

Torvald was born on 10 May 1972. Yesterday was his twenty-third birthday. I have brought him up on my own. It has been a struggle but I have never asked you for anything – until now.

Torvald is good at mathematics and computers and has a job in a bank. It is a good position, but he is at risk of losing it. This is because he is also mixed up in a terrible black-metal scene. They have burnt down churches and there have been stabbings and shootings. Torvald is fascinated by guns and knives and is becoming more and more sucked into this cult. Sometimes he has come home with bruises on his body and once he had to go to hospital with a knife wound. Whatever happens he is unable to resist these people. He is becoming silent and withdrawn from all except number puzzles and this evil scene. He needs to leave Norway.

He does not know who you are. I only told him that you were Swiss – what you told me. He once said that if he ever found you, he would kill you. I was frightened by his voice and said no more.

I read about your new bank in the newspaper. You are probably rich, but I am not asking you for money – only that you might be able to arrange something for Torvald to get him away from these people. I am sure he could be very successful in a new environment. He is very good at mathematics and he is valued for this at the bank where he works. I remember you were studying mathematics at Oxford.

Nicholas, please help us.

Yours sincerely,

Hilde Nielsen

I did not move a muscle for fifteen minutes after reading Hilde's letter. I sat in my chair at my desk and re-read it. I don't know how many times I read it. By the time I folded the letter, put it back in its envelope and put the envelope in the inside pocket of my jacket, I could probably have recited the entire text of the letter verbatim. I had no idea what to do next. What I did do was go to see Colin.

Colin and I knew each other's secrets. Not all of them – that's clear now – but enough, Colin had once said, to hang the other. He had been with me on Ios. He had turned to me for help when Anna turned up in London wanting to rob a bank. More recently, when I was starting Kellaway & Co. and needed to open a Swiss bank account, it was Colin's help I had sought, the technical knowledge of account-opening formalities and money transfers he had acquired during the fallow years of his career.

"I thought you knew everything there was to know about Switzerland," he had said.

"Not about this."

"Why do you need it?"

"The small problem of tax." It was a matter of justice, really, equity in the best sense of the word. What is not widely appreciated is that Britain was, for many years, a tax haven – at least if you were not British. If you could claim non-domicile status then you were able to get away with paying taxes only on your UK-sourced income. If your home country regarded you as resident in the UK, and subject to UK tax jurisdiction, you did not pay taxes at home either. Then hey presto! You'd arbitraged different countries' definitions of 'domicile' and 'residence' and saved yourself a pretty packet – especially if you were a Greek ship owner or a Russian oligarch, a French footballer or a Pakistani terrorist. It didn't apply to someone like me, someone of good old British stock. I was meant to bear the full tax burden. It's obvious why I didn't consider the system equitable. With the prospect of international funds and an international clientele at Kellaway & Co., I saw an opportunity to recalibrate the scales of justice. I would squirrel away in a tax-free Swiss account exactly – and not a penny more – the difference between my tax bill, had I been not domiciled in the UK, and my theoretical British tax bill had I declared everything to the Inland Revenue.

"Sounds perfectly reasonable to me," Colin had said.

I showed Colin the letter from Hilde. He read it very slowly.

"What," I asked, "do I do?"

"I don't know, Nick," he said. "This is a guy's worst nightmare, isn't it? Not only have you sired a kid, but it sounds like the bastard's grown up to be a psycho. Have you told Caroline?"

"No."

"You'll have to, Nick."

"A guy can't help it if a girl's contraception fails."

After discussing it for nearly an hour, we decided I would tell Caroline, let her read the letter. We decided that Claire should know as well. Caroline would, Colin reasoned, tell her anyway, even if I didn't take the initiative. Caroline and I would come round to dinner at the Witheridges' that evening. We would discuss the whole 'Torvald thing', as Colin put it, openly over a few bottles of wine, work out together what to do. It would be easier that way, Colin reasoned. "It could have been any of us, Nick. It was me in that fertility chapel, don't forget."

That evening, after Héloïse had gone upstairs to bed, the four of us devised a plan. I think, in retrospect, that it was Claire, well briefed by Colin, who was the plan's chief architect. Her cold, forensic analysis of the situation also, I think, blunted any potential outburst from Caroline. As Caroline and I walked home afterwards, the warm evening air smelling of flowers, I said, "I'm sorry, darling. Please forgive me."

Caroline took my hand, squeezed it, said, "There's no need even to ask. It was a long time ago."

"Caro, do you think we're right not to bring him to England?"

"Absolutely. No question about it."

On Sunday morning I began to put our plan into action. I phoned a friend who worked then for UBS in Zürich who, on the personal tally sheets that hang around City necks, owed me a major favour. It took considerable pressure, probably tipped the favour scales slightly in his direction, but he agreed to try. On Thursday he phoned to say I was clear to make the next move in the Torvald game.

I phoned Hilde on the Oslo number she had written at the top of her letter. The voice on the other end of the line was weighed down by stale aquavit and cigarettes and echoed in a dingy room that cried out for sunshine and fresh air. "I am alone," she said, "so we can talk freely, Nicholas."

Hilde listened as I outlined the plan. Essentially, it consisted of a work permit and a job in a Swiss bank on a salary worth nearly double what Torvald was earning in Norway.

"I will try," Hilde said, "and then I will let you know."

"Do you think he will agree?"

"There is a chance. Torvald always tells people he is half-Swiss. Are you sure you do not want to meet him?"

"I have agreed with my wife that I will not."

"Okay, then. A photograph, perhaps?"

"No. No, thank you."

When Hilde phoned back the next day she said, "Torvald said yes."

"Anything else?"

"Not much. He is not a very communicative boy. He just said it would be cool to live in a country called 'Helvete'."

When the conversation staggered to its end, when neither of us had anything left to say to the other and when I had replaced the receiver into its cradle, I wrote out a cheque for £10,000 and sent it to Hilde. She never cashed it.

8

Colin was away from home far more than I was. I put this to Caroline as evidence in my defence. Caroline had come up to London to spend a couple of days in the Mayfair flat and we were having dinner at Nobu. "I never hear Claire complaining," I argued, "and Héloïse seems just fine."

"Please at least have the courtesy to listen to me. This isn't about Claire and your blessèd Héloïse," she retorted. "It's about us. Us and *our* children…"

Colin's business thrived during the nineties. He had clients in the United States – big companies like Mobil, Exxon and Enron – and a growing number in Russia that few people had yet heard of. He met the Russians at places of their choosing: Moscow, Eze, Courchevel, Geneva, Cyprus… When he met his Russian clients in London he often spent the night afterwards in my flat to sleep off the effects. The first time he visited, he walked slowly round the rooms. "Am I drunk or mistaken, Nick," he eventually asked, "or is this the flat you were talking about in Santorini that night Kupferhoden threw the glass at you?" In the bedroom he paused before the painting of the elongated nude that hung above the bed. "That's not the choir girl, is it?"

After the Russian debt crisis broke in 1998, Colin was away even more often than before. Kellaway & Co. made a tidy fortune for its investors shorting the Rouble in the six weeks prior to the readjustment of its trading band on 17 August 1998. The irrational spike in volatility that summer was good for us in other markets too. Others, including big names with big computers and very rational Nobel Prize winners at the helm, were not so fortunate. Long Term Capital Management was only the most famous of the casualties. Colin's position was also different than ours. He was very long Russia.

Largely through his efforts, Colin's employer had become one of the major western bankers to the Russian oil industry. Colin owed his spectacular bonuses in the mid-nineties to those efforts. Another department in his bank, attracted by the high interest rates, invested heavily in Russian sovereign debt. Yet another department was long Russian stocks when the Moscow Stock Exchange plummeted. This accumulation of correlated risk positions, apparently lacking common oversight, had the potential to bring the bank down. "Even things John Meriwether had never thought of turned out to be correlated," Colin said, "things his merry computers hadn't modelled in a trillion years of black-hole scenarios." Then they discovered that some of the more creative players in the bank had, in the expectation of enhancing their bonus packages, reclassified large chunks of Russian exposure as Swiss or Dutch or French. True exposure to Russia had shot dramatically through the prudential country limits that the risk committee and the board had set.

Colin, the fluent Russian-speaker, earned his even larger bonuses over the following years trying to sort it all out, keeping the bankruptcy wolves from the door, flying between far-flung meetings with grumpy oligarchs and corrupt government officials. "He calls me at least once day," Claire said, "but it's always from a mobile and often I don't even know where he's calling from. Once I said, 'Colin, where are you?' and he went, 'I don't know. Some hotel room somewhere.'"

One bright Sunday morning – it was November 1999 and I had forgotten our twenty-first wedding anniversary not long before – I joined Caroline and Claire on a walk among the golden beech woods out in the Surrey hills. Héloïse came too. Héloïse was born on 20 February 1986, so in 1999 she would have been thirteen, just on the cusp of metamorphosing from gorgeous child into gorgeous teenager. Colin, who had flown in overnight from New York, decided to spend the morning in bed.

Caroline and Claire strode out ahead. Once they were out of earshot, Héloïse asked, "Uncle Nick, can I, like, ask you a question?"

"Of course."

"Okay, then. Here it is. Have you ever, like, slept with my mummy?"

"Héloïse! What a question!"

"It's all right, Uncle Nick. I know about these things. If I can't talk to my godfather, who *can* I talk to?"

"What do you think you know about?"

"I know you wanted to marry her."

"That is *not* true, Héloïse. It would never occur to me to marry Claire."

"Whatever... I also know Daddy slept with Aunty Caroline."

"Do you, now?"

"I know about sex, Uncle Nick. I mean, like, I've done it, you know."

"Hmm."

"And I know about Torvald."

"Who told you about that?"

"Nobody."

"Then how do you know?"

"Well, like, you know, I was listening that night you and Aunty Caroline came round and talked about packing him off to Switzerland. I mean, we have this, like, listening sort of thing. Mummy and Daddy used it to listen to me when I was a baby upstairs and they were, like, downstairs. I sort of like reversed it so when I'm upstairs I can hear what's going on downstairs."

We had lunch at The Stephen Langton in Friday Street. Safe in the knowledge that Claire was driving, I drank three pints of beer and was put in the back seat of the car, like a naughty little schoolboy, for the journey home. At some point before I fell asleep, Héloïse, the naughty little schoolgirl, took hold of my hand, folded the palm of her hand around my index finger and squeezed.

Colonel Charles Stoodleigh Carter died on 20 January 2001. He had risen that morning before six and at first light taken the dogs for a walk. The dogs returned home alone. They led Caroline's mother to her husband's body, lying on the damp grass not a hundred yards from the house. The pathologists recorded a heart attack as the cause of death. He was eighty-six. Caroline and I were in Norfolk before nightfall. I read all the obituaries that came my way, surprised by how little I found I knew about my father-in-law, by how little I had bothered to find out. "Darling," I said. "I didn't know your father had been awarded the VC."[72]

"Nor did I."

"What do you mean?"

"Just that. I knew he'd been wounded at Montecassino, but he never spoke of the circumstances. Certainly never about his medals."

"He wasn't embarrassed about them, was he?"

"He hated war, but, no, I'm sure he wasn't at all embarrassed about them. It was just that, well, he wasn't a self-publicist. It wasn't the way he did things."

It was a season of death and disappointment. A week after we buried Colonel Carter, my mother died. A fortnight later, Colin's mother, widowed almost as long ago as my own mother, passed away. Robert's girlfriend was killed in a car crash in Leeds. The pyres of foot and mouth disease turned Britain into Dante's *Inferno*, acrid smoke from burning corpses polluting the land. Jane Fonda, looking rather older than in *Barbarella*, announced she had become a Christian. The NASDAQ – the junior stock exchange in New York favoured by the dot-com stocks, shining hopes of the new millennium – peaked and slid into purgatory.

9

Caroline left me in that miserable spring of 2001. I suspected her mother's influence. There was no drama involved; nothing that in a rational world would have warranted the severity of her action. I had simply been unable to keep a promise to take Henry back to school after his Easter holidays.

"He'd really like you to do it, Nick," Caroline had said. "It's so much cooler than being dropped off at the school gates by his mother."

---

[72] The VC – the Victoria Cross – is Britain's (and many Commonwealth countries') highest military award. It is awarded for "conspicuous bravery, or some daring or pre-eminent act of valour of self-sacrifice, or extreme devotion to duty in the presence of the enemy". – Ed.

But *all* promises carry an implicit caveat: they are promises only unless an overriding business reason intervenes. 'City Rules', as we used to call them. Caroline, without a grumble, assumed my duties as chauffeur. When she returned to Weybridge that evening, she phoned me on my mobile. "Nick," she said, "you've got to stop playing Peter Pan. There are some big choices to make and until you've made them, you can stay up in London. I'll pack your things and get them sent to you."

Twenty-eight and a half years since Paestum, twenty-two and a half years of marriage, three kids and a wife more than amply provided for, and that was that: a ninety-second conversation as I walked along Curzon Street wondering what single malts I had in the flat, wondering whether it was an Islay evening or one for Speyside.

Nothing I threw at Caroline over the following weeks hit its target. Eventually, I gave up trying, decided to sit it out, wait for a little time to pass. I was, after all, not entirely uncomfortable. I had my work with the Lost Boys of Kellaway & Co. to keep me busy and word soon got round the ladies that I had a sexy flat in Mayfair and was generous with my credit card. Hey! What's an anti-fascist with lead in his pencil meant to do?

Then came the problem of the summer holidays.

We have a rule at Kellaway & Co. that every employee has to take a fortnight's break each year and that during that time there should be no contact with the office. If contact is unavoidable, it must be logged and signed by the person on holiday *and* the person he or she has contacted in the office. You might think this was a kind humanitarian policy of mine – a gentle, paternal insistence that everyone spend an uninterrupted two weeks of quality time with the family each year, away from the frantic pace of the office, recharging their batteries, vacuuming their upholstery, polishing their chrome work, filing the heads of their spark plugs, adjusting the balance of their wheels and whatever else one is meant to do to keep the machine on the road and performing to manufacturer's specification. Sometimes I portrayed it as such. In fact, it was a rule designed to ensure that anyone who might have his or her hand systematically in the till would be caught. It was not genius proof, but it was fool proof. Leaving a garden unattended for two weeks is usually enough time for the weeds to germinate, for most scams to come to light. As owner of Kellaway & Co., I could have exempted myself from the rule, but as a matter of principle, I didn't. I have a fiduciary responsibility for the funds we manage and I needed to be seen to take that seriously. As usual I, too, would take a summer holiday. I was, however, far too streetwise to take with me one of the dames mesmerised by the shine on my credit card.

It was Adam Heggie, my old housemate from Balham Days, who came up with the solution to my problem. I had not seen Adam for years – probably only twice since the morning he turned up at my Islington flat bearing Mao Tse-Tung and Freud. In the intervening years, Adam had married a woman who had fallen in love with his poetry. It lasted less than two years. He never remarried. He left his Iraqi employer soon after I left Balham and worked his way through a series of more mainstream banks, but his moves were not well thought out and his banking career stalled. Nevertheless, he was still at it, despite being over fifty, toiling away in the dark recesses of some retail bank's credit department. On the side, he had written a failed pornographic novel (*Sex with Fat Girls*), made a minor name for himself as a poet and, more recently, a somewhat larger name as the author of a polemic advocating mass euthanasia to solve the country's pension crisis. He would attract further notoriety with his publications on Saddam Hussein and on paedophilia and sexual rights for all, but the evening I ran into him those works were still in the future.

I was standing just inside the door of a Soho curry house, waiting to be shown to a table, when I felt a tap on my shoulder. "What," Adam said, "is the great Nicholas Kellaway doing down in a dive like this?"

"Adam," I exclaimed, grasping his right hand, my left on his shoulder, "you're still alive! I thought you'd been assassinated by a hit squad from Help the Aged."

We shared a table and, over biryanis and a couple of lagers, Adam introduced me to the arrangement he had used several times to solve the holiday problem, most recently for a spring break in Iraq, where, he said, they understood the concept. "You pay all the costs, airfares, hotel bills, food, extras, the lot. Plus something like, look, a thousand quid or so as a gratuity. There are agency fees on top, of course, but you can deal direct and avoid those." He put on his reading glasses, consulted his pocket diary, wrote two telephone numbers on a scrap of paper he dug out of his jacket pocket. "The top one's direct," he said. "Nice girl, Polish, about twenty-eight, PhD in English literature. Tell her Adam sent you. Look, take her out for a nice dinner and if you don't like what you see…" Adam shrugged his shoulders. "… no hard feelings. Then the bottom number's the agency. They've got a niche and they know their market."

"Not one of your fatsoes, is she?

"Careful there." Adam spread his hands out over the table between us, palms upwards as if comparing the weight of two different objects. He lifted his right hand. "Fact," he said, looking at it. Then he lifted his left hand and nodded to it, "Fiction." Then, looking at me, he added, "Don't muddle them, Nick." When I said nothing in response he added, "Are you still keeping that book of your dreams?"

"Occasionally. Nothing like the same regularity, though. I'm too busy."

"That's probably a good thing. For your mental health at least. Anyway, if fat's what you're looking for, this one's not for you. Compared to the ones I made up in *Fat Girls*, she's concentration-camp thin."

"Name?"

"Ewa. With a 'w', as in George Dubbya Bush. She's Polish. Surname of Brown. Her father was an American who defected."

"Ewa Brown. I like it. Flying off to South America with Ewa Brown. Maybe I'll grow a moustache for the occasion."[73]

"I think she's probably heard that one before."

Ewa Brown had bright blue eyes and hair streaked with blonde. "Short for sport," she said. She was athletic and flexible, tall – maybe three inches taller than me – and nicely built. She didn't smile much but her English, as you would expect given her paternal and educational pedigrees, was impeccable. And she boasted other attributes that were quite definitely peccable.

Ewa thought that two weeks touring Brazil sounded attractive. We agreed on a gratuity of £2000 on top of all costs. "Up front," she said, "and in cash. Then I don't charge VAT."

I went out to Weybridge, at a time when I knew Caroline and the kids would be away, to collect some things I thought I might need for the beach. I could have bought new beach wear, but – well – I

---

[73] Eva Anna Paula Braun (1912–1945) was Adolf Hitler's mistress and, for the last few hours of their lives, his wife. They married in Berlin in the early hours of 29 April 1945. The next day, 30 April 1945, in the afternoon, Mr and Mrs Hitler committed suicide. Mrs Hitler was thirty-three. Her husband was fifty-six. – Ed.

wanted to have a quick squint around the old house, to see if there had been any what you might call 'changes' during my enforced absence. Before locking up the house, leaving it just as I had found it, even Jan's old guitar still standing in its corner, I phoned Colin. He was, he said, home alone.

Colin was barefoot, wearing faded blue jeans and a navy-blue boating jacket over a grey polo shirt – the same clothes he had worn the last time I had seen him, on our booze cruise to Calais. We went to his study. "My space," he said. Three empty French beer bottles sat on the desk beside his old typewriter.

"You've still got that old thing? The same one you had at Oxford?"

"This?" Colin asked, touching the typewriter. "It's part of me. With these computers it's all work. With this baby," he caressed the side of his machine, "it's pure pleasure. I still have the Russian one as well."

As we sat in his study drinking beer, I exaggerated the pleasures of the single life in Mayfair, told him of my plans to do a Voltaire, to cultivate my Brazilian garden with Peccability Brown, repeated the joke about growing a moustache.

"D'you use your Swiss account to pay for these little trips?" Colin asked.

"No. Why should I?"

"Out of Caroline's sight. Offshore money. Tax free. Cheaper…"

I smiled. "I don't worry about that sort of thing these days. Funds go into Geneva. Nothing comes out. Safer that way."

"Probably right. No fingerprints. The taxman's getting more vigilant and there's political pressure on the Swiss. They pretend it's about the Nazis, but it's really nothing more than greed. 'As long as the State exists there is no Freedom.'"

"Lenin. *The State and Revolution*. 1917."

Colin nodded appreciatively, stretched back in his chair, took a swig from his bottle. "Well, well," he said, grinning. "So Fuck-a-Lass goes to Brazil. *Sex macht frei.*"

"What?"

"He who sleeps with the same woman twice has joined the bourgeoisie."

"What's all this about?"

"Nothing. Just another of those pot-head slogans from the good old bonobo days. Don't mind me. There are other roads to freedom, you know."

"Like money?"

"Money can't buy you love."

"But it helps."

"So does imagination and... and... death. And the old ruby-red grapefruit Revolution, of course. Roads to freedom, Fuckaway, roads to freedom... you remember that? 'Fuckolas Fuckaway'? Santorini? Kupferhoden? Tough German guy? He's dead, you know. Shot and left to rot on a Berlin bomb site."

"By the German security services," I said, hoping subtly to indicate insider knowledge.

"Ah. Is that it? Still the old Cold War certainties?" Colin looked at me, took a long swig of beer. "Nick, old man, I have it on the best of fucking authority that it was not the Pigs – as we'd've called them then."

"Who then?"

A long pause. Colin's next words may or may not have been an answer to my question, "Remember the name Anastasia Kuznetsova?"

"Anna Schmidt?"

"Maybe," Colin said after a long pause. "Anna lives in Brazil now. Can you imagine it? Anna Rotten in the country of her adopted father."

"Are you still in touch?"

Colin took a fat English–Russian dictionary out of his bookcase, reached into the space where it had stood, took a key that was taped to the underside of the shelf and opened one of the drawers in his desk with it. He pulled the drawer out to its full extent, removed a panel, a cleverly concealed false back to the drawer, and withdrew a small bundle of papers. He leafed through the papers and handed me a photograph. "Remember that?" he asked.

The picture was the one of himself, Nigel and me standing outside the Dionysian fertility chapel in Crete. On the back, Anna had written 'The Three Musketeers – Kreta, 1971'. She had sent me a copy of the same picture.

"Are you still in touch with Nigel?"

Colin nodded, continued looking through his private stash of photographs. "Still happily farming. He's not changed much. Except that he's balder than either of us now." He paused and looked up at me – probably to see if I'd caught the oblique reference to – the pun on – his old 'Balder' nickname. "Remember how you asked him whether his dad was a kulak?" He laughed at the memory. "You were hilarious, Fuckolas. You were looking at England and saw a textbook image of the Ukraine in the thirties. A right little Stalin you were. Utilitarianism writ large. 'Individual lives don't matter. It's the purity of the goal that counts.' Remember that? Nick Kellaway, Oxford, 1970. I suspect Nick Kellaway hasn't changed much either. It's just that your goalposts have shifted."

The second photograph Colin handed me was another of himself, older now, wearing sunglasses, his arm around the shoulder of a woman also wearing sunglasses. The woman's hair was dyed blonde, probably naturally grey. Earrings dangled from her earlobes. Colin and the woman seemed to be sitting on a bench with tropical vegetation in the background. I turned it over. On the back, Colin had written 'Florianópolis, 1995'. Colin winked his conspiratorial wink. "I've been to Brazil, too," he said.

"Who's the woman?" I asked. She didn't look like Anna Schmidt. But then, by 1995 nearly twenty years would have passed since I'd last seen Anna.

"D'you wanna guess? I'll give you a clue: it's not Jeff Skilling."

Before I could offer a name, Colin had handed me another picture. "French," he said. "Probably the most beautiful thing I've ever set eyes on." The picture was of the head and bare shoulders of a drop-dead gorgeous black girl.[74]

"'Once you've had black…'"

"Colin Witheridge. Durban. 1969. You remember. Well done." Colin began to hum the tune of 'House of the Rising Sun'. Then, after opening another two bottles of beer, he sang.

---

[74] Véronique Lalionne was born in Sénégal in 1976 or 1977. Her family immigrated to France in 1981 where she grew up in HLM tower blocks in the eastern *quartiers* of Paris. At the age of seventeen she won a major beauty contest and was spotted by, and began to work for, a number of leading *couturier* houses. She achieved national prominence in France as the face of a milk marketing campaign in 1996 and 1997 with the most provocative advertising seen on the streets of Paris since Myriam (*Demain j'enlève le bas*) had illuminated the nation's billboards. In 1998, she landed her first major film role, playing the prostitute in J.-P. Delmas' film *La Boussole de Poitiers*. Her subsequent and very public conversion to Islam, the religion of her Malinké forebears, and her espousal of the campaign for the rights of Muslim women in France to wear clothing appropriate to their religion shocked the French secular establishment. In 2000 Véronique Lalionne announced her intention to be the first female president of the Islamic Republic of France – 'The Sixth Republic' – before she was fifty. She has not been seen in public since early 2001. – Ed.

And all you need for travellin', man
Is a rucksack and a gun.
And the only time I'm satisfied's
In the House of the Risin' Sun.

It was only then, I think, that I realised Colin was drunk.

I chartered a plane, to avoid the possible complications of being seen at Heathrow, and flew to Brazil with Ewa Brown, my upper lip still clean-shaven. I travelled unarmed and with a new suitcase I bought for the trip instead of a battered old rucksack. Football, the national sport of Brazil, is a game of two halves, they say, and so was my holiday with Mrs Hitler: cool in Copacabana, naked in Niteroi, randy in Rio; pedestrian in Paraty, ignored in Iguaçu, mugged in Muriqui, garrotted in Ipanema.

CHAPTER EIGHT

"Nick. It's your wife on the phone."

"Caroline?"

"Is there another one?"

"Put her through, but don't go home before we've nailed down this trip to New York, okay?"

It was a few minutes before six on a Friday afternoon in September. We were gearing up Kellaway & Co.'s autumn campaign. I was booked on a Saturday flight to New York and the appointments in the diary started early on the Monday morning: Goldman Sachs, the Morgans (JP *and* Stanley), Cantor Fitzgerald, Citi, Lehman, Bear Stearns, Harriman's… We would then move on to a round of presentations to investment consultants with big pension fund accounts, followed by visits to our existing American clients and a big NASDAQ market maker who was setting up a fund of funds to supplement his order-flow income. It was, as usual, all extremely well orchestrated.

I had not seen Caroline for nearly five months, nor spoken to her since two days after my visit to Weybridge to pick up my swimming trunks, when she had phoned to tell me she'd had the locks changed.

I went into my office, closed the door, sat down behind my protective desk, counted to ten and picked up the phone. "Caro," I said, "good of you to phone."

"Nick," she said – no preliminary niceties, "Colin's disappeared."

"Sorry?"

"Colin's disappeared. He went on a business trip and he hasn't come home." Caroline sounded like a long-distance runner on the verge of collapse.

"Caro. Slow down. Where did he go?"

"He never checked out of his hotel room, and, when he didn't show for a few days, the hotel staff called the police. Most of his stuff was still in his room. Oh, Nick, you've got to come home. We've got to help Claire and Héloïse."

"When was all this?"

"Three days ago. Tuesday. That's when the police called."

"When did Claire last hear from Colin?"

"Saturday. Saturday morning. She's been phoning his mobile but it's switched off. Just come home, Nick. I don't want to do this on the phone."

"Darling, hang on a moment. Where did all this happen?"

"Geneva."

Eventually, I tossed a coin: heads, Weybridge; tails, New York. It came up heads, but I fudged the verdict. "Linda, could you change the New York flight to Sunday late afternoon, please?"

Only when I was on the train, letting the familiar motion of the iron wheels on the iron rails lull me into a partial sleep, did my thoughts move away from New York to Weybridge. It belatedly struck me that Caroline had asked me to come home. *Oh, Nick, you've got to come home. Just come home, Nick.* There we are in our bedroom, the Modigliani of Caroline that is neither of Caroline nor by Modigliani hanging on the wall above the bed. Caroline undresses, lets her clothes fall to the floor where she stands. She is telling me something Robert has done at school, that Amanda wants to start piano lessons, that Henry would like me to take him to his cricket match on Saturday morning. I kiss her as she speaks...

Colin often went to Geneva in those days. "It must have been amazing growing up there, Nick," he had said once. "You know, I don't need to be in London. We could base ourselves in Geneva. Héloïse could go to that school you went to. Sailing in the summer. Skiing in the winter. What a life! Claire would love it."

Colin went to Geneva mainly to meet his Russian clients. His job as an energy banker had given him his original contacts in the days of what was euphemistically called Russia's 'auto-privatisation'. Then, when one of his early contacts in the kleptocracy discovered that he not only had hard currency to lend, but that he also spoke Russian, word spread and his client base expanded rapidly. "I learned it back in my Oxford days," he said to them. "You know, language of the proletariat and all that." They laughed, knocked back their Swedish vodka and toasted the follies of youth.

Not phoning, not checking out of his hotel room, the people he dealt with? "The majority," Colin had said once, "are very nice people. It's just that when they're speaking a foreign language they can sound a bit gruff." *What about the minority? The Mensheviks were nice; but what about the Bolsheviks? The men of steel?* But not in Geneva, surely. They would do their dirty work elsewhere and keep Geneva clean.

Caroline opened the front door and gave me a single kiss on the cheek. "Thanks for coming, Nick," she said, as if I were an itinerant plumber.

Claire, Héloïse and Henry were sitting at the dining-room table. Empty teacups and a milky way of plates and crumbs, papers and Post-It notes were scattered across its surface. Héloïse was fifteen now, as gorgeous as ever, but like her mother she looked pale and anxious. Henry seemed unable to keep his eyes off her. He had just returned from backpacking in India. Caroline told me later that it was Henry who had asked her to phone me.

"Uncle Colin was in Geneva when he vanished, right?" Henry had argued. "Dad knows Geneva."

"That was a long time ago," Caroline had said.

"He should be here anyway," Henry had retorted. "Uncle Colin is his best friend." He had insisted I come home, said he would phone me himself if he had to.

The papers and Post-It notes on the dining-room table were the pieces of the jigsaw puzzle. Claire had been to Geneva and spoken to the police and the hotel staff. She had been up to London and gathered more pieces from Colin's secretary.

- On the morning of Wednesday, 29 August, a taxi had picked Colin up at his home and driven him to Heathrow. He had packed the night before and gone quietly, waking neither Claire nor Héloïse.
- He took the first flight to Geneva and went by taxi to the Hotel de la Paix. He checked in but, as it was early and his room not yet ready, he left his suitcase with the *concièrge* and went out, carrying only his briefcase.
- Colin's electronic office diary for that Wednesday showed a late morning meeting with a Russian client, lunch with another Russian at the Pavillon de Ruth and a meeting at four o'clock with a man who may have been a Central Asian. The two Russians confirmed that Colin had met them at the appointed times and places. The third man had not yet been traced.
- Sometime between five and six o'clock, Colin returned to his hotel, reclaimed his bag from the *concièrge* and carried it up to his room. He phoned Claire at six twenty-three, Geneva time.

- The hotel staff saw Colin leave the hotel on foot shortly after seven. He had changed from his suit and tie into casual clothes.
- The diary showed a dinner appointment at Le Béarn with two British energy traders based in Geneva. They confirmed the meeting and said that they and Colin had left the restaurant before ten o'clock, each going his separate way.
- The hotel staff did not recall Colin returning to the hotel that night. But he did sleep in his room. There was no evidence of anyone having been in the room with him. He took breakfast on his own, downstairs, the next morning. The breakfast bill was timed at seven forty. On Friday, the following day, the bill was timed at seven forty-three. The police commented, with evident approval, that this was the sign of a man following a disciplined routine.
- Colin's diary for Thursday, 30 August, was empty until lunchtime. For lunch he met an American, an employee in the finance department of a big oil company. He met a minor Saudi prince who was a personal client of his bank (though not on Colin's client list) and a Russian lawyer in the afternoon. All three confirmed that the meetings in the diary had taken place.
- The diary entry for dinner on Thursday read '19:30. Andropov. His place'. Mr Andropov's office confirmed that the boss had spent that evening at his Geneva home. They could not confirm the names of his guests, if any. The servants at the house said he had had only one guest. They described him as British and middle-aged, but did not know his name.
- Colin kept both of the appointments he had on the morning of Friday, 31 August, one at Meyer & Cie at eight fifteen, and another, late morning, with yet another Russian client. There was a long gap in the diary between the two appointments. Colin used his credit card to buy lunch, apparently, to judge by the amount of his bill, only for himself, at the Café de Paris, near Cornavin station. The time of the bill was two thirty.
- When the police spoke to the waiter at the Café de Paris, he identified Colin from the photo that he was shown and confirmed that Colin had taken lunch alone. He added that Colin had, for his last fifteen minutes in the restaurant, been

joined at his table by a woman. The waiter remembered bringing a glass for her to help Colin finish his bottle of wine – a good Burgundy. Colin and the woman had left together. The description of the woman provided by the waiter had been vague and she had not been traced.

- For Friday afternoon and all day Saturday, Sunday and Monday, Colin's diary showed 'Montreux?'. Colin had told Claire he would be away over the weekend because of a conference. Caroline and Claire had tracked down, through his website, an American who ran energy conferences in Montreux. He had no conferences organised for that weekend, but perhaps, he said, others did. Caroline and Claire had not yet pursued that line of enquiry. It seemed unlikely to yield anything.

- At two minutes to three on Friday afternoon, Colin used his credit card at Cornavin. The amount charged to his card was exactly the equivalent of two first-class return rail fares from Geneva to Montreux. Colin phoned Claire from his mobile phone at three forty-two. Although he did not say where he was, Claire had the distinct impression he was on a train.

- Colin's reservation at the Hotel de la Paix was for the nights of Wednesday, 29 August, to Monday, 3 September, inclusive. He did not sleep in the room on the night of Friday, 31 August, nor on any of the following nights. The room had been left neat and ordered and there was no evidence of unauthorised entry, but there was also no money, no credit card, no passport, no mobile phone, no computer in the room. Nor was his briefcase found. From two suits, a clean white shirt, three ties and a pair of leather shoes left in the wardrobe it was deduced that Colin had gone, to Montreux or wherever, in his casual clothes. The police had a description of the casual clothes that Colin had taken to Geneva from the two energy traders he had dined with on Wednesday evening, although their descriptions differed. One said his shirt was blue. The other said it was green. Claire said that Colin didn't have a green shirt.

- Colin phoned Claire on the morning of Saturday, 1 September, at ten thirty, English time; eleven thirty Swiss time. Claire told the police he sounded "Happy, relaxed, flippant, almost light-headed". The conversation lasted four minutes and was the last phone call logged for Colin's mobile. No other calls were made or received that Saturday morning. He told Claire that he would phone back in the evening to speak to Héloïse. He never made that call.

- Records showed that Colin had made, either from his mobile or the hotel room, seventeen other phone calls on Thursday and Friday in addition to his conversations with Claire. Nine were to his office in London, three were to numbers in Moscow, one to a number in Houston and the rest to local Swiss numbers, some landlines, some mobiles. Those numbers that could be traced related to appointments in his diary. He had received thirty incoming calls, mostly from his secretary in London.

- Colin had six appointments in his diary for Tuesday, 4 September 2001: one at UBS, one with an Arab diplomat, another with an Arab who described himself as a weather trader, two with Russian clients and one with an American. Each of those contacted, except the American, confirmed that he had not kept his appointment. The American could not be found. The company he allegedly worked for in Houston had no record of him. Nor did Colin catch the last BA flight from Geneva to Heathrow, on which he was booked.

- On Monday morning, the hotel alerted the Swiss police to the fact that Colin's room had not been used for three nights. The Swiss police contacted their British counterparts later that day. On Tuesday morning, 4 September, the British police contacted Claire. A man and woman, both in uniform, came unannounced to the door. Claire's first call, when the police had gone, was to Caroline. On Wednesday, Claire flew to Geneva.

2

"What do you think?" Caroline asked.

I knew what I thought, of course. Only one of the names on Claire's Post-It notes had meant anything to me, but that one was enough. Vladimir Ivanovich Andropov had not made his money playing Saturday night bingo or studying hard for his accountancy exams. There was trail leading from the oil fields of Siberia, by way of shadow companies in Cyprus and bank accounts in Geneva, to villas and yachts on the Côte d'Azur. Decaying bodies littered its hard shoulders. A *Financial Times* article shortly after Putin became president of Russia listed among the Russian government's top priorities 'Get Andropov' – if Andropov didn't get the government first.

Thursday, 30 August 2001. 19:30. Andropov. His place. Two days later, Colin had gone missing. When Héloïse, Claire and Henry had gone upstairs to bed and Caroline and I were left alone in the sitting room on opposite sides of the cold hearth, beneath Hodler's painting of the *Statue de la Bise* (then not yet exiled from the family home), I expressed my fears.

"Why the Russians?" Caroline asked. "Why not the Americans? He was thick with them as well. One of the Americans he met in Geneva was obviously lying about who he was. He went on those ski weekends in Chamonix, remember? You called them 'dubious'. That was an American outfit. You can't rule out the Americans."

"Americans don't do things like that."

"Don't they?"

Caroline dashed my hopes of being restored to my rightful position in bed. It had been a long day, she said, gave me another peck-for-the-plumber on the cheek. "There are too many things to deal with first, Nick. Sleep in Robert's room tonight." Three minutes later I found my bedroom door locked and a pair of my pyjamas on the floor outside. I took them, went to Robert's room, undressed and put on a pair of pyjamas that I had never worn. They had apparently belonged to Nicolae Ceaușescu and arrived anonymously in 1998, 'From one Nick to another'. I suspected Colin.

The bathroom at Robert's end of the corridor was in use. I waited. When the door was unlocked and opened, Héloïse emerged. She was wearing one of Amanda's dressing gowns. If she had anything on beneath it, it was not apparent. She seemed startled to see me. Her eyes and mouth opened wide.

"Uncle Nick," she said. "He's dead, isn't he?"

"You can't come to that conclusion, Héloïse."

She threw herself against me, put her arms around me.

"It's horrible. It's the Russians, isn't it, Uncle Nick?"

"Héloïse. Let's get some sleep and look at all this with clear heads in the morning. He'll probably turn up in the next few days and there will be some perfectly ordinary reason for why he's been out of touch. For now, let's just go to bed and drop off to sleep."

But for a minute, maybe two, Héloïse did not move. She stood holding tightly to me, her blonde head on my shoulder. Through Amanda's dressing gown and Ceauşescu's pyjamas, I could feel the contours of her body pressed against mine. Then, suddenly she pulled herself away, looked at me in astonishment, ran back to Amanda's room and locked the door. She had felt, pressing against her, the involuntary swelling of my erection.

Neither Saturday, Sunday nor Monday brought any further news of Colin. I rebooked my New York flight for Wednesday, cancelled the first three days of meetings, the ones with the banks and brokers. Claire and Héloïse continued to stay with us. We ran over the facts we knew, tried in vain to speak of other things. We phoned the number the police had given us for updates. At night Caroline kept her bedroom door locked. So did Héloïse. Henry had plans to go to South Wales to visit a friend. He would, he said, cancel the arrangement, but, when I discovered that the Welsh friend was a girl he had spent a week with on a beach in Kerala and recalled the looks he had given Héloïse, I encouraged him to make the trip. On Monday morning I drove him to Reading to catch the train west. "You'll let me know if you hear anything, won't you?" he said as he was getting out of the car.

"Of course we will."

When I returned home more papers and files had joined those already on the dining room table. Claire had brought them round from Colin's study. "I've got to be doing something," Claire said. "I can't just sit around. There are bank accounts here I knew nothing about." She was a forensic accountant, she said. She would go through them with a fine-tooth comb, looking for clues.

Clues. Pacing the sitting room floor. Colin's movements from Wednesday to Saturday memorised, plotted on maps and time charts. Colour-coded Post-It notes stuck to the wall. *Let's just go to bed, close our eyes Andropov to sleep.* Phone calls to Geneva that brought forth neither information nor confidence. Héloïse's suspicious glance. A suppressed scream. Crying out for oxygen. Waiting. Waiting. Waiting.

"Tomorrow," Claire said on Monday evening, "we'll look at the bank accounts. There are two Swiss accounts there I never even knew Colin had."

"Nick'll help you," Caroline offered. I had intended to go up to the office on Tuesday. "You were meant to be in New York, Nick," Caroline said, "so they won't miss you."

After Caroline and Héloïse went upstairs to their respective beds, Claire accepted my offer of a nightcap. I poured two generous measures of Laphraoig. After the first sip, she asked, "Nick, have you ever been into Colin's study?"

"A few times. Why?"

"When were you last in there?"

"Earlier in the summer. You were out playing tennis. Why do you ask?"

"This morning I just had this feeling… there's something different about it."

"Different? In what way?"

Claire sighed, sipped the whisky. "I'm probably just being silly. It's just that when I went in there to get some files, I had this funny impression like somebody…"

"So…"

Claire interrupted, "Then, when my brain was going like that, I thought, what if they've been in the other rooms as well? So I went looking around and up in our bedroom I had the same feeling. It was as if Colin had been back and taken some of his things."

"What's missing?"

"I don't know. Maybe nothing. How can I tell what's missing when I don't know what was there in the first place?"

"Did you tell the police?"

"Nick, do you think I'd know if Colin had a green shirt?"

"Another whisky?"

She stretched out the empty glass. Her hand was adorned only by a thin, gold wedding band. I remembered Héloïse asking, in the November woods above Friday Street, if I had wanted to marry Claire.

Tuesday morning after breakfast, Claire and I drove round to the Witheridges' house and went straight to Colin's study. "Everything's in this room," Claire said. "Where do we start? I've moved all the bank account and investment files. Work-related stuff's in that cabinet. That's just ordinary bills and stuff," she said pointing at another filing cabinet, "and that's full of stuff from his father. Inheritance. It's all beautifully filed but it's been untouched in there for twenty years. I can't believe how organised all this is. I was hardly ever in here. It was Colin's space." I noticed she used the past tense. She looked at the bookcase. "All these Russian books. He didn't want Russian books anywhere else in the house." In the clear light of morning she did not mention her concerns that the house had been tampered with. "Some of the desk drawers are locked. I have no idea where he keeps the key." Present tense again.

We started with what Claire called the 'work-related stuff'. There were copies of correspondence, Colin's employment contracts, payslips, bonus letters, appraisals. There were yellowing internal memoranda relating to the funds that went missing from Thomas Rotten's FMBB account in 1976, references, CVs, articles from newspapers and trade journals that had been carefully cut out and dated, a letter from Enron with joining instructions for a weekend in Chamonix. We found a pile of maps, including one of Moscow annotated with Xs and names, in Russian, beside them. We found copies of proposals Colin and colleagues had made to win business. Another file was labelled 'The Dirt'. We all had one of those, incriminating memos that could be brought out when a colleague needed to be knifed. But there was nothing, so far as I could see, that related to Andropov.

When Claire went to make tea, I looked for and found the key to the locked drawers taped to the underside of the bookshelf. I opened the drawer and removed the secret panel. The bundle of papers and photos, tied up in its elastic band, was still there. Was it thinner than when I had seen it earlier? At the top of the bundle I found the two pictures taken the summer we went to Crete, the *Three Musketeers* and the one I had taken of Colin and Anna by the church. 'To Colin, With love, Anna.' Colin was young. He would have been nineteen. Smiling eagerly, a very full head of hair bleached by saltwater and sun. It had been his first trip to the Mediterranean, his first journey south of the Alps.

Next in the bundle was an envelope. American stamp, illegible postmark. It was addressed to Colin at his office. No return address. Inside the envelope were two photographs. The first was of Anna, posing on what seemed to be a beach. There was sand in the background and the kind of grass that grows sparsely in the inhospitable environment of seashore dunes. Anna was naked, but discretely so. An arm was held across her breasts. Her other hand was splayed across her pubic hair. If she had not been posed like that by the photographer then the camera had caught Anna in a pose of uncharacteristic modesty. The photo had been inscribed in biro, 'For Colin. With Love, Anastasia'.

It was the second photo in the envelope, however, that took me more by surprise. Anna again, now fully clothed, laughing in the sunshine, a loaf of bread and four glasses of white wine on the table.

There was another girl in the photo. She had long black hair and was wearing reflective aviator sunglasses. My immediate reaction was *that's Janice Day!* It was not impossible, was it? Anna had called Jan her 'soulmate' and they had been together in Germany on the run for months. There were pictures of Andreas Baader, when *he* was on the run, sitting at café tables in the sun wearing his trademark Ray-Bans. How had Colin come to have this photo? Why had he not shown it to me? Or had my brain, searching for connections, made a connection too far? I looked again at the girl in the sunglasses: maybe it wasn't Jan after all. Janice Day would never have dyed her hair black.

I heard Claire returning with the tea. Without thinking, I thrust the photos and the rest of Colin's little bundle into a pocket inside my jacket.

"You got those drawers open," Claire said.

"Yeah. I found the key."

"Where was it?"

I showed her.

"How did you find that?"

"Luck."

There were other interesting things in the drawers I had unlocked, things I regretted Claire seeing. She looked at them stoically. We found a letter Caroline had written to Colin during the Easter vac of our second year at Oxford that I regretted reading. We found Colin's 1971 air ticket to Athens, his InterRail pass from 1972, a 1973 ticket to Odessa (via Moscow) tucked into a copy of *The Communist Manifesto*. The book was inscribed 'To Colin, Much love, Sochi, 16 August 1973', followed by a scribble that looked like the five-pointed Soviet star with one of its legs missing.

Before we decided to break for lunch, we also found an envelope that Colin must have picked up in a Moscow hotel containing two return tickets from Geneva to Montreux. The tickets were dated just over three years earlier, August 1998. The Russian envelope lay atop a pile of Swiss 1:25,000 maps, the brown series. What had been happening in August 1998?

"Colin had to cancel our holiday that summer. Something going on in Russia. We were going to go to Kenya," Claire said.

"The Russian debt crisis hit. 17th of August," I said. "Do you remember Colin taking a trip to Switzerland about then? The tickets are dated a week earlier."

"Not one trip in particular. He was always travelling. We could check his diary at work if they still have it."

"They'll still have it. Nothing electronic vanishes, ever."

We ate lunch with Héloïse and Caroline around our kitchen table. We spoke little. Tears began to drip quietly down Héloïse's cheeks. Without a word, she took her glass and her plate into the next room and switched on the television. A teenager wanting to be alone.

There was little more I could do. I wanted to get away for a few minutes to leaf through the bundle I had taken from Colin's secret compartment, to think about what else might have been hidden in Colin's study – in 'The Dirt' or elsewhere – that could potentially harm me. I needed to phone the office. True, I would have been in New York had Colin not vanished but I would have nevertheless been on the phone to London before my first meetings, checking our positions, forming an impression of who was doing what. As it was, I did not even know where the FTSE had opened, let alone how Kellaway & Co. was doing. There had been rumours…

Héloïse screamed. We ran into the TV room to find her standing in the middle of the room, the remote control in her quivering hand pointing at the black screen in front of her. "God! Mummy! Daddy's there." She threw herself against Claire. "God! I know he's in there."

Claire stroked Héloïse's back. "Where, dear?" she asked quietly. Héloïse stretched out the hand that clutched the remote, pointed at the television. I took the remote from her and pressed the red power button. The screen came to life just in time for us to see a plane fly out of the clear blue sky and crash into one of the towers of the New York World Trade Center, explode and disintegrate into a ball of flames.

That night, my exile ended.

"Nick," Caroline said, "there's a hell of a lot for you and me to sort out. This is…" She did not finish her sentence. She took my hand, pulled me towards her. She locked the bedroom door again that night, but this time I was on the inside. "We've got a lot to talk through," she said. But she spoke between kisses as she unbuttoned my shirt and unbuckled my belt. I wanted to say 'sex is the great healer', but that night I kept my own counsel.

In bed, Caroline held me tightly. When I entered her I came quickly, much too quickly, like an eager teenager. I would like to say that the images filling my head were of Caroline, images of the Temple of Hera at Paestum, of the time in Portugal when we sneaked out of our rented villa before dawn, went down onto the deserted beach and made love on the wet sand as the tide came in. Or of Anastasia posing naked or Jan at a café table with hair dyed dark, or even of Ewa, the concentration-camp whore. They weren't. The images in my head as I held Caroline's naked body next to mine and fucked her for the first time in five long months were of the hard fuselage of the hijacked aircraft thrusting at the tower, penetrating it, exploding in a great, furious orgasm of all-consuming fire.

3

Claire and Héloïse moved back to their own house on the morning of 12 September 2001. "We need to restore some normality," Claire muttered without conviction.

I caught a lunchtime train up to London. In my briefcase I had the bundle of photographs that I had borrowed from Colin's desk. It would be after five o'clock that afternoon before I would have the chance to look at them – even though little work was done at Kellaway & Co. that day as people replayed events, recalled impressions, remembered rumours, wondered about people they knew, asked who could have done it, how many were dead. One of our desks had been on the phone to an office in the World Trade Center when the first aircraft struck. "It was awful," Khalid, a fixed-income trader who'd been with us just six months, said. "We had just agreed a price and then there was this huge mother of a noise, then all this screaming and the line just went dead. Then there was nothing. Nothing. No way in hell she could've got out of there alive." The conversation was taped, Khalid said. Of course it was, all trading desk calls were taped. He offered to play it to me. I said no, maybe another time. "Do you think they'll honour the trade?" he asked.

At four o'clock, with New York closed, I told everyone in the office to go home. Their families needed them, I said. Linda came into my office to say goodnight fifteen minutes later. She said, "You were scheduled to be there, Nick."

"I know, but, you know, terrible as it is for those people in the World Trade Center and their families, most of New York's okay."

"I checked your itinerary. You'd've actually been in that tower."

"Lucky miss, then."

"Or else somebody's looking out for you."

"And not looking out for the ten thousand people who *were* in the towers? I'd prefer to put it down to luck, I think."

"Would you?"

"G'night, Linda. You should be getting home."

I closed my office door, took Colin's elastic-bound bundle from my briefcase and spread the contents across my desk. I was certain now that it was a thinner bundle than when Colin had shown it to me. What was I looking for? I'm not certain. The very fact that this package had been kept in his secret compartment was enough.

There were eleven photographs in the bundle and one used envelope containing two of the pictures. Two sheets of paper folded around the bundle protected the photos.

- The Three Musketeers – Kreta 1971.
- Colin and Anna Schmidt outside the chapel in Crete.
- Anna modestly naked. Any clues as to where it might have been taken? I was reasonably certain it was not our beach in Crete – or Santorini. Anna's hair is shorter on the unknown beach than in the Greek pictures. Had the picture been taken before or after? I opted for the latter. 'Anastasia'? We had not known her as Anastasia until the wanted poster of February 1972. Even then, Colin, like me, had believed the name did not match the mugshot. At least that's what he'd said.
- Anna and the dark-haired girl at a café table in the sun. Why had my first reaction been to think of Janice Day? To see Jan in that face beside Anna? Why, when I sat alone drinking whisky as a cure for insomnia on one of my nights of exile, had I been unable to shift my gaze from her guitar? It wasn't Jan. I compared the two pictures with a magnifying glass and concluded that Anna was older in the one at the café, possibly many years older. I also saw something now that I had not seen at first. There is a sign in the picture and the language on it is French.
- A picture of Héloïse. She is about five or six. She is standing in a garden beside a paddling pool and has no clothes on. The look on her face is of that of a much older child. It is a disturbing look, accusing the beholder. Why did Colin have pictures of his daughter in the nude in this secret bundle? I began to draw a very twenty-first century inference, retreated from it.

- Then, to my great surprise, two pictures of Caroline. In the first photo Caroline is standing beside a lock on the Thames, looking down into the water. It is winter. Caroline is pregnant and the angle of the photograph has caught Caroline's swollen belly in profile and from below, exaggerating its size. Perhaps she was bigger when she was pregnant than I recall. I remembered the day this one was taken: a Sunday afternoon in March 1979 at Sandford Lock near Oxford. Caroline is pregnant with Robert.

- In the second picture, Caroline is naked apart from a mortarboard cockily perched on her head and a commoner's gown loosely draped across her shoulders. I recognised the background. It is the Indian décor of her room at LMH. It took little effort to imagine the circumstances of the portrait being made.

- Another picture from Oxford: Anna and Jan in silly self-conscious poses, leaning against a wall beside a sign that reads 'Broad Street'. Had Colin taken Anna and Jan on a tour of Oxford? I cannot recall him mentioning it.

- A photograph of Jan on Port Meadow. A horse grazes innocently in the middle distance. Jan is walking towards the camera, smiling. Emma Wallace, walking beside her, is not smiling.

- A picture of me. I am holding a baby in my arms. I recalled Colin taking this photograph when we were walking Hampstead Heath. 1979. The baby is Robert. I remembered the call of the cuckoo.

- Finally, a photograph of Colin himself – black shorts, green polo shirt, Yankees' baseball cap, barefoot. In his left hand he holds a machete with a two-foot-long blade. With all that was going through my head I imagined for a moment that there was blood on the blade, but on closer examination my conclusion was less macabre: it is rust.

That was all. At least that was all the packet *now* contained. It *had* been tampered with since Colin had shown it to me. I was certain of that. At the very least the anonymous black girl and the middle-aged woman on the bench in Brazil were missing. Why had Colin removed those two pictures? Where were they? Why had he shown them to me in the first place? What else had he taken?

I gathered up the contents of the bundle, stretched the elastic band around it, locked it in my secure cabinet. I would find a way of replacing it in Colin's desk soon. There was nothing, I thought, that I needed to worry about there, nothing that might unduly embarrass me if it became public, nothing that, as Colin once said, would hang me. If there was anything like that, it would require another look through his study.

Just as I was about to close the office door on my way out, the phone rang. Had the call not come in on my private ex-directory number I would have simply locked the door and let the phone ring unanswered. I pressed the button next to the red flashing light. It was, alas, Uriah Heep, alias Edward Reader. His voice oozed down the phone line, out of the loudspeaker and onto every surface in the room like the fat that drips from a Victorian Christmas goose as it slowly roasts. After three long minutes I interrupted the oozing, asked, "Edward, what *is* the point of this call?"

"Ah, yes, Nick," he said, "I was coming to that. It's just that I hear that our mutual friend has gone AWOL."

"Yes."

"You'll keep me informed, won't you?"

Greasy little toad.

I left the office angry. Why should I keep Edward Reader 'informed'? A perverted voyeur lurking like some unwashed evil presence on the edge of others' emotions. Was this what all that research did to the brain? All that peddling, under the guise of being a literary agent, of the detritus of other people's shattered lives? I walked briskly along Curzon Street toward the flat, trying to think about anything that might remove Edward Reader from my head. Surely there was plenty of material available that day. Despite all that, Edward festered in my mind until I was turning the key in the lock.

I had rushed home the previous Friday evening direct from the office and there were a few things I needed to collect if I was going to be living in Weybridge again. As I stepped across the threshold into the flat I thought, *somebody's been in here.* I looked around. There was nothing concrete on which I could pin the feeling. Nothing, as far as I could see, was missing or even out of place. I dismissed the sense of intrusion as the product of too much thinking about Colin, as paranoia following events in the US, as the overflowing of a dim realisation that over the past few days the whole world order had changed – a new tide was flowing in and would not spare my Mayfair flat from its all-encompassing advance.

I was locked out of my bedroom again that night. Caroline, angry because I had come home late, accused me of trying to avoid the process of 'working things out'. Alone again in a room that was not mine, I fell asleep thinking about Colin's photographs. In the half-awake emptiness of the single bed they disturbed me more than I should have allowed. Jan on Port Meadow. Jan on Broad Street. Caroline naked. Caroline pregnant. Why had Colin kept those ones? Why was Caroline now locking me out of my bed? Were his pictures windows into a different world or simply a disorienting viewpoint on the familiar world I had created? A viewpoint that removed me from the centre and left me a hapless bystander, wallowing on its fringes?

Claire tried to interest the police in an examination of Colin's study. They arrived, asked a few questions, took a cursory look at a few items Claire thought might be of interest to them, made a few notes in their mini-flip-chart notebooks, drank coffee, departed, went on to fill in Home Office forms and log other crimes. It was Claire's frustration at their dilatory approach, as much as her inability to sit and wait, that pushed her to look into Colin's affairs herself. Over dinner on Thursday she told us, in her cool forensic accountant's voice, what she had found out about Colin's Geneva accounts.

In August 1998, a deposit of SFR 3.5 million had been made into one of the accounts. Over the following three years, almost all the funds in the account had then gradually been withdrawn. By August 2001, only SFR 40,000 remained. Then, on the Friday before he disappeared, Colin had deposited a further SFR 5.25 million into the account. Both the 2001 deposit and that of 1998 had been made in the form of a bearer CD issued by another Geneva bank.

Alarm bells rang. If Colin had run off with a mistress – the black girl in the photograph, Anna Schmidt, Emma Wallace, the woman on the bench in Brazil, anyone – I could keep him alive, one day to reappear, repentant, with his tail drooping like a naughty dog. If, on the other hand, he had been fool enough to defraud one of his Russian friends, his story might not have so happy an ending.

Colin had the detailed knowledge and the technology to move funds discreetly. That, quite possibly, was the real reason the Russians liked their English banker so much, the reason Andropov had invited him round for dinner *à deux* at 'His Place'. Colin had helped me, when I needed it, to open a very specific type of account in Switzerland. I knew, too, that he was not above taking part in a scheme to defraud. He had kept the internal FMBB memoranda on Thomas Rotten's missing money.

I offered to help Claire with the material in Colin's study at the weekend. "Sunday," she said. But it didn't happen.

4

On the evening of Friday, 14 September, at about six-thirty in the evening, a man was walking his dog in the woods behind Versoix, in a place near the French border marked on the map as Bois de Ste Marie. The dog, which was off its lead, began digging at a patch of ground fifteen metres from the path and would not return when called. The owner followed the dog into the undergrowth. The ground that had attracted the dog seemed to have been recently disturbed. Vegetation around it had been trampled. He saw, as the dog unearthed it, buried in a shallow hole, covered with a layer of earth and wrapped in heavy, semi-transparent plastic, what appeared to him to be part of a human body. He phoned the police and waited until they arrived.

On Saturday the Swiss police contacted their UK counterparts. They suspected that the plastic-wrapped remains might be those of the missing English banker Colin Witheridge. On Sunday, a policeman and a policewoman knocked on Claire's front door. On Monday morning, at Claire's request, I flew to Geneva to identify the body. I carried a sealed envelope that Claire had given me. It contained a lock of Héloïse's hair.

"Thank you for coming, Mr Kellaway." I had expected to be speaking in French, but the policeman sitting across the table addressed me in excellent, precise English. "I understand," he continued, "that you once lived in Geneva."

"That's right. From 1960 to 1970. My father worked at the ILO."

"Yes, indeed. Then after 1970 you were not in Geneva?"

"I was here for holidays, regularly, until my father died and my mother returned to England."

"1977."

"Yes."

"And then?"

"Other than transiting through the airport this is my first visit to Geneva since Christmas 1976."

"I am sorry, Mr Kellaway, for the circumstances of your return."
He turned a page of his file. "Did you know Mr Witheridge well?"

"Yes, I did. We met at university. We spent summer vacations together as students. He was best man at my wedding. I am godfather to his daughter. He lives…" I noticed my use of the present tense, noticed only then that the policeman had used the past tense "… less than 300 metres from me. So, yes."

"Does this mean anything to you?" The policeman slid a piece of paper across the table to me. On it was what appeared to be a Chinese character.

"No," I said after studying the paper and sliding it back across the table.

"Are you aware of any tattoos on Mr Witheridge's body?"

"No."

"Do you know whether Mr Witheridge was religious?"

"No," I said.

"No, you don't know; or no, he was not religious?"

"I am quite sure he is not religious."

"I apologise for asking this, have you ever seen Mr Witheridge naked?"

"Yes."

"Recently?"

"No. Not since… well, probably twenty years. May I ask why you're asking?"

The policeman's forefinger tapped the piece of paper with the Chinese character on it. "Our victim has this mark tattooed on him. It is the only tattoo he bears and it is in a very strange place. It is located midway between the navel and the area of the genitals."

"You should ask his wife."

"We shall, but I had hoped your answer might spare her some questions."

"I don't think Colin had a tattoo there twenty-five years ago."

"Our experts tell me it is an old tattoo."

"Do you know what the character signifies?"

"We will come to that. At present we are dealing with identification. You brought me a sample of hair, I think, Mr Kellaway."

I took the envelope Claire had given me from my briefcase. "Hair from his daughter," I said.

"I would have preferred hair from Mr Witheridge."

"The wife swears there is no way that anybody other than Colin

Witheridge could be the father of her daughter."

"Of course. I am sure," he said, "but nonetheless…"

I never was shown the body. That surprised me: on television the police always show the body to the next of kin or whoever they bring in to identify it. I was asked to keep silent about what I was told and shown, in order not to prejudice the police investigation. Indeed, a legal requirement of silence was formally imposed on me. Then, instead of showing me the body, the policeman passed a series of photographs from his black folder across the table to me one by one, taking each back and replacing it in the file before letting me see the next: the site in the woods where the body was found, the parcel wrapped in plastic and bound together with brown tape, the mutilated corpse unwrapped, a close-up of the tattoo on the margins of the victim's pubic hair, three close-ups of the dead face. Another policeman came in and asked me more questions, questions about Colin, about any thoughts I might have as to who could have done this to him, about his financial affairs, about his work, his clients, his friends, his relationship with his wife, any other women. I answered straightforwardly, where I could.

I flew home that afternoon with no shadow of doubt remaining that it was indeed Colin's body that the dog had unearthed. This was confirmed soon afterwards by the DNA analysis. At least, technically, the Swiss policeman told me over the phone, what it confirmed was that the donor of the hair in the envelope was the daughter of the body in the plastic parcel.

When my flight landed at Heathrow, I had the car take me direct to Colin and Claire's house. Caroline, who had spent the day there with Claire, opened the door to me. I nodded silently, solemnly. When Claire appeared ten seconds later I repeated the gesture. I think she was beyond tears. She simply returned the slight nod and whispered, "Thank you." Héloïse clung to Claire's arm and buried her blonde head against her mother's shoulder.

Caroline poured me a large measure of Colin's gin and topped it up with ice and tonic. I think both Caroline and Claire had had several drinks to fortify themselves against the news they must have known my return would bring. 'Dead Man's Gin', I remember thinking. The tune of the old ballad rattled like dry bones somewhere in the caverns of my mind. There, too, were the pictures again, the photographs I had seen in that antiseptic Geneva room, death laid out systematically piece by damned piece across the policeman's tidy table, images I had not yet spoken of to anyone. The silly grin on the dead face, the Chinese tattoo on the lower abdomen, Colin's severed head placed within the plastic package where his genitals should have been, secured there by the same heavy-duty tape that bound his plastic shroud...

It is odd how something you already know can hit you afresh, knock you down like an enormous tsunami crashing on a shore, knowing but yet not knowing that the wave is advancing. Colin was dead. My best friend for over thirty years was dead. I was nearly fifty. We had been nineteen when we had met in our first term at Oxford, in the anterooms of our adult lives. There would come a time for returning to the questioning trails of who and what had brought Colin to his gruesome end, returning to the dark forest paths that led from this desolate coastline into the uncharted interior. That would not, could not, be far off, but at that moment, as I sat on Colin's sofa, drinking Colin's gin, Colin's wife and Colin's daughter sitting huddled close together on another of his sofas opposite me, staring, all of us, into an empty space where Colin had once lived and breathed and had his being, the wave broke. It crashed with a simple, deafening message that echoed up and down the abandoned shore: Colin Witheridge is no more, Colin Witheridge is no more, Colin Witheridge is no more. Balder is dead.

"Colin had a tattoo," I said, when Claire returned from saying goodnight to Héloïse in her bedroom.

She nodded.

"Chinese character?"

She nodded again. "He had it when we met. You didn't know?"

I shook my head.

"I see," Claire said. "I thought..." The unfinished thought hovered between us.

"The police in Geneva..." I, in turn, was unsure how to complete my sentence.

Claire looked at me, the vacant stare replaced by an air of puzzlement. "What," she asked, "did they say?"

"They asked if Colin was religious."

"Colin said it meant something like 'new life' or 'resurrection'."

Caroline said, "I see."

She didn't really see because she did not yet know where on his body the tattoo had been. Or did she? A tremor ran up my spine. I tried to suppress the rogue images that were forming and invading my head.

"Religious?" Caroline prompted.

"I don't think so." Claire got up abruptly from her seat, dashed out to the lavatory. We heard her vomit, flush the toilet, return even paler than she had been before, sweat glistening on her brow.

Caroline offered to stay the night, but Claire insisted she would be fine. She and Héloïse would look after each other, she said. Her parents were in the house as well, keeping out of the way upstairs while Caroline and I were there. They would be fussing over her the moment we had gone.

Caroline took my hand as we walked home. "Nick," she said when we were nearly at our door, "you know that tattoo Colin had, the Chinese character for 'resurrection'?"

"What about it?" I did not want to talk about whatever knowledge Caroline might or might not have of the Chinese tattoo and its vicinity.

"It could also mean something else."

"Like?"

"The Paschal Greeting? The Easter responses?"

"So."

"Christ is risen? And the response: he is risen indeed?"

"Sorry, Caro. I'm not following you. Colin wasn't into religion and all that gobbledegook. What you *possibly* don't know is where the tattoo was. He had it on his groin. Some silly reference to 'erection' – not 'resurrection'. At best it was homage to the continuity of the species. The go-forth-and-multiply kind of religion. God knows what the bugger was thinking."

Caroline persisted, either ignoring or not noticing my use of 'possibly', "'Christ is risen. He is risen indeed.' The original? In Greek?"

"How the hell should I know? You're the one who went to Sunday School."

"*Christos anesti; alethos anesti.*"

"Say that again."

"*Christos anesti; alethos anesti.* The Greek for 'resurrection' is '*anastasis*'."

"Oh God!" I should have got there more quickly, much more quickly. "Anastasia," I exhaled. "Anna-Fucking-Stasia."

5

Kellaway & Co. (aka Peter Pan and the Lost Boys) actually did quite well out of 9/11. NASDAQ, the junior New York stock exchange, peaked in March 2001. Between that peak and when the markets closed on 10 September 2001, the NASDAQ fell from something over 5000 points to below 1700. Many a long shirt was lost. Kellaway & Co. had, however, presciently sold shares and begun to take short positions just before the peak. That was Fabrice's call and I rewarded him handsomely for it. Through the summer we extended our short bias to the main exchanges where we thought some individual shares might be particularly vulnerable. We shorted airlines and were, on the eve of 9/11, on the right side of a series of interesting commodity bets. We also shorted Enron – based on a passing remark Colin made about Jeff Skilling on the afternoon I had gone round to tell him about Eva Braun and my Brazilian holiday plans and found him drunk.

The London market – the FTSE – fell 5.7% on 11 September 2001 on the news from across the Atlantic. New York itself, of course, did not open that day. When it did open – on 17 September 2001, the Monday I flew to Geneva to identify Colin's body – the Dow Jones Industrial Average fell more than 7% and continued its slide through the week to record a cumulative loss over the first five days of post-9/11 trading of 14.3%. We made good money for our investors that week.[75] Then, on the next Monday, 24 September, I held an impromptu strategy meeting. Our conclusion was that the time had come to act on the countercyclical investors' old maxim, 'Buy on the bullets'. Was it the sober Presbyterian John Templeton who said, 'Buy when there's blood in the streets'? I'm not sure.

My fiftieth birthday fell on the Friday. Caroline and I spent the evening at home – just the two of us with a single bottle of Dom Perignon that failed to add sparkle to that time of dry dreams and

---

[75] Kellaway & Co. was investigated for insider trading shortly after the 11 September 2001 Al-Qaeda attacks on the United States. Although Kellaway & Co. was eventually exonerated by the investigating authorities, the extraordinary profits made by Kellaway & Co. at this time, together with the late cancellation of the trip to New York by Nick Kellaway and senior colleagues in his firm and the importance of Arab money in Kellaway & Co.'s funds, formed *prima facie* evidence for the firm's prior knowledge of the attacks. For a comprehensive survey of evidence for prior knowledge of the attacks, particularly in circles with Israeli or Arab connections, of information being systematically suppressed or buried, of government withholding information and of the general lack of critical questioning and analysis surrounding the events of 11 September 2001, refer to Paul Thompson, *The Terror Timeline: Year by Year, Day by Day, Minute by Minute: A Comprehensive Chronicle of the Road to 9/11 – and America's Response*, New York, 2004. – Ed.

rogue reality. We were in bed – together – before ten.

We spent the Saturday helping Claire as she continued to sort through the papers in Colin's study. When Caroline and Claire were in the kitchen making a pot of coffee, I returned the bundle of photos to the secret compartment in Colin's desk.

In the afternoon, just as I was coming to the conclusion that there was probably nothing in Colin's study that could damage me, Claire found a draft of the speech Colin would have given, had he still been alive, at a surprise birthday party he had planned for me. Claire paused in her methodical sorting, read it silently, and then passed it to me without comment. It did not have the makings of great oratory, but as I read it and heard the echoes of Colin's voice as he delivered it, tears began to roll down my cheeks. Héloïse walked into the room just then and asked, "What's wrong with Uncle Nick?" [76]

That night I dreamt vividly.

I am driving a car somewhere in South London. I know where I am meant to be going but I don't know why, nor do I know how to get there. There is very little traffic in the streets and that seems ominous to me. I drive past council tower blocks and long rows of dilapidated terraced housing. Other cars begin to follow me. I go the wrong way up one-way streets, through red lights, the wrong way round roundabouts. The others follow. Then I come to an unpaved street lined with crumbling Victorian mansions. At its end, there is a steep hill and a path leading into a late autumn wood, where the trees have lost all their leaves. I turn the car round on the forgotten, mossy lawns of the abandoned houses. The other cars follow. It is four-thirty in the afternoon and getting dark. I need to pick up Amanda from her school before the paedophiles get there.

When I arrive at the school the sun is shining. A long line of girls in pink dresses and carrying bouquets of flowers cheer our

----

[76] The lines from Adam Heggie's poem 'September 2001 – Reflections' (in his *Posthumous Poems*, 2004)

> *When Balder lay excarnate*
> *Outside the realms of time,*
> *All that really mattered*
> *Was scansion and the rhyme*

only begin to make sense when one considers that the subject may not be 9/11 but rather the death of Colin Witheridge, nicknamed 'Balder'. – Ed.

arrival. Amanda is sitting in the car beside me now. She is in flowing bridal white and a veil covers her face. I realise I am not dressed properly for her wedding and also that I have not prepared the speech that I know I must shortly give. I am paralysed by panic. The speech I find in my pocket is the one Colin was meant to have given at my funeral.

I am driving again. It is a bigger car now, maybe a Bentley, but I am still in South London when I am stopped by the police. They take the suitcase I bought to go to Brazil with Mrs Hitler from the boot of the car and open it. The policewoman looks like Héloïse. The case is full of women's cosmetics, hair rollers, curling irons, a long, coiled, orange rubber hose, a hand pump, sanitary towels, a gun, an unsheathed hunting knife. Héloïse picks out a bottle and holds it to the light to examine it. It is a clear, viscous liquid in a glass medicine bottle. She sets it down on the roof of the car.

"Fuckolas Fuckaway," she pronounces, "I am arresting you in connection with the murder of Colin Witheridge. You do not need to say anything, but anything you do say…"[77]

6

It was tea-time when they came to my flat. When I asked them if they would like a drink, the short, fat one cracked his knuckles and said he would like a gin and tonic, please, and the tall, thin one said he would take the same, please, but with no lime or lemon. They both wore dark suits, cheap, off the peg, thin lapelled, worn so often that they shone with a sleek and shiny sheen. Their unfashionable ties had seen younger days, had perhaps once belonged to their fathers. They sat only when I invited them to do so, side by side on the sofa, awkwardly, nervously adjusting and readjusting the position of their limbs. If you had turned off the sound you could have imagined yourself preparing to be interviewed by Laurel and Hardy. You would never – and I suppose that is the whole point – have imagined them to be spies.

"You said this was about Colin," I said.

"Yes," said Stan Laurel, "it is and, as I'm sure we don't really

<hr>

[77] This dream does not appear in *The Dream Diaries* as published by KISS. See E. Anstey and M. Bottreaux, 'The Unpublished Dreams: What Wichita's Dream Selection Left Out' in *Sex Today*, Vol. 20, Sydney, 2005. – Ed.

need to tell you, everything you hear today, the very fact that we have been here, our faces, everything, is subject to the Official Secrets Act."

"I've never signed the Official Secrets Act, I'm afraid."

Oliver Hardy said, "You don't need to." He placed an envelope on the table. "Your section 1 (1) notification. Of course, you..." He finished the sentence with his right hand. It was a large menacing hand: palm open, facing upwards, fingers spread, performing a slow, clockwise, circular motion. It was a hand that did not usually content itself with filling in forms in the dusty back offices of Laurel, Hardy & Partners.

"Are you going to tell me who killed Colin?"

"We are hoping," said Laurel, "that you will be able to help us there."

"Me?"

"Yes."

"Well, if you put it that way. My money would be on the Russians. Friends of Mr Andropov perhaps?"

"Would it? We..." Pause. "We don't think so. Severed genitals? Decapitation?" Another pause. "Not his style."

"Who then?"

"What we need first, Mr Kellaway, are some documents Mr Witheridge left in your care. In a sealed envelope."

According to Stan Laurel, Colin had been recruited during his first term at Oxford. The fact that he was reading Russian and a Labour Party member – even if, at first, a relatively inactive member – made him an interesting candidate, a candidate with potential. Under the tutelage of MI5, Colin moved politically towards the groups that competed for revolutionary purity around the fringes of the Labour Party. "You will recall that you and Mr Witheridge joined the Oxford Revolutionary Socialist Students on the same day." Colin's task was not to meddle, simply to keep a watch on things, to write the occasional report on individuals, "Including, as you know, on you, Mr Kellaway." Until that moment, of course, I had not known.

"You will recall," Laurel said – a wink from Hardy as Laurel spoke, "a Slovak refugee in Munich. You probably never imagined she was a protégée of Mr Witheridge's old tutor at Oxford, did you? The one who recruited him. Although you will remember the old tutor sending you to see an individual in Bonn. You'll remember this Reader chap, I believe."

"And a fight," said Hardy, "over a woman. A fist fight."

"A fight?"

"Mr Kellaway, please," said Laurel. "Do us the courtesy of not pretending. Amsterdam? I believe the woman in question is currently your wife."

Hardy added, "It was long before our time, but from what we understand, Mr Witheridge was not altogether well pleased…"

"… Which makes it all the more surprising that he should confide his documents to you. One of his little foibles, perhaps. He did have his little foibles, did our Mr Witheridge." Laurel smiled as if he thought I would understand what he meant by 'foibles', that I would sympathise with Her Majesty's Secret Service for having to deal with foibles. Foibles, of all things.

I offered my guests a second gin and tonic. My offer was declined by Laurel, accepted by Hardy. I made his strong, mine of pure tonic water. When I returned to the room, Laurel and Hardy were standing in a corner examining one of my nineteenth-century Persian lithographs. On the battlements of a stylised Moghul fort, a man in a red turban and a coat of many colours reclines with a woman. The woman, her veil and modesty in disarray, is in a state of rosy semi-undress. From an improbable position beneath the man's robes, an unsheathed pink dagger thrusts towards the exposed flesh of the woman's thighs. Tigers and elephants lurk among the palm trees of the jungle beyond the walls.

"Indian?" asked Laurel.

"Persian actually, but based on an Indian scene."

"Did your son enjoy his time in India this summer, Mr Kellaway?"

"… And his trip to Cardiff afterwards?"

Without responding, I handed Hardy his drink. Once they were seated again, Laurel produced a photograph from his briefcase and passed it to me. "Another of Mr Witheridge's foibles," he said. The picture was of Anna Schmidt, a different pose to the one in Colin's bundle, but to my eye taken on the same unknown beach.

"You know the woman?" Hardy asked.

"Yes."

"Name?"

"Anna."

"It's Anna, then?" A pause while Oliver Hardy sipped his gin, tested his teeth on the ice cube, hardened his voice and added a slice of sarcasm. "Good. We'll call her Anna. Just Anna. Not Anna

279

Schmidt or Anna Rotten or Anna Kowalski or Anna Kowatsch or two Annas short of a Rupee. Certainly not Anastasia Kuznetsova Soviet agent. Or maybe it was Stasi or maybe the Czechs or maybe none of the above. Listen, Mr Kellaway. 1972. Height of that Baader-Meinhof thing? Munich? Our German friends are keeping an eye on a house. They see two people walking away from it in the middle of the night. Then, a couple of minutes later..." Another pause, this time to crack his knuckles. "... the place explodes in a ball of fire. Gas leak? So they say. Accident? Maybe, but one of the two walking away answers to the description of your friend Anna here. Wearing clothes at the time, naturally. The people in the house were not identified for years, not until Gauck started doing his lustration thing, or whatever they called it, to the old Stasi files.[78] One of the dead was pregnant. Nine months pregnant."

"Why are you telling me this?"

"Just a moment, Mr Kellaway. Move forward. 1977. Easter. Royal Lancaster Hotel, London. A gunman kills three Arabs. Who is with him, Mr Kellaway?"

I did not reply.

"Why the sudden silence, Mr Kellaway? It was your friend Anna, of course, and where did they spend the night before, Anna and this Arab assassin? At your flat in Islington, wasn't it? Now, how did *that* come about? And then we know what happened later in the year, don't we? This gunman got on a Lufthansa flight out of Mallorca and ended up dead in Somalia."

"What are you trying to say?"

Hardy leaned back into the sofa, sipped his drink. By way of response to my question, Laurel produced another photograph. It was the one Colin had shown me in his study, the woman in sunglasses sitting beside Colin on a bench. I turned it over. There was the inscription in Colin's hand: *Florianópolis, 1995* – the same one I had seen earlier in the summer. Hardy asked, "Who's the woman?"

I said, "I don't know."

"But you've seen the picture before?"

"Yes."

---

[78] The German Federal Agency for the Records of the State Security Service of the former German Democratic Republic is often known, in short form, as the Gauck Authority, after Joachim Gauck (1940–), its head. 'Lustration' was a term used in Czechoslovakia not in East Germany. – Ed.

"Where?"

"Colin's study. Colin showed it to me." I saw an exchange of glances between my two interrogators that suggested they thought I had inadvertently made a significant admission.

"Perhaps," Hardy said, handing me another photo, "this will help you." The second photograph appeared to be of the same woman, but without the sunglasses. It was slightly blurred, apparently taken from a distance using a high-powered telephoto lens. When Colin showed me the Florianópolis photograph of himself with the woman in sunglasses, I had wondered, given our conversation, whether the woman might be Anna Schmidt, aged and unrecognisable from my memories of twenty-five or thirty years earlier, but the woman in the photograph had blue eyes and fair skin and Anna had been dark.

"I'm sorry," I said, "it doesn't."

"Well," Hardy smirked, "I'll give you a clue: it's not Jeff Skilling. Though, considering the amount of money you and Mr Witheridge's estate have been making out of Enron in the past few weeks, it wouldn't really be all that surprising if we found Mr Skilling in your wallet, would it now?"

I'll give you a clue: it's not Jeff Skilling. Colin's study had been bugged.

"And this?" Laurel handed me another photograph. It was the black woman from Colin's secret compartment.

"I don't know."

"Mr Kellaway," said Hardy, "you are lying to us. That's not a good idea." His right hand began to make its clockwise motion. I waited for the knuckle cracking ritual, but it did not come. "You are very lucky we got here before the Russians."

"I… I'm sorry. Do *you* know who she is?"

"We do."

"Who?"

"She was French. Secret service. Working here in London. 'Londonistan', the French call it. She was working among certain Muslim groups, a motley crew of Algerians, Moroccans, West Africans, what not. In June, July, she caught whispers of an impending attack on the US using hijacked aircraft. Paris transmitted the intelligence to Langley. The German brethren were picking up something similar, but it seems it all got lost in the noise. The circumstantial evidence suggests she may also have mentioned it to Mr Witheridge."

"Circumstantial?"

"Mr Witheridge does not appear to have passed on this intelligence to us. Somewhat remiss of him, of course. On three separate occasions he made phone calls to his broker with very specific instructions on stocks to buy, stocks to sell, stocks to short. Not just Enron. He circumvented his employer's usual compliance procedures by using a Swiss account. The last of these instructions was given in a phone call from Geneva on the morning of the 31st of August. You will recognise that as the day Mr Witheridge went missing. The positions he took proved very profitable for his estate."

"I see."

"I think we may agree with you."

"What do you mean?"

"What we mean is that, from an examination of Kellaway & Co.'s positions over the period leading up to 9/11, you may well have been in possession of the same intelligence."

"What! No, completely not true."

"Then you'll have no objection to an investigation of your trades over that period."

"None, none whatsoever. You can look at whatever you like."

"It will be very disruptive, Mr Kellaway. And not just to your daily office routines. I imagine a business like yours has to be careful of its reputation as well. Am I wrong there?"

"What are you saying?"

"You're in this up to your neck, Mr Kellaway." Hardy's hand began to describe flat circles again. Then he suddenly drew it across his neck in a single severing motion. "Wouldn't it just be altogether easier to hand over the envelopes? Colin's dead, after all. You've seen the body."

I didn't correct him on that point of detail. I simply said, "I told you, I have no papers. Search the flat. Look wherever you want."

Laurel smiled. "We've done that already, Mr Kellaway."

Hardy added, without a smile, "This flat, your office, your place in Surrey, Colin's house. We've had his house under watch, electronically, for some time. We need those papers, Mr Kellaway. It's your duty as a citizen of this country to hand them over. This is not a time for misplaced loyalties. Her Majesty's Government needs to know what's in that envelope."

They clearly didn't believe me. With what they took as my refusal to co-operate with their gentle methods, they seemed to have come to the end of their business with me. The tall, thin one began to move his limbs about awkwardly. The short, fat one cracked his knuckles one by one. I asked, "And the French agent?"

"What about her?"

"You said she *was* French. Past tense."

"Well spotted, sir. 'Was' is correct. She was found last week in a house in a place called Ferney-Voltaire. You probably know it: Route de Versoix, to be precise. It's in France, very near to the Swiss border. Very near, in fact, to where Colin..." He cracked another knuckle. "Nobody had been seen going in or out of the house for weeks and the neighbours were noticing – what shall we say? – an unpleasant odour."

After we had shaken hands in a meaningless formal gesture of farewell, with Hardy already out the door, Laurel turned to me, his face twisted in imitation of Lieutenant Colombo. "I was just wondering, sir. What does a man who's as rich as you are need with another five million Swiss Francs?"

"What?"

"I don't need to ask *how*, but just *why* did you take the money out of Colin's account after he was murdered?"

"I didn't."

"Didn't you? A transfer of five million Swissies from Colin's account in Geneva to your account in Liechtenstein? Two days later you withdrew the whole lot. A mix of cash and bearer CDs. Mean anything to you?"

"I don't have an account in Liechtenstein."

Stan Laurel looked down at me as if I were a naughty child. "Do us a favour, Mr Kellaway. Your Liechtenstein account has been on our radar for twenty-five years, and we *will* find those papers."

7

Dreams. Fast and furious. Bongo drums playing algorithms inside my skull. Robert, two-months old, screaming as I push his buggy across Hampstead Heath. Colin, knife held to his balls, screaming. Héloïse, a naked five-year old standing by a paddling pool, her face marred by tears. "Fuckolas Fuckaway," she screams, "you've killed my daddy."

Then, one night, I dream of Caroline. I am walking along the shore of the lake toward La Bise. The lake is as still as the surface of an enormous mirror. The sun on my back is warm. Caroline – or is it Marie-Claire? – walks beside me. We come to the house and then we are inside, on the other side of a door that used always to be locked, in a room with a bare wooden floor beneath our feet. Yellow morning brightness flows through an open window. It shines on a stack of suitcases and cabin trunks and brings with it a blackbird's song. Jan is there, wearing a crimson kaftan, with flowers laughing in her hair.

We are walking now in an immense garden, along a white farm track where no one has ever gone before, through golden, God-kissed fields. The towers of Rouëlbeau rise behind us as we walk east towards a row of poplar trees and a range of blue hills that dissolve into the sunrise. It is early summer, school has finished for the year, exams are behind us. A season of promise stretches ahead of us like the virgin path we tread. We speak softly. Caroline's voice is like the morning breeze, rustling the topmost leaves of the poplars. We talk of Saturday evenings to come and of the first bright Sunday morning after the dust of the Revolution has settled.

Nightingales sing and Jan says they are singing of liberty. Marie-Claire picks ripe cherries from fruit-laden trees as we pass. They are so red that they are almost black. She places one between my lips. It is sweet in the mouth and I long for more.

Then, suddenly, I was awake, more awake in that dark, Weybridge bedroom than I have ever been, completely alive in every muscle of my body, in every pore of my skin, overcome by an indescribable joy, by a feeling that everything was hopelessly wonderful, by a beauty that promised an everlasting, impossible extravagance. I found myself longing – an outrageous sense of longing – for a return not to the dream itself but to that exquisite feeing I had had when waking from it.

The moment passed quickly – very quickly. I sank back onto the mattress. I could hear Caroline's deep, rhythmic breathing beside me. As if from a broken water tap, my mind filled with dripping images of Colin and barely credible tales of envelopes and bank accounts and then with gruesome pictures of that grinning head. *God damn you, Colin Witheridge! Why the hell did you have to die in Geneva – of all places? Why did your bloody corpse have to pollute the sacred soil of my land? Why, from beyond your shitty little woodland grave, are you fucking with my mind?*

Who were these guys? MI5 as they claimed to be? Or some other rogues posing as officers of Her Majesty's Secret Service? After all, pretending to be somebody they are not is what spies do, isn't it? Was there anyone I could check with? Maybe Roger Moore or Sean Connery posing as James Bond? Yet when I considered the alternatives – friends of Vladimir Ivanovich Andropov or whoever had murdered Colin for his envelope or whatever – I found myself hoping that Laurel and Hardy were actually who they said they were: gentlemen practitioners in the service of the Crown.

I checked with Claire, she checked with the bank in Geneva and, yes, the funds – SFR 5,000,000 – *had* been transferred out of Colin's account on 5 September 2001, all properly documented and authorised. Claire, however, did not get details of the transfer's beneficiary when she phoned Geneva and, with even a remote possiblity of my name surfacing there, I decided not to ask her to phone again and put that question to the bank. I would have to play the long game. For how could I otherwise, just then, possibly trace an account in Liechtenstein? Phone up every bank in Vaduz and ask whether they happened to have an account in the name of Nicholas Kellaway through which SFR 5,000,000 had just passed? I might as well phone Andropov himself and ask him, since he stopped short of cutting off genitals and heads, what his recognised style of murder was.

On the morning of 15 October 2001 at eight-fifteen, I received confirmation of who my visitors had been. A team of twenty men – in suits and ties, garb rarely seen in my offices since their opening – arrived unannounced at the offices of Kellaway & Co. to begin an investigation into our trading over the past year. No mention, of course, of Laurel and Hardy or of Colin and his missing envelope. Scarcely even a hint that we were being accused of front-running Al-Qaeda's big American trade. *Bastards.* Impeccably polite bastards.

"No women," Fabrice observed after we had shown the investigators where they would work. "Not even an ugly one."

"Not many women work *here* either, Win-Win."

"True. You employ them, Nick. They just don't stay long."

"Okay, Fabrice, I hear you. Get Oil to close out her positions and focus on looking after these fuckers, will you?"

The men worked hard and in relays – the early shift on duty from six in the morning until two in the afternoon and the late shift taking over for the next eight hours – making life hell for everyone at Kellaway & Co. Oil came in every morning looking exhausted.

After our guests had been with us a week, Fabrice lost his cool. "This could never happen in France!" he screamed. "You live in a fucking police state and you just sit there and take it. Do something!" Caroline said something similar, but in different words, as I repeatedly broke the promise I had made to spend more time at home. I placed calls to the heads of the FSA and the SFO, to senior officials in the Bank of England and the Treasury, to my MP, to one of Gordon Brown's special advisors known to be dazzled by wealth and all that goes with it. The only response I got, ten days into the investigation, was from Oliver Hardy.

"Mr Kellaway," he said softly down the phone line, "wouldn't it be a little more pleasant if you just gave us the envelope?"

"I know nothing about your goddamn envelope."

"Have it your way, then, sir."

The investigation wound down in the week before Christmas. "Phase one, at least," the team leader said as he packed his slim briefcase. "Please pass my thanks to your staff. Everyone has been most co-operative."

When no investigators turned up the following morning, I called my staff together, passed on the authorities' thanks and added my own. Despite being harassed eighteen hours a day, we had made decent money for our investors over the quarter. With the entire firm exhausted from the effort, I declared the next three weeks to be a half-holiday – each person to work, on a rota, only fifty per cent of the days. I did not exempt myself from the new rule and went home mid-afternoon to Caroline and a little investigation of my own.

On Christmas Eve I took some hair from Robert's hairbrush and on Christmas Day itself I wiped a spoon that Robert had licked with a swab of cotton wool. I also found a used condom that could only have been Robert's. I put the samples into three separate plastic sandwich bags, the sandwich bags into a padded envelope and sent my little parcel to an address I had found on the internet.

It was early in the palindromic year of 2002, when the winter festivities had been packed away in their cardboard boxes and when we workers had returned to our desks, but school children had not yet taken their places again in their classrooms, that an unexpected crisis forced me to stay late in the office and then spend the night in the Mayfair flat. At eleven-fifteen I switched off the light.

When I was woken by the buzzer on the entry phone, the digital clock on the bedside table stood at 00:48. I tried to ignore the buzzing, dismissed it as a rancid drunk's silly prank; but the noise persisted, insisted. I got out of bed, wrapped myself in my dressing gown, went to the entry phone and barked some obscenity down the wires into the street.

"Uncle Nick. It's me. Héloïse."

Héloïse was drunk and cold. She had, it seemed, left her coat behind in a bar. I made her a cup of coffee and, when she had drunk it and eaten some shortbread I found in a tartan tin, showed her to the flat's spare bedroom – a place her father had often slept when he, too, had turned up drunk and cold. She told me, before I closed her bedroom door, that she had missed the last train home and that she had not contacted her mother since five the previous afternoon. I phoned Claire to tell her that Héloïse had arrived on my doorstep, that she was now safely asleep in the spare room.

It was 01:41 by the digital clock when I closed my door and turned my light off again. I remember thinking Caroline would be glad after all that I had had to stay up in London. God knows what would have become of poor Héloïse out on the vicious streets of the metropolis otherwise.

It was still dark when I awoke suddenly, but there was, marginally, more light in the room than there should have been. My bedroom door was open and I could see the glow of the never-dark London night in the corridor beyond. Gradually, I became aware that there was somebody in the room, standing beyond the foot my bed, at the chest of drawers where I kept my money and credit cards. I could vaguely make out the outline of a bulky, probably human, shape.

Now, those who believe themselves to be rich, famous or simply vulnerable can undergo training instructing you what to do in a variety of emergency situations. In my case, this training, repeated annually in the same month as my medical examination, was a compulsory condition of the firm that provided my kidnap and life insurance policies. In the situation where you wake and find a burglar in your room the advice is to lie still, feign sleep, let them take your money and whatever else you keep in your drawers. Press the red panic button on the bedside table only after the intruder has left the premises.

Instinct, however, overcame training. I reached for the light switch. It was no burglar. Héloïse stood at the end of my bed wrapped in the duvet from the bed in the spare room. "Héloïse!" I exclaimed. "What are you doing here?"

"Uncle Nick," she whispered. "I'm scared."

I said nothing, simply stared at her. She carelessly let the duvet drop to the floor. Héloïse, Colin's gorgeous daughter, stood naked less than a metre from the tips of my toes.

The results of the DNA test came back in the first week in February. I opened the envelope and pulled out the brief type-written report. The genetics laboratory had proved that, beyond any reasonable doubt, Robert was my son.

CHAPTER NINE

We moved to Knightsbridge in the spring of 2002. It was Caroline's idea, spawned one night when I was away, when Laurel and Hardy's friends on the evening shift were being paid honest taxpayers' money to work me overtime.

Straightforward? Well, it all became a bit more complicated than that. Selling my now unnecessary Mayfair flat became part of the deal. With it went my collection of Persian miniatures, auctioned through Christie's. A gallery in St James's sold the anonymous nude, who had hovered companionably over my big brass bed, to a rising Chinese pornographer. The flying carpets found their way onto our matrimonial Knightsbridge floors.

The second complication was Imogen, Caroline's sister. Imogen was going through a divorce. She had left her husband, a needy man who was generous to the point of personal bankruptcy, then found herself with nowhere to go when the bank foreclosed on what had been the family home. I agreed, when Caroline proposed it, that we would delay the sale of our Weybridge house and let Imogen stay there while matters sorted themselves out. "It'll only be for a few weeks," Caroline promised – and Imogen moved in the next day. Accompanying her were five children under ten, three dogs, a horse, six guinea pigs, a large goldfish tank and my mother-in-law.

I found the third complication in a cardboard box that the movers had mistakenly left in the room that was to become my Knightsbridge study. When I opened it I found copies of *Family Law* journal and the *Journal of Social Welfare and Family Law*, something called *Family Law: Issues, Debates, Policy*, a monograph on *Family Law Perspectives on the Human Rights Bill* and another on *The Yardstick of Equality of Division*. I had just begun to leaf through a paper titled *White v. White: Implications for Divorce in the Twenty-First Century* when Caroline walked in. I waved the paper in front of her. "What's all this about, Caro?" I asked.

She looked at the paper and the half-unpacked box at my feet. "Sorry. That should have gone to my room."

"What do you need all this for?"

Caroline smiled. "I *am* a lawyer, Nick."

"That was more than twenty years ago."

"So all the more to catch up on when I start practising again."

"What?"

Caroline kissed my cheek. "Nothing definite, but with the kids all flown the nest and everything…"

"Imogen?" I nodded at the paper in my hand.

Caroline's smile vanished and her lips tightened. "It won't do her much good. 50% of nothing is still nothing, I'm afraid."

The fourth complication was Phil Scott.

Phil Scott is a City legend. Born on a cattle station in the Queensland outback in 1935, Phil came to England in 1958 to do a physics doctorate, married an undergraduate who happened to be the daughter of a Conservative Member of Parliament (later ennobled) and abandoned his academic career in favour of a job at a merchant bank where his father-in-law just happened to be a director. He made a considerable amount of money, both for his firm and himself, through the sixties and seventies – decades when that was not, especially in Britain, a particularly easy thing to do.

By the latter half of the eighties, the entire panoply of the old City – where everyone who mattered knew everyone else who mattered and proclaimed that his word was his bond – was being swept away. Most of the old British merchant banks, together with stockbrokers and jobbers, were bought by continental universal banks, American investment banks and British clearing banks staffed by eager grammar-school boys who, though they didn't know what their bright new acquisitions did, were pleased to own a bit of the aristocracy of finance. Phil, who was by then not only chairman, but also the largest single shareholder in his firm, took advantage of the froth leading up to the Big Bang and sold. He worked his three-year earn-out period for the new owner and then retired to nurse his invalid wife.

Phil had been a widower for ten years when our move to Knightsbridge made him our neighbour. With his thinning white hair worn unfashionably long over the collar, red cheeks, jovial green eyes and baggy corduroy trousers, you would have marked Phil Scott down as an out-of-work Father Christmas. Not a once-famous banker. Not a wife thief. Not Santa Claws.

On the evening of the Monday we moved, we went next door to Phil's for dinner.

"You didn't tell me," I protested when Caroline told me she had accepted the invitation.

"Sorry."

"When did he invite us?"

"You'll like him. He reminds me of my dad."

"Christ! We move up to London to get away from your mother and find ourselves living next to your father."

"Nick. Stop a moment, please. You *know* that's not why we've moved, okay?"

So, tired from three days of moving house and scarcely speaking to one another, Caroline and I knocked on our neighbour's door. Phil had, fortunately, invited another couple as well: a banker, whom I knew by reputation, and his wife. They had arrived before us. Conversation flowed freely, conventionally. Caroline and I put on our model-couple show.

Phil himself had prepared the supper: a large pot of homemade minestrone, two large loaves of granary bread, cheeses laid out on a wooden board, Sainsbury's own-brand Valpolicella. When Phil began to expound his views on current City practices, living up to his reputation of being out of touch with twenty-first-century paradigms, the banker lapsed into silence, focused on his soup, pushed the last beans about with his spoon. It fell to me to mount the defence.

"Good, Nick," Phil said. "*Very* good. I don't agree with you, but you *are* eloquent. The City will need folk like you before long. The morality of money. Another glass of wine? You're not driving anywhere."

I held out my glass, said, "Money is the measure of all things."

Phil paused in the refilling of my wine glass. "Ah," he said, looking me in the eye, "in that case, my friend, you'll need a lot more than eloquence."

Antediluvian wanker.

Caroline added, as if she were on Phil's side rather than mine, "Money can't buy you love." Colin, the last time I saw him alive, had said the same thing: *money can't buy you love.*

"But," I replied, "it can buy you freedom. Controls. You can build the walls that keep other people, all the stuff and nonsense that the world's filled with, you can keep all that at bay. Then you create the space where you can be free. Free on your own terms."

"Is that," Phil asked, "really freedom?"

"The only kind of freedom you'll ever find outside your dreams."

Phil probed, "Freedom from suffering?"

"Inter alia."

In the moment of quiet that followed, I heard Caroline's voice whisper, "Or doubt."

Phil heard her too. He turned to face her. Was it in that empty moment that he began to plot and scheme, to sharpen his proselytizing claws? He nodded and, in a voice that was no louder than Caroline's had been, he said, "Suffering and doubt."

As we were leaving Caroline invited Phil to Sunday lunch.

"I would be absolutely delighted," Phil said. "But, my dear, it's your first Sunday in your new home."

"No problem at all," Caroline replied.

"Then," said Phil, "what I suggest is that you put an old-fashioned roast in the oven, you come with me to church and when we get back I help you do the veg. I'm no good at roasts but I'm very good at veg. I'm not having you slave over a hot stove all Sunday morning on my account."

To my enormous surprise, Caroline agreed. Agreed to the whole package. Agreed even to give Phil Scott total responsibility for buying, preparing and cooking the vegetables. "You can do the wine, Nick," she said.

The idea of Caroline going back to work was one thing. But church?

"Why not?" Caroline said. "I used to go to church when I was a kid. I did the whole works, choir, Sunday school, youth group, the lot."

"Your parents forced you into *all* that?"

"Not forced at all. I wanted to go. I…"

"And now, because you find you're living next to someone who reminds you of Daddy…"

"Get off it, Nick, will you? You don't have to come. I'll be okay in a church on my own."

2

I went to church. I sat next to Caroline. Phil Scott was on her far side. I watched Caroline carefully, watched her breast rise and fall as she breathed, watched her pulse beat in a vein in her neck. She seemed to be lost to me, in a trance between sleeping and waking, in that state captured by Byzantine icon painters where the face is poised indifferently between life and death. A great mosaic Victorian

Christ, modelled on those pre-Renaissance features and surrounded by his twelve apostles, gazed out at us from beyond the altar. I touched Caroline's fingers. She turned her head, smiled at me from a long way off. We stood to sing. Caroline squeezed my hand, returned – from wherever she had been – to the pew. Her voice tingled down my spine. She must have felt the shiver.

> *Behold him there! The risen lamb*
> *My perfect sinless righteousness;*
> *The great unchangeable I am,*
> *The King of glory and of grace!*
> *One with my Lord I cannot die,*
> *My soul is purchased with his blood;*
> *My life is safe with Christ on high,*
> *With Christ my saviour and my God,*
> *With Christ my saviour and my God.*

Caroline had smothered a leg of lamb in rosemary garlands and rock salt crystals and put it in the oven. Was shrivelled lamb a fitting food or sacrilege? Did I care? I opened two bottles of a decent *1990 Château Dassault St Emilion Grand Cru Classé*. Caroline complimented Phil on his vegetables. Phil complimented Caroline on her voice.

"I was in the choir," Caroline responded. "I used to do solos."

Conversation ebbed and flowed, most of it between Caroline and her substitute father. I contented myself with thoughts of the week ahead and the St Emilion; noticed as we passed the halfway mark on the second bottle that I was its main consumer, that neither Caroline nor Phil had yet finished their first glass. Phil, no doubt sensing my absence, tried to draw me back to the dining room.

"What," he asked, "did you make of church, Nick?"

I muttered a non-committal "Okay", added something about how unfortunate it was that it was all based on legends, on empirical impossibilities, then tried to think of something to alter the course on which the conversation was tacking, dangerously close to the wind.

The breeze filled Phil's sails. "That's exactly it, Nick. I agree with you completely: people don't rise from the dead. Ever. Dead is dead. Gone. Finished."

"So then…"

"So if *once* somebody did return from the dead, it would, to say the least, be interesting, because that's not what happens. That's not life as we know it, is it? But if the best-fit explanation for a certain set of events is that a geezer actually did rise from the dead then it bears some investigation. It might actually be quite significant. Then if you discover that before he died the bloke claimed to be the son of God and that he predicted his death and resurrection..."

Colin Witheridge, on the other hand, like the overwhelming majority of defunct humanity, remained resolutely dead. If the tattoo on his lower abdomen had had anything to do with resurrection it had, so far at least, done him precious little good.

Laurel and Hardy lapsed into deathlike silence. A brief message on the office voicemail, in the passive voice of bureaucracy, told me that, for the time being, it had been decided not to progress phase two of the Kellaway & Co. investigation. I was tempted to interpret this as a signal that somebody had found Colin's envelope misfiled somewhere in the bowels of Thames House. As events would prove, I was wrong in that. The spies were simply turning their attention to things that had become, in the new world order, more important than Colin's Russian dalliances.

Nor did the Swiss police appear to be any more lively or diligent or effective in their pursuit of Colin's killers. They seemed to have formed a ready conclusion that Colin had crossed one of his Russian clients, betrayed his secrets, stolen his money and fucked his favourite girlfriend. Disturbing the Russians, particularly if Andropov was involved, was something their superiors would not be keen on: the Russians were bringing considerable amounts of money into Geneva then, using it to buy real estate at inflated prices, stuffing it into bank accounts paying below-market rates of interest in exchange for absolute anonymity, and keeping the town's laundromats flush with business.

Only Claire kept the search for truth and justice alive. She suffocated her grief in disciplined routines and make-work projects. She sorted Colin's study, rearranged it, sorted it again. In bent paper clips and discarded envelopes she sought clues as to who had killed her husband. She seemed to have no idea that he had worked for MI5 on the side, no concept of what his long-standing links with Russia might imply. No Laurel or Hardy ever came to enlighten her and I, bound by the Official Secrets Act and cautioned by its agent's hand, did not take on the task.

Claire created theories, developed them, elaborated them. She discussed them with anybody who would give her an audience. She was, with unusual tact and sensitivity, accused of wasting police time. Caroline softly recommended to Claire that she see a psychotherapist to help her cope with her grief. Claire looked puzzled, said, "I'm doing just fine, Caroline. If I need help, I'll talk to you and Nick."

A month later, Claire phoned me at my office. I took the call. "Nick," she asked, "can I see you?"

"When?"

"Now. I'm in London."

"Sure, any time. This evening? I'm sure Caroline would be delighted to see you." It was during those weeks after Caroline and I had moved to Knightsbridge, but before we had sold the flat in Mayfair. I had not seen Claire since the move.

"It's *you* I want to see. I'm standing outside the flat. You can be here in ten minutes."

Claire was standing on the pavement when I arrived. The grey, gaunt look had gone. She was wearing make-up and her hair was freshly cut, washed and styled. She wore sunglasses, high leather boots and a Burberry tied at the waist. She carried a fat, black leather briefcase – the type lawyers take their sandwiches to work in and use to coax exorbitant fees from their intimidated clients.

"I think," she said, in cold tones resurrected from her days as a forensic accountant, as she pulled files and papers from the case and spread them across the table, "that you know the people who killed Colin."

"Me? Know them? What could possibly give you that idea?"

No answer. More papers emerged from the briefcase. Then she said, "I've always wondered what this place was like. I've never been here before, you know." Claire walked over to the amorous Persians on the battlements of Hindustan. After ninety long seconds in India, she turned, looked at me. A flat, uninterested look. "Héloïse thinks you want to marry me."

I laughed. "Amazing imagination these kids have. I mean…"

"She thinks you killed Colin because you want to marry me. 'Don't worry, Mummy,' she says, 'I'll protect you.'"

"Really, now," I laughed. "You're my best friend's wife. You're my wife's best friend…"

Claire echoed my laughter. But there was ice in her voice. In an arctic whisper she said, "And *you're* Héloïse's godfather…"

"Quite." I turned and said, "I'll make us some coffee." It was as if I only then heard what Claire had said, heard the seeds of an accusation germinating in the icy flatlands of her voice. I stopped, turned again, looked back at Claire, still standing in the corner beneath the Indian walls where a man in flowing robes had drawn his pink dagger. "What do you mean by that?"

Ludgate Hill runs almost due west from St Paul's Cathedral down to Ludgate Circus. Once upon a time, in the far-off days of make believe, the Fleet River flowed south through Ludgate Circus, making its sluggish way towards the Thames. Cross the erstwhile course of that river and you are in Fleet Street. In 2002, Reuters was still based in Fleet Street, but all the proper newspapers were gone, the printing presses silent, the printers gone the way of other unionised species and fairy-tale characters, the journalists dispersed to wherever they could find a connection for their laptops. Goldman Sachs had moved into the offices of the *Daily Express*.

My meeting there one afternoon ran long and late. I sent my colleagues back to Mayfair in a taxi and took a walk to clear my head. I walked east along Fleet Street, across Ludgate Circus, up Ludgate Hill towards St Paul's. Rain had been falling most of the day, often heavily. There were still dark clouds in the east, but the sky was clearing behind me. As I passed Ludgate Circus, the sun fell below the edge of the clouds and shone directly up the line of Ludgate Hill, illuminating the façade and dome of the cathedral at its head. I became aware of Phil Scott walking beside me. "Magnificent, isn't it?" he said. "D'you know the most curious thing about it? It's that golden cross on the top of Christopher Wren's splendid dome."

"Curious? Why?"

"Why? Well, they're everywhere aren't they, these crosses? I've even got one on the wall of my bedroom at home, but nobody ever thinks about them. Most people don't at least. A cross was an instrument of torture, a gruesome form of execution. It was, literally, excruciating. A bloke could hang there in utter agony for days before giving up the ghost. I mean, the guillotine is civilised by comparison. What would you think if I kept a guillotine in my bedroom, or an electric chair in the sitting room? What's curious is why anybody would cover a barbaric instrument of torture with gold and stick it on the top of such a magnificent building as St Paul's."

"Or hang it round her neck."

Caroline had fallen for it all by then. She'd done the Alpha course, read the book, sung the songs, eaten the body, drunk the blood. One evening I made the mistake of asking her what she was reading. Without looking up, she simply began to read aloud, "'The jailer brought them into his house and set a meal before them and the whole family was filled with joy, because they had come to believe in God.'" I didn't respond. After a long pause, Caroline looked up and said, "It's hard to describe, Nick. It was like coming home, like coming back from a long, weary exile. Coming in from a cold, damp night into a place where it was all bright and warm. It was like something I'd been looking for forever, without knowing that I was looking. Then, out of the blue, God found me. It feels like home, back where I belong."

Shit! I mean, how would *anybody* feel if his wife described their marriage as a 'cold, damp night' and a 'long, weary exile'? Caroline's unspoken motive for moving to Knightsbridge was to repair a marriage. I knew that and told myself it was an aim that I shared…

3

Even a quick glance at a chart of stock market movements in the early years of this millennium shows what was happening. What you see, when you eliminate the noise, is a steady fall from the heady peaks at the turn of the century. The graph continues to fall through 2001 and 2002 and into the first quarter of 2003. Then, as investors begin to buy on the bullets of the Iraq War, the graph begins to rise, the upward slope over the following years almost the mirror of the previous years' fall.

At Kellaway & Co. we began to use this graph in our reports to our clients and in our marketing from early 2002. We traced the fall of the underlying equity markets in black ink. Then, rising gently off the millennial peaks, ascending out over the dark chasm beneath, we drew another line and painted it gold. This fine filigree bridge represented the performance of Kellaway & Co.

Those were the glory days. Over the previous twenty-two years, from 1979 to the end of the millennium, any investor long equities or bonds had done fantastically well. Bankers and fund managers, persuading everyone that they were the masters of the universe, got rich just by being in the right job at the right time. From 2001 onwards it was different – skills were tested. Kellaway & Co. shone, outperforming every imaginable long-only fund. Consistently, quarter-by-quarter, our funds' returns ranked us in the top quintile among our peers. Money flowed in. We raised our minimum investment level requirements. We raised the fees we skimmed off our investors' portfolios. Still the money flowed in. The consistency of our performance was the marvel of the industry. Only very occasionally, and even then with utmost discretion, did we have to borrow from new investors to ensure our loyal, long-standing clients would continue to earn the returns which they had come to expect. It was done for the greater good and, over a longer time horizon, it benefited all our clients, old *and* new, because it kept the reputation of Kellaway & Co. soaring like an eagle.

In 2003, not long after the fall of Baghdad and before it was clear that equity markets were emerging from their gloomy abyss, I received an approach from the authorities in Geneva, proposing that Kellaway & Co. relocate from London to Geneva. They had worked up a comprehensive proposal. The basic incentive was a tax deal that extended not only to the corporate entity, Kellaway & Co., but also to the personal tax positions of each member of senior management. The move would not have been of any personal financial benefit to me. I had achieved a similar result for myself through the judicious use of my Swiss bank accounts. The benefit to the firm would have been marginal at best. It was already structured, as you would expect, to be pretty well tax-proof. But it would have worked wonders for the UK-domiciled members of my team.

What was really clever in Geneva's approach was the manner of its presentation: it was delivered by the Chairman of Meyer & Cie, Paul Meyer, the younger brother of my old friend Claude, over dinner in Kellaway & Co.'s private dining room. When I showed Paul into the room, his eyes were drawn immediately to the painting on the wall, the blurry grey painting of an unsmiling nude sitting on the floor in front of a bookcase, with her thighs spread and her knees drawn up beside her breasts. The way her big, grey eyes stared at you in the accusative had led one of my quants to christen the girl 'Minerva's Owl'.[79]

"That's not a Richter, is it?"

---

[79] Nick has, apparently, missed the reference here to a famous line in Hegel: "When philosophy paints its grey in grey, one form of life has become old, and by means of grey it cannot be rejuvenated, only known. The owl of Minerva takes its flight only when the shades of night are gathering." From G.W.F. Hegel's Preface to *The Philosophy of Right*, Berlin 1820 – here translated by S.W. Dyde, 1896. – Ed.

"It is indeed. *Studentin IV*, 1967. Very evocative of the era, don't you think?"

"I'm a few years younger than you, Nick."

"You're not offended by it, are you? We take it down and replace it with a pseudo-impressionist landscape when…"

"Me? Offended? No," he laughed, "it's nothing compared to what you can get nowadays on the internet, nothing compared…"

Paul, unusually for a Swiss private banker, had recently found himself in the news – at least he had been in the news if you count *Hello!* in that category. He had divorced his wife of twenty-three years and married his mistress, a famous skier eighteen years his junior. He was rumoured to have paid a significant sum to suppress a series of photographs of his new bride in poses not dissimilar to the one the student had found herself in in Richter's *Studentin IV*.[80]

"And," Paul said, by way of ultimate inducement as he laid the offer out over coffee, "you could live at La Bise. It's on the market."

"You're selling?"

"We sold it years ago, just after Mom died. Andropov bought it. He's hardly been there for the last year, operates out of Monaco now."

"Andropov?"

"Vladimir Ivanovich Andropov, the oil guy. Not altogether savoury. Ex-KGB, they say, like his namesake. If somebody like you doesn't buy it, it'll probably get turned it into some kind of boutique hotel. I'd rather it stayed in private hands."

I spoke to Caroline about moving to Geneva, but I had not advanced beyond my first "darling" before she said, "No way, Nick." Among the senior management of the firm, however, there was greater enthusiasm. Money sings a pretty tune.

I reported back to Paul three days after our meeting. He said, "Great. And, Nick, you might be interested to know that Andropov will hold off on the sale. I talked with him yesterday. The hotel guys

---

[80] No painting entitled *Studentin IV* appears in S. Pagé et al *Gerhard Richter: Catalogue Raisonné 1962-1993* (Ostflidern-Ruit, 1993). The picture described here is similar to a painting by Richter that does appear – as number 149 in the *Catalogue Raisoné, Studentin, 1967*. It is probable that the painting on the wall of the dining room at Kellaway & Co.'s Mayfair offices was a forgery. – Ed.

can be kept in the wings for a week or so. It suits him to have some competition. Good for the price."

On Friday evening, Caroline and I went out to Weybridge and arranged to see Claire on Saturday morning. Something had come to light, I said. I needed to check it against Colin's diary for the days before he disappeared.

When Caroline and I arrived for coffee, Claire had the relevant papers ready. It only took me thirty seconds to find what I was looking for: the entry for the evening of Thursday 29 August 2001. *7:30. Andropov. His Place.* Colin's last known dinner had been at La Bise.

"Did you find what you were looking for?" Claire asked.

"No. Sorry. Just a hunch, but… no."

"At least you're still thinking about it, Nick. Thank you for that."

On the way home Caroline asked, "What was all that about?"

"Nothing. I thought I had made a link, but I hadn't."

"We need to be a bit more careful with Claire. We can't just barge in on her with every little hunch."

But Claire barges in on us, I thought. I *said* nothing, however. Caroline seemed unaware of Claire's visit to the Mayfair rooftops of an ancient Hindustani caravanserai and, if Claire had not mentioned it, it seemed best to let her remain unaware of that little episode.

La Bise was just the pinnacle of the emotional aspect to Geneva's approach. Over that dinner *à deux* in Kellaway & Co.'s dining room, Paul Meyer evoked other memories, spoke of old friends, nostalgically referred to the 'good times', seemed unaware that for most of my teenage years I had been exiled from La Bise. "Claude's still in his château in the Médoc," he said.

"I was last in touch with him only six months ago. He sent me an email on my birthday, believe it or not."

"Then you won't know that his wife's unwell."

"Unwell?"

"Very sick, I'm afraid. Probably has – what – a month to live?"

Later, out of politeness, I asked about his other brother.

"We haven't heard from Oscar for years. Thirty years, I'd guess. We don't even know whether he's alive or dead." I had no reason to suspect him of lying.

Like Claude, Marie-Claire had produced six children. She had used the sperm of at least four different males to make them. Her fourth marriage – to a Greek ship-owner – had lasted the longest, but it, too, had ended in divorce. She was living in Paris again, in her father's old apartment in the sixteenth. Her latest consort was a Canadian ice-hockey player less than half her age. "She explains it," Paul said with a barely suppressed grin, "as altruism: teaching a little boy the facts of life."

"Are her parents still alive?"

"Her mother is. She lives in Nyon. The old man died a few years ago. He made his century, though. Died a week after his hundredth birthday. I've got his gun collection."

"*You* do?"

"Downstairs, in the bomb shelter. Just a temporary home. It's a rather impressive collection, actually. We're trying to find a permanent place for it. A Russian – Andropov, in fact – wanted to buy it. But we want the collection to stay in Switzerland. Marie-Claire's considering setting up a foundation if we can't get an existing museum to find proper space."

Eva Bocardo had left Italy. She had apparently told a journalist that she had slept with Berlusconi, or maybe it was the Pope or the head of the Cosa Nostra. "Anyway, somehow, things got a bit hot for her in Italy. She's in California now."

"Janice Day?" I ventured.

"I remember the name. Same year as you and Claude, right?"

"Yeah."

"I was three years below you, Nick. I hardly knew anyone in Claude's year, really. I only know about Eva because she banks with us."

Over coffee, I asked Paul why he wanted a competitor in Geneva.

"It would be good for Geneva, good for us. You're a competitor already. There are no borders in this business any more. We believe in the economic case for clusters. You know, Michael Porter and all that.[81] It seems to work. In a globalised world, the more hedge funds and private banks we have in Geneva, the better. Geneva's a good place for our kind of people. Creative people with loose feet and agile minds. The kind of people for whom the State has withered away. Have you read Richard Florida?"[82]

---

[81] Michael Eugene Porter (1947–) is a professor at Harvard Business School and regarded as an authority on corporate strategy and international competitiveness. His concept of 'clusters' is set out in *On Competition* (Harvard, 1998) and in 'Clusters and the New Economics of Competition' in *Harvard Business Review*, Nov/Dec, 1998. – Ed.

[82] Richard Florida (1957–) is an American social theorist specialising in urban renewal. – Ed.

Paul was in London again ten days after his pitch and it was over a second dinner – at our Knightsbridge house – that I told him we would be setting up a small office in Geneva and relocating one of my top traders there. The trader was personally keen on the move and it would suit me – both for trades that needed to be executed more discreetly than was advisable through an open London dealing room and because it would give me the excuse for an occasional visit to Switzerland. Over time, the Geneva office would grow. "But," I said, "we'll be keeping Kellaway & Co.'s main office in London."

"I'm sorry to hear that," Paul said. He turned to Caroline, a quizzical expression etched on his face. "You'd've loved living in Geneva."

"I'm quite happy in London, thank you."

Happy, perhaps; but that evening Caroline was feeling unwell and went to bed early. Paul and I retired to the drawing room for a whisky. After his first sip of the Lagavulin he said, "We've hired a young man by the name of Torvald Nielsen."

I made no attempt to conceal my surprise.

"Don't worry, Nick," Paul said. "Your secret is safe with me. I'm a Swiss private banker, after all."

"How did you know?"

"Another Swiss private banker."

"I see."

"He's been a tremendous hire for us, extraordinarily good with numbers. The brains behind all our trading programs. Good with things, too, a real craftsman. Could've been a master watchmaker. He's in the process of becoming a Swiss citizen, with my personal sponsorship. You've never met him, I gather?"

"No."

"Would you like to?"

"I don't think so."

"A lot of time has passed, Nick. He's quite like you. He wouldn't need to know in what capacity you're seeing him."

"Thank you, but no."

"Okay, but if you change your mind…"

Later that year, Paul and his young wife spent a long weekend with us in Knightsbridge. Caroline persuaded them to come with us to church on the Sunday morning. Phil Scott was, as it happened, preaching. He began his sermon with a description of walking up Ludgate Hill towards St Paul's, "…And there was my friend and neighbour, Nick Kellaway, just as the sun came out from behind the clouds, staring up at the golden cross sparkling in the sunlight against a terrifyingly dark sky behind..." It was, I suppose, a bit like being mentioned in dispatches.

Phil ran through his list of the means of execution: gas chamber, lethal injection, firing squad, hangman's noose, electric chair, guillotine, sharpened sword. "What is it about the cross on which Jesus died that it should have been turned into that something that decorates our churches and is worn around the necks of pretty girls? Why don't we focus our eyes exclusively on the resurrection, the historical fact of the glorious empty tomb? Why does this Roman instrument of torture mean so much to Christians? What is it...?"

Afterwards, Paul asked, "Was that the Phil Scott who used to be a banker?"

"Yes."

"He was a friend of my dad's."

"He lives next door to us."

"How extraordinary. He spent a week at La Bise with Dad just before he died. Dad was very grateful to him."

Running dog of an imperialist paper tiger.

In May 2004, I was in Geneva for a few days on business. Paul invited me to stay with him. I hired a car at the airport and drove out the *autoroute* towards Lausanne. Paul Meyer had built himself a spectacular villa on La Côte soon after he had married his second wife. From the balcony the view was over vineyards, across the lake where early summer sailboats drifted lazily and on to the snow of the Alpine peaks beyond. Paul handed me a glass of white wine. As I took a first sip, he said, "What you are drinking was grown within a hundred metres of where you're now standing."

"It's good. Do you own the vineyard?"

"No. A pity. But no."

"I remember your champagne. Do you still have that place?"

"No, it was the first to go. We've sold all the old properties now – except Crans. We held on to Malibu until after Mom died and then it went too. Real estate's too much of an encumbrance. Too – what – too twentieth century? If you want exposure to property, there are plenty of paper derivative instruments that are a hell of a lot less hassle. *You* know that."

"Les Sornettes?"

A short laugh. "I'd almost forgotten about that old place. It was sold I don't know how long ago. Went for a song. It was almost derelict." Paul raised his glass and sipped the wine. "Swiss wine has improved out of all recognition since you lived here. Even the Geneva *vignoble* is now world class. You'll remember what it was like in the sixties."

"In the sixties I drank anything I could pour into a glass."

"You weren't that bad, Nick. I remember you as a model student. Hell, you'd never have made Oxford if you'd been pissed all the time."

"What do you think Oxford was about?"

Paul ignored my comment. "I've been trying to persuade Claude to move back to Geneva, set up in a vineyard in Dardagny or somewhere. Maybe even out here. Be near family now that he's on his own. Three of his kids are living in Switzerland."

"How's he taking it?"

"Hard. Have you been in touch?"

"When she died, yes. The usual. Nothing since."

"You should go see him. Marie-Claire was there for a week last month. She's living in Geneva again, you know."

I said, "No, I didn't know that... I'll give Claude a call."

Paul opened a second bottle of wine...

I didn't phone Claude. I phoned Marie-Claire instead, had lunch with her the next day at La Perle du Lac before driving out to the airport to catch the flight back to Heathrow. I was astonished by how little she had changed. She had not put on the weight that usually comes with the years; her hair was still dark; her skin was still smooth; her voice had the same soft lilt; her eyes had not loss their sparkle, nor her smile its mischief. The kiss she placed on my cheek as she prepared to leave lingered, I thought, more than form required. She said, "Dionysus and Ariadne – remember that?"

"Of course."

"I keep the boat in Greece now. My last husband was Greek. I'm going out there next week: Delos, Mykonos, Naxos, Paros, Ios... Remember how you used to dream about all those little islands when we were in Corsica?"

I smiled at the memory.

"You made a list of seventy-five Greek islands. Want to come?"

"Marie-Claire, don't tempt me."

She gave me another kiss, lips to lips this time. Then she turned and I watched the hips move, just as I had done on the ski slopes above Crans many years before, as she walked away without looking back.

4

Paul opened a second bottle of white wine…

As the sun moved westward and the clouds gathered on the Jura, he tried again to persuade me to move Kellaway & Co.'s main operation to Geneva. I changed the subject, tried to put him on the defensive, asked about the progress of the American attack on the Swiss banking system.

"I suppose it gave them confidence to go after Iraq and Afghanistan," Paul replied, without a trace of irony in his voice. "Global reach and all that. You know, Nick, we had our own little Holocaust accounts drama at Meyer a few years back. It was most peculiar."

"What was that?"

"Well, we took in quite a lot of Jewish money in during the thirties. 'Meyer' sounds Jewish. It's not Jewish, as you know; Dad always said he was descended from Nero, the Roman emperor, but if Jewish was good for business, I guess my grandfather didn't see the point of disabusing anybody." After the war, Meyer & Cie had adopted a liberal policy of returning the money with limited proof, provided the claimant signed a legally binding agreement to return the funds if a better claimant turned up. If the other banks had done something similar, Paul maintained, Switzerland could have avoided all the American trouble of the previous ten years. "I mean, how rational was it to insist on a death certificate for someone who'd died at Auschwitz?"

"Quite."

"Anyway, we had very few claims, as you might imagine. The Nazis were efficient." Among the types of account Meyer & Cie had operated for Jews sending their money out of Germany was one that did not even nominally require the original depositor's death certificate when an inheriting survivor came to make a claim. All that was needed to withdraw funds was a twelve-digit number. If the account holder lost the number, he or she would, in principle, lose the money. Otherwise it was a highly secure system, suited to its time. A claimant, under the terms governing the account, would never even need to identify the name of the holder, would not even have to identify himself or herself.

Paul filled my glass, pausing to listen to the distant rumble of thunder in the hills behind the villa. Although everything before us was still bathed in sunlight, you could smell the rain approaching. "About 1978," he continued, "we began to get claims on these accounts. The first one that came in gave the name of the original account holder which strictly wasn't needed, but he gave the twelve-digit number, too, so we paid out. A couple of months later a second came in. Then a third. We'd never before had any claims on this type of account. Not a single one. What was really odd about it was that all twelve claims we had came from page three."

"Page three?"

The original record of the accounts, Paul explained, had been made in duplicate. One of these two original sets of papers was kept in a safe in the bank in Geneva. The other set had, since the early sixties, been held separately in a vault deep under the Valais mountains. At some point, the paper records were transferred to a modern, more manageable, system and in the course of doing so the originally recorded order of the accounts was rationalised and rearranged alphabetically. As a result, it took Meyer & Cie nearly ten years and twelve claims to suspect the connection to page three of the original handwritten accounts list.

"There were only a few of us in the bank who had access to these records, so it was Dad and me and another guy – a guy called Benno Winckli – who went up to the Valais to check the vault. The safe where these records were kept hadn't been opened since the documents were stored there. The original seal was intact. We opened it and, sure enough, page three was missing. Winckli went white as a ghost."

It was Winckli who had been responsible, much earlier in his career, for organising the documents to go to the Alpine vault. He swore that the paperwork was complete when it left the bank. Christian Meyer himself had taken over the operation at that point, delivered the documents personally to the mountains, watched as the vault was sealed. Paul and his father realised that either page three had gone missing in transit or the employee was lying. Christian Meyer was adamant that the former was impossible. Winckli's sudden pallor was taken as evidence against him.

"It was awkward," Paul said. "There was nothing in Winckli's lifestyle to suggest he'd benefited from extra money. He was sixty-two at the time. Meyer has always been a compassionate employer. We let him go on full pension. He didn't take it well, but what choice did we have?"

"And that was the end of the claims?"

"No. There's more to come. There was an attempt at a thirteenth claim, August 1989. I was on holiday at the time. A Russian-speaking individual, about our age, well-dressed, British passport, arrived at the bank unannounced. He had the twelve-digit number and a story that his grandparents had been Russian Jews living in Germany when Hitler came to power."

"You gave him the funds?"

"Actually, no. Thirteenth time lucky. My instructions were that, if anybody tried to claim on one of these accounts, they were to stall and contact management. When the staff on duty did this, the claimant panicked and fled."

"Without the money?"

"Exactly. Yesterday, because it was nagging me, I called up the memo that was written at the time. The curious thing is that the claimant said he was you."

"Me?"

"Well, not exactly. I exaggerate for effect. The memo records the name he gave – the name in the passport he produced – as Nicholas Carraway. 'Carraway' as in the spice, but with two Rs."

"Nicholas Carraway is the name of the narrator in *The Great Gatsby*."

"Good. I discovered that too. Courtesy of Google."

"Did you go to the police?"

"No. Too many risks. We circulated his picture to all staff, though."

"You got the guy's picture?"

"Not a very good one. Security camera."

"That was the last of the claims?"

"It was. We heard nothing else about our Jewish accounts until the Americans started claiming that we, the whole Swiss banking system, the whole of Switzerland even, had been one big Nazi money-laundering machine."

"Do you think you could send me the photo?"

"Sure, I don't see why not."

I made another trip to Geneva a fortnight after my lunch with Marie-Claire at the Perle du Lac. Memories and daydreams still fresh, I rang her number. The phone was routed through to her mobile.

"Sorry, Nick," she said, "I can't do lunch. I'm in Greece. At anchor in the lee of the island they call Naxos. Remember Dionysus and Ariadne? Gods and goddesses of their own little world. Pity you didn't come."

So, instead of a second lunch with Marie-Claire, I made an appointment at Chaudet & Cie, the bank where I kept my tax-equalising Swiss Francs. I had had the account for ten years by then, making, by a suitably circuitous route, regular deposits into it. I had not, however, visited the offices of Chaudet & Cie in my capacity as a client and, in the obvious absence of regular statements, had only my own calculations as to approximately how well my investment should be performing. In one sense, performance was irrelevant: every centime in the account would have ended up alienated in the Exchequer's coffers had it not been in Geneva. On the other hand, one cannot be in my profession, at least one cannot be *successful* in my profession, without being possessed of an intense desire to see every last penny perform.

I was ushered into a room that was elegant but restrained: a Persian rug on the floor, dark brown leather chairs, red roses in a pewter vase. I recognised the painting on the wall as a Hodler; not one of his best, but still an original. It was a room that spoke of timeless solidity. It reassured. We strove for the same look at Kellaway & Co. and I think we did it better.

The problem, however, became apparent the moment that Chaudet's bespectacled man, an expatriate Canadian, slid my passport back towards me across the polished desk between us and looked up from his file. His thick glasses magnified the size of his grey eyes. They seemed to fill the room. "I'm sorry, sir," he said. "These documents do not match the details we hold for this account." The language was precise, but the voice cloyed like synthetic maple syrup.

"I beg your pardon."

"We hold records with which to identify you and what you have shown me does not match them."

"Impossible."

"Each time the holder of this account has withdrawn funds he has been correctly identified."

"I've never been in here before."

"We may be a small Swiss bank but our systems are world-class. They have to be. That is why people bank with us. People in your circumstances, Mr Kellaway." He closed his file and his eyes.

I asked to see Jean-Luc Chaudet, the chairman. Big Eyes left the room, came back five minutes later, said, "Mr Chaudet is, unfortunately, not available."

"Then I'll wait until he is available."

"I do not think that would be a good idea, Mr Kellaway."

"Why not?"

"You will have to wait a long time. Mr Chaudet is in Zürich today and tomorrow morning he flies from there to Beijing."

From a phone box outside Cornavin station – I did not think it prudent to use either the hotel phone or my mobile – I phoned Chaudet & Cie. I got as far as the chairman's secretary. I asked for a meeting, offered to meet him that evening in Zürich, I tried to persuade with the fact Kellaway & Co. had more funds under management than did Chaudet & Cie. Nothing moved her. She was a good secretary; she would not enter my name into her boss's sacred diary.

5

I got my meeting with Jean-Luc Chaudet two weeks later. Paul Meyer arranged it for me. Jean-Luc received me at an apartment used to meet clients for whom even the semi-anonymous door beside the polished brass plaque was insufficiently discreet. We sat in well-padded armchairs, our feet resting on the thick pile of a Chinese carpet, beneath a mountain landscape by Alexandre Calame to remind us we were in Switzerland. A silent butler served us coffee from a silver salver, set the antique porcelain cups on mahogany side tables and then withdrew with an ostentatious closing of the double doors.

Jean-Luc Chaudet was fortyish, suntanned, hair cropped close, as alert as a hawk, probably rippling with muscle under his Saville Row suit and monogrammed shirt. The voice purred as efficiently as a well-oiled clock. "According to our records," he began when the introductory formalities had been disposed of and we had, as fellow owners of financial institutions, agreed to be on first-name terms, "you have been into our offices five times. Each time you have been properly identified. You opened the account. You have withdrawn money three times, paid to you each time in bearer CDs. You came in a fifth time, to open a safety deposit box. You did not withdraw any funds on that occasion."

Suddenly, it was clear to me what had been happening. I do not, however, think that I betrayed my sudden flash of illumination. We went through the formal procedures. We checked my signature against the one on the bank's records, my passport number against the one held by the bank, my biometric details against those that had been added during one of 'my' visits after Chaudet & Cie had upgraded its security system. "You don't need the biometrics for remote operations, of course; but until now all your withdrawals have been made in person."

Nothing matched.

"What's in the safety deposit box?" I asked.

"I don't know. Do you have the key?"

"No. Don't you?"

"It is a dual-key system. We have one. The client has one. You need both to open the safe. We don't keep a copy of the client's key."

"You don't need my signature, passport, all that?"

"For the box you need just the key. Terms of access are different than with the accounts. We will have to sort the account out later and it could take some time, I'm afraid."

I phoned Claire when I got back to London, told her that I thought Colin might have had a safety deposit box in Switzerland and arranged to see her at the weekend.

Claire had thrown nothing of Colin's away. She had kept his collection of keys in an old shoe box. One of the keys in the box matched the drawing that Jean-Luc Chaudet had given me of a typical client key.

The next Tuesday, I flew to Geneva again. Jean-Luc Chaudet himself inserted the bank's key into its slot while I put the one Claire had lent me into the other keyhole. The door swung open. "I'll leave you with your papers," he said.

There was only one item in 'my' safe. I took the large manila envelope, sat at the table in the secure room, opened the envelope, spread its contents out in front of me. On my far left were several pages, stapled together, covered on both sides in dense handwritten Cyrillic letters, paragraphs interspersed with what seemed to be names and numbers. All illegible to me – except for the numbers and signature on the lower right corner of each page. That signature was, near as damn it, mine.

Next was a long memo, typed in English: 'To whom it may concern'. It detailed a complex, highly lucrative scheme for removing from Russia funds that the Russian state was likely, under its emerging laws, to claim for itself. It named the beneficial owner of the scheme: Vladimir Ivanovich Andropov. It went on to chronicle Andropov's career, from junior officer in the old Soviet KGB serving in East Berlin, where he ran agents whose mission was to create havoc on the other side of the Wall and where he was recruited as a double agent by Her Majesty's Secret Intelligence Service, through his role (with financial assistance from his friends in London, since amply repaid) in the auto-privatisation of the former USSR's oil assets, to (last entry) his August 2001 decision to relocate his international headquarters from Geneva to Monaco.

Beside the memo on Andropov was an account of the prototype for his money laundering schemes: the Rotten heist of 1976. It was all just as Colin had explained it to me after the event: the stolen FMBB tested telex codes; the transfer of funds to Zürich to buy a chalet in the Alps for Rotten's daughter; the majority of the funds withdrawn from the bank in Zürich and re-deposited in a bank in Liechtenstein. It went on, however, to name the person who had paid Martin Broadwood-Kelly, the trade-unionist agitator, for the stolen codes and it also gave the name of the beneficial owner of the Liechtenstein account (with both the name of the bank and the account number set out). Both were the same person. Lest there be any doubt, my middle name was given as well: Nicholas Alfred Kellaway.

The fourth item in the envelope was a carbon copy of the Longfellow poem – 'Tegnér's Drapa' – that I had received anonymously in 1977 after Andreas Baader had been found dead in his Stammheim prison cell. Except that in this copy the poem's original 'Balder' had somehow replaced the 'Baader' of the 1977 version:

I heard a voice that cried
'Balder the Beautiful
Is dead, is dead!'
And through the misty air
Passed like a mournful cry
Of sunward sailing cranes.
I saw the pallid corpse
Of the dead sun
Borne through the northern sky.

To my amateur eye it seemed pretty clear that the memos on Andropov and Thomas Rotten had been typed on the same typewriter as the poem.

The next item was something that I was now expecting to find. Long ago, when I was a lad of ten out on an afternoon adventure to rescue a damsel in distress, I had stolen the brittle, yellowed paper from the old tower at La Bise. For fifteen years I had faithfully kept its runes hidden deep among my lists and dreams. Then Anna Schmidt had taken it from me the night she had stood at the foot of my bed offering me a trade. Page three. Christian Meyer's page three.

Then there were two playing cards from the same deck: the ace of spades and the king of hearts. Someone had scrawled 'Joe Ace' across the ace of spades in fat, American handwriting. The king of hearts had been printed without his head – nothing between the royal shoulders and the royal crown.

The last item was a single photograph, one I had seen before: Caroline Carter – the choir girl – in her rooms at LMH wearing a commoner's gown, a mortarboard and a wicked smile.

"Did you find anything?" Jean-Luc Chaudet asked when I rejoined him in the anteroom.

"Yes. I'm taking it with me. I don't need the box any more."

"You know, then, who has been accessing your account?"

"I think so."

"Will you be pressing charges?"

"I'll have to think carefully about that."

"I'm sure that's right, Nick. In the circumstances it could be more of a problem than it's worth."

I made a phone call to Claire the next day. "I'm sorry, Claire, the box was empty."

"The key?"

"I left it with the bank. No sense in paying them for an empty box."

I paused to think for a moment after phoning Claire, then left the office and went round the corner into Shepherd Market where I thought there still might be an old red phone box. In an age when mobile phones had become ubiquitous, these old phone boxes were well-nigh obsolete. Westminster Council kept a few on as a service for tourists who wanted to be photographed standing in one and for prostitutes who used them to advertise their services. Among his friends and fellow collectors, Henry had boasted a fine collection of illustrated calling cards gathered from London phone boxes – before

Caroline found it. She made Henry watch as she burned the entire collection of nubile bodies and specialist services on the bonfire at the foot of the Weybridge garden.

When I found the Shepherd Market phone had a dial tone, I phoned Liechtenstein. The voice on the end of the line was that of a Hollywood actor auditioning for the role of an SS officer in a 1950s war movie. He could only speak to me about the account, he said, after I had given him the password. I am good with numbers. I remembered the number Colin had used for the account in Geneva and fluently reeled it off to him. It worked.

"I'm sorry, sir, you have closed this account."

"Have I?"

"Yes, sir. In December 2001. You opened the account in December 1976 and closed it exactly twenty-five years later, exactly to the day." The tone of his voice indicated that he admired the extraordinary precision of 'my' timing.

It was what Laurel and Hardy would have expected me to do, wasn't it? Wait until a few months after their visit and then close the account they had told me they knew about. I should, I suppose, have phoned the number Laurel and Hardy had given me then, but, at the end of the proverbial day, what did it matter to me or even to MI5 and MI6 whether Vladimir Ivanovich Andropov was ripping off the Russian state or not? It might even be of benefit to the UK. Some of his illicit gains would likely – very likely if he was still an MI6 agent – make their way to Britain, in some mysterious manner enhancing our GDP and the international prestige of our elected politicians. Moreover, the questions coming in my direction, were I to resurface the matter of Colin's envelope, would have been rather awkward. Colin was dead, nothing could alter that. Not even his tattoo. Besides, Laurel and Hardy themselves might have been fakes. The phone number they had given me might have connected me with something altogether more sinister than MI5.

So, 'in the circumstances', as my discreet Swiss banking friends would have said, instead of making the phone call, I took everything – the Russian list, Andropov's résumé, the story of Anna's 1976 bank fraud, the carbon copy of Longfellow's poem, a 'page three' that did not come from *The Sun*, the defaced ace, *le roi d'Aquitaine à la tête abolie* and even the picture of Caroline – to the far end of our Weybridge garden and burned the lot on the spot where Henry's women had gone up in flames not long before. Had I not lit that innocent little bonfire that morning, I would have been – as my less discreet British banking friends would have said – 'fucked'. Colin Witheridge, pretending to be me as he withdrew money from my account, would have seen that outcome all too clearly. I am sure it would have brought a smile to his lips as he signed my name and pocketed all those certificates of deposit made out to 'The Bearer'.

For my fifty-third birthday Caroline gave me, among other things, Adam Heggie's third and final book of poetry[83] – the one published after his death that contains 'Toxic Iraqi Derivatives, Free at the Point of Delivery':

> *In Babylon did Tony Blair*
> *A state-owned pleasure dome decree*
> *Where Enkidu could shave his hair*
> *And fuck fine whores for free*

That evening, as we had a quiet dinner at home together, Caroline said she had discovered another link with Phil Scott. Phil had somehow discovered Caroline's maiden name and put that together with the facts that she had grown up in Norfolk and had spent time as a child in India. He asked whether she had any connection with Colonel Charles Carter. "Quite an inspiration to me your dad was," Phil had said. "Back in the seventies and eighties we used to be members of a group that met to pray for persecuted Christians behind the Iron Curtain. We became quite close as a group, sharing things, praying for each other's families." Then he had added, after a pause and with a broad smile, "Our wayward children."

Counter-revolutionary prick.

"Isn't that amazing?" Caroline said.

From: Paul Meyer
Date: 30 September 2004 05:58
To: Nick Kellaway
Subject: Thirteenth Claimant
Nick,
Apologies for the delay. Photo attached. Not great quality.
Best,
Paul

---

[83] Adam Heggie, *Posthumous Poems*, London, 2004.

This transmission is intended for the sole use of the individual and/or entity to whom it is addressed. It may contain confidential or privileged information, etc., etc.

I opened the attachment. The photograph was in black and white, very grainy, taken from an angle above and to the left of the subjects as they walked towards a door. The woman was walking behind the man and the wide-angle lens made her much smaller than he appeared. To a casual observer it would not have been clear whether they were together or had simply been caught together by the camera as they walked independently towards the door.

I studied the picture of the man. It showed his face only from the eyebrows upwards: angle and shadow obscured the rest. Even though I had once claimed Colin Witheridge as my best friend, I could not have been anywhere near certain that the man in the photograph was he. It was the woman's face, captured as she glanced up at the security camera, now staring out at me from my computer screen with a momentary look of apprehension frozen for all time in shades of pallid grey, that made me certain that the man walking out of Meyer & Cie was indeed Colin. The woman was Anna Schmidt.

CHAPTER TEN

Héloïse and Claire came to lunch on the same Saturday that the *Financial Times* ran the headline 'Andropov's villa bombed'. I had risen early, gone to the office and read everything I could find about it on the internet.

A bomb in a car parked outside Andropov's villa at Eze on the Côte d'Azur had exploded at four the previous afternoon. Two people died. Even though Vladimir Ivanovich himself, the presumed target, had survived unscathed, the articles read like obituaries, tracing Andropov's career from the KGB apparatchik in East Berlin to becoming one of the world's richest men. They referred to rumours of unconventional methods and rivals dying in mysterious circumstances. La Bise was mentioned by name as his former Geneva residence and the venue for his legendary parties.

With nobody claiming responsibility for the bombing, speculation as to who had done it was rife: competitors, Russian agents, Al-Qaeda... One blog even blamed the CIA. There was, however, not so much as a hint of a connection to the British Secret Intelligence Service or – which may or may not have been the same thing – to Colin Witheridge.

I returned home to find Héloïse in my entrance hall, inhaling the perfume from Caroline's roses. She was wearing a skimpy dress – the same bright green colour as the dressing gown she had wrapped around her silken body on the morning after the night she had appeared cold and drunk at my Mayfair door. "Mummy and I," she said, "have just been to Harvey Nicks." She pirouetted on shoes that matched the green of the dress. The hem line rose two inches up her thighs.

We joined Claire and Caroline in the sitting room. I opened a bottle of New Zealand Sauvignon Blanc and, as we sat swirling the pale liquid around our glasses, watching its sunny reflections of the good life, Claire told us of Héloïse's summer plans. She was going, Claire explained as Héloïse sat demurely looking at her shoes, to Crete with her university boyfriend, Jack. "Show Aunty Caroline and Uncle Nick that picture of Jack."

Jack-in-the-Picture was a pimple-cheeked lad with greasy dark hair that covered his no doubt equally pimply brow. He looked about fifteen. Caroline passed Jack back to Héloïse, her only comment an incredulous smile as she went toward the kitchen with Claire in her wake.

When they had left the room, Héloïse said, "Uncle Nick, I don't want you to get any wrong ideas about me. That photo I just showed you? That's not Jack." She produced another photograph from her handbag and passed it to me. Jack-in-the-Handbag was a black-and-white 1930s American movie gangster with a scar on his left cheek, a cigarette on his lower lip and a fedora perched cockily on his head. "That's *my* Jack," Héloïse said, looking at me now with the same triumphant morning-after sneer she had worn as she sat on a stool in my kitchen, drinking strong coffee and wearing nothing but a silk dressing gown. "Jack, my Jack, is thirty-eight. He's an investigative journalist. He has three kids, each by a different woman. And you know what, Uncle Nick? *He*'s a lean, mean fucking machine."

It was Héloïse who, before she and Claire left us that Saturday afternoon, showed me Henry's Facebook page. Why she did it I can only guess. The smirk on her lips as she scrolled through pages was a derivative of another morning-after look – the grin when she had stood up from the stool and the dressing gown, its belt deliberately untied, had fallen open. In Henry's pictures it had done more than just fall open.

When she and Claire had gone, I phoned Henry on his mobile. I told him there were pictures on Facebook that I thought he should remove.

"Why?" he asked. I imagined, from the agricultural slurry in his voice, that he was probably on drugs. Caroline had found a bottle of tablets in Henry's room a month earlier and had confronted him with them. "For God's sake, Mum," he had said, "it's only Mandy." Caroline had taken his answer as an attempt to shift blame to his sister. Henry had laughed at her, slammed the door in her face. We had not seen him since.

When I decided that Henry quite possibly *was* listening on the other end of the line, I told him he had a reputation to live up to. "You need to think of Héloïse's reputation as well."

"Yeah, right, Dad," he said.

"Henry, it's true. You really cannot put this kind of photo of her out there for the whole world to ogle at." There was no reply. "Henry?" I enquired of the silent phone line.

"Get off it, Dad. Don't be such a fucking fascist."

"Henry!"

"Henry, what? Truth's a fascist concept."

Ungrateful, revisionist fool.

Three minutes had not passed and my anger had not fallen below boiling point before the phone rang. I hoped it might be Henry, repentant and apologetic. "Yes," he would say, "you're right, Dad. I've deleted those gorgeous pictures of Héloïse. Sorry. You were right." I counted to ten and picked up the receiver. It was not Henry.

"Mr Kellaway," said the voice – a voice I had not heard for five years, but recognised instantly. "My apologies for phoning you at home. I was just wondering whether there was something you thought you might want to tell us. Anything about the envelope and that? You know, with all this Russian business and so forth."

"No."

"Ah," Hardy said. "A pity. Mr Witheridge's widow thinks you know the people who killed him and the daughter, you know, has some *very* interesting ideas about you. Did you know she calls you 'Fuckolas Fuckaway'? Not very polite, but rather amusing, don't you think?" I thought I could hear the knuckles crack.

2

In early 2006, Emma Somerwell (*née* Wallace) – head of modern languages at an expensive girls' school, co-author of a French textbook, author of several well-received illustrated children's books and of a few obscure academic monographs – published the collection of six short stories she had conceived a long time earlier. It was called *Jericho House.*[84]

Emma sent me a copy of her book, neatly wrapped up in brown paper and addressed by hand. On the title page she had written, *Nick, Some stories. There never has been and never will be anything else. Love, Emma.*

- 'The Blood-Red Cord' is an account of an Israeli attack on Jericho led by the 1960s revival rock group 'Joshua and the Children of Israel'. They sing 'House of the Rising Sun'

[84] E.J.F.W. Somerwell, *Jericho House*, London, 2006. – Ed.

('And all you need for travellin', man/ Is a rucksack and a gun/ And the only time I'm satisfied's/ In the House of the Rising Sun.') as they saunter round the fortified walls of the Palestinian city. The story is told from the standpoint of Rehab [sic] the Prostitute. The elite among the Canaanite inhabitants of Jericho, before their overthrow by Joshua & Co., had apparently practised the sacrifice of their women's first-born sons. As their moral compass evolved, however, they had developed a system under which a foetus taken from the womb of a temple prostitute could, for a fee, be substituted for the life of a noble first-born lad. Rehab hangs a red cord from her window on the east wall of Jericho, to ensure her house is spared when the rest of the town is destroyed. Because of such references as the University Press, The Bookbinders' Arms and the River Jordan boatyard, a pleasing ambiguity remains as to whether the Jericho of Emma's tale is the biblical town or the one in Oxford. Whisky Willie makes a cameo appearance as a maker of red ropes in the building where Rehab and friends ply their trade.

- 'The Oxford Compass' is the story of the wives of two well-known Oxford philosophers, thinly disguised as Denis de Lucinge and Raoul de Faucigny of the medieval Université Aliénor d'Aquitaine in Poitiers. The two philosophers go away to lecture on such matters as 'The ought of prudence and the ought of morality in the context of David Hume's Is/Ought Question', 'Meaning, Truth and the Construction of the Oppressive Society', 'The Villesalem Conundrum', 'Utilitarianism and the Concept of Conscience', 'The Is/Ought question in the light of what is deemed to exist', 'Nietzsche on the Love of One's Neighbour' and 'From Bonobos to Humans: the Application of Sociobiological Ethical Principles in Complex International Relations'. They stay away from Oxford/Poitiers for seven years. During that time the wives they have left behind entertain poets and troubadours and throw legendary parties.

When the philosopher husbands return to Oxford/Poitiers at the end of seven (or it may be 700) years, their wives are not at all pleased to see them. They use their well-honed charms to persuade two distinguished local psychiatrists to lock the husbands away in a prestigious Swiss mental

320

institution (Le Salvan-Cheiry), 'during which period of their lives they produced some of the most notable works of twentieth-century philosophy'.

- 'Oedipussy Regina' tells of a third-year Oxford modern languages undergraduate who finds herself, late one afternoon in the Michaelmas term, taking a solitary Rousseau-esque promenade through a desolate wasteland of marshes and bogs. Towards dusk, as a cold, thick mist rises from the damp land, the student loses her way. Eventually, she sees a light shining in the darkness and makes her way towards it. The light comes from the windows of an ancient church that stands forlorn in the abandoned marshlands. An English Heritage plaque tells her that the village the church once served was wiped out in the Black Death, and that the parish had never subsequently been resettled. As the girl approaches the church, she sees a beggar sitting in the porch. The student reaches down to him, takes his hand, helps him rise to his feet. She leads the vagrant around to the back of the church, away from the light, sits him on an ancient tomb and feeds him honey cakes and vintage champagne that she takes from her rucksack. (Again: 'And all you need for travellin', man/ Is a rucksack and a gun…/ And the only time I'm satisfied's/ In the House of the Rising Sun.') She removes the tramp's grimy clothes, washes them and then him, in a warm spring that gushes from the foundations of the old church. As the old man eats and drinks, the girl takes off her clothes and dances for him among the gravestones. In the frenzy of copulation that follows, the man suffers a stroke and is left paralysed. The student reaches into her rucksack, takes out a gun, fits a silencer to it, finishes the vagrant off. She dumps the body in the river, dresses herself, takes the tramp's clothes with her, returns to Oxford on the last bus, puts the dead man's clothes in a box.

Nine months later, the girl – now graduated from Oxford and living in Crete, where she works as a holiday rep for a German package tour company that has taken possession of the island following a defaulted debt – gives birth to a monster. The people of Crete try to kill the monster, but they cannot. They build a labyrinthine enclosure in which to keep the creature. The monster promises to do no harm if each year, on its birthday, they feed it a virgin. The people of Crete agree. Word spreads rapidly through alternative travel company websites and the labyrinth and its monster become a major tourist attraction. Tickets for the annual 'Sacrifice of the Virgin' ceremony are eagerly sought.[85] Television rights prove extremely lucrative. As the renown of the festival spreads, a small village in Portugal hires a firm of Los Angeles image consultants to re-imagine for the twenty-first century its own, rather tired, virgin experience. The Oxford woman, whom nobody knows to be the monster's mother, stays in Crete rather than returning to England, which is in terminal economic decline. She is elected to, and sits on, the prestigious 'Virgin Selection Committee'. After seven years in Crete, the Oxford woman opens, for the first time, the sealed box where she has kept the clothes that belonged to the dead beggar. Sewn on the inside of the old man's ragged overcoat is a name tag. She stares at it in disbelief, "That vagrant was my father."

- 'In Vino Veritas' is also set in Crete 'before the tourists came, when the ancient gods still stalked the sun-soaked slopes and students slept on sandy strands with sirens the sea swept in'. After an evening at a taverna on the beach, where wine and ouzo and marijuana are consumed in record quantities and crockery is smashed against the walls to save the bore of washing it up, a band of scantily clad females sets out on a traditional bacchanalian procession into the moonless night. During their revels they pass a church – a little chapel set on a rocky promontory at the far end of the beach. One of the women, a girl called Anna Kowalska, pauses.[86] She sees that the door to the chapel is ajar and that within a man sleeps on the stone ground before the iconostasis. She enters the church, wakes the sleeping man with her kisses, makes tender love to him, but then demands more and more and more. When the exhausted man can do no more, she cuts off his head and his genitals, drenches herself in his blood ('It felt good, that warm, fresh blood on her skin, soaking into her thirsty pores. It tasted salty in her

[85] See www.completevirginsacrificeexperience.com – Ed.
[86] See A. Kowalska, 'Sex, Race and Social Darwinism in the *Vernichtungslager* from the Herero to the Jews' in H.A. Frankland and F. Honeychurch (eds.) *250 Years of German Political Theory* (Oxford and Berlin, 1993). – Ed.

mouth. She could feel the truth as it enveloped her.'[87]), then rejoins her fellow maenads as they process down the beach and plunge their delirious bodies and satisfied minds into the dark depths of the all-enveloping sea.

- In the story called 'Joe's Ace', April, a first-year undergraduate at Magdalen, books an Easter holiday with Timetravellers Unlimited, an alternative travel company recently established in the Cornmarket, to go to Knossos for the time of Theseus's encounter with the Minotaur. Because of a technical malfunction in the timecraft, however, April is transported to another destination. She finds herself with six people – three men and three women – in a dark room where an old clock ticks with sober regularity. The six are completely oblivious to April's presence, but April can see them, hear them and touch them. She watches the six as they eat, drink and make love. She listens as they bicker, play card and dice games, tell stories they make up about the world beyond the dark room and discuss a murder they plan to commit.

Secure in her immateriality, April does things she would never have done in the flesh: she massages the strong shoulders of one of the men and then caresses the full breasts of the statuesque blonde woman who stands like a naked Nordic goddess on the threshold of a door that never opens. Little by little, like daylight in the high latitudes, April's presence dawns on the six. April is first aware that things are changing when, after she had spent the hours of sleep in one of the men's arms, he recounts his dream and the sex he has had in that other realm. "I haven't had a wet dream in years," he says and describes April with perfect accuracy – right down to the birthmark on her left thigh. An hour later, by the melancholy clock, one of the women suddenly jumps and claims she has seen the ghost of the one they intend to kill. She points to the chair where April is sitting and says, "She has a birthmark on her thigh just like the girl in your dream." April slowly materialises into the room. At first the six can only hear the high notes in her

---

[87] See E. Reader, *Das Gefühl und die Wahrheit: Competing Ideologies in the Berlin Kommunes, 1967–1977*, London, 1989. 'She could feel the truth as it enveloped her' is a direct quote from one of the case studies in this work. – Ed.

voice and can put their hand into her body as if into a bowl of jelly as it sets. Before the ominous clock strikes noon, April is as real as the others in room. "This," says the woman who saw April first as a ghost, "is a godsend. She can be the one we kill, whose death will give us the key to the door and to our freedom at last."

"If we kill you now," says another, "you will be back in Oxford for the first week of Trinity Term."

The man who fucked April in his dreams reaches for the carving knife, but April gets to it first and is about to stab him when the man raises a hand and says,

"Tell you what; let's play cards to see who dies." April plays the queen of hearts and Joe the ace of spades... April never does find out whether it is she or Joe who dies. Back in Oxford, Timetravellers Unlimited apologises for the malfunctioning timecraft and refunds the cost of the failed trip. April uses the money to pay for an abortion at an expensive Harley Street clinic.

- 'Sogol' is set in a chalet in the Alps high above the top end of Lake Geneva. A group of six girls – all recent Oxford graduates – have hired it for a reunion and a week's skiing over Christmas. On Christmas Eve a storm gets up and in the morning they awake to howling winds and a blizzard that in the course of the day turns into an ice-storm. A phone call advises the girls that they must not go out. The chalet is cut off from the real world and three men – the lamplighter, the local policeman and a man who said he was God – have already died because of the weather. The phone line is cut before the warning is finished. The electricity fails. The girls light candles and make a big fire in the hearth. They huddle around it to keep warm. A life-size portrait of Nero Redevivus watches over them from above the mantlepiece. They decide to tell stories to pass the time. The first tells the story of the Joe's Ace as if she were the time traveller from Magdalen College. The second tells the story of the maenads in the voice of the one who decapitated the man she found sleeping in front of the iconostasis. The third is the undergraduate who gave birth to her father's monster child. The fourth tells of the legendary parties she and a friend used to throw when their husbands were away on lecture tours in the United States. The fifth says she is a

Jewess, who can trace her lineage back to the time when the Israelites returned to Canaan from their bondage in Egypt. She relates a secret story that has been passed down the female line of 'a house that stood in Jericho and faced the rising sun'. Then all eyes are on the sixth woman. She alone has not told a story. Instead of telling a story, she slowly undresses in front of them. The five watch in silence. Her breasts are preternaturally enlarged like those of a primitive fertility goddess and eventually they can see, concealed until then beneath the swaddling layers of winter clothes, that she is pregnant. The pregnant girl, smiling like an icon, places a gentle hand on her belly. A sudden gust of wind causes the fire in the hearth to flare up. As if on a pre-arranged signal, the five rise up as one from their seats and kill the pregnant woman. They cut her open. They pluck the unborn child from the dead woman's womb and squeeze the enormous breasts until they sag like balloons forgotten after the party is over and the guests have all gone home. They boil the baby in the milk in a great cauldron set over the blazing fire. They sit down at the candlelit table. Only the Jewess, who can trace her matrilineal heritage to Rehab the prostitute, refuses to participate in the feast. "It's not kosher," she says, "to cook a kid in its mother's milk."

3

In the late spring of 2006, not long after *Jericho House* was published to critical if not popular acclaim, Caroline and I attended a formal dinner at one of the City livery halls in honour of a visiting American economist. The man of the moment gave a self-congratulatory, proselytising speech on the joys of increased capacity for risk-bearing in the new economic order. It contributed, he proclaimed, to the general good of mankind by enabling higher GDP growth than would otherwise have been feasible under contemporary demographic conditions. The City audience, proud of its role as the vanguard of well-being, basked in reflected glory. The economist's fee was, I have no doubt, commensurate with the light and warmth preached.

Fabrice had been on the event's organising committee and so, through the good offices of Linda, my secretary, I found myself seated next to Emma Wallace. Her husband, Tom Somerwell, was sitting at the high table with the speaker. Caroline had been placed at a table on the far side of the room. Emma had recently lost her job as a result of publishing *Jericho House*. The middle-class parents of her schoolgirl pupils had mounted a campaign against her. It was not appropriate, they had said, for somebody with *Jericho House* thoughts in her head to teach their daughters. Emma's dismissal had merited several column inches in the national newspapers over a period of two or three days. From the story, as reported, I had naïvely imagined that she would have had a good case against the school for unfair dismissal. Caroline had corrected that notion: the girls' rights to their presumed innocence would, she opined, trump any and all of the rights that Emma might claim had been violated.[88]

"I thought you were a family lawyer, darling," I had said.

"Protection of minors?" Caroline had answered. "Isn't that what family law's all about? That and making sure the wife gets her fair share in a divorce."

Emma did not seem to mind her dismissal. She and Tom had already amassed a significant fortune and the much-vaunted new economic order was contributing handsomely to further augmenting the general good of the Somerwell household. Tom was still making money aplenty and Emma was in demand elsewhere for precisely the reasons she was no longer in demand at the school.

"I've had my fill of teaching, anyway," she said, in the comforting, persuasive voice of a sat-nav woman, as we sat at the liveried table. "They're happy for me to teach Baudelaire, even Georges Bataille, but God forbid I should set anything original down on paper myself. It's like you're allowed to sit at home in your comfy armchair sipping chardonnay, watching people shoot and knife each other on television, but you're *not* permitted to go out and do it yourself. I mean the knifing and shooting, of course – not the chardonnay. You were stabbed once, weren't you, Nick? Do I remember that right?"

"A long time ago, Emma. 1977."

"Did they ever get the bloke who did it?"

"Not as far as I know."

"Knifed… shot… axed… you know, those are the euphemisms they use at Tom's bank when they fire someone. Probably the same where you've worked."

I nodded.

---

[88] See W.C. Batsworthy, *Power Narratives: Natural, Human and Civil Rights in a Post-Modern Context* (London, 2007). – Ed.

"Still, I'm not alone. Last year they hounded the chaplain out because she was teaching their daughters about the virgin birth. Now *that*, they thought, was a seriously dangerous notion. I mean, if you can get pregnant regardless, what's the point in preaching safe sex?"

Over salt-roasted sea bass on a bed of withered spinach, I told Emma that I had read her book and she laughed, "My meta-narrative for an age in which there are no meta-narratives." Then, more quietly, she said, "You probably recognised some of the sources."

"Some."

"All the stories have their origins in the Jericho House, of course. I'm thinking of doing a second volume, you know, something like *Jericho House Revisited*. Six more stories. In what was published I didn't even touch on the poster of Eve and the Cobra or that story about the workman raping that German girl in the front room. What about *Acéphale*?"

"How will you decide whether to do it?" I asked.

"Edward's encouraging me."

"Edward?"

"Edward Reader. You probably don't remember him, he's my agent. I had something based on the Garden of Eden painting and that German girl in the draft, except that I turned the rapist into a graduate with psychotic eyes and got the council to employ him as a town planner. He was wandering about with a clipboard when he saw a girl in the front room of the Jericho House lying naked on the floor beneath the poster. It went from there. Edward had me take all that out, save it for the sequel."

"I remember the poster. It was…"

"… And 'Joe's Ace', he completely changed that. The way I originally wrote it, the way we originally conceived it in the Jericho House, Sill and I, it was much longer. It started off with some fantasy of Sill's about having sex with a man she found lying asleep on a mountain in the Alps. In his dreams. About her being in his dreams; the object of his dreams. Or maybe she'd killed him in order to indulge in a little bit of necromancy. There were different versions. Sometimes it was six feral lesbians on an Alpine walking holiday who found the poor bloke. I called it 'On Blueberry Hill' originally…"

"'Joe's Ace'… the title rings a bell, but I can't think from where."

"Nick, do you remember that night at the Nietzsche Society when we did 'The Sixth Must Die'? I used some of that in 'Sogol'."

"Did I also detect the night when…"

"What was that woman's name?"

"Jan."

"No, not Jan. I haven't forgotten *her*. The other American, the one who was there the night we did 'The Sixth Must Die', who took you on after Jan and Sill had gone."

"Sylvia," I offered.

"That's her. Sylvia Spurway. The one whose stag we killed. Are you still in touch?"

"Just Christmas cards."

"And Jan? Since you mention her... she was your friend originally, wasn't she?"

I gave Emma the concise version. I ignored all the dead-end byways that had been fancifully built around Jan's trail in the seventies, bypassed Edward Reader's delving into the Stasi files, omitted Tom O'Neil's research and said simply that I believed Jan had died in a house fire in Munich in 1972.

"I heard," said Emma, "that she became a gangster's moll and helped him rob banks somewhere out in the Midwest."

"I've heard a lot of Janice Day legends over the years, but never that one."

"So the house fire in Munich then?"

"Probably."

"Was that German girl involved?"

"I don't know. I know she didn't die in it."

"How? Is she still alive?"

"Absolutely no idea." I stayed away – thought I was keeping Emma's imagination away – from Anna's visit to my Islington flat, from the tattoo on Colin's lower abdomen, from the picture of Anna caught on camera as *she* tried to rob a bank. Anna Schmidt *and* Colin Witheridge. What followed made me wonder whether I *had* kept my thoughts to myself. Or perhaps Emma was just thinking about her own Janice Day legend.

"So how old would Jan have been when she died?"

"Twenty," I replied.

"That's *very* young. Even Bonnie Parker was twenty-three."

"Bonnie Parker?"

"The Bonnie of *Bonnie and Clyde*? You know, 'Hey boy, what you doin' with my mama's car?' Great opening scene. The rest of the film's shit, though. Warren Beatty going on about not being much of a lover boy? Give me a break! Of course Bonnie and Clyde were fucking the pants off each other. That's where all the excitement came from. The bank jobs were just side shows – they were ambushed and shot to pieces because they were fucking without a licence."

Sitting beside me in the back of the car as it drove us home from the City, Caroline asked, "How was your evening?"

"Fine."

"You seemed to be in deep conversation with the woman next to you."

"Did I? Possibly… it was Emma Somerwell. Emma Wallace. St Anne's? The year above us?"

"The one who's written those books on Nietzsche?"

"I think so."

"I've read some of her stuff."

"Really?"

"Murder as the route to personal freedom… morality after the death of God, after we've killed God…" Caroline took my hand and looked out at the Temple on our right as the car drove along The Embankment. "I suppose," she said, more to the barristers in their chambers than to me, "there *was* a Nietzsche moment."

"Was?"

"The Saturday after Good Friday… when Jesus was in the tomb… before the Resurrection."

4

The good times rolled. Money was being made hand over fist. Only an unimaginative eejit with less than half a brain could have failed to get rich. Sure, there were prophets of doom, Jeremiahs howling from the sidelines, the vintners of sour grapes calling foul, but hey, the graveyards of finance contain many a tombstone of those who were right before their time.

In truth there was no choice. Chuck Prince was right: if you had chosen to dance, you had to dance as long as the music was still being played.[89] If you didn't dance, your competitors would eat your

---

[89] Charles O. 'Chuck' Prince III (1950–), then chairman and chief executive officer of Citigroup, said on 9 July 2007: "When the music stops, in terms of liquidity, things will be complicated. But as long as the music is playing, you've got to get up and dance. We're still dancing." Mr Prince resigned his post in November 2007. He is understood to have left the company with vested Citigroup stock worth nearly $100 million, a pay package of $38 million that continued to be paid and an annual pension of $1.75 million. – Ed.

dance card, lure your clients away with the promise of higher returns, lure your employees away with the promise of bigger bonuses, steal your children and sell them to Oliver Wyman or whoever turned out to be the highest bidder on the day. All you could do was be vigilant, watch the charts, the signs and the omens, listen to the rumours, trust your well-honed instincts to get out when you could, without losing the silk shirt off your back. At Kellaway & Co. we knew we were the best, confident of our abilities, certain we would know when to go short again. It was the little guys who would suffer, the guys who should have stuck to estate agency and tiddlywinks, the guys who should never have dreamt of mixing it with the big beasts.

5 June 2007

Dear Nicholas

I've been writing this letter for thirty years.

What we did that night in Houston back in 1976 was WRONG. For years I wished I'd plunged the knife straight into your heart.

I could not stay in that house after you'd been there. I could not sleep in that bed any more. It had been Johnny's and my bed. After he was killed I used to lie in it, thinking about him and crying myself to sleep. And then you defiled it, joining our bodies together like we never ever should of [sic] done.

I left my job. I moved back to my parents. My father wanted to get an International Arrest Warrant out on you and get you hauled back to Texas and tried for Rape. He said no jury in Texas would have acquitted you for the Rape of a girl who's [sic] husband had just died for his Country in Vietnam and you would spend the rest of your days in a Texas prison. They do not treat rapists kindly in the jails back there. I said NO. He said he'd go to England and get his hands on you personally. I said NO.

Later that year I moved to Dallas to be near the Church Johnny and I got married in. I didn't tell anyone up there what you'd done to me. They'd known Johnny. It helped that they'd known Johnny. Folks were kind and loving. One of the elders in the Church found me a job in his Company. After a couple of years I was almost ready to forgive you and ask the Lord's forgiveness for any part I might have played and for my hardness of heart.

Then two things happened. My father HAD flown over to London. He found you outside of one of your drinking dens and stabbed you in the heart. For two years he kept silent about the hole [sic] thing and then in 1979 he told me he had killed you. So I had that to deal with. He died some years back and before he did he came to terms with what you'd done and what he'd done. He knew, too, by then that you had survived the attack. I learned from Polly Page that you were still alive and told him. Polly said you'd had Sexual Intercourse with her too and that I shouldn't take what you'd done to me personally. Polly said it was all just a little game you played to compensate for your introverted bookworm teenage years when you were scared of girls and couldn't form normal relationships with them. I don't buy all those Psychology Excuses.

Then another thing happened and I realised how EVIL your game really was. Dave Hill came back to Dallas. Dave's from Oklahoma originally. He's been married before. When he was still in High School in Oklahoma he got a girl pregnant and they had to get married. That's how it was back then.

They were two angry teenagers living with a screaming baby on a trailer park outside of Tulsa. His first wife was deep into drugs and so they had to take the baby away to protect her. By GOD's mercy Dave realised he had to do something. He left his wife and got his kid back and ran off to Dallas. He got a job and within a few years he was very successful and running his own Company employing more than a hundred people. He finished High School in evening classes and started on his College Degree. He went through a long list of women because he could never hold on to the same one for more than a couple of months. He went back to drink. He did coke. He cheated on his Company Accounts so he wouldn't have to pay so much TAX. I'm telling you all this because I don't want you to think he doesn't know what goes on just because he's the Pastor of a big Church in California.

A friend of Dave's brought him to Church. That was the Church where Johnny and me married. He heard the Gospel, sought the foregiveness [sic] of his sins through Jesus' substitutionary sacrifice and gave his life to the LORD. He wrote to the IRS and over the next couple of years paid the taxes he'd cheated on. He made reparations wherever he could. He and his daughter moved to a house that was near to the Church so he could serve there more easily. He tried to find his wife. But she was dead of a Heroin Overdose.

Dave wasn't at the wedding because by then he had decided to go to seminary and he was away on a course. But his daughter was there. She was just barely fifteen at the time. I remember seeing her as I walked up the aisle. She was sitting there in a sparkling bright yellow dress pretty as an angel with a great big happy smile. Maybe you don't remember Myrtille Hill. Maybe to you she was just one of those many little pieces you played your Games with. She remembered you though. She could describe every moment. How she told you how much she liked your English Accent, like something out of the Movies she said, and how thrilled she was when the Best Man of all people started paying attention to her. How you told her you were staying in the hotel upstairs and said you had to go up to the room to get something she might like to see and then asked her if she would like maybe to come with you. How she went with you, totally trusting and innocent.

331

Myrtille told her dad, of course. She told me too when I started going out with Dave. That was 1979. She was twenty-one by then and she could describe the whole thing just like it had happened the day before. Every thought that I had of writing you a letter and telling you I had forgiven you went up in smoke. Maybe I had forgiven you what you did to me and Johnny but I could NOT forgive you what you did to Myrtille.

Myrtille became my daughter when Dave and I married in 1981 even though she is only seven years younger than me. We stayed in Dallas for four years after we were married. Dave was an associate pastor at the Church.

Myrtille was still living with us then. She helped me look after my own children and she was a wonderful blessing to me. At one point I had three children under eighteen months and I do not know what I would have done without her. Then we had a calling to a Church in California.

My eldest guy is called Johnny. John Morris Hill. That was Dave's idea. The twins are Matthew and Mark. They have all grown up and left home now. They are all fine Christian young men for which we praise the LORD. Johnny's married with two little girls of his own. I have four other grandchildren because Myrtille has two guys and two lovely girls. My life turned out to be a very fulfilling one. Surrounded by all these Blessings, I think I had almost forgotten about you. Then your name came up again.

Matthew, who is studying commerce and accountancy, was home for the Holidays. At dinner one night he said ,"Mom, wasn't a guy called Nick Kellaway Johnny Morris's best friend as a kid and best man at your wedding?" I said YES.

"Mom," he said, "this guy is seriously rich. He ran a seminar on edge [sic] funds at school. He's one of the richest guys in England. Our professors were so, like, in awe that one of them introduced him as 'SIR Nicholas Kellaway'. I Googled him. It's got to be the same guy. His résumé says he grew up in Switzerland and went to the International School in Geneva. That's where you and Johnny went, isn't it, Mom?" I thought: Nick Kellaway is one of the richest guys in England. I sat there wondering how many people you had walked over and what pact you had made with the Devil.

Dave came to me where I was sitting on the edge of the bed, crying. He put his arm around me. I screamed and ran to the other side of the room. It was just like you were in the room with me. You were looking at pictures of Johnny with me. You were telling me that Johnny had been your best friend and how you had camped out in the woods at Rulebow [sic] and laughed about ghosts. You were putting your arm around me and brushing my hair from my face and wiping my tears. I had dreams that night and for weeks afterwards. You were always there. You were unbuttoning the yellow dress Dave had bought Myrtille for the wedding. You were dancing naked in those woods you used to go to with Johnny except Johnny wasn't there and you were drenched in Myrtille's blood and Myrtille was lying dead on the cold earth. You were lying on the floor of my house in Houston and I was screaming and stabbing you again and again with a knife but no blood flowed and you just laughed and laughed and said what a good Game you thought it was.

Dave took me to see a Counsellor. We went six times. Dave always came with me. We worked it out that I had never really forgiven you for what you had done to me and Myrtille. It was still there gnawing away at me, giving the Devil a foothold in my Soul. In not forgiving you I was giving myself a moral superiority that I am not entitled to independent of Christ. For ALL have sinned and fallen short of the glory of GOD. When Jesus taught his disciples to pray, he said forgive us our sins AS we forgive those who sin against us. We prayed that I might be able to forgive you. We prayed that I might live in the reality of my own forgiveness, that I might be able to let go of my false pride and claim the grace and promises of GOD through the cross of Christ.

Dave and I put you on our prayer rota. You are still on it. We pray for you on the 29th of each month. Dave said he thought I would not be able to obtain my full release in Christ's grace until I had talked everything through with Myrtille. The last thing I wanted to do was bring Myrtille back into this and to re-open her pain. I said NO. But Dave phoned her anyway and Myrtille flew out to California There were tears. Lots of tears. Then we prayed.

We prayed for ourselves and we prayed for you. None of the three of us has any idea how long we knelt there crying and praying and confessing our sins. But then, suddenly, it was all over. It was a physical feeling just like a big weight being lifted off my chest. I could breathe again. The same thing came to Dave and Myrtille at exactly the same time. We were, all three of us, kneeling at the foot of the cross of Calvary. Jesus had taken away our burdens two thousand years ago. We were experiencing the lightness and the joy and the peace of the resurrection.

We pray that one day you might experience this too.

Very truly yours,

Sally Hill

Surely this was a joke! The letter had to be a forgery, some perverted prank. I mean Sally Pinkerton married to cute, little Blueberry Pie's pointy-headed Ku Klux Klan daddy? Give me a break! It was about as likely as the perpetual virginity of Bonnie Parker. But, then, Christians do coincidences.

I re-read the letter, alighted on *SIR* Nicholas Kellaway, remembered the lecture, wondered with a weak inward smile whether the flustered professor had the gift of prophecy. Caroline came into the room. "Who's the letter from?" she asked. By 2007, handwritten personal letters had become rare, something worthy of comment. Any important communication came by email nowadays.

I ignored the unknown joker and said, "Sally. Johnny Morris's widow."

"That's nice," Caroline said casually. "You haven't heard from her for a long time."

"More than thirty years. She remarried apparently, had three sons, all grown up and flown the nest now."

"When their children grow up, people do seem to want to reconnect with the friends of their own childhood. Will you write back to her?"

"Of course," I said, although I had no intention of replying. Not then at least. Probably never.

When Caroline, in her usual corner of the sofa, tucked her legs under herself, put on her reading glasses and picked up a book, I went to my study, ostensibly to check something on my Bloomberg screens. I would shred the letter in due course or burn it on the ashes of Colin's envelope and Henry's whores, but, since I could not do that immediately, I would have to find a safe interim hiding place for it.

I unlocked the drawer where I kept my dreams and lists concealed beneath a pile of stationery picked up from hotel bedrooms. Sally's letter came to rest between my Big Five list and one I had begun a few years later, in 1971, and pompously labelled 'Lifetime Total'. The Big Five: Janice Day, Sally Pinkerton, Marie-Claire Dufraisse, Polly Page, Eva-Maria Bocardo-Griffin; four of the names with tidy ticks beside them. Then, very slowly, I ran my eyes down the other list: Priscilla McGinley, Karen O'Neil, Hilde Nielsen, Rosa Luxemburg, Sylvia Spurway, Caroline Carter…

"Fancy a game of Scrabble?" Caroline was standing in the doorway. My lists on the desk were openly visible. I leaned forward to hide them. I must have looked at her blankly, for the next thing she said was: "Are you okay?"

"Yes, of course. I'll just put these things away. What did you say?"

"Scrabble?"

Scrabble! Did anyone under the age of ninety play Scrabble? Had Caroline never sat opposite Heggie's lines, mechanically reading them through again and again, as the Central Line trundled from

Notting Hill to Bank? [90] Possibly not. My wealth had spared her such indignities in life. It had built the walls around our lives that kept all the shit out.

The knife went in. The pain shot up through my brain. *The knife was in the Europa bag.* Scrabble!

Et tu, Caroline?

"Scrabble. Yes, what a good idea. Be with you in a moment."

5

"Let me," said the preacher in his pulpit, "pick out a few of the phrases in this morning's reading: 'When you hear of war and revolutions... Nation will rise against nation and kingdom against kingdom... There will be great earthquakes, famines and pestilences in various places, and fearful events and great signs in heaven... They will lay hands on you and persecute you... You will be betrayed by parents, brother, relatives and friends, and they will put some of you to death... All men will hate you because of me.' Jesus is telling his disciples all this to reassure them, to show them he is in control and to urge them to stand firm. You can't help wondering, you

---

[90] See Adam Heggie's 'How They Brought the Good News★ from Perivale to Epping' in *Riding the Central Line to Bank* (London, 1987):

> *When God came down to Ealing,*
> *One Friday afternoon,*
> *He travelled on the Central Line*
> *And made the ladies swoon.*
> *He told his ancient story*
> *Of Eve and Adam's plight:*
> *From their reign in youthful glory*
> *To the trivial and trite;*
> *From splendid God-lit garden*
> *To grubbing in the shite;*
> *How they started out by fucking*
> *One steamy August night*
> *And ended playing Scrabble*
> *By winter's fading light.*

★ About God being found dead, nailed to a tree in Hanger Hill Park.

This poem was featured in London Underground tube carriages as one of the 'Poems on the Underground' in 1999. – Ed.

know, if this is what Jesus says to *reassure* his disciples, what he would say if he ever wanted to *scare* them. But Christianity is not a passport to the soft life. It's not a wish-fulfilment formula. Jesus has not promised us a rose garden. He has not even promised us a pair of rose-tinted spectacles. What God has promised us is that he will be with us always. The very last words from Matthew's Gospel tell us 'I will be with you always, to the very end of the age'. Or, another example from among many, the well-known words from the twenty-third Psalm: 'Even though I walk through the valley of the shadow of death, I will fear no evil, for you are with me.' Now let's look more closely at what Jesus is saying here in today's reading and why it really is reassurance..."

Phil Scott was sitting on my right, next to the aisle. Caroline was on my left. Both had their eyes fixed on the preacher, their ears listening intently to his sermon. It was the Sunday after Sally's letter had arrived and, as I sat there, my thoughts drifted to its hiding place under stationery from the Moscow Kempinski and the Bangkok Oriental, between the 'Big Five' and the 'Lifetime Total'.

I had been going to church with Caroline for over two years. I had even bought myself a Bible, a rare and particularly authoritative 1631 edition of the Authorised Version.[91] It might cause English eyebrows to rise and French lips to suppress a grin into an exaggerated frown, but church was by no means bad for my reputation as an honest custodian of rich men's investments. Like Imogen's continued residence at my Weybridge house and the occasional game of Scrabble, churchgoing was also part of keeping the marriage fabric in good repair. Sometimes, though not today, I almost succumbed to belief. The elegance of it all appealed to me. For mathematicians and physicists, elegance is an indicator of something interesting. As you would do for a mathematical system, you accept a few quite reasonable axioms and then the whole thing runs to its own seductive logic...

The voice of an Australian chainsaw revving up for an orgy of destruction in my sacred grove: "In your belief system, Nick," Phil whines, "I imagine

---

[91] An edition of the Bible printed by Barker and Lucas in 1631 omitted a small, three-letter word from Exodus 20:14 such that the seventh commandment came to read "Thou shalt commit adultery". The edition was recalled shortly after printing and destroyed. Only eleven copies are known to have escaped destruction and, since the whereabouts of all eleven is known, the copy bought by Nick Kellaway was almost certainly a forgery. Or is he simply making up the story about owning this Bible? – Ed.

that's all there is, matter: a closed material system. In my world, there's matter as well, of course, but it's ultimately an open system. There's also Mind. And Mind – God – is the ultimate reality. You infer one belief system from the evidence and I infer something different; and I think, with all due respect, Nick, that my way of looking at things is a better fit with the evidence than yours is – a finer explanatory scheme, a more elegant integrative hypothesis. God's got the better arguments here, old boy. In the beginning, that's roughly 13.4 billion years ago, God created the heavens and the earth, the space-time continuum, matter, stuff, Sally's tits and Blueberry Pie in a nice yellow crust pastry..." I believe in Texas, in the silent elevator that lifts us up to the heavenly realms of the fourteenth floor (actually the thirteenth if you were in a less superstitious state – or even the twelfth if you were in Europe), in the door that shuts behind us with the thud of its automatic lock, in the revelation of unbuttoned buttons and unzipped zippers, in the smooth breasts and incredibly soft skin on the inside of Number Seven's thighs, in the holy hymns sung by warm lips, in the redeeming blood of a sacrificial virgin... I have, sir, no need for your G-hypothesis: coito ergo sum...

Caroline left for Weybridge immediately after church. Imogen had phoned and asked her for her help with their dying mother. Caroline had arranged a week off work – though in theory she only worked, was only paid for, three days a week. "Imogen's hardly got two hours' straight sleep for a fortnight."

"Darling," I had offered – again, "we can easily get contract nurses in round the clock."

Caroline had sighed. "I know. It'll probably come to that eventually, but not yet. I'd actually *like* to help. While she's still able to recognise me and talk to me and hold my hand. She's my mother."

Phil stood with me on the pavement as we waved Caroline off. When her car was out of sight, I asked Phil whether I could buy him lunch. "Caro and I had," I said, "a table booked at the Brasserie St Quentin."

Phil declined. I had forgotten one of his principles: never do anything that causes somebody to work on a Sunday. "Society as a whole," he reasoned, "is better off when things aren't pushed to extremes. It needs rhythms with rest built in, just as companies should aim for healthy sustainable profits and not be forced into short-term profit maximisation." Phil wouldn't even buy Monday's *Financial Times* because journalists had worked the previous day to produce it. "Have lunch with me instead, Nick. Cold roast beef. There's plenty for two."

I accepted the invitation, said I'd bring a bottle of wine. In my *cave* I found two bottles of *1999 Frederic Magnien Charmes-Chambertin Grand Cru* that Phil would appreciate, though he would never buy anything equivalent for himself. I phoned, at Phil's urging, to cancel my lunch reservation and I removed Sally's letter from its comfortable position between the lists and put it in my jacket pocket. After we had finished lunch, I poured the last of the wine into our glasses. We carried them to the armchairs on either side of the framed needlepoint that Phil's wife had made in the weeks before she died, standing where a fire would have smouldered had it been winter. Within five minutes, Phil was asleep, snoring gently.

I let myself out and, without calling in at my own house, went to Hyde Park for a brisk walk. From there I crossed Park Lane and made my way to Curzon Street. Only Fabrice was in the office. Most people try to get their work done on Sunday morning to be home, or with their mates at the pub, for lunch. Fabrice, however, spent more time in the office than most people – more time even than me. He had only a robotic dog at home – though office rumour claimed he was about to upgrade his domestic menagerie, that he had placed an order for a custom-built robotic woman with an up-market specialist manufacturer in Japan.

I waited until Fabrice left an hour later, took Sally's letter out of my pocket and read it through again. *Sir Nicholas Kellaway.* Then I fed it to the hungry shredder.

On 27 June 2007, the entire staff of Kellaway & Co. abandoned their trading screens to tune into Gordon Brown quitting the Treasury. He went across the park to Buckingham Palace, kissed the Queen's ring, or whatever he had to do to receive the Crown's constitutional magic, and returned across the park to the coveted house that Tony Blair had just vacated.

> *When Jesus walked on water*
> *With his good friend Tony Blair*
> *Tony did it better*
> *And walked upon the air.*[92]

Régime Change had been effected.

---

[92] From Adam Heggie, *Posthumous Poems*, London, 2004. – Ed.

338

I have no way of knowing whether Tony Blair ever read Heggie's poetry or of knowing what his thoughts were as he left ten years in Downing Street behind. Perhaps, just perhaps, he thought *après moi le déluge*. If so, he was right. Rain fell heavily across southern England throughout the next month. The Severn and the Thames flooded. Parts of Oxford were under water for weeks. London was threatened. Then came the financial floodwaters, the effects of the reign of debt. They did not subside as readily as the muddy waters in Oxford and I, by then, was *hors de combat*, unable to man the sandbags and the barricades.

CHAPTER ELEVEN

Four weeks later, on the evening of 25 July 2007, I was sitting in my office with the *Financial Times* spread across the desk in front of me. One of the four screens in the array beside me, open at Northern Rock's website, betrayed my previous activity. That day, Northern Rock had announced bullish interim results. Fabrice, however, had pointed out a little note buried deep in the hyperbole: Northern Rock's cost of funding itself in the wholesale market was rising. Sometimes Fabrice, with his instinct for spotting human and corporate weaknesses, honed among the syndicates of Marseille, picked up things that the whole army of Kellaway & Co.'s expensive quants, glistening brightly in their Ph.D.s, never noticed. Late that afternoon, we doubled our short on the stock. It was a good call.

At eight-thirteen, my phone rang. I was hoping for a call from Robert in response to a message I had left on his answer phone. I was also expecting to hear from Caroline. Earlier in the day she had answered another summons from Imogen and gone to Weybridge: their mother had taken a turn for the worse.

It was neither Robert nor Caroline on the phone.

The voice on the other end of the line was hesitant, betraying a slight tremor. An American voice, a voice for long summer evenings on the back porch as you sit, cold beer in hand, listening to the corn grow in the bottom forty. A female voice.

"Is that Mr Nicholas Kellaway?"

"Speaking."

"Hello, Nick. My name is Barbara McIntosh."

I was about to hang up. But there was something in the slow, deliberate tones of the voice of the woman on the phone – something in the pregnant pause after she had announced her name – that caused me, in turn, to hesitate.

"I'm really sorry to disturb you this late in the evening, Nick," she said. "You knew me a long time ago, back when we were kids in Geneva together."

"Did I?"

"My name then was Janice Day."

"God Almighty!"

"Do you remember me?"

Did I remember her? Did I remember her! Did I remember the voice that sang 'Puff the Magic Dragon'? Did I remember the afternoon I saw her lying beside the lake? Did I remember those few weeks in Oxford, the kiss as we crossed Magdalen Bridge? Did I remember her? A better question would have been did I believe her? The answer to *that* question was no. I did not believe her. Not then at least. As I listened I thought, *There's something not quite right about this voice, this accent...*

"Nick, I know it's been a long time, but I need your help."

"Mine?"

"Yes."

"What can I do?"

"Can we meet?"

"Yes, of course," I answered.

"I've booked a table at the Mezza Luna."

"God! Does it still exist?"

"Well, they took the booking."

It was a quick decision. As far as I could recall, I had never mentioned to anybody our dinner at La Mezza Luna in the autumn of 1971 just before Jan disappeared. This had to be either Jan or someone to whom she had spoken.

I agreed to meet the woman with the American voice for lunch the next day and decided in that same moment not to tell anyone, not even Caroline, what I was doing. If this was an impostor I could always walk away, tell no one that I had been a fool caught – I thought of 'Sally's' letter – in a prankster's emotional trap. We were to meet, after all, in a London restaurant in broad daylight, an improbable place for a physical ambush. And if it was Jan...

I checked my calendar in Outlook and then phoned Downing Street. I advised the whisky-tumbler voice that answered that Mr Nicholas Kellaway regretted that he would be unable to keep his appointment the following day. My absence would, I knew, be noticed by those who cared about these things, by the keepers of the List of the Great and the Good and those who are paid to spend their days worrying over the next set of Queen's Birthday Honours. *Sir Nicholas Kellaway?* I might have to wait a little longer for that. It was a risk that I was prepared to take. Frankly, I knew I would not be missed in any substantive way. Other earls of private equity, dukes of investment banking and hedge-fund princelings would be there saying whatever it was the City and those who lived on its lucrative fringes wanted to be heard in the court of the new king.

When I phoned Caroline's mobile, I could hear restaurant sounds in the background. "I've taken Imogen out for dinner," Caroline explained. "I got an agency nurse in."

"How's your mum?" I asked.

"Not good."

"When will you be home?"

"Late, I'm afraid. Don't wait up. We've just got to the restaurant, haven't even ordered yet. If you want it, there's some poached salmon and a bottle of white wine in the fridge. A nice Chablis. I had a glass at lunch."

"What does the weekend hold?"

"I don't know. I should probably come back down here."

"It's that bad, is it?"

"'Fraid so."

Then I made another phone call – to the number I had jotted down from the caller display when Janice Day or Barbara McIntosh, or whoever it was, had phoned. I let it ring for a long time but there was no reply, no anodyne voice requesting me to leave a message, nothing. Later, the police would trace the call to a phone booth in Knightsbridge, the one that stands outside the entrance to the tube – but that was later.

I woke earlier than usual the next morning. The first fingers of the new day were just beginning to explore the edges of the heavy bedroom curtains. Normally, I would have got up quietly and gone to my study, flicked through the screens to see what the markets had done to our positions while I slept and made phone calls to the Middle East or China. That morning, however, I lay in bed. Caroline lay asleep beside me, naked and uncovered because the night was warm.

There were two women in the bedroom. There was Caroline in bed beside me and I *could* say that the other was the painting that is neither by Modigliani nor of Caroline, yet both at the same time; Caroline when I first knew her, my brown-eyed girl in an Oxford room rich with Indian silks and Parisian velvets, a room scented with sandalwood and steaming lapsang souchong and oranges and lemons that came all the way from Tesco. But that would be another lie. The painting was sold long ago to pay for the tea and oranges. The other woman, as I lay half awake, was the road not taken.

I slipped quietly from the bed, put on my dressing gown and

closed the bedroom door behind me. I shaved and showered and dressed with precision and care. I checked that Jan's old guitar still stood untroubled in its corner and walked past the painting of the Temple of Hera at Paestum that hangs above our mantelpiece. I ate an apple for my first breakfast. There would be more breakfast in the office later. The enormous mirror that fills our entrance hall reflected yesterday's red roses. The air was heavy with their rich perfume. I met Phil Scott outside the door. He was on his way to buy a newspaper.

I frittered away the morning, flicking aimlessly from screen to screen. I interrupted others who were trying to put in a normal day's work, people who had to let me interrupt them because I was the boss and paid their salaries and bonuses. I tried to read a backlog of reports and correspondence, abandoned them, threw them in the bin. I suspect that the police have since investigated my activity on the internet that morning. They will have found that I googled 'Janice Day' and 'Barbara McIntosh'. I found nothing that I felt was linked to the voice on the phone. I looked up Andreas Baader, Ulrike Meinhof, Gudrun Ensslin, Priscilla McGinley, Anastasia Kuznetsova… I learned that Brigitte Mohnhaupt had been released from prison in March. Then I googled myself, trawled the internet's references to Kellaway & Co. and followed various links from them. I looked at dozens of references to myself. Nowhere could I find a record of my ex-directory private landline, the number that had rung the previous evening at eight-thirteen.

Just after eleven I phoned Caroline.

"I'm going back down to Weybridge this afternoon," she said. "I think I probably ought to stay a few days. Imogen's shattered and this could go on for weeks."

"I may have to go abroad tomorrow."

"Oh. I'd missed that."

"It's just come up."

"Right."

"Just Geneva or Zürich."

"You'll enjoy that. Especially if it's Geneva."

A few minutes after noon, I went down to the street to find a cab. I would like to say that, as I climbed into the back of the anonymous taxi, there was a little child blowing soap bubbles through a plastic ring, dancing joyously among them as they floated on the currents of the soft summer air. But there wasn't. This was Mayfair. This was 2007 – 26 July 2007. I doubt any of the passers-by would have recollected, even five minutes later, seeing a man in a dark-blue suit hail a passing cab, give the driver the name of an obscure, stubby little street around the back of Paddington Station and nervously straighten the knot in his pale-blue tie as the taxi driver pulled out into the slow-moving traffic. The moment was, however, caught on CCTV.

2

"You sure this is the right place?" The cabbie had drawn up outside the faded front of what they used to call a 'greasy spoon'. I did not recognise it, but was that unusual after a lifetime and a half? The sign said *La Mezza Luna*.

"Yup, this is it."

Jan… Barbara… the woman had arrived before me. She was sitting at a table towards the back of the room, facing the door, and stood as I approached. Grey hair was combed back from her face. She wore a frilly white blouse, the kind that Laura Ashley used to sell in the eighties, and a dark red skirt that fell in many pleats to the middle of her calves. A pair of half-moon reading glasses dangled at her breast from a thin silver chain around her neck. She said, "Hello, Nick," and air-kissed me on both cheeks. "Very good of you to come."

"It's been thirty-six years."

She smiled. "A long time."

But was it Janice Day? I still wasn't certain. There was a certain familiarity about the woman's face. It could, I thought, have been Janice Day, changed over nearly four decades of course. Equally, it could have been the face of someone else I knew, of someone I had seen in a photograph, or of an actress on television. For a fleeting moment I saw my grandmother's face on the day she took me to lay flowers on her husband's grave. I imagined a tentative scent of lavender and mothballs on the cheek that had just touched mine.

The clothes the woman wore were too loose fitting for me to form an accurate impression of her body. I would have thought that that once-famous figure would have grown comfortably plump with age. Yet, as far as I could tell, the body beneath the clothes was slim. The unringed fingers were thin and the veins on the back of her hands were prominent. From certain angles, when the muscles in her face relaxed, her cheeks looked almost gaunt. I looked for, but could not detect, any trace of a dimple. The eyes, it's true, were bluish-grey, but they were not the pale-blue they were in my memory, not the blue that is bluer than robins' eggs. For a few seconds I wished I hadn't come: even if this person were Janice Day, I preferred the one who lived in my mind.

But I stayed. I sat on the Formica seat of the aluminium chair, took the grease-stained menu the sullen waiter handed to me, looked again into the eyes. "It's very nice to see you again, Jan," I said. "We have a lot to catch up on."

"Thirty-six years squeezed into a business man's lunch hour." Was there a gentle, lightly mocking irony in her voice? Or was it a veiled request for more than an hour? And if more than an hour, why? What then? How long? It sounded seductive. It sounded like Jan.

"How long have you been in London?" I asked.

"I got in yesterday morning. Overnight from Chicago." That accounted, I thought, for the tired look. There was no reason for me to suspect, just then, that she was lying.

Neither the woman nor I ate much. Perhaps it was because the lasagne that was served to us was dry, hot and crispy on the outside but cold and untouched by La Mezza Luna's microwaves at its centre. Or perhaps, for my part, it was because I was too pre-occupied looking at the face opposite, listening to the voice. I learned that the woman had googled me, worked through the articles she had found on the internet, noticed factual inaccuracies about my childhood in my *Wikipedia* entry. She had watched an abridged YouTube version of a speech that I had given in Davos a few months earlier. I answered her questions about me, questions that glided along the harmless surface of life, questions about Caroline, about the children and what they were doing now that they had grown up and left home. I turned the questions back to her.

"Married, yes. Children, no." She gently pressed her teeth into her lower lip. Did I imagine in the silence that followed that I could hear a wistful longing that things had worked out otherwise? Did I hear a guitar and a distant voice? "We live in Montana, up near the Canadian border. Our land was always too dry and barren. Guess some of that just rubbed off on Joe and me."

Later, "You changed your name?"

She smiled. "It's what happens to women, Nick. They marry and take their husband's name."

"Barbara?"

"Barbara was always my name. Barbara Janice Day. When we settled in Montana it seemed like a good time to go over to Barbara, 'Barb'. I've never been 'Barbara', always 'Barb'. 'Barbara' wouldn't work out there where the wind freezes long words before you get them out of your mouth." I had never recorded 'Barbara' among the facts I'd collected about Janice Day.

"Leaving Jan behind?" I ventured cautiously.

"I guess. In a way." She shrugged, turning the conversation back to me.

Now, rarely do I have much difficulty talking about myself and about Kellaway & Co., so I was ensnared readily enough in Barbara-Jan's listening trap. When she declined coffee, looked at her watch and abruptly announced she had another appointment, I suddenly realised that – other than that she was alive and claimed to be married, childless and living in Montana – I had learned nothing about Janice Day, nothing about the missing years, nothing about yesterday's plea for help.

In the taxi on my way to the Mezza Luna I had decided to tread warily, to let the woman lead the conversation and not to mention her request for help until she did – or until I was 100% certain that the woman really was Jan. When you're rich you suspect 'help' to be a euphemism for 'money'. I still wasn't sure that this woman was Jan; but I was inching towards belief, wanting to believe, and just then I wanted her to stay. I abandoned my tactics. "On the phone," I said, "you mentioned needing help."

Jan didn't respond. She was fumbling for something in her handbag, her 'purse' I suppose she would have called it.

"Jan," I persisted. "You asked me for help."

She looked up. Was the hunted, frightened look in my imagination, or was it really there? "I'm sorry, Nick. Let's forget I mentioned it. It's been nice having lunch, but it's been thirty-six years and you can't turn back the clock."

I reached across the table and gently took her hand. Was it when I held her hand and felt no resistance that I believed the woman was Jan? In that moment, at least, I believed her. "Where," I asked, "are you staying?"

She was staying, she said, in a hotel on Sussex Gardens, less than a five-minute walk from La Mezza Luna. I protested, perhaps too vigorously, that she couldn't possibly stay there, proposed she stay for the rest of her time in London with Caroline and me. "It's a big house," I said, "we have plenty of room."

Jan declined. I insisted. Eventually, with apparent reluctance, she agreed and made it seem like she was doing me a favour rather than the other way round. I said we would hail a cab in the street, collect her things from her hotel and go straight to Knightsbridge. I did not want to let her go again. Not after thirty-six years. Not yet at least.

"Nick," she said, "I can't. I've got an appointment."

She made to get up and leave.

"Well, come over afterwards, then."

I scribbled out the address. I would later learn that that was not needed: she already had the address written in a little booklet in her handbag. She took the paper on which I had written my address and nodded, the almost imperceptible little nod that would eventually take her to a place of no return. She said that she would come at seven, kissed me on both cheeks as she had done when I arrived and left me in the restaurant to pay.

"I paid last time," she said.

"Did you?"

"Damn right. It was your birthday. Your twenty-first. My treat."

It had been my twentieth birthday in 1971, not my twenty-first. If any body language or facial twitch betrayed that I had picked up the mistake, the woman did not notice it. She was already on her way to the door.

Four minutes later, out into the street, there was no sign of the woman. I wondered whether she would come to Knightsbridge, whether I would ever see her again. I deeply feared that if the woman actually was Jan, I would not. If she was an impostor, I probably would.

3

I spent a useless afternoon in my office. Most of the time my door was closed, sealing me away from the rest of the firm. That was unusual and I could sense, when I walked out onto the floor, a sense of uncertainty and nervousness. In the course of the afternoon, the staff at Kellaway & Co. worked out that I had skipped the meeting at Downing Street and began to speculate among themselves. Some of my more charitable employees spread the word that my mother-in-law was dying and attributed my curious behaviour to that. Others added my curious behaviour to the nervous state of the markets to produce a secret lunch and the imminent sale of the business.

That afternoon, I didn't give a shit what they thought. I retreated behind my closed door and tried, with help of Bloomberg and Google, to invent ways to speed up the clock. The police would later ask my reasons for visiting each website I looked at that afternoon. Some were obvious. I looked at HBOS's website. Kellaway & Co. was sitting on healthy short positions in that stock. We had no inside information, we were simply shorting British banks that, like Northern Rock and HBOS, had a high loan-to-deposit ratio. Underlying our short position on the Royal Bank of Scotland, however, I explained candidly, were stories as well as statistics. On the cocktail-party circuit we had picked up that, with the acquisition of ABN-AMRO, the bosses in Edinburgh were intent on becoming the biggest bank in the world and that their teams in London and Connecticut were obliging them by competing with each other to see which could book the greater number of assets. A perfectly sensible basis for selling RBS short.

I looked up Montana on *Wikipedia*. I read about the retreating glaciers in Glacier National Park and then about Al Gore and his views on climate change. A posting from 'Montana Mountain Man' poured vitriol on Mr Gore, accusing him of being a stooge of something called the Bilderberg Group and the Club of Rome, secret societies that forged temperature statistics and did all sorts of other 'communistic' things.

I looked at the websites of several hotels in Geneva, as well as at the pages posted by the Compagnie Générale de Navigation on the technical details – the *fiches techniques* – of each of its ships plying the waters of Leman, and at several pages on Ferdinand Hodler, who had painted the unfinished picture of Geneva hanging on my office wall.

I took a call from one of the hedge-fund captains who had gone to the Downing Street meeting, a man with a red, carnivorous voice and a world-class collection of Edo-period ivory *katbori netsuke*. "Nick," he said, "I'd've thought someone with your ambitions would never've missed a thing like that."

A managing director at Citicorp called, a man who in the past had often provided useful, off-the-record tips on what might be happening in the realm of mergers and acquisitions. We'd had lunch at White's three weeks earlier. He had said then, "Nick, you know, it's hell out there." Now he was saying, "It's like Dante: each circle in hell is worse than the one before. The next one's civil disorder, rioting and looting in the streets. In the one after that they blame the Jews."

"But Prince Charles is still dancing?"

"Yeah, whatever."

When he had hung up I looked at various screens on the US sub-prime mortgage market, then went out onto the floor to talk to Fabrice about one of our trickier positions. "80% of it's gone," he said. "We can't get a price on the rest."

"Take a bigger loss if you have to. Up to 40%. Tell me if you need to go more."

I phoned Caroline. She was back in Weybridge and said she would be staying there until Saturday evening, possibly longer. She was too distracted, I think, to pay much attention to my saying that I would be putting an old school friend up in one of our spare rooms, that I might still have to go to Switzerland. Amanda, she said, was planning to come down to Weybridge on Friday because she wanted to see her grandmother before, well, before... Caroline did not complete her sentence. We both knew the words that she had chosen not to say. Implicit was the suggestion that I too should make the pilgrimage to my mother-in-law's bedside.

When I heard the doorbell ring I looked at my watch. It was ten to seven. During the course of the afternoon I had banished thoughts of scams and impostors, persuaded myself that the woman at La Mezza Luna had been genuine and restored the pale-blue colour to her eyes. I took it now as a good omen that Jan had arrived early.

I straightened my tie in front of the hall mirror and noticed only then that Caroline had replaced the morning's red roses with white ones. As far as I could recall Caroline had never before ordered white roses. Another omen? A random mutation in the great chain of evolution that would at last bring Hodler's unfinished flowers into bloom? I opened the door.

A man stood on my doorstep. My heart, which had been edging its way up into my throat, plummeted into the pit of my stomach. The man wore the flowing white robes of Araby and an embroidered skullcap to match. His beard had suffered attacks of moth and rust and in the voice I diagnosed Birmingham and an acute case of irritable vowel disorder. He said, "Mr Philip Scott, I presume."

I directed him next door and returned to my perch on the edge of a sofa. I think I almost cried. As the hour struck seven I cursed myself for letting Jan go again, for allowing her to walk out of La

Mezza Luna alone. I saw her again walking away from me into that dark and stormy Bulwer-Lytton night, away from me across the summer afternoon lawns at La Bise. I saw her disappear from the moonlit walls of Rouëlbeau. I saw her lift her skirts, stick out her tongue and run away, lost to me among the tombstones and the trees.

4

Jan eventually arrived by cab at ten past seven. She was carrying her big handbag and pulled a small suitcase on wheels. Her clothes were the ones she'd worn at lunch, but the dangling schoolmistress spectacles were gone. I greeted her with kisses on the cheeks. She bent to take off her shoes.

"Leave them on," I said, "it's okay."

"At home we take our shoes off, so I'll do the same here." Jan stepped barefoot onto the Persian rug that covers the polished wooden floor. Her toenails were painted a deep shade of scarlet.

I watched her as she looked up to the great chandelier that hangs from the ceiling, at the painting of flat Norfolk fields and the distant church spire beneath banks of clouds gathering, grey and ominous, in the big sky, at the white roses in their antique Sèvres vase. She caught me watching her in the mirror, the big mirror in front of which a moment earlier I had straightened my pale-blue tie for the second time in twenty minutes. "This is magnificent, Nick."

I threw my arms open, encompassing everything in the room, the room itself, the house... what else? I've thought about that spontaneous gesture often since, its echoes of a make-believe story told by the waters of Leman forty years earlier. Was it simply a gesture of welcome? Or was it something more? Did Jan read my wide open arms as saying something like 'all this could have been yours'? I don't know.

In the sitting room, Jan walked over to the mantelpiece and with her finger delicately touched the gold carriage-clock by which the shepherds of Paestum keep time. "How in the world," she asked, still smiling, "did you turn innocent little quadratic equations into all this?"

"None of this is real," I said breezily.

"It looks pretty damn real to me." Jan sat on the deep Knole sofa that faces the ruined temples and tucked one of her bare feet under her thigh. I offered her a drink.

"Sure. A diet coke or something?"

"I was going to have a gin and tonic. Sure you won't join me?"

"Okay." Then she saw it. She stood up and walked over to the corner where her old guitar stood, alternately looking at it and me. "Nick," she asked eventually, "is this what I think it is?"

"Your guitar."

"*My* guitar?"

"Yes."

"My God. You've kept it all these years!"

All my doubts were gone: this *was* Janice Day. I smiled. I think I had possibly never smiled quite as deeply as I did just then in my entire fifty-six years.

Only later in the evening, much later, after we had eaten the dinner I had ordered in and drunk the wine I had brought up from my cellar (a *2003 Yvorne Clos du Rocher*); after she had told me of the hard, barren life on the high plains where the winds hit hard and heavy up there on the Canadian borderline; after she had dangled into the conversation a few tantalising morsels about her flight from Oxford to Berlin; after I had held her hand across the table, longing to take more but restraining myself with every ounce of civilised self-control I could muster; after she had agreed that it would be nice to see Geneva again… only then did she go to the corner of the room, pick up her old guitar, stroke it, tune it and play a few chords. Then, as if magically to erase thirty-six years, to take us back to a time when there was a girl with pale-blue eyes and frosted blonde hair that hung long and rolled and flowed over her shoulders and all down the swell of her breast, she sang. She sang 'Farewell Angelina', so softly that I had to strain to hear her voice.

> *There's no need for anger*
> *There's no need for blame*
> *There's nothing to prove*
> *Ev'rything's still the same*
> *Just a table standing empty*
> *By the edge of the sea…*

When she had finished there was a deep silence. You could dimly hear the noise from the streets of London beyond the drawn curtains and the triple-glazed windows, you could hear the clock ticking in the next room, but nothing disturbed *our* silence. An impenetrable silence that spoke more than words. A minute? Three? Ten? Until Jan said, "If we're starting early tomorrow, I'd better go get some shuteye."

I showed Jan up to the bedroom Caroline calls 'the Swiss room' because of its old prints, antique maps and Victorian paintings of the Alps. She said goodnight and thank you, kissed me first on the cheek and then lightly on my lips. Then, abruptly, she asked, "Did you ever hear anything more of Anna Schmidt?"

"No," I lied. Even now I don't know why I lied. Perhaps it was simply that I did not want thoughts of another woman spoiling the end of the evening, spoiling whatever might have happened in the seconds after that kiss. Whatever the reason, I *did* lie and later, when our stories became more tangled in their telling, it was a lie that I felt I had to maintain.

Another goodnight. Another thank you. Did I then hear a sigh before Jan closed the door behind herself? I heard her turn the key in the lock.

I still had work to do if I was to put flesh on the skeleton of my plans. I went to my study and turned on the computer. Forty-five minutes later I was satisfied that I had done the best I could in the circumstances. It was just after eleven-thirty.

I phoned Caroline's mobile. My call went straight through to voicemail. I left a short message, enough to let her know I was thinking of her and her mother, enough to let her know I would be flying to Geneva the next morning.

As I hung up, I saw Jan standing in the doorway. She was wearing the green dressing gown that Héloïse had once wrapped around her silken body.

"What are all these?" she asked pointing at my array of screens.

"Bloomberg screens. They keep me up to date with my markets."

"Even at home? At eleven-thirty at night?"

"I'm afraid so."

"Is one of these just an ordinary computer?"

"This one."

"Would it be okay, Nick, if I used it for a few minutes when you're finished?"

"Sure. I'll just clear this stuff up." My passport, printouts from the computer and other things I had assembled for the trip to Geneva lay on the desk.

"Don't worry about it. They won't be in my way. What time do you want me up in the morning?"

The question doused the hope Jan had stirred in my loins when she appeared in my study door. I took my iPod with me to my bed, plugged the earpiece into my ear and found the song I was looking for, the boot-leg one that Bob Dylan had sung in the taverns of Greenwich Village in the sixties. I played it through, went back to the beginning and listened again.

The machine guns are roaring
The puppets heave rocks
The fiends nail time bombs
To the hands of clocks
Call me any name you like
I will never deny it
Farewell Angelina
The sky is erupting
I must go where it's quiet.

5

We got to the Hôtel des Bergues in Geneva early on Friday afternoon and went straight out again without unpacking our cases, leaving Jan's guitar locked away in her room. We walked across the Pont du Mont-Blanc, caught the tram to Grange-Canal and went into the grounds of La Grande Boissière. Jan said, "I can't believe it's been nearly forty years since I was last here."

Pink, low-rise blocks of flats had been built along one side of the avenue leading into Ecolint. On its other side, trees had been felled to make way for a car park. New buildings had appeared within the grounds, but the buildings of my memory had survived the changes. They were still the same – smaller perhaps, but they had the same shapes, were still coloured with faded ochre stucco and dark green shutters. The doors were locked, but we peered in through the windows at what had been the dining-room-cum-assembly-hall.

"I remember," I said, "you sitting on this window ledge at break, trying to catch the rays."

"I remember *you* selling doughnuts at break."

"I didn't do that!"

"Yes, you did." After a pause and a smile to ensure that I would take no offence, she added, "Taking in the money even then."

We walked over to the top of the Greek Theatre. It seemed to have been cleaned, restored – as if being prepared to accommodate an upmarket corporate event, to host young executives wearing 'smart-casual' rather than the vanguard of the Revolution wearing flowers in their hair.

"You used to play your guitar down there."

Jan walked down the empty steps. I joined her at the bottom, on the mosaic representation of the world. The world we had once had at our feet.

When we had drunk our fill of Ecolint, and were walking away along the path to Grange-Canal, I suggested we go to the Auberge, share a carafe of Fendant, sing and dance a few stanzas from 'Those were the Days' and remember other tunes from the time of flowers. But the Auberge – our beloved tavern – was gone, its site occupied by an American pizza joint.

We rode the number twelve tram to its terminus in Carouge and then back again as far as Place Neuve. The old orange trams, where you could stand on the platform outside as they rattled and clanked from Moillesulaz to Carouge and back again, had been replaced by sleek, hermetically sealed tubes swishing along the rails. The number one tram – *La Ceinture* – had vanished altogether.

From Place Neuve we sought out the Landolt, where Lenin had carved his name on a bar-room table and where I, his self-nominated disciple, had bought champagne to celebrate the success of the anti-war crowd in bringing Lyndon Johnson's presidency to an end. But the Landolt, we found, had been replaced by a Japanese restaurant. Can you do Revolution with salmon teriyaki and hot sake in little stoneware cups? Jan laughed. "*Nobody* serves Revolution any more, Nick. Not with chopsticks *or* Kalashnikovs."

We crossed the Parc des Bastions and passed Calvin and his gang of opium dealers pinned to their wall. We went up through the old town, coming down again where La Vie en Rose had been. No hint of its beckoning pink light remained. Au Grand Passage had metamorphosed into Globus and on the other side of the Place Molard there was no sign of the old Café du Commerce. Where the Café des Négociants had stood, a pseudo-English pub, trading under the name of Lord Nelson and sporting the shiny copper vessels of its own internal micro-brewery, attracted the passing tourist trade.

After dinner at the Café de Paris – Jan's choice – we wandered through the new pedestrian underpass into the station. We recalled the names of the villages strung out along the north shore of the lake as we looked up at the departure boards. "Remember," I asked, "how we took the train once out to Marie-Claire's and went sailing on the lake? You dived in for a swim."

"Did I?"

"And I jumped in after you."

From a different memory, Jan mused, "Once, I was in Frankfurt alone one cold night just before Christmas, looking at all the places trains were going and thinking I could just jump on one and wake up in the morning in a whole nother world. Geneva... Oxford... anywhere. There was a time when I could've turned the clock back."

Jan gently kissed me goodnight in the hotel corridor and twenty minutes later I was in bed in my room with the lights out. But I couldn't sleep. Switching the bedside light on again, I began to flick through the brochures and magazines hotels provide for solitary insomniacs. In one of the magazines I found a two-page advertisement for the Hôtel-Restaurant de la Bise and recognised it as the old Meyer residence on the lake. It had been sold, as Paul Meyer had told me, by Andropov and the new owners had converted it into a restaurant with, the ad said, rooms upstairs and a helipad in the grounds. The reviews quoted were, as you would expect in an advertisement, lavish in their praise. Michelin had awarded a star.

The internal photographs bore no resemblance to anything I remembered about La Bise and there was only one photograph showing the exterior. It had been taken from the lake at dusk. Beneath strings of twinkling lights, eternally young men and women – bronzed skins, black clothes – stood drinking champagne on the dock where Jan had once sunbathed. Listening carefully, I could hear the golden music of a previous generation's summer party tinkling in the distant evening air. I wondered whether the new proprietors had kept the soft, green light at the end of the jetty.

6

On Saturday morning, Jan and I played tourists and after lunch we went back to the hotel to fetch Jan's guitar.

"My folks gave me this for my fourteenth birthday," Jan said, caressing the wood of the guitar.

"I remember."

"I don't have hardly anything from my parents. Just a pair of earrings and a letter from my mom. Her last letter to me. The only one she ever wrote me in her native language."

"*You've* got that?"

"Yes." Jan looked at me curiously, but neither of us pursued the thread of the conversation. There would be plenty of time, I thought, to ask Jan how she had come to have the letter Emma Wallace had claimed to have in *her* possesion five years after Jan had gone missing. Just then I did not want her mother's youthful orgies interrupting the prospect of my perfect Saturday afternoon in Geneva with Jan.

We crossed the Pont du Mont-Blanc, found an unoccupied patch of grass in the Jardin Anglais and kicked off our shoes. Jan played the songs I asked of her, sang the lyrics when she could remember them. She sang '*Guantamera*' and 'Puff the Magic Dragon'. "God," she said, "I haven't sung these songs for ages."

She sang 'House of the Rising Sun'. We lost ourselves in the music, Jan in the singing of it, me in listening to its echoes. A woman with a walking stick, wrinkles on her skin and stars in her eyes, exclaimed, "*Ah, les années soixante-huit. Oh, les beaux jours!*" and blew us a kiss.

I asked Jan to sing '*Le Temps des Cerises*'.

"What?"

"*Le Temps des Cerises?*"

"I don't know that one. Sorry."

We were sitting on a bench near the *jet d'eau*, the guitar beside us, when Jan, without prompting, said, "I'm leaving Joe." She was leaving him, she said, because he was violent, because he drank, because when he drank he became more violent, and because the older he got, the more he drank. He would drive Jan from the house with screeching black-metal music played at full volume. When Jan complained, he said, "Why the hell not? There's not a goddamn soul around for fucking miles." He listened to Rush Limbaugh on the radio. They no longer had a television because when Senator Barack Obama had appeared on it, he had mistaken a gun for the remote and shot him.

Joe McIntosh used to go out for days in his pick-up truck with his cans of beer and dehydrated food, with his fishing rods and his beloved guns. Once, when he returned covered in bloodstains, Jan asked Joe what he had shot. He replied, "A moose, two deer, a nigger, a democrat and three ducks." Joe smoked some of the meat in the smokehouse he had built back in their early idealistic days, when self-sufficiency was still a cherished goal rather than a life sentence to solitary confinement. When, at suppers that winter, they ate the meat, Joe referred to it as 'smoked socialist'.

After the Al-Qaeda attacks in 2001, Joe began to stockpile an arsenal of weapons and ammunition. "Freedom to defend my home and my family," Jan reported him saying. He stopped any pretence of working on the ranch, leaving Jan to grind a living from the cold soil, ignored or mocked her efforts, and satisfied his periodic need for sex at a brothel seventy miles away, except when he was "too drunk to find his truck and had to make do with a little squirt between my legs."

I formed the clear impression that Jan's request for my help, in that phone call three days earlier, and her decision to leave Joe McIntosh were related, although she did not say so. In fact, she never mentioned her call for help at all during those days in Geneva. Nor did I ever ask her about it. Nor ask, "Why me?"

"So," Jan continued, "one morning when he was too hung-over to wake up, I just took the truck up to Calgary and got on a plane to London."

"Calgary?"

"Yeah. In Canada. It's our closest decent airport."

"I thought you said you'd flown in from Chicago."

"No. Calgary."

Later, when we were walking back into town thinking about where to eat dinner, I proposed the Hôtel-Restaurant de la Bise.

"Do I remember it?" Jan asked.

"You will. It's the Meyers' old house. It was converted into a restaurant a few years ago."

"Meyers?" Did Jan flinch? Or has memory conjured that footnote from a future that had not then yet happened?

"Three brothers? Oscar, Claude and Paul? Their father owned a private bank. Big house on the lake just below where you lived in La Capite." I could have said more, but I left it at that.

"A restaurant?"

"I saw it in a magazine at the hotel. It's got good reviews."

"You sure it's the old Meyer place?"

"Positive."

Jan appeared to think about my proposition before saying, "It's too difficult to get all the way out there."

"Why? We can take a taxi. Even better, I'll hire a car."

"Too much, Nick. No."

"Of course it isn't. We can keep the car and drive around tomorrow. When were you last up on top of Salève?"

We went over to the Ile Rousseau and sat at the feet of the philosopher while we waited for the car to be delivered. Pigeons still perched on his head. "'Modesty,'" I quoted, "'only begins with the knowledge of evil.'"

Jan turned and looked me squarely in the face. "That's from Rousseau, isn't it?"

I nodded. "I heard it first from you. In Oxford."

"From me? What a memory you have!"

"You were telling me a story about Anna Schmidt in the Jericho House…"

Jan turned her gaze back to the river, clear and fast-flowing as it escaped the lake. "Anna," she said, a blank, impenetrable look in her eyes, "was a very special person. Then…"

It was to see Anna, Jan said, as Sill had told me years before, that she had gone to Berlin in 1971. She had returned through the November rain to the Jericho House from my college rooms, found a letter from Anna and decided there and then to go to Berlin for a few days. Sill had said she would like to come too. "And why shouldn't Sill come along, just because she didn't have any money? I had more than enough. When I told the guy who'd knocked me up that I wasn't going to marry him and go back to Pakistan as his third wife, he gave me ten times more than I needed for the abortion. He had no idea what they cost."

"Abortion?"

A distant smile. "It was a very long time ago, but, yes, Nick, that's what I'd come to London for." She turned to look at me again. The smile became less distant. "That's what I loved about you, Nick, you were such an innocent. Lost in your books and equations and all those eager theories of Revolution. Completely innocent. I could escape from all the sordid realities with you."

It took Sill and Jan several days to track Anna down once they arrived in Berlin. They called at the address in Kreuzberg that Anna had given them. The students who lived in the squat treated them with suspicion, especially Jan, because she was American but spoke fluent German. Anna, they said, had not been seen since before the summer, had told people she was going to Greece. Nobody knew whether she'd returned to Berlin. She'd spoken of a *Wanderjahr*. One of the students suggested another address, another squat where Jan and Sill spent the next few nights. By day, they wandered around the streets of West Berlin like homeless tourists. In the long evenings, they listened to political debates and the fine tuning of revolutionary arguments. Sill was in her element. Jan drank white wine and smoked marijuana.

On their fourth night in Berlin, Sill and Jan met Anna in the dark recesses of a bar hard up against the Wall. "I had to get to you, make you stop asking questions about me," Anna said. In the days that followed they found themselves in the company of those semi-mythical figures whose names had been covertly whispered in small-hour talk in the communes; the ones who had gone underground, on the run, the Outlaws. One of them wanted to sleep with Jan. Jan resisted. Sill said there was no way in hell Jan should give in to him, but then Sill went to Bonn and Jan went to his bed. "It was just like everyone was screwing everyone, so what was the big deal? I just, like, went with the flow." Once the bedroom door was locked behind them, the man turned violent. He shouted anti-American obscenities as he ripped Jan's clothes off her. He drew blood when he bit her shoulder. He refused to wear the condom that Jan had brought and she was not on the pill.

"It was the first time I'd slept with a man since the abortion," Jan said with a blank passivity. 'Slept' seemed to be stretching the euphemism too far.

When it became obvious to the communards what had happened, a well-meaning type tried to get the two of them to sit down as part of the collective, in a circle holding hands and, Jan mocked, "systematically analyse our sexual difficulties in the fullness of our socio-autobiographical complexity." Jan was having none of it.

She went to Anna and Anna took her to a wizened old Indian medicine man who gave her a dark, evil-smelling potion to drink, "an old-fashioned, morning-after pill." Jan felt as though her insides were dissolving in acid. She thought she would die. Anna, however, would not let her go to hospital, would not permit her to see a doctor. Anna put her arms around Jan, held her tightly, said she was sorry a hundred times. She wiped Jan's tears, said she would sort it all out, promised Jan she would be fine, made her drink herbal teas sweetened with honey and gave her toast and cherry jam to eat.

Later, rumours began to circulate, among those who vaguely called themselves students, that the body of one of the Outlaws had been found near Tempelhof, on an old bombsite. He had been killed by a single bullet to the back of the head. In the squats, they said that his murder bore the hallmark of an extra-judicial execution. The capitalist state was moving against them. Preparations were made for a siege. People went about in threes and fours, never alone. Soon, television and newspapers were carrying the story. Details of how the Outlaw had died were omitted. What was published neither confirmed nor denied the virulent rumours that, before he had died, the martyr had been tortured and had had his genitals removed with a blunt knife.

Later, Jan saw the media photos of the dead man's face. She recognised him as the one who had fucked her. He had told Jan his name was Peter, but the journalists identified him as Karl-Heinz Kupferhoden. His body was discovered in the precise spot where Anna had told Jan it would be found.

Jan was in East Berlin when Kupferhoden's body was found. She had travelled there on an American passport, but not her own. It was one Anna had given her after Jan's own passport had gone missing one night. As Janice Melinda Rose, with an American-made backpack on her shoulders, Jan had gone several times into the East. She picked up envelopes and brought them back to West Berlin. Once she was told to go to Dresden, meet an East German boy with the incongruous name of Mike, deliver him to a woman in Prague called Else, travel on alone to Bratislava and from there to Vienna, where Anna met her off the train and fed her cakes and hot chocolate piled high with whipped cream. That night, Anna told Jan that the police were looking for her in connection with Kupferhoden's death.

"But," Jan protested, "I had nothing to do with his death."

"Anna said, 'That's not how it looks to the police. Not after what they heard from your friends in the squat.' Then she said she'd protect me as long as I did what she said." Anna wrapped her arms around Jan and before they went to sleep, in a big Vienna double bed piled high with whipped-cream duvets, she took a pistol from her bag and placed it under the pillow.

"God, was I scared, Nick. Shit scared."

Anna arranged for Jan to stay in a house in a bourgeois suburb of Munich. Two men and two women lived in the house. They were all young professionals. One of the men worked as a municipal accountant, the other for an electricity company. The women were both teachers. One of them was pregnant and it was unclear – even to the woman – which of the two men, if either, was the father. They were polite and very generous to Jan and over the next few months she went there often. She even had a brief affair with the accountant, the pregnant teacher sometimes joining them in bed.

"I wasn't the only one they took in," Jan said. "Sometimes a guy would come, maybe a couple, stay a night or two and then move on. Then one afternoon Anna phoned when I was in the house alone. She said something was wrong and asked me to meet her at Augsburg station." Anna had Jan drive from Augsburg back to Munich and park the car – a blue BMW registered in Hamburg – a hundred metres away from the house which Jan had left only a few hours earlier. She told Jan to stay with the car. Anna continued on foot. It was while she was standing by the car smoking a cigarette that Jan was seen by a vigilant neighbour, the source of the description – of the stolen car *and* Jan – circulated by the Bavarian police two days later.

Anna returned to the car twenty minutes later. "They won't bother you again," she said.

"They never did bother me," Jan responded airily. "They were good to me."

"Back to Augsburg," was all Anna said as Jan was driving off. Then Jan heard the explosion and saw the fireball.

"I looked over at Anna. She was sitting there with her face all tight and her jaw muscles working away. I sort of whispered, 'Anna, what's going on?' but she didn't say anything. It was like putting two and two together and getting three and all Anna was saying was, 'Turn left, turn right,' kind of shit. I slammed on the brakes and screamed at her, 'We can't drive off like this. We've got to do something. Call the fire department, the police…' Anna pulled her pistol out of her pocket and said, you know, very quietly, 'Darling, I am the police.' She told me to get out of the car and then slid across into the driver's seat – the pistol was still in her hand – and before she drove off she just casually leaned out of the window and went, 'Do be careful whom you talk to about this, okay? They'll need someone to pin this on and, if you're not careful, you might find yourself as the chief suspect.'"

"Shit. Are you serious?" I asked.

Jan shrugged.

A couple of teenagers – t-shirts, jeans, expensive running shoes, silver chains serving as a belt around the girl's waist – strayed onto the island. As oblivious to our presence on the bench as they were to Rousseau's on his pedestal, they stopped by the railing and locked themselves in a deep embrace. I watched the boy slide a hand inside the chains, inside the girl's jeans and down over the skin of her buttocks.

"It was a long time ago," Jan said.

"Still. What did she mean by saying she was the police?"

"I don't know. Enforcer of some kind. Who knows? Not real police, couldn't have been."

"Did you ever ask?"

Jan turned away from the teenagers and said, "I never saw Anna again."

Perhaps I should have told Jan then that Anna had turned up in London four and a half years later, that she had stolen from a Brazilian businessman's bank account, that she had accepted a yellowed, handwritten sheet of paper in return for letting me shag her. I could have gone on to tell her how Anna had used that piece of paper to rob Meyer & Cie, how she had been caught on camera running from the bank when her scam was uncovered, how Anna's accomplice was my friend and British master spy, Colin Witheridge, off on one of his Bonnie-and-Clyde foibles. I could even have told her that, according to that same Colin Witheridge, Anna had still been alive and living in Brazil as recently as 2001. But I didn't. In my silence I maintained *my* lie. "What," I asked, "did you do?"

"I guess I just kept a low profile. I was this American kid bumming around Europe, Janice Melinda Rose. I met up with groups of kids, mostly Americans, travelled around with them a bit. Stayed in youth hostels. Moved on. You know how it was. I got stopped a couple of times, of course. They were stopping everybody in Germany then, especially kids. I would almost shit myself when they were looking through my passport, but they always just let me go. I went up to the Swiss border once with a couple of guys, thinking I'd cross over and get away from it all, but when I saw the border guards stopping people, even people going out of Germany, rummaging through the trunks of the cars and stuff, I just panicked and walked away. Then I heard on television that they'd arrested Sill, and there I was thinking all along that Sill was back in Oxford doing finals. That really freaked me out. I locked myself away in my room and didn't come out for three days."

Eventually, Jan's money began to run out. She was in Munich again then and it was easy to get jobs in the run-up to the Olympics. When the sportsmen arrived in town, she began hanging around with the American team. She had been out on the town with the Americans when they came back to the compound one night after

363

the gates had been locked. "We found some guys who seemed to be from one of the Arab teams and they said they'd been locked out, too. One of the guys gave me the creeps. He kept looking at me and saying he'd seen me before somewhere, asking if I'd been in Prague in the winter. Did I know someone there called Else? That kind of thing. I denied it all, of course." They all climbed the perimeter fence together.

In the aftermath of the Palestinians' massacre of the Israelis, a description of Jan was again circulated by the police. It was a different description to the one that had done the rounds after the Munich house fire. No connection was made to the woman who had been seen standing by the Hamburg-registered BMW that night, nor to the women wanted for questioning in connection with Kupferhoden's murder. This time the police had a name: Janice Rose.

Jan destroyed her false American passport, got rid of any clothes that had even a suggestion of American origin and replaced them with German ones. She resurrected the German identity that Anna had given her when she was first staying in the Munich house – "in case the pigs start sniffing you out like a ripe truffle," Anna had said. It proved unnecessary. "They don't ask for your ID when you're, like, serving litre mugs of beer and turning tricks for drunken Joes. They just don't."

A squeal came from the amorous teenagers. The boy's hand had moved up the girl's back under her red t-shirt and unfastened her bra. She pushed him away in protective protest. It was only as she released herself from the explorer's hands that I saw the front of her t-shirt. Spread across the liberated teenage tits was a black twenty-first-century fashion statement: the star and Kalashnikov of the Red Army Faction.

"It was," Jan said, "a long time ago."

7

We drove out along the lake road in the hired black Mercedes C-class. When we turned down the lane that leads to La Bise, Jan said, "It doesn't look like it's changed all that much."

Inside, however, the house *had* changed. The bright colours of an Alpine spring, the paintings of snowy mountains – the Matterhorn, Piz Buin, the Wildstrübel, the meadows above

Montreux, the richness of dark wood, the patina left behind by the daily lives of a family once happy: all gone. In its 2007 reincarnation, La Bise had returned in minimalist ivories, greys, browns. Lighting emerged from unseen sources. Plants without flowers grew in pots of old pewter. Pictures in bare wooden frames seemed to have been painted by the same decorator who had spread the paint across the surfaces of the walls on which they hung.

Pale tables were laid with squares of dark slate. A single, white rose lay between rows of sparkling crystal. The menus were in Russian as well as in English and French. Jan's menu had no prices on it. The ones on mine were in both Euros and Swiss Francs. Our waiter was a dyed-blonde Eastern European, past his prime, ostentatiously homosexual, entirely clad in black, conscientiously part of the décor.

We drank champagne. It was not from the old Meyer vineyards, of course, but it was of good quality nonetheless. When the waiter came and said *"Je vous écoute"*, Jan asked me to order for her. We ate foie gras with slivers of artichoke heart encased in the lightest imaginable brioche and then, because this was all about nostalgia, a plate of *filets de perche du lac* – although the lake in which the fish had once swum was almost certainly not the one that lapped beyond the open window. The sommelier offered us his finest wines. I passed them up, ordered a bottle of Fendant from the Valais, then later, another.

"You won't be able to drive back," Jan protested.

"We'll worry about that," I said, "when we come to it. They probably still do taxis around here."

Jan smiled. She looked much younger when she smiled. "Okay," she said. "You're the boss."

We ate an intricate pattern of white and dark chocolate for dessert, drank our coffee, nibbled the handmade chocolate truffles that came with it, sipped a pear liqueur. "The ad in the magazine said they had rooms here," I said.

"We have rooms already."

"So? Let's just ask."

When the waiter came to see whether we wanted another round of liqueurs, I asked him about rooms for the night. He frowned, said he was doubtful (*"Un samedi au fin de juillet? Ça m'étonnera."*) but went away to enquire. When he returned he said, *"Il nous reste qu'une seule chambre ce soir, monsieur."*

I looked at Jan. She did not look up. I did, however, detect that very slight nod. At least I think I did.

The waiter showed us up to the room. *"Monsieur n'a pas de bagages?"*

"Non."

"Ni madame?"

"Non plus."

"Alors, je vous souhaite une très bonne nuit, monsieur."

Only one room left, no baggage, goodnight. I closed the door behind him and turned the key in the lock.

The bedroom shared the minimalist makeover with the dining room downstairs: white, ivory, grey, beige. Here the dominant colour was white. The room even smelled white. The Ukrainian maid's armoury probably included an aerosol can with a lily-of-the-valley scent that she sprayed on the fluffy duvet lying across the big bed between its polished brass ends. Hodler's white flowers by the *Statue de la Bise.* A bridal dress translucent in the medieval moonlight. Whipped cream atop a steaming mug of hot Vienna chocolate.

> *Whatever colors you have in your mind,*
> *I'll show them to you and you'll see them shine.*
> *Lay, lady, lay, lay across my big brass bed.*
> *Why wait any longer for the world to begin?*

Jan did not protest when I put my arms around her, did not resist when I kissed her. Gradually, she began to return the kisses. Her body seemed to come alive, to press against mine. I unbuttoned the top button of her shirt. Then the second. I felt Jan's lips on my neck. My fingers moved to the third button, the same button I had reached on that wet, Oxford evening thirty-six years earlier.

Abruptly, Janice Day pulled away from me. She gasped, "Pardon me," and escaped into the bathroom. She locked the door behind herself, leaving me standing between the white door and the whipped-cream bed.

The picture on the wall was of a grey sea beneath a grey sky. A plaque set into the frame read: *J.-P. Delmas. Arcachon. Septembre, 1951.* Testimony to a seaside holiday that disappointed? Perhaps. Or maybe it was just two shades of grey separated where they met by a line of darker grey. Perhaps J.-P. Delmas had never been to Arcachon, had just imagined a land by the ocean where there are no mountains to climb. I listened to the flush of the lavatory behind the locked door. I heard water running, heard water splashing in water. I heard Jan moving. Something metallic fell onto the tiled floor...

Then there was silence. Thirty-six years ago, Jan had said, "Not tonight, Nick." I had lent her my umbrella and she had left her guitar with me because the night had been wet. The lavatory flushed again. I heard the key turn. The door opened.

Earlier this year, in the spring of 2008, nine months after I had gone to Geneva with Jan, nine months after that night at La Bise, I went to Geneva again, telling myself it was purely for research purposes, to gather the background smells I needed to write this story. The frontier police let me into Switzerland without question, without a flicker of recognition: my name was on neither their wanted list nor their unwanted list. I took a taxi to the Hôtel des Bergues but, when the doorman opened the taxi door and I got out, I turned and walked the other way up the Rue du Mont-Blanc – past the Anglican Church and the Café de Paris and McDonald's – through the underpass and up into Cornavin Station; seeing Colin as he ate his last lunch, bought his last train ticket and made his last journey, following Jan's shadow as she walked the same path, with me at her side, six years later. The departures board showed a train to Montreux leaving in two minutes. In a souvenir-shop window, Jan's reflection moved towards the platform.

I retraced my steps to the Quai de Bergues and walked across the narrow bridge to the island. Rousseau's head had been polished. It was the first time I had seen it free of pigeon shit. Perhaps the twenty-first century has invented a paint, equivalent to the one that keeps urban graffiti at bay, to keep the crania of philosophers clean and notions of liberty safely sealed within. I sat on the bench where I had sat with Jan and recalled the teenage lovers as clearly as I did Jan's account of the fire in Munich. I wondered how long it had taken *him* to part the Kalashnikov from the chest, to unfasten the chains, to do *his* little anti-fascist squirt between *her* legs.

I took the tram to the Ecolint. It was morning break when I arrived and schoolchildren milled about the courtyard. If anyone was selling doughnuts, I did not see them. At the top of the Greek Theatre, a student – probably a monitor taking his surveillance duties seriously – asked me politely whether I was looking for someone. I told him I was an old boy. The American teenager, however, did not understand that English expression and escorted me past the lodge and out through the gates.

I rode the tram from Grange-Canal to Place Neuve. This time I went into the Japanese restaurant that had replaced the Landolt, asked about the table on which Lenin had carved his name. It was gone, I was told. I could find it in a museum. My informant didn't know which museum but thought it might be in Zürich or Moscow, he wasn't sure.[93] I wondered whether Marie-Claire's inherited gun collection would now ever find a museum home.

I conveyed Caroline's regards to Calvin and Knox, to Farel and Bèze. I wondered who was following whom, wondered which of the four was Mr Tambourine Man. I walked back through the old town, past the cannons opposite Les Armures, through the square in front of the cathedral, through the Place du Bourg du Four, down to Place Molard and out past the monument to the Sisters of the Confederation and the floral clock. It was a joyless journey past places that had become no more than words on a stranger's map. Caroline had been oddly right: you need to travel with someone with whom you can share memories. I found, I think, the patch of grass on which Jan and I had sung songs from the sixties. I sat on the bench by the *jet d'eau* where Jan had told me why she was leaving Joe McIntosh and then related one of her disjointed instalments about life on the run in Germany in 1972.

Jan got a job as a waitress at the *Oktoberfest*, she had told me, as the white water fell in diaphanous curtains onto the surface of the blue lake. They dressed her in a traditional Bavarian costume that emphasised the fullness of her breasts. They paid her well. Customers gave her big tips because of the size of her tits. "I'd paid a lot of money for them," she said, "so I thought I might as well use them. In those days I could always get a job when somebody needed a pair of boobs."

She had paused in her story there, got up from the bench and stood facing me, towering over me like a disappointed schoolmistress, her reading glasses dangling from the chain around her neck. She had said, "That's when I saw you, Nick. If you'd've been alone and sober I'd've come over and asked you to help me there and then. I totally would've. I was so goddamn desperate. But you were with Colin and both of you sons of bitches were so goddamn drunk. I was so mad at you, terrified what the two of you would do if you'd've recognised me. I hid in the washroom." Another pause, then, "It was a bad decision, Nick. I should've taken the risk."

---

[93] The table on which Lenin allegedly carved his name in Cyrillic capital letters has not found a home in any known museum. There is, in fact, considerable mystery as to what happened to the famous table and some have even questioned whether it ever existed. For a full account of recent speculation about the table, refer to *La Tribune de Genève*, 3 August 2006, '*Où Est la Table de Lénine?*' – Ed.

Had Jan, just possibly, been telling the truth at that moment? That she would have asked me for help if I'd been sober? That she thought it had been a bad decision to hide in the women's loos? I still wonder. I got up from the bench and walked along the waterfront to the *Statue de la Bise*. I said goodbye to my stone muse, found a taxi at a taxi-stand in the Eaux-Vives and asked the driver to take me to the airport. I resolved never again to return to Geneva.

Something metallic falls onto the tiled bathroom floor. Then there seems to be no sound, no movement behind the locked door for a very long time before the lavatory flushes again. I hear the key turn. The white door opens. Jan steps into the room. She is naked. She is thin but for a roll of fat that clings like an awkward belt around her waist. She is smaller than I remember her. She is grey. Her pubic hair is grey. Her skin is grey. Eyes once pale blue have turned grey. There is a long, unpleasant scar from a past operation across her belly. Those breasts that were once the eighth wonder of the world sag like grey balloons, wilted and forgotten after the party is over. Are the little scars on them where they took the implants out when they became too uncomfortable with age? A large birthmark discolours her left thigh. My eyes scan the woman again from head to toe. Grindstone grey. The only colour is in the red paint on the toenails. The impostor comes towards me. She says, "If we're going to do this thing, let's get on with it."

8

I awoke before Jan did. She lay on the far side of the super-king-sized bed, everything but a few strands of hair hidden beneath the white duvet, snoring lightly. I rolled away from her. A shaft of daylight entered the room between the two halves of the curtains. It formed a line across the white armchair, across the black lacquer table on which the magazines lay, onto the wall opposite. Tiny motes of dust sparkled as they floated into the light and were extinguished as they drifted again into the shadows.

I slipped from the bed. My clothes had fallen on the floor at Jan's side of the bed. To retrieve them would have been to risk waking her. I was not yet ready for that, so I left my clothes where I presumed they still lay and walked the few steps to the window.

Through the gap where the two halves of the curtains did not quite meet I could see the lake. In the foreground was the dock. It was empty, too early in the day to attract sunbathers and party folk clad in evening black. In the distance, across the water, I could see a sliver of Geneva. Then I saw something that I had never seen in all the years I had lived in Geneva: I saw the *jet d'eau* come to life. The great fountain sprang up from the deep loins of the lake. Then, just as suddenly, it was turned off again. For a moment the spray lingered in the air. Then that, too, was gone and it was just another lonely Sunday morning in Geneva.

I looked back at the big brass bed where Jan lay naked but out of sight under the duvet. I had climbed the ultimate summit. I had claimed my trophy. I had completed my list. According to the script I should be jumping over the moon, dancing a jig on the Meyers' dock, walking out across the waters of Leman. In fact, I felt as flat as the dark grey line two-thirds of the way down J.-P. Delmas's painting of Arcachon. For the first time in decades I felt a craving for a cigarette, just a few deep puffs on one of my old Sobranie Black Russians.

Jan stirred and, without waking, threw the duvet off. She lay on her back, her grey nakedness fully exposed. What was it she had said as she'd unbuttoned my shirt, unbuckled my belt, unzipped my trousers: "'Imagination is just one weapon in the fight against reality'"? But no spark from all the years of imagination had ignited the fire.

It had been a very mediocre coupling, too tentative at first, too hasty in its finale. She had rolled away almost immediately afterwards, had lain briefly on her back, staring blankly at the ceiling, before saying she was very tired. She had then pulled the duvet up to her chin and fallen quickly asleep. I had slept badly, haunted by half-dreamed dreams and an elusive far-off smell of light rain falling on an urban graveyard.

It was only after I had showered and dressed, when I was standing at the window again waiting for Jan to finish in the bathroom, that I identified the room where we had slept as Oscar's. Oscar's bedroom, where he and I had fought on a Thursday afternoon more than forty-five years earlier. Children lashing out at a world that deviated from our dreams. I remembered where his desk had been, his bed, his wardrobe, his toy guns. We had both drawn blood, I with the aid of his brother's toy locomotive.

I left the window, sat in an armchair and picked up a magazine.

Jan emerged from the bathroom, a towel turban on her head but otherwise casually naked. Scarcely looking up from the magazine I was leafing through, I said, "This was Oscar's room."

I did not expect an answer. I had not posed a question, but Jan, absently, answered, "Yes." She was looking, as she spoke, at the autumnal seas at Arcachon.

Oscar had arrived at the 1972 Oktoberfest a couple of days after Colin and I had left Munich. He came to the Löwenbräu tent late in the evening, pretending to be drunk. He put an arm around Jan's waist when she served him his beer, winked at the manager and whisked her away. "Simple as that," Jan said.

They went to Jan's lodgings, took a few of her things but left most behind, including her German identity papers. If anyone came looking for Jan, the evidence remaining in her room would suggest that her absence was not intended to be permanent. "That was Oscar's idea. 'Get a few days ahead of them,' he said."

Oscar and Jan crossed into Austria under cover of darkness the next night. Jan's lack of a passport gave Oscar an excuse to plot a silly route out of Germany. "Like some ridiculous thing out of *The Sound of Music*," Jan said without a smile. Two days later, they crossed into Switzerland through the Silvretta range where Christian Meyer had taken each of his sons in turn for what psychologists term 'bonding sessions'. Oscar, whose English was less than fluent when he was young, called them 'bondage sessions'. They travelled westward across Switzerland by train.

Oscar put Jan up in the old family chalet at Les Sornettes. After she had been there for a few days, he came up from Geneva and said he feared the net was closing. Either the police or some wild assassins hired by the Baader-Meinhof Group – or possibly both – were following her and would eventually work out where she was hiding. "Maybe he just made that up," Jan said. "Who knows!"

Jan would be safer, according to Oscar, in the United States. There was more space to hide there than in Europe and she could blend into the population more easily. "Oscar called it the 'New World'. He liked the sound of the words. He kept on repeating them – 'New World. New World'."

Early one morning while it was still dark, Oscar arrived at the chalet with a fake Canadian passport. The name in the passport was Barbara Palmer, born in Regina, Saskatchewan, on 22 December 1950. The photograph in it was of Janice Day, based on one taken at the automatic photo booth outside Grand Passage during Jan's last year at Ecolint. Oscar had kept it in a drawer in his bedside table since the evening it was taken.

Later that day, Oscar and Jan flew from Geneva to Paris. There Oscar put 'Barbara Palmer' on an Air France flight to Montreal. "I drifted around for a few years. If anyone was looking for me I guess they weren't looking too hard and then, before I knew it, the driftin' days were through and I was Mrs Joseph B. McIntosh out in the boonies of Montana. A home out in the wind."

A bowl of red cherries sat on the breakfast table. While we waited for the croissants and coffee, I popped a cherry into my mouth. It was sharp and bitter, there, like much of the house, for decoration only.

I paid the bill at the reception desk: dinner, room, breakfast. Jan and I had been the only ones at breakfast. Either the waiter had lied to me about there only being one room left or all the other Sunday morning guests were still enjoying their big brass beds, still seeking those elusive goosebumps on the skin of eternity. The bill was considerably more expensive than I had expected. The Hôtel-Restaurant de la Bise had charged me for a bottle of vintage Krug when all we'd had was two flutes of house champagne and the room rate was at least double the price advertised in the Hôtel des Bergues' magazine. But I did not have the energy to complain about being diddled. I tapped my PIN into the handheld terminal.

The pretty girl behind the desk handed me my credit card and the receipt. "Have a nice day," she said in English. As I inserted the card into my wallet, it suddenly struck me what the receptionist had said. *A Nice Day. J.A. Nice Day. Janice Day.*

"Thank you," I replied as I put the wallet back in my pocket. "I've already had that."

Jan stood by the car, facing the sun, eyes shielded by sunglasses, wearing yesterday's clothes. She looked at her watch. Time, perhaps, to begin again without the weight of history bearing down on us?

"Where to?" I asked and when I received no reply added, "What about driving round the lake? We could drive up to Les Sornettes."

"Not now. Maybe later."

"Then where to now?"

"You decide."

I drove up the hill towards La Capite. "We'll take a spin past your old house."

Jan turned her face towards me. "No, Nick," she said, a momentary panic in her voice, "I don't want that."

So when we reached La Capite, I avoided the road that went past Jan's old house and turned left on the one that runs north, straight down the hill to join the main Evian road that comes up from Vésenaz. From that road, as you go down the hill, you can see the woods of Rouëlbeau, ahead and to the right below you.

"I used to go there a lot when I was a kid. We used to camp in the ruins overnight. There was no proper road anywhere near it then."

Jan said nothing.

"Mind if I just take a spin past and have a quick squint?"

Again, no response from my passenger, so, when I saw a narrow but paved road that I thought might lead us closer to Rouëlbeau, I took it. The Chemin des Combes ran east, towards the sun, across flat fields that in medieval times had been marshes, but also the Duke of Faucigny's only outlet to the waters of Lake Geneva. The fortress at Rouëlbeau, now to our left, had been built to protect that route. The dark forested ridge of Les Voirons rose ahead of us in the distance. Closer to us a row of poplar trees was backlit by the morning sun. To our right a vineyard climbed the slope towards La Capite. It all seemed so much tamer, so much more suburban, than when Johnny Morris and I used to come here. Beyond the woods of Rouëlbeau, I saw the tall floodlights of a sports stadium and the aluminium sheds of light industry.

An unmade farm track led to Rouëlbeau. A sign said 'Trafic agricole seul autorisé'. I turned along it, although a Mercedes C-class could scarcely be classified as agricultural traffic. I saw at once what had happened to the enchanted forest and a shiver of horror ran down my back.

A large part of the woods, the corner we were approaching, had been ripped away. The stone ramparts – looking so very small and fragile now – had been cleansed of their vegetation. A corrugated plastic roof sheltered the old stonework from the elements, metal scaffolding poles holding up the roof and supporting the ancient walls. Fencing had been erected to keep trespassers out. Rouëlbeau had become an archaeological dig. The past was being stripped bare. The legends were gone. The palimpsest on which each generation had written its own story had been analysed, found wanting and shredded. Even in the bright morning sunlight, my once-magic Rouëlbeau looked desiccated, grey and uninviting.

I parked the hired Mercedes next to a makeshift green building.

There was another car parked at the archaeologists' shed, a silver Opel registered in the Canton of Vaud, but no sign of activity. The doors of the hut were locked and the generator beside it stood silent and idle. Jan said quietly, "I could see this place from my bedroom window when I was a kid."

"Didn't you ever come down here?"

"I came once," she said. "Only once."

A flash of light caught my eye. It was like the glint of the sun off a mirror. It came from somewhere on the hill that rises towards La Capite, towards where Jan had lived. I turned my head instinctively towards the flash. Jan continued to stare through the car windscreen. Her face seemed to be frozen; she seemed to address her words to the derelict woodland and the history lying naked before us. "It was in the dead of night. A warm summer's night. A full moon."

Another flash, but this flash didn't come from the 2007 vintage ripening on the hillside to the south of us. It came from 1967, almost exactly forty years earlier, from a time when Rouëlbeau was still intact, when Johnny Morris and I camped in these innocent woods and lay on our backs as the embers of the campfire died, watching the harvest moon play tricks among the branches of trees as we listened to the philharmonic of the night. Quietly, to match the stillness in Jan's voice, I said, "Jan?"

"I lost my virginity that night."

"What?"

"Surely I don't need to explain."

"I mean, who?"

"You really don't know who it was?"

"No idea."

"Really?"

"Really."

"Oscar. It was Oscar Meyer." She sighed. The blank stare again. "It was always Oscar."

9

Jan got out and walked around the back of the Mercedes to the archaeologists' hut. I joined her as she looked at a sun-faded history of Rouëlbeau and description of *la fouille* nailed to wall by the Archaeological Service of the Republic and Canton of Geneva. Jan looked at me, smiled and said, "I think we've got the place to ourselves this morning." The absent gaze and the quiet voice were gone, buried, to be excavated by a future generation of students digging with nail files and toothbrushes.

Jan walked towards the ruins. I followed. We passed an abandoned metal barbecue filled with the ash of charcoal briquettes and the drippings of meat eaten long ago. Beside the barbecue was a black plastic bucket in which someone had once mixed cement. Crushed beer cans littered the ground beside it.

We came to the first moat. It was dry. White butterflies darted in and out among the weeds that grew where the earth had been disturbed and then forgotten. The path led along the bank between the outer moat and the inner one, past thistles and stumps of trees. Archaeological dust dulled the sharp green of the nettles. A duck flew up from the bulrushes in the second moat. A light breeze blew in from the lake and then fell still again. The violated walls of Rouëlbeau rose to our left. One of the round medieval towers seemed to have been rebuilt. The archaeologists appeared to be preparing to reconstruct another. An orange power cable led to it from the generator by the hut. One day, I wondered, will they open all this as a tourist site, charge admission fees and provide headsets through which you can listen to a commentary (in the language of your choice) on what life was like for campers and ghosts in 1967?

I caught up with Jan at a point where we came to a track. One muddy day, the archaeologists must have brought their earth-moving equipment along here: the caterpillar tracks had sunk deeply into the earth. The rutted imprints led up a ramp to the left that penetrated the north end of the old east wall of the castle, ending atop a man-made hill that was probably the archaeologists' spoil tip.

"Let's go up there," I said. "We'll get a good view of whatever it is they're doing here."

Jan lagged behind. I heard her say, "Nick." I turned. "You don't get it, do you?"

"What?"

"You don't have a clue."

I stared at her. She had stopped walking up the slope. She was holding her sunglasses in her left hand, looking at me with a quizzical, almost pitying, look on her face. "About what?" I asked.

"Oscar and me."

"What?"

"I married Oscar. Oscar *is* Joe McIntosh."

"What! How?"

If my burbled exclamations had a meaning, Jan misinterpreted them. She said, "*Day of the Jackal* kind of thing. He found a gravestone for a kid born in 1948. Got his birth certificate, got the driving licence, got the passport. When we got married Barbara Palmer became Barbara McIntosh. Nick, it's like…"

Jan saw them before I did. I turned to see what she was looking at. Two men were coming over the top of the mound, each carrying a gun. Now, I knew nothing about guns then, but these were what I imagined heavy-duty assault rifles to be like, Kalashnikovs, AK-47s, whatever other aliases they might go by. The kind of thing menacingly spread across the star in the old RAF logo to let you know that the coming Revolution would not be some derivative of a genteel bourgeois tea-party.

The older man's chin was covered with white stubble. His hair was pulled back from his face into a ponytail. He wore an army surplus jacket with the gold, red and black bars of the German flag sewn onto the shoulder. The younger man was covered from neck to ankle in khaki camouflage fatigues. The bottoms of his trousers were tucked into the tops of black boots, like the ones you see Nazis wearing in war films. His head was shaved and his face was streaked with war paint.

The younger man trained his gun on Jan and me as the elder walked slowly down the hill towards us. He was chewing gum. His gait was an exaggerated John Wayne swagger. Then he spoke and I recognised the green, corrosive voice at once.

"Well," Oscar drawled like a caricature of a sixties' comic-book villain. "What have we here? Mrs Barbara McIntosh all the way from the badlands of Montana, and…" Oscar slapped me across the jaw, "… little Limey Farthole." He walked past me towards Jan. "Has," he said, "our rich little benefactor been treating you okay, Miss Day?"

Jan did not answer him, did not move. Oscar walked back up to me. "My most sincere apologies," he said, "for touching your rich little face, Farthole."

"Oscar. I…"

"Shut it, Farthole! You say another goddamn word and my man over there'll put an ounce of lead into that little egghead of yours." The bald golem on the hill stiffened. He seemed keen to test his index finger on the trigger. Oscar turned to Jan, "What shall we do with the little son of a bitch, Barb?"

Again, Jan did not reply.

"Remember that weenie roast I told you about, Barb?"

No reply.

"Christ! Are you gonna just stand there like a fuckin' statue?"

Oscar turned to his golem. "Tie his hands and gag him," he said. The silent, blue-eyed soldier laid down his gun and did as he was ordered, took a piece of cloth from one of his pockets, put it into my mouth, tied it tightly behind my head. He tied my wrists behind my back. "Take his pants off." The boy obediently unbuckled my belt, unzipped the zipper, put his hands inside the waistband, pushed my trousers down. "And his underpants before he shits them. There's some unfinished business here, ain't there, Farthole?"

Jan began to protest. "Oscar…"

"Shut it, wench." The golem pulled my underpants down to join my trousers, around my ankles. Oscar came over to me, grabbed my genitals with his right hand and squeezed. The pain shot up my spine.

Oscar lay his Kalashnikov on the ground and pulled a long hunting knife from the sheath that hung from his belt. "Shall we see if we can make Little Farthole sing? Always liked singing, didn't you? Do you remember those little lists you used to make up? Best singer: number one – Janice Day. Best tits: number one – Janice Day. Remember all that shit? Barb, come here and show him your tits. Try and get some blood into this puny little dick before we cut it off."

The noise of a car engine and a car door closing not far away. Oscar said to the boy, "Go see who it is and get them to scam." Thirty-five years of living in America seemed not to have improved Oscar's grasp of the vernacular.

The boy went, carrying his weapon. Oscar picked up his gun, cocked his ear and sniffed the air like a hunting dog. There were other guns lying on the ground: five, maybe six, rifles. We waited, each silent.

The boy returned. "Police."

Oscar turned to me. "Is this your doing, Farthole?" The gag prevented a reply.

"How many?"

"Two cars," the boy said.

"Rope his legs and tie him to a tree."

The golem did as he was commanded. He wrapped a nylon climbing rope around my ankles, tied it through the rope around my wrists and then pulled me tight against a tree. Oscar approached Jan and whispered in her ear. There was another noise on the far side of the woods where the boy had seen the police cars. Oscar sent the boy to investigate again and then kissed Jan's cheek. "Love ya, babe." He picked up a rifle from the pile and threw it to Jan. She caught it in one hand, ran her other hand along it, released and then refastened the safety catch. She kept her eyes from meeting mine.

Oscar said, "You have it? Everything?"

Jan nodded.

"Ready, then?"

Jan nodded again. That little, scarcely perceptible nod.

"Over there." With a jerk of his neck, Oscar's unshaven chin motioned to the wall on the opposite side of the archaeologists' site.

Jan used her feet and the butt of the rifle to break down the fence that barred the way into the excavations. She walked across the dig, across the space where my enchanted clearing in the woods had once been, and climbed onto the ancient battlements. Oscar took shelter behind another wall.

We did not need to wait long. After ninety seconds or so, the shooting began. Later I learned from the police that it was the boy with the painted face who had fired the first shot. At the time, I could not tell where it had come from. The sound of more shots followed, gunfire responding from beyond the perimeter of the woods. I saw Oscar fire into the trees beyond his wall. His fire, too, was answered. He fired again into the woods then turned and pointed his rifle at me. A single shot hit my left arm. At first there was no pain. Then a sensation like fire spread up my arm towards my brain. I saw blood beginning to flow from both sides of my forearm.

I looked for Jan, saw her crouched low behind her stone wall. Oscar fired another bullet at me. It hit my naked leg just above the knee. I slumped forward but the rope that tied me to the tree kept me from falling onto the ground. I could feel my head becoming lighter, consciousness beginning to drain away.

As I struggled to lift my head, I saw Jan stand up on her wall, look back into the enclosure and aim her rifle. There was a blank, impenetrable stare in her eyes – the look I had seen on her face as she lay in bed in Oscar's room at La Bise, gazing at something beyond the ceiling. She squeezed the trigger and a volley of bullets flew at Oscar as he aimed a third shot at me. I heard his scream, watched him topple from his wall.

Another shot. Two. Three. I stopped counting. I didn't know where they were coming from. As I drifted away, I watched Jan fall

378

to her knees, watched her lose her grip on her gun, watched it drop from her hands. Like a broken rag doll, she tumbled down into the excavations, down into the medieval courtyard where children once played, into a time of blackbirds and nightingales when cherries tasted sweet and guns were toys, into a time when sunshine sparkled on the lake and blossom gathered in the hedgerows became flowers in your hair. She fell from the walls of Rouëlbeau at precisely the spot where I had seen her standing in the moonlight forty years earlier. I watched her shirt turn from white to red.

Nicholas Kellaway
London, July 2008

CHAPTER TWELVE

Tuesday, 29 July 2008

I completed my manuscript on Tuesday, 29 July 2008 – on schedule, exactly a year after the shootings at Rouëlbeau. I had it printed out on A4 paper (font twelve, Times New Roman, double-spaced, single-sided), put into a box and couriered to Edward Reader's office.

Edward Reader? Yes, you might well ask. What can I say? Ed had been roughly contemporary with me at both Ecolint and Oxford. His website suggested familiarity with the world of finance. His doctorate in twentieth-century German history promised expertise in a field that I would likely have to research. He had acted as literary agent for Emma Wallace for *Jericho House* and Emma heartily recommended him. And hey, Edward Reader was the only literary agent I even vaguely knew, though 'knew', even so qualified, was far too strong a word. I had heard Ed's voice on the phone often enough, but I had not seen him in the flesh since the Escalade dinner at the old Leicester Square Swiss Centre in 1975. And from that distant evening only the voice remained in the memory.

The same pattern – the voice of a faceless weasel gnawing at the other end of a rusty steel pipe – repeated itself in the weeks after I was shot. No sooner had I been repatriated to England than Ed was on the phone suggesting, then almost begging, that I write an account of the path leading to Rouëlbeau. There had been considerable media coverage and, given my resulting prominence as the country's best-known hedge-fund manager – a profession then being dragged into a lurid red spotlight – Ed was confident, he said, that he would be able to interest the best publishers in the land.

At first I said no. All I wanted was to regain my strength and resume my life running Kellaway & Co. It was Emma Wallace who persuaded me that I could do both. Under her guidance, I began to find scenes in the recesses of my memory and make verbal sketches of them. The activity helped to fill the blank canvases of my convalescence. Then, as I began to recover from my bullet wounds, I threw myself into the task, setting myself routines and keeping rigorously to them, trying to create order and meaning from a palette of colours extracted from the carcasses of burnt-out dreams. It was not always easy. There were continents of unexplored memories across which I had to trek. There were mountains to climb and dark valleys to discover and traverse. The path was often ill-defined, overgrown and tangled, but I kept going, scribbling and hacking away with my Mont-Blanc machete, working towards the goal of completing the manuscript by the first anniversary of that Sunday in Switzerland.

Despite what I told Ed and Emma, I had absolutely no intention of publishing. The document would be strictly for myself – my emotional catharsis. I would use Ed's and Emma's skills strictly for my own therapeutic ends.

Edward Reader phoned in early August a week after getting my narrative. "Nick," he said, "you're going to have to murder your darlings."

"What?"

"Sorry. Editor speak. Arthur Quiller-Couch, in fact. The chap who did the *Oxford Book of English Verse*. 'Murder your darlings' was his phrase. There are too many bits here that don't contribute to the story – whatever we decide the story might be. They need to go. 'Your darlings' in old Q's terminology. There are far too many loose ends and too many people. People nobody remembers any more. I mean, who nowadays remembers Gudrun Ensslin or Uschi Obermaier? I'm going to have to footnote all these obscure references if anyone's going to make sense of it."

"Uschi *who*?"

"Uschi Obermaier. She's in your book, Nick."

"She's not. I've never even heard of her."

"She's there. Believe me, I've just read it."

"I've *never* heard of her."

"So you said. Whatever. Anyway. Characters just drift in and drift out. There are so many of them *you've* even forgotten at least one of them. We don't know why they're there in the first place and we never learn what becomes of them."

"That's just how life is; over fifty-seven years most people do just drift in and out. I've got ten Rolodexes full of people. I don't even know who most of them were, much less what's happened to them."

"Sure. I understand all that, but, if we take this forward, we're going to be marketing it as fiction, and fiction readers have certain expectations, legitimate expectations if I may say, that you will solve the mysteries you create. They need the whole thing to be drawn together. A feeling of completeness and satisfaction when they come to the last page."

"How many people's lives are like that?"

"That's exactly why they need to get it from books."

"Ed, this is my life we're dealing with – not some detective novel."

"A detective novel, Nick? Is that how you see it?"

"Come off it. That's how I *don't* see it."

"How *do* you see it?"

"What d'you mean?"

"Well, we've got to fit this into some recognisable genre and, I must say, I find it hard to know what I'm dealing with here."

"Go on."

"What's the whole thing about? A spy thriller? Maybe, in a strange way. Some sort of priapic odyssey? Is it the sex wars at the end of the twentieth century? The quest for some elusive concept of Liberty? Or the Ideal Woman? Or maybe it's about the loss of innocence? Some kind of *Bildungsroman* – but with no epiphany to your story. No learning. No fundamental change in the main character's life."

"Listen, Ed. I'm only the narrator here, the observer. You *do* find out what happens to the main character."

"Who is...?"

"Janice Day."

Ed did not respond. Did I hear him shuffling papers? Another phone was ringing in his office. When it stopped, he said, "Okay, but there are other things. We never find out who murdered Colin Witheridge for a start. We never learn anything about Anastasia or Anna or whoever she's meant to be. The character fascinates me, but... And then there's that black girl found dead in Ferney-Voltaire. She..."

"Listen, Ed. With due respect. I just don't know. The police, MI5... they don't even know who killed Colin. Their imagination stops at dinner with Andropov."

"Can you make a link between Colin and Jan? Sort of to tie it all together."

"There was no link."

"Nothing? What about Oxford?"

"Their paths crossed. Jericho House. After that, nothing."

"What happened to Anastasia?"

"No idea." Silence again. More paper shuffling. "Who," I continued, "was the third one you mentioned?"

"The black girl, the French spy. You don't even give her a name."

"She was just a photograph."

"Not giving her a name might be considered racist."

"Ed, do whatever the fuck you want with her. Make her Colin's Amsterdam prostitute. Make her the original one from Durban. Make her some beautiful Muslim terrorist. Make her the director of the Milk Marketing Board. Shit, edit her out if she's embarrassing."

"I'm only trying to help, Nick. We just *do* need a final chapter."

"You've got it already."

Ed sighed. "Okay, tell you what, let me go away and come up with a few ideas. See what you think of them."

"Ideas?"

"A nice rounded ending. The type of thing novel readers expect, especially female readers. 70% of people who read novels are women, you know. We'll need to make the whole thing a lot less male in the process."

"What's that mean?"

"If you…"

"Ed, this is *not* fiction."

"Just let me see what I can do. And, Nick, why don't we call the black girl something like Veronica?"

"Okay. Véronique, then."

"Véronique?"

"She's French, remember?"

"I remember."

"Or, if she's become one of *your* darlings, Ed, why don't you just follow your old friend Q's advice and kill her off."

"According to your novel, somebody already took care of that."

2

Sunday, 29 July 2007

Paul Meyer and his trophy wife had gone trekking in Ladakh. His neighbours out among the vineyards of La Côte knew when they were due to return, so, when a middle-aged American male arrived and let himself into Paul Meyer's villa, the vigilant villagers phoned the police.

The American – long grey hair drawn back into a ponytail, cut-off blue jeans, well-worn running shoes without socks – opened the door. He told the police that he spoke no French, said he was a friend of Paul Meyer, that Paul had invited him to stay in the house and keep an eye on it while he, Paul, was in India. He showed them a US passport in the name of Joseph Benito McIntosh. One of the watchful neighbours had reported seeing a woman in the house. When the police asked about the woman, Mr McIntosh laughed. He was alone in the house, he said, but if the Swiss authorities were in the business of supplying women to visiting Americans then he would accept one with gratitude.

The police left, but they remained suspicious of the American. The Meyers had not mentioned him to any of their neighbours and Mr McIntosh was not the type to whom they would have expected Paul Meyer to lend his villa. If there were any doubts on that score, the ponytail tipped the scales. The police accordingly mounted a discreet round-the-clock watch. It was, after all, the residence of the chairman of one of Switzerland's most prestigious private banks and a woman who had been the darling of the World Cup slalom races.

At six forty-two on the morning of Sunday, 29 July 2007, a silver-grey Opel Astra with Vaud registration plates arrived at the wrought-iron gates at the bottom of Paul Meyer's drive. It was driven by a light-skinned male. Head shaved, probably mid-thirties. The automatic gates slid open as the vehicle approached. The car drove in. When the Opel reached the house, the garage door rose. It slid shut again behind the car once it had entered. The policeman on duty phoned Lausanne to trace the vehicle's ownership. The response was superficially reassuring: the car belonged to Meyer & Cie.

Just over an hour later, at ten to eight, the Opel left Paul Meyer's garage. The driver was now wearing a military style cap, a khaki camouflage jacket and streaks of black and green paint on his face. The American with the ponytail sat in the seat beside him. He wore a German military surplus jacket and reflective aviator sunglasses.

The car drove down to the *autoroute* and there turned west towards Geneva. The policeman followed as far as the Versoix exit, where another unmarked police car, manned by two officers, picked up the car's tail and followed it as it entered Geneva, crossed the Pont du Mont-Blanc, turned along the south side of the lake and then up through Cologny.

They continued following the car when, beyond La Capite, it

turned right into the small Chemin des Combes. When the Opel turned left down a farm track towards the archaeological excavations at Rouëlbeau, the police did not follow: they would have been too conspicuous. That was a mistake. But only in hindsight.

In less than five minutes the police had set up their observation post on the hill to the south of the Rouëlbeau woods. From there they saw the two men return to the car on foot from the archaeological site and unload what appeared to be six assault rifles. The two men carried the guns up the spoil tip on the far side of the excavations. The watching policemen called for reinforcements.

The first batch of reinforcements, including three marksmen with high-powered rifles and long-distance sights, were just in place when a black Mercedes approached Rouëlbeau. It parked next to the Opel and a man and a woman eventually got out. They looked briefly at the notice pinned to the side of the archaeologists' shed and then walked along the ditches that had once been the castle's moats, the woman leading the way. They paused and seemed to discuss something before walking up the spoil mound.

The policemen watched as the newcomers met the riflemen, the American moving towards them while the younger man covered him with his gun. There were no handshakes or other physical signs of greeting. A discussion ensued. From a distance, it appeared to be a heated discussion primarily between the woman and J.B. McIntosh. His skinhead accomplice then gagged the newly arrived male, tied his hands behind his back and removed his trousers. J.B. McIntosh brandished a knife that glinted in the sunlight.

The officer in charge of the operation went to his car, turned his key in the ignition and radioed his men to prepare for action. Plan A, as he later told it, was to use loudhailers to demand that the armed men lay down their weapons and release their hostage. Guns would only be used when diplomacy failed, but at that point he did not have all his 'Plan B' forces in place and, in accordance with accepted health and safety procedures, he did not initiate 'Plan A' before the fall-back was ready.

A moment after the officer's radio message, the police saw the younger man go down the mound into the trees. He was carrying his gun. Ninety seconds later, they saw him emerge on the far side of the woods. He scanned the fields, first with his naked eye, then with binoculars. He disappeared back into the woods, reappeared on the mound again briefly, where he tied the hostage to a tree, before going back through the woods to emerge again at its north-western edge. From there he fired his rifle in the direction of the two unmarked police cars. Bullets hit the field and road in front of the cars. Two bullets, ricocheting from the ground, penetrated the bodywork of one of the two police cars. A policeman was hit in the leg and because he was on his radio at the time, the entire besieging force knew immediately that one of their colleagues had been shot. One of the police marksmen, stationed at a point a hundred metres to the south of the two police cars but with a clear view of the rifleman, returned fire. They saw the khaki man fall to the ground.

The policemen on the hill then heard more gunfire coming from the excavations. When a marksman spotted the woman standing on the ramparts, aiming her rifle into the enclosure where the hostage was held, he fired at her. Seconds later, the woman was seen falling from the rampart, towards the inside of the old fort.

The gunfire stopped when the woman fell. Through their loudhailers, the police demanded that the people in the woods put down their weapons and come into the open with their hands above their heads. There was no response. After twenty minutes of silence from the woods the police began to advance cautiously towards Rouëlbeau. Just outside the western perimeter of the woods they found the body of the younger man. Subsequent ballistics analysis determined that he had been killed by a single bullet to the skull fired by a police marksman.

The woman, lying at the foot of the ruined southern rampart, had been shot by another police marksman. Two bullets had entered her abdomen, but she was still alive when the police reached her.

J.B. McIntosh was dead. He had been killed by the gun found on the ground beside the woman.

The hostage, the British banker Nicholas Kellaway, although the police did not yet know who he was, was found gagged and tied to a tree. He had taken three bullets and had lost a worrying amount of blood. He was unconscious but breathing.

3

Oscar's third bullet: "Two centimetres from death," the surgeon said. But it was some days later he told me that – when he was saying goodbye before discharging me.

When I briefly regained consciousness from the operation that saved my life, I was in a white room, staring at a white ceiling, watching helplessly as it blackened and crumbled towards me. I had to get up and run – or die smothered by the falling ceiling. My muscles failed to respond. I opened my mouth to scream, but where my voice should have been there were only other people's white whispers.

A hand took mine. A familiar face sheltered me from the crumbling ceiling. Soft lips touched my forehead. *Caroline? Darling?* "Shhh," she said, "it's okay. You're going to make it, Nick." A tube in my throat gagged me. A black nurse in a white uniform injected a plastic bag full of clear liquid. A machine gurgled, whirred and pumped.

When I woke again, both the tube in my mouth and Caroline were gone. Phil Scott was sitting in the chair by the machine, his head slumped forward onto his chest in sleep. "Phil," I gasped, "what are you doing here?" I watched him wake, stand, come towards me and put his hand gently on my sheet-covered shoulder. "Where's Caro?" I asked.

"Back at the hotel, getting some rest."

"Getting some rest," I repeated and saw the flat, grey horizon that hung on Oscar Meyer's bedroom wall at La Bise.

Jan's blood soaks into the white sheets as she lies dying in my hospital bed. She lies close to me and I try to touch her breast, but a cancer that reeks of rotten fish has eaten it away. She has become Sill and, in a distant whisper, Sill's dying voice thinly recites Heggie's 'Mesopotamian Lullaby'. The black nurse covers us with a shroud of pale-blue alpine flowers. It smells of disinfectant and salt-water gargle and a priest says a prayer for those who have succumbed to the plague.

Darkness. Darkness. Then it was not completely dark. There were pale lights in the distance and blue and red on the nodules and dials of the machines. A green line made a ragged path across a screen. I looked for the Bloomberg but there wasn't one.

The machine whirred and moved towards me. It opened its jaws and clamped its teeth around my thighs. I screamed. The nurse wiped the sweat from my face, held a glass of water to my lips, injected the little bag that held the liquid flowing into my veins.

"Jan... Jan!"

No reply. But she's alive, isn't she? She's lying in a hospital bed, maybe just through the thin partition wall from my white room. I'll see her again soon and she'll smile her dimpled smile... Something metallic falls to the floor. The door opens. The woman comes into the room. "If," she says, "we're going to do this thing..." My eyes scan the naked body and fix on a large birthmark that discolours the left thigh. *An imposter. This is an imposter!* Jan did not have a birthmark on her thigh. I'd have seen it that day on Marie-Claire's boat, that day when she lay on the dock at La Bise... Surely, even in the most desperate quest for perfection, memory could not have airbrushed...

"The woman died, Nick. She died in the ambulance. Three dead. You're the only survivor." Whose voice is that? Whose voice is this howling in the wilderness?

Colours began to seep back into the world. When Caroline was alone with me in the room, I began to tell her what had happened. She would learn everything in due course anyway: the autopsy would find my DNA in the woman's body. So I told her about that as well, hoping she might think I had taken sufficient punishment already. In retrospect, perhaps I should have kept quiet and relied upon the Swiss authorities to do the same.

I watched as colour drained away again. Caroline's eyes clouded. Tears formed and ran down both cheeks. She turned to the white wall, fiddled with something in her black handbag, stood and walked out the door.

Phil was sitting in the chair where Caroline had sat previously. "You're a bastard, Kellaway," he said. "A complete bastard." He crossed his legs and hid behind *The Economist* and the machine that gurgled and pumped.

Other visitors arrived. Robert and Henry flew out to Geneva to see how I was doing. Amanda came with Jason, her fiancé. While Henry and Robert would soon grow bored of the hospital room, make excuses and wander away, taking Jason with them, Amanda sat diligently by my bedside for hours at a time. She was there beside me, reading while I dozed, when Claude Meyer and Marie-Claire Dufraisse arrived. I had had no idea that they were living together in a one-bedroom apartment in Dardagny. Beneath the drawn masks of sympathy, they were ecstatically happy.

389

Since I would now be unable to go, Caroline had offered Amanda, Jason and some of their friends the Corfu villa we had rented for the last two weeks of August. Marie-Claire said, "You must go, dear. Claude and I will be there with my boat. Your father was a great sailor when he was your age, weren't you, Nick." The mischievous smile.

Claude had genuinely heard nothing from Oscar since the mid-seventies. That was not so for Paul. When the news of what had happened at Rouëlbeau reached them, Paul and his wife flew back early from India. Paul, however, did not come to see me in hospital. I have charitably put that omission down to the fact that he needed to spend a considerable amount of time answering police questions. Paul, it turned out, had been in regular if infrequent contact with Oscar. He knew Oscar had married Jan, knew that they called themselves Mr and Mrs McIntosh and had even been to see them in Montana. I imagine they thought their secret was safe with Paul Meyer: he was, after all, a Swiss banker. And Paul *had* given Oscar the keys to his villa. He and Jan had visited him there on several occasions and he thought nothing of letting his eldest brother stay there while he and his wife went off on their summer holiday.

The police were also interested in Paul's connections to Oscar's golem. Even before Paul had returned from India, the police had established that the dead man with the shaven head had worked for Meyer & Cie, that he was in effect the chairman's *factotum*. It was the *factotum* who had done hours of work on old Mr Dufraisse's gun collection, undoing the disabling of 1968, readying them for action. Paul admitted the golem had worked under his instructions. He faced a number of questions.

Another surprise visitor was Emma Wallace. She was spending the summer in Switzerland, putting the final touches to *Jericho House Revisited*. "It's uncanny," she said, "how the chalet's sitting room is so like the one I imagined for 'Sogol'. It's like I'm sitting there waiting for the snow storm and the phone call saying God has died." She had read about the ambush in *La Suisse*, she said, and come straight to the hospital. I took what she said at face value. It was only more than a year later that I realised Emma's first visit had preceded the police releasing my name as the victim of the Rouëlbeau ambush.

Then, when I was lying somewhere between sleep and wakefulness and the room was empty of well-wishers, Sylvia Spurway, my postmodern economist from Summertown, walked

390

in. Emma had contacted her. She touched my cheek in the manner Gudrun Ensslin had once done in her long-ago Oxford bed. It was by that hesitant fingertip and the Nietzsche Society voice that I recognised the old woman – smiling at me through her thick, tinted glasses – as someone who had once been Sylvia. She was living in Geneva, working for the WTO – the World Trade Organisation. "I fulfilled that dream," she said.

"That dream?"

"To live here again. In Geneva." The WTO had, sometime before long 2007, taken over the lakeside premises occupied by the International Labour Office when my father had worked there. "A sign of the times," Sylvia pointed out. A wistful sigh. Then, as she was leaving me to my morphine dreams, she said, "I was sorry to hear about Jan's death. I guess *that* dream didn't quite work out for you."

A veritable party was underway around my hospital bed when yet another unexpected visitor turned up. Emma had come for a second visit. Marie-Claire and Claude were again trying to persuade Amanda and Jason to join them on the old *Phalanstère* off Corfu. Phil Scott was talking to Robert and Henry about Jesus and people who died. I was waiting for a quiet moment to ask one of them where Caroline was. The nurse came into the room. A big woman, overweight and poorly dressed, walked several paces behind her. Tears stained her broad cheeks. The nurse said to me, "Madame wishes to say good-day. She is the mother of one of the people at Rouëlbeau."

I looked with distaste at the fat woman, at her stained and threadbare cardigan, at her puffy eyes, red from crying. I did not know her. There had been some mistake, I was sure. I did not even recognise the lilting voice when she spoke. "I am so sorry," she said. "It is a mother's loss, but it is also Mr Kellaway who has lost a son." She looked around the sterile hospital room for an understanding face and found only well-dressed incomprehension. "Please excuse me. I need to introduce myself, don't I? I am Hilde Nielsen." When there was still no sign of recognition she added, "Torvald's mother."

4

The police over in the Boulevard Carl-Vogt had their theories. In them there was no place for accident or coincidence or the unfortunate conjunction of malevolent stars. I appeared as a passive and innocent victim of an elaborate scam – lured into it by a former schoolmate whom I trusted. In *their* narrative, however, she belonged to a sophisticated gang of fraudsters and bank robbers. Their corroborating evidence turned on two things they found in Jan's handbag. The first was a note, on paper from The Oriental in Bangkok, of my Swiss bank account numbers and all the security information needed to access them remotely. Jan had found them, the police suggested, during the evening when she had had unrestricted access to my study while I listened to 'Farewell Angelina' on my iPod.

The good people who solve riddles and puzzles at the Hôtel de Police interpreted the night Jan and I spent together at La Bise, and, indeed, the whole trip to Geneva, as an integral part of the plot – a classic honey-trap, even if the bait was a fifty-six-year-old woman. They produced their second piece of evidence: an unopened pack of condoms, also taken from Jan's handbag, to support the theory. When I questioned why a woman of Jan's age would be carrying condoms, they said, "Protection from disease." I attributed significance to the fact that she had not opened that little box.

The police found two other things, fragile links to her mother, in Jan's handbag: the letter Ursula had written to Jan in German in November 1971 and a pair of tarnished silver earrings in the shape of swastikas. I disclaimed all knowledge of both items when asked and the police did not demur when later I asked for a photocopy of the letter and a photograph of the earrings.

In the emerging official version of reality, the police operation at Rouëlbeau had, conveniently, been a success: the wounded hostage had been freed, was alive and making a decent recovery and a cunning attack on the sanctity of Swiss banking had been thwarted. I went along with the story. What would I gain through challenging it? I was, however, unconvinced by it. Jan had, after all, come to me for help. I had believed her, believed that she needed and wanted my help. The police had not seen how genuine Jan's pleasure at being with me had been. Contrary to police theories, I knew that the idea of sex had been mine, not Jan's, that it had been mine since my list-making days at school. The idea of visiting Rouëlbeau the next morning had been mine, too. Nor had the police seen the horror on Jan's face when Oscar and Torvald had appeared from among the trees. What could have come more naturally to Oscar, when he found the guns in the old Dufraisse collection to be in working order, than to go try them out in the woods where he had once tested the Swiss Army guns from his father's cabinet? And who more obvious to take with him than his brother's *factotum* who had mended the weapons, who shared his taste for black-metal music? Most fundamentally, the police had no coherent explanation as to why Jan had turned her gun on Oscar, why she had died defending me. Even if there had been a scam going on, Jan's heart was, I knew, not wholly engaged in it.

Oh, of course, Jan *had* told me lies, but the basics were true. Oscar *had* found the grave of a dead child in an Oakland cemetery and assumed the identity of Joseph Benito McIntosh. He *had* married Janice Day in 1975 and on their marriage certificate Jan's maiden name *was* given as Barbara Palmer. They *had* lived their entire married lives in Montana, though the ranch where nothing would grow was fiction. They lived in the suburbs of Billings. Joe McIntosh worked for the utility company and Barbara McIntosh was a much-loved elementary school teacher. They had two grown-up children, a boy and a girl.

Jan had also lied to me about her flight into London. She had flown in from neither Calgary nor Chicago. Airline records showed that she had arrived from Geneva three days before she phoned me. The British police, who in due course spent a long time asking me questions, found that CCTV cameras had picked Jan up in the street outside my house twice during those days.

The Swiss police found traces of Jan's DNA in Paul Meyer's villa; she was probably the woman the neighbour had spotted there. Paul Meyer eventually admitted that Jan had been to Geneva at least four times since 1972. On one visit, in 2001 – while Oscar was away attending to other business, accompanied, as it happened, by Torvald Nielsen – Paul had driven Jan into Geneva specifically to reminisce with her about her schooldays at Ecolint. They had sought out her old haunts in Grange-Canal and found everything changed. Jan knew, then, that the Auberge was gone when she had pretended to be surprised by its demise, but her lie had given us a sense of joint discovery and shared disappointment that happy first afternoon in Geneva and I was grateful for that.

In the course of my research, I tried to verify what Jan had told me about her life on the run in Germany in 1971 and 1972. In this I was greatly helped by Edward Reader. Karl-Heinz Kupferhoden's death is well documented. It is still an article of faith among the German Left that Kupferhoden was the victim of an extra-judicial state execution. Jan could have learned the manner of his death and the place his body was found from any number of sources and adapted them to her story. There was no proof one way or the other.

The Munich house fire is also fully documented. Edward Reader found the police identikit photo of the woman seen loitering by the stolen BMW shortly before the explosion. It shows an unsmiling girl with long hair. It could be Janice Day, but it could equally be Gudrun Ensslin or Brigitte Mohnhaupt or Rosa Luxemburg or any 100,000 German girls who cultivated that look back in those wild days. It is not a good picture and I imagine that it was not of much help to the Bavarian police at the time.

We did not find any convincing record of a female accomplice to the American athletes who helped the Palestinian terrorists access the Israeli compound at the 1972 Munich Olympics.

Germany had still been a divided country in 1972 and there was no official West German presence in Prague – or any East Bloc countries – then. If there had been a woman called Else there, issuing West German visas to Palestinian terrorists and running an underground railroad for escaping East Germans, then her trail had gone cold. When I asked Ed how he had given me that name – Else – in 1990, long before Jan reappeared, he said he couldn't recall, said that it was perhaps something he'd found in the Stasi files, that he'd worked through so many of them in 1990, that he did remember one on me – and traces of one on Caroline... It seemed a minor point and I felt no need to press him.

Curiously, one aspect of Jan's tales that had seemed least credible when she told it did, according to Ed, have an odd ring of truth about it: the boy from Dresden called Mike. Apparently, as an act of defiance against the occupying Russians, East German parents often christened their children with ostentatiously American names. Mike could have been one of those, but I did not have a surname and we made no attempt to trace him.

Ed's contacts in Germany also enabled him to establish that Stasi had not only kept a file on Janice Day, but also one on Janice Rose, the alias that Anna Schmidt had conferred on her. Like the Janice Day file and the one on Caroline, Janice Rose's file had gone missing. It was unclear whether Stasi knew that the two Janices were one and the same person. Stasi had been very thorough at keeping records, but less good at making connections among the random fragments in their enormous store of data.

And that mistress of aliases? Anna Schmidt? Anastasia

Kuznetsova? Anna Rotten? Whatever you wish to call her – nothing. Beyond a pencil drawing that may or may not have been our Anna on the website of an American soldier, I could find no trace of her. Nor, claimed Ed, could he. We knew, from the photograph on Meyer & Cie's security camera, that she had been with Colin in Geneva in August 1989. Not long before he died in 2001, Colin had implied that Anna was still alive and living in Brazil, but Colin was our only link to these latter-day sightings and our ability to access Anna's secrets, which were undoubtedly legion, seemed to have gone with Colin to his grave.

As part of our wider research, we did look again into Colin's murder. Claire let Ed look through the papers that she had gathered and now stored in a locked metal box. I went through them again a few days later. They told me nothing I did not already know. In fact they told me less. There was nothing I could connect to Colin's alleged parallel career as a spy and, as I looked over the material again, I began to question whether it had ever existed. Not only was it utterly out of character, but there also seemed so little time to slip a sideline in espionage through the paper-thin cracks in an international banker's diary, so little opportunity to be in two places at the same time.

Those doubts led me to another question: who had Laurel and Hardy really been? In pursuit of an answer I actually made contact with MI5 and MI6. It's not difficult to get to their front doors in this age of supposedly open government, but as you can imagine, I did not get very far beyond the electronic doorstep. If the relevant records are ever declassified and made public, I will be long dead before it happens. "A pity," Ed remarked, "you burned Colin's envelope."

For the record, I did investigate the black woman in one of Colin's hidden photographs. As Laurel and Hardy had said, the decomposing body of a black woman *had* been found in a flat in Ferney-Voltaire about the time Colin disappeared. The Geneva newspapers had reported it at the time but they had offered no name and implied that the French authorities were ignorant of her identity. It seemed unlikely that I would ever find anyone who could confirm or deny that the woman in Ferney, or the one in Colin's desk (or, if they were not the same person, both), had been in the employ of the French Secret Service. No French equivalent of Laurel and Hardy ever came to drink my gin and tonic.

The Swiss authorities are very good at keeping journalists at bay.

The early articles that appeared in the local press, under headlines such as 'Trois mort à Rouëlbeau' and 'Massacre à La Capite', were consequently light on detail. Names were withheld, but – alas! – the wounded hostage was identified as a 'banquier de Londres'. A posse of British journalists flew to Geneva. For thirty-six hours, a reinforced police presence at the hospital kept them out and my name a secret. Then one of them managed to get all the way into my room.

Caroline and Phil had just arrived. Caroline sat slumped in the chair, while Phil stood solemnly at the foot of my bed. "Nick," Phil announced, "there's something we need to tell you."

I looked towards Caroline. She was staring at her shoes and absently rubbing her thumb and forefinger together. A cascade of hair hid her face from me. I heard conversation – English voices – in the corridor beyond the open door. Then Phil was speaking again,

"We haven't wanted to burden you with this while you were still so sedated. But you're coming round now and you need to know. Nick..." Phil paused and looked at Caroline. Caroline looked up, nodded. "... Caroline took a call on Monday evening back at the hotel. It was Imogen saying that their mother had taken a turn for the worse. She had stopped taking fluids and was asking for Caroline..."

Caroline stood, came to the bed where I lay propped up on pillows, kissed my forehead and held my hand. "Nick," she said, "Mummy died four hours ago."

I think I was meant to feel, through the manner in which the news was delivered, some of the emotional complexities of the situation: not only had Caroline's mother died, but Caroline had chosen to stay with her unfaithful husband rather than be at her dying mother's bedside. For a moment I am sure that I *did* feel what people are meant to feel when confronted with things like this. My heart was beating faster than its normal rate. I could see that on the monitor to which I was still attached. I saw that Caroline was crying and there were tears of empathy on my cheeks as I squeezed her hand.

If ever I doubt my memory of this moment, I have the photograph by way of reminder: naked to the waist, bandages on my abdomen and wounded arm, tubes and wires going in and out of me, stubble on my unshaven chin and tears dribbling from my eyes. Jack Diamond's picture, taken on his mobile phone, was on the internet by Thursday evening.

Jack Diamond got in because he came with Héloïse Witheridge and Héloïse got in because she was with Amanda, whom she had had the good fortune to meet just outside the hospital. Jack's story was an 'exclusive' on the front page of Friday's *Daily Telegraph*. Every British paper – even *The Sun* and the *Financial Times* – carried a derivative story on Saturday.

Jack Diamond's follow-up ramble appeared in the *News of the World* on Sunday. Despite being labelled 'investigative journalism', it was short on details as to what had happened at Rouëlbeau: those were still being closely guarded by the Swiss police. It was, however, very long on background, on Kellaway & Co., on 'the shadowy world of hedge funds' and on me. Although the article made no attempt to link me with the dead woman at Rouëlbeau – Jan's name had not yet been released – it did cast me as 'one of the City's most notorious philanderers' with 'a predilection for young blondes'. Héloïse's hand was evident, too, in the references to her father ('... the death in strangely similar circumstances of Colin Witheridge, another London banker and close friend of Nick Kellaway, whose body was found near Geneva in 2001...') that were used to compensate for the lack of detail about more recent events.

Kellaway & Co. issued a press release the next day confirming that I had been wounded in an accident in Switzerland, but that I expected to be back at my desk within a week. Such a timeframe was utterly unrealistic. A week was long enough, my communications consultant thought, for the worst of the Rouëlbeau story to subside. He was, of course, wrong.

5

Things fell apart while I was away.

I was back in England, but still at home, when Northern Rock collapsed. On the TV in my bedroom, I watched Robert Peston laboriously commenting on the queues outside Northern Rock's branches, ordinary people, egged-on by the BBC, patiently (or, in genteel Cheltenham, not so patiently) waiting to get their money back.

To me as a banker, this was an extraordinary sight. Physical runs on a bank happened in the dustbowls of the American Midwest in the depths of the Depression. They were the stuff of the legend, like Bonnie and Clyde and Butch Cassidy and the Sundance Kid. I had read about bank runs in novels and history books, where they were presented as morality tales, incontrovertible evidence against the fragmented American banking system, or, if the writer was Marxist, against capitalism itself. But in the UK? In the twenty-first century? There had not been a run on a proper British bank since 1866 when Overend, Gurney & Company closed its doors. And then there had been no BBC to let the world watch what was happening in real time. These pictures were not ones a profoundly image-conscious government could tolerate. They would have to do something.

We in mortgaged Britain were not alone. The US sub-prime mortgage market had been squeaking for several months. Sub-prime mortgages had been encouraged by government policy there, as a means of spreading the American dream to less privileged members of society. The vehicle was our old friend debt. An erstwhile-uncreditworthy member of the lumpenproleteriat could borrow 110% of the cost of a house, spend the excess funds on the dream's accessories and not have to worry about payments on the loan (principal *or* interest) for two years. You know what? Folks down in the backwoods of Arkansas and the slums of Detroit thought this seemed like a pretty damned good idea. Then the whiz kids on Wall Street got hold of the loans, bundled them up into securities with fancy names, valued them using the default-rate metrics of an earlier generation of mortgages and sold them to hedge funds and banks that, as a result of world trade imbalances and the gap growing between the poor and the rich, had more cash than brains.

In the spring of 2007, New Century Financial Corporation, a major sub-prime lender that had not been sufficiently savvy to offload its loans onto gullible Europeans, filed for Chapter Eleven bankruptcy protection. Shortly before I was shot, the good people who ran the Bear Stearns hedge funds told the world that there was very little left in their funds. In August, the German banks IKB and Sachsen Landesbank collapsed into the arms of unsuspecting suitors under the weight of their sub-prime exposure. BNP-Paribas in France suspended trading in more than $2 billion worth of its asset-backed funds for want of credible market prices and Barclays had to seek £1.6 billion in emergency loans from the Bank of England. The European Central Bank felt it necessary to inject over €200 billion into the Eurozone's banking system to preserve liquidity. Although they never, to the best of my knowledge, appeared in the financial press, rumours circulated in quiet corners of the City, where people know more than they say in public, that one weekend in August the

Fed had come very close indeed to losing one of the biggest American banks outright.

By the autumn, the little American dreamers were beginning to claim big scalps: UBS in Switzerland announced sub-prime related losses of $3.4 billion and its chairman and chief executive officer resigned; Chuck the dancing prince resigned as chairman and CEO of Citigroup. There would be many more receding hairlines to go before the rout was over and bonuses restored.

As events had developed over the summer, Kellaway & Co. had taken an interest in, among other things, Northern Rock's future. Our short position in Northern Rock stock was performing well as the company's share price drifted steadily downwards. In late August, we put on another Northern Rock trade: we wrote credit-default swaps on Northern Rock deposits. By the time the queues began to form, our credit-default swaps were trading at stratospheric prices in the secondary market. Were we staring a massive – fund-destroying – loss in the face? We didn't think so. We doubled our bet. We sold a second tranche of our Northern Rock credit-default swaps into the market. Risky? You might have thought so if you were one of the cloth-cap punters seeking redemption outside one of Northern Rock's branches; though I don't expect much of our product was actually bought by the man on the Biker omnibus. Most of it probably ended up in the hands of professionals who held it as a naked credit-default swap in the mistaken belief that it was an easy way to profit from Northern Rock's woes. Profitable? For the investors at Kellaway & Co., very, very profitable.

Our analysis was based on the fact that the company was based in Newcastle. Northern Rock was an icon in the North East of England. Newcastle United's footballers wore its name on their jerseys. The North East was Labour heartland. Tony Blair's constituency had been only a few miles south of Newcastle and other prominent Labour party politicians also had their seats in the region. There was no way this Labour Government would stand by and watch its supporters in the North East lose their life savings because of the unbridled capitalist policies of Northern Rock's management. The politicians would, ultimately, trump the Bank of England's shrill – and economically correct – cries of 'moral hazard'. We reckoned we would never pay out on the credit-default swaps we had written.

And we were right. On 17 September 2007, Alistair Darling, the Chancellor of the Exchequer, announced that the British government would guarantee deposits in Northern Rock. Fabrice phoned me at home, told me to turn my television on, burbled with irrepressible joy.

How did Kellaway & Co. square writing credit-default swaps on Northern Rock deposits at the same time as shorting the stock? Again, that was part of our political analysis. Somebody would have to pay for what had happened to the North East's banking icon and, to any Labour Party stalwart, the first in line would be the capitalists, evil once again, who held Northern Rock's equity. By the time the end drew nigh, Sid the Shareholder and his mates would have sold out, the shares would be in the hands of American vulture funds and Ted the Taxpayer, footing the bill for the government's largesse to Northern Rock's depositors, would be the next government's problem. We called government policy – and its distinction between classes of debt and equity holders – exactly right. We dubbed our strategy 'Class Warfare Revisited'.

We had played the class game before. During the previous winter, 2006–7, we had bought the equity tranche – the toxic effluent – in some of the most notorious, late-generation, sub-prime CDOs then being issued by Wall Street. We held no illusions about making money on these purchases, although in the end, because we managed to extract a proportion of the investment bank's fee in return for our essential services and because we were able to offload the shit into various Luxembourg toilet funds before the fan was turned on, we actually almost broke even on that part of our strategy. The point of that facilitating leg of Kellaway & Co.'s plan, however, was to enable the issuance of the higher tiers in these deals that the generous people at the credit agencies were still blithely giving excellent ratings. These, in particular the top AAA-rated tranches, we shorted mercilessly. On those trades we were making fabulous profits. It was in the warmth of those profits that I was basking when the phone call came in from Janice Day on the evening of 25 July 2007.

During the autumn of 2007 and into 2008, the looming credit-cum-economic crisis in North America and Europe was serving to emphasise the eastward shift in the world's geo-economic centre of gravity. We set up a company in Mauritius to mount an assault on India and, in December 2007, Kellaway & Co. took the decision to open an office in Shanghai, sending two of our investment officers to China and recruiting a local team over the next few months. In our December strategy meeting, we agreed that, if it proved beneficial for symbolic reasons, I would move to China. I didn't consult

Caroline on this. She had her head filled with other things: church, charities, preparations for Amanda's wedding, the increasingly big divorce cases her firm was handling... Anyway, I never imagined Kellaway & Co. would have to resort to symbolic acts.

In January 2008 we bought, for a very reasonable price – because it was suffering from cash-flow problems – a little company in the business of writing longevity swaps. Longevity swaps are an alternative to Adam Heggie's more robust solution to the problem of ageing populations. They can be used by pension funds wanting to protect themselves against the risk of its pensioners living too long. The credit crunch was, we reckoned, not so severe that it would defuse the demographic time-bomb by lowering life expectancy in the way Russia's end-of-Communism crisis had done. In fact, we thought matters in the pension world would probably get worse as indebted companies and over-leveraged governments lost their room to manoeuvre. The current crisis was brought to you courtesy of the blessings of owning your own home. The next one will come from the blessings of healthy old age, unless it comes first from profligate governments, without an ounce of commercial or financial sense to temper their politics, once again telling banks what and to whom they must lend.

As I write this, it is still early days, but Kellaway & Co. is very pleased with this little investment so far. In June 2008, less than six months after we bought the longevity-swap business, we were offered three times what we had paid for it. We announced very publicly that Kellaway & Co. is here for the long term and we do not need cash, thank you, our liquidity position is just fine. We declined to sell. It was the right decision, but a difficult one. Everything was not quite as it seemed.

Trouble came from the liability side and in some respects we were fortunate to make it though the year after Rouëlbeau. The problem began with my investors. News that I had been shot scared some of them shitless. Press releases and excellent performance figures did little to quell their irrational turbulence. A few panicked and demanded redemption. With a little assistance from our broker-dealers and other banks, we met the claims, but then, rather than settling down as the weeks passed and I recovered from my injuries, my investors became more agitated, began to behave not unlike the little people in Newcastle. Mohammed and Abdullah, the Arab brothers who were my oldest and largest investors, brought forward our regular meeting scheduled for December and came to see me in early November. Annabel, whom I had not seen since the night in my old Mayfair flat when I introduced her to the joys of investing, requested an appointment.

Caroline and I received the once-famous model and her 'financial advisor' at our Knightsbridge house and Caroline personally served the tea and biscuits. An hour later Annabel kissed us airily on the cheeks, lowered herself into her chauffeured Bentley and, exuding a rather depressing, perfumed, middle-aged stability, went away seemingly reassured. Her 'financial advisor', however, was frowning deeply as he climbed into the back seat of the car beside her, but, then, that's what 'financial advisors' are meant to do and I'm sure the man wanted to look the part.

When the Arab brothers returned to the Gulf, they left their funds under my management, but the storms had not abated yet. The Arabs' tone had been ominous: cool, cosmopolitan civility had replaced the enthusiasm of being let loose in a Bangkok brothel. Mohammed had daintily suggested that what we were seeing was only the tip of the iceberg, had darkly inferred that I was being given just one more chance to sail the good ship Kellaway into clearer waters, before they scuttled me and sent me to join the *Titanic*, treasure-laden on the deep bed beneath the market's waves.

The problems soon spread to Kellaway & Co.'s once-faithful lenders. One by one they began to reduce or withdraw lines of credit. The pain was at its worst in the weeks leading up to the collapse of Bear Stearns, where, a JP Morgan banker subsequently told me, "Credit analysis was a spectator sport."

Bear Stearns died on the weekend of 15/16 March 2008. On the following Monday, in what commentators called 'a febrile market' (whatever that means), rumours, apparently originating in the Department of Health, began to circulate that HBOS was in such liquidity difficulties that it had postponed the closing and funding of one of its hospital loans. More rumours started and more HBOS stock was sold short. On the morning of 19 March, the price of HBOS shares fell 20% on opening. Although the regulators say they are intolerant of traders who start rumours and then deal off the back of them, there is little they can do if the rumour-mongering trader in question is sitting at his computer screen in a distant tropical beachside jurisdiction watching from afar as the edifices of capitalism crumble. The excitement was tangible – even in our London dealing room – even in my sleep that night when my old mate Che Guevara came down from his poster on a long-abandoned bedroom wall and insolently blew smoke rings with the smoke from his Havana cigar into the face of his CIA tormentors.

Hey! Che! Señor Guevara! What's the point of all these mosquito-infested jungles of bloody Bolivia, then? Today you can do it under the palm trees of a five-star beach with Miss Annabel Nonikaz on your knee and a glass of *Perrier-Jouët Belle Epoque* in your hand. Run the guns of liberation ashore under cover of a moonless night? Ha! Mao-Tse Tung? Andreas Baader? Eat your fucking hearts out! Power flows from the barrel of a flaming-red twin-turbo 600-horse-power Ferrari 360 Modena – and from a well-connected laptop.

Alas – or perhaps fortunately – the champagne and young Annabel, Baader, Che and the Ferrari were only a dream. When I opened my eyelids and turned on *my* computer in the clear light of morning, Marx, Engels, Lenin and all the holy saints were only bugs in the software, just harmless viruses spawning in a .exe attachment to a rogue email. Kellaway & Co. called a benediction down on the Department of Health and the distant rogue traders and took the profits from our long-standing HBOS short.

Bear Stearns and HBOS were the nadir. Or so it seemed. Matters began to ease in spring 2008: confidence returned to the markets; stock markets rose; lines of credit were restored. From the specific perspective of Kellaway & Co. another event was of considerable assistance: a persistent thorn in my flesh was extracted.

6

After his article in *News of the World* on 5 August 2007, Jack Diamond did not lay down his poison pen. Rather, he milked the Rouëlbeau shootings, and such inside information as Héloïse and a hired snoop provided him, to create a series of speculative articles that served to put both me and my firm under an unwelcome spotlight. He cast doubts on the probity of my record without actually saying I had done anything wrong. He asked questions about Kellaway & Co.'s early days, asked how we had shown such consistent returns while sitting on a trade so bad that it drove one of our employees to suicide. He resurrected the gains I had made for my employer in 1992 when Sterling was ejected from the ERM, casting me as someone who profiteered against the interests of the country. He stated that Kellaway & Co. had been investigated for trading on inside information at the time of the 9/11 attacks without saying that the investigation had totally exonerated us. He raked over the lifeless coals of Colin's murder, hinted (hints from an undisclosed source in questionable quotation marks) that I had somehow been involved or, at least, that I might have known those who killed him. He noted that Caroline had been Colin's girlfriend at Oxford before she had been mine. He even cast me, totally without justification, as a climate-change-denier. Investors and lenders never mentioned Jack Diamond's articles, but I knew when I met them that they had read them and swallowed the poison.

The lawyer advising us said, "Take out an injunction. On the basis of what he has published so far, you'll have no trouble stopping next Sunday's article. If he's hacked your phone, as appears likely, we'll have a case in court."

"No," I said. "It'll only lend credence to what he's writing. It would be like oil to the fire. Shit, I know plenty of guys who've crossed the press. The papers make them pay hell for it and there's fuck all anybody can do. Anyhow, everybody knows the papers aren't interested in facts. They publish anything that'll titillate their readers. I don't want to be another rich bastard lacerated for their bloody amusement. No, we pay him no attention and dismiss him as a teenage scribbler when people ask."

Fabrice, who had insisted on being present at the meeting, shouted, "Nick! This country's crazy. You are crazy. This guy is killing us."

"We could make it a super-injunction," the lawyer added, "whereby it would be unlawful even to mention that you had taken out an injunction. A bit more costly, but…"

"No," I persisted, "No injunction. Super or otherwise."

Of course, I wanted to gag Jack Diamond more – much more – than either of them, but I couldn't. The reason? That line in the original *News of the World* article: 'a predilection for young blondes'. One whisper of legal action by me and the counterattack would begin with a full expansion of that sentence, illustrated by one of the nude photographs with which Héloïse was beginning to make a name for herself. No injunction could stop Héloïse pressing charges. You can do anything in twenty-first century Britain: you can evade taxes, profiteer against the interests of your country, deny climate change, fail to give warnings of murderous terrorist attacks; you can be a serial adulterer, a purveyor of unclean investments, an accomplice to murder. Any – all – of that is socially commendable compared to being labelled a paedophile. It would be Héloïse's word against mine; she might even withdraw her charge a few days later, but not until after Sally and Myrtille had retracted their forgiveness and joined Héloïse in a class action demanding my extradition to Texas. Not until after the damage had been done and my image had been shredded more thoroughly than Arthur Andersen's Enron papers. After the *Financial Times* had run a photo of me being shoved into the back of a police car as a policewoman humiliatingly pushed my head down. After I had been paraded, exhausted and downcast, in a straightjacket and handcuffs, before the jury of tabloid cameramen. Even if the case went to court and I was found innocent there, I would have lost. In an era where bankers had become bad people, there was no doubt where market perception would decree truth to lie. I would be forced to seek asylum in France.

"No," I repeated. "No injunction."

The lawyer looked away from me, towards Richter's candle – no doubt wondering, as part of his fee calculation, how much it was worth. Then he gathered up his papers, sweeping them across the polished table into neat little piles, straightening the piles one by one before putting them meticulously into clear plastic folders. He filed the folders in his fat briefcase. Snapping the briefcase closed, he held out his hand – for me to shake it or to collect his fee? I opted for the former course of action.

"Linda will see you out," I said.

When the lawyer had left the room, Fabrice walked to the far end of the table where he had been sitting throughout the meeting, leaned over a sheet of paper and scribbled on it, his jaw muscles working furiously as he wrote. He folded the paper three times and handed it to me. His dark brown eyes bored two neat holes into my skull. "Remember," he said, "that guy who would wouldn't do Libor for me?"

"The one from..." I named the bank that had employed him, a big respectable bank.

"Remember what happened to him?"

"Can't say that I do. He left... no... hang on... He drowned. Drowned on his summer holiday, didn't he? In St Tropez, wasn't it?"

Fabrice's eyelids closed slowly and I thought I detected a slight jerk of the neck before the eyes reopened and again locked onto mine.

I opened the folded piece of paper. A telephone number – a London 0208 number – was scrawled across it.

"Kosovar," Fabrice said, "but formerly of the Boulevard Mortier in Paris. Very discreet. Accurate. A real professional. Not expensive. Tell him, 'Chez Fonfon. Nine. Nine. Ninety-nine.' He won't even ask your name."

From time to time that autumn and winter, I saw Héloïse. She called on me ostensibly to see how I was recovering, bringing me (her 'favourite godfather') chocolates and flowers, kissing me on the forehead when she left. We spent Christmas in Weybridge with Imogen and entourage (then *still* in residence in my house) and Caroline invited Claire and Héloïse to join us. Around the hearth, after the Queen's speech, Héloïse said, "Uncle Nick, Jack would like to meet you. Meet you properly, like."

"No."

"You'll have to meet him eventually," she said. "He's coming to Amanda's wedding."

"I'm not inviting him."

"Aunty Caroline already has."

Early in the new year, the day after Claire had flown back to India, Héloïse advertised herself on page three of *The Sun*. It was an absolutely gorgeous photograph. Caroline had seen the picture before I got home from the office. "Nick," she said, "can't you do something with that girl? She's your goddaughter."

I arranged to have lunch with Héloïse. We met at Le Gavroche. I had mixed emotions about the impression we would create among our fellow lunchers. On the one hand I was delighted by the surreptitious, but obviously envious, glances directed towards our table; on the other hand, I feared that the sight of me, only recently recovered from my gunshot wounds, dining with the girl who had just graced page three of *The Sun*, would revive Jack Diamond's rumours that had been dormant over the season of goodwill. And I wouldn't have put it past Héloïse to come with a team of undercover paparazzi in tow.

Over coffee I made Héloïse my offer. "Here's the deal. Jack Diamond doesn't come to Amanda's wedding. He publishes no more articles that mention either me or my firm. You, yourself, never mention me to anyone again, neither in writing nor orally, not in public or in private. Within a week of your last exam finishing you leave this country and you stay away for at least two years. From today, no pictures of you appear anywhere, including online, including Facebook, from now until August 2010."

Héloïse smiled beatifically as I outlined the offer. When I had finished, she asked, "What's in it for me? The other side of the bargain?"

"Two million pounds. One million the day after Amanda's wedding and the rest on the 31st of July 2010."

Another lovely smile. "Is that all?"

I nodded. It was a very generous offer.

"Then all I can say is, like, no way. You're gonna have to do better than that, Uncle Nick. I mean, like, even with only half of what you've got now, you'll still be filthy rich. This is worth a hell of a lot more to you than two million stinking quid. You know it and I know it. You've gotta do better."

I told Caroline that evening that I'd had my talk with Héloïse and that, although I had extracted no promises, she would consider my advice. I was more frank about my conversation with Héloïse when I saw Emma Wallace the next day.

Since her surprise visit to the hospital in Geneva, Emma had strongly encouraged me to write. When, in late September, I finally agreed with Edward Reader to put pen to paper, Emma became my style guru. I began by reading her some of the passages that I had written and listening to her comments. Sometimes she would probe, push me to delve deeper into dreams and memories, mainly of Janice Day but also of others, cause me to remember things lost decades earlier. She pursued links where I thought there were none. "How often did Colin meet Jan?" she asked once.

"Only when she was staying with you at the Jericho House, as far as I know."

"He never mentioned seeing her again later?"

"No, not that I recall. Why?"

"Well. He saw Anna Schmidt. We know that. And Anna and Jan were close."

"Jan never saw Anna after the Munich fire."

A week later, Ed sent me a copy of the Bavarian police's picture of the girl by the blue BMW on the night of the 1972 fire and used it to cast doubt on Jan's stories of her life on the run. Emma and I decided to ignore the doubts and for me simply to recount Jan's version of events. Increasingly, I sought Emma's advice on what to include and what to omit.

The day after lunch at Le Gavroche the decision before me was whether to leave Héloïse, the blackmailer, out of my narrative altogether, or, if I included my little blonde persecutor, how to treat her. You have already seen the result: a teenager appearing like Venus before the Phrygian shepherd, standing on the Persian rug at the foot of my bed while I, her rescuer and deliverer, sleep the sleep of innocence. This was, basically, Emma's suggestion. There were echoes here, Emma said, of Anna Schmidt's tactics in my Islington bedroom in 1976; echoes too of Karen O'Neil's oriental rugs and alabaster vases and the derivative Moghul miniatures on the walls of my Mayfair flat. Anna was an evil terrorist and bank robber, you will recall. Karen was the devious wife of a CIA spy and a corrupter of the flower of British youth. Like Héloïse's name, Anna and Karen were also both foreign.

7

News of Jack Diamond's death appeared on the screens on the morning of Tuesday, 25 March 2008. Fabrice rushed into my office. "Look at this, boss!" He had an impressive grin stuck to his face.

The emerging story was that Jack Diamond, freelance investigative journalist, had been shot dead in Palermo on Easter Sunday evening. He had been in Sicily working on a Mafia story and was shot in his hotel bedroom as he slept. A woman had been in bed with him. She too was dead.

I picked up my phone and dialled Héloïse's mobile number. The call went straight through to voicemail. I left a simple message, asking Héloïse to phone me. My next three calls to Héloïse also only got her voicemail. I left no more messages, but Héloïse would – if she could – see from her register of missed calls that I had been calling. With no reply from Héloïse by early afternoon, I decided to phone Caroline. Caroline had no idea where Héloïse might be. It was the middle of university Easter holidays. "She *might* have gone with…" She did not finish her sentence. She could be anywhere, she said. "We must phone Claire. I've got an emergency number in India."

"Wait. They'll release the name of the woman soon, after they contact the next of kin."

"Nick," Caroline said, "in Claire's absence, that's us."

No call came that afternoon, neither from the police nor from Héloïse nor from Claire. In the evening, I tried making enquiries with the police, phoning them to ask the name of a person, as yet publicly unidentified, who has just been murdered in a foreign country. Whoever you are, whatever story you tell, true or otherwise, you don't get very far along that track.

Caroline slept very close to me that night, but neither of us slept well. At one point, when we were both awake, she said, "I don't know what Claire's going to do. First Colin, now Héloïse."

The dead woman's name was released late the following afternoon. She was a Milan-based photographer. Jack Diamond had been working with her on his Mafia story, using her *inter alia* as an interpreter. She had been last seen taking pictures outside Palermo cathedral after Easter Mass.

Héloïse returned my calls on Thursday morning. "You bastard!" she screamed.

"Héloïse, I'm sorry. I didn't like the man, but I had nothing to with his death."

"You bastard! You filthy bastard!"

"Héloïse. He was with another woman. In bed. She had a wad of €50 notes stuffed up her…"

"I don't give a shit if he was in bed with the pope. You're a complete bastard, Fuckaway."

"Héloïse…"

"I'll get you for this, Fuckolas. First my dad and now…"

I hung up. I would speak to Héloïse another time, when the news wasn't fresh, when she was behaving more rationally. I did not have Jack Diamond's blood on my hands. I had not phoned the number of the Kosovar that Fabrice had given me. There was nothing to link me to Jack Diamond's murder, nor to Colin's.

I next saw Héloïse at Amanda's wedding. Héloïse is difficult to miss. I first spotted her as I walked Amanda towards the altar to give her away. She was standing at the aisle end of her pew, on the bride's side of the church, next to Claire, clad, in contravention of all tradition, in a sequin-spangled black dress so skimpy that I imagine it would have been acceptable to the photographers who do the shoots for page three of *The Sun*. Tattooed above her left breast, where her Scottish grandmother would have pinned a silver brooch to a tweed jacket, was a playing card – the jack of diamonds.

The wedding reception was held in a marquee on our Weybridge lawn and it was during a lull in the proceedings that I eventually spoke to Héloïse. I found her, with an ardent admirer close at hand, at the far end of the garden, at the place where I had once burned the secrets from her father's Swiss safety deposit box, where Caroline had burned Henry's phone-box whores.

"Could I have a word, please?" I asked.

"Sure, Uncle Nick." She dismissed the spotted admirer.

Instead of beginning the conversation I had planned in the days after Jack Diamond had been killed, I took a simpler course. The tattoo had changed my mind. I renewed my offer of two million pounds, restated my conditions – minus those that involved Jack and minus keeping her picture out of Facebook. I exempted Facebook, provided that in any pictures there she appeared decently clothed. I told her, in quasi-legal sentences, that I was writing a book and in it would be going public about what had happened when she was fifteen and, as a consequence, this was the last time I would make the offer. I was only renewing it now, I told her, out of family affection. It was, I suppose, a sort of private injunction, enforced by the niggling doubt that Uncle Nick really might have friends in Sicily.

Héloïse looked down into the ashes of dead fires, stared at them for a long minute, maybe more. Then, without raising her gaze, she softly said, "What are you going to do after the divorce? Are you going to marry Mummy?"

"Don't change the subject, Héloïse. This is about you."

She looked up, a tender, vulnerable look in her eyes that called to mind... well... Emma's scene of the teenager in my bedroom. "I'm not changing the subject," she said quietly. "I've got it all on tape."

"What?"

"My little machine, you know. You were downstairs drinking whisky with Daddy and I was up in my bedroom listening to you, like with the Torvald thing."

"You *taped* that?"

"Not that, but other things. Like the stuff about you and Mummy."

"What 'stuff'?"

"I've memorised the words." There were tears forming in her eyes now. "You were like 'Colin, you've gotta believe me. Those early days in Balham were utter hell. I wasn't thinking of Caroline. She was gone and I didn't really give a shit. Not really. All I wanted – all I ever wanted – was to marry Claire.' That's what you said, exactly. Word for word."

The knot forming in my gut exploded in a burst of laughter.

Was *that* why Héloïse had been persecuting me all these years? Why, as Claire had once darkly inferred, she had offered her body as a shield to protect her mother? "Come off it. You're not serious?"

Héloïse nodded.

"God," I shook my head slowly, "how long's this been going on for?"

Héloïse looked puzzled. Mine was not the reaction she had expected.

"That had nothing to do with your mother. It was another girl. A rich French girl with a boat on the Med. Her name was Marie-Claire, like the magazine. 'All I ever wanted was Marie-Claire.' Not '*to* marry Claire'. I hadn't met your mother when I was living in Balham. Nor *even* had your dad." I saw Phil Scott walking towards us and gave Héloïse a godfatherly pat on her sequined bottom. "Come on," I said, "let's get back to the party. People with perverted minds'll begin to wonder what we're doing up here."

It took Héloïse less than two days to accept my offer. She would, she said when she phoned on Monday morning, spend her two years of exile in Australia. "Mummy says I need to get as far away from you as I can."

8

"All I wanted – all I ever wanted – was Marie-Claire."

I remembered, after Héloïse had reminded me, that evening with Colin. I remembered it as clearly as if it had been yesterday. I remembered saying the words Héloïse had taped and misunderstood, but, try as hard as I might, I could not remember when it had been. I had spent many an evening drinking whisky with Colin.

I poured myself a large Lagavulin. Images of the summer of '73 swirled around with the smoky liquid mirror in the tumbler. There is the narrow Corsican cove that Marie-Claire and I have to ourselves as we play at being gods and goddesses, as we run the guns of liberation into the beach, as we make love on the sand. The Romance of the Revolution. Then, suddenly, the urban desolation of Balham. There I am in the damp back room as hopes that Marie-Claire will come to London die under the winter's dust and the rusting ironmongery and crowded nettles, die under the weight of the dark Northern Line commute, die as the fluorescent lights flicker out to the accompaniment of Adam Heggie's lugubrious poetry about the coal miners' strike. Masturbating to keep the summer images alive. What would my life have been like had I chucked in the offer of a graduate trainee job at Harriman's and stayed for ever on the *Phalanstère*, really had become a gun-runner in the cause of Freedom?

I re-read the chapters I had written about Marie-Claire. Edward had advised me to get rid of her. "She has nothing to do with your story about Janice Day," he had said. I suppose, in the words of his later advice, he would have called her my 'darling' and told me to murder her. But I kept Marie-Claire alive. I nurtured her with whispered phrases half remembered. I inserted – between two bottles of Paul Meyer's wine – the lunch I had had with her at the Perle du Lac. I described the 1971 Escalade dinner at her Geneva flat and the night I had heard her fucking on the other side of the wall at the Meyer's chalet in Crans.

Emma read the changes I made and said, "We create the past in order to control the future." I felt a pang of envy for Claude, living simply in Dardagny, cultivating his vineyard with Marie-Claire.

I imagine Emma, who has experience of the emotions released through writing and knows all about the hazy line between fact and fantasy, sensed something of my unspoken thoughts and feelings. "Why don't you," she said, looking up at the ruins of Paestum after a long pause, "rework your early days with Caroline? Maybe make something more of that day at the beginning of your second year at Oxford when she came running across the Parks to you. What did she look like? How did it feel to see her again? That sort of thing."

Emma was right, of course. I had to do something with Héloïse's corrosive suggestions of a looming divorce and a fifty-fifty split of my assets, do something more than just let them fester as if they were an unwritten chapter in a third-rate novel. I took Caroline out to dinner and, after we had drunk a bottle of wine, bluntly put the question to her.

"Nick!" she exclaimed, laying down her knife and fork. "For goodness' sake! Whatever put that into your head?"

"Sorry, darling. It's just…"

"Nick. Come on. Look at me. I'm *never* going to divorce you."

We skipped pudding. Caroline had me call for the bill and a taxi. In the back of the cab she held my hand. Once we were in the house, standing in front of the Temple of Hera, the goddess of women and marriage, she began to unbutton my shirt. We made love on the Persian rug in front of the hearth, slowly, erotically, as if time had been shed with our clothes and we were twenty-one again.

Afterwards, as we lay close, side by side, looking up at the ceiling, she said, "Believe me, Nick. No divorce. Ever." Then, after a moment and a lingering kiss, she added, "Love's not *just* a feeling, you know. It *is* a feeling. A wonderful feeling. But it's much more than that. It's a promise, 'to love and to cherish 'til death do us part'. My covenant."

Just then, and for the next few days, I did believe her. Then the doubts Héloïse had sown began to germinate again. There was actually some sense in the notion, wasn't there? Although Caroline had stood by me after Rouëlbeau, to the point of staying with me even when her mother was dying, I had been unfaithful – and not only then. Had she really any idea how often?

Since I had been able to get up and about again, our ways had diverged. I was juggling to keep my firm on a straight path through the financial storm and write a book at the same time. My cup brimmed over with reconstructed dreams: Janice Day, Oscar Meyer, Johnny Morris, Blueberry Hill, Colin Witheridge, Anna Schmidt... they were the ones I was living with. I heard more of Edward Reader's voice on the phone than I did those of my children. I was spending more quality time with Emma Wallace than I was with Caroline.

And Caroline? Church, prayer meetings, charity committees. "I'm just a hodman for the Kingdom of Heaven," she said once, with that false modesty the English find so endearing, "helping build a little stretch of the walls of the New Jerusalem." And, on the side, handling lurid divorce cases with higher and higher payouts for the spouse who'd stayed at home and raised the children. What were Héloïse's words at Le Gavroche? "I mean, even with only half of what you've got now, you'll still be filthy rich." A fifty-fifty split? I'd still be well into the ranks of the *Sunday Times* Rich List with half my wealth, though much farther down the pecking order. Whose money was it, anyway? Who had earned it with his own blood, sweat and tears?

Even though she had made a professional career out of divorce, Caroline's Anglican belief system was ostensibly against it. When asked once by one of our dinner guests about the tension this created for her, she replied, "I don't instigate the divorce. In fact, as a matter of principle, I do my best to get the couple back together, but if the divorce is going to happen anyway *then* I turn my attention to getting the best deal I can for the woman."

But are Anglicans really against divorce or is that just the position for external consumption? The Church of England knows in its gut that it wouldn't exist if it weren't for divorce. The whole Anglican Communion is a perpetual memorial to Henry VIII's divorce from Catherine of Aragon. When the stakes are high enough, divorce is back on the agenda. What richer prize did the Church of England have in its sites in the spring of 2008 than half a famous fortune? Were they tempted by the prospect of paving the streets of their little Jerusalem with ingots of solid gold? Whispers from charity chairmen. Nods and winks from penniless but persuasive priests. Even Phil Scott co-opted to the cause...

Something would have to be done to stop them.

9

At eight-thirteen, with uncanny precision, the phone rang.

Caroline was in Hampshire on a church retreat and I had decided to stay in the office rather than spend the evening in an empty house. I had filed away Kellaway & Co. business and had twenty or so A4 pages from my manuscript spread across the desk in front of me. A moment earlier I had been on my hands and knees in front of the Hodler, where it stood propped against the wall. It would be collected the next day and sent to a museum in Switzerland to be displayed alongside a plaque that read *Donation de Kellaway & Co.* I had wanted a last look at those unfinished white flowers around the base of the *Statue de la Bise*.

The Hodler's place on the wall had been taken by a painting of a highly distorted London skyline. The artist claimed that the wobbly bank towers represented the credit crisis. It could have been painted by a five-year old with a grudge. It had been an ill-advised purchase – even if it really did have excellent investment value.

When the call came I had one of my screens open at a Google map of Oxford. I was trying to remember exactly where the Jericho House had been, what streets I had walked along to get to it. I could ask Emma; but it would provide me more authentic background touches, I had just decided, if I went to Oxford and looked for it myself. I pushed the button to activate the speaker phone and said, "Kellaway."

The voice on the other end of the line was hesitant. It betrayed a slight tremor, an American voice speaking slowly and deliberately. A voice that spoke of unfinished condominiums, see-through office blocks and repossessed houses lining the Interstate. Intonations honed by hanging around the malls with the rest of the gang because in a little burg out there on the high plains there ain't fuck all else to do. A female voice.

"Is that Mr Nicholas Kellaway?"

"Speaking."

"My name is Pam McIntosh."

"Pam?"

"I'm sorry, sir. Pam's a nickname. You've probably heard me referred to as Priscilla. Priscilla Anastasia McIntosh. I hope I'm not disturbing you."

I had heard of Jan's children. I had learned they existed while I was still in hospital in Geneva, the first indication that everything Jan had told me might not be 100% accurate. I had been intrigued that they both had been given the same initials. The boy was called Peter Augustus McIntosh, named after the brother who had drowned in Argentina while out sailing with Jan. The girl, two years younger, was Priscilla Anastasia. When they no longer had any need for them, the police sent Jan's guitar, the letter from Ursula, the swastika earrings and the other things Jan had had with her in Geneva (but not the condoms nor the details of my Swiss bank account) to them in the States.

My instinct had been to make contact, but Caroline had dissuaded me. "Don't you think that might be a little bit insensitive just now?"

Later, when I was well into writing Jan's story, Emma and I had speculated over her children's names. "Why 'Anastasia' and not 'Anna'?" I had asked. "Jan and Anna were close, fair enough, but we always knew her as 'Anna'. 'Anastasia Kuznetsova'? A Russian name. The girl we knew was German." Emma offered no credible explanation.

When, as my book progressed, I had thought again about contacting Jan's children, Emma had taken the same stand as Caroline. "It wouldn't be right," she had said. "They'll contact you when they're ready."

One of them just had. It had taken nearly eleven months.

"Pete and I never knew anything about our parents. I mean nothing about where they'd come from and stuff. I don't think we ever

415

asked. I guess we just kinda thought they were ordinary Americans like everybody else out in Montana."

After the notoriety of the Rouëlbeau shootings had died down, Pam began to do research. Pete wasn't interested, he wanted to leave the whole 'dirty episode' behind and get on with life, but Pam devoted herself to the task. Money that came to her from a Christian Meyer fund, when her identity became known, meant she that was amply provided for.

Pam had met Jan's brother and sister and their children and grandchildren. She'd made a trip to Buenos Aires with her new uncle and been shown the places that Happy Day and family had known in the early sixties. She had made contact with her grandmother's relatives in Germany and, of course, she was now a fully incorporated member of the Meyer clan in Switzerland. Claude and Marie-Claire had seen her when they were in the United States.

"I'm planning the trip to Europe, now, and I was wondering, Mr Kellaway, if it wouldn't be too painful, whether I could meet with you?"

"Of course, no problem. When are you coming?"

"I'm not really sure yet, sir. I'd like to see Oxford and I guess that's not too far from London. Mainly, though, I'm going to be travelling in Germany and Switzerland, the countries of my ancestors. It depends on when Aunty Anastasia can see me."

"Anastasia?"

"The person I'm called for? My middle name?"

"Anna Schmidt? Anastasia Kuznetsova?"

"Yeah. I guess. Anastasia Something anyway. She's got a different last name now. Married name, probably. Let me see. It's in my notes somewhere… I'm going to write all this up into a book so I have tons of notes… oh, shit…"

10

I spent the next day in my study at home reading every Anna Schmidt passage I had written. Anna alive? If Anna's availability was a factor in when Pam would be coming to this country, did that imply she might even be living in England?

I went through the notes I had made with Edward Reader when we concluded that our chances of finding Anna had gone with Colin to his gruesome woodland grave. Nothing I found in my files served to change that conclusion.

But now, what about this phone call now from someone claiming to be Jan's daughter?

Yes, I did try to trace the call when it ended so abruptly. I found it had been made from a call box on Broadway in Boystown, Chicago. Why, in this day of ubiquitous cell phones, had she done that? Was it a hoax, not really Jan's daughter after all? Why else phone from a public phone box? Why hadn't she gone to find more money and rung back? Unless it wasn't that she'd run out of coins. Sinister possibilities flooded my mind. Maybe it was better if I treated the call as a hoax, but I wasn't ready to do that just yet.

I phoned the number of the McIntosh house in Billings. Not surprisingly, the number had been disconnected. I phoned Claude and, because of the one-hour time difference, woke him with the call. I imagined I could hear Marie-Claire in bed beside him. Yes, he *had* seen Jan's daughter. He and Marie-Claire had been in California and had met Pam in San Francisco. They had taken her to dinner at Fisherman's Wharf. A charming girl, physically very like her mother at that age. No, he did not have an e-mail address or phone number. No, he did not know about a planned trip to Europe. No, he'd never heard of Anna Schmidt or Anastasia Kuznetsova...

I phoned Emma the next morning. She listened in silence as I told her about the call from Pam. "Why aren't you saying anything?" I asked when the silence ran on after I had put a direct question to her.

"I'm thinking, that's all."

Emma's thinking, however, produced no results. By the time Caroline came home from Hampshire, I had exhausted all the forking avenues that held any promise of leading me through the woods to Anna or Pam and there seemed no point in telling Caroline about the call from the phone box in Chicago, particularly since Caroline came through the door with Phil Scott.

When the three of us went out for dinner, conversation turned, as it often does with Phil, to metaphysics. "When I was doing physics back in the sixties," he said in response to a remark of Caroline's about her Hampshire retreat, "the big story was that the universe had always been there and always would be. Then, when evidence began to point to something different, a beginning, people didn't like it. They resisted it because they thought that if you allowed that, the next thing you'd get was the God squad jumping on the bandwagon. You know, they were right. If the Judeo-Christian narrative is correct, the Big Bang some 13.4 billion years ago is exactly the sort of thing you'd expect. You'd expect time to be created. Eternity's not just some space-time continuum going on and on *ad infinitum*. It's something qualitatively different. God's realm. It interacts with our – created – time and space, but it's different. That is... Blah, blah..."

Sanctimonious twat.

"...Blah, blah, blah... anthropic principle."

"The what?"

"The anthropic principle? The observation – the possibly rather uncomfortable observation – that the universe, and specifically the four fundamental constants of physics, seem to be fine-tuned to bring about carbon-based life. If the gravitational constant or the strength of electromagnetism or either of the two constants specifying the strength of the nuclear forces were just the tiniest bit different from what we've got, then there would be no life. No us. Do you have any idea what the chances are – mathematically – of a coincidence like this happening? It's something like zero point zero followed by fifty eight more zeros until you eventually get to a one. There would be..."

Old Fart.

We were home again in time to see the ten o'clock news. While Caroline prepared herself for bed, I took my old undergraduate copy of A.J. Ayer's 'Language, Truth and Logic' down from the bookshelf, poured myself a whisky and settled into my armchair.

The fifth item on the news came from Moscow. "The Russian police today released the identity of the Briton killed in Saturday's bomb explosion." The picture of the devastated dacha was the same one that had been shown on Sunday's newscast when the news of the attack, attributed to Chechen terrorists, had first broken. I had ignored it then: you can't get emotionally involved with every terrorist outrage and murder. "He is forty-six-year-old London businessman, Jonathan Loxbeare..." The picture of Mr Loxbeare replaced the ruins of the dacha.

I lurched forward in my seat, dropping Freddie Ayer onto the floor and almost spilling the whisky. The likeness was unmistakeable. I knew the man, but I did not know him as Jonathan Loxbeare. He had come to my Mayfair flat in 2001 – after 9/11, after Colin's death. He had drunk my gin and tonic and admired my Persian miniatures. He had not given me a name but he had said he came from MI5. I had baptised him Stanley Laurel.

I had to wait just thirty-six hours for contact from the dead man's partner. I asked Linda to close the door and took the call waiting on my ex-directory line. I recognised Oliver Hardy's voice immediately. I thought I could even hear the knuckles crack.

"You've seen the news from Moscow?"

"Yes."

"Colin's envelope?"

"There is no envelope."

"Your lack of co-operation is getting people killed, Mr Kellaway."

"There's no envelope."

"We'll see about that."

The line went dead. There was no envelope, not any more. But I couldn't tell Hardy that, couldn't tell him I had destroyed it. They do things to people who do things like that, things that make death by Chechen big bang seem appealing. I swung round in my chair and looked up at the City, wobbling in lurid impasto across my wall. Somewhere out there – beyond the crumbling towers of finance, beyond the mountains of Switzerland and the beaches of Corsica, beyond the distant horizon where time meets eternity – the first drumbeats of a plan were beginning to emerge from the jungle.

CHAPTER THIRTEEN

The first of the photographs came in on the afternoon of Thursday, 14 August 2008. It arrived on my computer screen at work from an untraceable email account. I studied the picture for a couple of minutes before deleting it and then deleting it again from the deleted-items box.

Five months earlier we had discovered an image, arguably less pornographic than the one I had just received, on the computer of one of my American traders, the moron responsible for some of our worst asset-backed losses, a man his colleagues nicknamed 'House'. I had fired him on the spot, in the middle of the crowded dealing room, with the offending picture rigid on his frozen screen in front of him. Balentin the Vulgar had laughed, just a nervous little snort of a laugh. I had immediately fired him as well. He had fucked up his options on the VIX. Fifteen minutes to clear their desks, under Fabrice's close supervision, and, a special instruction for Volatility, no farewell kiss from the bright pink lipstick smeared on the oil trader's face. Oil had blushed.

It had felt good to shoot someone, to feel my finger on the trigger. It had felt good where it mattered, down in the root of my loins. I had walked casually away from the scene of death and then over to talk to a group of meditative quants before sauntering back past Oil's desk. She had looked up at me and smiled. It had been a cautious, uncertain smile, but it had nonetheless brought the dimple to her cheek. And with the dimple had come a rush of complicated memories that I'd tried to delete with the photo.

For my 2008 compulsory annual fortnight away from the office, Caroline and I hired the villa in Corfu that we had been unable to occupy the previous summer and chartered a plane to fly us out. Quite a number of interesting people, who do not go to Scotland after the Twelfth to shoot things, spend the second half of August in Corfu. For much of the last year I had been in seclusion: recuperating, writing, guiding my firm through turbulent markets, keeping my investors happy, marrying off my daughter... By August 2008, the storm in Jack Diamond's teacup was several months behind me. I hoped it had been forgotten or at least brushed aside as irrelevant, imagined that the fraternity of wealth would trump the sorority of gossip. I was eager to re-establish contacts.

My confidence in the resilience of the Agios Stefanos crowd proved, however, to be misplaced. We saw them on the beach, out on their boats, in shops, in tavernas. But it was their backs and shoulders we saw and they were made of ice. There was one spontaneous invitation for a quiet drink and that was withdrawn by text message two hours later. There were no invitations to the round of parties we knew were taking place and the response to our own invitation was pathetically weak. People who would once have queued all night in the driving rain of an English January for a ticket to one of my parties would not dirty their dainty fingers touching the invitations Caroline sent round. "Better the devil you *don't* know," said one of the few who did arrive on the night. She nodded in the direction of a massive yacht, the brightly illuminated competing devil, out to sea. *Legs like you've never even imagined. Not even in your most spectacular dreams. And you, my old friend Colin Witheridge, you and your laughing ghost are out there as well, cavorting with your friend the devil, fluently chatting up all those gorgeous, long-legged Russian blondes.*

The result of our blackballing was that Caroline and I spent much more time than we had expected in one another's company. I had brought a copy of my manuscript of Jan's story to Corfu, but when I tried to persuade Caroline to read it, she declined. "Can't we just have a holiday together?" she pleaded. "Sometimes it's like you've been off living with that woman for the whole of the last year."

I looked down at Caroline on her sun lounger, eyes hidden behind her reading sunglasses, her nose in a paperback. I had not heard a whisper of complaint from her all year and now... I turned and walked away.

"Where are you off to?" she called after me.

"For a swim," I shouted back, without turning round.

I don't know how long I was gone. I swam a furious, thrashing crawl out to sea until I felt a pain in my thigh where the bullet wound had been. I floated on my back, drifting with the current, to regain my breath. I found a cove between the rocks with six foot of coarse sand at its head. The warm salt water lapped at my legs as I stretched out on the little beach. My body lay still, drinking in the sun as my brain reprocessed the email photograph which I had deleted before leaving London and thought thoughts that were not its own.

When I woke, it was late afternoon and my cove was in shadow. The sleep-wrought erection subsided as I waded out to sea and then swam back around the headlands to Caroline.

"Where have you been?"

I shrugged off the arms she threw around me. "I'm cold. I need to get some clothes on."

I showered, dressed slowly and spent twenty minutes on the phone with Fabrice. It was dusk when I returned. Caroline had opened a bottle of wine and set it on the poolside table. Two waiting glasses stood empty beside it. "I'm sorry, Nick," she sighed as she filled them. "It's just… well… I'll read it when we're back in London."

Lazy cunt.

The second photo came in at twelve thirty-nine on Tuesday 2 September. It was similar to the first but subtly, and importantly, different.

When the first image had arrived, my first startled thought had been that the woman in the photograph was Janice Day. The position of the male in the picture meant that he was unrecognisable and probably, I had imagined, unimportant. If the woman was Janice Day, it was Jan when she was much younger, probably in her late teens or early twenties. The fullness of the famous breasts had been emphasised for the photographer's lens. But as I had studied the image before double deleting it, I had decided that the model had not been Jan. True, there *was* a blurry likeness. I had even wondered for a moment whether the woman might have been Jan's daughter. According to Claude, Pam was physically very like her mother, but in the end I'd convinced myself that the differences were more significant than the similarities and dismissed my initial reaction as the product of too much thinking and writing about Jan over the past year.

The second photo changed all that. The woman's face was much more distinct. It was, beyond doubt, Janice Day. What startled me now, however, was the man. A mere anonymous adjunct to the pornographer's art in the first picture, he was now fully part of the scene. I gaped at the sparkling blue eyes, familiar hairline, the tousled mop of hair, the freckles, the art of being in two places at the same time… There could be no mistake. Colin Fucking Witheridge.

The third email was timed at nine minutes past one on the

afternoon of Friday, 5 September. It was sent to my private email address rather than the one at Kellaway & Co. I opened the attachment with some trepidation. The picture that filled the screen was one I had seen before – in physical form. Colin had shown it to me in his study the last time I saw him alive, in the summer of 2001, just before I went to Brazil with Ewa Brown. He had said "Anna lives in Brazil now" as he handed it to me. On the reverse of the picture he had written *Florianópolis, 1995*. I had seen it again when Laurel and Hardy visited me later in the year. It was the picture of Colin and a then unidentified middle-aged woman in sunglasses. Now, primed by the previous two photographs and with the benefit of the previous summer's encounter, I saw instantly who the woman was. It was the woman I had met for lunch at La Mezza Luna. The woman who said she had once been Janice Day.

2

Sunday, 7 September 2008 – The weight of encouraging US home ownership becomes too much for poor Freddie Mac and Fannie Mae to bear. They own or guarantee some $6 trillion of mortgage debt. When they cry for help the government bails them out. Cost to the US taxpayer (or, rather, those long-suffering Chinese who own America's debt)? I'm afraid, sir, that is as yet unquantifiable.

Borrow more! Spend more! Keep the old economy ticking along. See, the government does it, so you can too!

Complacent revisionist pricks.

Tuesday 9, September 2008 – Another photograph arrives, the fourth in the series. It is of Oscar Meyer in his Joe McIntosh disguise. He stands with his left foot resting on a rock. In his right hand he holds the barrel of a rifle, the butt of which rests on the ground. He is smiling for the camera. A woman stands beside him, on the other side of the rock. She too is smiling for the photographer. She resembles Emma Wallace, but I am unsure whether it is Emma. It seems unlikely, but in this mad September of 2008 anything is possible. The background is blurred but I can see a pine-covered hillside with snow-capped mountains beyond. The sky is heavily overcast. Do I recognise the peaks? The cloud level is too low for me to be sure.

Wednesday, 10 September 2008 – I go out to Canary Wharf for a meeting at Lehman and run into Paul Meyer in the lobby. It's the first time I've seen him since before Rouëlbeau. He says, "I'm sorry about what happened last summer." He invites me to use the chalet in Crans-Montana over Christmas. He and his wife will be skiing at Whistler with American clients. "Canada," he says, as if I might not know where Whistler is. "The United States itself is a little too uncomfortable for Swiss bankers these days."

"Whatever happened to Les Sornettes?"

Paul looks puzzled by my question, asks, "You prefer Les Sornettes to Crans?"

"No," I reply, "just curious."

He doesn't answer my question.

Thursday, 11 September 2008 – Caroline tries to engage me in a religious discussion. At first I ignore her, concealing myself in the *Financial Times*, but when she persists I tell her bluntly that I don't want to have anything to do with paedophiles, suicide bombers and the rest of the fucking God squad.

"Don't be so stupid, Nick," she says. "You're hiding behind Osama bin Laden's skirts. You know full well that's not what following Christ is about. You can't hide from God."

Friday, 12 September 2008 – I try to phone Emma Wallace. I have not spoken to Emma since the day before I delivered my manuscript to Edward Reader six weeks ago. On her home number I reach only an answer-phone asking me to leave a message. Her mobile, too, goes straight to voicemail. I try Tom's office. They tell me he has left the firm, retired on 31 August. *Good time to cash the chips in, eh?* No, they are not permitted to give me his private phone number, but they do tell me they think he and his wife have gone abroad. Maybe South America. Emma has told me nothing about any such plans.

I make a mental note to ask Ed, when I next speak to him, if he knows where Emma is. I've not spoken to Ed since the beginning of August when he told me was going to come up with ideas for another chapter to Jan's story.

Saturday, 13 September 2008 – Caroline has still not kept her promise to read my manuscript. All her attention has been consumed by a big divorce case. "I may," she tells me with an ominous note of triumph creeping into her legal voice, "get the wife even more than 50%. The husband's been a real bastard, affairs since the day they got back from their honeymoon and even now spending a packet on a mistress in Rome." Whether she reads my narrative or not matters less to me with each passing day.

Late in the evening, when there is no serious reading time left, Caroline comes into the drawing room carrying a white cardboard box that once held six bottles of Pécharmant. It now contains the copy of my book I printed out for Caroline before we flew to Corfu.

"Tell me what it's about," she asks. "You know, the quick synopsis you send to publishers to whet their appetite."

I pour myself another glass of whisky before saying, "It's not for publication."

"Tell me anyway."

There are two ways I can answer that. I can tell Caroline to fuck off, or I can give her my standard response: it's about Janice Day. The dead woman Caroline thinks I've been living with for the past year. The smoky embers somewhere deep in the Lagavulin, however, lead me to other words. "We've been a fortunate generation, you know," I say, contemplating my drink. "We were born after the horrors of the War and we were young in the halcyon days, after the Pill but before AIDS and internet porn. Our generation had the best music ever and then we came of age on the morning when finance was coming out of its dark ages. Now we're rich and not too old to embark on something new as the evening shit hits the fan."

"Sounds almost poetic." Caroline sets the box down on the floor. "What do you want to do?"

"I don't know. Maybe teach our grandchildren Chinese. What about you? What do you think we should do?"

"Maybe repent of our sins?"

Bitch.

Sunday, 14 September 2008 – Phil Scott is preaching at church this morning. Caroline does not even ask me to go with her. I am in my study pretending to look at papers which I have brought home from the office when she sticks her head round the corner to say she is going. After I hear the front door close, I open the drawer that contains my lists and the notebooks of my dreams, the successor to the drawer Anna Schmidt must have rummaged in when she found the Gothic list of Meyer & Cie bank accounts. Since those days I have added stationery collected from hotel bedrooms around the world to the papers in this drawer. I quickly find something that will serve my purposes nicely.

During the afternoon, Caroline says, "I have to be in Weybridge next weekend. I'm seeing three estate agents." Imogen moved out in February to combine her meagre assets with the rather more substantial assets of a stockbroker now prematurely retired and breeding horses in Dorset. Weybridge is to be sold. "I don't suppose you'll be able to come, with the markets going crazy like this every weekend."

"No. I'll come."

I must go. It's part of the plan.

Monday, 15 September 2008 – The landlord rings his bell and calls time. The party's over and everyone must go home. Lehman Brothers files for Chapter Eleven bankruptcy protection. Merrill Lynch sells itself to Bank of America for $50 billion.

Tuesday, 16 September 2008 – The US Federal Reserve spends $85 billion bailing out the world's largest insurance company, AIG. The resulting 80% US government shareholding allows us a sigh of relief. Kellaway & Co. holds some useful put options that AIG has written. We want somebody to answer our knock when we stand at the door and ask for our money. The US taxpayer will do nicely.

Wednesday, 17 September 2008 – To rescue HBOS, the UK's largest mortgage lender, Lloyds Bank announces a £12 billion offer to acquire its dying rival. The government's arm-twisting is evident in a rare smile from Gordon Brown and a cameo appearance by Shriti Vadera. Some anonymous straight face says that Lloyds will face no investigation into market dominance.

In the early evening, I take a call from Dante Aligheri. He is phoning, it seems, from one of his infernal circles where alcohol is drunk in copious quantities. "What do you give it?" he asks. "Ten years? That's what it took last time: 1929 to 1939. What odds will you give me on bombs dropping on Canary Wharf by 2017?" When I don't play along with his casino futures, he adds, "I'm offering the same odds on French bombs as on German bombs, Nick. Even better odds on American bombs."

Thursday, 18 September 2008 – The SEC outlaws short selling in 950 stocks on US markets for a month. The FSA bans short selling in twenty-nine London-quoted financial stocks for four months. Fabrice throws his Blackberry at the wall and screams, "How's an honest man meant to make a decent living in this fucked-up country?"

Friday, 19 September 2008 – The fifth email from my anonymous source arrives at one-nineteen in the afternoon. It is another photograph: Anna Schmidt comes to life on my computer screen. Her hair is piled loosely on her head. She holds it there with one hand. Several strands escape. There is a band of leather around her neck and another around the bicep of the arm nearest to the photographer. From the leather band around her neck a red cord dangles between her naked breasts. I examine the picture closely: I think it may be a very cleverly photoshopped fake, the kind they use to make presidents and prime ministers more appealing to women voters. But I am not sure.

I look again at the photograph of Oscar and the woman who might be Emma Wallace. I think I detect a faint white line around her as if her image has been added later to the original photograph. My doubts grow when I detect an even thicker white line around the non-descript rock on which Oscar arrogantly rests his booted foot.

In the middle of the afternoon, when I am out on the trading floor, my brain suddenly recalls that I saw a picture of Anna Schmidt in that pose when I was researching my book, except it was a pencil drawing not a photograph.

"Are you okay, boss?" Fabrice asks.

"Sure. Go on. Something just occurred to me that I've gotta deal with." As soon as Fabrice finishes running me through the figures swimming across his screen, I go back to my office, close the door and Google 'Thomas Rotten Diaz', the soldier on whose website I had seen the drawing of Anna. I cannot find it. The website is gone, or at least it has hidden itself from Google.

That evening, after Caroline has gone to bed, I go back to the drawer where I keep the lists and dreams and souvenir hotel stationery. I take a sheet of Moscow Kempinski letterhead and put it in my briefcase. Colin would probably have been there often on his trips to Russia. I have stayed there only once: 1997. Colin would still have been alive then.

Saturday, 20 September 2008 – "Claire's gone to Sydney to see Héloïse," Caroline tells me as we're driving to Weybridge. "I've no idea why that girl's run off to Australia."

After Caroline goes to the estate agent, I walk round to the Witheridge's house and let myself in. In Colin's study I find what I am looking for. Claire has thrown away many things over the last seven years, but not Colin's old typewriters. I put the Kempinski paper into the machine and begin to type the list: *Andropov's People*. Vladmir Ivanovich Andropov: the man Colin dined with at La Bise just before he disappeared. According to the papers Colin left for me in a Swiss safe deposit box, he was a Soviet operative in Berlin from 1966 to 1973. The same papers told me he was recruited by MI6 in 1971. Those dates provide the frame for my list.

When I began planning the list, the first name I came up with was Rudi Dutschke. At first, Dutschke seemed to fit perfectly. He was East German originally and, conveniently, he escaped to the West the day before the Berlin Wall was built. He was the best-known left-wing student leader in Germany in his day and he had featured prominently in Edward Reader's telephone lectures on the German background to Janice Day's story. As I thought about it though, Rudi Dutschke seemed too obvious. If not Dutschke, then what about the guy who shot him? Josef Bachmann... I type the first name on the list, watch it emerge from Colin's typewriter.

An interesting twist to history as we know it.

The second name came easily: Karl-Heinz Kurras – the policeman who shot and killed Benno Ohnesorg when the Shah of Iran visited Berlin in 1967. He, too, would probably be dead by now.

Another interesting little footnote to the Cold War.

The Shah connection led me to the third of Andropov's people: Tom O'Neil, Connemara leprechaun, collector of Persian rugs and husband of a deliciously adulterous wife. The loyal CIA Middle Eastern hand becomes, as I type his name, a Soviet double agent.

We invent the past in order to capture the future.

Who else? Colin Witheridge himself? No, Colin would never have put his own name on the list, even if he *had* been working for Andropov. He would never have let his talent for being in two places at the same time stretch quite that far. Anna Schmidt? Anastasia Kuznetsova? Again, too obvious and, if I heard Pam McIntosh correctly before the line went dead, Anna might still be alive.

My plan calls for only one living person on the list.

I remember Tom O'Neil's wife in my Mayfair flat in the story I told to a group of German lefties in a taverna on Santorini. I remember also, as I type the name, the man that Jan claimed Anna had killed in Berlin in 1971. Colin, too, had told me that earlier, when I sat drinking beer with him as he erotically caressed his typewriter before going to Switzerland to die. Then, I'd not understood what he was saying: I was too preoccupied with the prospect of going to Brazil with Mrs Hitler. The fourth name appears: Karl-Heinz Kupferhoden.

With love from Fuckolas Fuckaway.

The fifth name? I am into my stride now, reliving everything I have dreamt and written over the past year. She went back and forth across the Berlin Wall. She was in Prague with a mysterious woman called Else at or about the time the Palestinian terrorists got their permits there to go to the Munich Olympics. Stasi kept a file on her. Early doubts I had about including her were dispelled when the second photo from my anonymous source arrived. The keys on Colin's old typewriter bang out the name with a ferocity that will make her stand out among Andropov's lesser mortals: Janice Day.

There is a house in New Orleans,
They call the Rising Sun...

The sixth name would explain everything, wouldn't it? It would account for her trip to Eastern Europe in 1971 and her holiday in Moscow in 1974. The fertile minds at the Secret Intelligence Services would, doubtless, find other dots from the past forty years to connect. Some old Oxonian boffin deep in the archives where they keep Colin's reports on our student days would recall the words of the prophets written on the Northgate Hall and pronounce that someone with *that* sex drive could never become a hod-carrying Christian. It was all done with mirrors, all part of a cleverly crafted cover. It would explain why Stasi had a file on her and, perhaps most importantly of all, why I have held back Colin's envelope for seven years after his death. It would set the hares running when they found her body.

Very slowly, one by one, the deadly hammers hit the black ribbon and spell out the name onto the Kempinsky's paper: Caroline Carter.

As soon as five of you are together, the sixth must always die.

I turn the platen knob and remove the list from Colin's typewriter. I put the list in a manila envelope. I take both ribbon spools and the ribbon between them and put them in another envelope. I wipe the typewriter clean and replace it where I found it. I wipe other surfaces that I may have touched. I reset the alarm and let myself out of the house.

At home, I put the envelope containing Andropov's people in my safe and lock my morning's work away. It's a cheap safe; the professionals will have no trouble breaking into it.

By the time Caroline comes home, I am preparing lunch.

Sunday, 21 September 2008 – Caroline is right: weekends this September are proving to be busy. This one sees the end of investment banking altogether. Bear Stearns, Lehman Brothers and Merrill Lynch are already gone and now Goldman Sachs and Morgan Stanley announce that they will become commercial banks. After what Hank Paulson did to Lehman, being a commercial bank looks a safer bet. It has taken only a week for the best game in town to collapse altogether.

Monday, 22 September 2008 – Lehman was a good friend to my firm and we are having temporary problems raising credit elsewhere. Several of our funds hold too many assets for which the market will not currently give us prices. Under pressure from Fabrice, I agree to setting conditions and delays when our clients come in seeking redemption. Come they do.

Tuesday, 23 September 2008 – Warren Buffett buys 9% of Goldman Sachs. Fabrice says, "Why don't you phone Omaha and see if he'd like 9% of us as well? Cash offers only."

"Fuck off, Win-Win."

Wednesday, 24 September 2008 – I make a different phone call, leaning casually against the railing on Lambeth Bridge, midway between the spooks in Thames House and the archbishop in his palace over the river. My call is answered after one ring.

"*Oui.*"

"*Chez Fonfon,*" I say, enunciating clearly. "Nine. Nine. Ninety-nine."

"Details, please."

I give him name, address, preferred date and a payment method worthy of Colin Witheridge in his prime.

"Okay."

"How much?"

The man names his price. I can detect now the Balkan accent lingering in the shadows of the Provençal French. I agree the price. The line goes dead. The entire conversation has taken less than ninety seconds. This is so goddamn easy. And it's so cheap – compared, at least, to what I will be saving.

I take the pay-as-you-go Swiss SIM card out of the phone and drop it in the river. The phone itself follows. So do the ribbon spools from Colin's typewriter.

Thursday, 25 September 2008 – Washington Mutual collapses into the arms of the Federal Deposit Insurance Corporation, which sells on the lender's banking assets to J.P. Morgan Chase for $1.2 billion. Fabrice says Kellaway & Co. is desperate for liquidity. "Something must give, damn it."

When I arrive home late in the evening, Caroline says Claire has phoned from Sydney. There are tears in her eyes as she tells me what Claire has told her: Henry is living with Héloïse. "That girl's not good for Henry," she says. The relationship has been obvious on

Facebook, complete with photographs, for a month. Caroline and I don't do Facebook and we haven't seen or heard from Henry since Amanda's wedding.

Friday, 26 September 2008 – You can smell the panic in the dealing room as rumours eddy. Fortis is down to its last euro and about to be nationalised. Dexia and Hypo Bank face similar peril. The days of Bradford & Bingley and Wachovia are history. The entire Irish banking system is bankrupt. Iceland has been removed from the map. Maybe Iceland is a typo for Ireland. Will anyone own up to missing either Ireland or Iceland?

3

Despite the economic storm clouds gathering around us, I kept my promise to Caroline. She had booked us a weekend at a Sussex country-house hotel to mark my fifty-seventh birthday and drove us down late on the Friday afternoon. For most of the journey I slept in the seat beside her.

Caroline could not have foreseen, in May when she booked the weekend, what September 2008 would bring to the global financial markets. Neither could she have forecast the weather we had that weekend. The summer in England had, despite the many hopes pinned on climate change, been disappointingly grey and cool. Excessive rain at the beginning of September had brought a repeat of the previous summer's floods and farmers had warned of a wheat shortage because they would not be able to bring in the harvest before the grain sprouted in the ear.

Then, on the weekend the British government nationalised the Bradford & Bingley Building Society and the US government put $700 billion of taxpayers' money at the disposal of derelict American banks, the Sussex sun shone from a brilliant sky from daybreak to dusk. Caroline said the morning mist and the smell of the air reminded her of India, waxed lyrical about her childhood there, suggested we spend the month of November in a palace in Rajasthan in such an off-hand manner that I wondered whether she had been living on another planet over the past weeks as Earth crumbled to dust around us. Then she changed her mind, or maybe she was in two minds, perhaps the wild side of the imagination can be in two places at the same time, perhaps it was something she had learned in the arms of Colin Witheridge. She said the rising mists and scents of

432

wood smoke and rotting autumn leaves evoked the essence of England.

"It's not many people's England any more," I said gently.

"It's still mine," Caroline replied.

From mid-morning until well into the late afternoon, the day was unseasonably warm. We went for a long walk. We tramped up a sunken lane where crisp leaves fallen from the coppiced chestnuts lay, along a path trodden by the men of the parish a thousand years before the Romans came. The mist lingering in a time-forgotten hollow smelled of apples fermenting on the damp earth where they'd fallen. Caroline found a sprig of blackberries to which the frost and the devil had not yet got and declared them the sweetest she had ever tasted. A herd of Friesians plodded across a meadow, not a mad cow among them: restored, healed, forgiven, chewing the cud. A flock of sheep, replenished after the foot-and-mouth plague, grazed on a hillside.

We ate lunch at a pub that fortuitously sprang up beside us, drank too much beer, fell asleep on a grassy South Downs slope from which we could glimpse a tiny fragment of sea sparkling to the south. There is a point in this gentle, mythic land where you can see four counties and the sea. Caroline could not remember where it was. I'd never heard of it. Perhaps, I said, it is in a novel, in an historical romance orbiting around a fatally flawed love, or in a hymn like 'Jerusalem'.

We phoned the hotel and they sent a car to fetch us. We sat in the back seat and held hands, from time to time whispering secretively to each other like a pair of lovers on an illicit escapade. The driver watched us in his rear-view mirror. He would remember us when he was asked.

From our bedroom window, we watched the parlour lights come on in the Queen Anne farmhouse in the vale below, home farm long ago to this once-stately home. We heard bells summon the faithful few to evensong and spent the hour before dinner reading poetry to each other from old books we found on the shelves of the hotel library alongside Colonel Mustard and the lead pipe. Heads poked round the corner of the door, saw us sitting close together and withdrew discreetly, unaware that our verses were out of rhyme, our seasons out of synch.

From a volume of American poetry, Caroline read her Emily Dickinson:

Hope is a thing with feathers
That perches in the soul
And sings the tune without the words
And never stops at all.

I took the anthology from Caroline's hands – it was the same edition I'd once found, leaning intimately against 'The Age of Innocence' on Karen O'Neil's La Gradelle shelves – and excavated familiar lines from Robert Frost:

Two roads diverged in a yellow wood,
And sorry I could not travel both…

We played a game of Scrabble. I'm sure someone saw us playing by the softly fading evening light. I won – and ordered champagne to celebrate my impending birthday. We ate well, drank an excellent Burgundy to wash the venison down, were conspicuously happy. No other guest in the dining room that weekend could possibly have imagined that we had been married for thirty-one years.

Afterwards, upstairs, in a bed that was neither brass nor big, I had my celebration fuck. There used to be a saying in the City, which worried me when I was in my late thirties, that over the age of forty a man has to choose between making money and making love. It's not true. Success breeds success. Success in bed leads to success on the trading floor and vice versa, but when one begins to ebb, the other soon follows it out to the lost depths of the great sea that swallows all. I wonder whether, through the thin walls of the old house, anyone heard our noisy copulation, like I once heard Marie-Claire. I hope so.

We slept soundly, untroubled by the markets and all that would be unleashed the next week, and on Sunday morning, instead of taking the mossy path down to the cold stones of the parish church when its bells began to toll, Caroline read me the passage commended to her for 28 September in her book of daily devotions:

Jesus said, "There was a man who had two sons. The younger one said to his father, 'Father, give me my share of the estate'. So he divided his property between them.

Not long after that, the younger son got together all he had, set off for a distant country and then squandered his wealth in wild living. After he had spent everything, there was a severe famine in that whole country, and he began to be in need. So he went and hired himself out to a citizen of that country, who sent him to his fields to feed pigs. He longed to fill his stomach with the pods that the pigs were eating, but no one gave him anything.

When he came to his senses, he said, 'How many of my father's hired men have food to spare and here I am starving to death! I will set out and go back to my father and say to him: Father, I have sinned against heaven and against you. I am no longer worthy to be called your son; make me like one of your hired men.' So he got up and went to this father.

But while he was still a long way off, his father saw him and was filled with compassion for him; he ran to his son, threw his arms around him and kissed him.

The son said to him, 'Father, I have sinned against heaven and against you. I am no longer worthy to be called your son.'

But the father said to his servant, 'Quick! Bring the best robe and put it on him. Put a ring on his finger and sandals on his feet. Bring the fattened calf and kill it. Let's have a feast and celebrate. For this son of mine was dead and is alive again; he was lost and is found.' So they began to celebrate."

When she stopped reading, I looked up and saw that Caroline's eyelids had closed. When she opened them she turned her head towards me and said, "Don't you think it's time to come home, Nick? Let God put a robe around your shoulders and a ring on your finger. What's stopping you?"

I did not respond. Instead, I reached out to my bedside table, took hold of the book I had brought up from the library. It was an old first edition of *The Great Gatsby* – disembodied eyes and red lips staring out from a night sky – from a time when our country-house hotel was still owned by the family that had built it when the conquering Normans settled down, untroubled by the ravages of inheritance tax, filled with parties not unlike Jay Gatsby's across the Atlantic and those of the Meyers by Lake Geneva, afloat on a sea of financial wizardry tame in comparison to what we've done over the last twenty years.

I read Caroline three paragraphs from the end of the book, words F. Scott Fitzgerald put in the mouth of my American namesake, Nick Carraway, the bondman who quit:

And as I sat there brooding on the old, unknown world, I thought of

Gatsby's wonder when he first picked out the green light at the end of Daisy's dock. He had come a long way to this blue lawn, and his dream must have seemed so close that he could hardly fail to grasp it. He did not know that it was already behind him, somewhere back in that vast obscurity beyond the city, where the dark fields of the republic rolled on under the night.

Gatsby believed in the green light, the orgastic future that year by year recedes before us. It eluded us then, but that's no matter – tomorrow we will run faster, stretch out our arms further... And one fine morning –

So we beat on, boats against the current, borne back ceaselessly into the past.

I opened the curtains and the window and let the sun shine in. When I got back in bed, Caroline took my hand, pressed it and said, "'For *me* to live is Christ and to die is gain.'" *Does she have some preternatural inkling of what is about to happen?*

"Would you really die for your faith?" I asked.

"I'd like to think I would. Though for now, it's probably better that I stay alive, for you, for the kids, for... that was St Paul's conclusion as well after he'd written 'For me to live is Christ and to die is gain'. The rest is... well... just dust on the nettles." *No, I don't think she does.*

"How does it go on?"

"What?"

"That poem. That dust on the nettles thing."

"'I like'," Caroline quoted, "'the dust on the nettles, never lost except to prove the sweetness of a shower.'" After a few seconds of deep quiet she added, "God can do amazing things with dust, Nick. Believe me: Jesus is the most important..."

"More important than me?" I asked, rubbing her thigh to interrupt the flow of the inevitable words.

Caroline smiled that ethereal distant smile that had in our early years driven me wild with desire, but that now was simply a mild irritant. "Different," she said, "but, ultimately, yes; more important than either of us."

After a while, after we had run fingers over the tingly bits of each other's bodies, after I had seduced Caroline Carter once again, while we were listening to the sounds of morning coming in through the open window, sipping post-coital coffee and wondering what miracles the Sunday papers held in store, I said, without thinking about what the future held, "We'll go there someday."

"Where?"

"The United States. I'd love to drive across the country. Ohio, Indiana, Illinois, Iowa, Nebraska, Wyoming, Montana…" The list of names rolled off my tongue, as they had once rolled off Colin's, like a slow night train clattering its poetic way across the endless cornfields, like Claude Meyer's litany of the meadows and cabins and peaks of the Valaisanne mountains, like an anonymous Belgian girl's rhythmic recital of the islands that float on the wine-dark sea between Piraeus and Kastelorizo, like Jan's wonder at the liberating list of stations strung out like a glittering necklace along the north shore of dark Leman.

"I think," Caroline said quietly, "I'd rather go to Jaiselmer."

4

Caroline dropped me at the station to catch a late evening train up to London. She needed to spend the next few days in Weybridge preparing the Surrey house for sale. I wanted to be in the office by six on Monday morning so I would spend the night in town. Whatever the markets would bring, it promised to be an interesting day.

On Friday, before I left for Sussex, I had asked the team to be in by a quarter past six on Monday. I knew quite a few would be there well before the appointed hour. We needed to determine how to position ourselves on the basis of the weekend's events before the markets opened in Europe. We expected little lead from Asia but we had kept a skeleton staff in overnight nonetheless in case something happened. I should have been there myself – but life is full of little compromises. The night watchmen were scheduled to brief us at six-twenty in the board room. As usual there would be ample fresh coffee, croissants, Danish pastries and orange juice on the sideboard.

I spent the train journey up to Waterloo listening to messages and picking up email traffic on my Blackberry. I had ordered a three-page analysis of events of the previous forty-eight hours to be prepared and delivered by hand to my Knightsbridge address by nine o'clock on Sunday evening. It was waiting for me on the entrance hall floor when I pushed the front door open.

After reading the briefing through twice and deciding how we would play the next day, I made a phone call. It was Hardy's voice on the answer machine. "Look," I said after the tone, "sorry to phone so late on a Sunday. It's just... well, I thought you ought to know. I've got the envelope."

We watched our screens as the Monday morning markets came to life: stock prices, bond yields, foreign exchange futures, oil, wheat... the roulette wheel spinning... last bets being placed... someone in the far corner of the dealing room played Dylan's song 'The Times They Are A-Changin'" through the normally hermetically muted speakers of his computer.

At ten past nine, Fabrice came into my office, his Gallic grin as wide as the Champs-Elysées. He gave me a high five. Once again, Kellaway & Co. had called it precisely right.

"But it's unstable as hell," I said. "Be vigilant."

"Don't worry, boss," he replied. "Fat tails make fat cats."

"What?"

"Boss, when equilibrium comes back to the markets, you and I will starve."

At ten o'clock the sixth email arrived. I opened the attachment.

Three women sat in conversation at an outdoor café table. A carafe of white wine stood on the table, six glasses surrounding it. There was writing in French on the red parasol over the table. Each of the three women had a cigarette in her right hand. Two men hovered in the half-distance beyond the table. The photograph had been taken on one of those cameras that stamps the time and date on the pictures it takes: *16:15, 31 August 2001*. Of course, the time is not necessarily the local time in the place the photograph was taken. Owners of these cameras rarely change the settings from their home time zone.

It took me no time at all to realise that the time and date placed the picture on the afternoon Colin travelled from Geneva to Montreux. A quarter past four on 31 August 2001 was precisely one hour and seventeen minutes after Colin Witheridge's last known position, when he used his credit card to buy a ticket from Geneva to Montreux before disappearing.

Colin was, of course, one of the two men in the middle distance. I had no problem at all recognising the other four actors. The other man, the one standing beside Colin, was Oscar Meyer, complete with ponytail. The women were Janice Day, Emma Wallace and Anna Schmidt.

When shall we three meet again?

I was still staring at my computer screen when Linda broke into my thoughts to say that there was a call waiting.

"Not now," I said.

"It's Edward Reader."

"Okay."

She put the call through.

"Ed," I said. "Morning."

"Good morning, Nick. Thanks for taking the call. How's the world of finance?"

"Interesting."

"Good, good. Well, my screen has provided me with some interest as well this morning. I seem to have been blind-copied on an email of which you are the addressee. I don't know whether you've seen it yet. It's got an interesting attachment and I think we should have a chat, but not on the phone."

"Do you want lunch at White's?" I asked.

"Oh, Nick, that would be lovely. When?"

"Today?"

"Yes, today. Why not? Splendid. I've never been to White's, you know. This will be a real treat, thank you."

Sycophantic bastard.

I walked over to White's, arriving five minutes before the time I had set. I had not seen Edward Reader since 1975 and had only the dimmest recollection of what he had looked like even then, but the staff at the club would sort that out. That's what they're there for.

Edward arrived ten minutes later. He carried an old-fashioned leather laptop case – unnecessarily commodious for modern laptops – and wore a suit that was as stylish as the ones Laurel and Hardy had worn when they came to tell me Colin Witheridge had been a spy and that they were looking for his envelope; a white shirt that was too loose around the collar and too long in the sleeve; a tie that was too broad and too bright – something a graduate trainee might have thought fashionable in the seventies – and buttoned cuffs rather than cufflinks. He had a severely receding hairline and a jaw like Richard Nixon's. He was the sweaty type of person HM Revenue and Customs might send round to see whether Kellaway & Co. was behaving. I would not have recognised him, but the voice was the one I had heard on the phone.

I took the man upstairs, played the host. We filled our plates from the central table and sat to eat under Sir Joshua Reynolds' portrait of Charles James Fox. Edward declined a glass of wine, put off perhaps by the watchful gaze of Queen Charlotte.

When we had started on our second plates, Ed asked, "Do you recognise those people in the photograph?"

"I think so." I gave him the five names.

"I see," he said. "Do you know where it was taken?"

"No. Somewhere French speaking. I have an idea but it's not comfortable."

"Very interesting. Might it be useful for a final chapter, Nick?"

"Ed," I said, perhaps too loudly for our surroundings, "this isn't bloody fiction." I spelt it out. The date stamp on the photographs. The date Colin had disappeared. His purchase of a ticket – two tickets – from Geneva to Montreux. After that it was speculation – I spared Edward that. I did not want to let my imagination run away with untested theories and wild nightmares. Nor his.

"Do you think the photograph's a fake? A mock-up?"

"You know, I just hope it is." I told him about the previous emails from the same anonymous source.

"I've brought my laptop with me," Ed said. "We can blow the picture up and have a closer look at it."

"I think I should go to the police."

Police? It was that word tripping off my tongue that caught me off guard. The wine drinkers at Ed's summer café and Queen Charlotte and all White's worthies faded, overlaid with another image. The police *would* be calling soon. What, I would ask, had happened? A knock on the door? A knife? A gun? Rough calloused hands tightening around the windpipe? Had they raped her first? Had they cut out the vital organs while they were still fresh to sell them on the secondary market? Had they videoed the whole operation and uploaded it to You Tube? What about the envelope? Had the police found that? The manila envelope in my safe? Andropov's people? Andropov's six people at the Moscow Kempinsky?

"Are you all right, Nick? You've gone a bit pale."

"Yes. Sorry. A lot on."

"Of course," Ed continued, "before involving the police, though, don't you think it would be better to be sure that the picture's real? That you're not dealing with a joke, with some warped sort of fiction."

When we had finished lunch, I took Ed across the head of the staircase to the Gaming Room. The Gaming Room is the most famous room in White's. It was here that eighteenth-century fortunes were lost and won on an aristocrat's throw of a die, here that entire slave-plantation islands traded hands on the turn of a card, here that a woman with a fine collarbone could command for an hour's work what the average working-man could not earn in five years. The room was empty. The table was bare. It was all redundant now. The action had moved east to the City, then farther east to Canary Wharf, was moving farther east still to the erstwhile socialist dreamlands of Moscow and Shanghai.

Ed laid his computer on the green baize covering the table and opened the attachment that had brought us here, expanding the picture until you could scarcely distinguish anything. I confirmed the identity of those in the photograph: Colin Witheridge, Oscar Meyer, Janice Day, Emma Wallace and Anna Schmidt. We looked for flaws in the workmanship, for indications that what we were looking at was a photomontage. Several times we thought we saw telltale signs of clever artifice, but it was all wishful thinking. The five *had* been together on the afternoon of 31 August 2001 and now I had a rough idea of where they had met.

Colin had purchased his train ticket at 14:58. The direct train from Geneva to Montreux takes about an hour. If you have to change at Lausanne it takes about an hour and twenty minutes. The 15:10 and 15:36 departures (assuming the timetables I'd found on line that morning had been in force in 2001) from Geneva would have put Colin in Montreux between 16:30 and 16:45. The photograph was date stamped '16:15'. There were two possibilities: either the timing was wrong, the camera's clock set, say, to UK time rather than Central European time; or Colin had got off the train at one of its intermediate stops. All I had to do was find the café with the red umbrellas somewhere along the north shore of Lake Geneva, somewhere between Nyon and Montreux, and I would know where the five had met.

But why? Why this frantic dealing-room urgency in my brain? Three of the five were dead and one had been missing for more than thirty years. The fifth, Emma Wallace, was a public figure in England, a well-known author. I saw her regularly; spoke to her even more frequently. All I needed to do was wait for her to return from South America. I did not need to do all this today – of all days.

Six glasses? I counted them again. In 'Sogol', Emma's final story in *Jericho House*, the five rose as one and killed the sixth, the one they

441

discovered to be pregnant. Who was the sixth here at the Swiss café? The photographer? Emma had set her story in a snowbound chalet high above the top end of Lake Geneva, one where Nero had hung on the wall above the fireplace.

And the sixth must always die.

Ed said, "Nick, old chap, could you point me in the direction of the gents'? The old bladder's not what it once was." I pointed him the way.

There was another possibility, wasn't there? That the date stamp on the photograph was wrong, that the picture had been taken some time before, perhaps a long time before, Colin had died? That seemed, as I let the thought settle, the most likely explanation. One that I might be able to live with, even though it left a trail of dangling questions – including who the sender of the anonymous emails was and why he or she had put such a provocative date on this latest image. Why had it been sent to Edward Reader as well as me? Did that point to somebody who knew that Ed knew me, knew he was acting as my literary agent?

I returned to the Gaming Room. The computer stood open on the table, but Ed had not yet come back from the lavatory. *The little shit must be emptying more than his bladder.*

Lost in speculation, I drifted to the window. *Where?* and *How?* and *What?* are questions for the science lab and dealing room. Outside that environment the question is always that of the irritating child: *Why?* Why had the five – those five – been meeting anyway? Why Oscar? Why had I been excluded? I was, after all, the common link: Ecolint with Oscar and Jan; Oxford with Emma and Colin; Greece with Anna. It should have been my circle. My circle with me at its centre.

Whose was the sixth glass? A gruesome thought flashed across the screen in my brain, down my spine and convulsed the muscles around my stomach. It couldn't have been, couldn't possibly have been, Caroline. Could it? "Murder your darlings, Nick." That was Edward Reader's advice. Nay, his command. From no less an authority than Q himself. The knife surgically plunged into the abdomen, ripping out the kidneys, the liver, the heart, the foetus... All along I had thought the model for the pregnant girl had been Jan, that the model for all the girls in *Jericho House* had been Jan. How vigorously Caroline had refused to abort Robert and Henry! And now, darling... half my assets! Abort half my wealth! 50% of *me*! Parade *me* on a circus stage? A divorce court fool? A penniless homunculus? Never!

4

I looked at my watch. To steady myself, I counted the seconds as they ticked by. Twelve minutes had passed since Edward had asked me for directions to the men's room. I decided to go find him. As I passed in front of the abandoned laptop open on the table, the black screen flickered to life and then died again. I retraced my steps. The same thing happened again. I looked more closely and saw a small plastic disc stuck to the wall opposite the computer. There was a red dot in the middle of it. I cut the laser beam again and left my body blocking its path. The monitor came to life. The picture of the famous five – Colin, Oscar, Jan, Emma and Anna – appeared. I stared at it again, instinctively searching for more clues, for a reason for my exclusion. Each one of them looked happy. A happy reunion of old friends.

Then, abruptly, the scene changed. I was looking now at the picture I had double deleted before going to Corfu. Janice Day, pornographer's model. Fifteen seconds later, Colin joined Jan on the screen – the second photograph from the anonymous source. The programme had been set to 'simple slide show' and I watched as Jan and Colin appeared clothed and in their right minds and sitting on a bench in Florianópolis. Were they still at it in 1995? Then I noticed something I had not seen before: the earrings dangling from Jan's ears were in the shape of swastikas.

"Maybe Oscar killed Colin." It was Ed's voice.

"What?" I span round. There was no sign of Ed in the Gaming Room.

"It would make sense, you know," said the rusty, whining, weasel voice. "Oscar found Colin shagging his wife and he killed him for it. Cut off his balls and his head for good measure. I mean, it's what he tried to do with you when you fucked Jan in Geneva last year, isn't it?"

"What are you talking about?"

"It would make a great chapter in your novel, Nick."

"Fuck off."

Imaginary bespittled dwarf of reaction.

The picture of Anna appeared, the one that so resembled the pencil drawing I had found on an American soldier's website alongside a collection of evil-looking guns and the lyrics of a song by a Norwegian black-metal band. Wasn't that the kind of music

Hilde had said Torvald liked? Maybe it was those guns that Oscar and Torvald had used. Maybe they had found them on the now-vanished website, downloaded them and carried them out to Rouëlbeau. In fifteen seconds, the five are at their café table again. The six glasses are still on the table by the carafe of white wine.

The next photographs narrowed the location even further. Colin Witheridge has Anna Schmidt in his arms, holding her tightly to himself, but not in such a way that I fail to see their beaming faces. To one side stands Janice Day; she too is smiling. To the other side of Colin and Anna is a sign in the blue-and-white of the Swiss railways: 'Montreux'.

Then there are six. The five from the café plus Edward Reader. They stand in a formal group, smiling stiffly, facing the camera, waiting for the little red light to stop flashing and the shutter to open. Whoever had set the camera on the tripod had not centred the lens well. The group of six is in the lower left-hand corner. In the upper right is a dark wooden chalet. I recognise the place: Claude and I spent the half-term weekend there in October 1969. We were there again the following May, planning our trip to California, drinking kirsch and telling stories of madmen who slaked their thirst with blood from the slit throats of little boys. The place Paul said the Meyers had sold long ago: Les Sornettes.

I had seen a version of the picture that appeared next on my computer at Kellaway & Co. It was the one of Oscar Meyer holding the barrel of a rifle, with Emma Wallace standing beside him. Was this the rifle Torvald had downloaded? The one that Oscar had used to shoot me? And Emma? What was Emma Wallace doing there? After Oscar had fired those bullets at me, Emma had turned up at my hospital bedside. She had arrived *before* the police had released my identity. She had been staying, she had said, in a holiday chalet above Montreux putting the finishing touches to *Jericho House Revisited*. The sitting room of the chalet had reminded her of the setting she had invented for the telling of the six *Jericho House* tales when the girls were snowbound. Invented?

When the call came that God had died.

We move on.

There was a Nietzsche moment. A moment when God was dead. The hours after Good Friday when Jesus was in the tomb...

A subtly different version of Oscar and Emma replaced its predecessor. The rock nondescript rock around which I had thought I detected a white line was replaced by a naked body. The edge of the picture cuts the lower half of the body off and, due to the way the body slumps, the head is invisible. Oscar's boot rests between the dead man's shoulder blades.

We move on. All I have to do to stop this is to move *my* body out of the line of the laser beam. Move. Move, Kellaway, and the ending will not come. Edward Reader's final chapter will never be written. Fact and fiction will be kept forever separate. But I do not move and Colin appears on the screen. The flash from the camera has picked out nothing but his naked body, the red reflection in his eyes and the copy of *La Suisse* that he holds across his chest, one hand holding either side of the newspaper. I can check the date later, but I don't need to. I already know it – within a few days. Knowing – fearing – what comes next, my eyes are drawn down below the lower edge of the newspaper. The photograph stops short of Colin's genitals; but it has captured, indistinctly in the shadow of the paper, the tattoo that in Chinese stands for Anastasia.

The slide show moves relentlessly forward. Today's people die and tomorrow's are born. Fifteen seconds a frame, that's what you get, then you're moved on. Edward Reader holds a large machete in his hand. He wears a white boiler suit and yellow rubber gloves. There is red blood on the white of the suit.

5

I close the computer, put it in its case and run down the stairs carrying it. I ask the man at the door whether he has seen my guest.

"He left, oh, must be nearly half an hour ago, Mr Kellaway."

I make my way back to the office. I am not thinking where I am going. My feet know the route perfectly, I have walked it a thousand times. A bus hits me as I cross Piccadilly. I am not hurt, just a light nudge. I get up, pick the computer case off the tarmac. The driver, coming out of his cab, swears at me. *Fucking pleb.* I ignore him, walk through the traffic, along the pavement. I have gone a hundred yards before I notice that there is blood on my hand. I have torn the sleeve of my suit at the elbow. The shirt beneath is red with more blood. I will wash it off before I phone the police.

The police? *They* will be phoning *me*, won't they? The ordinary police who investigate the little murders of daily life will phone and so will Hardy and his lot, unable to resist my message about Colin's envelope. Perhaps, even now, they've found *both* the envelope and the body in the kitchen – or the conservatory or the hall or wherever Fonfon's Kosovars have done the deed – and are bickering over whose jurisdiction covers the crime.

By the time I reached Curzon Street, I had convinced myself that it was all just some kind of game, a charade scripted and acted by Emma and Edward. I imagined them laughing now, up in the gods, as the punters down in the expensive seats mistook their play for reality and gasped in horror. In a moment the curtain would fall, the lights go up and Lehman would still be plying its gentlemanly trade, Goldman would still be an investment bank and the Bradford & Bingley Building Society would still be as solid as the bricks and mortar of a Yorkshire terraced house. Johnny Morris would never have broken our Rouëlbeau vow of silence nor gone to Vietnam, Andropov would never have bought La Bise, governments would be debt free, bell curves would be strictly enforced by international legislation, Caroline would still be alive, pregnant with our first child, smiling and welcoming me at the door when I came home from an honest day's work at the office…

I stepped into the building. What if Edward Reader did kill Colin? What if that whole group – Oscar Meyer, Janice Day, Anna Schmidt, Emma Wallace and Edward Reader – had all killed Colin? One of those Agatha Christie murder kits you buy in a cardboard box to entertain bored dinner guests? A house party in the Meyers' old chalet at Les Sornettes gone horribly wrong? What if 'Joe Ace' – the name scribbled on a playing card in the vault of a Geneva bank – the title of one of Emma's *Jericho House* tales – was code for the gang that played the fatal game? Their initials: Janice, Oscar, Emma, Anna, Colin, Edward… What if they wanted to be found? Don't psychologists say that many criminals harbour a desire to be caught, long to have their deeds exposed, revel in the horror they inspire as if it were a form of public adulation? What if they wanted *me* to be their public?

Soon after I had been shot, Emma had arrived at the hospital and said she was staying at a chalet above Montreux. Edward had been on the phone before many more days had passed. It was the two of them – Edward and Emma – who had encouraged me to write my narrative over the past year. Only the two of them. I had followed where they led, ignoring Caroline when she tried to dissuade me, pushing her farther and farther away into her divorce cases and charity committees.

446

What game had Emma and Edward been playing over the past twelve months? Oscar and Jan were, of course, as dead as Colin. I had seen all three bodies. No, not all three bodies. I had only seen *pictures* of Colin's corpse. What if Colin wasn't really dead? Spies do that sort of thing, don't they? They pretend to be dead and then re-emerge with a new identity. I've seen them do it on television. What if the pictures the police had shown me were just clever fakes? What if this was his ultimate revenge for my fucking Caroline in the ruins at Paestum? Revenge served cold, long after the heat of his Amsterdam punches? What if he had run away with Anna, across all the states of the Midwest, on a Bonnie and Clyde fucking spree? Ohio, Indiana, Illinois, Iowa, Nebraska, Wyoming, Montana... Where did Jan fit into all this? Where had I been? Why had *I* not been there? Why the hell had I not been there?

When I reached my office, Linda handed me a pile of notes. The top one said 'Pam McIntosh phoned'.

"Who's this?"

"She's on your list of…"

"Okay."

Pam McIntosh. Jan's daughter, of course.

"Did she leave a number?"

"No. Said she'd phone back this afternoon."

Why today? Of all possible days, why today?

Fabrice came into my office three steps behind me and closed the door. "Where the fuck have you been? You left your fucking Blackberry on your fucking desk."

"What's up?"

"Up? Shit. Nothing's 'up'."

The Footsie was down more than 4%. New York had opened down and was continuing to fall. Worse would come before the day ended. The market disliked the compromises that had been hastily tacked on the Americans' $700 billion bank rescue plan. Opinion polls said voters hated the whole concept of a bank rescue, hated anything that appeared to offer monetary salvation to the rich of Wall Street, whose greed they believed had caused the crisis in the first place, hated bankers and all species of *homo financiensis* known and unknown. *Their* stock was way, way down. Rumours were beginning to eddy across the trading room screens that Congress would, despite diluting it, still reject Hank Paulson's rescue plan ('He's a goddamn banker just like the rest of them, ain't he?') and

447

let the whole Wall Street mess drown into its own excrement; that Europe was about to bail out another bank that had exploited lax Irish regulation; that the Republican presidential candidate was on the verge of a nervous breakdown. There were rumours, too, Fabrice said, about Kellaway & Co.

"What?"

Fabrice shrugged his shoulders and sighed. "That our lines of credit are frozen, that the Arabs are pulling their funds, that we're sitting on more sub-prime shit than the Royal Bank of Bloody Scotland, that Revenue is going to haul you in for tax fraud... for God's sake, Nick, it's like Chinese fucking whispers."

"Okay," I said. "Give me a few minutes. I've got some stuff to do."

"More important than *this*?" Fabrice threw his arms wide open and his big mouth sagged into his chin, a despairing gesture that encompassed the whole of Kellaway & Co. and much, much more beyond our walls.

"Possibly."

When the door slams behind Fabrice's retreating tread, I sit down at my desk beneath the wobbly towers of finance. Maybe... maybe they're not solid concrete, steel and glass office blocks after all. Maybe it's just a pack of pricks deflating after collective orgasm. Maybe... it really isn't a good painting.

I open Ed's computer. I want to make sure that I have not lost the pictures when the computer fell onto the street. For a moment I irrationally hope that they have vanished, been wiped out, swept away, forgotten forever. But nothing is ever really lost, is it? I boot up the computer. While I am waiting, I phone Ed's office. He should, if he has gone straight back from White's, be there by now.

"Edward Reader, please."

"I'm sorry, sir. Mr Reader left the company on the 31st of August."

Bastard.

I hang up, turn back to the computer screen and swear at it. I double click on the 'My Pictures' icon. There are two folders in it. I click on the first. Jan and Colin on the bench in Florianópolis in 1995. A slide show. The pictures I saw in the Gaming Room. Fifteen seconds a frame.

I open the second file. The first picture is of my house in Weybridge. Caroline stands on the front door step. She is wearing jeans and a t-shirt and holds a watering can in her hand. The second is my street in Knightsbridge. The photographer has caught Phil Scott walking past my house on the way to his. In the third, I see Janice Day beside the telephone kiosk near Knightsbridge tube station. There is someone inside the phone box and Jan seems to be waiting her turn. In the fourth I am paying the taxi driver through the window of his cab outside the Mezza Luna. In the fifth I am putting Jan's guitar into the boot of the car that took us to Heathrow. The last is a close-up of Caroline. It has been taken on a high-power telephoto lens and makes the choir girl disintegrate into a million dots. There are only six photographs in this file.

Linda comes in and says, "Are you all right, Nick?"

"Yeah. Tough day."

"I've got that Pam McIntosh on the phone again."

"Okay," I say, "put her through."

I close my door and sit behind my desk.

"Oh, hi, Mr Kellaway. Thanks for taking the call. It's just that I was…"

I listen to the voice, encourage it when it falters. There is something comforting about it – like the warmth inside the shopping mall after school, when you're hanging out with the other kids while outside the wind howls and blows snow and sagebrush in from the west; like the fire in the hearth at Les Sornettes when Claude and I told each other stories, before the call came to say that God had died and we were cut off from the world. Is there something of her mother in Pam's voice? Something of Jan when she arrived from Buenos Aires and sat in the back row in class sucking the ends of her long blonde hair? Perhaps, just now, I need to let myself believe that there is.

"… I was in England back in July. We sort of started out here. I was gonna call you, but I chickened out. I guess I was just kinda, like, too scared or something. I mean, you know, you being there when they were killed, like."

"You *should've* got in touch."

"I know. Anyway, I took the train out to Oxford and saw the place that Mom and Aunty Priscilla and Aunty Anastasia used to call the Jericho House. The guys who live there now let me in to have a look 'round and stuff. There's a book out about it, you know, and these guys had no idea they were living in, like, *the* house. They were just so excited. It was amazing. It was so cool…"

"… cool…"

"… and then I met with the author."

"You met the author?"

"Yeah. It was so cool. She's called Emma Somerwell and she's just such a sweet little old lady."

"How did you meet?"

"It was really amazing. I was staying with Aunty Anastasia in her chalet in Switzerland." The voice rises at the end of the sentence, the affectation of contemporary youth that still sounds to me like uncertainty, like a need for parental affirmation.

"Yes," I say, as if I know all about Aunty Anastasia and her Swiss chalet. And I do, really, don't I? She, Colin and I plotted how to extract the money from her Brazilian godfather, the money she used to buy the place. Then she came over to my place in Islington and I fucked her. Though, of course, I denied it when Colin accused me…

"It's this quaint old chalet overlooking Lake Geneva. It used to belong to my grandparents. It's really fun – all these links I'm discovering. Mom and Dad were staying there for a bit during the summer they died in that accident. They'd also, like, been over there for a vacation in 2001 and Pete and I never even knew where they'd been. I guess we weren't even interested enough to ask then. What was it you asked me?"

"The author."

"Yeah. That was just awesome. I mean, she and her husband just, you know, turned up one day. I don't think Aunty Anastasia was expecting them or anything."

"When was that?"

"Oh, I don't know. Two or three weeks ago? Anyway, she gave me a copy. She even signed it: 'To Pam. With love and in fond memory of your mother.' I haven't read it yet, though. Then, you know…"

I listen. I speak calmly. I listen again. Pam, tentatively, suggests we meet.

"Yes, of course. You're right. It would be much nicer to meet and have a proper chat. Perhaps you would let me buy you dinner. Your mother and I…"

"Yes. That'd be great, Mr Kellaway. There's so much I want to learn about. It'll have to be today, though. I'm leaving London tomorrow."

"Tomorrow? Leaving?"

"Yeah. I'm going to Corsica."

"Corsica?"

"Yeah. Marie-Claire – I guess I should call her Aunty Marie-Claire, it's taking time getting used to all this new family. Anyway, she's lending me and my friends her boat for a couple of weeks. I'm, like, picking it up on Wednesday morning."

"Where are you now?"

"In a phone box by Knightsbridge subway station."

"That's close to where I live. Would you like to meet at my house? Or maybe at a pub?"

"Your house'd be great. I know where you live. I walked past it yesterday. You'll have no trouble recognising me: long blonde hair. You know, folks say I look just like my mom did when she was my age. I've got this green backpack and an old guitar. It used to be my mom's. I never even knew she played the guitar."

"What about my house in an hour from now?"

"Sure. See ya."

Fuck. Fuck. Fuck.

The line goes dead.

6

I turn to Ed's computer again. I delete all the emails. There are not many. I delete both folders in *My Pictures*. I delete everything in every *Deleted Items* box. They will be able to resurrect it all, of course. The password is 'Anastasia'. But first they'll have to find the computer.

As I put the computer into its case, I see a folded piece of paper. It falls out and lands on the floor. I realise, as I bend to pick it up, that my hand and elbow ache from the encounter with the Piccadilly bus. That seems a very long time ago – as long ago as the bright morning I went to Rouëlbeau with Jan; longer ago than the afternoon when she lay on the dock at La Bise; much longer ago than the day I watched the eagle fly out over the abyss of freedom. The flow of blood from my arm has stopped. Somehow I will clean it up and change my shirt before I meet Pam.

I watched her shirt turn from white to red.

I unfold the paper and recognise the handwriting that covers both sides. It is the same handwriting I have seen in the margins of my developing *magnum opus* over the past year.

If they killed him, why did they do it? Had he threatened to talk? Perhaps they learned he worked for MI5 and had been spying on them for years. All that time he had passed himself off as a true friend and loyal member of the gang he was actually reporting back to HM the Queen on every single reunion – Les Sornettes 2001, Florianópolis 1995, Berlin 1989, Castelfiori 1983, Montana 1977. Maybe he was just super numerary. A recession was coming, efficiency measures needed to be taken and five was company, but six was a crowd. Like in Nietzsche, the sixth must always die. Murder to achieve the same sense of liberation that those who murdered God had felt. Through one man's death comes freedom for the others, right? They drew lots and it fell to Colin to go. Doesn't explain why they had to slice off his genitals, though, does it? What, then, do we say? Maybe Oscar was jealous because he'd screwed Jan.

"Screwed Jan? Colin?" Nick asked, aghast.

What's this? Am I now just a character in Emma's fiction? A minor imaginary character with an insignificant walk-on part in one of her bizarre short stories? The kind of person Edward Reader would want Emma to kill off before she sent her manuscript to the publisher? What of Jan and Oscar? Colin and Anna? Are we all just ghosts in Emma's Nietzschean dreams, wiling away our unemployed, off-stage hours in a world of Bloomberg screens and put options, of credit default swaps and collateralised debt obligations?

I read on.

"Screwed Jan? Colin?" Nick asked, aghast.

"Well," Emma replied, "it would fit wouldn't it? It was something Colin would want to do, isn't it? You'd screwed Caroline, his beloved choir girl. How better to score a point, to get revenge, than to fuck the bird you were always on about?"

"You're not serious, Emma."

"Run with it. Oscar finds out. Castrates him. Beheads him. It's what he was going to do to you after you'd slept with her, wasn't it?"

"There's no proof."

"Does there need to be, Nick? This is a novel. It's fiction. You make it up as you go along. A bit like photomontage… a bit like… well, like life, I imagine. It was many years ago, somewhere in a yellow wood, that I lost track of life… Do you want me to read you the last story in Jericho House Revisited? *It's called 'The Sixth Roll of the Die'."*

"Please."

Emma began to read: "'It was the girl they called The Resurrection who cast the sixth and final die, while the one they used to call Salvation stood naked in the doorway and kept a watchful eye. As the black dots on the bone-white cube settled on the green, a dark voice very calmly said, "Let's see what's to be seen. For now the time has surely come, to do as we all promised back in 1971." Then Reconciliation stretched out a languid arm, "Let's grant the dead man one last wish before we do his body harm." Liberation stood against the wooden cross and said, "Let's drink a final toast today to freedom and the dead." While Alienation's body lay lifeless on the ground, a green voice said, "We'll leave it at Montreux lost and found…"'"

I put Emma's paper into the case with Ed's computer and walked out onto the floor. As I approached Fabrice's workstation, he was shouting obscenities into the mouthpiece of that thing that sticks out of his ear. He stopped when he saw me, looked at me like a child caught with his red hand in the biscuit tin.

"Fabrice," I said. "I may be gone for some time."

"Nick, you can't. Not today. The markets are crazy."

I looked at his face, the yellowed armpits of his shirt, the big, twisted mouth. "I've been thinking about it over lunch. The old adages? 'Sell in May and go away'? And the other one, 'Don't come back 'til St Leger's day'? And what about the bullets? 'Buy on the bullets'?" I heard my voice rise at the end of my sentences – yesterday's earth-bound certainties taking wing as an endless symphony of tomorrow's questions, fleeting questions to which there are no longer answers, brightly coloured butterfly questions, eagles soaring above the void – an intonation like Pam's. Pam with the long blonde hair, the green backpack and the old guitar. I would be seeing her soon.

"What are you saying, Nick?"

"What I'm saying is go long financials and short the goddamn Euro."

The mouth gaped open. Echoes of distant words full of inarticulate phonemes began to emerge from the cavern in Fabrice's face. "You're crazy, Nick. Have you gone fucking crazy? What kind of trade is that?"

"Do it, Fabrice. I'm the boss around here. The fucking boss. I own you."

I walked along Curzon Street. Beside a dustbin where they collect the rubbish from the Hilton, I set the computer case on the ground. Perhaps it would become, as the vigilant authorities are always threatening, the object of a controlled explosion. Or perhaps a tramp, on his way to find a church door and shelter from the cold, would pick it up and carry it away, sell it in a pub round the back of the Elephant and Castle and treat himself and his mates to a pint on the proceeds.

The sun shone brightly as I crossed Hyde Park. A group of oriental tourists followed a man who carried a red flag. Two aspiring paparazzi in leather jackets knelt, trained their long black lenses on a squirrel that frolicked in the fallen leaves and then ran away, lost to sight among the trees. A flock of geese flew overhead. A little child, too young to go to school, blew soap bubbles that caught the afternoon light and broke it into watery rainbows. She tried to capture her creations in her tiny hands as they drifted and danced, as they lived and died, on the gentle currents of the autumn breeze.

My heart pounded in my chest, raced ahead to its tryst, backwards through the years, over the summits and down the valleys, back to that dock and its soft green light, where the gentle waters of Lake Geneva lap, where the angel with the rainbow voice lies and waits for me. They say we should travel light, my friend, with our rucksacks and our guns. Then perhaps one warm night, when with muffled oars we row the guns ashore and hear the songs of liberation lingering low in the purple air – perhaps on such a starlit night, I'll reach out and touch her arm and feel the goosebumps of eternity.

IMPORTANT NOTICE

Dust on the Nettles is a work of imagination. In it there are background (off-stage as it were) references to historical people and to real events, places, books, poetry, music, paintings, corporations, websites and so forth. I have tried to be accurate in these background references. The characters in *Dust on the Nettles* are, however, entirely fictional and any resemblance to real persons, either living or dead, is unintentional and purely coincidental. Characters on stage talk about and refer to both real and imaginary people, corporations, paintings, books, poetry, websites and events. On occasion, the fictional characters' perceptions of, and opinions about, real (as well as imaginary) events, people, places and so on, may not be entirely accurate. This is part of the fiction. Imaginary events sometimes take place in real places; but the characters also venture into imaginary, fictional places. You will, for example, not find, at the time of writing at least, a restaurant near London's Paddington Station called La Mezza Luna (I borrowed the name from a pizzeria in Rome), a place called Les Sornettes in the hills above Montreux, nor (despite occasional appearances to the contrary) an Acephelion in Athens.

I have salted *Dust on the Nettles* with allusions to various works of literature. I have, in particular, drawn on imagery and phrases from four works published during a twelve-year period in the first quarter of the last century: Alain-Fournier, *Le Grand Meaulnes*, 1914; Edith Wharton, *The Age of Innocence*, 1920; T.S. Eliot, *The Waste Land*, 1922 and F. Scott Fitzgerald, *The Great Gatsby*, 1925. Towards the end of the book, I quote the last three paragraphs from *The Great Gatsby* in full. The references to Balder, the Norse fertility god, were inspired by C.S. Lewis's reaction (described in *Surprised by Joy*, 1955) to a poem by Henry Wadsworth Longfellow. Part of the poem, Longfellow's 'Tegnér's Drapa' (1850), is quoted - once with, as noted in the footnote, a minor alteration. Other snatches of poetry quoted include Emily Dickinson's 'Hope is the Thing with Feathers' (1861) and a couple of lines from each of Hilaire Belloc's 'The

Modern Traveller' (1898) and Robert Frost's 'The Road not Taken' (1916). 'The Road not Taken' also provides the background to one of the recurring motifs in the book, though not perhaps quite as the poet would have intended it. I also, of course, quote from Edward Thomas's 'Tall Nettles'. In Chapter 4.3, the lines beginning '*Yo soy un hombre sincero...*' are from the popular Cuban song '*Guantanamera*', based on José Martí's poem '*Versos Sencillos*' (1899). Phrases from Shakespeare and the Bible, many in common English-language usage, have found their way into the text. At several points in *Dust on the Nettles* I quote from the New International Version (NIV) of the Bible (Psalm 23 verse 4; Matthew 19 verse 24; Matthew 28 verse 20; Luke 15 verses 11 to 24; Luke 21 from verses 9 to 12 and verses 16 and 17; Acts 16 verse 34 and Philippians 1 verse 21). These quotations are taken from the Holy Bible, New International Version Anglicised, Copyright © 1979, 1984 Biblica, formerly International Bible Society. Used by permission of Hodder & Stoughton Ltd, an Hachette UK company. (All rights reserved. 'NIV' is a registered trademark of Biblica. UK trademark number 1448790.) The opening lines of 4.3 are taken from Edward Bulwer-Lytton's 1830 novel *Paul Clifford*. The quotation from Friedrich Nietzsche in 4.5 is taken from *The Gay Science* (*Die fröhliche Wissenschaft* - 1st edition 1882; 2nd edition 1887) as (as noted in the footnote) translated by Walter Kaufmann (New York, 1974). In 9.2, I quote lines from a hymn ('Before the Throne of God Above') written in 1863 by Charitie Bancroft and in 6.7 from the entry for 15 August 1665 in Samuel Pepys' diary. Many of the items in the bullet-point list in 6.1 come from a lecture I gave in Warsaw in November 2007 when I had just completed the first outline draft of this book. The excerpts from Hansard in chapter 6 contain parliamentary information licensed under the Open Parliament Licence v1.0.

I found the quotation from Andreas Baader that appears at the very beginning of *Dust on the Nettles* in Stephan Aust, *The Baader-Meinhof Complex* (English edition, 2008), a very useful source of information on the German Red Army Faction (*Rote Armee Fraktion*) of the 1970s, and the one from Lester Thurow in Stefan Stern's article 'Fat Cat Pay Packages Show No Signs of Causing Indigestion' in the *Financial Times* of 31 October 2006. Some of the Communist/New Left slogans and insults that litter the text are made up but many are real. One of my favourites ('bespittled dwarf of reaction') *is* real: it was used by Polish Communists to denigrate the Nationalist Second World War resistance. I owe it to Timothy

Snyder, *Bloodlands*, 2010. I first found the lyrics from Dimmu Borgir's 'Progenies of the Great Apocalypse' on Thomas Rotten-Diaz's website. It is instructive to read them. I have not quoted them in *Dust on the Nettles* since I did not receive a response to my request for permission.

Much of the early chapters of *Dust on the Nettles* is set against the backdrop of the 1960s and 70s. Nick Kellaway's worldview is formed during that era. There are references in the text to the films of those decades, such as *Le Grand Meaulnes, Butch Cassidy and the Sundance Kid, The Graduate, Fellini's Roma, Chitty Chitty Bang Bang* and *The Sound of Music*. A line from the opening scene of *Bonnie and Clyde* is quoted. For many of those who were young in the 60s and early 70s, echoes of the music of those times are among their most abiding memories. Faces and places may grow dim but the background music plays on. An important strand feeding into that music was the revival and adaptation of American folk songs and ballads. 'House of the Rising Sun', quoted in various forms and places in *Dust on the Nettles*, is one such traditional ballad. It has been recorded by various singers, including Glenn Yarbrough in 1957, Pete Seeger in 1958, Joan Baez in 1960, Bob Dylan in 1961, Nina Simone in 1962 and The Animals in 1964. Another is the cowboy ballad 'Streets of Laredo'. As 'Streets of Geneva' it becomes a banker's ballad in *Dust on the Nettles*. Music echoes from that era include (in no particular order and without in any way trying to make this Kellaway-esque list comprehensive) the voices of Woody Guthrie; Pete Seeger; Joan Baez; Mary Hopkins (particularly her 1968 recording of Gene Raskin's 'Those were the Days', his adaptation of an earlier Russian song), Scott McKenzie ('San Francisco (Be Sure to Wear Flowers in Your Hair)', written by John Phillips of the Mamas and the Papas); Crosby, Stills, Nash and Young; The Beatles; Peter, Paul and Mary (especially, in *Dust on the Nettles*, 'Puff the Magic Dragon'); The Mamas and the Papas ('California Dreamin''); Simon and Garfunkel; The Eagles; Fleetwood Mac; Leonard Cohen; Carole King ('You've Got a Friend'); James Taylor; Lori Lieberman ('Killing me Softly'); Judy Collins; Joni Mitchell; Neil Diamond (including 'Sweet Caroline'), Gordon Lightfoot, Tom Paxton, Van Morrison, Olivia Newton-John, Kris Kristofferson, Johnny Cash and Bob Dylan. Lines from Bob Dylan's lyrics from 'Farewell Angelina' (copyright © 1965,1966 by Warner Bros, Inc; renewed 1993,1994 by Special Rider Music) and 'Lay, Lady, Lay' (copyright © 1969 by Big Sky Music; renewed 1997 by Big Sky Music) are quoted; by permission and on the payment of a USD 200 fee. In a less opaque world, where it was not so difficult (and costly) to obtain permission to quote copyrighted song lyrics in print, these echoes would have been louder and *Dust on the Nettles* richer.